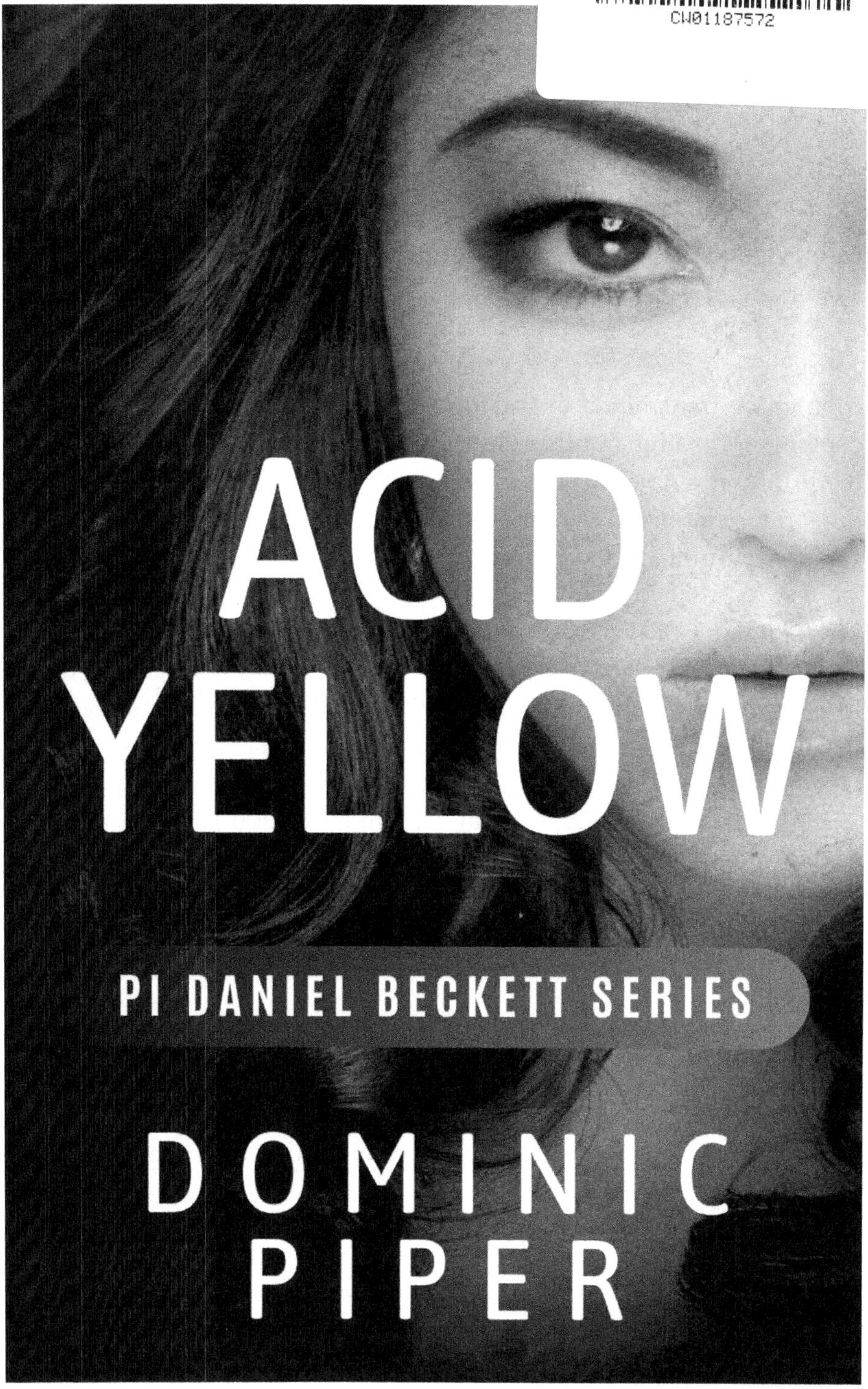
ACID
YELLOW
PI DANIEL BECKETT SERIES
DOMINIC
PIPER

ACID YELLOW

First edition published by Opium Den Publishing 2024

OPIUM DEN PUBLISHING

Paperback Cover and Formatting by The Book Khaleesi

Credits: Image of the Fazioli Piano, NYT Line
https://www.fazioli.com/en/special-models/m-liminal-2/

PI DANIEL BECKETT SERIES
by Dominic Piper

Kiss Me When I'm Dead
Death is the New Black
Femme Fatale
Bitter Almonds & Jasmine
Acid Yellow

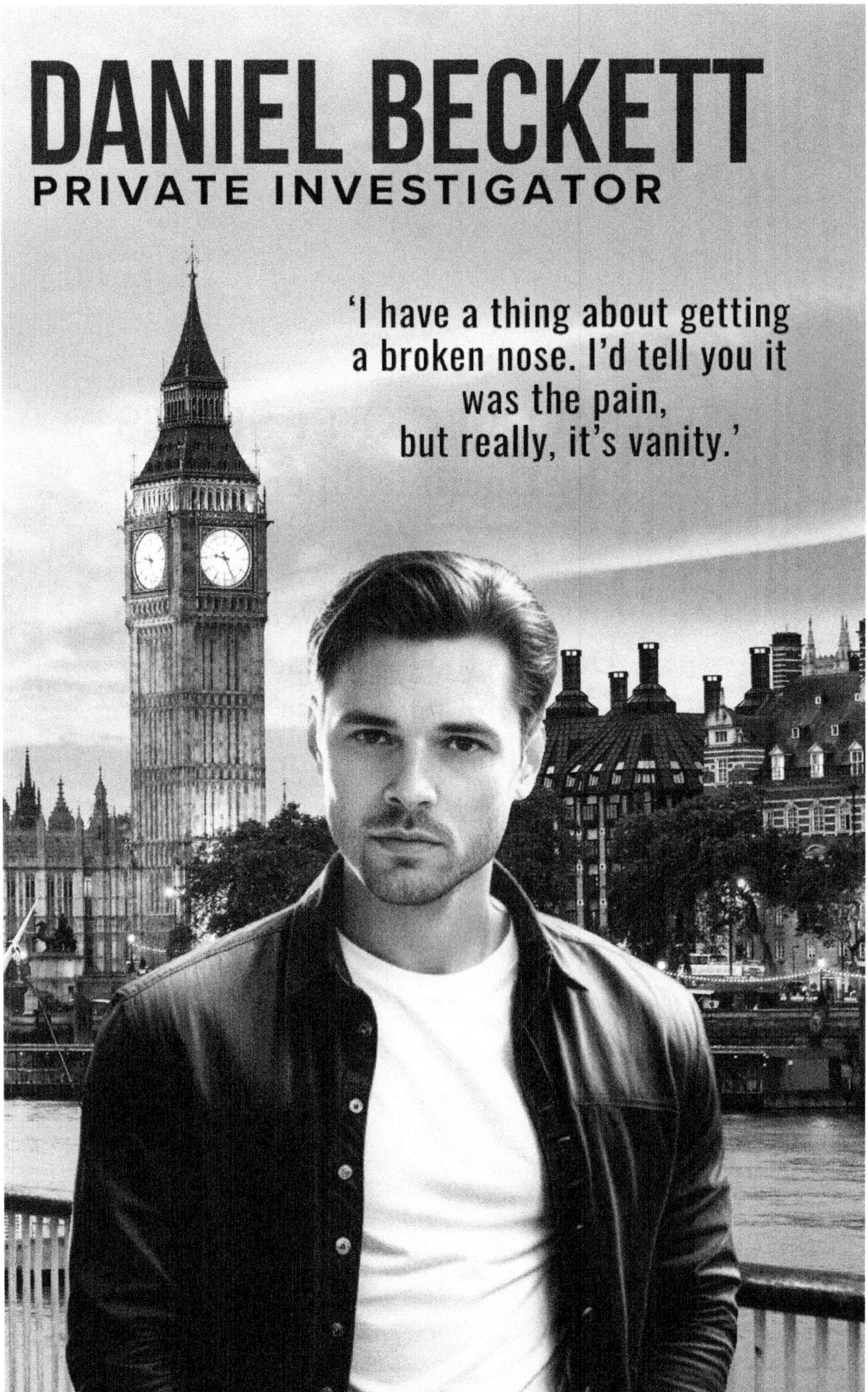
DANIEL BECKETT
PRIVATE INVESTIGATOR
'I have a thing about getting a broken nose. I'd tell you it was the pain, but really, it's vanity.'

ACID YELLOW

Dominic Piper

1

CHANCE MEETING

It's hard to tell her age.

Her hair is jet black and reaches down to her shoulders. It's swept back off her forehead, and there's a striking and decorous white streak that runs down the centre and I don't think it's a fancy dye job. Whatever, it's an arresting look; it's like a pop culture mash-up of Audrey McDonald in *La Dolce Vita* and Rogue from *X-Men*.

White (or grey) hair is an unreliable age marker at the best of times, but I'm guessing she's somewhere between forty-five and fifty-five, though I could be wrong. She could be older. Or younger.

Pale, flawless skin, violet eyeshadow, dark red matt lipstick, a short black shoulderless cocktail dress over a well-proportioned, voluptuous figure and five-inch heels which she doesn't need as she's tall, but they make her legs look great. Our eyes meet. She walks towards me. She's slightly tipsy.

'I thought if I waited for someone to introduce us, I'd be waiting all night. I'm Suzanna Leishman. Hi.'

'Daniel Beckett. Please to meet you, Suzanna.'

We shake hands.

'I saw you glancing at me earlier, Daniel, but as it was only thirteen or fourteen times over the space of about twenty minutes, I was afraid you might think I was a little forward forcing myself on you like this.'

She smiles. I'm hooked. Perfume is pleasant and floral; ylang ylang, bergamot, heliotrope – it's Roja's A Goodnight Kiss.

'That's *exactly* what I thought. I may have to call someone and have you ejected.'

'Manhandled. Grabbed by an upper arm. Pushed into the street.'

'At the very least. I'd probably join in.'

'Perhaps I should make a habit of being forward.'

'Perhaps you should.'

'The consequences sound exhilarating.'

'If you like that sort of thing.'

'The jury is still out, Daniel.'

Another bewitching smile. Meaningful eye contact. I'm already exhausted. Thankfully, a waiter appears with a champagne tray. We both take a glass. I down half of mine immediately, as my mouth is suddenly a little dry.

'Thirsty?' The question accompanied by a raised eyebrow.

'It's this terrible heat.'

'Not helped by this terrible cool air conditioning. I take it you're a guest of Manfredo.'

She's right. This is Manfredo Moretti's sixty-fifth birthday bash. He's hired The Buddha-Bar in Knightsbridge, an expensive and exclusive restaurant/bar famed for its mixology and Wagyu Beef fillet with Truffle Butter. If you can afford the minimum spend of approximately twenty thousand, it's a fab and groovy place to celebrate whatever it is you're celebrating.

The décor is mainly modern chinoiserie; kaleidoscopic, pan-Asian and jaw-dropping, with gold Buddhas all over the walls and lots of red and magenta lighting.

If you hire it, you can even choose your own music selection for the evening. In Manfredo's case, it's an unrelenting streaming of The Doors and all their works. There are about a hundred and fifty people here. It's pretty packed and smells of potent cocktails, expensive perfume, and exotic spices.

A woman in her twenties sidles past and almost pushes me into Ms Leishman. We move to the left. We're closer now; a stimulating foot away from each other. She says something, but I don't catch it due to the volume of "Woman is a Devil". She leans in, one hand on my shoulder, her mouth by my ear, her right breast touching my chest. I resist placing a hand on her hip.

'How do you know him? Manfredo, I mean,' she asks.

That's a good question. Manfredo Moretti is an antique dealer, specialising in the rapid buying and selling of silver hip flasks, goblets, and other expensive collectables from the eighteenth-century. Well, someone has to do it.

He'd made his first million by the time he was thirty. A year ago, he became suspicious that his wife Janja (his fourth), was cheating on him (again). She was, but this time it was a little more serious.

She was cheating on him with a renowned blackmailer and embezzler, an exotically named Galician called Bieito Iago Ferreira. Bieito was filming himself and Janja having sex and posting the results on a popular porn site based in Belize (it was called Womanfuck, so ten points for good taste and subtlety).

He would send Manfredo the link, then ask for a sum of money for it to be removed. Janja was in on it. Just a hunch, but I don't think she loved Manfredo anymore. I suspect it was the humiliation more than the money that got him, and he was concerned about his business image.

From a professional point of view, what they were doing seemed to be a little mad, and under different circumstances would have given him excellent grounds for divorce, but I can understand how the unhinged complexity of it would even give a bright spark like Manfredo pause for thought.

In a bizarre situation like that, it would be a waste of time asking Bieito to please stop it.

The other option, paying up until Bieito had enough money to live in the style to which he and Janja had become accustomed, would obviously be a no-no. Blackmailers are ravenous creatures.

I had an expensive online meeting with Doug Teng, a computer hacker / cybercrime / counter-surveillance / technology-melting expert and financial fleece artist, with whom I've worked for several years.

His solution was to trace and track and hack the origin of these films, so we had a tag on Bieito's 'home' or 'homes' in net terms. A month-long task for a police cybercrime unit, it took Doug seven minutes. He told me he was watching *John Wick 2* and eating a bag of Joe & Seph's gourmet caramel and almond popcorn while he did it. He knows I like inconsequential detail.

Once we'd broken in, we discovered an Aladdin's cave of similar scams, downloaded them onto one of Doug's laptops and a memory stick, leaving conspicuous proof of our dirty deed on Bieito's computer.

The next day, I gave Bieito a friendly anonymous call and told him that unless he quit pronto, the stick would be immediately FedExed to Interpol's cyber-enabled crime division, who'd been interested in speaking to him for several years.

The shakedown stopped and the money was immediately returned to a temporary online bank account and thence to Manfredo. I sent the memory stick to Interpol anyway, because why not?

'Manfredo? Oh, I bought an eighteenth-century silver sugar caster from him last year, and we became firm friends.'

'For some reason I don't believe you.' The music seems to have got louder and she has to raise her voice.

'Do you think I'd lie to you, Suzanna?'

'I've no idea *what* you'd do to me, Daniel.'

"20th Century Fox" is playing. I can hear Manfredo's voice above the hubbub, and watch as he navigates his way through the mob. 'I'll be with you in a minute, *cara mia*,' he says to someone. Then, nodding in my direction, 'I have to talk to this gentleman.'

He heads towards us holding a couple of Helldorados. He looks a little drunk. A striking red-haired girl in a black one-shoulder bodycon dress approaches, kisses me on the mouth and walks away.

Suzanna smiles at me. 'So, Manfredo believes you to be a gentleman.'

'Well, he has been drinking, Suzanna.'

A few feet away, someone smashes a glass and says, 'Shit! *Shit*!' A woman laughs. "End of the Night" starts playing.

Manfredo nods to a waiter to take our near-empty champagne flutes and presses the Helldorados into our hands. These cocktails are a strong, sweet, tasty mix of tequila, rum, whisky, Aztec chocolate bitters and mango syrup. Suzanna and I take a sip at the same time. Her eyes widen with the alcohol hit. Manfredo puts an arm around my shoulder. Strong cologne. Pomélo Paradis by Atelier.

'This man,' he tells no one in particular, while glaring drunkenly at the floor, 'Saved my life. He saved my *life*! I owe him everything! He is – he is so *clever*. He has integrity, he has focus, he's as smart as a wolf and he is a bastard.'

He starts to get a little tearful. 'I don't know what – I don't know what I'm doing sometimes. In my life, you know? I have everything, yet I have nothing, you understand? Tell her, Daniel, my friend. Tell her what you did for me.' He does a double-take at Suzanna, as if noticing her for the first time. She looks at me as if for help. 'I'll get him to tell you,' continues Manfredo. 'It is incredible. Incredible.'

'I don't think that's a good idea, Manfredo,' I say.

'No. No. You're right. You're quite right. It is not. Anyway, I don't want to think of things like that right now. It's my birthday. Is it my birthday? Yes. It is. Yes. Do you know how old I am?'

'Twenty-two.'

'Ha ha. Inside. Yes. Oh, yeah. I'm going downstairs to dance.' He turns to Suzanna. There are tears in his eyes. 'Look at this woman, Daniel,' he slurs. 'Look at her. She is beautiful. Look at her ravishing mouth. Look at her fine bust. You must worship them, my friend. You must worship *her*.

'You must take her to the heights of ecstasy, again and again and again. And then one more time. And then another time for luck. And maybe another time after that! And then when you are drained like some crazy sex swamp, you do it again! I'm drunk. I'm going to find someone and do a drunken confession. No holds barred!'

He disappears into the throng. Suzanna shakes her head in wonderment.

'You've got lipstick on your mouth from that redhead,' she says, an amused grin on her face. With the ringless ring finger of her left hand, she dabs away at my mouth until she's satisfied it's all gone. She inspects her fingertip. 'Nice shade. I think it's Melon d'Or by YSL. Did you know her? The redhead, I mean?'

'Never seen her before.'

'Very pretty. Lovely curves.'

'Great legs.'

'Your type?'

'Not this evening.'

'So, to get back to you looking at me all of the time. What caught your attention?'

'I'm *far* too refined to answer a question like that, Suzanna.'

'Oh, come *on*. Flatter me. You never know *where* it might lead.'

'I'm afraid it was your eye-catching figure.'

'Any particular feature?'

I lean forward and whisper it to her.

She raises her eyebrows. Bites her lower lip. Laughs. 'You're refreshingly crude.'

'You obviously bring out the worst in me.'

'I certainly hope so.'

She finishes her Helldorado and takes a small step closer. Another small brush of a breast, this time against my forearm. Blood pressure now 140 over 90.

'So how do *you* know Manfredo, Suzanna?'

'I'm a lawyer. I represent his company from time to time. I'm a partner in a law firm called Aakster, Leishman & Cussane. Corporate. Employment law, business growth, technology, tax. Very boring. And what about you? I'm dying to know why Manfredo was in such thrall.'

'I'm a private investigator.'

'Really? Hm. Somehow that makes sense. I had a feeling you weren't a hedge fund manager. Just call it female intuition. You've still got…hold on.'

With a forefinger, she gently dabs away some residual lipstick on my mouth.

'There. All gone. I don't think Melon D'Or was your shade, anyway.'

'What would you recommend?'

'Difficult. I think Banned Red by NARS is more your style. Coincidentally, that's what I'm wearing this evening. Let's see.'

She leans forwards and plants half a dozen of the gentlest kisses on my mouth, then leans back to inspect her handiwork. 'Much better.'

'Maybe another application,' I say. 'Just to be sure. A little more pressure, perhaps.'

'Yes. I think so.'

As it's a party, no one really pays attention as we melt into each other, her arms around my neck and her breasts flattened against my chest. I truly try to stop myself, but I find I'm grabbing her ass and squeezing it.

She moans, and I can feel the slow, subtle, insistent, intoxicating rhythm of her hips.

Then she gasps and pulls away, slightly red-faced and breathless. 'How many times was it that Manfredo said you should take me to the heights of ecstasy?'

'I can't remember now. I think it may have been five times. Maybe six.'

'Are you sure? I thought it was more. Were the heights of ecstasy before or after the worship of my ravishing mouth and fine bust?'

'I think it was the worship of your fine mouth and bust, then the worship of you, *then* taking you to the heights of ecstasy.'

'I'm sure we could mix and match,' she says, her eyes sparkling. 'Taking me to the heights of ecstasy while ravishing my fine bust could be an option.'

'I'm not sure that ravishing your fine bust came into it.'

'No? Now I'm disappointed.'

'I think Manfredo used "ravishing" to describe your mouth,' I say. 'I can see why.'

'So, ravishing my fine bust would not interest you.'

'On the contrary. It's all I've been thinking about for the last ten minutes.'

'Same here. And don't forget the manhandling.'

'As if I would.'

'I'm starting to feel that terrible heat you mentioned.'

'I saw an extinguisher on the way in.'

'One may not be enough.'

'I'll see if I can find a bar with a sub-zero plunge pool.'

Another kiss, then we hit the pavement.

* * *

The cab ride back to Covent Garden is murder and I almost feel embarrassed for the driver. Suzanna sits to my left. I squeeze her thigh as she pants, kisses my neck, explores the front of my chinos with her hand, and murmurs well-bred obscenities.

'Mm. You shouldn't let me misbehave like this, Daniel. I feel quite ashamed of myself. Where are we going?'

'I don't know. I thought we'd leave it to the driver.'

'Tell me something bad,' she purrs.

'The Beatles have split up.'

'Oh, no.'

When we get out at Exeter Street, she looks around. 'Oh! We're in Covent Garden. You live in Covent Garden. Wow.'

We're halfway up the stairs to the third floor before she needs another snog break. She's a great kisser, alternating between fiery passion and soft submission. She starts undoing the buttons of my shirt. 'You could have had me on the floor of The Buddha-Bar,' she whispers. 'I wouldn't have cared. I like being the centre of attention.'

'I'll keep that in mind the next time we're both there.'

'Perhaps we could hire it for the evening. Just the two of us.'

'You pay the minimum spend and it's a deal.'

We finally arrive outside the door to my flat. By the time I'm attempting to open both enhanced Yale cylinder locks at approximately the same time (if the second one isn't opened within three seconds of the first, the first one locks itself again), she's got my shirt off and is running her hands down both of my arms, squeezing the muscles. I can feel her warmth against my back and I can smell her sweat.

Once we're inside, I grab her upper arms. I know she'll like this. 'Turn. Hands flat against the wall.'

'Is this a private detective thing? A merciless frisking?'

I laugh. 'No. It's an amusingly depraved sexual dominance thing.'

'Even better. I think you better unzip me.'

She turns her back to me and places her hands flat against the wall, about a foot above her head. I place a hand on her shoulder and quickly tug the zip of her dress all the way down to her coccyx. A soft sigh escapes from her mouth.

She performs an alluring wiggle, and the dress falls to the floor. She steps out of it. She reaches behind her back and undoes the clasp of her bra with one hand. Then the bra is on the floor next to the dress. She turns to face me, her hands covering her breasts.

'Aren't you going to offer me anything to drink, Daniel?'

'What d'you fancy?'

'I don't know. Something cold. The only problem is that I don't have any hands free to hold a glass. My modesty. I'm sure you understand.' She smiles and licks her lips. 'Though I *am* thirsty.'

I take her wrists in my hands and pull them to the side, pinning them against the wall. She looks down at her breasts and looks up at me. 'Well, that's *that* problem solved. Perhaps we could start the manhandling now. If you're not too busy, Daniel.'

'No need to rush things. Maybe a little worship to start. Which would you prefer first? Fine bust or ravishing mouth?'

'You're a detective. Can't you tell?'

2

SANSUYU

When Suzanna wakes me up for the third time, I take a look at my alarm clock. It's eleven minutes past five. To be honest, I'm surprised I can still comprehend digital displays after all I've been through.

I realise that I'm still mildly curious about her age. I had her down as being mid-forties to mid-fifties when we met, and I'm still no wiser.

Whatever she is, she has a phenomenal sex drive and tremendous energy. Maybe she works out or does Pilates or something.

I can't really remember how much I had to drink last night, but despite the interrupted sleep, I don't feel any hangover symptoms at all. And I start wondering about Suzanna; doesn't she have a headache? She looks absolutely fine if a tad tousled.

Is she working today? What was she? A lawyer? I hope she's not in court this morning, she may have trouble concentrating. Personally, I don't think I'm going to go back to sleep now, even if she'd let me. She sits up on her haunches and runs a hand through her hair. She sees me watching her.

'I like being looked at like that, Daniel. Don't stop. I like being appreciated in that way. I've had a fantastic night with you, but don't think I'm finished with you yet. I feel – I don't know – I feel kind of stoned, you know? Tingling all over. Like I've been taking something.'

'I thought we'd only just started, to be honest.'

She laughs. 'I adore this bed. I've never seen anything like it. It's so big. And it's so *firm.* Are those genuine antique brass top rails on the ends?'

'Reproduction. I had it custom made. It's basically a super king size futon base with a super king size futon mattress. The top rails were just something I wanted.'

'I'll bet.'

This makes me laugh. 'What's that meant to mean?'

'Like you don't know.'

'I genuinely have no idea what you're talking about.'

'Sometimes a woman may need something to hang on to. Something to grip. Something to keep her in place. Some support.'

She demonstrates. I run a finger down her back.

'That's it. Be very gentle.'

'You've changed your tune from last night, or whenever it was.'

'Stop it! You'll make me blush. You've been wondering how old I am, haven't you?'

'Not at all.'

'I'm fifty-seven.'

'I want my money back.'

'Sorry. No refunds.'

'I should have asked for a receipt.'

'Seriously. Does it bother you?'

'Why would it bother me?'

'I don't know. I guess it would bother some men. Don't tell me that age is just a number. I hate that phrase. But then you're somewhere in your early to mid-thirties, I would guess. Maybe it's not so bad for you. You'd doubtless think differently if you were twenty-one.'

'Maybe. Maybe not.' I rest a hand on her bottom and squeeze. She flinches, then arches her back.

Her skin is covered in goose pimples. Suddenly, she lets go of the rails, twists around and lies on her back, her arms stretched above her head for maximum effect. She's breathtakingly sexy. Her Banned Red lipstick needs a reapplication.

'I got married when I was still a student. I was twenty, can you believe it? I don't think my husband ever really appreciated what he had. I'm talking about *me,* in case you were wondering. Just my modest, conceited, egotistical opinion, of course.

'I would have done *anything* – I was a great fantasist – but he didn't have the sexual imagination and I didn't have the – the *audacity,* the *confidence,* the *maturity* to ask.

'We were divorced when I was fifty-three. I felt like I'd been asleep for years. I've been asleep since the divorce, as well. I think my career helped while away the hours and the frustration. He didn't like it that I was a partner in a law firm while he only worked for one. He never said as much, but I knew it was true.

'We never had children, and I'm rather glad about that. It never interested me. I'm not that sort of person and I never have been. I've been using HRT for a few months. Perhaps you realised. It's a real eye-opener. I'm not dumb. I know the health risks. But it enabled me to enjoy last night like I did. And I really *did* enjoy it. I really want to do this with you again, Daniel, if you're OK with it. It was a revelation.'

'I'll see if I have any cancellations.'

She smiles. 'I want to experiment. Make up for lost time. There are a lot of things I want to do. A couple of things last night were firsts for me, and I loved them. Particularly the second one. And I was ready for them. It's finding the right man to pick as a lover. Someone who isn't shocked easily. Someone who can take me in hand. Am I talking too much? Tell me if I'm talking too much.'

'It's OK. I'm not really listening.'

She runs her hands down the sides of her body. 'Someone with intelligence, experience, and ability. It's not easy. I'm very choosy and I was lucky with you. *Intuition féminine. Désir à première vue.* Otherwise, I wouldn't have approached you. You had the looks as well. You certainly have the body.

'I've read a lot, you know? About what's out there. About the avant-garde, the adventurous. I've always been a voracious reader. Some things excite and appeal, some don't. There's one kink in particular that interests me...'

'Are you going to share this with me? A brief text would be fine.'

'No. I don't know you well enough. Maybe another time if and when we see each other again. It depends. I'll know when it's the right time. It may be a bridge too far. I don't know. You may think I'm too weird and you might be right. I'm a little ashamed thinking about it, but I'm also excited. Very excited.'

'Now I'm completely disinterested.'

'Mm. I can tell. I don't know that *kink* is the right word, really. Some people see it as a lifestyle thing, though it can also be casual. Lifestyle sounds a little too regimented for me, too formalised.

'Others refer to it as a fetish. I'm still studying it if *studying* is the right word. But, patience, Daniel. I don't want to scare you off, and I'm not one hundred per cent sure that I'm ready for it, but it stirred something in me when I read about it.'

'Well at least I've got something to look forward to.'

'Maybe you have. Maybe you haven't. Did you think I behaved like a gauche teenager last night? I was worried.'

'I was about to call the whole thing off.'

'Come here.'

We kiss for a while and soon her body is responding once more. Then a quick jolt and it's over for her. I must try HRT myself. She dozes for a while. I gaze at her body, then stare at the ceiling, listening to the world wake up outside, as much as any of it can be heard through triple-glazed ballistic glass.

I decide to get up and make coffee. I think the noise of the Siemens broke her out of her catnap and she's wide awake when I return to the bedroom.

'This is made from Bourbon Espresso beans. It's still quite hot. Be careful.'

She sips her coffee and looks serious. 'Do you think I should stop shaving my armpits? I saw a photograph of Sophia Loren when she was young, and she didn't shave them. It looked sexy. Would you like it?'

'Most definitely.'

'Then I'll stop. No time like the present. Can I ask you something?'

'Of course, Suzanna.'

'Your private investigation work. What sort of things do you do? Do you specialise? This coffee is fantastic. What was it again?'

'Bourbon Espresso. Specialise? No. I just do whatever comes up. It's a Zen-like approach. The sound of one case clapping.'

'But seriously. Tell me about a few things.'

I take a sip of coffee and sigh. 'I can't be specific, but, um, tracking down missing persons, dealing with blackmailers, extortion, kidnapping, cybercrime. Even murder. And those were the mundane things. A lot of them were firsts for me, but you soon pick things up.'

'How did you learn how to do it? Were you in the police?'

'No. All my knowledge and skill comes from podcasts and graphic novels.'

'I thought you weren't ex-police. I've worked with police, and you don't have their vibe.'

'I'll take that as a compliment.'

'Is it dangerous? The work, I mean? Do you ever get assaulted or anything?'

'Nothing too serious.'

'I noticed a few scars on your body. Were they from your work?'

'Yoga.'

'I knew it. What were you doing for Manfredo Moretti?'

'I can't really discuss it. Client confidentiality.'

'Silly of me to ask. But that's a good sign. He seemed very impressed with you. What was it he said? "He has integrity, he has focus, he's as smart as a wolf and he is a bastard". Do you work for some big company? Do you have a partner?'

'I'm on my own. Sometimes I solicit discreet specialist help.'

She carefully places her coffee on the bedside table. 'Come and sit next to me. I promise I won't take advantage. Unless you insist.' She props several pillows against the brass rails and sits up. I sit next to her. She flicks her hair back into shape. She smells marvellous. I place a hand on her thigh and rub slowly.

'I'm going to have to get back to my flat before I go into work today. I'll reluctantly take a shower here first, if that's OK.'

'Reluctantly?'

'I like the way I'm smelling right now, don't you? I'll get changed for work when I get home. But it's still early. Is it good for cabs around here?'

'Always. The Strand is a minute away. What time do you have to be in?'

'Not until eleven. Just some admin. Emails. No meetings until this afternoon. I live in Westminster and work in Dyer's Buildings off Holborn.'

She frowns. 'I noticed that you had a Sansuyu compact stereo system in your living room, lounge, or whatever that room was.'

'Do you want me to put some post-coital music on?'

'What do you know about Sansuyu, Daniel?'

I shrug. 'I used to think they were Japanese, but they're Korean, aren't they? Like Samsung or LG. A big multinational electronics conglomerate. Smartphones, televisions, music systems, tablets, semiconductors, memory chips, movies. Undoubtedly a lot of things I don't know about. Gigantic profits, I understand.'

'That's about it. They're a big presence in this country now. Have been for some time, actually.'

'Are Sansuyu a client of your law firm?'

'Yes. Yes, they are. But it's not quite to do with that. It's a tad more personal. I'd like you to meet someone there if you're interested and have the time. Do you have a lot on at the moment?'

'Manfredo Moretti was my most recent case. It was all tied up a few days ago. Right now, I'm free.'

'That's good. This concerns their CEO. A very important woman. Her name is Mi-Cha Jeong, pronounced j-o-n-g, but spelt j-e-o-n-g.' She rolls her eyes. 'I warn you, the Korean name thing is a bit confusing when they live and work here or in America. Took me a while to work it out. In Korea, they place the family name first, so she'd be known as Jeong Mi-Cha or Jeong Mi Cha with a gap replacing the hyphen.

'To make things even worse, the two parts of the forename are often contracted to just one word in the West, so the hyphen would be removed from Mi-Cha, and she'd be known as Micha. Micha Jeong. But sometimes if the hyphen isn't used and there's just a gap, the second part of the forename often gets turned into a middle name or initial, which they don't have in Korea. So, she could find herself called Mi C. Jeong over here, which is a bit ridiculous.'

'I've got a headache just thinking about it.'

'Just think of her as Micha Jeong. That's what she calls herself now. Mi-Cha, by the way, means "Beautiful Daughter". I think you'd like her. She may come across as a bit serious and intense sometimes, but she's just from a different culture, that's all. She may not get your jokes and references every time, despite being pretty westernised. She's actually quite lovely when you get to know her.

'As you're a man, you may detect a chill in the air until she gets acquainted with you and trusts you, though me recommending you will help things along, and you may even find she's very open from the off.

'There are a few reasons for the chill. One is that she comes from what is still a fairly patriarchal society. I personally blame Confucianism. It's a culture where woman's obedience to men has been around for aeons: "To the father when young, to the husband when married, to the son in old age".

'Feminism and/or women's rights are a relatively new thing in South Korea. Despite her brains and seniority, I'm sure she's experienced quite a lot of struggle.

'Even now, women workers are expected to get the coffee and cigarettes for their bosses *and* their male co-workers, if you can believe that. There's a lot of workplace sexual discrimination and a high level of sexual violence against women in South Korean society as a whole.

'It's hard to believe, but some women are pressured into having plastic surgery to please their employers. Misogyny has always been a problem. And it's taken a step back recently with the latest president. Thinks feminism is to blame for low birth rates. Thinking of banning the ministry for gender equality.

'And young men think that the advancement of women is a threat to their own financial security. They also think that it is *they* who are the victims of gender discrimination. So, poisonous gender politics and fluctuating attitudes. It won't have been easy for her.

'How old is she?'

'Mid-thirties, same as you. Oh, and she's pregnant. Five or six months, I think. Not married. Not sure about the history of this or who the father might be. Once again, no one's really bothered here, but there's a stigma attached to unmarried mothers in South Korea. No legal protection, social exclusion, lots of shame.

'If you're a single woman and you're pregnant over there, there's enormous pressure to get married or have an abortion. Your family may well cut you off, you can lose your job, your home, and any kids are treated like crap. But it's already better than it was ten years ago.'

'So, what would you like me to meet her about?'

'I don't know how au fait you are with the world of classical music. Have you ever heard of Kiaraa Jeong?'

'Let me think. No. A relative?'

'Older sister. She was a famous classical pianist. World renowned. Sell-out concerts, CD sales through the roof, you name it. Like Micha, she was permanently based in the UK.'

'Was?'

'There's no nice way of putting this. Roughly two years ago, she was kidnapped. A ransom was paid, but they raped and murdered her anyway. I'm surprised you haven't heard about it. It was big news at the time.'

'I think I did, now you mention it. It was the name that was unfamiliar. Or maybe I'd never heard it spoken out loud. Where did this happen?'

'Here in London. It gets worse. I don't know the full details, but her body was mutilated and stuffed in the boot of a car. Enfield, I think it was. Near there, anyway.'

'How was it…' I stop myself. No one wants to remind themselves of gory mutilation details. If this goes ahead, I can always find out the specifics some other way. 'What about the police?'

'It looks like they drew a blank. Or are still drawing a blank if you wish. There was a huge murder hunt and I presume the investigation is still ongoing. No statute of limitations for murder, you see.

'Micha has hired three detective agencies to investigate it so far.

Not all at the same time, I hasten to add. She was disappointed with the first and stopped using them after a month. The second lot lasted longer until she couldn't stand listening to their "litany of failure", as she put it. The third came up with a lot of theories, possible leads, and endless promises, but, once again, no results. I think they've been out of the picture for about six weeks.'

'Can we backtrack a bit? Who paid the ransom and how much was it?'

'Micha paid it. It was three million. Her career has made her a very wealthy woman. I think the police would have advised against it if they knew about it. But you'd have to talk to her about what happened if she chooses to discuss it with you. I wasn't involved in it in any way and I'm not cognisant of all of the details.'

'What makes you think she'll want to hire another investigator? She must be sick to death of them by now.'

She takes a deep breath. I avert my eyes. 'Just lawyer instinct. She may not even know it herself yet. I probably connect with her a couple of times a month. They're usually brief meetings; me giving her things to sign and then I'm away. Sometimes legal advice on whatever's currently going on with the company.

'I think she's profoundly sad, though she hides it most of the time. You can often feel it as soon as you enter her office. It's not always like that. The day before yesterday she was very funny, bouncy and positive. I think that's her professionalism more than anything else.

'She's quite tough. Occasionally frosty, but she can be remarkably droll, and has a sharp sense of humour. We don't talk about a great deal of personal stuff, and we *definitely* don't talk about her sister.

'But last week we were discussing some securities law compliance. This is tedious at the best of times, and I felt her attention starting to go. Then she suddenly burst into tears. Securities law compliance is boring but it's not *that* boring.

'I never do this, but I took her hand, and gave her a hug. It was a little, er, *awkward* because of her condition, as it were, and the fact that she's smaller than me. I thought she wasn't going to stop sobbing. It was starting to make *me* cry.

'Finally, she disengaged herself, wiped the tears away and sat down. She was staring straight ahead, as if she was in shock. I got us a couple of coffees, dragged a chair over and sat next to her, not saying anything.

'Then she started talking about Kiaraa. How the police had made no progress whatsoever in two years. How she felt she was to blame in some screwed-up way because she paid the ransom. How the detective agencies had let her down and cost her a fortune.

'She didn't care about the money, but it still annoyed her. She said the whole thing was burning a hole in her every day. She wanted whoever murdered her sister to be brought to justice and punished, but she was beginning to think it would never happen and there would be no rest for her sister and no rest for her.'

'Why no rest for her sister?'

'I don't think Micha is particularly superstitious, but there are a lot of myths in Korean culture that involve people who've met untimely deaths, particularly if they have been killed away from their place of birth. One is the wanderer ghost.

'They drift between the worlds of the living and the dead, sometimes causing harm to people, sometimes assisting those who may endeavour to avenge their deaths, sometimes helping to dispel the grief of those that are left behind.

'Some say that they will only find peace when their death has been unquestionably avenged. The Koreans call them *Gaekgwi*. They are feared. I think the legend originates in the fifteenth century.

'Micha is afraid that her sister might have become one of those. She knows it's silly and it's just a story, but it keeps preying on her mind.

'It's a funny thing. There were aspects of Korean society, culture, whatever, that neither of them liked. Particularly the attitude to women there. They'd both lived in the UK for three years before the murder. They liked it here. And then...'

'Should I speak to her? Do you want to set up a meeting? How do you want this to go?'

'I've only just thought of it, so I don't know. I'll have to get it straight in my head. Maybe she won't want to get her hopes up again.

But to be realistic, what else can she do? I feel sorry for her. There was nothing I could do to help, and it frustrated me. The fact that she's pregnant made it all the more poignant.

'It doesn't – this is stupid – it doesn't seem to have cheered her up. The thought of having a baby, you know? Something tells me that she wants it all cleared up before the baby is born. I just think it's worth a try.'

'Like the others, I can't guarantee anything,' I say. 'But my suggestion is – have a word with her. We can take it from there.'

'If it's OK with you, I'll give her a call later on today. No time like the present and all that rot. As soon as I know anything I'll call you back. That's assuming you want me to have your mobile number. I'm sure you don't want me pestering you for sex at all hours and texting vulgar selfies.'

'I've got a business card with my number on. You can pick one up on your way out.'

She thumps me on the chest. 'I need cheering up now. All that talk about Micha and Kiaraa and ghosts. What time is it?'

'I've no idea. Night and day have merged into one hyper-erotic slurry.'

'Can we stand up? I'd like you to hold me from behind.'

She gets up and stands a few feet away from the door. I stand behind her and place my hands on her hips. She laces her fingers behind her neck. I can't imagine what this will look like from the front. Oh, yes I can.

'Can you hold me just beneath my breasts? Don't touch them.'

'I wouldn't dream of it.'

We stand there for maybe two or three minutes. The only sound is her soft breathing.

After a while: 'Doing nothing like this is, for some reason, very exciting. Very interesting. Hm.'

'Exercises your self-control.'

'Maybe. Can I see you tonight?' she asks.

'We can go out to dinner if you like.'

'No. I want to come here. We can order something in. Better still,

I'll bring something we can eat. I'm sure I can rustle up something dramatic, devastating and epicurean. Something to drink, too. You can touch them now.'

'Like this?'

'Mm. That's it. That feels amazing. Oh. Don't move. This is incredibly erotic. Just standing here like this. You like it too, don't you? I can tell.'

'So will you tell me tonight?'

'Tell you what?'

'About the kink you're a little ashamed of.'

'Oh, no. I'm much too bashful. Maybe one day, Daniel. We'll see.'

'You're awful, Suzanna.'

'I'm starting to be. You should buy me lingerie, you know. Women expect it from their lovers, or so I hear.'

'I'll look into it. What type?'

'I'll leave that to your discretion. And to your imagination. Something indelicate, I think. Now. Let's get on with that cheering up.'

KIARAA JEONG
WORLD-FAMOUS CLASSICAL MUSICIAN

3

THUNDERBIRD THREE

The Sansuyu Building is a 650-foot skyscraper on the north side of Leadenhall Street, right in the centre of London's financial district.

Known locally as Thunderbird Three due to its tubular shape, pointed peak, slightly red concrete shade and its trio of stylish (and totally unnecessary) flying buttresses, it was built in 2002, the allusion to a rocket from a 1960s puppet show presumably lost on its architects, though as I'm approaching it, it's immediately apparent how the nickname originated.

This seems to be quite the thing with recently built skyscrapers in London. All that architectural hard work, innovation and skill, and they end up being called things like The Shard, Cheesegrater, Helter-Skelter, Can of Ham, Stealth Bomber, The Scalpel and The Gherkin. I think Thunderbird Three beats all those hands down, though, just for the absurdity and wit behind it.

It has forty-five floors, and a large basement car park for Sansuyu employees. Although Sansuyu own the building, they only occupy the top ten floors, the others being leased or rented to a variety of insurance companies, banks, and other financial institutions.

At the moment, it's the fifth highest building in London.

Leadenhall Street is packed full of glass and concrete structures like this (plus the odd thirteenth-century church), but the main thing you notice as you walk along is the relentless building work going on: construction, refurbishment, demolition, and the constant drilling and brain-searing loudness of unidentifiable power tools doing their jarring thing.

Add to this the choking dust and pungent industrial aromas, and the fact that you have to keep stepping into the road to avoid closed-off areas of the pavement, and you have a chaotic thoroughfare that any visitor to the capital would be delighted to visit once they'd taken in Buckingham Palace and Madame Tussauds. I've been here a minute and I've already got a bad taste in my mouth, like I've been licking the dust off the pavement.

I find a coffee bar conveniently situated right next to an acupuncture clinic, order an Americano, and sit outside, watching some guys in hard hats and hi-vis orange outfits leering/catcalling at passing female office workers or whatever they are. One girl steps into the road to avoid them and almost gets run down by a HEJ Coffee van that says 'Caffeine Response Unit' on the side.

I've arranged to meet Suzanna in the foyer of Thunderbird Three at two p.m. That's seventeen minutes from now. She spoke to Ms Jeong this morning and suggested a meeting. She agreed immediately and without any prevarication, so Suzanna's lawyer instinct was correct. Quick work.

This could indicate a number of things: she wanted to get it out of the way; she was doing it out of politeness to Suzanna; she was desperate to get closure regarding her sister; or she was curious to meet a focussed bastard who was as smart as a wolf with integrity, or whatever Manfredo said that obviously impressed Suzanna so much.

We decided that Suzanna would personally introduce me to her and then leave. Two reasons for this. Firstly, it's Korean business etiquette and secondly, Ms Jeong may be reluctant to discuss highly confidential and potentially upsetting matters with someone else present, even if it's one of her lawyers, which is fair enough, I guess.

Suzanna also made some other suggestions. The first was that I take some sort of notebook with me and jot things down during the meeting. I told her that I usually relied on my excellent memory, but she said that making notes would indicate to Ms Jeong that I was taking the matter seriously, so OK.

I bought a Leuchtterm1917 A5 notebook in port red and a Schaeffer Rollerball pen in matt black. Those two items just scream 'serious' in my opinion. They're now nestling in my fashionable JJZSL messenger bag, the only items in there.

She also suggested that I wear whatever I usually wear, which today is black chinos, a charcoal grey t-shirt, and a black leather Pierotucci single-breasted jacket which I picked up in Florence a few years back.

This combo not only makes me look cool AF, but will serve to distance me, at least visually, from the sort of grinning/sincere/besuited/shirt and tie/huge watch/pungent aftershave types she'll have been dealing with from the big investigation companies.

It might work, it might not.

I spent this morning recovering from Suzanna and doing a little preliminary research on Kiaraa Jeong or Jeong Kiaraa (when she was back in Korea).

The world of classical piano is not one I'm particularly familiar with, but it didn't take long before the enormity of her abduction and murder began to manifest itself. And that this was a woman, and a young woman at that.

I started to feel anger but supressed it. Anger stops concentration and focus.

I sat in front of the computer with a coffee and looked for images. You have to start somewhere. Typing her name into Google produced a mind-boggling amount of stuff. It was at that point that I realised that, in her field at least, she was enormously famous, though at the same time it was understandable that if you weren't into classical music/classical piano, you might never have heard of her.

There was an entrancing photograph of her wearing a striking yellow dress which I expanded so I could get a good look at her. Impossible to tell when it was taken, but she looked mid-twenties at the time.

Slim and attractive, with long lustrous black hair that, in that photograph, seemed to almost reach her elbows. A pretty, guileless, heart-shaped face, beautiful, amused eyes, a wide smile, full, sensual lips with an appealing sexy downturn at the edges, and skin as white as marble.

Very little makeup: a dusting of bronze eyeshadow, some pale pink lipstick and that was it. Maybe a touch of blusher beneath her cheekbones, or a photographic touch-up of some kind. She was standing against a white sheet of photographer's backdrop paper, and the shot made it obvious that was the case, as you could see the sides of the sheet and the roll at the top.

A side-on view, she was leaning backwards against a black plastic saddle stool, legs crossed at the ankle, both hands resting against the seat, looking straight at the camera, a favourite photographer's pose.

What was that photograph for? Some sort of publicity shot? A magazine article?

I did a quick scan of the other photographs, then found her Wikipedia page. She was born in Seoul, in the neighbourhood of Myeongdong, now a famous shopping district. Father was an electrical contractor, mother was an amateur violinist of some repute.

She was a champion athlete in school and college, specialising in javelin and hurdles. She began piano lessons when she was three. First performance in front of an audience was at the age of nine at the Seoul Arts Centre.

She won fourth prize at the ARD International Competition in Munich when she was fourteen and first prize at the International Chopin Competition in Darmstadt when she was sixteen.

From then on, it was award after award and a scholarship to study at the Conservatoire de Paris, or the Conservatoire National Supérieur de Musique et de Danse de Paris, as it likes to be known.

Then it was on to the Lucerne School of Music in Switzerland, The College of Music, Drama and Media in Hanover and The Guildhall School of Music and Drama in London.

If all that wasn't enough, she attended courses for concert performance in Naples, Winterthur, and Stuttgart. I assume she had a special room where her many certificates were displayed.

Back to Korea for the start of her performance career proper, then a whirlwind of concerts in Holland, Sweden, Mexico, China, Ukraine, Norway, Romania, Albania, Argentina, Australia, and America.

From there, she progressed to performing at major festivals and concerts; the Dubrovnik Summer Festival, the Cheltenham Music Festival, the Bad Kissingen Summer Festival, the Prague Spring Festival and many, many others.

She'd played with the Berlin Symphony Orchestra, the Seoul Philharmonic, the China Philharmonic Orchestra, the Greensboro Symphony Orchestra, and the German Radio Philharmonic of Saarbrücken, and had given concerts at Carnegie Hall, the Symphony Hall in Osaka, the Vienna Musikverein, and the Boston Symphony Hall.

She was also a prolific and best-selling recording artist, who seemed to be signed exclusively to Lysander Records, a company founded in Germany in 1971 by someone called Jürgen Eierkuchen, that specialised in classical and jazz recordings, plus audiobooks.

And in case she was ever short of some ready cash, she was sponsored by Bulgari and regularly did ads for them.

I found one of them: a black V-neck taffeta dress, side-swept shoulder length hair, minimal makeup, a sultry pose with her left hand resting on her right shoulder. She was wearing one of their Mediterranean Sapphire necklaces. These are extremely expensive, and I wondered if she was allowed to keep it after the shoot. I decided she probably was.

Eighteen solo albums over sixteen years (whenever did she find the time?): six Chopin, three J.S. Bach, two A. Scarlatti, three Clementi, one Debussy, one Cécile Chaminade and two Erik Satie. Plus, a piano duet album with a wonderfully named Greek pianist called Phoenix Raptis, and two albums with the New York Philharmonic.

Then a profile-raising world tour taking in fifty-six countries. She must have been sick to death of staying in luxury hotels.

She and her agent were in preliminary talks with Mezzo TV in France about a documentary on her career so far, to be made sometime next year.

The last thing she did was to give a masterclass at the Académie Internationale d'Été de Nice.

Then some fuck kidnapped, raped, and murdered her.

She was thirty-four.

There was nothing at all on her personal life, but a quick look at the pages of similar artistes showed that this was typical for a musician of her ilk; this was fame, but it wasn't prurient, showbizzy fame.

I turned the computer off and stared out of the window.

I didn't know Kiaraa Jeong, and now I never would, but I felt a little rattled. All that achievement and then she's carelessly snuffed out. Or maybe not carelessly.

We'll see.

I made a point of not searching for details of her kidnapping and murder. First of all, I might not get the gig, and second of all, I didn't want my potential opinions coloured by sensational and/or inaccurate media reporting.

When I walk into the foyer of the Sansuyu Building, Suzanna is already there, looking delightful and professional in a long-sleeved burgundy crepe midi dress with a matching wide buckle belt at the waist.

We quickly reference last night's activities with the briefest flicker of eye contact before air-kissing like we're work colleagues. She's wearing a different perfume which I can't identify.

The foyer is shockingly large, spectacularly space age, and smells like it was constructed and decorated a few hours ago.

The reception desk is ghost white with pale blue underlighting and easily accommodates the seven grey-suited Sansuyu staff seated behind it: three females and four males.

On the wall behind them is the company name in pink neon set against a photograph of some delicate yellow flowers on a cut branch. To my left is a gigantic ultra-hi-res television screen blasting Sansuyu's achievements and products in a never-ending promo loop, and to my right another big screen with the words 'Innovation', 'Improvement', 'Entertainment', 'Finance', 'Integrity' and 'Telecommunications' coming and going in different colours.

Suzanna hands me an ID badge with my name on it. I clip it to my messenger bag. 'They know we're here,' she says. 'Someone will escort us to the forty-fifth floor in a few minutes. Let's take a seat. Oh. There was something I forgot to mention.' She lowers her voice. 'About six years ago, Micha and her sister lost both parents. They were shot dead in a store robbery that went bad. Try not to bring the subject up.'

'Fuck.'

'Indeed.'

We sit next to each other on a colossal green furry sofa that is so soft and spongy that you feel it'll swallow you up if you make a wrong move.

'You smell lovely, Suzanna. What's the perfume?'

'It's Roja, like I was wearing last night. This time it's Chypré Extraordinaire. I love their perfumes. So sensual.'

'Orange blossom in there somewhere.'

'That's right. Geranium and cumin, too. Did I tell you what Sansuyu means? You never know. It may come up in conversation.'

'You didn't.'

'It's the Korean name for the cornelian cherry flower or Chinese dogwood. You see it everywhere in the spring in Korea. Lovely golden blossoms. See the flower photograph behind the reception desk? That's it. They say that a tea made from the flowers can cure erectile dysfunction.'

'I'll order some online when I get home.'

'It also means "immortality".'

She produces an iPhone and starts texting.

My mobile pings.

It's been very uncomfortable for me to sit down today.

Why is that?

You know why.

Tell me about the kink you were ashamed of, Suzanna.

Patience, Daniel.

She turns and gives me a look that makes my insides turn to jelly.

In a few moments, one of the reception guys walks towards us, smiling. His gold ID badge says that he's Chan-Yeol Choi. We stand and he bows briefly then shakes our hands. One of the female reception staff, a plump and graceful young woman of about twenty, stands a few feet behind him smiling, but I don't really understand why she's there.

'Hello again, Ms Leishman. Good afternoon, Mr Beckett. Welcome to Sansuyu. I'm Chan-Yeol Choi, senior daytime reception co-ordinator. If you would like to come with me to the elevator, I shall accompany you both to the forty-fifth floor.'

The female reception girl smiles, bows and returns to her post. We follow Chan-Yeol and get into the largest lift I think I've been in. Unfortunately, I don't have my tape measure with me, but I would guess it's about fourteen by twelve and approximately ten feet high. We could play basketball in here.

Our man presses a button, and the doors swiftly and silently close. When they open again a couple of seconds later, I think something's gone wrong, but incredibly we've arrived at the forty-fifth floor in total silence, without any discernible motion and at some insane speed. Suzanna smiles at my conspicuous bafflement; she's done this before, of course.

Chan-Yeol walks with us to another immense and imposing reception area, this one with a very good-looking Korean woman of about Suzanna's age behind the desk who gets up to greet us. No grey uniform this time, instead, a smart dark blue trouser suit over a sugar pink blouse. Four-inch black stiletto heels.

She nods at Chan-Yeol, who tells us he was enchanted to greet us and reverses into the lift.

She walks towards us, shakes Suzanna's hand and then mine. Green eyeshadow. Deep maroon lipstick. No perfume. Twinkling eyes. Knowing smile. Scandalous cleavage. Glam and sexy. Wedding ring. I bow slightly but notice that Suzanna didn't.

'Hello again, Ms Leishman. Always a pleasure to see you. And this must be Mr Beckett.' She glances at Suzanna and raises her eyebrows in mock amazement. 'Oh! So handsome! A red-blooded deportment!'

They both laugh. I don't know what's going on.

'Can I get you anything to drink once you're inside?' she asks. 'Coffee? Tea? Mineral water? Dr Pepper? Bacchus-D?'

'Not for me, thank you, Aera,' replies Suzanna. 'I'll be leaving shortly.'

'I'll have a coffee, please,' I say. 'Black with a dash of milk. No sugar. Thanks very much.'

Aera frowns slightly before nodding her head, then I get a seductive megawatt smile. I realise I'm feeling slight anxiety and disorientation about the etiquette required in just about everything here. Was it rude of me to ask for no sugar? Well, I'm sure everyone understands. What's Bacchus-D?

'I'll just let Micha know you're here.' She taps a black state-of-the-art timepiece on her wrist with a middle finger and says something *sotto voce* in Korean. I don't hear a reply, but she nods her head. 'OK. You can go in now. Here. Let me. Do enjoy your meeting.'

She opens a pair of glass doors and we're in. And there's Ms Jeong, walking towards us hand outstretched and a big smile on her face. This is not one of her sad days, presumably.

She shakes hands with Suzanna and then with me. Then she holds Suzanna's shoulders, kisses her on both cheeks and gives her a quick, shy hug. She says something under her breath which I don't catch, but which ends with 'my dear'. Then she steps back and becomes more formal.

'Hello, Suzanna. Thank you for coming. And you must be Mr Beckett. I am so pleased to meet you.' I can see her take in my clothing and general appearance for a second, then a quick, charming downturn of the mouth which is her smile style, and a brusque nod of satisfaction. I guess I passed *that* test, whatever it was.

I wasn't sure what to expect, but I can feel my heart racing. This is an unbelievably attractive woman. She has a fresh, head-turning beauty that resembles that of her sister, and although she has the same heart-shaped face, her features are somehow more sensual and sybaritic, the beautiful, big eyes more knowing; wicked even.

You can never be sure, but she looks like she'd be a fun date. She has a cute, captivating smile and her skin is darker and more beautifully golden than Kiaraa's (though it occurs to me that her sister's skin tone may have been lightened for her promo pics).

I'm smitten.

Her black hair is styled in a short, layered pixie cut that flatters her face shape and looks like an expensive salon job. As Suzanna mentioned, she's very obviously pregnant, maybe five months or more, her bump still high, and she's wearing a charming, figure-flattering and fashionable green midi wrap maternity dress with a white flower pattern and an empire waist. She's medium height, maybe five five or five six.

I know she's about a decade older, but she looks like she's in her mid-twenties. It feels a little weird admiring the full, high, disproportionately large breasts which are obviously the result of her pregnancy, but I do it anyway; I'm sure this is perfectly normal and is a variety of virtuous aesthetic appreciation.

She's wearing Rose D'Arabie by Armani, and there's a Murakami-Hublot Black Ceramic Rainbow watch on her wrist. Flowery dress, flowery perfume, flowery watch.

'As I told you on the telephone, Micha,' says Suzanna. 'Mr Beckett came highly recommended by one of our top clients. He is professional, discreet and a man of great integrity. You will be discussing highly confidential matters, so naturally I will take my leave of you now. I'll be in touch regarding the Luxembourg expansion. Perhaps we will see an end to it on the horizon!'

Micha laughs. She's constantly rubbing her bump. 'I shall look forward to it!' she says, in a manner that makes it plain that she won't, and which amuses both of them.

'Enjoy your meeting, Micha. I'm sure Mr Beckett will be of great assistance to you.'

'I hope so. Goodbye, Suzanna.'

Another affectionate hug and kiss and Suzanna turns to leave, but not before slapping my senses with another lascivious half-second of eye contact.

'Come, Mr Beckett. Let us sit down and chat.'

I follow her in, looking at her bottom and her legs. Well, at least I've got eternal damnation to look forward to.

MICHA JEONG
CEO OF A SOUTH KOREAN MULTINATIONAL
SANSUYU
미래 만들기

4

GLACÉ CHERRIES & CHOCOLATE TRUFFLES

Micha's office is, unsurprisingly, as big as everything else in this building and almost occupies the entire floor. Looking out of one of the many windows, I can see The Shard, The Gherkin, Tower Bridge, and a breathtaking view of the River Thames reaching out as far as Tilbury Docks and Southend-on-Sea. We're so high up, that on a clear day you could probably spot Belgium and The Netherlands if you knew in which direction to look.

The floor is unpolished black granite, with a dozen thick white fur rugs scattered around in a random fashion. Three big coffee tables, each with brightly coloured sumptuous sofas on each side, all covered with countless scatter cushions, and, on the floor, two enormous blocks of rough-sculpted clear crystal, easily seven feet tall. They look like a pair of transparent Easter Island statues that are about to kiss.

Down the far end of the office is a white marble dining table that seats ten with a big bunch of deep purple roses in a green bottle vase in the centre. I can smell the flowers from where I'm standing; a touch of honey fragrance if I'm not mistaken. I can hear jazzy guitar music playing, but the volume is so low that I can't tell what it is, and I can't see any speakers to detect where it's coming from.

There's a sizeable coffee station with a Sage Barista Pro Coffee Machine, a Nespresso Gran Lattissima, three silver Tom Dixon cafetières, a selection of Sansuyu promo mugs in bright yellow and a cupboard that probably contains all the grains and beans. Maybe even the spoons.

If this is all for Micha, I'm surprised she's not bouncing off the walls. Are you allowed to drink loads of coffee when you're pregnant? It's all very fab, modernist, and cool. You could live in here.

Surprisingly her desk, actually a stone-topped charcoal grey dining table, is relatively small, about five feet across, with just enough room for her 24-inch iMac, a spectacularly large Sansuyu ultrawide monitor, a Hewlett Packard DeskJet, an iPhone holder shaped like a black high heel, a stack of magazines, a couple of books, half a packet of Polo Mints, a big jar of glacé cherries and a box of Lauden chocolate truffles. I'm surprised stuff isn't falling onto the floor.

Behind the desk, a black Herman Miller Aeron office chair. I've seen these before. Very comfortable, very expensive, very good for back pain. There's a powder blue velvet scarf slung over the back.

There's a lot of big colourful art on the walls, but I don't recognise any of it, apart from one of Harland Miller's spoof Penguin Books canvases.

Next to that, there's an eye-catching, impressionistic nude in plum, red and turquoise. The model has a voluptuous figure like Suzanna's.

I suddenly get inspired, and decide to visit Lipstick & Leather, an exclusive fetish wear boutique in Soho, owned by a former client of mine. Well, Suzanna did mention the word 'indelicate' during her request for lingerie.

Micha follows my gaze. 'Mariano Tosetti. An Italian artist. A very good investment. You like it?' She smiles. 'Apart from the subject matter, I mean.'

'Striking. A little too large for my flat, though.'

'Where do you live, Mr Beckett?'

'Covent Garden. You don't have to call me Mr Beckett. Daniel will do.'

'Then you must call me Micha. Shall we sit down? I like Covent Garden. Many nice shops and restaurants. Les Néréides and agnès b are my favourites for attire. And there's the Royal Opera House, of course. Can I take your jacket?'

I take it off and hand it to her, and she carefully drapes it over the back of the Herman Miller chair, covering her scarf. I place my messenger bag on the floor.

'Oh. Before I forget,' I say.

Suzanna told me to hand her my business card with both hands and rotate it so the details can be read straight away.

Mine is an unusual design: silvery metal with miniature micro-grilles on the top and bottom. It's meant to be memorable, or something.

She bows, takes it with both hands, reads it and smiles.

'Thank you. I see someone has been coaching you!' She looks amused. 'I wonder who?' She places the card on a corner of her desk. 'But it is good. You are polite. Here.' She scoops up a business card and hands it to me. Gold-plated wood with the Sansuyu flower on the front. Probably a bespoke job by l'arbre. I read it, look suitably impressed, and slide it into my wallet.

We sit opposite each other on a matching pair of plush red sofas which are either side of a wide, rectangular, glass-topped coffee table. She's rather awkward when she starts to sit down and I almost get up to help her, but then she settles. She grabs a big green velvet cushion and stuffs it behind her back.

She smiles at me, her eyes bright and amused, as if she's trying not to laugh. I don't know how I'm meant to respond, so I smile back.

'Did Aera ask you if you wanted something to drink, Daniel?'

'Yes, she did. I, um...'

As if on cue, Aera appears with a coffee tray; two flowery Noritake cups and saucers, brown sugar lumps, a small jug of milk and a large cafetière. She places the tray on the coffee table, smiles at Micha, raises her eyebrows at me like we're an item and pours out two coffees, white for me, black for Micha. I get another enigmatic eyebrow raise and then she's gone.

Micha watches her leave while dropping four sugar lumps into her coffee. 'A handsome woman, yes? I think you would say "curves in all the right places". She is a widow. Four years now. Her husband was an embedded firmware engineer.'

'Oh, really,' I say, as if I know what that is and can talk about it for hours.

'She is my personal assistant. She looks out for me.'

If Aera's in charge of the refreshments, why is there all this coffee gear in here?

I watch Micha as she lifts her cup. Her movements are feminine, precise, and delicate. She makes shy eye contact from time to time. I guess she's trying to assess me in some way.

We sit and drink. She smiles again. I smile back. Is she nervous? Then she starts laughing, placing her fingertips against her lips. Once again, I'm not sure how to respond, so I laugh, too. She looks as if she's the possessor of some big secret that she's not going to tell me about.

'You are having an affair with Suzanna Leishman, Daniel.'

This is a statement of fact. Did Suzanna tell her? Ah well. I better come clean. I try to appear honest, truthful, reasonable, and casual. It's a look I practise in the mirror whenever I have some free time.

'Yes. Yes, I am. How did you know? Did she mention it?'

'No. She did not mention it. I just saw the way she looked at you. Two separate occasions, each one only lasting a fraction of a second, but that was enough.'

'I thought *I* was meant to be the detective.'

This gets a laugh. 'Also, the way she walked when she came in and when she left. I have met her on many occasions and know her well. Her whole demeanour was different today. She was more *feminine,* more *earthy* somehow. Is that right? Earthy? Her face looked different, and her body moved in an atypical way. She was acting like a woman in the first flush of a sexual relationship. Just an impression. Is it rude of me to say this?'

'Not at all. You're disturbingly perceptive.'

'Please don't think that I am concerned that she may have recommended you because you are lovers, Daniel. Suzanna is a woman of great rectitude and virtue. I know that she would never take such a course. I mentioned it because I didn't want to pretend that I didn't know.' A quick giggle. 'Does that make sense? How long has it been going on?'

'About fourteen hours, give or take a few minutes.'

This amuses her greatly. 'Ah, *that* explains it! I am glad. I am very fond of her. She is very good-looking and a very nice person. I also venerate her dress sense. She has advised me on couture on several occasions. And she is an outstanding lawyer.

'I know that she has not been with anyone for a while. We have little chats every now and then, woman to woman, and I could feel that she felt frustrated with that aspect of her life, although she did not express it in so many words. We are professional women after all.'

'Well, I'm only glad I could assist her with that aspect of her life. It's all part of being a private investigator.'

She likes this. She sips her coffee and smiles at me. 'If you don't mind me saying, there is quite an age gap between the two of you. I would say at least twenty years. Do you find that a problem?'

I lean forwards with a confidential expression on my face. 'I do. I can't keep up. Her libido is off the charts. I was going to ask if you had any spare Korean ginseng.'

She laughs once more. I'm glad I can make her laugh. I like her. I think this is going well.

'I'm *very* nosey!"

'Really? I hadn't noticed.'

'Who knows? I may get even *more* nosey!'

'I just hope you're discreet.'

'Oh, I'm always discreet, Daniel. Your secrets are safe with me. The more intimate they are, the safer they are.'

She sighs. She looks more relaxed. 'I suppose I'm interviewing you, aren't I. It seems silly. You are maybe here to help me with something important and I'm interviewing you as if you'd come for a job. I suppose I should ask you if you want to ask *me* something!'

'What are the holidays like?'

'No holidays! Fifteen-hour days and one weekend off a year. You know how us Koreans are.' She leans forwards. 'But I have good instincts about people, Daniel. And I feel comfortable in your presence. I wanted to talk to you about this and that to get a feel for your honour and your confidence. And I can feel your, your *intent*. Is that the right word? When Suzanna told me about you, I was afraid that you'd be like the other investigators, but you are not like them. You are different.'

'I suppose none of the others were having an affair with one of your lawyers.'

A quick laugh. 'That is true. Is that your preferred method for getting recommendations?'

'Every single time. By the way, if there are any other female members of your workforce who need some TLC, you must let me know.'

'I'll be sure to. Actually, I can think of one…' She nods towards the reception area.

'Really?' I look at my watch. 'How long is this meeting going to take?'

She claps her hands together and laughs delightedly. 'I can call her in if you like.'

'Maybe later. I don't want to get too distracted.'

'That would never do!'

'Although if you insist…'

'Ha! Can you tell me how much you charge, Daniel? I think we should get that out of the way before we progress.'

'Certainly. I charge a thousand a day plus non-negotiable expenses.'

'That is cheaper than the others. Can you explain why that is?'

'They have big overheads: buildings, heating bills, beautiful secretaries, expensive suits, acrid aftershave. Also, I don't know what I'm doing.'

She sits up. She smiles. She rubs her bump once more. 'Yes. Yes. I can see that Suzanna's judgement was correct. I can also see why she is attracted to you. You are quite charming and self-effacing. But I can also feel that you are confident in your abilities. You do not need to brag. Let us see what happens, shall we, Daniel? I think I would like to hire you. When can you start?'

'Right now. I have a feeling that time is of the essence.'

'Excellent. And you are quite right. It is. I would like my head of security, Mr Baek-Hayeon Bahk, to join us later on. He was intimately involved in this matter, and it may be useful for you to speak to him. I have known him for a long time. We were colleagues back in Seoul. He is very trustworthy. You can communicate freely with him.'

'I'll look forward to meeting him.'

I think I've passed the audition. Was that an audition? I rather think it was. She's very sharp. I'll have to be careful. I open my messenger bag and take out my notebook and pen. She looks at them with approval.

I'm going to veer away from the subject a little and meander around to ease her gently into things. I know the sort of investigators she's been dealing with, and it would have been all "Now, madam, if we can just start from the beginning". My sixth sense tells me she wouldn't like this approach.

'Just out of curiosity, could you tell me what were the names of the other private investigation companies you used? Suzanna told me there were three but didn't give details.'

'Certainly. The first one was called Teece Investigative Services. Mr Teece had been in the Metropolitan Police Service for thirty-five years. I did not use them for long. I felt that this kind of investigation was out of Mr Teece and his associates' world of experience.

'The second one was called Fenwick & Fenwick. It was a father and son business. Both ex-police again. The son dealt with me. Very overbearing manner. Horrible aftershave or cologne. Tried to exude a confidence that I don't think he really had. Imperious. Promises, promises. But at the end of the day, out of his depth.'

'What about the third?'

'Bespoke Investigations. They were the most recent. They are in a big building quite near here. Fenchurch Street. High prices. I think they were more used to divorce cases and suchlike. They were always telling me that they were close to a breakthrough, but it never came. Also, I did not like the attitude of the principal investigator, Mr Lockford.

'He had also been a policeman, but not in London. Is Lincoln a place? Then it was there. He kept telling me that there were things that I did not understand, as if I was not very bright.

'Also, I did not like the way he spoke to me and looked at me. It upset me. Once, he tried to rub my back. He said his wife had liked it when she was pregnant. That was the end of his tenure.'

'I might hire him myself.'

I pretend to write the names of these companies in my notebook. This is a new experience for me. I smile at her. 'Did you ever come across agencies like those three when you lived in Korea?'

'Hm. Not really. In fact, it was a felony crime to charge for that sort of work. South Korea used to be the only member state of the OECD where running a private detective service was illegal.'

'I didn't know.'

'Even the term "private detective" was banned, as was the term "intelligence service agent". I think the term "private detective" has only been officially allowed quite recently. People used to use the term "private investigator" to get around it, like a scam. It's very confusing. I believe they're trying to regulate the industry over there now. I don't really know the history behind this. The data seems to fluctuate constantly.'

Now a tiny bump back in the right direction. 'Tell me about Kiaraa.'

'She is, she *was* older than me by three years. She always showed musical talent, even as a toddler. I preferred breaking things!'

'What sort of things?'

'I never liked dolls. I always liked robots. There were robot toys that you could change into spaceships and cars. Kind of like *Transformers*, you know? I loved playing with them. Having adventures. But I wanted to see how they worked. I used to take them apart, and if they would not come apart, I used to use something to *make* them come apart, a hammer, a saucepan, anything. Then I would try to put them back together.'

'Did it work?'

She grins. 'Generally, not. I was always getting told off. My parents were not rich. I didn't understand how much things cost. I like to think it was the scientist in me trying to get out.

'Eventually, I went to Ewha Womans University in Seoul. I was in the ELTEC College of Engineering. I studied computer science and engineering and then nanoscience, then I studied for a PhD in SKKU, that's Sungkyunkwan University. And here I am today; creating the future!'

'So did you and Kiaraa get on when you were kids?'

'Well, three years is quite an age gap when you are young, but yes, we did. We hung out together quite a lot, more when we were teenagers, yes? Even though she was older than me, she used to always ask my advice about clothes and makeup and how to talk to boys. I was more popular with boys when I was in school, and she was always asking me how I did it.'

'What was your secret?'

'No secret! Just – I don't know – what would you say? I knew how to twist them around my little finger! It was intuitive, I guess. I was terrible. I was a terrible tease. I could always tell when they liked me.

'By the time I was fourteen, boys used to call the house all the time and if my dad or my mom answered the telephone they would hang up. It would drive my folks mad. But Kiaraa caught up with me eventually. She was beautiful and elegant and funny and when she was studying in Paris, she was quite the charmer, as I used to call it. Lots of affairs with, um…' She smiles. 'She was, you know…'

I let this hang in the air for a couple of seconds. 'What?'

'You know. Both sexes.'

'Ah. OK.'

'Do you think that is not a good thing?'

'It's the work of Satan.'

She smiles. 'It was a big secret for a long, long time. She mentioned it for the first time in an interview with the BBC a few years back. She always kept it from our parents, though. They would not have approved. She'd mentioned it in a few interviews, in fact, but she would never have done that when they were alive. It was not a big thing for her, just part of life. Kind of gay stuff isn't illegal in South Korea, but it was much easier for her to blossom in Europe, if you know what I mean.'

'But she spoke to you about it.'

'We talked to each other about everything. We always had done.'

'What did you think of her career?'

'I was *so* proud! If I was somewhere and people started talking about her and they didn't know, I'd always say "That's my sister!".'

And now she bursts into tears. Oh, God.

'I'm sorry. I'm sorry.'

'Forget it.'

She stands up and scoops a handful of paper tissues from a box on her desk, then sits down again, blows her nose, and mops her eyes. The tears run down her face in a slow trickle. She sniffs. She sniffs again.

'I take it you know what happened to my sister, at least to a degree.'

'Suzanna gave me the basics.'

Suddenly, her tone becomes glacial. 'I want whoever murdered her to be caught and punished. I'm almost six months pregnant. They have done the tests. It will be a girl. I will name her after my sister. I do not want her to be born into a world where my sister's murderer or murderers are still at large. I will not stop, do you understand?' Her voice becomes shaky. 'I will not stop. It has been two years. Two years since it happened. I cannot believe that whoever did it is still out there. Still out there thinking they have got away with it. Living whatever sort of life they live. Laughing and joking.'

Tears, head shaking, tissues being picked apart. I want to sit next to her and put my arm around her. The crying would stop, she'd look up at me, and without a word being spoken our lips would meet.

I must get a therapist… maybe two.

'Laughing and joking,' she repeats.

I give her a couple of moments to recover.

I want another coffee.

She looks at me and smiles. 'Sorry. I don't know – it just happens sometimes.'

'I understand.'

'I'm not like this. I'm…'

'Believe me, I'll do everything I can to hunt them down, Micha. Listen. I'll need to speak to whoever's in charge of the murder investigation.'

'Yes. Yes, of course. It's Detective Chief Inspector Hugh Sallow. He is Homicide and Major Crime Command. They are in Putney. I know he is not pleased that I have used private companies. I suspect he thinks that it reflects badly on him, but I think he understands all the same.

'He was very angry about the whole affair. What they did to her, I mean. He will talk to you if I ask him to. There are details about Kiaraa's death that you will have to get from him. I cannot bring myself to discuss them or even think about them.

'I sometimes think he is even holding things back from *me*, but I don't think it is malicious or patronising. I will text him now and ask him to call me. You can never ring him up, there's always a message. Very vexatious.'

She picks up her mobile. I watch the concentration on her face as she taps away at ultra-high-speed using just her middle finger. I wish I could do that.

'I made a big donation to a police charity he favours. Police Care UK. Do you know it? Furnishes financial and practical support to police and their families. Provides counselling and psychotherapy. That is why I am sure he will speak to you. It is manipulative of me, I know. It is how things are often done in Korea.'

She places her mobile on the table and gives her face a final mop.

'There. Now I am ready. I have cried enough for today. I must look like a mess. What must you think? I would never let employees see me like this. I will be professional now. You may ask me anything about this matter. What I cannot answer in detail, or with the correct perspective, Mr Bahk will be able to. But as I said, some details upset me greatly, and I may leave the room for a short while as they are discussed.'

She walks to her desk once more and presses a small piece of pear-shaped blue plastic, which I have to assume is an intercom of some sort. 'Aera. Could you send Mr Bahk in, please?'

5

SOME COOL GUY

At first glance, Baek-Hayeon Bahk looks like he's in his late twenties, though his close-cut steel-grey hair and fierce demeanour tells me he can't be, and you could probably add ten years or so to my assessment.

He's stocky, five eight or nine, weighs about a hundred and ninety pounds and his posture tells me it's all muscle and that he's ex-military. When Aera shows him in, he strides straight towards me, shakes my hand and bows. I bow back. His eye contact is serious, curious, intimidating.

He wears a uniform like the reception staff, but his is dark blue, not grey, and he doesn't have an ID badge. He looks at Micha, as if for permission to speak. She nods at him.

'Good afternoon, Mr Beckett. I am Baek-Hayeon Bahk. I am chief security director for Sansuyu UK & Ireland.' He smiles, though it's more like a grimace, and a little scary. He points a stubby finger at me. 'Now *you* are more what I expect a private investigator to look like!' He turns to Micha. 'Some cool guy, eh? Just like the movies.'

Micha nods and grins. 'Like Han Suk-kyu in *Double Agent* and *Shiri*!'

They both have a nervous, stressed laugh at this, whatever it is. I must look these films up, if films they are.

'I make a point of dressing to impress,' I say, smiling at them.

'Dressing to impress. That's good,' says Baek-Hayeon. He narrows his eyes. 'Those other guys we've seen. I keep it to myself, but – out of shape, you know? Flabby. Gross. Sleazy. Not interested. Old blasé ex-police. Money, money. Also, I felt they didn't take us seriously. Hard to put a finger on. Maybe because we are foreign, you know?'

'You're *foreign*? I'm leaving right now.'

More overwrought laughter. They're both pretty tense. Micha suggests that we sit at the dining table. She moves the purple roses down one end. That honey scent isn't so pleasant when you're this close.

Both sit directly opposite me. Strong eye contact. I place my notebook on the table and get ready to write.

'Please go ahead, Daniel,' says Micha. 'Whoever can answer your questions will answer them, if that is OK with you.'

'Sure. Tell me about the night that Kiaraa was kidnapped.'

Now there's a definite chill in the air and all the laughter and informality evaporates. Micha's posture instantly becomes more rigid. She interlaces her fingers beneath her bump and stares straight ahead, as if in shock.

This is exactly how Suzanna described her behaviour during their meeting last week and I wonder if she needs therapy of some sort.

After a few tense seconds have passed, she and Baek-Hayeon exchange tormented glances. Who will speak first? Who wants to? Will anyone? Shall I make coffee then flirt with Aera for a few minutes? Baek-Hayeon finds a spot on the floor to investigate. It's Micha who composes herself and makes a shaky start.

'Two years ago, almost to the day,' she says. 'Kiaraa had been out to dinner with some friends.'

'Which restaurant?'

'Abd El Wahab in Pont Street, Knightsbridge. Lebanese.'

'Do you have the date, please?'

'September the 12th.'

'Who was she there with?'

'Nozomi Terada. Gordon Hepburn. Odette Fournier and her husband Mathéo. Sheila Hulme.'

'Tell me about them. A sentence each.'

'Nozomi Terada is a first violinist with the NHK Symphony Orchestra. Odette Fournier...' She pauses for a moment, then resumes. 'Odette Fournier is the director of a textile company which is based in Paris and London. Her husband Mathéo is a book publisher: non-fiction, political and philosophical subject matter.

'Gordon Hepburn is a classical tenor, but I don't know who he sings with. He is quite famous in his field. He is Scottish. Sheila Hulme works for the UK branch of Lysander Records, Kiaraa's record company. Oh, I think Mr Hepburn is with the same label. He is also with the same agent, Devika Pussett at Cadence.'

'Was this a purely social event?'

'Yes, it was. It was Nozomi Terada's last night out in the country before she returned to Japan. It was she who booked the restaurant. It was a favourite of hers when she was in London, and it was a favourite of Kiaraa's.'

'Did everyone leave together?'

'No. Kiaraa was feeling tired. She hadn't been playing, but she'd been in a recording studio all day in St John's Wood, I think listening to some recent work before they released it. Something to do with Dolby Atmos. It adds height channels to sound, though in my opinion, is not as good as our ProLab XZ90 system. She left a good hour before everybody else, at approximately ten-thirty p.m.'

'How did she intend to get home? A cab?'

'She walked. She only lived a couple of streets away. She owns – owned a house in Chesham Place. Number 37.'

Chesham Place. Belgravia. Georgian. Expensive. Posh. Lots of embassies. The sort of houses you'd walk past and wonder how much they cost and who could afford them.

I scribble the address down. 'Well, that must have been a walk of, what, five minutes?'

'That's right. Not far at all. She lives, *lived* almost across the road from the Embassy of Spain.'

'Did she tell everyone else she was going straight home?'

'Yes.'

'And they all knew how long that would take?'

'Almost certainly. One or two of them would have been to her house on occasion. Dinner parties. It did not happen often, though. She preferred to socialise elsewhere. She regarded her home as her sanctuary.'

'Did she live alone?'

'She did.'

'Housekeeper? Cleaner?'

'Some company came to clean once a month. She was always present when they were there, if she was in the country of course. If she was not, they didn't come.'

'Did the police speak to the people she'd had dinner with?'

'Yes. They were unable to help, according to Detective Chief Inspector Sallow. He said that he'd spent an hour with each of them, and another detective, a woman detective, had also interviewed them.

'Nozomi Terada rescheduled her flight home so that she could speak to both officers. They spent the same amount of time with Kiaraa's agent, Devika Pussett. They also spoke to me, of course. Mr Sallow was determined to be exhaustive. He said it was as if Kiaraa had disappeared into thin air after she'd left Abd El Wahab. He was most perplexed, I think, though he tried to conceal it.'

'So, to the best of your knowledge,' I say, 'She didn't get as far as her house, if that's where she was going.'

'That is correct,' says Micha. 'Her bed had not been slept in. There is an internal smart alarm system – a Yuhwa TT7992. One of ours. She would have disabled it upon entering the house. It would have recorded the time she came in.

'When we checked, the last time it had been set was 7.44 that evening, about the time she would have gone out. It indicated that she had not come back.'

'Is there any chance that it could have had some sort of malfunction?'

Baek-Hayeon Bahk sits up and looks shocked. 'It is a top-of-the range Sansuyu alarm system, Mr Beckett!' he says indignantly. 'It would not fail. Impossible. I was personally involved in the software design.'

Micha smiles and taps his forearm to calm him down. 'That is true,

Daniel. It is a failsafe system, but we ran three comprehensive checks and there was no sign of a defect.'

'Would you mind if I had someone take a look at it?'

She frowns. 'Who?'

'Just a sometime colleague. Someone who could bypass a system like that and make it look as if it had not been tampered with. If there's a fault, or evidence of unauthorised interference, he'll spot it.'

They both look astonished, particularly Baek-Hayeon, who's obviously taking this as a personal affront.

'Certainly,' says Micha. 'If you think it might help.'

'I would like to meet the person who could circumvent such a system in that manner,' says Baek-Hayeon, recovering slightly. 'It would be most informative and useful, I suspect.'

'I'll see what I can do. But I warn you, he'll take it as a consultation and will charge you. He doesn't come cheap.'

'It could be that there is a design fault in the software, Mr Beckett. If that is the case, I would like to know what it is.'

'No problem.' I turn to Micha. 'Just out of curiosity, what's going on with the house now? Does someone else live there? Is it rented out?'

'No. It is as she left it. All the utilities have been switched off apart from the electricity. The alarms, you understand. I have not been inside since the police took a look around. That was almost two years ago now. I can't face it. I can't face it and I can't sell it. It's mine now. All of it is mine. Her recording royalties, everything. Our parents died six years ago, so I'm her sole heir. I really wish I wasn't. Excuse me.'

She gets up and heads towards a cleverly camouflaged door on the far side of the office. I think it's a bathroom. She goes inside and closes the door behind her.

Two things have already piqued my interest.

That little pause after she mentioned Odette Fournier.

Also, Micha's a wealthy woman, but she's considerably wealthier now. Does that make her a suspect? It seems unlikely, but you never can tell.

'You are not an army man? Or should I say an ex-army man?' asks Baek-Hayeon.

He looks anxious. It's as if he's appealing to me to make normal conversation.

'No. I'm not.'

He nods as if he already knew this. 'I was a soldier in the Korean Army – what you would call a colonel – serving in the 11th Special Forces Brigade. Our special pocket patch emblem is the Golden Bat. I always, ah, wished that I had been in the 3rd Special Forces Brigade. Their emblem is the Flying Tiger. I always thought that was better than the Golden Bat. I am a veteran of the East Timorese crisis.'

'Must have been tough.'

He turns his head to the right and tugs at his shirt collar to reveal a three-inch scar at the base of his neck. 'Bullet graze. A .223 Remington fired from a Daewoo K2 assault rifle. One of my own people. Friendly fire. I was incandescent with rage,' His eyes bulge madly. 'Another centimetre and I'd have been dead.'

Thankfully, Micha returns. She seems OK. But she's been crying, and she can tell I've spotted it.

'I'm sorry.'

'It's OK.'

She composes herself and continues. 'Kiaraa was expected at a meeting at her agent's the next day at nine-thirty a.m. This would have been the 13th of September. When she didn't turn up, the agent tried to get her on her mobile, but to no avail.

'So, Devika – her agent – rang Odette Fournier, presumably as she was present at the dinner the previous night, but Odette had not heard from Kiaraa. Then Devika rang me. I did not know about the dinner. Apparently, Odette said Kiaraa had been feeling tired after the recording studio, like I told you. So, I thought that she was still tired and had forgotten to call her agent to cancel the meeting.

'Less than an hour later, I got the first phone call. This was ten-thirty a.m.'

Baek-Hayeon now takes over. 'The telephone call was from someone calling themselves Mr Munro, though I have my reservations about that being their real name.'

'He had what you would call a regionless UK accent,' says Micha.

'Unplaceable. I am not an expert on British accents from all the regions, but I would say it was not distinctive, at least not to me. Not cockney or Scottish or anything like that. You might say well-spoken, I think. His age was difficult to establish, but I would say over forty years.'

'You didn't record these calls, by any chance?'

'No. We did not.'

This was when the serious stuff started. This Mr Munro told Micha that he had kidnapped Kiaraa and wanted three million in cash for her safe return. If the money was not delivered in forty-eight hours, he would kill her, and it would not be a good death, and he would enjoy doing it.

Under no circumstances was she to contact the police. If she did that, he said, he would know, and Kiaraa was dead, and it would be Micha's fault. She would have to live with it for the rest of her life.

He was, she said, very business-like. He told her he'd call again in four hours. Until then, she should think hard, and prepare herself to organise the cash.

'I was stupid, I know,' says Micha, 'But it was so incredible, I thought it had to be a crank call. I cut him off. I tried to call Kiaraa just for my peace of mind, but she was still not answering her mobile.'

When the second call came, Mr Munro put Kiaraa on, or, at least, allowed her to be heard. There was no doubt whatsoever in Micha's mind that it was her. She was sobbing, mumbling, possibly drugged or incapacitated in some other way. She sounded terrified.

Micha heard her being slapped or punched and some men talking in the background. There was also some laughter. Munro repeated his demand. He said he would call again in another four hours, and she had better be ready with the arrangements. He sounded calm and confident.

'How many men did you hear in the background?'

'There was Mr Munro who was doing all the talking and, I think, two other voices. Two men. I mentioned that to the police. Unplaceable accents again. Difficult to be accurate, though. It could have been just one other man. My focus was on Kiaraa.'

By now Micha was extremely concerned. She called Baek-Hayeon into her office and explained the situation to him.

'Why didn't you immediately call the police?' I ask.

A quick exchange of glances. Baek-Hayeon silently asks Micha's permission to answer this question. His expression is grim.

'The, the KNPA, Mr Beckett, the Korean National Police Agency that is, has the reputation of being one of the most effective police organisations in the world. But like many citizens there, we have no confidence in them, related to long-term reports of corruption.

'I am sure that it is not the case that the whole agency is corrupt, but that suspicion of the police, well, we carry it with us, do you understand? We know this view is largely wrong, especially when we are in foreign countries, but it is ingrained, nonetheless. The KNPA have a chequered history. There are even reports of police brutality. So...'

'So, our first instinct,' continues Micha, 'Was to deal with a matter like this by ourselves. And as the man, Mr Munro, said that he would kill Kiaraa, and it would not be a good death, it seemed that involving the police would be unwise, maybe even disastrous, especially after I heard Kiaraa being, being *maltreated* like that.

'I believed what he said. Was it panic? I don't know. His tone of voice made me believe the truth of it. I suppose it's foolish, but we are a big, powerful company. We felt – *I* felt – we could deal with anything.'

Well, too late now. Already, I hate these guys.

That hint of weak, illogical emotional blackmail in there that criminals of this type always resort to: if anything happens to the victim, it'll be *your* fault, not mine. *You* killed them, not me. It's pathetic, but it pushes all the right buttons.

I wonder; did Munro know about the Korean attitude to police? Was his research that deep? Was he dumb? Was he smart?

And how would he know if Micha called the cops? Was that just baseless dramatic bullshit? Something you couldn't risk calling his bluff on? Or was it the truth?

'Can we just go back a bit? This guy's voice. Munro. Did you pick up an intelligence or directness in the way he spoke to you? Any sort of professionalism? Not as a criminal, more in the sense of you could imagine him being a teacher, or you could imagine him being a company director, a manager. An impression, no matter how vague.'

She frowns and stares at the dining table. I watch her eyes. She's looking increasingly upset with each moment that passes.

'I have tried to forget, Daniel. This is not easy. To recall in the way you want. But maybe – this is silly – maybe someone who liked bossing people around. In a job, perhaps. Someone who thought they were better than everyone else. Someone self-important. Someone who might be a workplace bully. Someone who you would not want to work under. Pompous. Someone who, underneath all the bluster, was a coward. Not a nice man. But educated, possibly. Yes. Educated.'

Baek-Hayeon looks both baffled and mildly contemptuous. I think he prefers blacks and whites, not nebulous conjecture.

'Perhaps,' she continues, 'Someone who wanted to be in charge of things but had never been in charge of things. I had not thought of it in this way before, and I may be overthinking now. Once you start expressing ambiguities, it can lead you down the wrong path. You have to think of how difficult it would be for you, Daniel, to assess the personality of some random person in South Korea from just listening to them speak.'

'I'm sure. So, what did you do next?'

'The third time Mr Munro called – this was six-thirty p.m. – I told him that one of my managers – I didn't want to give Baek-Hayeon's proper title in case it alarmed him – would help me deal with his demands as I was not confident that I could do it all on my own. I played the helpless woman. Some instinct told me that this would seem feasible to him.

'I told him I would be getting the money the following morning. It would take some time as I had to deal with three different banks. He seemed to accept this. It was true, but I was afraid he might have doubts and harm Kiaraa. I handed him over to Baek-Hayeon to make the arrangements.'

'It was a black-and-white situation, as far as I was concerned,' says Baek-Hayeon, his confidence returning. 'You give these men the money they want, and you get Kiaraa back unharmed. It is what I would have done if I were in their shoes. Why create more trouble for yourself?

'I did not perceive for one single moment that they would resort to murder after receiving the money. Why do it? Who needs that sort of trouble?'

'Not necessarily true, I'm afraid, Baek-Hayeon. Just that comment about Kiaraa's death being Micha's fault if she didn't pay up rings alarm bells. Guilt-tripping, victim blaming, however you want to spin it. It's sadistic. It's rubbing salt in the wound. It's cheap manipulation.

'It shows a lack of compassion and indicates someone who thinks nothing of adding additional suffering to an already bad situation. That makes them unpredictable and dangerous, maybe sociopathic, or worse.

'You must put that comment out of your mind, Micha, by the way. In no way was any of this your fault. Did you pass on Mr Munro's telephone number to the police?'

'Yes, I did,' she replies, looking disconcerted despite my assurances. 'It was actually three telephone numbers. A different one for each call. He didn't bother to conceal the numbers. The police said that the lines no longer existed. They said that they were probably pay-as-you-go mobiles that were discarded after each call.'

'Did they follow that up?'

'No. I don't know. Maybe. One of the detectives said they would investigate, but I did not hear anything about it again, so presumably nothing came of it. The detective did not seem too optimistic.'

'Do you still have a record of those numbers somewhere?'

'Yes. I wrote them down.'

'Good. I'd like a copy of them before I go. OK, Baek-Hayeon. Tell me about their arrangements for delivering the ransom.'

'Mr Munro informed me that there would be a white Fiat Ducato panel van parked in Elder Street, the day after we had arranged the cash situation. That would be the 15th of September.'

'Where is Elder Street?'

'It's not far from here,' he says, nodding to himself. 'Ten minutes by car. Roughly north-east of the City of London. Off Commercial Street. Spitalfields zone. London E1. Mr Munro said that the van would be parked there between eleven-fifteen and eleven twenty-five a.m., not a minute earlier and not a minute later. If I was late, or too early, or did not show up, he would brutally kill Kiaraa. Those were his exact words.'

Brutally. Nice touch. Scary. Piles on the tension.

'Like Micha, I believed him,' he continues. 'I have experience of violent men and think I can detect a bluff. The van would have its back doors wide open, ready for me.

'I was to arrive in that precise time window, place the money in four suitcases in the rear of the Fiat, and then leave immediately without looking back. I was not to close the doors. It was an unequivocal instruction. I found that rather odd, but I was not about to disobey their orders. That might have had catastrophic consequences.'

'That's odd. Wasn't there a risk that someone might steal the money?'

'My thoughts exactly, Mr Beckett. When I first saw the van, I assumed that the doors were being left open for my convenience, but also so that any lurking thieves would think that the driver was nearby and not attempt to steal the van.

'As for not closing them when the money had been deposited, perhaps the same reasoning was behind it. I presume that those doors would not have been open for long, particularly if the criminals were nearby. This was a quiet, well-to-do road, and not, I suspect, a haven for opportunistic thieves. And of course, no one would know what was in the suitcases.

'So. The kidnappers would count the money, make sure it was all there, then they would call us to let us know where we could pick up Kiaraa from.'

'You said four suitcases. Was that enough for three million in cash?'

'He was very specific about that. He told me that three million weighs about 60 kg using new £50 notes. The money could then be fitted in four large suitcases, if packed neatly and precisely.

'The reason it had to be new notes was that used notes would use up too much space. I thought all criminals wanted used notes because of tracing, serial numbers etcetera, but maybe that's just in the movies.'

Are we dealing with experienced professional criminals here?

Laundering, let alone *spending* three million in new fifties would be a major pain unless you had the contacts. So, we're looking at someone running the whole show who's smart, skilled, capable, and has good organisational skills. Just got a little closer to you, fucker. Hi, there.

'Oh. I forgot,' says Baek-Hayeon. 'He even suggested the best suitcases for the job.' He shakes his head with disbelief. 'And where to buy them.'

'Tell me about that.'

'He said that myself and Micha should go to the John Lewis department store in Oxford Street. We should go at different times in different vehicles and even park in different car parks. They suggested leaving an hour between our respective visits. I went first as Micha was with her financiers earlier in the day. Visiting the banks, I mean.

'I was to buy a couple of Samsonite Upscape 4-Wheel 84cm Expandable large suitcases in black, then drive back to our underground car park here. They were very cumbersome to get out of the shop. I was most disgruntled. Micha commented on that, also.'

'Hold on. They actually had those suitcases in stock? In that colour?'

'Yes, they did. For some reason it was quite a relief that I was able to purchase the exact ones.'

So, someone did a recce in that store and had up-to-date information about what was for sale. Or perhaps they did it online. Why would they do that? For a start, they wanted confirmation that their marks would take orders and obey them, no matter how trivial or eccentric. That would also cover the different vehicles/car parks thing, and the van doors being left open after the drop. They were, in a sense, training them. And the suitcases had to be the required size, of course.

But it's also a possibility that he/they got off on manipulation and domination. Is Munro or whoever a covert-aggressor? A narcissist? A psychopath, even?

Controlling the little things is usually a sign of wanting a little power boost; a quick fix of authority when you have none. I'm drifting into psychobabble here, but my gut instinct tells me that Munro is a failure. Though at what, I have no idea.

'It took me almost three hours with the banks,' says Micha. 'Eventually, I only used two of them. I arranged to have the money delivered directly to my office here by our favoured courier service that afternoon. That was the 14th of September, as I said.

'Then, as ordered, I went to that department store and bought two Samsonite Upscape 4-Wheel 84cm Expandable large suitcases in pink. They were in stock, too. Like Baek-Hayeon observed, very cumbersome. I had never bought two suitcases at the same time before. A lady had to help me get them to my car.'

'I think,' says Baek-Hayeon, 'That they would have asked for more money, but that would have made the logistics a little more difficult for us. More suitcases, more time, more risk, more hassle, more suspicion from the banks who might tell someone. I could be mistaken, of course.'

'So, the money arrived, you put it in the suitcases and the next day made the drop.'

'That is correct. Elder Street is a small cul-de-sac with an iron barrier gate down one end blocking your way. A narrow road. Very awkward to park. You could not turn around easily, so had to reverse out when you'd finished. No parking on one side, residential parking, permit only, on the other. Lots of spaces, though. No evidence of traffic wardens or police. At least not when I was there. The van was facing the barrier gate.'

'Security cameras?'

'There was some sort of company down the far end of the road. I did not inspect it closely and I do not know what it was called or what its business was. They had two cameras, both aimed at what looked like the entrance to a garage. The van would have been out of their range by quite a distance, but they were facing the wrong way in any case. I did not see any others. Any other security cameras, that is.'

'What happened next?'

'I got there at 11.17 precisely. September 15th. The white Fiat Ducato van was there, outside number 45. You could not miss it. It was the only van of any type in the road. Its back doors were wide open, and it was empty inside. The street was deserted.

'There were about seven or eight cars parked. There did not appear to be anyone sitting in them. I can't recall the makes of these other cars. I am no expert when it comes to identifying foreign motor vehicles. So. I took the suitcases out of my car, put them in the van, left the doors open as instructed, got back in my car, reversed out and drove away.'

I'll bet anything that one of those parked cars had a spy cam in it. Aimed at the van, watching. It's what I would have done.

'Did the van have a registration number?'

'The registration plate is situated on the back doors of vans of that type, so as they were open, it would not have been visible when I entered the street or when I left it. Besides, my entire focus was on the time window. Ten minutes only, as I said. Less, really. I had tunnel vision without a doubt. Not surprising.'

'Was this a new van? Say, less than five years old?'

'I would say so, yes. Looked very clean. Very new. Clean wheels. Clean tyres. No dents. No dirt. There was a little damage to one of the bumpers, but nothing major. Bumpers on vans like that look very solid, but they are not. I had a Hyundai i800 once. Brand new. Burnt orange. I reversed into a plastic pillar and the bumper cracked in three places.'

'What side was the damage on?'

'Um. That would have been the left side.'

'How many cracks?'

'Just one. Quite thin. Possibly nineteen or twenty centimetres long. You could see a little of the yellow polystyrene foam core beneath. I think someone had attempted to repair the damage, but you could still see it.'

'Tell me about the interior. As much as you can remember.'

'Clean white interior. Spotless. Spacious. Black panels down each side. The more I think about it, the more I think it was brand new. The police were more interested in people that I might have seen in the van or lurking around it, though, not so much what it looked like inside.'

'Did it *smell* new? Like a showroom vehicle?'

He thinks for a moment. 'Yes. That type of *fresh plastic* smell, I think you would call it. Like a new stereo, maybe. But at the same time there were no other distinctive odours. No food smells. No cigarettes.'

'Was it a hassle for you to get four large suitcases in your car? To get them out quickly? What do you drive?'

'I drive a blue SsangYong Korando. Plenty of room and room to spare. Too large a vehicle for that road, really. Difficult to reverse out.'

'So, he came back here,' says Micha. 'And we waited.'

'I was confident that things would go as planned,' says Baek-Hayeon.

When the call came at two p.m., it was the same voice. Munro, or whoever he was, told Micha that everything was in order. Kiaraa was now free to go. She was tied up in the back seat of a red Renault Megane in the car park of Enfield Golf Club. He told Micha that it was a pleasure to do business with such a beautiful lady.

Immediately: how did he know she was a beautiful lady, for beautiful she most certainly is? Was it just a phrase he used when talking to any female? Had he seen her somewhere? Had he been stalking her? I must check to see if her image appears anywhere where a scumbag like this could get easy access to it.

Baek-Hayeon pats Micha's forearm. 'I think *I* should continue the narrative with Mr Beckett at this point, Micha,' he says.

'Of course,' she replies. I get a fragile smile. 'I will just go and have some chit-chat with Aera for a few minutes.'

And she leaves. Baek-Hayeon stands up, straightens his suit jacket, runs a hand through his hair, wipes nothing off both of his sleeves, looks out of one of the windows, sits down again and gives me one of his alarming grimaces. Now what?

6

FISHING FOR COMPLIMENTS

The first thing that's going through my head is wouldn't it be marvellous if we could all go back in time, and as soon as Mr Munro bestowed that first phone call on Micha, she got in touch with me. But wishful thinking isn't going to bring Kiaraa back.

To Micha's credit, I'm not picking up any rancour from her about the three million she's lost. It's clearly of no importance to her whatsoever. But it interests me that the kidnappers knew she could acquire that amount of cash in forty-eight hours. They'd done their research on her. Or one of them knew her.

Baek-Hayeon Bahk seems like a straight shooter, but he was clearly out of his depth dealing with a situation like that.

There was a chance, I suppose, that things could have gone the black-and-white way he'd imagined – you pay the money, you get her back – but there's no guarantee that paying a kidnapping ransom will be one hundred per cent effective and you have to remember that you're dealing with criminals, who are never the brightest or most moral of bunnies.

The money thing is interesting, though; knowing how much new high-denomination banknotes weigh, how many suitcases they can be stuffed in, and which specific suitcases to buy. Certainly not general knowledge. Are we looking at someone who'd done this before?

Perhaps many times? Or were they beginners and just making it up as they went along?

Then there's the question of letting Micha hear Kiaraa being the subject of violence during the second phone call. It would certainly reinforce the idea that these were serious guys, but it was an unprofessional thing do that early on in a kidnap situation and makes it more likely that they were novices, at least in the abduction game. Or they just didn't care.

If you were a pro, you'd want to give the impression that the kidnapee was, for the moment, safe and unharmed; that there was a good chance that they'd be released in the same state. That would be the best way to get your money. But if I'd heard that sort of savagery, I'd be under no illusions about the probable outcome of the whole thing.

Also, and this may be nothing, if I was the driver of that Fiat van, I'd have to make damn sure that there would be somewhere for me to park at the allotted time, otherwise the whole operation would fall apart. How would I do that?

At the very least, I'd have to do a walk-through every day for a week or so before the drop to get an idea of the parking situation, unless, of course, I already knew it. Perhaps I lived in that road or in one of the adjacent roads. Perhaps I walked down that road every morning at the same time to get to work. These are unlikely scenarios, however.

If I was unfamiliar with the road, if I wasn't a local, I'd have to stagger the times I was present, maybe even changing my appearance, so I was not a familiar face to any lurking traffic wardens, workers, or residents. Whatever, I could not leave finding a parking spot to chance. Certainly something to think about. Or maybe not. Maybe it was dumb luck.

Another alternative would be to brazen it out and stick a few traffic cones in the space that I wanted. Or have an accomplice park another vehicle there and drive off when he saw me arrive. Also, leaving the back doors of the van open throughout the drop was an interesting MO. Lots of possible reasons, but one thing it tells me was that the kidnappers were in the vicinity, and they were cocky.

Mr Munro is an appealing puzzle. Let's assume he was the main man. Well-spoken, educated, over forty, fairly good planning, logistical and organisational skills, ruthless, sadistic, manipulative, and criminal. And an asshole; let's not forget that. Uses a different mobile for each call, but that's a no-brainer, I'd have done the same myself.

Then there's Micha's impression and my psychobabble. A coward. Bossy. Resentful. Fearful. Vain. Powerless. A failure. All qualities that could push you towards crime, but equally could not.

He knew Micha's direct line, though he could have got that from Kiaraa. Would the Sansuyu switchboard have given that number out for any reason? I'll have to check. Maybe there were a few 'rehearsal' calls, but this is two years ago now and I don't know how long records are kept for, or if they're even kept at all. Kiaraa could also have been the source of Munro's description of Micha as beautiful, but I somehow don't think that would have been the case.

Munro also knew who Kiaraa was. Now that's interesting in itself. I'd never heard of her, though she was plainly popular in her field. Is he a classical music fan, or did he read about her in a dentist's waiting room and think 'Yes'? Did he research her family, or did he get lucky?

Then there's the small matter of Kiaraa being lifted on her way back home from a restaurant she was familiar with after leaving a private dinner that under half a dozen people, apart from her agent, knew about.

Who else was aware of this gathering? Was it in the papers? Was it mentioned in some social media account or other? Was there someone parked outside the restaurant, waiting? Were they *in* the restaurant, sitting at the next table? Had they been planning this for a long time and were prepared for a decent opportunity? I'm beginning to wonder if I can keep all these threads in my head by the time that Micha returns.

Assuming that Kiaraa was heading directly from the restaurant to her home, it's quite handy that this happened almost two years ago to the day. It means the light will be the same at around ten-thirty tonight.

I'm going to have to retrace her possible steps and take a detailed look around the area. A visit to Elder Street may also bear fruit, though I'm sure the police will have given it a good scouring.

I'm also going to have to find out as much as I can about Kiaraa

Jeong and her life. Small, possibly inconsequential things. Things that the police would be unlikely to concern themselves with.

Baek-Hayeon sits down opposite me and folds his arms. He scowls. 'I didn't want her to go through all of this again, to hear it all again. I'm sure she goes through it over and over again in her mind all of the time. I know from experience that traumatic events can get their claws into your brain and not let go. Also, I suspect you would like her mind to be clear when she resumes this meeting.'

'Of course. Let's hear about when you went to the golf club.'

He takes a deep breath then purses his lips. He doesn't like talking about this. He's troubled. 'I used my mobile telephone to navigate to the Enfield Golf Club. I was not sure what I would find there. By that I mean I did not know whether such a place would be busy at that time of day.

'As soon as I drove into the parking area, I saw the car. The red Renault Megane. It was on its own at the far end of the car park by some large grey bins. There were only three other cars there, all unattended.'

'Do you remember what kind of cars they were?'

'Yes, I do. This time, I made a point of it. They were nowhere near the Megane. They were near the entrance to the car park. They were where you would park if you were going into the club. There was a dark orange Toyota, a white Kia Sportage and a metallic blue Ford, possibly a Ford Puma, but I wasn't one hundred per cent positive.'

'That's very useful. Keep going.'

'Everything was quiet and there was nobody about. I parked a few spaces away from the Megane and got out. I could not see Kiaraa in the back seat. My heart sank. I thought we had been lied to. Then I remembered that Mr Munro said she would be tied up, so I thought that maybe she had fallen over inside the car and could not be seen from the outside.

'I was very cautious. Booby traps, you know? Easily improvised, especially in a motor vehicle: door, steering wheel, clutch, an interesting-looking package on the passenger seat. I looked inside the car, and it was obvious that there was no one within.

'I carefully tried the doors, but they were all locked. I was looking for doors that were partially open. That is one sign of a booby trap: concealed trigger mechanisms, always a danger. Then I tried the boot, but that was firmly locked, too. I squatted down, placed my ear next to it and counted to fifty, but heard nothing. I decided to break the lock. I always carry a Leatherman multi-tool. I forced the lock with the primary blade. Then I opened the boot.'

He stops his narrative and looks out of the window. He's clenching his jaw over and over again. He decides to get it all out of the way in one burst, and I can't say I blame him. 'Kiaraa was in the boot of the car. She was dead. Naked. Foetal position. Ankles and wrists tied. Multiple stab wounds. Many minor cuts. Bruises. Some red and livid, some darker and older. And...her fingers and thumbs had been cut off. From what I could see, they were not present in the boot. I stepped back. I did not touch anything. I called the police straight away. This was now a murder case.'

'Did the fingers and thumbs turn up?'

'They did not. This occurrence was particularly distressing to Micha. Unless it is totally ineluctable, I would not bring up this topic with her.'

Both of us take a deep breath, almost simultaneously. OK. Munro and/or his cohorts are dangerous vicious psychopaths.

'Naturally, the police would not fully confide in me,' he continues. 'But I think there were elements of the case that they were not troubling Ms Jeong with either, and they asked me to keep what I had seen to myself.

'The police officer I spoke to said that many details in a case like this were kept from relatives, the press etcetera. I think sometimes it can be to set a trap, do you understand? If someone – say a suspect – talks about something that they should not or could not know about.'

'I get it. What happened then?'

'As soon as I had spoken to the police, I called Ms Jeong to tell her the bad news. The police wanted to call her first, but I thought it would be better if the news came from me. They did not agree, but I did it anyway. The police are not experts on everything, and I was now as close to a family member that Ms Jeong had in this country.

'The police sent two officers, a female detective sergeant and a male detective constable, to be with her while I waited in the car park. They spoke of sending some sort of counsellor to be with her, but I'm not sure that happened in the end.

'I went and stood by the car. There was nothing I could do, obviously, but I felt that...someone...should be near to Kiaraa; someone she knew, as it were, someone who was close to being family. Then the police arrived, and the car park and the club became a crime scene.

'Then they took the, er, they took the body away and all the usual protocol, you understand? This may be my paranoia raising its ugly head, but I felt as if the police were observing me as if I was a suspect. But I stood my ground and met their gaze. I had been a soldier, after all, and they were only police.

'Then I drove to the police station to make my statement. I followed one of the police cars. It seemed like a long drive, Mr Beckett. A long drive.'

'Just a couple of things. As far as you know, did the police check out that white Fiat Ducato? Search for it? The one you put the money in?'

'Yes. They were unable to trace it. I don't know if they are still looking.'

'And what about the residents of Elder Street?'

'I believe there was a thorough house-to-house enquiry. I do not think it bore fruit. I am not surprised. I do not think that the kidnappers would have operated outside their own doorstep. On the other hand, perhaps the police were hoping that someone might have seen someone or something. I understand that the residents of adjacent roads were interviewed also.'

He frowns, looks rattled, then recovers. 'I have to say, Mr Beckett, quite confidentially, that I would be pleased to get my hands on these people.'

'I'm sure you would, Baek-Hayeon.' I hand him one of my business cards. 'That'll be all for the moment and I'm sorry you had to relive those details. I know all of this was two years ago, but if anything pops into your mind that you think might be useful, anything at all, no matter how inconsequential, give me a call, any time of the day or night.'

'I will be sure to, Mr Beckett. I will fetch Ms Jeong. Very pleasurable to meet you. I sincerely hope you can succeed where others have failed. For all the weaknesses of the KNPA, I find myself wondering how they would have dealt with a case like this. Savagely, I suspect. My best wishes to you and good luck. Oh!' He hands me his business card. 'For you. You can always call me if you need anything.'

A brief bone-crusher handshake and off he goes to reception. I stuff his card in my wallet.

When Micha returns a couple of minutes later, she looks a little calmer. She's holding a smart white Sansuyu carrier bag with that photograph of the Chinese dogwood branch on the side. She places the bag on the coffee table, and we sit opposite each other on the comfy sofas once more.

'So now you know,' she says.

'Now I know.'

She smiles at me, but tears start to prick her eyes again.

'There are a few more things I need from you, Micha. Firstly, you said that you hadn't been in Kiaraa's house for close on two years. I'd like to have a look inside. I'll do it tonight. Do you have the keys?'

'Yes. There is a passcode required also for the keypad entry lock. It has remained the same since she lived there. I could not see any point in changing it. I will write it down for you in a moment.

'There is also a second alarm inside. The one we mentioned. The Yuhwa TT7992. On the wall to your right as you go through the front door. That also has a code number which must be entered within thirty seconds of the front door being opened. Remember, there is no gas or water now. And you wanted those mobile telephone numbers. Oh. And there is something else.'

She hands me the carrier bag. 'This may be of no use to you, but I thought you should have it for background information perhaps. There are some of Kiaraa's CDs in a little bag, plus her Blu-ray.

'Also, a programme for one of her concerts in Wigmore Hall in London, an interview with her in *Classical Music Magazine* and another in *Vanity Fair*. She is on the cover on both of those. It – I don't know – it may help you get to know her. Something might, um, inspire you.

Could I please ask you to return them to me when you have finished with them?'

'Of course. And thanks. I've got one question about what you said earlier. Kiaraa's agent knew about that dinner that Kiaraa attended. How did she know?'

'Oh. That would have been...did I tell you that Gordon Hepburn was with the same agent? He had had a meeting with her earlier that day and had mentioned it in passing.'

'But when Kiaraa didn't make that nine-thirty meeting the next day, it was Odette Fournier that the agent rang. As opposed to, say, you.'

'Well, she would probably have known that Odette would have been at that dinner, and, um...' She widens her eyes at me.

'Oh. OK. I get it. In case I ever get to speak to any of these people, does Madame Fournier's husband know about this? In fact, do *any* of that crowd know?'

'I don't know. I don't think so. Only Devika. And me, of course. I think it would be discreet not to mention it unless it is brought up. Kiaraa and Devika Pussett, her agent, were very close. They had been good friends for several years. She would have confided in her, but not anyone else.'

'Were there any other relationships you were aware of? Apart from Odette, I mean?'

'I know she was involved with a man, and it had been going on for quite a while by the time she passed away. I do not know who he was, however. A mystery man. It wasn't as if she was keeping it a big secret. Sometimes with her relationships I got a name, other times I didn't. It just never really came up in conversation, whereas Odette did once or twice for various reasons. She and Odette quarrelled sometimes.'

'About what?'

'Silly things. Lovers' tiffs, I think you would say. I suspect it was a fiery relationship. Intense and unrestrained. Kiaraa did not do things by halves in any aspect of her life.'

'Did the police know about Odette?'

'Yes. I told them. And I told them about the mystery man.'

'What did they think about that?'

'I don't know. It was never referred to again. Not to me, at least. One of the women police officers said that they would be questioning everyone they spoke to about this person and looking for evidence of a relationship in Kiaraa's personal effects and correspondence, but sometimes leads like that can be difficult to follow up, particularly if someone wished to keep parts of their private life a secret from others.

'The thing with Odette and the mystery man; I think they were going on concurrently. Kiaraa would have seen no problem with that. Morally, I mean. The different sides of her sexuality were strictly separated. She would not have seen one as being unfaithful to the other. She may have kept it a secret from Odette because she didn't want to hurt her. Who can tell?

'Mr Sallow said he mentioned the mystery man to her, and she seemed a little caught off balance, but not particularly upset or surprised. She knew Kiaraa too well for that, I think. I suspect they had a similar outlook on such matters. After all, Odette was cheating on her husband with Kiaraa.

'There was another man I knew about by name, but that finished about three, four years before Kiaraa died. It was Lucas Quaresma, the violinist. He was from Argentina.'

'As far as you know, is there any way that that dinner could have been in the public domain? Could it have been on social media?'

'Very doubtful. It was not Kiaraa's way, and her friends were similarly media shy.'

'What about the restaurant itself?'

'Kiaraa had been there many times for several years before her death. I don't think they would dream of publicising her visits. I have been there myself. They are very attentive and discreet. They would not have wished to lose a customer like her. They liked her. Everyone who knew her liked her.'

'Munro called you on your direct line. How would he have known that number?'

'I truly don't know. If he had called the switchboard here, they would have asked him who he was and why he wanted to speak to me. It would not have been easy. Even then, he would have been connected to Aera, who would have done a second screening before passing the call on to me.

'This is intentional. I do not have the time to take unnecessary telephone calls. I am – I am impossible to get hold of, you might say.

'My direct number is something else entirely. At present, fourteen people have it. Business only. Kiaraa was an exception to that decree, as is Mr Bahk. Perhaps Mr Munro obtained it from her under duress. That would seem to be the only credible explanation.'

'I'd like the names of the other people who have that number. Who they are, where they are, and a telephone contact if possible. Oh. And while I'm here, I'd like the contact numbers for the other dinner party people: Gordon Hepburn, Nozomi Terada, Odette and Mathéo Fournier and Sheila Hulme. I may not need to interview them all, but that information might come in useful.'

'Sheila Hulme, yes, but not the others. I'll ring Devika and see what she can do. I did exchange addresses with Gordon Hepburn, Odette Fournier and a conductor called Henri Mercier at the funeral – I think all three wanted some sort of link to Kiaraa for differing reasons, or perhaps they were being kind – but for some reason we did not exchange telephone numbers.

'I got a Christmas card from Monsieur Mercier last year and the year before. He seemed very nice. He is quite ill now, I understand.'

'And I'd like you to check with the switchboard to see if there were any calls from those three mobile numbers before the ransom request. Even ones that were curtailed after a second or two. Ask them to go back three months. No. Six months.'

She gets up and walks over to her desk. She takes a small notebook from a black leather shoulder bag, opens it up, then burns up the keyboard of her iMac for a couple of minutes. She rips a sheet of paper from an A4 pad and starts writing. It's quite a pleasure to look at her controlled, calm, meticulous movements, and the expression of concentration on her face. I find I'm smiling.

She sits next to me and places the sheet of paper on the table. Her proximity and the Rose D'Arabie perfume are distracting. She points at each item on the sheet.

'Those are the three defunct mobile numbers that Mr Munro used. Sheila Hulme's number is underneath. That is the pass code for the keypad entry lock at Kiaraa's house. This is the pass code for the internal alarm. Remember, thirty seconds or there will be mayhem. Those are the names, positions and contact numbers for the individuals who have my direct telephone number. Oh.'

She gets up and rummages around in the leather shoulder bag once more, returning with a set of keys hanging from a jewelled treble clef key ring.

'These are the front door keys to the house. I'll put these and this sheet in your carrier bag.'

'Great. Oh, and a couple of kind of vague things. What did you think about Munro making you buy those pink suitcases, when Baek-Hayeon was instructed to buy black ones?'

She frowns. 'I hadn't thought about it. Not at all. I suppose it was because pink is a girl's colour. Is that significant?'

'Probably not. You said that when you spoke to Munro for the third time, regarding the ransom, you played the helpless woman. You said that some instinct told you that it would seem logical to him.'

'Yes. I mean, you get a lot of practice at that, growing up in Korea. You can feel when a man wants you to behave in a submissive way. I don't mean submissive in a *sexual* way. I mean...'

'Yeah. I understand. Go on.'

'It may not be their words. It may just be their tone of voice, their inflections. It's very subtle. It would not be something that you, for example, would pick up on if you heard it. I was trying to appease him, I guess. I thought it would make things run smoothly. You might say that I was *humouring* him, even though I thought he was foolish.'

'Also, when Munro had received the money, he told you it was a pleasure for him to do business with such a beautiful lady. What did you make of that?'

She shakes her head dismissively. 'It was just the way he talked. It was all "my dear" and similar phrases. There was a slight air of condescension. Now I think of it, it irked me, I suppose. I'm a scientist and businesswoman. I hold four university degrees. I felt it was mildly disrespectful, as if he was…as if he was putting me in my place by his language. Does that make sense to you?'

'And back to the "beautiful" thing: is it easy to find photographs of you on the net?'

'Oh. Um. Well, the only thing that comes to mind is the Sansuyu website. I don't do interviews or anything like that. Let me show you.'

We walk over to her desk. She touches the base of the ultrawide computer screen with a single finger, and it instantly lights up. I wish mine did that; I have to tap the mouse a thousand times.

A burst of breakneck typing and the website appears. A couple of clicks and there's a page showing photographs of the nine members of the key executive team of Sansuyu UK & Ireland with Micha at the top.

Underneath the photograph 'Dr Mi Cha Jeong, Representative Director, CEO, President'.

She clicks her photograph, and it expands. It's a professional head-and-shoulders shot. Her hair is longer and she's wearing a dark green blouse. There's a Valentino leather choker around her neck. She's smiling and the smile reaches her eyes. Red lipstick, eyeshadow that matches the blouse and a hint of bronze blusher highlighting her cheekbones. She looks breathtakingly beautiful.

'That's it. I think that's the only photograph of me on the net. We don't go in for lots of photographs of our staff. It's a security thing. I'm sure that Baek-Hayeon would be able to explain it to you in more depth, if you wished it.'

'Can anyone access this page?'

'Of course. It's our official site. But I don't see how someone could have looked at that photograph and thought "beautiful",' she shrugs. 'It's just a typical key people shot. All companies like ours have them.'

I turn my head as slowly as possible until I'm looking straight at her, then raise an eyebrow and grin. She can't keep up the pretence a second longer and bursts out laughing, then slaps her hand across her mouth. She suddenly looks fifteen.

'Tell me, Micha. Was "Fishing for Compliments" one of your degree subjects? Perhaps the PhD?'

'Oh!' She hits me on the arm. 'You're so mean!'

'"Mean" is my middle name. I'm going to leave you now. I'll be in touch as soon as I have something positive to report. You have my number if you want to call me. I'll see myself out. Take it easy with the glacé cherries. Don't forget those other telephone numbers. Don't forget to speak to the switchboard. When DCI Sallow gets in touch, make it seem that I'm different from the other guys. He might even fall for it.'

'He will because it is the truth. Already, you have asked much that the other investigators and the police did not. Do not hesitate to contact me if you need any other information. I will be available for you at all times.'

I put my jacket on, grab my messenger bag and the Sansuyu carrier and shake her hand.

'OK. Well. I'll see you soon, I'm sure. Very nice to meet you, Micha.'

'And you. And thank you, Daniel.'

'I haven't done anything yet!'

Her eyes fill with tears once more. 'Oh, but you have, Daniel. You have.'

As I'm passing through the reception zone, I hand Aera one of my business cards.

'I gave one of these to Micha, Aera, but in case she loses it, here's a spare.'

She gets it straight away. 'Of course, Mr Beckett. I am most obliged. It would not do if she were to mislay your contact details. Can she call or text you any time of the day or night if she needs anything? Anything at all?'

'Of course, Aera. I'll be very keen to hear from her.'

'I'm sure she'll be very keen to get in touch.'

'I certainly hope so.'

'I think it is a foregone conclusion, Mr Beckett.'

'One thing, Aera – I'm a little confused. Are we still talking about your boss?'

She wriggles her bottom in her seat. A purse of the lips and a dismissive wave of the hand. 'Now you are embarrassing me!'

'Well, I wouldn't want to do that. Have a nice day, Aera.'

A sideways glance which is both demure and sexy, and she's back to her work. Then she stops and writes something on a piece of paper and hands it to me. It's her mobile number.

'Belt and braces, Mr Beckett.'

'Pays to be prudent, Aera.'

'Just being professional, Mr Beckett.'

I think that went quite well, whatever it was.

7

ORNELLAIA BIANCO IN THE FRIDGE

Even though I'm laden with bags of one sort or another, I want to visit Elder Street. I look at my watch. It's still only three-thirty, so I've got plenty of time before it starts to get dark. After five minutes, I manage to flag down a cab in St Mary Axe, in the shadow of The Gherkin.

'Elder Street, please.'

The cab driver nods, accelerates to the end of the road, and takes a stomach-lurching left into Camomile Street, where we come to an abrupt halt due to a traffic delay caused by some totally unpredictable roadworks. He keeps looking at me in his rear-view mirror.

'This was meant to be cleared up last August.'

'Oh, really.'

'I never see anyone working here. It's as if they lost interest.'

'Christ.'

I'm tapping my mobile, looking up Elder Street. It's an interesting mishmash and I don't think I'd ever heard of it before. For a start, it's a bit of a millionaires' row; a quick check shows the average house price to be two and a half million. The driver is still looking at me in his mirror.

'Didn't I pick you up yesterday?'

Most of the houses have three floors and a basement.

'I don't know. Where from?'

Mainly residential by the look of things, but a few buildings are used for businesses.

'Outside The Buddha-Bar. Knightsbridge. With your, er, with your lady friend.'

All Georgian listed buildings, which would explain the prices and the fact they've been saved from the local redevelopment destruction.

'Oh, yes. That was me.'

They were built in the 1720s for the families of Huguenot silk merchants.

'Nice-looking place, The Buddha-Bar. Never been inside, though. Famous cocktails, they say. I couldn't help overhearing, mate. The two of you, I mean. You've got a right one there, if you don't mind me saying.'

The whole area used to be one of the poorest and most overcrowded slums in London, whole families living in one room.

'I'm sorry – what was that?'

'You were both quite involved, shall we say, with each other. Not surprised you don't remember me, to be honest. I'm amazed my windows weren't steaming up!'

Families were so poor that they couldn't afford to bury corpses and just left them to rot somewhere in the house.

'Yeah, well. It had been quite an evening.' I'm on conversational autopilot.

'Very elegant lady.' He allows himself a tiny smirk. 'Very vocal, you might say. Is she an actress of, er, some sort?'

'Lawyer.'

'You're kidding. Looking like that?'

'Traffic's moving.'

He drops me off in Commercial Street near the south side of Elder Street. He looks peeved when he doesn't get a tip, as they always do. He forfeited it with those 'right one there' and 'very vocal' comments.

Despite the gentrification and developments, this area is still largely Graffiti City, peppered with run-down shops, fast food joints and buildings which look like they're falling apart. A couple of chi-chi bistros and branches of Taylor Taylor and Planet Organic forecast the future. I can smell chips and open drains.

There's no way into Elder Street from Commercial Street, and if you were in a vehicle, you'd have to drive across from Folgate Street, which itself comes to a dead end after a while.

Many smaller roads are closed due to construction/demolition work. It must be as confusing as hell if you're delivering a pizza around here.

So, it's a narrow cul-de-sac with an iron barrier gate down the high street end, as described by Baek-Hayeon. There are quite a few of these gates in this area, and all of them can be unlocked for emergency access. A 20-mph speed limit. Old-fashioned black streetlamps. A blue plaque on the wall of one house where the artist Mark Gertler used to live.

Many of the houses have bricked-up windows from the window tax days. People leave their drinks cans and takeaway coffee cups on the windowsills. Lots of colourful hanging baskets, always a sign of affluence.

There are two visible security cameras down one end, angled to cover the entrance of some company or other, but which would leave most of the street free from surveillance worries. Not a single pedestrian in sight.

Conspicuous bell box alarms on every house, but a total absence of video doorbells, which would have come in useful for the police.

I read somewhere that the more affluent an area is, the less likely you are to see video doorbells. Perhaps they spoil the look of the place or are thought of as being vulgar. Perhaps that's one of the reasons the kidnappers chose this road.

Nine cars parked, space for another twelve. Double yellow lines on one side, resident permit holders only on the other. People will be coming home from work in a few hours.

This would be a moderately risky road for unauthorised parking, particularly if you were organising a kidnapping payoff. Those double yellows would mean a traffic warden presence from time to time, maybe even the police, and they'd both be checking out the resident side of the street for permit-free vehicles. Getting a ticket or, worse, a clamping, would be disastrous for your operation. What were they thinking?

Add to that the fact that you'd have to reverse out, with all the hassle/collision risks that entails, plus the possibility of getting blocked in. It's certainly an odd choice of road.

I'm a little confused, in fact. If I was planning this operation, the last place I'd choose would be a quiet, narrow, one-way, largely residential, posh dead-end street like this. Maybe they're just stupid. Once again, something tells me they were first-timers, and had dumb luck on their side, unless there's something I'm not seeing.

I check out number 45, outside which the Fiat Ducato was parked. Despite this having happened two years ago, I crouch down and take an optimistic look at the floor, to see if there's something there that someone missed. Some useful case-solving physical clue that one of the kidnappers dropped that's inexplicably and illogically still in place. Nothing. Thought as much.

A few feet from where I'm standing, there's a brand new silver Audi Q5. Does it belong to the house? Number 45 has a couple of Flamingo Willows in terracotta pots outside the front door, and an ADT bell box above the lintel. Two hanging baskets on the wall, each filled with yellow petunias. A window on the second floor is open. I wonder what sort of people live here?

As if in answer, a woman pops her head out of the open window.

'Hello! Can I help you? Are you lost?'

'Yes. I'm looking for Buckingham Palace.'

For a moment, just a *moment,* she takes this seriously. Then she laughs. 'Oh, don't be so silly.'

'Could I speak to you? I'm a detective. My neck is starting to ache from looking upwards.'

'Are you the police?'

'Private sector.'

'Is it about that girl? The pianist?'

'It is.'

'Long time ago now.'

'I know.'

'Terrible thing.'

'Yes.'

'Hold on. I'm coming down.'

Well, this might be something. Or it may be nothing. Just as I'm thinking 'How long can it possibly take her to get down here?' the door opens. She reaches out to shake my hand.

'Hello. I'm Penny.'

'Daniel Beckett. Hi, Penny.'

Late thirties/early forties. Slim. Attractive. No makeup. No perfume. Nice teeth. Artfully tousled blonde hair. Striking green eyes. Faded one-inch scar on the left side of her forehead. Wearing a man's blue cotton shirt that's much too big for her with the sleeves rolled up and no bra underneath. Khaki cargo shorts. Bare feet. Clipped RP accent, but a soft, agreeable voice so it's not grating. White stuff, possibly plaster, over her hands, arms and spattered over the shirt. What *has* she been doing?

'Um,' she says. 'I don't know what...ohhh.'

She spots an empty can of Pepsi Max on one of her windowsills. She picks it up. 'Such a nuisance. Do you have any, er...'

I hand her one of my business cards. She holds it in between a finger and thumb and looks amused.

'Gosh. Stylish. Do you want to come in? Have a confab?'

I follow her inside, looking at the backs of her legs. A slightly self-conscious, sexy walk. Nice hair bounce. I was curious about what these places looked like inside, but we're walking so fast towards the back of the house I can only get an impression.

The high wide white spotless hallway has grey wooden floors, Art Deco chandeliers, three big terracotta pots containing unidentifiable spiky plants and an enormous delaminated antique mirror propped up against the wall on my left.

On the opposite side from the plants and mirror, a couple of photographic prints in black frames. One looks like the work of Paolo Pellegrin, but the other is unfamiliar. We pass three closed doors, two on the left, one on the right. The smell of recent decoration. These houses are much bigger than they seem from the outside, so now the prices make more sense.

The kitchen is black, white, and chrome with a long breakfast bar that seats four. Low-hanging ceiling lights in hammered copper. Blackened wood flooring and lots of cupboards. Shelves with stacked white crockery that looks unused. A purple azalea in a jute pot. An unopened bottle of Cazcabel Coffee Liqueur. A glass bowl full of limes. French windows leading to a well-stocked garden with a brass sundial. She dumps the Pepsi can in a stainless-steel bin.

'Sorry about the mess. Coffee? It's Waitrose. Sumatra Mandheling.'

'Thanks. Black with a dash of milk, no sugar.'

'Of course. Take a seat.'

I sit down at a kitchen table that seems to have been made from a large slab of driftwood, and take a look around. Mess? What mess? This place looks like a pristine upmarket kitchen showroom.

There's a print of *The Knight and the Maiden* by Sven Richard Bergh on the wall next to a small window. She boils a kettle and spoons coffee grains into a big MOGGA cafetière. I wonder what she wants to talk about.

She sits opposite me, placing two steaming coffee mugs on a couple of cork coasters. A half-second of eye contact. 'I've only got hazelnut milk. I hope that's OK.'

'That's fine, Penny. Thank you.'

She waves her hands in the air. 'I must look a fright. It's plaster of Paris. Just a hobby. Plant pots and things. Picture frames. Useless, really. So, what are you doing here? Is anything happening with that girl? I didn't see anything in the papers. Awful. Truly awful.'

'It's still unsolved. I've been hired to investigate it. I'd heard about the circumstances of the ransom payment, and thought I'd take a look at the...'

'I know! That van was parked right outside this house!'

'Did you live here then?'

'Yes. We've been here seven years. Or eight years. Can't remember. A policeman came to speak to me. He spoke to everyone in the road. But no one saw anything. I mean, one doesn't peer out of the window looking for unfamiliar vehicles all day long. I *did* tell him.'

'What was his name?

'Kendall? Keeble? Something like that. It *was* two years ago. You mustn't expect miracles! Oh – it was Kinnaird. Yes. Kinnaird. At least I think it was. Isn't that Scottish? He didn't *sound* Scottish. I love Scotland. Have you been to East Lothian? Unearthly. I had relatives there. Dead now.

'I think he was a detective sergeant. Overweight. Double chin. A big man. Rather ugly. As tall as you or perhaps taller. Rather intimidating, in fact. His size, I mean. He sort of filled the room. Blinked excessively, like a nervous tic, you know?' She demonstrates. 'Shifty. Sly eyes. Fat hands. Fat face, too.

'Had one of those little beards and moustaches that men have here.' She makes a circle around her open mouth with her finger and thumb. 'When they're trying to pretend their face hasn't become a tad shapeless from the fat. Does that sound terribly bitchy?

'Don't recall his first name if I ever knew it. I made him show me his warrant card, though for all I knew it may have been a forgery! How do they expect people to know what to look for? They should give you a thing. You know. But then people would know how to forge one, so that would be a waste of time, too. I suppose the sensible option would be to never let anyone inside your house at all.'

'What happened when he spoke to you?'

'How on earth did you ever start doing this? Detective work, I mean?'

'One thing led to another. You know how it is.'

'Oh, *yes*. Well, it's better than knowing what you're going to be doing when you're seventy. I hate predictability. I like the unknown. The unexpected. A life around the corner. People always think I must have studied art.'

'Do they? Did you?'

'No. I've got a bachelor's degree in Anglo-Saxon, Norse, and Celtic. Not much use for anything, really. Would you like something to drink? I've got a bottle of Ornellaia Bianco in the fridge.'

'Thank you, but no. I try to avoid drinking while I'm working.'

'Of course. How silly. My husband's always saying that I'm scatterbrained.'

'Did the police speak to him as well? Did he see anything?'

'Who?'

'Your husband.'

'My husband? Andrew? Goodness, no. He works in HK. Hong Kong. It's just me and the children. Well, I say that. They're away at school, so it's just me, really. Hibernating away! They're seven and nine now. My children, I mean. Boys. Andrew wanted them to go to the school he went to, so…'

What an odd life. Husband off doing the right job three thousand miles away, kids off at the right school God knows where, and here she is on her own producing plant pots from plaster of Paris that, presumably, no one ever sees.

'Would you mind telling me what happened when the police detective spoke to you, Penny? I know it was a long time ago. You don't have to be that accurate. Anything will do.'

She takes a sip of coffee and points at my Sansuyu carrier bag. 'Have you been shopping?'

I feel a little surge of adrenaline. This is going to be one of *those* interviews. I flash her a sincere smile.

'Shopping? No. It's just some stuff from an electronics company.'

'That's the Sansuyu logo thingy on the side, isn't it? We have one of their televisions. Oh. And the washing machine, I think.' Her eyes widen. 'Oh, of *course*! It was the *sister*, wasn't it. Some sort of big cheese in that company. Paid the ransom and then they murdered her. The pianist, I mean. Not the sister. Terrible. All that money gone to waste. I'll bet she was livid.

'Oh. Is that where you've been? Is she your client? That big reddish building with all the glass. It's near the Guild Church of St Katharine Cree. I worship there sometimes. It's a tad depressing. All old people. Smells of sandwiches. A man was sick on the floor there once. I *did* complain...'

'You're quite right. She is my client.' I lean forwards. 'But I'd be grateful if you could keep it to yourself. It's very hush-hush at the moment.'

'Oh, of course. Diplomacy required. My father was a diplomat. Pitcairn Islands. Well. You know. I'll help you all I can. Making the streets safe and so on.'

'What was the first thing that the detective spoke to you about?'

'He said that he was investigating the murder of, er…'

'Kiaraa Jeong. That was her name.'

'Yes. Quite a mouthful! He said that the police were trying to track down what they thought was a pretty new white van connected with the murder that had been parked in this street. Right outside my house, in fact. Did I say that already? At the time, I assumed it was a getaway van or whatever they call them.'

'Did he show you a photograph of it?'

'The van? Yes. Yes, he did. It was a Fiat of some sort. Awful. I have to say, I was surprised that the criminals had chosen a new vehicle. I thought they'd have chosen one that was a tad more lived-in looking. Needed a clean, perhaps. But then they probably wanted whoever was doing the payoff to spot it straight away and not have to go hunting around for it. Is your coffee OK?'

'Very nice, thank you.'

'Do tell me if you want another. It's no trouble.' She fiddles with her hair. 'I can't quite recall, but I don't think he mentioned at the time that that van was related to the ransom money collection, just that it was connected to the murder case. I think the white Fiat van/ransom thing came out later, possibly in the newspapers. I can't remember now.'

'That's likely. There would be several reasons that they wouldn't want people to know the whole story at certain stages in the investigation. They're still keeping a lot back. It's normal procedure until the crime is solved.'

She slaps her hands on the table. 'I'm going tell you something. You and he could not be more different. Manner, appearance, clothing, everything. And you're a private detective, is that right? Is that what you are?'

'Last time I checked.'

She likes this and laughs. 'Like, um, like a private detective on a television show.'

'Exactly like that.'

'Or in a film.'

She's funny. 'Like that, too. It's a curse.'

'This is very exciting. I'm going to be exceedingly forward. Shoot me down in flames if you wish. Could you take me out to dinner? I haven't been out anywhere for three months. Longer. In fact, I've barely spoken to another adult in that time, either. Apart from at the shops. Going a tad stir crazy! Cabin fever. Antsy. Horrid.'

I've got to laugh. I hope it doesn't make me seem too cruel. 'Er, yes. I mean, um, I can't do it straight away. I've got this case to deal with, and...'

'Oh, no no no no no. I didn't mean *tonight* or anything. How silly. I'm Penny, by the way. Did I tell you that?'

'You did. Do you have anywhere in mind, Penny?'

'Well, actually *yes*. There's a fantastic new Japanese restaurant in Soho that I noticed when I was out shopping a few weeks ago. It's called Tengoku No Aji. I looked inside. Through the window, I mean. Lots of juniper bonsais and orange lanterns and they serve these delicious-looking dishes on square marble slabs instead of plates. Looks fab. It's in Frith Street. Opposite Ronnie Scott's.'

'OK, Penny. I'd be delighted. Text me your number and I'll give you a call as soon as I've finished with this case. Shouldn't be too long.' He said optimistically.

This is surreal. But I'm getting a little tremor of satisfaction and excitement. And she's good-looking and charming. And her husband's in Hong Kong.

'Thank you! I won't let you down. I scrub up pretty well when I can be bothered.'

'I'm sure you do, Penny. I'll look forward to it.'

'Me too. I *do* like dressing up. I sort of – I suppose I'm telling you this as you're a stranger – I haven't really been feeling too glamorous or fanciable lately. Too much info? Do tell me if it is.'

I smile at her. 'Perhaps I should buy you some sexy lingerie; that usually does the trick, or so I've heard.'

She shrieks with laughter, then calms down. 'Really? I mean – is that a thing? Do – do detectives do that?'

'It's one of my major expenses.'

'Well, now you're pulling my leg.' She sits up. Her whole demeanour has changed. She stares at the floor. 'I'm a size ten.'

'I could tell.'

'Really? Just by *looking*? Well. Gosh. Anyway. The lack of adult company notwithstanding, it's such a bother cooking for oneself all of the time. Gets to be a bore. You're not *married* or anything are you? I wouldn't want to...'

'I'm on my honeymoon right at this moment. My bride's waiting outside on her motorbike.'

This gets a laugh. She's more relaxed now that's out of the way. I can see the cogs turning as she tries to remember what she was talking about.

'So. Yes. Anyway. The detective showed me a photograph of the van, but as I said, I couldn't help. Then he asked me if I'd seen anyone who looked suspicious lurking around, or any other strange or unfamiliar vehicles. Once again, I couldn't assist. This is a somewhat quiet road most of the time, as I'm sure you've noticed. But people still manage to leave their rubbish on one's windowsills.'

'How soon after the murder was this? Do you remember?'

'It must have been about ten days. Something like that. Or was it? Might have been six days. Can't really recollect. Terrible memory. Long time ago now. Would you like a chocolate? I've got some delish Tinkture Rose Gin truffles. Oh. And some cherry ganache chocs from Fortnum's.'

'Maybe later. What else did he ask?'

'If anyone I didn't know had called at the house. I said no. I thought it was a rather silly question. What did he expect? The kidnappers to knock on the door and ask if I minded if they parked their ransom van outside?'

'Was that it?'

'Basically, yes. But then he started going all around the houses. Reiterating. Asking me the same questions over and over again. I was getting impatient, and I wanted him to go, but it began to feel as if I couldn't get rid of him. I thought he'd be busy, you know? With the murder? But he was hanging around, d'you know what I mean?

'Kept asking me questions about myself. Personal questions. It was like someone without a friendly nature pretending to be friendly and failing rather gravely. Rather redundant questions about house security.

'He had a little snigger when I told him that Andrew was in HK. He said that he could tell, whatever that meant. This will sound a tad curious, but it felt as if he didn't like me. Most strange. Do you think I'm likeable?'

'Exceedingly.'

'Really?'

'Yes,' I smile at her. 'Likeable and charming.'

'Goodness. I'm going goose-pimply. How strange.' She quickly adjusts her sitting position. She places her hands flat on the table. 'Then he started going on about the case. The murder case. All these ghastly details. That poor girl. Gruesome. I'm sure he shouldn't have been telling me half of it. I think he was trying to impress me. That's not true. I *know* he was. It made me feel very uncomfortable.'

'What sort of things was he telling you?'

'He was saying that he was going to catch who did it. Like a macho thing, you know? Because of what the kidnappers had done. How they found her naked in the boot of a car. All these terrible, gory details. Awful things. I started to get rather tearful and then he stopped, as if he'd said too much, as if it wasn't having the desired effect.'

'What effect do you think he was he going for?' Though I already know the answer.

'Well, I think, probably, that I might invite him up to the bedroom, you know? I mean – that was *definitely* never on the cards. It wasn't said in so many words, but I just knew that was what he was thinking. To be frank, it made me want to vomit.

'He spoke in such a way that he could backpedal at any moment. Pretend that I'd misunderstood. Quite sly, really. It was as if he was skilled in it, do you know what I mean? Deniable suggestive remarks, you might say. Done it in the past, perhaps.

'But it was mixed in with a sort of contempt, like I said before. Rather aggressive, really. I was quite upset when he left. In fact, I had rather a cry. Quite a bit of a cry, in fact. Not like me at all. Lots of things.

Everything. All piling up. Silly. Horrid. The whole thing, I – it left me quite unsettled.'

'You should have reported him.'

'Well, I suppose so. But I wouldn't have known who to report him *to*. And it was the *police*. And they were investigating a *murder*. It was *pretty serious stuff*. You assume it's *you*. I just...'

There are tears in her eyes. I place my hand on hers. 'OK. That's fine, Penny. Don't worry about it now. It's over. It was two years ago. You mustn't dwell on it.' She slides her hand from beneath mine, grasps my fingers and squeezes.

'Was there anything else you remember him saying that stuck in your mind? About the murder, I mean.'

'Hm.' She taps the table surface with a middle finger. 'Well, there was something that I thought was a little unusual. Obviously, you assume that the police would have sympathy for someone like – who was it?'

'Kiaraa Jeong.'

'That's right. Very hard to remember that name, for some reason. Doesn't roll off the tongue, I suppose. Yes. Sympathy. Might have just been me, but he didn't seem very sympathetic. As if it was her fault, you know? As if she was *asking* to be murdered. Mad. I thought that was very odd, that lack of compassion.'

'Perhaps you get blasé after a while in his job,' I say. 'You have to push normal emotions to one side.'

'Yes. Yes, I suppose that's what it was. Still peculiar, though.'

We let this hang in the air for a few moments. I can't think of anything else to ask her. We look at each other and smile. I take a deep breath and stand to leave.

'That's it for the moment, Penny. I'm going to leave you to your plaster of Paris. Thank you for the coffee and your help.' I shake her hand. 'And I'll give you a call to arrange our visit to Tengoku No Aji. As a special treat, I'll let you do the ordering.'

'Ha ha. Famous last words! They have a cocktail bar there as well. What's your favourite cocktail?'

She sees me to the front door. I can feel her eyes on my back as I walk towards Commercial Street. I drop the two cherry ganache chocolates she gave me into my Sansuyu carrier. She texts me with her mobile number before I've gone a hundred yards. This is looking promising. And that detective. Kinnaird. It's a flimsy thread, but it may be worth tugging.

I get a cab straight away, and thankfully it's not my friend from earlier.

'Old Compton Street, please. Lipstick & Leather. Do you know it?'

'The, er, *unconventional* lingerie place? Sure. Get in. Wife's birthday?'

'Certainly not.'

'Ha ha. Some things are best kept secret, mate!'

We share a couple of conspiratorial gestures and off we go.

8

LIPSTICK & LEATHER

She holds it at arm's length, her expression both curious and captivated.

'Am I naïve? I don't understand how this is lingerie.'

'That depends on what your definition of lingerie is, Suzanna.'

'What's yours?'

'Women's intimate and alluring apparel.'

'Well, this is *certainly* lingerie in that case.'

'I'm glad you agree.'

'Just a first impression, but I fear the wearer's breasts may be totally exposed.'

'It's called a body harness. I described you and your figure to the manager. A former client. She's trustworthy and has very good taste. This was one of her suggestions.'

'I'm sure you were mortified. I think I should like to visit this place. You'd have to come with me, of course. I'd be embarrassed to go on my own.'

I had considered getting something for Penny while I was grazing in Lipstick & Leather, but I don't want to scare her. I think I'll stick to Fleur of England, for the moment at least. Far more her style.

'What were her other suggestions?' asks Suzanna.

'They're in the bag.'

'Are they leather, too?'

'No. Only that one. Wait until you try them on. You'll see.'

'I think I should shower first. How did it go with Micha?'

'She knows about us.'

'*What?*'

'She can read you like a book. And then there was your "We've Been Shagging" t-shirt.'

'I knew I should have left that at home. Was she OK about it? What did she say about me?'

'She said you were a good-looking woman and a very nice person.'

'A very nice person? Did you tell her the truth?'

'I'm keeping that to myself for the moment.'

'What else did she say?'

'She was fond of you, and thought you were a good lawyer.'

'Anything else?'

'She was curious about the age gap between us and wondered if it was a problem.'

'And how did you respond?'

'I told her that I had to have spinal traction after our night together.'

'Ha. I like the idea that she knows about us.'

'Oh, *do* you.'

'It's silly, but it's kind of good for my image.'

'In some weird, twisted aphrodisiacal way.'

I help her off with her work clothing, unzipping the burgundy midi dress which she steps out of and folds neatly over a chair.

'Exactly that,' she says. 'It's a fascinating feeling.'

I watch as she removes her heels, underwear and stockings, and admire the dimples on her lower back. I seem to remember they're called The Dimples of Venus. Something to do with making it easier to reach orgasm. I must look it up.

'There is also a *soupçon* of eccentric exhibitionism rearing its ugly head, I think,' she continues. 'Talking of which, I like it that I'm naked and you're fully dressed.'

'You're naked? I hadn't noticed.'

'Oh yeah?'

'Well…'

'Maybe it makes me feel more confident about myself that someone else knows. Quite invigorating. Stimulating. It certainly makes me feel sexy. So, when are you going to start working for her?'

'I've already started. In fact, I'll be going out later on tonight to check something out. Go and have your shower. You'll get cold standing around like that. It's already having an effect.'

She places her arms around my neck. Her mouth is on mine immediately. Then she pulls away. 'Not distracting you, am I?'

I grab her shoulders. 'That would never happen.'

'It feels like you're lying.'

'Really?'

'Mm-hm. I'm a lawyer. I can always tell when someone's not telling the truth. Especially when there's *prima facie* physical evidence.'

'I'm going to hide your HRT gel.'

'I don't think I need it anymore. Certainly not this second. Do you *fancy* Micha? I'm curious.'

'Would you like it if I did?'

'Yes. But I'm not sure why. Oh God. What are you doing to me? It feels like you're inside my head, interfering with my moral compass.'

'Shower. Now. Quickly.'

'Bastard.'

I find the list of defunct mobile numbers that Micha gave to me and decide to give Doug Teng a call.

His mobile rings for what seems like an age before he answers. It sounds as if he's in some insane games arcade; there's a constant barrage of gunfire, screaming, and explosions in the background.

'Hey, Mr Beckett. How's Covent Garden this evening? And how was, er, Elder Street before that? And Leadenhall Street before that? Really weird breakup when you were there. Really clear signal, then it fragmented in a way I hadn't seen before for a couple of seconds, then back to normal again but fainter. Weirder than weird. Might have been me, of course. Doubt it, though. Never is.'

'Are you stalking me, Doug?'

'Just trying out this new iPhone tracking software I'm working on. You're always going from place to place so you're a really good subject. Or should that be guinea pig. Don't expect payment. Limited range at the moment, but this will even track mobiles that are switched off or have been destroyed or are fitted with anti-manipulation vapourware. To a degree, anyway. It'll be in the form of an app you can operate from your mobile. The Buddha-Bar yesterday, I see. You should see the one in Paris. Mind-blowing interior. Great toilets. Sticky floor, though.'

'Leadenhall Street. I was in a high-speed lift. Took maybe two or three seconds to get from the ground floor to the forty-fifth.'

'Ah. Got it. What was it like inside?'

'Silver with a blue ceiling and blue floor lighting. Orange digital display. About ten by twelve feet. Maybe nine feet high.'

'No. I meant the Buddha-Bar.'

'Um...' I can hardly remember. Suzanna's fault. 'Nice decor. Strong cocktails. There was a big floating Buddha.'

'Cool. So. The lift. That'll be one of the new generation of Ollida elevators. They use that new carbon fibre cable. Replaced the old DX class.

'This type kills microbes and stuff. Annihilates fingerprints on the walls. Probably zaps cockroaches, too. Wages war on defenceless countries. They've got IoT. That means they can work out traffic history, where they need to be next to save energy, all that sort of shit. Did you feel ill when you got out? Nosebleed or anything?'

'No. I didn't even think we'd moved.'

'Well, that's really useful. How can I help?'

'I'm going to give you three pre-paid mobile numbers. All dead. Last used about two years ago. It's unlikely you'll be able to trace the owners, but if you can manage it, I'd like to know where and when they were bought. The police may have looked into this, but I've no idea how far they got.'

'Do you want me to try and locate the owners anyway? I mean, the phones may have been physically destroyed, but...'

'Sure. Anything you can get on them. But they were used in a kidnapping which turned bad, so I would imagine they'd have been ultra-careful at both ends of the operation.'

'Okeydoke. I'll see if I can pick up an IMEI for them just for the hell of it. I may be able to discover the purchase point, but – two years. Don't expect miracles. These places come and go, or they move premises, whatever...'

'That won't necessarily matter. Can this be an ASAP?'

'Sure. Fifteen hundred. This is harder than you might think. These companies like to protect their client's privacy, extraordinary as that may seem.'

'Well, hold that estimate. I may have some more stuff for you in a couple of days, so you can add it all together and give me a discount.'

'OK. I'll get back to you as soon as I can. Sorry – did you just use the D word? That's *blasphemy*, man.'

'Oh, and I may need you to look at a Yuhwa TT7992 security system later on tonight. Probably nothing. Just want to check if someone's been fiddling with it.'

'That's a Sansuyu, isn't it? Won the ISAK Home Security Platinum Award last year and the year before. So, no problem. Like cracking a sparrow's egg with Thor's hammer. I'll send my Thunder Crash Bomb app to your mobile. Let's hope you've got the space. That'll be another five hundred, but the app's free for you, as it's you. You're welcome. Give us a call when you're in proximity. Oh, and probably remove the app when you're finished, in case you get killed and the police look at your mobile for clues. You know the drill.'

'Right. I'll be in touch. What's the background noise?'

'*The Raid 2*. Seen it? Fuckin' delivers. Hey…'

'See you, Doug.'

When Suzanna returns a few minutes later, I lose the power of speech. I must remember to send Zulmé at Lipstick & Leather a bottle of champagne. Two bottles of champagne. I must also ask her out to dinner. It's been a year. I don't know if she's currently attached, but nothing would stop her going to Hélène Darroze at the Connaught.

'I didn't know you'd bought me nylon stockings as well. And a latex bodysuit. And these heels! Five inches! Was all this from the same shop? Look at me. I look *obscene*! Isn't this what they call fetish wear? Can we eat later?'

'You don't want to watch some TV first?'

'Get in the bedroom.'

* * *

A cab drops me at the junction of Sloane Street and Pont Street just before ten. I want to get a feel for the whole area and what it would have been like for Kiaraa, walking home from that restaurant. That's assuming she was going home in the first place. And going home on her own, knowingly or otherwise.

It's already been dark for a few hours and it's busy. To my left is a lit-up cabman's shelter with three driverless cabs parked along the taxi rank. A solitary cab driver leans against the wall of the shelter having a cigarette, yawning, and sipping a coffee.

Small tree-filled parks on each side of the road. Some people are standing in them doing God knows what. Mixed-sex groups of four or five mill around on the pavement doing nothing. Six women walk by, talking in Bulgarian and laughing.

I keep walking and watching.

Wide pavements, parking restrictions, regular bright streetlamps, Belisha beacons, traffic lights, couples, families, solitaries, two cops, joggers, cars, minicabs, black cabs, buses, apartment windows open with music pouring out: altogether a relatively safe section of road for a lone female.

In a hundred yards, upmarket shops and services start sprouting: Anya Hindmarch, Forever Rose, Carine Gilson, Jeeves, Agent Provocateur, The Fold, Jeroboam's, THG Paris and the Anya Café. All shut, but the pavements are thoroughly flooded with their internal and external lighting.

Thinking of Suzanna, and maybe Penny, I take a look in the AP window. A couple of exotic mannequins, each dressed for the mannequin boudoir, one in a black and pink corset with an ouvert thong, the other in a red high-neck bra, with matching waspie and a high-waisted brief. The corset would suit Suzanna and so would the thong. Eight people walk by as I stand there, staring like an idiot.

I cross the road to look in the window of Carine Gilson. The mannequins aren't quite as foxy as AP, but the prices certainly are: two and a half thousand for an ivory silk kimono and almost three hundred for a single silk and tulle brief. Well-designed and sophisticated couture, but out of the two, I think Suzanna's more of an Agent Provocateur girl. Or perhaps she's found her spiritual home with Lipstick & Leather.

Maybe half a dozen people on this side of the road. Two women in their twenties stop to see what I'm looking at, then laugh and walk away. I hear one of them say 'fuckin' loser'.

Across the road again, and right next door to Abd El Wahab is a hair and beauty salon called Neville. Shut, like everything else, but blazing with light from the ground-floor interior and from the first and second floors.

The restaurant itself is full, bright, and busy. I had considered popping in and having a word with the manager, if he or she was there, but I don't think it would be a good time, and I'm not really here for that.

A few yards down the road on the same side is The Hari, a luxury eight-storey hotel that illuminates the street outside 24/7, and another, smaller hotel right across the road. Well-lit flats and houses on both sides. Traffic lights winking on and off. More crowds. So far so good.

There are a fair amount of security cameras here. I wonder if any of them caught Kiaraa as she walked along. Most, though, are aimed at building entrances and not the pavements or the road. Maybe DCI Sallow will be able to help me there.

As I reach a crossroads, I get a little confused. When I look at the street signs, Chesham Place seems to be everywhere. It's to my left, my right, and it's also straight ahead. It also seems to be on the left- and right-hand sides of a small fenced-off triangle of leafy parkland, one of many communal gardens in the area that only certain residents would have access to.

There's a gate that gets you inside this one, but you'd need a key to open it. I wonder if Kiaraa had one. Did she sit in that garden when the weather was nice? Did people know her? Talk to her? Know who she was? What she did? Was someone watching her as she sat?

Over a dozen four-storey houses, including the French Embassy, overlook this lively crossroads, as does The Hari and another couple of hotels.

As soon as the lights change, I cross over, almost getting clipped by a cyclist to whom traffic lights mean zilch.

Once I'm in Chesham Place, I pass the German Embassy on my left. Big building, lots of lights, a large number of people coming and going. I check my watch: ten-fifteen.

These are moderately narrow and busy roads, all controlled zones, and you wouldn't be able to stop, let alone park, without creating traffic mayhem.

So, the likelihood of cruising a solitary female here and whisking her away in your vehicle without someone noticing would be remote, but not impossible.

However, I have to factor in the inappropriate and puzzling location for the ransom payoff. Once again, were these people both stupid and lucky?

How would I do this?

If I knew about the meal, I'd get the restaurant computer hacked and look at the reservations. I'd have to know how many people were going to attend and what their names were; any of them could have booked it.

I'd have to know how long the average meal lasted. Some restaurants will tell you that they want the table back at a certain time, but not all of them. If the Abd El Wahab was one of those, I'd book a table under a fake ID to get an idea.

But even if I knew the time they might leave and go home, there was an unpredictable event: Kiaraa leaving early because she was tired. I, or my accomplices, would have to be observing/parking near/driving past the restaurant in shifts to cover that type of unpredictability. Or have the place bugged. Specifically, have Kiaraa's table bugged for unexpected occurrences.

But I'd have to know which table she was sitting at, or maybe bug all of them, just to be on the safe side. This would also involve breaking into the restaurant in the early hours to set everything up in a way that even the most fastidious cleaner would miss. And even then, ambient restaurant noise might be a problem.

What if she was not alone when she walked back? What if she was feeling lazy and flagged down a cab? What if two or three of her pals were going back to her place for a nightcap?

If even *one* of those events occurred, I'd have to abandon the operation.

It would be quite an undertaking, and I'd probably need the assistance of at least five other people and a techie, plus two or three motor vehicles.

But this is assuming I knew about the meal in the first place. And, like Elder Street, this is a bad location for purpose.

The other possibility is a text message emanating from the restaurant.

She's leaving now.

But it was a small gathering. Who could have done that without drawing attention to themselves?

If it was me I'd have that text composed and ready to send, just in case.

An unlikely scenario, though just possible.

Could it have been chance? Luck? Our kidnapper/s just happened to be walking down/driving past Pont Street/Chesham Place, spotted her and abducted her? Did she know him/her/them?

Whoever it was couldn't credibly be offering her a lift when she was sixty seconds away from her home. And she'd be smart enough not to get in a car with a strange man. Assuming it was a man.

Or perhaps she wasn't smart enough. Perhaps she was smart but not street-smart.

But then Seoul, where she grew up, has some pretty rough neighbourhoods. Where was it she came from? Myeongdong? I must ask Micha what it was like. May come in useful. Though judging by Kiaraa's early career start, she might have led a sheltered life whatever type of neighbourhood it was.

Was it someone pretending to be a fan? Was it a *real* fan she'd met before? A fan she trusted? A fan who wanted to play her a new classical CD he had in his car? Then out came the chloroform?

My mobile makes a noise like glass wind chimes. It's Doug's Thunder Crash Bomb app. I take a look. White background with a lime green Hanzi character, which probably means something funny or obscene.

I keep walking, looking for number 37, until I spot the red and yellow of the Spanish flag on the other side of the road. That must be the embassy that Micha mentioned. The Embassy of Finland is next door. This means that I'm getting warm. If only these roads had logical house numbering. Even *visible* house numbering would be better than nothing.

I stop, look from left to right, until I realise that, like an idiot, I'm standing right outside 37. So, a highly illuminated, short walk from the restaurant, lots of people around, the whole area buzzing with life.

Like all the other houses in this road, Kiaraa's is a well-kept white stucco affair. Probably built in the middle of the nineteenth century. Three storeys and a basement. Both houses either side of it are the same. From the outside it looks very clean. I assume that Micha pays for the exterior maintenance and the local window cleaner, if such a person exists.

There are six steps up to the front door, which is flanked by a pair of redwood planter boxes with no plants in them. Predictably, there is no sign of life or light inside, and every window, from the basement to the third floor, has closed wooden shutters in natural ash.

I tap the nine-digit passcode into the keypad entry lock. It's a Yuhwa ZZ662. Four quiet bleeps, a pause, five more quiet bleeps and a click. Presumably that's a good sign. I unlock the Yale and the mortice and I'm in.

As soon as I've closed the door behind me, I look for the second alarm system, which Micha said would be on the wall to my right.

It's a scary creature. About the size of an iPad, I can tell it's angry. A second ago, it was showing the time, date, and temperature, but now virtually the whole screen is filled with a bright red digital display, counting down from thirty.

Feeling slightly panicky, I tap the code number in and almost jump out of my skin as a soft female voice says something right in my ear, right in my *head* in Korean that ends with 'Kiaraa'. She must have directional ceiling speakers in here, probably the Sansuyu version of the Holosonics Audio Spotlight.

I assume this is the security system welcoming her home. Immediately after this, the house lights come on, then there's some soft electronic music that lasts for thirty seconds. Then the hall lights dim very slightly. I stand still, waiting for something else to happen, but I think that's it.

I give Doug a call.

'OK, man. Tap the app. Once it's open, you'll see six green squares. Tap the top right one, count to ten, then tap the bottom middle one. Done? Now. See the grid? Good. Aim your mobile at the Yuhwa TT7992 screen as if you're going to take a pic of it. Now tap the black circle at the bottom. OK. All done. I'll take a look and get back to you.'

'That was *it*?'

'No. There's another hour and a half of stuff to do yet and I'll need to see a bank reference and your passport. Of *course* that was it.'

I delete the app from my mobile as requested. There's a lot of junk mail on the floor; two years' worth, in fact.

Before I do anything else, I crouch down and sift through it, looking for real letters or anything else that might be useful, but there's nothing. It took me ten minutes.

I stand and take a deep breath. My thighs hurt. When you're hunting around an unfamiliar place, looking for God knows what (when there's no time limit or risk factors in play), it's always better to be relaxed and follow your nose. It's an approach that occasionally works, so I stick with it.

I take a slow walk around the entrance hall. Some nice art and a faint smell of tuberose and gardenia. Is that the ghost of a scent that she used to wear?

I suddenly get the odd feeling that she's watching me, wondering who I am, wondering what I'm doing here. Despite its size, the hall is pretty sparse; just a single small table with an empty Fornasetti Farfalle vase on the top.

I look up the stairs. Dark, so I assume it's only the downstairs lights have come on. I can hear radiators ticking, so something has decided that it's cool enough for the heating to be fired up. I'll have to give Micha a call to see what I have to do when I leave. Will she be asleep?

I pop down to the basement. County-sized gadget-stuffed kitchen in yellow marble with a partial view of the garden, dining room with a grey Art Deco table that seats twelve, utility room with washing machine, spin dryer and cleaning stuff, and a small but opulent toilet with a pouting *L'Avventura* poster on the wall, a *Yellow Submarine* toilet lid and a copy of *The Piano Teacher* by Elfriede Jelinek on top of a small bamboo laundry basket.

Returning to the hall, I decide to check out the second floor first and work downwards. There's a little bank of light switches at the bottom of the stairs, so I push all of them. This illuminates the staircase and what I can see of the first-floor landing. I take the stairs two at a time.

Right then, Kiaraa Jeong. Let's take a look at your life.

9

THE GHOST OF A SCENT

The second floor doesn't seem as if it was used much. There's a guest bedroom with an ensuite bathroom in coral. No scents, no smells, dead air. The bed has been made up. Everything looks brand new.

There's a stack of magazines on the floor: *The New Yorker, Cherry Chu, Puss Puss, Hunger, Allure Korea, 1814 Magazine, Côté Sud*. All two or three years old. A wardrobe containing copper coat hangers and a single red kimono, made by Sakurai Soji of Japan. An unused dressing table with empty drawers. I take a look under the bed for the hell of it, but there's nothing there. I bang my head on the way up.

Next to this is what seems like a room that was in the process of being turned into an office. There's an oak veneer desk, a pink ergonomic swivel chair, two empty pine bookshelves and a tall metal CD rack with no CDs. A small faux-Chesterfield brown leather sofa with a copy of *Cloud Computing for Dummies* resting on one of the arms, open at page thirty-three. A Mondrian mug on the windowsill. Same dead air as the other room.

There's a spare room bereft of any furnishings at all, but with a luxurious thick pile blue carpet. A spacious bathroom with a shower and two sinks, a separate toilet and next door to that, a small empty storage cupboard/room.

I think this house was too big for Kiaraa's needs. Maybe she, or some advisor, saw it as an investment.

Now down to the first floor.

There are four closed doors here. I decide to investigate the closest one.

I open the door and turn the light on. What's inside takes my breath away. An amazing-looking, white-walled, spacious room with pine flooring, and in the centre, the most incredible piano, the most incredible *musical instrument* I think I've ever seen in my life.

This thing belongs in an art gallery. It's a grand piano, for sure, but it looks like one that was somehow beamed here from the distant future.

It's a beautifully designed sleek and organic work of art in black, silver and plexiglass, and I'm almost afraid to approach it.

I sit down on the black leather piano stool. It's too low for me and was obviously adjusted to make it comfortable for Kiaraa.

There's a name above the keys, Fazioli, and to the right, it says NYT Line, whatever that is.

There's some sheet music on the transparent stand, "Piano Sonata in G Minor, Op.2 No.1: II. Presto" by Hélène de Montgeroult, a composer I've never heard of. Was that the last thing she played? Is that why it's still here?

I don't know why, but I feel compelled to strike Middle C on the keyboard. I keep my finger pressed down. The note seems to resonate for a long time before it fades.

I assume this room is built for acoustics in some way, probably soundproofed as well. I lift my finger off the key.

I can smell tuberose and gardenia – a little stronger this time – and once again experience an odd sense of Kiaraa watching and frowning.

Who are you? What are you doing? Why are you touching my piano?

There's no furniture in here apart from the piano stool and no sheet music in sight apart from what's on the music stand. Maybe she didn't need it. Maybe she relied on memory.

I look at the prints on the wall. *In The Tepidarium* by Godward and *A Favourite Custom* by Alma-Tadema.

As I get closer I realise they're not prints, they're the originals. It's only a guess, but I reckon her ransom could have been paid a few times over by selling just one of these.

But there would have been no time, of course.

The room next door must be the master bedroom. Big and luxurious. That perfume smell is more noticeable in here.

A thick, white carpet, a big bed covered by an orange and purple quilt, large red pillows, a wide dressing table weighed down with a ton of cosmetics and perfumes and a bedside table piled with books.

I take a quick look; *Literature and Evil* by Georges Bataille, *A Natural History of the Piano* by Stuart Isacoff, *La Dame aux Camélias* by Dumas, *The Open Door* by Charlotte Riddell, *Hi-Nikki* by Nobuyoshi Araki, *Against Nature* by Huysmans, *Puppet on a Chain* by Alistair MacLean, and *Poems* by Robert Southey.

I flick through the Araki book. It's a thick tome of photographs, almost a diary, one photograph taken each day over the course of a year: dolls, flowers, tomatoes, street scenes, women, meals, clouds.

Some of these would make great prints.

Talking of which, she has some really good-looking framed photography on the walls in here; one's definitely an Irina Ionesco, but I don't recognise any of the others.

I feel uncomfortable rummaging through the drawers of her dressing table, but it has to be done. It's pretty untidy and chaotic, and I'm guessing that the police have already been here and weren't fussed about leaving everything as it was. I look up and catch my reflection in the big Art Nouveau dressing table mirror. I don't look *too* sleazy, which I suppose is something.

Nothing particularly unusual: hair brushes, combs, perfume, knickers, bras, stockings, tights, an unopened five-pack of black uni-ball pens, a tube of Gucci Rouge à Lèvres matte lipstick, a tub of Miso Pretty plum lip gloss, a garnet and emerald ring, an unused Van Gogh diary, a gold and black Coco de Mer Intimate Wand, a half-used tube of Absinthe Purifying Hand Cream, two spare watch straps, a three-pin plug, a 40-pack of Durex 'Surprise Me' condoms, copper nail clippers, an unopened pack of Flucloxacillin, a crystal nail file, a packet of Azurette birth control pills with three left, a tape measure, an empty bottle of Rose Musk eau de parfum by Elegantes, an unopened box of a drug called mirtazapine, a packet of M&S ladder-resist black tights, and a well-thumbed copy of *The Diary of a Chambermaid* by Octave Mirbeau.

There's an inscription on the dust jacket of this last item: 'To my darling Kiaraa. Hope you like. Celestine reminds me of you!!! All my love, Conceição.' I wonder who this is? Conceição is a female name, common in Brazil. Another thing to ask Micha about.

Now her wardrobe. This takes up an entire wall. It's so big you could live in it. I don't want to spend too long on this, so the first thing I do is open all the doors, stand back, and take a cool, calm and collected look in the hope that I'll get inspired. This rarely happens.

For some reason, I start thinking about Penny from Elder Street again. Never found out her surname. I wonder what *her* wardrobe is like; what sort of clothes she likes to wear when she's not elbow-deep in plaster of Paris wearing a man's shirt and khaki shorts.

I'll be interested to see how she dresses when we go on our date, if that's what it is. I think it is. It was interesting how my jokey lingerie comment became a thing really quickly with her giving me her dress size. I think I know what she'll look good in. She'll be shocked and surprised, maybe embarrassed, but I think she'll appreciate the gesture. It'll be fun. And funny. I think she needs a laugh. What did she say? *I haven't really been feeling too glamorous or fanciable lately*. Well, we'll see about that. I've got lingerie on the brain at the moment. Isn't there a term for that? Undoubtedly some sort of fetishism. I'll look it up later.

The main part of the wardrobe is in two distinct sections. I take a look at the left side first. Lots of things on hangers: dresses, blouses, skirts, many of them a striking bright yellow like the dress she was wearing in that photograph I found on Google. Obviously a favourite colour of hers.

I slowly run a hand across the contents. Casual stuff, I'm guessing. Day to day. Pretty conservative. Some party clothing. No smell of her perfume in here, but a slight lavender fragrance, perhaps moth repellent.

I stop from time to time to take an item out and look at the label.

A Kika Vargas floral maxi dress, an Alessandra Rich polka dot midi dress, a green and orange stretch minidress by Farai with sexy cut-outs at the front, and a knockout rainbow pattern Valentino sequinned minidress with a one-shoulder neckline. I'll bet she looked great in these. So. Her tastes were often designer, fun and very expensive.

The vast collection of shoes in this section are in the same ballpark: a pair of Jimmy Choo glitter pumps, Mach & Mach double bow mules in purple, Christian Louboutin crimson suede ankle boots decorated with two pin-up figures and some more Louboutin, this time a pair of So Kate lime green pumps.

I don't know Kiaraa's height, but all the heels here are four, five and six inches. I somehow imagine she did a lot of teetering. There are also two pairs of Givenchy TK-360 sneakers, one pair in burgundy, the other in navy blue.

The right-hand side of the wardrobe couldn't be more different. A black Cucculelli Shaheen strapless gown embellished with a multitude of sequins and crystal beads, a beautiful Marchesa V-neck dress in charcoal and a round-neck Zuhair Murad daisy gown with a boned top and tulle skirt, and an off-the-shoulder Galvan London maxi dress in dark blue velvet.

There are also half a dozen very costly, short and medium dresses that don't look as if they're worn much. This lot have to be for performance, though she undoubtedly hires stuff when she's on world tours.

The shoe rack at the bottom confirms my thesis; two pairs of Louboutin slingback pumps in black leather, two pairs of Manolo Blahnik embellished pumps in black satin, some green Bottega Veneta mesh stretch sandals and a pair of Mach & Mach black stilettos.

I wonder if there's a problem using the foot pedals on a piano when you're wearing four- or five-inch high heels like this. Does it make the calf muscles ache?

But it hardly matters now. None of these items will ever be worn again, at least not by Kiaraa.

There's a small alcove down the far end of the wardrobe which contains more perfume. One bottle of Saharian Wind by Mancera, one of Eilish by Billie Eilish and three bottles of Estée Lauder Tuberose Gardenia.

I spray the Estée Lauder into the air. That's it. That's the ghostly scent I keep smelling everywhere. Obviously her favourite.

Put that back, I hear her say.

Kiaraa also owned a lot of sexy lingerie; once again, top-of-the-range stuff, usually black, sometimes red, rarely white. Lots of La Perla, mainly bras, knickers, and black camisoles, a Bordelle bodice bra with matching cincher brief, a black latex mini dress by Bondara, suspenders and playsuits by Myla, two bodysuits by Coco de Mer, a leather body harness which has had the label cut off, some extremely uncomfortable-looking seven-inch heels and that's just the tip of the iceberg.

I may be wrong, but it seems to me that there's leakage here from her taste in lingerie to what she can get away with wearing on stage. I think she'd have been pleased to overhear people saying 'Did you *see* what she was *wearing*? Oh, my *God*!' after some Bach recital or whatever.

Definitely an envelope-pusher, our Kiaraa. She liked to shake things up, if at all possible. She seemed fun, and I wish I'd known her.

I think of Penny from Elder Street again. Then I think of Aera. I don't know Aera's surname, either.

What am I going to do about her while the investigation is going on? I haven't thought that far forward yet. I think I can play the Penny situation by ear. The Aera situation (if there is one) is delicate on a lot of levels and will have to be handled differently.

There's a small, barely visible compartment in the back of the wardrobe behind the lingerie section, but it's locked. I push everything out of the way so I can get a good look at it. It needs a key, which I don't have, but I'm curious, so I get out my burglar's tools and pick the lock.

Two drawers silently slide out on their own, but it's nothing dramatic, just a selection of sex toys, BDSM stuff and a few items of more extreme lingerie, plus a neatly folded black PVC halter dress, which squeaks like a vinyl mouse as I attempt to ease it back into its packet.

There're also a couple of magazines: *Skin Two* and *KFS*. I have a quick flick through each: *Skin Two* is an upmarket fetish fashion magazine, lots of latex, rubber and leather being modelled, as well as interviews with couture corsetry designers, articles about goth weekends, and classy-looking ads for bespoke leather whips.

KFS contains more of the same but with a greater emphasis on erotic fiction, art, sex toys and lots of ads for dominatrices and swingers' clubs.

I flick through each magazine, looking for anything she may have circled or highlighted, or maybe a page that falls open, but there's nothing. In fact, both of these magazines smell and feel unused and unread. Judging by the dates, they'd have been pretty recent at the time of her abduction, so maybe she hadn't got around to looking at them.

I suppose I was searching for any clues that she might have entered some underground kink culture, but I think this sort of reading was just simple curiosity/entertainment on her part.

I replace both mags, gently push the drawers back in and lock up. I imagine the police missed this, or it would have been chiselled open and the magazines taken.

There's nothing very shocking or significant about this stuff. It only reflects interests that a lot of young women have.

It does make me wonder, though: who was this stuff being hidden from? Micha? A cleaner? A lover who wasn't into that sort of thing?

Or was she just naturally cautious; once again, a reaction to the conservatism of her background in Korea.

I wonder if she gives these magazines to whoever designs her stagewear and says *this is what I'm going for*.

The en suite bathroom is almost as big as the bedroom itself. Distressed, espresso-stained wooden floor, probably spruce, a freestanding copper bath surrounded by hexagonal white tiles, two black marble sinks and a matching bidet, grey-veined white marble walls, a large walk-in shower in silver travertine and a lot of shelves that are holding either neatly folded towels, or seashells and pieces of coral.

On one of them, a small, framed photograph of a young-looking Kiaraa with three female friends. They're all laughing. She's holding a white plastic rucksack with the word 'Dalki' on it in red.

One wall is entirely mirrored. There's even a television attached to the wall that can be seen from the bath (unless you're facing the wrong way). A small white chair with a slightly damp-corrugated copy of *Bon* magazine resting on it.

More shelves next to the sinks, and if it isn't more seashells, it's bottle after bottle of exotic bath oils and bubble baths: Temple Spa, Neom, Diptyque, Susanne Kaufmann, Made by Yoke, Mandala & Rose and L'Occitane.

There are also three Rituals aromatherapy diffusers dotted around. Kiaraa liked to pamper herself and why not; she had a stressful job.

I wonder if she had her fingers massaged. I wonder if she had her fingers *insured*.

The last room I check out on the first floor is yet another bedroom. This one looks as if it was used more regularly than the one upstairs.

There's a bookshelf with a Roxel Hi-Fi, four CDs (Ekaterina Kishchuk, Angel Olsen, Paris Combo, Baby Woodrose), a handful of books (all in Korean), a magazine called *Gratuitous Type*, another called *Noble Rot*. A bottle of Cîroc pineapple vodka and four Richard Brendon shot glasses.

There's a small bedside table on which rests a wooden duck, a bottle of Alba di Seoul cologne, a fashion magazine called *W Korea* and a book called *High-Speed Atomic Force Microscopy in Biology* by Toshio Ando.

The spacious ensuite bathroom is full of shampoos, conditioners, soaps, body oils, bubble baths, two tubes of O HUI cleansing foam and a half-full bottle of Rose D'Arabie by Armani. Presumably, Micha must have been a guest here from time to time.

Three out of the four walls are entirely mirrored. There are two freestanding cast-iron bathtubs, a black leather chaise longue and a red three-seater sofa.

Wooden floors again and a thick orange rug. A fair-sized print of *L'Odalisque* by Mariano Fortuny on the un-mirrored wall, but the paper's become a little ruched and discoloured, presumably from steam damage.

I'm getting nowhere with this, though I feel I'm starting to know Kiaraa a little better. I decide to go downstairs and take a look at the rooms down there.

The sitting room holds no real surprises or superb case-solving clues. No art on the walls in here. I scan her bookshelves, even looking behind the rows of books for...something. The books sneer at me, giving nothing away: *The Moon and Sixpence* by W. Somerset Maugham, *The Second Sex* by Simone de Beauvoir, *Cats & Plants* by Stephen Eichhorn, *A Woman's Life* by Maupassant, *Lost Hearts* by M.R. James, *The Art of Piano Playing* by Heinrich Neuhaus, *Heretic* by Ayaan Hirsi Ali, *Rêves d'Orient* by Serge Moati.

I spend fifteen minutes flicking through each book in turn, hoping that something enthralling will fall out, but it's another dead end.

On the coffee table, there's a sleek and sizeable book called *The Dream of a Sound*, about Fazioli, the company that made that futuristic piano upstairs, and another called *100 Interiors Around the World*, an upmarket interior design book with lots of Post-it notes stuck in various pages.

It seems that Kiaraa was planning some home improvements and was looking for inspiration.

Seeming rather out of step with the rest of the room is what appears to be an antique chest of drawers in red mahogany. Even though it's only three feet high, there are ten drawers, each one about three inches deep. I carefully pull out the top one.

It contains a large and beautifully laid out collection of fossils, each one in its own plastic compartment with its name on a small card at the bottom. Ammonites, brachiopods, corals, bivalves, echinoderms, and that's just the animals. Kiaraa was obviously a keen amateur palaeontologist.

Knowing her as I do so far, it's almost touching; the enthusiastic schoolgirl collector peeking out from behind the sophisticated, successful woman with the space-age piano, high heels and PVC dresses.

I take a look at each drawer, but they all contain roughly the same sort of thing. I attempt to make a futile connection between her abduction and these neatly displayed samples, but nothing comes.

There's a gigantic 85-inch Sansuyu 4K HDR Smart TV with several Blu-rays stacked next to it: *Paris – An Insider's Guide, The Handmaiden, The Seventh Veil, Take Care of my Cat, While You Were Sleeping, Cinema Paradiso,* and a couple of Bond films. But nothing really of interest in the whole room, or if there is, I haven't spotted it.

I try her office next.

A big, smart ebony desk, supporting an iMac 27-inch which I turn on. She has the same Herman Miller office chair as Micha. There's an old-fashioned, rather beautiful, and highly ornate oak bureau, which looks like an antique but is probably a recent reproduction. There are prints of *Odalisque à la culotte rouge* by Matisse and *Femme d'Orient* by Adrien Tanoux.

Interesting. That's three odalisque-themed prints so far, plus the Moati book in the sitting room. Just her taste in art or something else? From what I recall, an odalisque was a girl who served the concubines in a harem.

Sometimes, they became concubines themselves if they were considered beautiful enough. It's a well-known art genre and much of it seemed to be an excuse for the artist to paint a reclining naked woman. Maybe I'm overanalysing. Maybe I'm clutching at straws.

There are shelves groaning with thick sheet music folders, all alphabetically tagged on their spines in different colours. A tall, sturdy bookcase with books on music theory, composer biographies, musician biographies and other music-related stuff.

On the windowsill, a miniature bust of the composer Alessandro Scarlatti, which I'm only able to identify as his name is printed on the base. A Boss DB-90 metronome. Two small CD racks with maybe twenty classical CDs in each one. I take each jewel case apart and flick through the booklets. Nothing.

Two big blue ceramic plant pots with no plants and a small purple velvet sofa with two yellow cushions. That's it.

The bureau is locked. I decide to take a look inside, using my burglar's tools again to pop the lock. I pull down the writing flap and check all the pigeonholes and both small cupboards. Then I break into the drawers. But it's a disappointment. Bills, receipts, accountancy stuff, insurance, bank letters, tax things, concert programmes, old flight bookings.

I spend ten minutes speed-reading each item, but to no avail. I was really looking for creepy/disturbing fan mail, but there's nothing like that at all. Of the four small drawers, two are filled with more admin paraphernalia and two are empty.

I decide to have a more detailed search of the bedrooms, but just as I'm leaving the office, something makes me stop.

It's that bureau. My subconscious is telling me to take another look. But for what? I've checked every item in there.

I stand and give it the once-over. I grab both sides and carefully drag it away from the wall. It's heavy. I walk around it. I pat my hands over it. There's an inexplicably large gap between the writing flap and the highest of the drawers, which I noticed earlier, but didn't pay much attention to.

This gap is covered in a multiplicity of baroque carvings. No particular theme; animals, plants, abstract patterns, creepers, flowers. But there are just too many of them compared to the rest of the bureau surface. Are these rather beautiful designs intended to be purely ornamental, or are they there as a distraction?

I've read about furniture with secret compartments but never actually encountered one in real life. Until, I think, now. From what I recall, you have to be really careful. If you touch the wrong area or press the wrong hidden button, you can make things worse for yourself.

I gently run my fingers across the wood, following the tendril-like patterns, hoping they'll be friendly and lead me to something. Doesn't work.

I go down to the kitchen and start opening the cupboards until I find a torch. It's a hefty black super bright LED hand-held that was hiding under the sink. I switch it on. It works. Good. I was afraid the batteries would be dead. I take it back up to the office. I crouch down by the bureau and aim the beam at the little wooden curlicues beneath the writing flap.

There are two sunflower patterns that are slightly raised compared to the leafy background ones. I get the torch beam as close as I can to the surface and look for minute differences in the outlines, gaps that shouldn't be there, anything that looks wrong.

But that's where the designer of this damn thing would want you to look. That's why the sunflowers are so conspicuous. They'd *want* you to press the centre of the flower, it's the obvious thing to do.

I aim the torch from different angles; from above, from the side, from beneath. I can feel the sweat running down the sides of my body. And then, purely by chance, I see it. Like one of those 'spot the difference' puzzles in a children's comic, there's a carving of a bird, a sparrow perhaps, on the far right. The same bird appears on the left-hand side, but there's a very slight disparity.

It's the beak. The bird on the left has a distinct line separating the upper and lower mandibles. The bird on the right doesn't have this. I aim the torch at the bird on the left. Well, the worst thing that can happen is that the whole thing self-destructs, taking me with it.

I use the end of one of my keys and gently press it against the upper part of the beak. Nothing. I press a little more firmly. Still nothing. I try the lower part of the beak. I press firmly and keep pressing. There's a dull click. Then silence. Where did that click come from?

Another click, and the whole section beneath the writing flap moves forwards a centimetre.

I attempt to wedge my fingernails into each side so I can pull out whatever it is. There must be an easier way than this, but at the moment I can't work out what it is.

I put an enormous amount of pressure on it. My forearms ache and shake. Then slowly, I can feel it moving forwards. I keep up the pressure. I get a feeling that to stop now would have unwanted consequences. As I expected, it's a hidden drawer. As wide as the bureau, 7 inches high and 18 inches deep.

By the time it's all the way out, I hear two loud internal clicks. Hopefully, this means that it's locked into position. I cautiously take one hand away and then the other. It stays where it is. I take a deep breath and inspect the contents.

Two bunches of letters, both tied up with red ribbons. A beautiful fossil leaf plate measuring about 9 inches by 7 with three petrified ginkgo leaves on each side. A Daewoo K5 semi-automatic pistol. A small PMC ammo box containing twenty 9mm rounds. An A4 folder containing two sets of extremely explicit, erotic photographs of Kiaraa, one set in black and white, the other in colour.

And finally, a small item measuring no more than 3½ inches across and 2¼ inches down. It's made from a thin, silvery metal with miniature micro-grilles on the top and bottom.

It's one of my business cards.

10

CANNABICH238

This is impossible, of course.

As far as can be ascertained, no one has been in this house for close on two years. I'd never met Kiaraa and certainly didn't give her one of my cards.

So, the question is, who did? And when? And why?

I call Micha.

'Hello, Daniel. Is everything OK?'

I can't let her know about any of this. Not yet anyway.

'Everything's fine, Micha. I hope this isn't too late for you. I'm in Kiaraa's house. I just need to ask you… you mentioned that you hadn't been here since the police took a look around shortly after her abduction.'

'That is correct. Why do you ask?'

'No particular reason. So absolutely no one has been in here for about two years?'

'The house has been locked and the alarm system switched on, so no. They do a remote electronic check on the alarm system every two weeks, but apart from that…'

So, she was given my business card at least two years ago.

'I found a book that she'd received. A gift. It was from someone called Conceição. Do you know who that was?'

'Yes. That was Conceição Teixeira. She is a Brazilian soprano. She and Kiaraa were close about five years ago. I hadn't heard anything about her for some time before Kiaraa passed away.'

'OK. There's an iMac here I'm going to need access to. Also, is there an email account that you know of? One she used regularly? I'd like to look at her emails, if at all possible.'

'Oh. Can you hold on for a moment? I'm in bed. I'm just going to go in another room and get something.'

I look for a piece of paper. There's a cookery book on the surface that's falling apart anyway, so I rip out one of the pages and flatten it on the table in front of me. It's a recipe for grilled octopus with ancho chili sauce.

While I'm waiting, I get a text from Doug Teng.

Re: the Yuhwa TT7992. Last use was you. Before that, two years, one week and nine days ago at 19.44 and 28 seconds. No malfunctions and no sign of tampering. Trio of mobiles still ongoing.

So that means that Micha's guess was correct. Kiaraa left the house to go out to dinner, set the alarm and never returned.

Oh well, it was worth a try.

'Have you got a pen, Daniel?'

'Sure. Go on.'

'First of all, the password for her iMac is cannabich238. She had a Gmail account which was the one she used for most things. She certainly used it to communicate with me and I think with her agent and friends. It's jeongkiaraa@gmail.com. The password was daquin998, and I assume it still is.

'I believe the police had a look at that account at the beginning of their investigation. There was an old AOL account which she still used from time to time, but I don't think the police were concerned with that one for some reason. Same as the Gmail account, really: jeongkiaraa@aol.com. I don't know the password, though.'

'Great. Oh, and the heating came on once I'd keyed the passcode into the TT7992. How do I turn it off?'

'Don't worry. It'll turn itself off. It only comes on for fifteen minutes when someone neutralises that internal alarm. There's some clever reason for that, but I can't remember what it is. I can find out if you like.'

I reply to Doug's text.

jeongkiaraa@gmail.com and jeongkiaraa@aol.com

Passwords ASAFP please. Extra bonus and the chance to win your dream holiday.

'Don't worry. That's really useful, Micha, and thanks. Go back to sleep now.'

'I wasn't asleep, Daniel.'

'Well, go back to whatever you were doing.'

'Just reading.' Her voice is soft, drowsy. She sounds like a different woman. 'Oh. Switchboard. I forgot. It's a Sansuyu Jindo 5 system, so retains a record of all incoming and outgoing calls for five years. Those three mobile numbers did not appear before the ransom calls. I – oh.'

'You OK?'

'Um, just aches and pains. A lot of body changes at the moment. It's just a bit weird being pregnant.'

'I can relate.'

'Ha. You know Healthy Beauty? *Geongangmi*? It's a big thing for young Korean women. Kiaraa and I used to go to classes here in London, run by Choe Mi-Ok. Really cool. Weightlifting and strength training. Builds good muscles. Makes the body look toned and powerful.

'Kiaraa was really into it. She looked like a super-strong athlete, but still kept her womanish curves. I stopped when I got pregnant. I miss it. You should have seen me. I suspect you would have been appreciative. I liked my body being tight. I'm sure I'll do it again one day.'

'I'm sure you will. Oh. One small thing. Myeongdong, where you and Kiaraa grew up. What sort of place was it? We can talk about it tomorrow if you're tired.'

'It's OK. I – I like listening to you talk. You have a nice voice. Well, it was like anywhere else, really. Had its rough areas, you know? It was only when all the shops came along that it became more, um, genteel. Is genteel correct?'

'Sure. So, would you say that Kiaraa was pretty street-smart?'

'Mm?'

'Kiaraa. Would you say that she could sense danger when it was about? When she was walking around London, for example?'

A bit of a pause. 'Oh. Um, yes. I think so. I'm sorry. I was... I was drifting away there.'

'OK. I'll call you tomorrow. Thanks for your help, Micha.'

'You're very welcome, Daniel. Goodnight.'

I click her off.

I take a look at my watch. Still only five to eleven. I feel like I've been here for a couple of days. Come on, Doug. How long can this take? An image of Micha's pre-pregnancy super-tight body pops into my consciousness. I bat it away. I have to work.

I go upstairs to the office and search for some sort of carrier. All that stuff in the hidden drawer is coming with me; I just hope I can work out how to close it again. There's a Barbour messenger bag on the floor next to one of the shelves. That'll do.

I place the gun, ammo, letters, ginkgo fossil, business card and erotic photographs inside the bag and dump it by the front door so I don't forget about it.

I close the hidden drawer and spend five minutes looking for others like it, tap-tapping, patting, listening, lifting, though I can't imagine I'll find anything quite as intimate/interesting/informative as the stuff in the bag.

There's nothing. If there are any more hidden buttons, switches, or compartments, then whoever designed this was too smart for me, which is always possible. Perhaps one secret compartment was enough.

Doug gets back to me.

Gmail password daquin998

AOL password malikova223

Excellent. I thought the Gmail password might have changed, hence the double-check, but it's the same one that Micha gave to me. I sit down at the iMac, enter the password, and start with Kiaraa's Gmail account first.

I'm looking for a link to my business card being in the secret drawer. I cut to the chase and type 'Beckett' in the search fields for new, old, deleted and spam. Nothing. Then I try 'Daniel'. Still nothing.

Private may bring up too much stuff, so I try 'investigator' and 'detective'. Nothing there, either.

Last resort: 'private'. Quite a lot of stuff, including a lot of emails from a company called Private Parties, which looks like a high-end porn site purportedly featuring real people, uploading their athletic antics for the delight of well-heeled subscribers like Kiaraa. There's her account link, but it needs a password, so I leave it.

I skim through six or seven pages of emails, but apart from some junk mail from a company called Private Sex Style Japan (more porn) and a saucy Australian enterprise called Xtreme PrivateGirl Lingerie, there's nothing there that might relate to me. I check the AOL account next, trying 'Beckett' once again.

I get a result straight away. I sit back in the seat and laugh. This is all I need. Intriguing, all the same. And it could even be a breakthrough of sorts. It's a message to Kiaraa from two and a half years ago, and it's from a former client of mine who became a semi-regular lover.

My Dearest Kiaraa

I think we have made great progress over the last five months, and I was pleased to learn that you think of me as a friend, and not just as a therapist. I hope the business card I gave you will be of some use. Daniel Beckett is a hyper-competent investigator with astute attention to detail. He helped me during a very difficult time in my life and I can recommend him wholeheartedly. Do keep in touch, my dear.

All my love
Aziza

Aziza, or Dr Aziza Elserafie MBChB MRCPsych FRCPsych as she's known to her friends, is a renowned Wimpole Street psychiatrist. She hired me to deal with a complex marital situation that involved a rat of a husband who was running two separate families and a mistress, none of whom she knew about. I helped her take him to the cleaners and then some.

I started sleeping with her shortly afterwards, and it's an arrangement that has been going on intermittently for almost three years, though she is a little dissatisfied with the irregularity of it and never fails to describe her dissatisfaction in explicit and penetrating detail if she gets the chance, which I think I may be about to give her.

I did try to allow it to fizzle out at one point, and failed. Despite myself, it's hard to keep away from her, purely on a physical level. She's Egyptian, in her mid-fifties, strikingly and seductively attractive with a ravishing figure and an uninhibited, hedonistic, deviant nature that oozes from her every word and gesture, though I sometimes wonder if it's only me that sees it; she may be a sorceress.

Or I may need to become one of her patients.

I can't imagine what she would have been seeing Kiaraa for, and it's unlikely that she would tell me, despite Kiaraa being deceased. I may attempt some cynical manipulation; there has to be a way around her often-liberal interpretation of the Hippocratic Oath.

Those mirtazapine pills might have come from her, but they can be used for a lot of stuff, depression, OCD and panic attacks, so don't really give me very much. Also, the box hadn't been opened, so Kiaraa may not have actually been taking them.

What Aziza *has* to tell me, though, is why she gave Kiaraa one of my business cards. Was she in trouble? If so, was that trouble the cause of, or related to, her kidnapping? Her murder? Hyper-competent investigator, eh? Maybe I should up my charges.

I spend a further fifteen minutes trawling through the iMac, looking for anything else that might prove useful. Nothing jumps out. Kiaraa liked collecting photographs that she'd dragged off the net, but they're mainly of film stars, particularly Tom Cruise and Jennifer Lawrence, and lots of a K-pop band called Blackpink and another called Le Sserafim.

I take a final casual stroll around the whole house, touching things, moving things, inspecting things, but don't see anything that I haven't seen already. I can always come back if the mood takes me. I sling the messenger bag over my shoulder, reset the internal alarm, lock the front door behind me and leave.

I walk back in the direction of the cab rank that I passed earlier, making the incorrect assumption that I'll easily be able to get a taxi there, so I walk up Sloane Street, heading towards Knightsbridge tube. Five stops on the Piccadilly line to Leicester Square where I'll get off and walk back to Exeter Street in my customary convoluted way.

It strikes me that it was just over twenty-four hours ago that I met Suzanna at The Buddha-Bar, which is barely a minute's walk away from that tube station. Seems like a year ago.

Not a bad day, considering I've only been at it since two p.m. Met the client, got the kidnapping background info, learnt that the (three?) kidnappers/murderers were psycho vermin who called women 'my dear' and chose pink suitcases for them, made an engaging impact with Aera, visited Elder Street, got a dinner date planned with Plaster of Paris Penny, got Doug Teng tracking those mobile numbers and learned quite a bit about Kiaraa, her interests, her life and her pals. Oh, and had a ride in a very fast lift.

On top of that, I'll hopefully be speaking to DCI Sallow fairly soon, which may bear fruit. Or it may not. Police are notoriously unpredictable when it comes to talking to people like me, though I'm sure Micha's charity donation will smooth the way.

That DS that Penny spoke to is also something to consider. What was his name? Kinnaird? Scottish name but not Scottish. Sounded like a creep, which is what he may well have been, but that was unusual behaviour to display in the course of a murder inquiry. I'll keep it in mind.

Something about this case – and I don't know what it is yet – is putting me in a bad mood.

As I sit down in the tube compartment, I consider opening the messenger bag and taking a look at the contents of Kiaraa's secret drawer, then decide to do it later, particularly with regard to the gun, which may alarm the other passengers.

The introduction of Aziza into all of this was certainly a surprise. It must be a year since I saw her last. She seemed to be on very friendly terms with Kiaraa, which meant that the murder would have come as a great shock, so I'll have to be delicate. Would she have been questioned by the police? Perhaps she approached the police herself, offering to help.

Just one kiss.

And now the gun. Interesting that it was a Daewoo, the very make that Baek-Hayeon Bahk was an unintended victim of during his combat years. Did he somehow obtain it for Kiaraa? He would have to have smuggled it into this country for her. Unless he got it here, of course. But that's unlikely. The K5 is made primarily for the Korean military, though you can also get them in America.

One kiss each then we'll leave you alone.

Did Micha know about this gun? Did she ask Baek-Hayeon to get it for her sister? Does she have one herself? Why – *why* would a world-famous classical pianist need a gun? And if it comes to that, why would her psychotherapist think that she needed a private detective?

Come on. It's not as if we're gonna feel your tits.

And who were those letters from? At first glance, I thought 'love letters'. Maybe it was the ribbon they were tied up with. Maybe it's because they were hidden in her secret drawer. And the ginkgo fossil. Was that an expensive item? I have no idea.

I think that's what she wants. Is that what you want, love? You want us to feel your tits? Is that what you'd like?

Was that fossil a gift from the person who wrote the letters? Is it rare? Or – I can't concentrate. What the *fuck* is going on here? I look over my shoulder. A couple of guys; kids, really. Late teens. Tough, aggressive pricks. Intimidating a twenty-something young woman sitting on her own. One sits next to her, blocking her in, the other sits opposite her.

I think that's what she wants. She seems a bit of a ho to me.

I get up and sit down across from the mouthy fat one who's doing the blocking in. I can smell the lager on his breath. Carling Black Label.

'Someone sitting there, mate,' he says.

Yeah, yeah.

I lean forward so I'm speaking into his left ear. 'I've just got to tell you something about her.'

'What? Who the fuck...'

I place a hand on his knee, my thumb pushing downwards into the flesh on the inside of the thigh, two inches back from the base of the femur, thirty-degree angle. He glances at my hand, sneers, looks indignant, then his face is red, his eyes bulging and bloodshot. I speak quickly and quietly, just under the rattle of the carriage.

'Look at me. I know how much this hurts. In ten seconds, it'll get much worse. In fifteen seconds, you'll be crying for your mother. You. Your friend. Off this train. Right now. Next stop. Understand? Go.'

He nods, his face now purple and twitching. He stands up with difficulty and almost falls on top of me.

'Come on, Steve,' he says to his pal.

'What?'

'Come *on*.'

I look at the woman. She's close to tears. 'OK?' I ask.

She nods her head. She looks stunned. I keep an eye on my new friends as they get off at Hyde Park Corner, which I'm sure isn't where they were heading, but there're a couple of good bars nearby. Though I don't think those two'll get into either of them. At least I didn't have to use the gun.

* * *

'I wondered where you'd got to. I was going to ring for a male escort.'

'Just the one?'

'Well, it's a weekday. I didn't want to go crazy.'

Suzanna is wearing a dark green silk robe that she must have found behind my bedroom door. Belongs to Linda, who works as a sales assistant in The Body Shop in Regent Street. It's a little too small for Suzanna around the bust, but otherwise fits OK. I kiss her neck and hold her waist, pulling her towards me. She gasps and says, 'Oh.'

'Just some work I had to do on Micha's case. Took a little longer than I thought it would.'

'Not a nine-to-five job, is it. What you do, I mean.'

'Usually not. That robe looks good on you.'

'There's a bottle of Perrier Jouet in your fridge. Shall I open it?'

'Sure. There are some glasses in the kitchen.'

'I know. I've been nosing around while you were gone. There's a lovely set of Waterford trumpet flutes. You have good taste.'

'Not my taste. A friend's.'

I take the gun and bullets out of the messenger bag, wrap them in a tea towel and hide them at the back of the wardrobe in my bedroom under a pile of t-shirts. Suzanna returns with the champagne and we both head to the television room. We stand opposite each other.

'Some interesting items in that Lipstick & Leather bag,' she says. 'I had no idea. I thought it would just be lingerie.'

'I thought I'd spoil you.'

'Well, you certainly did that.' She takes a sip of champagne and nods towards an item resting on a table next to the stereo. 'You'll have to show me how that works.'

'There's a little booklet that comes with it.'

'I'd prefer a demonstration.'

'I might have a window next Thursday afternoon.'

She undoes the sash belt, and the front of the robe falls open. 'I have a meeting then. Could it be sooner?'

I slide the robe off her shoulders and use it to pull her towards me, gripping it tightly beneath her breasts. Our mouths are close, but we don't kiss.

'Any day in particular, Suzanna?'

'I'll have to consult my diary. Wait. I've just had a cancellation. Are you free in five minutes?'

'I'll just check with my people.'

She takes her champagne into the bedroom. 'Let me know when they get back to you. I'm in a bit of a hurry.'

11

THE WORK OF A PROFESSIONAL

The next morning after Suzanna has left for work, I sit in the kitchen with my second cup of Bourbon Espresso and watch as the sun makes slow-moving stripes across the table from the reinforced steel bars on the window. And so to day one of the investigation.

I've placed all the items from Kiaraa's secret drawer in front of me and stare at them, giving them ten seconds to magically rearrange themselves into something useful and logical. It doesn't happen.

I pick up the Daewoo K5 and sniff the end of the barrel. A faint smell of Napier gun oil. A full, thirteen-round magazine. There are signs that this gun has been used, but it isn't recent use. There's a version of this model called a DP51, though it's a commercial variant and not used by the armed forces like this one is. Has to have come from Baek-Hayeon, but we'll see. I take a photograph of it with my mobile.

Next, the letters.

I untie one of the bunches and take a single letter out of its envelope. I sniff it. A very weak odour of oud, cistus, patchouli and amyris. It's Oud Exquisite by Elegantes. Expensive.

The letter is brief, on a single cream sheet of watermarked Crown Mill paper. The writer used purple ink from a fountain pen with a reverse oblique nib; that almost always indicates someone who's left-handed. I look at the bottom first. I was hoping for a real name, but it just says 'Chaton'. This is French for 'kitten'. Looks like a female hand. Could this be from Odette Fournier?

Angel

Even as I start to write this, I get a thrill knowing that you will be reading it. I get a thrill knowing that when you read it you will be excited. I like writing to you and am glad I have started it. It is different from conversing by telephone. More romantic, perhaps? You are away for so much. Even when you are here it is so hard that I can't see you whenever I want to. My torment is great. All my inhibitions disappear when we are together. I have such excitement. You have corrupted me. That it is a secret from the man makes it even more arousing and wicked. (SMLLMC) Think of me before you sleep, as I do of you.

Chaton

Of course, this letter may not be from Odette at all, but I somehow feel it is. I'll have to speak to her.

Secret affairs can have all sorts of repercussions. Micha didn't seem to think that anyone at that dinner knew about Kiaraa and Odette, but you never know, and maybe Kiaraa told Odette something that might come in useful.

SMLLMC?

I speed-read all of the letters. There are sixteen in all. Looking at the post marks (all from London W11), they were written over a three-week period, ending just before Kiaraa's murder. I keep the dates in my head in case they become significant.

Each letter has the same theme: unconcealed frustration, declarations of undying love, powerful sexual obsession.

If Odette was behind these, perhaps that last dinner would have been thrilling for both of them, sitting there with Odette's husband present, sharing this exquisite secret.

Unless he knew and wasn't too bothered.

Many of these letters are explicit, and all the more erotic from being written in that breathless, syrupy style with its occasional odd inflection.

I can quite understand why they were hidden in that secret drawer. Whoever wrote them must have been devastated by her death. And if the whole thing between them was clandestine, who could they talk to about it?

I run my fingers over the smooth surface of the ginkgo fossil. Come on. Who are you from? Are you from the writer of those letters? Or someone else? Presumably it was from an individual who was aware of her interest in palaeontology, perhaps a fan.

Once again, I get a sense of Kiaraa watching me sort through her most private things and smiling at my confusion.

I take a £20 note from my wallet for size comparison, place the fossil next to it and take five photographs with my mobile. Then I call a company called Fossilia UK, who deal in the buying and selling of such items. I speak to a Mr Toby Bauguess and ask if I can email the photographs to him and get a rough idea of how much the fossil might be worth.

He tells me that he'd have to see it in person to give an accurate assessment, but for the moment that will do. I send the email.

Now the A4 folder. I tip both sets of photographs onto the table to avoid touching them more than is necessary. Some photographic paper is susceptible to staining/damage from barely discernible fingertip sweat. I lightly tap the corner of one of them with a middle finger to test its moisture uptake. Seems OK.

There are nine photographs in the first set, all 10 by 13 inches, and Kiaraa is naked in each. Grainy black and white. Unusual, often haunting lighting. Certainly the work of a professional.

I think of the older photograph of her I saw yesterday: the yellow dress, the long hair, the perfect skin, the wide smile. In these photographs she isn't smiling, and her hair is shorter, more like the pixie cut that Micha favours. In fact, if it wasn't for the slight facial differences and the downturn of the mouth, this could actually *be* Micha, though without the subtle tell-tale signs of a five-month pregnancy.

I can see why Kiaraa would be a great subject for a photographer specialising in this style of portrait. Symmetrical features, extraordinarily beautiful eyes, a sexy mouth, and great bone structure.

Her body is lithe and toned, the hips wide, the breasts almost nonexistent, and it's plain that this last feature was to the photographer's taste. Either that or it's a feature that she knew looked good/sexy and wanted to emphasize. Somehow, it doesn't make her look androgynous, but more incontestably feminine.

Every photograph accentuates the fact. Three of them have her lying on her back, stretching, arching her spine, and looking sideways into the camera, unsmiling, the nipples dark and prominent. In one of these her legs are wide apart, and she's digging her scarlet fingernails deeply into her thigh flesh; eyes tightly shut, teeth clenched.

In another, she's wearing black hold-up stockings and black velvet heels, a hand draped over one breast, head turned slightly to the side, eyes smouldering, staring straight at the camera. Looks like part of a high-quality boudoir shoot. My favourite so far.

In four of them, she's sitting or standing, hands clasped behind her head, back arched, chest thrust forward and once again that no-nonsense, challenging, erotic glare at the camera. It may be fanciful, but it's as if she's saying 'Yes. It's me. You didn't expect *this*, did you'.

The final two photographs have her standing with her back against a brick wall, looking at the floor, arms spread outwards, legs tightly crossed at the ankles, the quasi-crucifixion pose accentuating the sleek animalistic muscularity of her body, in particular the abs and the pecs. All that *geongangmi* seemed to have paid off.

Now I'm wondering what Micha's body looks like, despite her pregnancy, but I assure myself that this is a natural thing to think under the circumstances, and I am in no way deviant.

Kiaraa's skin looks different in these two, and on closer inspection it appears as if it's been oiled. These shots are also dramatically lit from beneath, so giant jet-black shadows of her body are cast on the wall behind her. Looks very 1920s/Man Ray influenced, though I'm no photography expert.

I place all of them in a row on the table. These are incredibly sexy, slick, elegant images. You could imagine them in some unimaginably expensive Taschen coffee table book. Nine. Why nine? I flip one over and take a look at the back, hoping for a photographer's stamp, but there isn't one. There is, however, a small #3 written in red ink on the bottom left-hand corner.

I take a look at the back of all of them. Numbered one to ten, but seven is missing. Was this given to someone as a gift? Perhaps to 'Chaton'? It could be that more are missing, but that hardly matters at the moment.

The second set are in colour. Same size as the others. Once again the numbering on the back of these prints goes as far as ten, but this time there are three photographs missing: one, four and seven. And this set is a different kettle of fish altogether. We've definitely drifted into the world of kink here; something that was hinted at in Kiaraa's belongings back at her house and has now materialised in photographic reality.

Unlike the monochrome set, these look as if they're mostly the product of different sessions, but something about the technique, the professionalism, and the way the camera is *appreciating* her, for want of a better word, tells me that the same photographer took these.

She's on her back, naked, her wrists tied with black rope and raised above her head, which is turned to her left. Teeth clenched and eyes tightly shut once more. There's a frog tie connecting the tops of her thighs to her ankles, resulting in what must have been an uncomfortably wide spreading of the legs.

Now she's standing next to a grand piano, but it's not the ultramodern one I saw in her house. One leg raised and planted on a plush velvet piano stool. She's wearing a black harness bra but nothing else.

She holds a rattan cane in both hands and bends it close to snapping point in front of her belly. She's looking straight into the lens and smirking, her expression contemptuous and superior. Looks like she's been oiled again.

More rope bondage. Red rope this time. She sits on a wooden bench, head down, thighs tied together. Tight, exquisite latticework around the breasts, her wrists bound together with handcuff knots.

Some sort of special effect on her skin. Looks golden. One great photograph.

Now she's naked once more, lying on her front on a pile of large Mondrian-esque cushions. Her head is turned to the side so you can see it's her. Her expression is blank. A leather collar around her neck, her wrists bound with rope behind her back, a rattan cane resting across her buttocks. The photographer's backdrop paper is a highly intense yellow. Almost too much, but it somehow blends well with the other primaries in the photograph.

Now a few that look like they've walked straight out of the pages of *Skin Two* or *KFS*. She looks incredible in these. Glam, striking makeup, long blonde wig, the first one in a black latex cupless crop top and matching thong, the second in a low-cut red latex suspender dress. In the latter, she's blindfolded and holding a flogger whip.

The third looks like a bit of fun or an outtake. She's only wearing a black latex underbust corset and impossible heels, but she's teetering, laughing, her hand across her mouth, as if she's enjoying the whole thing and can't keep it inside anymore. Maybe she fell over after it was taken. That vivid yellow backdrop paper makes another appearance.

And so it goes on, getting more and more extreme with each shot.

I take a look at my watch. I've only been looking at these for four minutes, but it feels like an hour. Why is that? I must look it up.

I wonder why she had these done. A record for herself of when she was looking this good? Souvenirs for her lovers? A dark side of herself that she wanted to explore? A deviant streak that she wanted to share with somebody (is that why four are missing)?

Are there digital versions? If so, where are they and what did she want them for? They certainly didn't crop up in the photo file on her computer unless they were hidden in some crafty way, which is always possible.

Was she sending them to strangers who may not have known who she was? Was she an exhibitionist? Did she get a buzz out of showing them to people? Did she get a buzz out of having them taken? Was it in some way liberating?

And who, for that matter, took them? A friend? A lover? A pro photographer?

The last option seems the most likely, though it's not impossible to do stuff like this if you're an enthusiastic amateur with all the gear, motivation, and the right influences.

Finally, are these photographs somehow connected to why she was abducted and subsequently murdered? And if so, how?

I don't know what to do with them. I guess I should give them to Micha, but part of me wants to get them framed and put them on the wall. Each one is absolutely, dazzlingly beautiful.

I adjust the ceiling lights and take a photograph of each one with my mobile; may come in useful.

As I stare at them, an insane part of my brain is thinking, 'I'd like to meet her', then the sane part says 'Hey. She's dead. Remember? What's wrong with you? Get help!'

My business card seems out of place in this little collection. She could easily have kept it in a wallet or purse. After all, it only has my name and mobile number on it. I could have been anybody. OK, it could be connected to the gun and the ammunition, and at a stretch it could be connected to the letters, but its presence seems unnecessary. I may be overthinking.

I look at my watch. Time to bite the bullet. I make another coffee, sit back down with my selection of erotic photographs, fossil, gun, bullets and love letters, call my contact and wait for someone to pick up.

'Dr Elserafie's practice. Good morning. How may I help you?'

'Hi. I wonder if you'd be so kind to put me through to Dr Elserafie. My name's Daniel Beckett.'

'May I ask what it's about?'

'It's about her golf club membership. It's in arrears.'

Slight pause. 'Thank you. Um. I'm just going to put you on hold.'

Five seconds of "The Girl from Ipanema".

'Very amusing, Daniel.'

'How are you, Aziza?'

'I have not seen you for almost a year. Is this how it goes? You pick my brain about some psychiatric matter, you take me to your bed and ravish me and then I have to wait until the next time I am of use to you? Have you ever heard of the phrase "crawling up the walls"? I frequently hear it from my most disturbed patients. I fear you may have a Cluster C personality disorder.'

'I'm sure it hasn't been a year. I…'

'Nine months, fifteen days and ten hours. That's a year as far as I am concerned. I am very busy today. Booked solid. I have no spare time to speak to you. What is it about?'

'I don't think I can discuss it on the phone. It's both complex and confidential. It's about a former client of yours.'

'A client of *mine*? How do *you* know who my clients are?'

'It's about Kiaraa Jeong.' And a quick lie: 'Her sister told me that you had been treating her.'

Long silence. Probably about a minute. A solitary ant walks across the kitchen table. Where can that have come from? I'm on the third floor. Are there more?

She clears her throat. 'Such a loss. I wept. I enjoyed her company.'

'I've been hired to find out who was responsible for her death. I need to speak to you.'

'You will take me out to dinner tonight. I'll leave the choice of restaurant to you. Text me when you have arranged it. Then we will return to your flat and you will make love to me in the usual protracted and barbaric way that I loathe and that disgusts me. My first appointment tomorrow is at eleven am, so you may exhaust me until the early hours. Am I making myself crystal clear, Daniel?'

'A bit subtle, but I think I've got the gist of it.'

'How would you like me to dress?'

'I'll leave it to you.'

'How would you like me to dress?'

'I really don't mind.'

'How would you like me to dress?'

'Tight skirt, tight blouse, stockings not tights, suspender belt, four-inch heels, indecent and immoral black lingerie which you will buy today from La Perla in Sloane Street. Be as brazen as you like in your choices. Go wild. Surprise me.'

She sounds a little breathless. 'Yes. Yes. That's good. I'll go there during my lunch break. Goodbye, Daniel. *Prendre vos commandes est un plaisir.*'

I take a deep breath and call Le Jardin d'Épicure in Covent Garden, as I know Aziza likes French brasserie and bistro food and it has a good bar. It's also a few minutes' walk away from my flat, which, under the circumstances, will be pretty essential. They're not in yet, so I leave a message for a table booking which I know they'll reply to.

Just as I'm heading to the shower my mobile starts ringing.

'Daniel? It's Micha. I have some news. Mr, er, Detective Chief Inspector Sallow responded to my message. He is on holiday for two weeks from tomorrow but agreed to give you an interview this morning or, if necessary, this afternoon, though I think he'd prefer this morning.

'I think I mentioned before that he was Homicide and Major Crime Command, but he is not in their headquarters at present. He has been at work since eight this morning and said you may visit at any time as long as it doesn't take too long.' There's a laugh in her voice. 'He likes to let me know that he's always busy.'

She gives me the address. Putney Bridge Road, opposite Bective Place. That'll be East Putney tube station. District Line. Too much of a pain. I'll get a cab.

'That's really useful, Micha, and this morning will be fine for me. Any news from Kiaraa's agent about Odette Fournier?'

'Not yet. Her work hours seem to be very erratic. Sometimes she doesn't get into work until midday. I could not get hold of her yesterday. I left a message...'

'She obviously doesn't work the Korean way. Alright. And I'll need a quick meeting with Baek-Hayeon about a minor point. Will he be in today?'

'He is in every day. Just ask for him at reception. I'll let him know you're coming, but it may be useful for you to text him once you're on your way. I am not in the office today, however, if you were hoping to check in with me. I'm leaving shortly. I am travelling to Brussels with one of our smartphone designers. I will be back this evening at Heathrow at twenty-thirty. What are you speaking to Baek-Hayeon about?'

I have to lie. Come on, subconscious, throw something up. 'I wanted to go over his account of the ransom drop-off. Since we last met, I've been to Elder Street and spoken to one of the residents there. She remembered the case and was interviewed by the police.'

'You have been there already?'

'Yesterday, after I'd seen you.'

'And then Kiaraa's house last night. You *have* been busy.'

'I'm hoping you'll recommend me to your female friends.'

'Ha. I think they would like you.'

'Not if they knew me.'

'That's probably why they'd like you.'

'That's too clever for me.'

* * *

When the cab drops me at Bective Place, I look around Putney Bridge Road for something that looks like a police station, but there's nothing.

Across from where I'm standing is a brand new four-storey block of smart office buildings; 8,000 square feet, it says on a big sign outside. Seems like they're still pitching for companies to fill it.

There's a postman with a trolley across the road, so I run over to ask directions, but as I'm halfway across, I see a brief flash of a police uniform on the first floor, so this must be it. I look at my watch. 10.46.

There are a pair of doors on the corner of the building, which hiss open as I approach. There's a reception desk with no one behind it and an unopened box of printer paper on the floor. Strong smell of fresh concrete and paint. I stand around like an idiot for about thirty seconds until what I assume to be a young female police officer comes in, eyeballs me, ignores me, walks over to one of the two lifts, and presses a button. I'll have to swallow my male pride and ask for help.

'Excuse me. I'm looking for DCI Sallow, Homicide and…'

'I know. I work with him. I'm a DC. Come with me.'

I stand next to her as the lift ascends. She runs a hand through her hair, looks up at me and smiles briefly. She checks something on her mobile. Red hair, lovely face. Hardly any time. Sod it.

'Hi. My name's Daniel. Would you like to come out to dinner one night?'

We arrive at the third floor. She looks astonished. We get out. I get a hard, suspicious stare.

'Are you kidding me? Has somebody here put you up to this?'

I fish out a business card. 'I know this is a bit sudden. I just felt compelled. I'm a private investigator. Send me a text if you're interested and I'll sort something nice out. What's your name?'

She looks at my card as if it's an alien artefact. Then there's disbelief mixed with humour in her eyes. 'Scarlett?' she says, as if she's not sure.

'OK. Nice to meet you, Scarlett. Where is, er…'

'The office down the end with the door open.'

'Thanks. Don't forget.'

As I walk away I can hear her laugh out loud. Well, we'll see.

'DCI Sallow?'

'Mr Beckett, I presume. Come in. Would you like something to drink? Coffee? Tea?'

We shake hands. Strong grip. Cautious eye contact.

'Coffee would be great, thanks. Dash of milk, no sugar.'

Detective Chief Inspector Hugh Sallow is a tall, rugged-looking black guy in his mid-forties. Hair already grey and receding. Grey eyes, as well. Deep scar on the back of the left thumb. Probably a ligament operation. Wedding ring. Remnants of a Birmingham accent. Paul Smith black wool suit. Silk navy tie with small multi-coloured spots. Hugo Boss chronograph watch.

Not the first designer-clad cop I've come across. I always wonder if they get pissed when they get a rip in their expensive jacket while chasing villains. Does it make them more careful? More cautious? Less effective?

'So,' he says, as he makes the coffee. 'Fourth time lucky for Ms Jeong.'

'Could be.'

My mobile trembles. It's a text from Aera.

Just wishing you good fortune in your work today. A.

I may be in later today, Aera. Pls do not sit in that provocative manner when I arrive. It affects my concentration.

She replies instantly: **blushes**

'She said you weren't ex-police like the others. Came highly recommended. I'll be honest with you, Mr Beckett. I don't like dealing with private investigators who used to be in the job. Either they're cocky and think you're a mug for remaining in the force on the shit pay, or they come across as sad and apologetic, like they know you're thinking they're wankjugs and you're wondering how they fucked up and had to join the private sector. No offence.'

Wankjugs? 'What were the three other investigators like?'

'I'm sure Micha told you about them. Two of them, Lockford from Bespoke Investigations and Fenwick Jnr from Fenwick & Fenwick were the former sort, Teece the latter. I looked Teece up to confirm how perceptive I was. Bounced out for taking bribes. Getting close to his pension, too. What a mug. Takes all sorts. Have a seat.'

'Thanks. I won't take up too much of your time. I'm sure you're busy.'

'What were you talking to DC Sackville about?'

That must be Scarlett. 'Just asking directions.'

'OK.' He shrugs and smiles. 'Everyone fancies her. Waste of time. She's a bit aloof. Intelligent girl, though. Into the force straight out of university. Did English Lit, I think. She was involved in the case, too. Trying to track down that bloody Fiat van, among other things. I assume you know about the van.

'And she also took part in the frustrating hassling of Economic Crime Command. If something spectacular comes up while I'm away, you can always give her a bell here. I'll give you her direct number.'

He waves a hand at the walls and terrible furniture. 'Sorry about the state of this place, by the way. Looks shit, I know. The main HQ is having the heating replaced so they're redecorating it at the same time. This is just for a month or two, I sincerely hope. Bit of a pain. Parking's terrible. Oh, and we don't have access to the mainframe computer here, so you'll have to rely on my memory for a lot of stuff, I'm afraid.'

'Micha Jeong said you were going on holiday tomorrow.'

'Taking the family to Innsbruck. Austria. Broaden the kids' horizons. Ever been there?'

'Can't say I have.' Apart from four years ago. Stayed one night in the Nala hotel. ZEN room. Nice bar. Had a Glühwein. Very sweet.

He sits down opposite me, taking in my general appearance just like I've been doing to him. He glances at his Boss watch. Subtle.

'OK. First of all, Mr Beckett, I have to tell you that the murder of Kiaraa Jeong is an active, ongoing case for us, despite the fact it happened two years ago. I don't want you to think that we've stopped investigating it.

'Unsolved murders are never officially closed and murder as a crime is not subject to a statute of limitations. At the present time, we have, however, got nowhere with this case. It happens, you know?'

'Sure.'

'I fully understand why Micha Jeong has reached out to people like yourself and I'm prepared to give you as much assistance as I can within reason. I would ask you not to repeat anything that we discuss today with anyone else.

'I would also ask you to inform me personally of any discoveries you may make that would help with the solving of this crime. I said exactly that to the other investigators so don't think you're getting special treatment.' He laughs. 'That's the small print over with. Now let's see what's what.'

12

OPERATION IVORY

I'll have to tread carefully with this guy. He's most likely speaking to me because of the money that Micha slung to the Police Care UK charity.

He probably feels uneasy about it, particularly in the light of his remark about the detective from Bespoke Investigations being thrown out for taking bribes. You could argue that he himself has been bribed, and he must suspect that Micha told me about her generous donation.

To add to that, I can tell immediately that this case upsets him in some way, and that it's not wholly connected to the fact that he and his team have made no headway.

I get the impression that he wants to talk to someone about it in a way that he can't with his colleagues and was reluctant to with the other private investigators. He has to watch what he says, and it bugs him.

He drinks some coffee and taps his fingers on the table. He turns his head from side to side. He stares at the ceiling. I bet he gets migraines. I can tell he's the sort of officer who'll respond best to a no-nonsense Q&A session, so that's what he'll get. I'll also give him space to speculate.

'Who do you think did this?' I ask.

He purses his lips. He's tense as fuck. I'll give it five seconds before he cracks.

It's three.

He slams his hand down so hard on the desk that my ears ring. His coffee spills. I hope that watch has good shockproofing.

'Cunts. Cunts did this, Mr Beckett.'

I'm beginning to like him.

He rubs his hand. That must have hurt. He tears off some sheets of kitchen roll and mops up the coffee mess. 'I want to get my hands on the people that murdered that woman and rip them to fucking pieces.

'I've got two girls. Nine and eleven. It fucks me off, I mean *really* fucks me off that they're going to grow up in a country where people like that are floating around, doing whatever the fuck they like.

'And it fucks me off that I'm restrained from doing what's necessary when I catch them. And I will catch them. I want to look them in the eye. I want to teach them a lesson they'll never forget.

'I'm going to tell you the state Kiaraa Jeong's corpse was in, just so you understand my rage and just so you understand the sort of human garbage we're dealing with here, and the sort of people you may find *you're* dealing with.

'I could be in Shit Street just telling you about this, and I'll be in Shit Street telling you some other stuff, but to be honest, I don't really care anymore as far as this case is concerned, and if I have to confide in someone from the private sector, I'm going to do it.

'The other guys that Micha hired; I didn't feel comfortable talking to them in this way. Ex-cops. You know how I felt about that. But I have no problem with breaking the rules when it suits me. I never have had.

'There's pressure on me to dump this case. Dump isn't the right word. Reprioritise. Use my time on things that are more recent, that may be more easily solved. I get it, I really do. Unsolved murder cases like this are never officially closed, but there's a point where investigative effort simply stops, unless new information comes to light. That's where you might come in. Or you might not.

'As you know, I'm going on holiday tomorrow for two weeks. Nothing would please me more than to come back and find someone like you had hung these fuckers out to dry. I don't see it happening, but you never can tell. What did Mr Bahk tell you about the condition of her body?'

'He said that she was naked, tied up, multiple stab wounds, bruises, minor cuts and her fingers and thumbs had been cut off.'

'Mm. She'd been stabbed thirty-six times. We call that overkilling. Just once would probably have done the trick, but that wasn't enough for the killer or killers. Many causes: extreme anger, resentment, psychopathy, we'll never know until we find the culprit or culprits and question them.

'That kind of male rage – and I'm assuming it was a male, it *feels* like it was a male – is infantile in origin. You'd be looking at someone who, in many ways, hasn't grown up. Probably lots of undiagnosed problems. But still capable of functioning in society, capable of fitting in.

'Now, the fingers and thumbs. The initial post-mortem examinations suggested that these were cut off using some sort of tool. Bit of a messy job. I hadn't heard of anything like it before. Certainly hadn't *seen* anything like it before. Don't want to see anything like it again.

'After two weeks, one of our forensic clever clogs confirmed it had to have been done using a heavy-duty wire cutter or cable cutter, as opposed to, say, a bone cutter like vets use, or a saw, or a pipe cutter, or cutting pliers, or some sort of knife. Minute traces of molybdenum from the blades was the icing on the cake, apparently.

'The post-mortem also showed that the digits were cut off when she was still alive. Can you imagine? Considering who she was? What she did? Just think about that for a moment. Pure fucking sadism. Pure evil. I hope to God she passed out after the first one.

'Anyway, once I knew the type of tool, I passed that info to our investigative team. It might have come in useful. Didn't, as it turned out, but there you go. Might turn out to be of use to you.'

'So, you and your investigative team didn't know about the wire/cable cutters until two weeks after the body was found.'

'That's right. Initially, we had no accurate idea of how something like that might have been done. Could have been a hammer and chisel for all we knew. Or an axe.'

'How soon after the body was discovered did your guys start questioning the residents of Elder Street and the surrounding roads?'

'Can't remember exactly. I didn't organise that part of it. Wouldn't have been more than a couple of days, though.'

'How much detail did they give out about what had happened to her?'

'They told all the people they questioned that she had been stabbed to death full stop. My orders. Anything else, any more details, would have been counterproductive; too upsetting and pretty irrelevant, really.

'We wanted people to remember things clearly, which they tend not to do if we put bloodcurdling images into their heads. Unsettles people.

'The other thing is, of course, that we don't give out every single detail in the hope of catching someone out, d'you know what I mean? Could even be a friend or relative. Someone who knows something they shouldn't know might pop their head above the parapet. Close relatives we generally give the whole picture to, unless your gut instinct tells you to avoid it. It's never perfect. We're only human.'

'Why are you telling *me* all this stuff?'

'Maybe it feels right. Who the fuck knows? Gut instinct again. I think now's the time to do it.'

'Did Micha see the body?'

'Yup. She and her security guy. He'd already seen Kiaraa in the car, of course. I think he was there to hold Micha's hand, really. Stop her passing out. He looked more rattled than she did. Went quite pale, I recall. Thought he was going to blub. Military type. You'd think he'd have seen it all.

'We made her look as presentable as we could under the circumstances. Not easy, but we have experience. So, there're a few injury details that she doesn't know about, or him. Like I said, sometimes doesn't pay to give too much info in a case like this, even to nearest and dearest.'

'It must have been frustrating, having to wait two weeks for that information about the cutters.'

'Par for the course. Forensics, you know? Lots of staff cuts. Get in the queue. And this is London, after all. Plenty homicides. Hundred and fifty a year on average. And it *was* frustrating, but that's police work for you.

'Told her sister about the fingers, obviously, but I didn't tell her that Kiaraa was alive when it happened. Another visit to Shit Street for me there, but I just...she was upset enough, you know? Maybe one day.'

That detail about the fingers and thumbs being removed while she was still alive gives me a cold feeling in the pit of my stomach. I've come across people who would do something like that and they're rarely sane.

'Did you make any headway on exactly what type of cutter it was? Make? Model? The sort of person who would use it?'

He shakes his head. 'They're a popular tool and there are thousands of different types made in the UK. None of them leave distinctive, traceable marks. Many of them have the molybdenum coating on the cutting edges.

'They're used in heavy industry, by electricians, jewellers, kids who've lost the key for their bike lock cable, people cutting through vape coils; the list is endless. I've got a couple at home, just for household stuff.'

'The stabbing. What sort of knife?'

'Eight-inch blade. Double-edged stainless steel. Could have been a hunting knife. We didn't find it. Had five officers and three dogs having a good look around the golf club and surrounds, but it was a waste of time. Had to do it, though. Procedure.

'Oh – another thing about the overkilling, Mr Beckett. She would almost certainly have bled to death from the fingers and thumbs being removed, according to our doc. There was probably no need for the rest of it. Make of that what you will. One of this gang had issues, I suspect.'

'Micha said she heard three separate male voices when Munro made the second call. That was when they let her hear Kiaraa being maltreated.'

'That's right. I've been working on the assumption that there were at least three of them. She wasn't sure, though, and you can't always trust the memory of someone who's suffered that type of trauma.'

'Sounds a bit unprofessional,' I say. 'If I was making that call, I'd tell my cohorts to keep it down.'

'True. Made me think it was a mixture of pro and amateur. Didn't occur to the guys in the background to shut up. Could mean nothing, of course.'

'Any CCTV footage between the restaurant and her home that night?'

'No. You have to remember that most of the buildings in that area, hotels, embassies and so on, have their cameras aimed at their front entrances, not at the street. We didn't get any lucky breaks.'

'I walked the route last night. What about traffic cameras?'

'Checked them and the traffic light ones. The Gatso RLC 36 units only react to certain types of vehicle movement; someone skipping a red light, stuff like that.

'And then there was the rape. We found two separate DNA samples. Micha was in such a state I could hardly bring myself to tell her, and when I did she kind of went catatonic. It's one of those duties you hate, know what I mean? I had to phrase it in such a way that I didn't put some unnecessarily horrific vision of Kiaraa's last hours into her head. Not easy.

'I can still remember her face when I told her, y'know?' He sighs and looks out of the window. Terrible view. A petrol station and a half-demolished block of 1950s flats. I can hear a muffled bass boom from a passing car, and two dogs arguing with each other.

'I take it that those two DNA profiles didn't match any you had on file.'

'We had a look, obviously. I take it you're familiar with the Criminal Justice and Police Act 2001?'

'It's my bedside reading.'

He smirks and nods. 'Well, since that Act, we've been able to retain DNA samples from people charged with a crime even if they're subsequently acquitted.

'And since the Criminal Justice Act 2003 we can take samples for any recordable offence, even if the person involved hasn't been charged, or, like before, was charged and then acquitted.'

'So, how many samples are there on file?'

'The National Criminal Intelligence DNA Database has samples from over three and a half million people.'

'Is it possible that a match could not have been found? Computer glitch?'

Tough stare. 'It's a failsafe system. It has to be.'

'Is there any way you could hand over the relevant DNA data to me?'

He answers my question by laughing.

'Back to the post-mortem for a second,' I say. 'Was there any sign of drugs that might have been used to capture her or keep her subdued?'

'Flunitrazepam. Rohypnol, the rape drug. Liquid. Administered orally. I presume she was given it to subdue her shortly after she was lifted. Small trace of alcohol in her system consistent with what we know about the dinner she'd been to. She'd had two glasses of white wine.'

'Anything like a wound to the head? Any sign of an assault that could have been used to knock her out before abducting her?'

'There were so many wounds and bruises that it was impossible to pinpoint the one that initially disabled her if that's what happened. She could have – I dunno – she could have been stunned in some physical way that didn't leave a mark. Or much of a mark. If you push someone against a brick wall with enough force they'll lose consciousness. Done it myself. Accidentally, of course...'

'Could the overkilling have been done to distract/deflect from any physical evidence of an initial assault?'

'Once again, possible. But we're not mugs. That wouldn't fool us for long. Personally, I don't think that would explain the overkilling.'

'D'you think that someone she knew might have politely invited her into their car? No fuss? No struggle?'

'Not impossible. But she was a short distance away from her home, so it would have been a bit weird. Unless it was pissing down, which it wasn't that night. Even then…'

'If that had happened,' I say. 'We know that it wasn't any of the people that she'd been having dinner with. Did they have any theories?'

'I asked them if she had any close friends or acquaintances who lived in the vicinity who may have given her a lift or whisked her off to a club.

'None of them thought that those scenarios seemed likely, and neither do I. She wasn't a clubber and even if she was, she was tired that night. That's why she left early.'

'OK. Why do you think they picked her to kidnap?'

'I think they knew who she was. I think they also knew who Micha was and how much she was worth as an individual. There was money in that family. It was likely that someone somewhere would be able to arrange things and arrange them quickly. Speed is of the essence in kidnappings, hence the forty-eight-hour payment window.

'Micha told me that neither sister mentioned the other in any media. It was an agreement they had. So, their relationship was not in the public domain. But I'm sure if you dug deep enough…'

'Did you check that there might have been an article or interview somewhere that mentioned Micha and her probable financial status, and/or her relationship to Kiaraa?'

He presses the tips of his fingers into his eyeballs. 'I got two of my officers to pursue that line of enquiry, plus a friend who works in the PNC had a look as a favour to me. Micha popped up from time to time, but it was all work-related stuff and no personal monetary details.

'She did appear on a rich list of people in her industry a few years ago, but we really had to dig to find that. It was in a specialist magazine published in France. *Le Nouvel Economiste* or something.

'Another possibility is that they may have thought she'd have access to Kiaraa's money, but that kind of doesn't make sense.' He scratches his head. 'I mean, I've got a younger brother. I wouldn't be able to extract money from his bank account that easily, I don't think, particularly if he wasn't available to OK it.'

'They didn't give Micha much time to sort it out,' I say. 'Which may indicate that they knew exactly how much she was worth.'

'You could be right. But they're criminals, Mr Beckett. Not usually the brightest bunch in my experience, and they might have got lucky.'

He leans forwards. 'I've given this a lot of thought. The reason that we've both been going around in circles for a couple of minutes is because both women involved in this were extremely affluent individuals. It's an unusual situation. It would be more normal if someone snatched the kid or wife of some millionaire businessman.'

'They got the money. Why did they kill her?'

'There's always a risk of a kidnapping ending in murder. She could identify them in some way. She'd seen them, heard them. They had no honour. No decency. They were amoral. Like I said, they were cunts.

'Murder after rape is also a thing, you know? No one's going to report a rape to the police if they're dead. It removes a huge source of stress for the rapist or rapists.

'You might say that having committed murder would be a little stressful, but some of these people don't think in the way you or I would. Some of them are just nutcases or simpletons. Or psychopaths.

'Maybe rape was not what they had in mind when they planned the kidnapping, but things must have changed. Maybe one of them was a loose cannon who couldn't control himself.'

'But you discovered two DNA samples.'

'You may not like this, but I'm just being pragmatic. Once the first one had done it, why shouldn't the other one have a go? After all, they were going to have to kill her now anyway, so why not? In for a penny...

'It may be that it was going to be the first and possibly last time that men like that were going to encounter a woman who looked like she did, so they took the opportunity while it was available. They struck while the iron was hot, so to speak.'

Something else is coming off this. It was putting me in a bad mood earlier on and the feeling is still there. I'll run part of it past him.

'D'you think they hated her? Could that have been a motive for the rape? Rape is rarely about sex.'

'*Hated* her? They didn't *know* her. Well...'

'Maybe they hated her because she was successful, talented, beautiful, rich, and foreign. They hated her on principle. They wanted to exercise power over her. They had their money, now they could do *this*. Icing on the cake, as you'd say.'

'I understand what you mean, but I don't think it holds water, Mr Beckett. Kidnapping is one thing, but as soon as the rest happened, the pressure on the police to catch them would have multiplied enormously.

'If the money had been paid and they'd safely returned her, neither of us would be sitting here talking about it two years later. But we are. On the plus side, I think they would know that someone, somewhere, still has their eye on them, whoever they are. They can never rest easy.'

'Maybe they think they've got away with it.'

'They haven't.'

'How do you know?'

'After seeing her body, I can't let myself think that people that fucking insane won't make some mistake somewhere along the line. There might be something they've done that they think is exceedingly clever that we'll eventually crack. Or maybe you'll crack it.

'I can't allow myself to think that they might die tomorrow in a road traffic accident or die of some disease or die of old age before I've got them locked up, shitting themselves and crying.'

He takes a few gulps of his cold coffee. He has a nervous tic beneath his left eye. The longer we talk, the more agitated he gets. He describes what he'll have done to the culprits once they're in prison. It isn't pretty.

I discover that each of the dinner guests (also Micha, Bahk and Devika Pusset) was interviewed twice, each time for an hour, once by Sallow and once by DI Judith Skeete. Apparently the psychologists believe that interviewees respond differently to a female interrogator, and this can often throw up some memory/opinion that didn't manifest itself when the interviewer was male.

'And I hate to say it,' he says, laughing. 'DI Skeete is much better at it than me. Much better. We can't all be brilliant at everything.

'Personally, I didn't think any of those people were involved in her kidnapping, but it was a useful process, and not a waste of time.

'We learned a few things about Kiaraa Jeong that may have come in useful. Not many things, but a few things. Funny bunch, though, that dinner party lot. Very arty. A bit snobby. Different reactions. Some got a bit shirty, some got extremely upset, some got angry, some got indignant.

'We also grilled all the officers who were on the scene shortly after her body was discovered, and even the guys with the dogs who searched the area around the golf club. Sometimes officers like that may have noticed something that they thought was irrelevant at the time.'

'Mr Bahk said he wasn't sure if you were still searching for the white Fiat Ducato panel van.'

'It's on the back burner. It seems to have vanished into thin air. The registration would have been handy, but that would have been on the back doors, which, as we know, were wide open before and after the drop. Even if they were closed, Mr Bahk was so stressed that I don't think he'd have noticed if Donald Duck was hanging off them.

'But even if he'd seen a registration, they may have used fake plates. It's what I'd have done. It could be that they had it crushed into the size of an Oxo cube and chucked in the Thames. There are a lot of dodgy scrap metal places in London and in the Greater London area who would have disposed of it ASAP, no questions asked. We checked with all the usual suspects. Zip. Bugs me a bit, that van, I have to say.

'And before you ask, there was no record of a white Fiat Ducato or one of any other colour having been stolen in the six months up to the kidnapping. Not surprising. They've got excellent anti-theft systems, mainly because they're generally commercial vehicles.'

'What about ones that had been bought legally?'

'One million three hundred thousand five hundred and eighty-four in the six years preceding the murder. That's sales in Europe alone. It goes without saying that we couldn't contact every owner.

'What we *did* do was to check if any of those vans had been purchased by known felons, even people with speeding or parking tickets. Nothing. Well, one bloke with a speeding ticket in Cheltenham three years and two months ago. We got in touch with him. *That's* how desperate we were.

'We also put the word out to every company who could do a professional spray job on a van like that, short notice or otherwise, no matter how small the company or garage was. Even tried the bent ones. Negative again.'

'Have you got the photograph of that van that you showed to the inhabitants of Elder Street?'

'Sure. Hold on. We posted it on our website and did a lot of TV appeals, local flyposting as well. *Did you see this van?* That sort of thing.'

He opens a filing cabinet, riffles around for about thirty seconds and hands me an 8 by 12-inch glossy photograph of a white Fiat Ducato.

'Can I keep this?'

He sits down. 'Don't see why not. I can run another off if I need to.'

I slide it into my messenger bag, which is getting more useful by the hour.

'What about the red Renault Megane that her body was found in?'

'Stolen the previous day from a TikTok software engineer who lived in Wimbledon. Name of, er, Junaid Razzaq. He reported it missing the morning of the day they used it. We took it apart and forensicked the shit out of it. Nothing. Whoever drove it and used it was being very careful.

'I don't think that the thief was travelling around with a corpse in the boot, if that's what you're wondering. I think someone drove it straight from Wimbledon to the golf club, where another vehicle with Kiaraa's body in it was waiting. Forensics didn't think that her body had been in the Megane for very long.'

'I had a brief look at Elder Street yesterday,' I say. 'Just curious, really. Funny little road. Spoke to one of the residents. Couldn't help really, but she was impressed by the professionalism of your detective sergeant. McKinnon or something? Kinderman? Her memory wasn't too good.'

'That would be DS Kinnaird. Rowan Kinnaird. He did a lot of the initial house-to-house. Later on in the investigation, he was also involved in attempting to track down that Fiat van. I can't remember why his duties were changed, or I didn't know in the first place, but the house-to-house would have been a finite task. He was working under DI Caroline McHale, not me. Spent a lot of time on the van, I seem to recall. Pretty good work, too. But it was all for nothing, as it turned out.'

'Oh. OK. Well, at least you can tell him that he made a good impression, even if it was two years ago.'

'Well, I don't really see much of him now. He got a transfer.'

'What – outside London?'

'No. Agar Street. Charing Cross Station.'

'So, now the money. Any rumours of sudden big spenders out there?'

'What – from my army of informers? Doesn't happen like that, Mr Beckett. This isn't a TV show or some sleazy pulp novel. But that's an interesting thing. You probably know that they didn't want used notes because of the suitcase capacity. Used notes would have taken longer to get together as well, which they also wouldn't want.'

'So, at some point, there was three million out there in traceable form.'

'It would seem so. Unless they were able to break it up by spending it really quickly, but you'd need a lot of people for that. Plus, a lot of time, plus trustworthy cohorts who wouldn't squeal.

'The other possibility is that they were in contact with high-end currency smugglers who would know how to launder it in super-quick time, or maybe invest it with some dodgy brokers. But that's not my expertise.

'I sent an email, several emails, to various officers at Economic Crime Command and it was on their watch list, and I assume it still is. And, like I said, DC Sackville was also on their case.'

I stand. 'OK. I'm not going to use up any more of your time. This has been very helpful.'

We shake hands. He nods his head. His expression softens. 'I'll walk down to the ground floor with you. Make sure you don't get bothered by any more female police officers.'

As we make our way down the stairs, he stops, looking straight ahead. 'Micha Jeong and her security guy. They should've called us straight away. Nothing like hindsight, is there. The UK is a world leader in kidnap response. We would never advise paying a ransom.'

We start walking again.

I realise that a part of my brain is looking out for DC Scarlett Sackville. 'She and Bahk are from South Korea,' I say. 'They have a sceptical attitude to the police and all their works.'

'They thought they were being smart.'

'Why do you think the kidnappers stopped at three million? It's possible they could have got a lot more.'

'Maybe they knew that, maybe they didn't. Maybe it was just a nice round figure. Or maybe they thought it was pushing it to ask for more. Too much hassle. God knows. Maybe it was going to be one and a half million at first, then they reckoned if they could handle two suitcases of cash, they could handle four. A little bit more risk, a bit more of a thrill perhaps, but if everything went as planned...

'I don't think the wealth of either sister was common knowledge. Or even their existence, for that matter. I'd never heard of either of them, but then I've got no interest in classical music or hi-tech televisions. Had you heard of them?'

I shake my head. 'You said you thought the kidnappers were a mix of pro and amateur. If you had to pick one or the other...'

'That'd be difficult. Sometimes I think they were pros, sometimes I don't. You?'

'At first I did. The way the demands were made, the mobile phones, the suitcases, the amount of money you could stuff in them, the narrow window for the ransom drop-off, but then that Elder Street location. Bad choice. A narrow, well-populated cul-de-sac that you could get trapped in, windows everywhere; it was dumb.'

'But maybe not that dumb. Virtually no CCTV and not a single video doorbell. Oh, I forgot to tell you. We called this Operation Ivory.'

'Piano keys.'

'That's it. Clever. Not my idea, though. DC Sackville's. If you need to leave a message for me, just use that as a reference and I'll know what it's about. "Ivory" will be enough. Don't know what you've done before, Mr Beckett, but I think you're going to find this a very difficult job.'

'Well, we'll see. Have a nice holiday. Take a trip out to Neuschwanstein Castle. Your kids'll love it.'

'I thought you'd never been to Innsbruck.'

'I must have read about it in a book.'

'Sorry I blasted off a bit earlier, but I think that in itself may help you. Let me know what you find. Say hello to Micha. Tell her I played ball.'

'I'll tell her you got the rubber truncheon out.'

'Never in the mornings. That's a late-night thing. Good luck, Mr Beckett. I reckon you're going to need it. And, er, be careful out there, as they say. I think we're dealing with major nutjobs. Keep your wits about you.'

'Thanks, Dad.'

He laughs. 'These guys haven't been troubled by the law for two years. They're probably feeling pretty pleased with themselves right now. If they think someone's breathing down their necks, if they think it's all going to fall apart, they may take drastic action. Frightened, desperate criminals are capable of anything. Cornered rats. They don't have to have a sane motive. Watch yourself. I kid you not.'

He pats me on the back, and he's gone.

I step into the street and there's someone getting out of a black cab right outside the building, so I get in. Happens about once a year, so I always savour it when it does.

'Leadenhall Street, please.'

'Certainly, sir.'

It's a female cab driver. What are the chances? I think it's something like two per cent of black cab drivers are women. I don't make a smart/corny comment, I'm sure she gets them all the time.

Almost as soon as she drives off, my mobile informs me I've got a text.

OK. I'll run with this. But we meet for a drink before we have dinner. Somewhere central. Scarlett.

Nice and romantic. Just how I like it. I text her back.

Fine. We can meet at Bar Termini in Old Compton Street, then maybe try Blacklock Soho in Great Windmill Street for dinner? I'll text you specifics when booked. Bring handcuffs. Daniel.

She replies with a laughing emoji. Good.

'Been helping the police with their enquiries?' asks the driver.

'Vomiting on a Sunday.'

'You look the type.'

'Flattery will get you nowhere.'

13

CHERRY BULLET'S BIGGEST FAN

I fired off a text to Baek-Hayeon Bahk to let him know I was on my way. I'm pleased to see that the Sansuyu foyer has lost none of its visual shock value. The reception desk underlighting has changed since yesterday from pale blue to pale pink. Does this have some meaning? Time of day? Receptionist mood?

This time, the excessively large OLED television screen is showing slow-motion film of flowers flowering, hot air balloons hovering and surfers surfing. The picture quality is so in-your-face-hyper-realistic it makes me feel slightly nauseous and all the blues look weird.

Once again, Chan-Yeol Choi strides out to meet and greet and hands me an ID badge. I pin it on my jacket. A different female member of the reception staff wearing pink eyeshadow and white lipstick stands a couple of feet behind him, smiling. Can it only have been twenty-four hours ago I was here last?

'Good morning, Mr Beckett. So pleased to see you again. The weather outside is better than yesterday, though I understand there may be showers later. If you'd like to follow me, I will accompany you to the forty-fourth floor.'

We get in the lift. The smiling reception lady bows and returns to her post. This time, I take a sneaky look at my watch to see how long the journey takes. It's just under three seconds. When we get to the forty-fourth, Baek-Hayeon is waiting. Chan-Yeol dissolves back into the lift. Baek-Hayeon and I shake hands.

'Good morning, Mr Beckett. I hope you are well. Let us retire to my office.'

Baek-Hayeon has a reception area like Micha's but there's no receptionist. Maybe they're on their coffee break. His office is, understandably, smaller than his boss's, but is still pretty impressive, the same fabulous views over London, the same expensive, stylish furniture.

I'd half expected lots of military stuff on display, but there's only a rather ornate antique knife or small sword in a Perspex case on his desk with an inscription in Korean on the wooden base. Could be about fifteen inches long. There's a big Toulouse-Lautrec print of *La Goulue* on one wall and a row of four scary but stylised Korean shamanistic masks on the other.

Two bookshelves with lots of books about insects, particularly butterflies and moths, a book called *Wasp Farm*, a hardback of *Dracula* by Bram Stoker, three paperbacks by Ernest Hemingway and lots of books in Korean. I can hear some sort of classical piano music in the background, but the volume is too low for me to identify it. Baek-Hayeon waves a hand towards his coffee station. He's got a black Jura coffee machine and a Smeg Dolce & Gabbana espresso machine.

'Can I get you a coffee, Mr Beckett?

'Thank you. Dash of milk, no sugar.'

'Please take a seat. How are things coming along? I know you have not been on track with this for very long, but I get the impression you are a fast worker.'

I sink into one of the two leather sofas. 'I've spoken to a few people. Had a look at Kiaraa's house.' I watch his face when I say that. No reaction.

'Oh. And before I forget,' he says. 'Mrs Seung has a message for you from Micha. A letter, I think she said.'

'Who's Mrs Seung?'

'You have met her. Micha's personal assistant.'

'Oh. Aera. OK. I'll pop up as soon as I've finished here.'

He walks over, places my coffee in front of me and sits on the other side of the coffee table.

'I saw you admiring that knife, Mr Beckett. A work of art, is it not? It is a jangdo. Very ornamental. Very sharp. Have you heard of these? Presented to me by my fellow officers when I left the army. An antique. Often carried by women for self-defence in the olden days. And for suicide, when necessary.'

'I've heard of them but have never seen one.'

'Great craftsmanship. Very popular during the Joseon Dynasty. Delicate engraving. It could be useful for tricky situations in warfare.'

He frowns. 'Yes. Kiaraa's house. It is hardly my business, but I have advised Ms Jeong that she should sell that property. She cannot keep it forever. Memories, yes? But I don't think she will consider it until the mystery of her sister is resolved. I have decided not to mention it again.' He leans forwards, his face sombre. 'I don't think it was received very well.'

'I think one thing at a time, don't you?'

He nods his head.

'I want to show you something.' I take my mobile out of my pocket and get the photograph of the Daewoo K5 semi-automatic on the screen. I shove it over to Baek-Hayeon, who picks it up and stares at it.

'Look familiar?'

I wonder how he's going to squirm out of this one. I give him one of my most non-judgemental, understanding, I-know-there's-a-good-reason-for-this stares, but it's wasted on him as he's squinting at the screen in a million different ways.

While he's running the gamut of perplexed expressions and changing the picture size, I refresh my memory about UK handgun laws. Stricter than strict, especially since the nineties, and a stiff prison sentence for possession without a licence.

Smuggling a handgun into the country is just as bad, not to mention being extremely difficult. Not impossible, just extremely difficult, but once you'd got the gun here, getting hold of 9mm bullets would be no problem at all.

And the Daewoo K5 is made from steel, for those who want to

make things a little more difficult for themselves and enjoy the sound of loud airport alarms going off.

Would Baek-Hayeon have the wherewithal to do such a thing? Would he want to? As an ex-soldier, does he feel naked without a gun? Is it his friend? Does he not care about the consequences of being caught? Was it for his own use, or did he bring it over specifically for Kiaraa?

Journeying almost three thousand miles with a semi-automatic in your luggage must pile on the stress. Maybe he took Valium to counter it.

Which reminds me. That packet of mirtazapine that I found in Kiaraa's place. That drug is used for anxiety as well as depression and all the other stuff. Is that why she had them? It was an unopened packet, but she could have had more.

Baek-Hayeon nods grimly and pushes my mobile back to me. 'Yes. That is my gun. There is a little nick next to the 'P' of 'Parabellum' on the side. That is how I know.'

'I take it you know where I found this?'

'I make the assumption that it was somewhere in Kiaraa's house. Micha informed me that you were planning a visit. But, um, I am surprised. I know that the police did a thorough search of those premises after she was murdered, and they did not turn it up. Presumably it was well hidden.'

'It was. First of all, how did it come to be in her possession?'

'She asked me if she could borrow it.'

'When was this?'

'Around two-and-a-bit years ago. In fact, I think it was the 1st of August.'

Almost six weeks before she was kidnapped.

'Did she tell you why?'

'No. I assumed it was for protection. She asked me not to mention the affair to Micha. Do you know what happened to their parents?'

'Shot dead in some sort of store.'

'Correct. It was in a branch of E-Mart. It is a famous supermarket chain. There was an altercation between the shooter, a disturbed young man, and some other shoppers. No one knew what it was about. He started firing and the parents were unfortunate collateral damage.

'The police arrived eventually and shot the young man. The whole episode was traumatic for both young women as you can imagine. Micha has had an aversion to guns ever since. And there was another reason why Kiaraa may have required a firearm.'

'Tell me.'

'When she was still in Seoul, there was a friend of hers who was threatened by a mugger who had a gun. This girl was not a musician. I think she was training to be a glaciologist. Anyway, this man was waving the gun around, asking for money, and it went off and killed the girl. I don't think it was intentional. There were witnesses who saw everything. But Kiaraa was greatly upset. I think she believed that if her friend had had a gun, she might still be alive.'

'Did it worry you that your gun had been lost for over two years?'

'Of course. But who could I tell? The police? Part of me hoped that it would be somewhere safe, that Kiaraa would show caution and care. I was in a quandary. It has never been out of my thoughts. The fact that you have discovered it has given me tremendous relief.'

'To backtrack a little, how did you get a Korean army handgun into this country?'

'It was an odd circumstance. I had been working here at Sansuyu for two years and had to go back to Seoul. General security business connected with hi-tech car park security and cybernated registration recognition.

'There was equipment to be brought back to the UK. We used a converted passenger aircraft. It was a private flight. A Boeing. I was on board. I realised that my handgun – it was from my army days – was in one of my flight bags. I cannot remember why. I should not have had it. It was just a place I stored it as I did not often use that bag.

'At Incheon International Airport, we drove straight onto the tarmac and avoided the usual rigmarole. I was going to hand it over when we got to Heathrow airport, but with all the fuss and bother it was overlooked.'

'Did Kiaraa know you had a gun?'

'No. No one did. When she asked I was apprehensive, but she was…she could be persuasive. I felt it was not my place to ask why. Maybe she suspected I might have had a gun and that I was the gentleman to ask. I had spoken to her about my time as a soldier once or twice.

'You have to remember, Mr Beckett, that she was not a stranger to me. I had met her on many occasions over the years and had worked with her sister for a long, long time. You could say she was like family. You will report me now? I like my job, but I will gladly leave it.'

'I'm not the police, Baek-Hayeon. I just wanted to know why she had it and what she wanted with it. So, you have absolutely no idea.'

'No.'

'How did she seem when she asked you for it?'

'Seem? She seemed normal, as far as I could tell, Mr Beckett. It was a casual request, as if she was asking me if I had a pen she could borrow.'

'What about when you gave it to her. Were you careful?'

'I saw her three weeks after her request. She came in here to see Micha. I think she had been in Tallinn in, um, Estonia for a few weeks. On her way out, she popped into my office, and I handed her the gun in a red leather music case. I thought it would look convincing. I'm afraid I also believed it was witty. She did not ask for ammunition, but I put in a box anyway.'

'Why did you do that? There were already thirteen rounds in the gun, and you gave her another twenty. That's thirty-three bullets. What did you think she was going to do? Take down a SWAT team?'

He looks shamefaced. 'I don't know. I really don't know. Perhaps I was trying to impress her. I had always had a soft spot for her.' He shakes his head. 'I suppose you would say it was a moment of madness. I was trying to be a big man. Mr Cool.' He grins for a moment, but it's soon gone.

'Where did you get the extra ammunition from?'

'A contact at our embassy here. An old friend from the 11th Special Forces Brigade. I know it was foolish, but I have always been a bit of a rule-breaker.'

'Now I know she travelled around the world a lot,' I say. 'But smuggling a gun like that in and out of God knows how many passport controls would be an impossibility. That means we're stuck with her and the gun here in the UK, which is where she'd made her home.

'So, we have to assume that either she wanted it to protect herself against someone or something in this country, or she was the aggressor; she wanted to threaten or kill someone with it. Off the top of your head, which seems the most likely?'

'Well, as she was a woman...'

'Forget her being a woman. Think of her personality, not her sex.'

He taps his fingers on his knees. 'She was a determined, focussed individual who had very strong views about what she wanted from life, so I would say either option was possible. That is to say, I would not discount the latter option. Does that answer your question, Mr Beckett?'

'Could she use a gun? Would she be confident with it?'

'Not that specific type of gun, maybe, but generally I think yes. For example, when she was younger she was a habitué of shooting ranges back in Seoul. BB guns. They are very popular with young women, these ranges. When I last checked, there were about thirty of them in Seoul and perhaps fifty plus nationwide. A BB gun would have the same shape as an automatic pistol, though not the same weight or kick-back, obviously.'

'Why are they popular with young women?'

'Mainly stress relief, as I understand it. From work as well as other things. Some young women bring their own target sheet with a photograph on it of some man who has been sexually harassing them at work.

'Many women use these ranges during the day when they are not so busy. Some young women use their lunch hours to practise. She would not have had regular practice with a real handgun. Just a BB. I don't think she would ever have fired a conventional gun. I could be mistaken, of course, but it's very unlikely. There are extensive gun laws in Korea. But she would have known the basics.'

'What – aim and pull the trigger?'

'Something like that. I asked her if she needed me to tell her what to do, but she said it was OK. It is not impossible that she could have joined some other sort of gun club where real pistols were used. They are very exclusive and expensive, but she had the wherewithal.

'There is a shooting range in Seoul, for example, where you can use real firearms that have been seen in Korean movies. They even have what they call Bond Girl guns for women to use: Smith & Wesson M637, Walther PPK, Glock G19.

'But if she did join a club, I did not know about it, and I do not think she would have had the time, to be totally honest. For what it's worth, my instinct is that she wanted the gun for self-defence, after what had happened to her friend.'

I take a deep breath. I was hoping that something more interesting would result from this meeting, but you can't have everything.

'You said that Kiaraa was like family. What did you know about her apart from the fact she was a famous classical pianist and wanted to borrow a gun?'

'Well, maybe I use family in a different way from you, Mr Beckett. In Korea, colleagues working for the same company have ties that can be difficult to understand sometimes, particularly in countries like your own.

'It wasn't so long ago that South Korea was a poor country. Everyone pulled together to change that. So, we all have a connection that is tied to our work and the way we approach it.

'When you start work in a company like Sansuyu, you enter what could be called a training camp. There are team-building programs. It can be very intense. You learn company ideology, values, many things. There is even a company song that you have to learn, just like they have in Japan. We have borrowed a lot of ideas from Japan and the Japanese.

'Anyway, you start to think of your co-workers as your family. Sometimes the company can be more important than your real family. That is what I meant. So, a close relative of someone like Micha kind of becomes family, too. That is how I thought of Kiaraa. It may be that I thought of her as a cousin; something like that.

'If you speak to other employees here, you will find the same thing. Mrs Seung, Aera upstairs; she would say something similar. She was devastated when Kiaraa was taken from us. She probably only met her on half a dozen occasions, but…'

'So, despite this family connection, would it be true to say that you didn't really know that much about her? There is nothing that you would, perhaps, be reluctant to tell me?'

'I knew she was what Micha would call "quite the charmer". Do you understand what is meant by that, Mr Beckett? It is a very old-fashioned term, I think. Very odd. But I think Micha used it in an unusual way, in an affectionate way.'

'She explained.'

'It amused me that Micha used it to describe her sister; her sister's *predilections*. But that is not particularly scurrilous, in my book. Everyone is different. Like there are many different types of animals and plants in the world, there are just as many different types of people.' He finishes off his coffee. 'I think she liked the fame that was a side effect of her profession. The, um, popularity and prestige. Only my impression.'

He laughs. 'I think she liked being handed big bunches of flowers at the end of concerts. I think she enjoyed it that she was well-known and loved all over the world. I think she liked to be on magazine covers and all the rest of it. She liked to be interviewed so that she could talk about things which interested her. Apart from classical music and playing the piano, I mean.'

'Such as?'

'I don't know all the details, but I know she liked modern photography. Photographers like JeeYoung Lee and Hein-Kuhn Oh. She was fond of Lee Ufan, the artist. She liked K-Pop. Do you know that?'

'I'm Cherry Bullet's biggest fan.'

'Ha! Yes. Kiaraa was in something called the Korean Women's Associations United. I don't even know if it still exists.'

'What was that?'

'Very distasteful. Its origin, I mean. A labour organiser called Kwon In Suk was sexually abused and tortured by police because of her efforts to help women in jobs. In the 1980s, I think. She inspired women to form the KWAU.

'Once again, you can see our attitude to the police appearing.' He taps his fingers against his chin for a moment. 'Oh, yes. She liked fossils.

Ammonites. Lycophytes. That kind of thing. Collecting them. I think she did an interview with some magazine about that. It was a girlhood hobby that she maintained.

'I think she spent a lot of money on clothes. Micha mentioned it jocularly. But part of that was to do with her profession. She wore very impressive, elegant clothes for her concerts, but I cannot be sure if they were her own or were rented.'

'And that's it as far as you know.'

'I can't think of anything else. As I said, I did not really know her that well. We did…we did not go out for a drink or anything. Most of my information about her was vicarious. Generally, I admired her as one might admire a famous sportsperson.'

But his eyes and body language tell me that he was a lot fonder of her than that.

We both stand and shake hands. 'This has been very useful, Baek-Hayeon. Rest assured, I'll get your gun back to you as soon as I can. And don't worry. I won't mention anything about this to Micha.'

As we walk to the lift, he looks downcast. 'I had put this out of my mind for so long and now it seems as if it is all back. Do you know what I mean? It is very sad-making. Very sad-making.'

'I'm sure it is.'

'Kiaraa had quite a presence. Sometimes, even now, I feel as if she is still with us in some way. Do you understand?'

As the lift here took a little under three seconds to travel forty-four floors, I'm curious about how long it takes to travel one floor. Perhaps it can be calculated in negative terms, like minus fifty seconds or something.

When the doors open, Aera is there to greet me. I'm beginning to think everyone here has some sort of sixth sense. No trouser suit today, instead a body-hugging black silk blouse and a dark blue knee-length pleated skirt. Black stockings or tights. The four-inch black heels, green eyeshadow, dark red lipstick and scandalous cleavage remain. Is it my imagination, or is it a little more scandalous today? My mouth feels a little dry.

'Hello, Mr Beckett. How charming to see you again.'

'And you, Aera. I must say, you're looking very alluring today. That's a striking combination you're wearing. Really shows off your figure. In fact, I'm starting to feel rather faint. A few more minutes of this sort of stimulus and I'll be asking for a glass of water.'

She laughs. It's a low, libidinous sound. 'Oh, stop it!'

'It's true. And you're wearing perfume today. Quite bewitching. May I just come a little closer to see if I recognise it?'

She rolls her eyes with fake exasperation, pushes her chest out and purses her lips. If she was a cat, she'd purr.

'Patchouli, musk, vanilla; it's Magnolia Sensuel, isn't it? Really suits you. I've actually forgotten why I'm here. Do I work here? Am I late for a meeting? A PowerPoint presentation? An induction?'

She gives me a friendly punch on the shoulder. 'You should not talk like that, Mr Beckett. You could give a girl the wrong idea.'

'And thank you for your text this morning. Very encouraging.'

'And thank you for yours. Though I'm quite sure I don't sit in a provocative manner.'

'I would tell you *why* it's provocative, but I'm far too well-mannered. I wouldn't want to make you blush again with my crude descriptions and salacious fantasies.'

She laughs and speedily fans her face with her left hand. 'Very warm in here today. Have you noticed?'

This makes me laugh. 'Baek-Hayeon said you had a message from Micha for me.'

'Yes. It was just before she left for the airport.' She turns and heads for her desk. Swaying walk. Sexy bottom. She turns and faces me as she leans forwards to open a drawer. More cleavage. Brief but meaningful eye contact. I imagine kissing her and biting her neck.

She returns with a small blue envelope which I open immediately. It's a telephone number for Odette Fournier. Beneath that are numbers for record company honcho Sheila Hulme, agent Devika Pussett, opera guy Gordon Hepburn (but he's in New Zealand at the moment), and then Nozomi Terada, who is back in Japan and has not been in the UK for a couple of years. Well, it's Odette Fournier who's top of my list at the moment, so that's fine.

'Good news, Mr Beckett?'

'Just a few phone numbers I needed for my enquiries. Thank you for this. I have to leave you now.'

'Lunch with Ms Leishman?' she says pointedly.

'Why do you ask, Aera?'

'I like her. She is most delightful.' Fleeting eye contact. 'Do you know, it's a strange coincidence, we share the same birthday, November the 17th. Same day, same year. We are exactly the same age.'

'That's interesting. I would have thought you were much younger.' I'm deplorable.

She sits and flicks her hand at me in an offhand way. 'Go away now. I have work to do. I cannot have distractions.'

'Am I distracting you?'

'The elevator is over there, Mr Beckett. Quickly, now.'

'Until the next time, Aera.'

'I shall reluctantly look forward to it, Mr Beckett.'

'I shall think of nothing else, Aera.'

As I turn my back on her and leave for the lift, I can tell she's smiling. I'm definitely going to sleep with her.

14

RHAPSODY IN BLUE

Once I'm back in my flat, the first thing I do is to give Penny a call. I make a large cup of High Voltage coffee and sit at the kitchen table, where Kiaraa's secret drawer stuff still lies.

Those photographs of her still give off their explosive erotic assault and I'm finding it difficult to drag my eyes away from them. I bought a large *pane e salame* from Rosetta on my way back and put it on a plate as a reward for completing my next round of chores.

DCI Sallow said that his detectives started questioning the residents of Elder Street a couple of days after Kiaraa's body was found. He was a little vague, but then it was a long time ago, he told me he didn't have access to the main database in Putney, and I'm sure he's had a lot to do since then. I need to clear up that vagueness for a couple of reasons that may or may not be important.

Operation Ivory, indeed. I wonder if Kiaraa would have liked that.

Penny seemed to think that she got her cop visit about ten days after the murder, but again: two years. And she herself said her memory wasn't too good.

'Penny? It's Daniel. The detective.'

'Oh, hi! Wow. Just thinking about you. Is it about the restaurant? I haven't had a chance to go out clothes shopping quite yet.'

'No, it's not about that.' I put a laugh into my voice. 'You must be patient. And don't rush buying clothes. Take your time. I'm sure you'll make excellent choices.'

'I was wondering whether to get a dress or just a skirt and top.'

I visualise her in both. 'I think a dress would be nice. Be casual. They don't fuss with dress codes in Tengoku No Aji, I'm sure.'

'You may be right. Gosh.'

'Listen, Penny. I've just been visiting the police. I wanted to ask you something. I know it was a while ago, but that police officer that called on you. Detective Sergeant Kinnaird.'

'Oh, yes. Horrid chap. It *was* Kinnaird, was it? Couldn't quite recall. Ghastly memory.'

'Do you remember the exact date he called on you?'

'Um. Oh, gosh. No, I don't. I can – I can probably find out. Might take a while. I keep diaries. Not long detailed ones with all my thoughts and yearnings ha ha. Nothing like that. Just odd things. Birthdays. Events. Appointments. I'd have put something in like "Police visit!" something like that. I can never remember where I've squirrelled them away.'

'Would you mind seeing if you can dig that one up? I just need to, um, coordinate the dates for my investigation. It would be really helpful.'

'Of course. Exciting! I feel like a gangster's moll.'

'And one more thing. If you don't mind talking about this, you told me yesterday that DS Kinnaird told you about some ghastly details regarding the murder case. Terrible, gory, gruesome details, I think you said.'

She pauses. This is painful for her.

'Yes. Put it all away in a little box in my brain now. Very disquieting at the time. I think I told you. I don't like to…' She sounds as if she's on the verge of tears.

'I'll understand if you don't want to talk about it, Penny.'

Though what I mean is 'I absolutely insist that you talk about it, to put it very mildly.' I attempt to put that message into my voice, accompanied by a hint of disappointment, regret and melancholy. It's a lethal cocktail of cynical manipulation. Sometimes it even works.

A longer pause this time. Her voice is different. 'It – it was how she'd died. I think it was in the papers that she'd been stabbed. One tends to think of a single knife thrust, do you know what I mean?'

'Of course.'

'But he told me that she'd been stabbed over and over again. Can't remember the number now. Twenty or thirty times, perhaps. Such a dreadful image to ponder. Frightful violence. Maniacal.'

So, Kinnaird went against his boss's wishes and gave her too much information just so he could impress her, it would seem. That's an odd way of going about things. I can hear that she's muffled her phone in some way. Is she sobbing? I wait for a few moments so she can recover. I may need a little more from her, but I'll wait until she's found her diary.

'It's OK, Penny. It's OK. You've done very well. I know that was hard for you to say and to remember. Put it out of your mind now. Go back to thinking about Tengoku No Aji and what you're going to order.'

She sniffs. 'Sorry. Childish.'

'Not at all. Really. Oh. Penny. I realised that I still don't know what your surname is.'

'Coryton-Ward.'

'OK. See you later, Mrs Coryton-Ward.'

'Oh, don't call me that! It makes me feel…you know.'

'Won't happen again, Penny. Speak soon.'

Did I just say 'Speak soon'? As soon as I click her off, my ring tone starts and for a second I think she's calling me back.

'Hey, Mr Beckett. Now a lesser person than me would attach a two hundred quid difficulty surcharge to this one, but as it's you…'

'Your generosity never ceases to astound me, Doug. What did you get?'

'OK. You referred to these mobiles as one, two and three. Someone's been clever here, but not quite clever enough. Borderline lazy, even. But enough of my detecting speculations, that's your job. Or is it? I think I've been doing your work for you in this instance. Are you still seeing that girl from Vietnam, by the way? Rangsei, was it?'

'Rachany. And she was from Cambodia. And no.'

'What happened?'

'You can read all about it in my never-to-be-published autobiography.'

'Cambodia. Shit. Went there once. Rained. Now. All three mobiles were bought on the same day exactly two years and ten days ago. Mobile 1 was bought in a branch of Carphone Warehouse in Wood Green High Street, right next door to a KFC. Mobile 2 was bought in the Westbury Avenue branch of FoneTech, which is a company I'd never heard of, but it's right across the road from a fish and chips and kebab place called The Tasty, which has a nice ring to it. The Tasty. "I'm off to The Tasty for a doner and chips. Catch you later".

'Now mobile 3 was the time-consuming one. I couldn't find any record of the place where that particular number was sold from, so just on a hunch I did a mega-sweep of all the mobile wholesale suppliers in North London, East London, and Middlesex. This is why it was time-consuming. I had a couple of crashes, too, which never usually happens. Just bad luck. I'm not perfect.'

'That's not what your charges indicate. Did you find it?'

'Yep. A wholesaler called DeltaMobile in Walthamstow had sold that number to a branch of Mobiles R Us in Seven Sisters Road.'

'Any fast-food joints nearby? If there are, I think we have a breakthrough.'

'Funnily enough, yes. It *was* right next door to a place called, simply, Manor Kebab. I say *was*, because the whole Mobiles R Us chain went out of business eighteen months ago, which is hardly surprising with a name like that, and it's the reason I had a problem tracking it down. A lot of these places seem to be fly-by-night. No idea why that should be. Anyway, this was where it all tied together. Have you spotted it yet? Clue: we're *not* looking for a compulsive junk food takeaway fan.'

'You're going to have to show off, Doug.'

'OK. The late unlamented Mobiles R Us branch was *right next* to the entrance to Manor House tube station, on the Piccadilly Line, yeah?'

'Got it.'

'So, I got inspired, retraced my virtual steps and found out that FoneTech, where mobile 2 was bought, is a three-minute walk from

Turnpike Lane tube station, and Carphone Warehouse, where mobile 1 was purchased, is a two-minute walk from Wood Green tube station.

'All three stations right next to each other on the Piccadilly Line, one after another. So, I don't know in what order the purchaser did this, whoever they were, but it looks like they hopped on and off that tube line and bought a phone at each one of those three adjacent stops to avoid looking suspicious. Paranoid little devils, eh?

'Oh. Couldn't help with the IMEI for those numbers, and a buyer name would be out of the question without starting on the banks, but I reckon they'd have paid cash anyway.'

'That's fantastic, Doug. Cheque's in the post.'

'That's funny. Can I use that?'

'I'm going to need your help on something else soon, but I'm not sure what it is yet.'

'I'll need a little more ambiguity.'

'Touché.'

Well, this is something and it's still only day one. I fire up the computer and Google 'Enfield Golf Club nearest tube station'. It looks as if both Oakwood and Southgate tube stations are roughly equidistant from the golf club. Both are on the same branch of the Piccadilly Line and are only three or four stops from where the northernmost mobile-buying station, Turnpike Lane, is situated. Certainly not walking distance, but only a ten-to-fifteen-minute drive if that. It could be that the purchaser (assuming it was a single individual) parked at Wood Green and used the tube for the next two stops.

So, what does this mean? Are our kidnappers/murderers from this general area or did they pick it at random? It certainly connects the dumping of Kiaraa's body and the purchase of the phones, at least geographically, but I'll need something more before I start crowing about it.

I can see why they did the stop-hopping, but they were still lazy, sloppy, cutting corners. If I was doing that, I'd have bought mobile 1 from a random populous location in London and the other two from somewhere a little further away but not too time-wasting to get to: Windsor or Guildford, places like that.

They'd obviously have bought the mobiles before the ransom calls were made, and if they were thinking straight, they'd have chosen somewhere else to dump Kiaraa's body.

But, as DCI Sallow said, criminals are not the brightest bunch.

Perhaps the logistics of the whole operation were complicated enough for them already, and the careful and cautious purchase of PAYG mobiles which were to be inevitably discarded/destroyed seemed to be an irrelevance.

Or they didn't think they'd have someone like Doug Teng on their trail.

While it occurs to me, I text Doug with a request for the Enfield Golf Club membership file, going back five years. May be useful.

I type Odette Fournier's number into my mobile and give her a call. I've no idea what I'm going to say, but spontaneity is sometimes the best way to sound convincing and sincere. She doesn't answer.

I leave a message asking her to call me, explaining that I'm working for Micha Jeong and would like to have a chat with her. I try to sound friendly and upbeat, and hope I've worded things so it doesn't sound too sinister, upsetting, or ominous. I want her to get back to me. I just hope she's in the country at the moment.

I realise that I left the Sansuyu carrier bag in my hallway. I place it on the table, slide the secret drawer contents out of the way and take a look at each item. Looking at stuff like this is frequently a waste of time, but even if one tiny thing pops out it can all be worthwhile.

The magazines first.

Kiaraa gets the cover of *Vanity Fair*. I check a few past issues. As far as they're concerned she's up there with Robert Downey Jr, Priyanka Chopra Jonas, Scarlett Johansson, Taylor Swift, Johnny Depp and Emily Blunt.

This issue came out a month or so before her murder. A startling, beautiful photograph of her standing next to a white Yamaha baby grand, wearing a medium length, blue-black, pleated dress with a bateau neckline.

Hairstyle is the same pixie cut as the secret drawer photographs, but it's been dyed blue to match the dress. Looks great. Just a guess, but this could have been taken around the same time as her nudes.

Blue eyeshadow, red lipstick, no nail polish, and no jewellery, apart from a pair of sapphire and diamond Bulgari earrings. Her fingernails are moderately long, which is a surprise. I thought she'd have them cut short, but what do I know? Perhaps she files them down before she goes on stage.

She's smiling, and there's an amused twinkle in her eyes. She looks confident, assured, seductive and bewitching.

At the bottom of the page: "Rhapsody in Blue. A revealing talk with Kiaraa Jeong about life, music, liberty, fashion, hand moisturiser and Erik Satie."

I can't take my eyes off the photograph. If you saw this cover in a shop, you'd buy the magazine without hesitation. I'm sure that's the idea.

I flick through the pages until I get to the interview. Words by Wendy Hamler, photography by Carolyn Kraft, styled by Richard T. Straka.

At the top, there's a photograph of her lying stretched out on a cream leather sofa. Short black shoulderless leather dress, pink cross-stitching down the side, fingers clasped above her head. Hair still blue. All white thighs and small boobs. Bare legs and feet. A smouldering sideways look straight into the camera lens. Dress by Di Pasqua & Soldati. Ring by Sauveterre.

Kiaraa Jeong doesn't dress like a classical pianist. But how should *a classical pianist dress, particularly if she's a woman? Kiaraa has strong views about this. 'There's a culture of keeping the classics in the past, where some people think they belong,' she says. 'This extends to the way that its performers should appear on stage. But how long will this go on for? Will we still be dressing like lords and ladies from the nineteenth century in two hundred years?*

'No one likes change, and the conservatism in the classics runs deep. I reject that and I'm not the only one. I've been called "that Korean attention whore" and worse. Someone referred to the clothes I wear during performance as "her stripper clothes". That should give you an idea of the mindset of the classical music establishment and, I'm sad to say, some of

its followers. I'm not the only female classical musician who likes to look glam when she performs. There are many of us now and I think it's great.'

Korean attention whore? Doug would say that sounded like a great band name.

Another photograph. Grainy black and white. Sitting at a grand piano, this time a Blüthner. Side-on view. An incredible, intense pose, as if she's in the middle of some dramatic/complicated passage. Arms arched. Fingers splayed. Body tensed. Head down. Face obscured. A short, barely-there backless dress. Fantastic shoulder and back muscles. She's wearing the black leather slingback pumps I saw in her wardrobe. A foot on one of the pedals. A toned calf muscle flexed. Dress by Gutiérrez. Shoes by Louboutin.

And then:

'Kiaraa, who is originally from Seoul in South Korea, is no stranger to controversy. Since coming out as bisexual two years ago, she has been on the receiving end of a considerable amount of online abuse. She actually finds it amusing. 'Perhaps we should all stop listening to Tchaikovsky, Saint-Saëns, Poulenc, and Leonard Bernstein! I'm from a culture where anything that is not strictly heterosexual is frowned upon.

'Whatever the mudslinging is here (we spoke to her in London), it's nothing compared to what it used to be like in Korea. So, I'm immune. I was uptight about it for a long time, and it was only after my parents died that I was able to become who I was. That sounds very California, but it's true. They were lovely people, but it would have upset them too much. They were from a different culture, and I have always been grateful for their support and their belief in me.'

A third photograph. Slightly soft focus. Lying on her front on a white fur rug, once again looking straight into the lens. Serious expression. Wearing a pink lace and mesh body. The pink goes well with the blue hair. Legs crossed. Looking like an upmarket lingerie model. Flamingo Pink Body by Vaillancourt. Bracelet by Slezák & Zima.

And then:

Her recent world tour, taking in fifty-six countries, was a resounding success, and she is now one of the most highly paid concert pianists in the world. Despite her busy schedule (not to mention her recording commitments), she still finds time to promote her feminist beliefs.

When she was younger, she was an active member of the Korean Women's Associations United, an umbrella organisation concerned with multiple women's issues. Does this still feature in her life?

'Not so much now,' she explains. 'Geographical reasons and pressure of work, as they say, though I am a patron. I've lived in the UK for quite a while and still support women's causes whenever I get the time. There is so much work to do, wherever in the world you may happen to be. It's always an uphill struggle, but one worth taking on, I think.'

I speed-read the rest, but it's mainly about hand care, problems with skin peeling, her aversion to having finger and hand massages (she prefers to use expensive moisturiser and do it herself), her irritation with people coughing and/or talking in auditoriums during her performances and a new lecture/performance Blu-ray she's making about the composer Erik Satie.

I pick up the Blu-ray that Micha gave me. This is it.

She mentions how she is a big fan of Satie's work, has already recorded two albums of his material and hopes to do more. But she never did. Her Wikipedia page only mentioned two albums by that particular composer.

She's also asked about her name. I remember Suzanna telling me that Micha meant Beautiful Daughter. Kiaraa's name has many meanings, and she jokes about it. It can mean bright, a first ray of sun, and even God's precious gift, and she comments that you never get Korean girls' names which mean sinister, envious, flirty, or daughter of Satan.

Despite the seriousness of some of the topics, there's a wit and warmth that shines through the entire interview. Even if you weren't a fan of this type of music, I can imagine that a chance encounter with this issue would leave you with a terrible crush on her.

Now *Classical Music Magazine*. This is a thick, expensive item that comes out every two months.

Once again, she gets the cover. She's toned down the sex an iota for this one: a stylish red sleeveless dress, a triple strand of white pearls, hands on hips, wholesome expression, big smile. Hair back to its normal colour, a little longer and tied back in a ponytail.

At the bottom of the cover: ***Kiaraa Jeong Exclusive Interview – Bach, Clementi and the problems with baroque.***

Understandably, the interview is far more concerned with the music than the *Vanity Fair* article and there's only one accompanying photograph, which looks like it's from the same session as the one on the cover.

CMM: Tell us about your current recording activities.

KJ: I'm recording – or should that be attempting – The Well-Tempered Clavier *by Bach. It's an enormous undertaking; forty-eight preludes and fugues to be released on four CDs and simultaneously for MP3 download. If things go as planned, I'll be doing a mini tour of several European capitals to coincide with its release.*

CMM: Obviously, you are aware of other performances and recordings of these pieces. Do you listen to them or even think *about them while you are preparing your own interpretation? Is there ever a point where you think "How will I ever top so-and-so?"*

KJ: (laughs) I don't think of playing as a competition! I admire and respect other pianists and have no desire to compete or emulate. The Well-Tempered Clavier *is a vast work, and certainly an important one. It is more a matter of seeking out new possibilities and readings while sticking to the composer's original intentions. You have to remember that it was written to be played on harpsichord or clavichord, so performing it on the piano has its own challenges. I love Kimiko Douglas-Ishizaka's performance and, of course, Angela Hewitt's. None of us are setting up stall and saying "Buy my version! It's the best!" It's more a case of saying "Look what I have done with these pieces. I hope you like it."*

CMM: Do you listen to much music that is not classical?

KJ: Oh, sure. I like all sorts. I like Ekaterina Kishchuk and Kotringo and Kyary Pamyu Pamyu. Oh, and Noémie Wolfs. And K-Pop, of course. I love Blackpink and Orange Caramel and Twice and Exo. They have a futuristic outlook! I like heavy bands like Abacination, who are a Dutch, no, Belgian post death metal band. I love their style. Sometimes you just have to listen to something that blasts the cobwebs out, you know? Salt The Wound are like that, and Anaal Nathrakh. And I like some jazz pianists, like Toshiko Ashioki, Kei Akagi and Cleo Brown. You can learn a lot from them, even though it's different music, yes?'

She talks at length about Scarlatti, Couperin, Clementi, trills, rubato, pianos, her dislike of Bluetooth page-turning devices (she doesn't trust them and never uses them) and her frustration at not being able to teach as much as she'd like, but there's little here that gives an insight into her personal life/troubles in that way that the *Vanity Fair* interview did.

Except for one thing.

CMM: What do you think about the rise of all these videos on sites like YouTube featuring female pianists like yourself under headings like 'Most Beautiful Women in Classical Music' or 'Top Ten Hot Classical Pianists?' Do you think it objectifies women? Makes people take musicians like yourself less seriously?

KJ: Of course not. Male musicians working in any genre can wear what they like without attracting those sorts of comments and so should we. I wear clothes that make me feel good; clothes that I think I look good in. Words like 'hot' or 'sexy' are an irrelevance. We're female and this is the twenty-first century. YouTube, for example, is a great way of getting the classics to a large audience and it gives a phenomenal boost to CD and download sales and, of course, interest in the concerts and the subsequent interest in the composers. I can't stop people cutting my filmed performances together with those of artistes like Lola Astanova, Yuja Wang, Felicja Zawadzka or Khatia Buniatshvili. In fact, I think they're fun and look cool and I'm flattered by the attention. She laughs. *Felicja and I have spoken about doing a duet so we can try and out-hot each other! Obviously, you'll get comments from less liberal sources, but generally it's a good thing.*

CMM: So, no negative feedback at all?

KJ: There's always some negative feedback, but thankfully it's not about the quality of the music. Most of it you can shrug off. Some of it rankles a bit and can be upsetting. I've mentioned it before, but I did get called "a Korean attention whore" by some guy and I was also called "a Japanese slut in a short skirt" about a year ago by someone calling themselves 'a friend of the classics'. I mean – I don't mind the slut in a short skirt bit, but Japanese? *Really?'*

I pick up the Blu-ray.

The cover is startling; it would demand your attention even if you weren't interested in the music. It's a head-and-shoulders shot. It's plain that she's wearing some sort of shoulderless dress, but you can only just spot it.

The photograph has been cut off about six inches below her collarbone so at first glance she could conceivably have been naked when it was taken. There's no getting away from it; that toned, chiselled *geongangmi* look is pretty damn steamy. Her hair is long, lustrous, and slightly wavy. She looks directly at the camera, humour in her eyes and her lips slightly parted. You can imagine kissing her. I think she'd close her eyes.

Her stripper clothes.

Korean attention whore.

A Japanese slut in a short skirt.

On a hunch, I text those three phrases to Doug Teng and request a major www sweep, starting with YouTube and extending to social media and beyond. This could take forever and may not bear fruit, but it feels like the right thing to do. I let him know that the sweeps are connected to Kiaraa Jeong, a Korean classical pianist, in case that comes in handy. Doug replies immediately.

Korean Attention Whore! One fuck of a band name, man. Deathgrind for sure. Or maybe Deathrash. On it.

When Sallow was telling me about the rape I started to get an odd feeling about all of this and I'm getting it again, but it's still a little hazy. I need a Campari and soda. I sit back in my seat, close my eyes, cross my arms, and attempt to let everything soak into my brain. Then it's all screwed when my mobile goes off again.

'Am I speaking to Daniel Beckett?'

Female. French. No prizes for guessing who this is. 'Yes. How can I help you?'

'This is Odette Fournier. I understand you wanted to communicate with me.'

15

SLOW & PAINFUL

My *pane e salame* is beckoning to me. I'll be with you soon, I promise.

'And so, you think talking to me would help you in some way? I have already communicated with the police. I cannot possibly see why my speaking to you could be of any use.'

She has a charming Parisian accent, but a terse way of speaking that makes you think she's in the middle of some important meeting and wants you off the phone yesterday. I persevere.

'I'm sure you're aware that the police have been treating Kiaraa's murder as a high priority case for two years and have got nowhere. At the moment, I don't know whether we're dealing with criminals who are very clever or just very lucky. At present, I think it's the latter.'

'But what can I tell you?'

'I won't know until I speak to you. That is sometimes how these things work. This is the first day I've been working on this, and I've already pieced together elements that I think the police may have missed.' Total bullshit, but it sounds good. I almost believe it myself. Perhaps it's true.

'Such as?'

This conversation is like swimming through treacle. 'Can I make an appointment to see you tomorrow?'

'I'm busy tomorrow. Besides, I did not know her that well. I met her through my husband, who is a patron of The Viennese Music Association. He is a patron of many musical associations. We went to one of her recitals there. Vienna, I mean. I think it was a couple of years ago and we were made acquainted. We were not particularly close.'

Big gamble. 'She kept your letters.'

Long silence. Could be worse. She could cut me off. 'I see. You will have to come to my office. I cannot see you at my London home. Do you know where I am? My company, I mean?'

'You're in Grafton Street, opposite the Givenchy store.'

'There is an entrance next to the Epok shop. You'll see the button for the buzzer. Press once. Tomorrow morning. Eleven a.m. prompt.'

'I…' But she's gone. Well, that's something, at least – the little mystery of the letters solved. Unless we're not talking about the same letters.

Finally, I can start eating my *pane e salame.* I take it and a coffee into the TV room and slide the Blu-ray into the player. Just as it's booting up, I get a text from Aera.

Thank you for noticing my perfume this morning, Mr Beckett. Very gratifying. Apparently, it's made for a desirable woman with a secret, seductive side.

I can see why you wear it, Aera. And it's not all I noticed.

What can you mean, Mr Beckett?

I'm unable to respond. I'm afraid the content would melt my mobile.

I must work now. You must stop these texts. You are putting ideas into my head.

Then you must stop your bewitching responses. You are a she-devil.

Hm!

I take a bite of my lunch and click on 'play'. Over Jean Cocteau's 1920 sketch of a seated Satie, credits slowly appear and disappear.

Lysander Records
Kiaraa Jeong, piano
Erik Satie (1866 – 1925)

Director: Claudy Broeder
Producer for Lysander Records: Christopher Turner
Piano: Fazioli M. Liminal
Thanks to the Musée d'Art Moderne, Paris

Then a leisurely fade to black, followed by a shocking cut to that amazing piano that I saw in Kiaraa's house. It's in the centre of an enormous white art gallery, on a stone floor in front of a colourful Raoul Dufy. The ceiling lights have been dimmed.

The click of high heels and there she is. My chewing is put on hold. It's the first time I've seen her as a living, breathing woman and she's breathtakingly lovely.

She's wearing a cherry red midi dress with an open back and matching suede pumps. She sits down at the piano and looks straight ahead. She says nothing.

A caption: 'Gymnopédie No. 1 (1888)'

As she starts playing, I realise that I know this piece of music, though I had no idea what it was called or who composed it. It's a slow, atmospheric, almost meditative piece, with a quirky, stately, dissonant melody that is constantly taking unexpected directions.

But it's Kiaraa that I'm hypnotised by.

Once I've got over the seductive shock of her clothing and the way it accentuates the astounding, sleek curves of her body, I start taking in the whole performance.

It's as if the melody is playing *her*, rather than the other way around.

Each note, each chord seems to elicit a physical response from her, whether it's a tilt of the head, a stretch of the torso, an arching of the spine, a pursing of the lips, a half-smile, a modest frown, a moue of concentration, a flick of the wrist as her fingers leave the keys, or the understated ripple of muscles on her thighs and calves from the manipulation of the foot pedals.

Even during a slow number like this, her whole body is involved in the process of playing. You just *know* her stomach muscles are contracting as much as those in her forearms. It's a riveting, sensual experience to see her perform and I suddenly understand why she was so *huge*. Even if you didn't like this sort of music, you'd pay to see this. The whole performance is a work of art.

Then it stops. The final chord hangs in the air. Her fingers leave the keyboard, and she rests her hands on her thighs. She's still. Then she turns, faces the camera and smiles. It's a warm, approachable smile, perhaps not the stern, serious one you may have been expecting.

Her voice is soft, cultured, and English-accented, with little hints of a cosmopolitan Europeanism popping out every now and then. If you only heard her speak, you'd never guess where she was from. Her delivery is straight to camera, humorous.

'"Behave yourself, please: a monkey is watching you."

"Avoid any sacrilegious excitement."

"Do not eat too much."

"With inane but appropriate naïvety."

"Like a nightingale with toothache."'

She smiles. My heart flutters.

'Even today,' she continues, 'Erik Satie's jokey and unconventional performance indications are considered eccentric, even shocking, just as they were when he was alive.

'The piece I have just performed, "Gymnopédie No. 1", certainly one of Satie's best-known compositions, comes with the instruction *"Lent et douloureux"* – "Slow and painful". His intent was to create an open-mindedness in the performer, to make them undermine their traditional teachings, to alert them to the modernism of what they were playing and, in a sense, to reject the past and flout convention.

'This does not mean that, as a player, you can interpret the pieces in any way that you wish, but it certainly means that you have to think carefully, laterally, about how you're going to play them. There is humour in these often mystifying and impenetrable instructions, but there is also a more serious intent: to re-examine and alter the creative link between composer and performer.'

I sit back and fold my arms. There's something about her delivery that's both mesmerising and soothing; you want to let her voice wash over you, sedate you.

She continues:

'Born in Honfleur in the Calvados department in north-western France, Satie's cultural background was idiosyncratic and bohemian. He worked as a café pianist, playing at the Chat Noir and Auberge du Clou in Montmartre.

'His piano work, probably the best known of all the music that came from Paris in the late nineteenth and early twentieth centuries, is still difficult to classify; drifting in and out of "classical", "experimental", "popular", "anti-virtuousic" and "revolutionary". Stravinsky described him as the oddest man he had ever known!

'He was a friend of Debussy, collaborated with Picasso and Cocteau, and took inspiration from the avant-garde as well as from street music, particularly the omnipresent barrel organ.

'His interests also took in opera, theatre, journalism, ballet, writing and art, making him, in effect, an early multimedia artist. He's also seen as an originator of ambient music, which he called "furniture music", something that could enhance day-to-day living without demanding too much attention from the listener.'

She runs through the influence that Satie has on modern music as well as his musical environment during his most creative period; how the innovational Parisian arts scene shaped and formed his outlook and his composing.

It's fascinating. Or is it Kiaraa who's fascinating?

Then she returns to the keyboard to play three connected pieces called *Véritables Préludes flasques (pour un chien),* the first part of which is hammered out with such ferocity that it makes me jump.

Looking at her slight frame, it's difficult to imagine where the power is coming from (unless it's the *geongangmi* once more). As a non-musician, I'm just thinking 'How does she *do* that?'

She runs through a few more of Satie's biographical details; his affair with artist and artist's muse Suzanne Valadon, his only known relationship with a woman. Seems he was unlucky in love. I'm sure his eccentricity and poverty didn't help.

I start thinking of Kiaraa's various relationships, at least the ones I know about. Odette Fournier, Conceição Teixeira the Brazilian soprano,

Lucas Quaresma the Argentinian violinist and of course the mystery man, whoever he may be.

It's all very urbane, ephemeral, disconnected, and perhaps par for the course for someone like her: rich, beautiful, famous, spending most of her time jetting around the world giving concerts, staying in luxury hotels, slogging away in recording studios.

Relationships may have been difficult for her. Did she, during her travels, come across someone who thought it would be a good idea to kidnap her? Was it someone she had an affair with somewhere along the way?

But then Micha's description of the kidnapper's voice and speech didn't make it seem like he was Kiaraa's type, though I could be wrong.

I'm still in the dark, here.

No wonder the police were/are having problems.

I watch her play another piece. This time it's called "Sonatine bureaucratique". Uptempo, complex; you can feel her joy as her fingers dance up and down the keyboard. Then Sallow's matter-of-fact description crashes into my consciousness.

One of our forensic clever clogs confirmed it had to have been done using a heavy-duty wire cutter or cable cutter.

And while she was still fucking alive.

I wonder about the shock she experienced during the initial stage of the abduction. Did it occur to her what was happening?

Is this a joke? Are these friends of mine having a laugh? My friends from the restaurant? What is this?

Then:

Is no one going to help me?

I'm sitting here, drinking coffee, basking in the glow of that face, that skill, that talent. Like a tidal wave, the chill, the *hell* of her awful, final hours washes over me. I realise that I'm grinding my teeth.

Those brief candles of false hope your brain is kind enough to transmit during woundings/torture/panic/despair: *this is not really happening, you're delirious/hallucinating/having a nightmare/still at home.*

They're sadistic, those little flashes, and they just last long enough for the comedown to be terminally disheartening, the hope bogus and brutal and you stupid enough to believe in it, even for a millisecond. I've been there myself. It's awful.

Then something else occurs to me. It seems so obvious that the finger removal was connected to Kiaraa's occupation that perhaps it's *too* obvious. Sure, there was certainly an element of sadism there, but what if there was a more practical reason? What if she'd scratched/clawed someone's face or hand while they were manhandling her?

If that had happened, there could have been tissue beneath her fingernails that could be used for genetic analysis. I've heard of hands being removed at the wrist for this reason. Sallow said that the two DNA profiles that forensics found had no matches, but it's conceivable that a third possible kidnapper had their genetic profile on the NCI database.

It could be that the removal of *all* Kiaraa's digits was a smokescreen to protect that person from identification; make it seem that it was about her occupation. But I don't hold out much hope of finding someone with a big scratch across their cheek two years on. Still, it's something to keep in mind.

I let the film run its course, finish my lunch, and open the small bag containing the CDs. There are two of them: *Inventions & Sinfonias* by J.S. Bach and *Preludes & Sonatas* by Muzio Clementi.

The cover of the Bach CD is stark, monochrome and mesmerising. A grainy three-quarter shot, she's leaning with her back against a whitewashed brick wall, head turned to face the viewer, a smouldering and mildly contemptuous look on her face, lips slightly parted, hair a tousled wolf cut.

She's wearing a soft white cotton shirt, which is tactfully unbuttoned to the navel to discreetly show off her fit, small-breasted allure. If the photographer was going for 'blatantly post-coital', he or she has certainly succeeded. You almost expect to see a cigarette dangling from her lips.

There are more photographs like this in the attached CD booklet and they're unquestionably from the same session. In one of them, she's photographed against the same brick wall, but now she's sitting on the floor, glancing to her left, sexy, indifferent, cooler than cool, her arms resting upon her knees, fingers dangling.

A blue stonewashed denim jacket this time, once again unbuttoned all the way down with nothing beneath; revealing but not revealing. Sawn-off jeans, no shoes. Different eye makeup, darker, and looking like it's been daubed on her face by someone's fingers. It looks like a shoot from an upmarket fashion magazine.

The Clementi cover, by contrast, is a different kettle of fish entirely and makes me smile at both its audacity and lack of subtlety.

Someone, I decide, is having a laugh here.

Full colour this time, and she's standing, leaning against the side of her futuristic Fazioli grand piano, supporting herself on the balls of her hands, legs crossed at the ankles and her head turned a little to the side. Hair is a mussed-up bob. She's laughing and it lights up her face.

White heels are maybe five inches, but it's the pale bronze shoulderless bodycon dress that draws the eye. Someone has taken the trouble to find a shade that exactly matches Kiaraa's skin tone, so for a nanosecond it looks like she's naked, until your brain realises you've been conned.

Or should that be bodyconned…

I flick through the booklet, looking for more of these photographs for research purposes only, and as I guessed, they've taken it even further.

Each pose, some with the piano, some without, demonstrates her pleasure in the way she looks and the knowledge of the effect that these photographs will have on those that view them.

She wants to flaunt, provoke, and arouse, and it's worked. They remind me of the nudes she had taken; the smugness and appealing immodesty of her facial expressions are almost identical.

I take the CDs into the kitchen and place them next to her secret photographs.

Yes. Different projects, different clothing, different hair, different poses, different makeup, but a style that is common to all.

I'm pretty certain that whoever took her CD covers also took the nudes. Please, *please* let there be a name somewhere amongst all these pages.

The credits turn out not to be at the end of the Bach booklet but, irritatingly, are right in the centre.

Piano Technician: Rosalia Sal
Booklet Editing & Translations: Ozren Jurković
Stylist: Angelina Auricht
Hair: Peverell Rochefort
Photography: Florian Pöck

The Clementi booklet has the same personnel, but with a different hair credit and a different stylist.

I get on the computer and Google Pöck's name. He's everywhere. He's one of those people you've never heard of whose work is featured in high-end magazines worldwide, particularly in Europe.

He's worked on campaigns for Versace, Burberry, Dior, Chanel, L'Oréal, Victoria's Secret, Monsoon, Givenchy, Comme des Garçons and many, many more. Magazine gigs include *Vogue, Femina, Artells, Harper's BAZAAR, Garage, Model Throwdown, Vanity Fair, Minus10mag, Dazed & Confused, Ylle, Top Notch,* and *Puss Puss* (didn't I see one of those in Kiaraa's place?).

His site is jammed with examples of his work, much of it featuring instantly recognisable fashion models and celebrities. It seems he's also not above doing boudoir, of all things, though I imagine this is a deluxe version for the cognoscenti, i.e. mind-bogglingly expensive.

He has a female associate, Jasna Løvstrøm, who, among other things, takes over this part of the business for women who would prefer a female photographer. He also does conventional portrait photography, but only, it would seem, if you're a famous actor, musician, writer, or model.

He's published five books of his photographs and has won nineteen awards, including the Sony World Photography Award, the Spotlight Award, the Fine Art Nude category at the International Photography Awards and the British Photographic Portrait Prize.

I click around looking for his work with Kiaraa but can't find anything. Maybe he took it all down when she died.

There's a link to the boudoir photography section. The photographs are tasteful and professional, simultaneously earthy and romantic, full of costly and sexy lingerie, enticing nudity or near nudity, and subtle hints of creative kinkiness.

The ages of the women seem to range from twenties to fifties, with a wide range of body types on display. Whether they're full-figured or slim and toned, the results are beautifully and fantastically erotic.

When the subjects are naked, there's often a discreetly placed hand or arm in the way, or they're lying on their front on a fur rug or similar. But this is not always the case. Many are thoroughly revealing and lascivious, the poses both audacious and mouth-watering, but still photographed with the same stylish professionalism.

These women all look good – quite beautiful actually – so either they're really professionals having us on, or a stylist comes as part of the deal. Or perhaps it's Pöck's photographic skill. For some reason, I think of Penny having a session like this done. I'd pay for it just to see her face when it was suggested.

He even does what he calls *maternité*, shots of women in various stages of pregnancy, mostly naked, sometimes artfully draped with lingerie, all with soft chiaroscuro lighting. I'd never heard of this as a 'thing', but why not? And in Pöck's hands, all of them are charming, attractive works of art, and not a little seductive and overpowering.

You can click through the pages of his books. I pick one at random, called *Déshonorabilité*. This is full of stark in-your-face fetish BDSM leather latex sex toy kink photography: severe, assertive, beautiful women strapped to chairs or each other with leather and rope restraints, blindfolded, breasts bared, nipples clamped, sneering, defiant, scary. The photograph of Kiaraa in the cupless crop top pops into my mind.

There are Jessica Rabbit lookalikes in tight-fitting long black rubber dresses and impossible heels. Another woman, excessively voluptuous, wearing only stilettos, black vinyl stockings and matching sixteen button gloves, is bent double, growling at the camera. The lingerie I bought Suzanna suddenly seems staid and conservative.

Another book, *Ordonnance Restrictive*, features women of varying body types who have been the subject of dramatic and provocative rope bondage. Some are overtly and crudely sexual, others are impressive works of art. The book seems to focus on breast bondage in the main (often with additional ropework around the crotch, wrists, thighs and ankles), but despite this, many of the models are petite and small-breasted.

One woman, possibly Japanese, features in many of the photographs, her breasts latticed in a variety of complex patterns, though the aim seems to be to enhance their beauty, not to cause discomfort, pleasurable or otherwise. I'm afraid I keep looking at her nipples. She has the same body type as Kiaraa, and the shots resemble those I found in Kiaraa's collection, right down to the red rope. Presumably Pöck hires a shibari specialist for these shoots, as this looks like highly skilled work.

Finally, I look at *Chose Extrême*. Even though many of the women here are naked, this is more like a collection of outrageous and avant-garde fashion shoots, and, indeed, the magazines the work was done for are referenced at the bottom of each page and the models are also named.

The women in these photographs lie on the floor watching television in hotel rooms, they cane other women dressed as housemaids, they look bored and smoke with the Eiffel Tower in the background, they lie, blindfolded, apparently unconscious, at the foot of a horse.

They hang around on street corners at night, wearing white wedding dresses and smoking. They stand, naked, drinking luminous cocktails at sophisticated parties, chatting to older women who are fully dressed. They wear stainless steel chastity belts and push-up leather bras, and count paper money.

The whole métier seems to exist in some alluring demi-monde that would never occur in reality, but in these photographs seems entirely plausible. There's no getting away from it; Pöck is really good.

There's a photograph of him sitting on a bed draped around two models who are wearing matching green cami pyjama tops and shorts. They're all drinking champagne and grinning. Some job he has there. Looks to be in his late fifties. Long, shaggy grey hair, rimless circular glasses. Good-looking with a weapons-grade smirk. He was born in Waidhofen an der Ybbs in Lower Austria. Studied Medical Biology at Salzburg University.

I decide to give him a call. Is this a waste of time? Maybe, maybe not. It's certainly an aspect of Kiaraa's life that the police would have overlooked, so it might turn something up.

There's what looks like a landline contact number on his website, so I try that. It rings and rings. Just as I'm about to give up, a jaded and impatient female voice answers. Swedish? Might be Jasna Løvstrøm.

'Yeah?'

I introduce myself and ask to speak to Florian. I can hear thundering, thumping music in the background, then I hear her shouting.

'Florian? You've got a fucking *detective* on the phone here.'

He says something, but I can't make it out.

'It's not *me* he wants to talk to, it's *you*,' she yells. 'What? How the *fuck* should I know what he wants?' She turns her attention to me. 'Are you the fucking *police*?'

Definitely Swedish. From Stockholm, judging by the inflections.

'No. I'm...I'm private. A private detective.'

She passes this information on to Florian, who yells something at her.

'If you're the police, he won't speak to you. He *hates* the police. If you're a private detective, he doesn't need one. That's it. Have a nice day. 'Bye.'

She hangs up. I take a deep breath and try again. More ringing. Finally, someone answers. Male voice this time. Austrian accent. I jump in at high speed before he has a chance to cut me off.

'Is that Florian Pöck? My name's Daniel Beckett. I'm a private investigator. I'm investigating the murder of Kiaraa Jeong. I found the photographs you took of her. The nudes. I need to talk to you.'

Let's hope mentioning the nudes grabs his attention. Let's hope it was him who actually took them. He shouts at whoever she is to turn the music off. She moans. *Not in the middle of a fucking track!* It stops. I hear a different female voice. Italian. *I was enjoying that, Flori-aaaan!*

'What do you mean you *found* them? Were they on the floor in a lavatory or something? Did you find them in an old jacket pocket or something? Down the back of a sofa or something? Did someone leave them on the underground or something? In the laundromat? Where, where, how could you *find* them?'

'I found them in her house. She…'

'What do you mean you're investigating? Where have you come from?'

'Her sister has hired me. Micha Jeong. She…'

'To do what? To investigate *me*?'

I start thinking of that Satie performance indication – *slow and painful*.

Another deep breath. 'No. To investigate her sister's murder.'

'I don't know her sister.'

'Nevertheless, she has hired me to look into Kiaraa's murder. Can I come and see you sometime? Maybe tomorrow p.m.?'

'I'm busy right now.'

'That's fine. I was talking about tomorrow. Shall we say one p.m.?'

Total silence.

A sigh.

'I don't like to have to think about this, you know?'

Was that the hint of a sob in his voice?

'I know. No one does.'

Five seconds of silence. Another sigh. 'Two fucking years now. More.'

'That's right.'

'Are you going to catch them?'

'Yes.'

'Hm. OK. Well. Do you know where my studio is?'

'It says 81-85 D'Arblay Street W1 on your website.'

'That's right. The Wardour Street end. Next to That Touch of Ink, the tattoo parlour. Two doorbells. It's the one that doesn't look like it should be working is the one you push. You won't hear the bell, but we will. One push will be enough. More than that and it drives me crazy, you know? Door is covered in artless graffiti. Keeps the punks out. Did it myself. Far superior to the real graffiti artists and I wasn't even trying. They all think they're Basquiat and *he* was overrated. OK. Make it one o'clock. I'm working tomorrow, but you can come in and hang around until I've finished. It's all a bit unpredictable. Sound OK? Daniel Beckett. Daniel Beckett. Sounds familiar. Do I know you from somewhere?'

'I don't think so.'

'Anyway. Tomorrow.'

Click.

I suppose I better take a shower and get ready for my date with Dr Aziza Elserafie MBChB MRCPsych FRCPsych. It's been a long day. I just hope I've got the energy for what is to come.

16

TAKING THE BLUE PILL

'I'll have a Manhattan, my dear. You may wish to write this down. I'd like it to have three fluid ounces of Basil Hayden's Dark Rye Whisky, one and a half fluid ounces of Carpana Antica Formula Vermouth, two dashes of Angostura, one dash of Peychaud's and to be garnished with two maraschino cherries. That's two. I'd like it served in a large champagne coupe and do, *do* make sure that the glass is chilled. *Merci bien*. Daniel?'

I smile at the waitress, who looks a little rattled as she scribbles away.

'I'll have a Vodka Gimlet with two measures of vodka, please.'

She seems relieved at the simplicity of my order. 'Any particular vodka, monsieur?'

'I'll leave it to your discretion, mademoiselle.'

A nod from the waitress and then we're alone.

'Did you find her attractive?'

'The waitress?'

'Who else did you think I was talking about? She is French. From Perpignan judging by her accent. Your type, I think. Petite and busty. Good legs. Impudent ass. Quizzical, flirtatious expression. Seductive pout. Father fixated. Conflict between the ego and super-ego resulting in narcissistic neurosis.'

She can always make me laugh. I shake my head and recover. 'You look fabulous, Aziza.'

A terse smile. 'I'm sorry. I am at war with myself today. My inner critic is particularly harsh, and my self-doubt is unrelenting in its barbarous assault. And thank you for your comment. The clothes are to your liking? I spent an hour trying on different items before I came out this evening.

'Even though it was me that suggested that you order me what to wear, I was able to sublimate that and pretend that it was *solely* your suggestion.

'Of course, Anna Freud said that denial was a mechanism of the immature mind. I disagree. What did *she* know about sexual acquiescence and transference of fetishism in the twenty-first century?' She shrugs. 'A famous surname doesn't mean you know everything about psychoanalysis.'

'That's my family motto.'

I get a lovely smile as she drops the faux-haughty/feigned jealousy/fake psychobabble act for a couple of seconds. For some reason I'm not qualified to comment on, it entertains and stimulates her to pretend she's not confident, assertive, and desirable. I wonder if there's a name for that.

As requested, she's wearing a tight-fitting dark plum silk blouse with a breathtaking plunge neck, a green cotton skirt that stops just above the knee, black stockings and black four-inch heels.

There's a yellow gold flame necklace around her neck and a matching Cartier Tank Française watch on her wrist. As usual, her fingers are adorned with a variety of gemstone rings: pink topaz, black tourmaline, malachite, snowflake obsidian, and mandarin garnet.

Her hair, inky black flecked with grey, usually tied back in a tight bun for work, has been let down and falls over her shoulders. Add to that the soft olive skin, the full, sensual mouth, the marvellous cheekbones, and the big, beautiful kohl-rimmed brown eyes you could get lost in, and she brings a new meaning to the words 'dazzling' and 'exotic'. She looks great. She knows this, of course, but you have to keep telling her. It's part of the game we play.

'Tight clothing always suits you, Aziza. You have the figure for it.'

'Are you just saying that to flatter me, Daniel?'

'Yes.'

'You can lie to me if you wish.'

'Your outrageously fabulous curves would not arouse a dead man.'

She raises an eyebrow; her mouth opens slightly, and she sighs as the compliment washes over her. 'I have put on exactly eight and a half pounds since I saw you last, Daniel. I think you can see where most of it went. I always watch your eyes and I can see where they are looking.

'I would like to say that being visually devoured by you is unpleasant, but I cannot. You know that I find it stimulating. If this restaurant had rooms to rent upstairs, we would be in one of them right at this very moment and you could do much more than just *visually* devour me.'

'Before we have anything to eat? I'm shocked.'

'In fact, I rather like the idea. Renting a room by the hour has always appealed to me. I think we should go to Japan and stay in one of their love hotels. I believe that a short stay can be anything between two and four hours. They have *adult vending machines*,' she says, looking a little crazed.

'Oh, no.'

'Obviously, I haven't researched it, but I understand that the Hotel Metro in Yokohama and the Design Hotel W Zip Club in Nagoya come highly recommended.'

'You *haven't* researched it?'

'Maybe some casual reading.'

'If we went to Japan, we'd be staying in a hotel anyway.'

'I know. But we could still visit *un hôtel d'amour*. Maybe just for a few nights. Staying at a love hotel has two advantages. Firstly, the reception staff would know exactly why you were there. They would look at you in a certain way. I think I would like that.

'Secondly, you would be able to hear people in the other rooms. Hear them making love as you made love. It would be a heady experience, and one I would be open to. Also, and I believe it goes without *saying*, the people in the other rooms would be able to hear *you*. They would hear every single uninhibited squeal of delight. Every gasp, moan, shriek, scream and howl. Every earth-shattering spasm.'

'Sounds very appealing, but I don't think the receptionists can be actually *seen* when you book in. It's all very discreet. Or so I'm told.'

'Whatever. There is an area in Tokyo called Love Hotel Hill, which I have also casually and inadvertently read about by accident. There are many of them there. I think it would be very pleasing to try out more than one of them. It would be like choosing chocolates from a Fortnum & Mason selection box.'

'Excellent metaphor.'

'Did you know that they have vending machines in Japan that sell used panties?'

'I think I saw one of those in Harrods.'

'Would you buy a pair of mine?'

'Just one pair?'

'Perhaps seven. One for each day of the week. You could keep them in a jacket pocket. You would be carrying my sexuality around with you wherever you went. I could sign them for you. Perhaps add a vulgar sentence or two or a profane quote. Something by de Sade or Bataille.'

'If you did that I could never wash them.'

Her eyes widen. 'I would not want you to. My God. Just the thought of it! It may well be a new fetish. I must give it a name. Perhaps there's an academic paper in it.'

The waitress arrives with our drinks. Aziza pinches the stem of her glass to make sure it's chilled. It is. She indicates her satisfaction and takes a few sips, fluttering her eyelashes with pleasure as the alcohol hits. She holds her glass out to me.

'Try.'

I take a sip and make a face. Too many bitters for my taste. 'Tart.'

'You may call me that later on.'

'I was going to anyway.'

'"Bitch" would not go amiss, either.'

'Now you're going too far.'

She laughs. 'You didn't say that the last time we met, *mon sauvage débauché*.'

'I was distracted by your intoxicating allure.'

She flicks her hair back. 'I went to La Perla as you suggested, Daniel. Much as I should enjoy literally showing you what I bought right here in this bistro, I...'

The waitress is back. I realise I'm looking at her in a different way thanks to Aziza. 'Seductive pout' was spot on.

'Would you like to order, madame? Monsieur?'

She gets an icy smile. 'Not yet, my dear. If you would be so kind as to give us a few more minutes.'

'Of course, madame.'

'Should we order champagne, Daniel, or have another cocktail first?'

'Another cocktail. What were you about to take out of your bag?'

'Ah, yes. The La Perla catalogue. I shall show you what I purchased. What I am wearing right at this moment.'

She produces the catalogue, flicks through it until she finds the page she wants, places it flat on the table and twists it around so that I can see it.

She taps the page twice with her forefinger. 'So. Firstly, I bought this black push-up bra in French lace. They measured me. It turns out I am now an FF cup, as I can see you've already noticed. I literally spilled out of the F cup when I tried it on. I thought of you as it happened; thought of the expression on your face. I almost bought the F cup just to torment you,' She turns a few more pages. 'And this black Lycra thong with embroidered tulle. In my mind's eye, I could see you smiling as I tried it on.' She looks up, a single eyebrow raised, lips pursed, for comment.

'I'm afraid I'm speechless, Aziza.'

'They did not have a suspender belt I liked, so I went to Plaisirs Interdits in Knightsbridge and bought a rather shocking Bordelle sanglé suspender in black leather and a pair of black nylon seamed stockings. I think you'll be pleased with the overall result, it is rather formidable. I hope you don't think I've been too *wicked*.'

'Heaven forbid.'

'I wouldn't want to be *chastened.*'

'Well now you're just fibbing.'

We both order Coquilles St Jacques in pesto for our starter. Aziza decides upon the Chevreau grillé Provençale for her main course and I choose the Choucroute. Another Mega-Manhattan, another double Vodka Gimlet, one bottle of Lombardi Hyménée champagne (2012 vintage) and a bottle of Bourgogne Aligoté.

I leave the alcohol ordering to Aziza. She seems to know what she's doing. She pours us both a glass of the champagne. We clink glasses like a pair of sophisticates.

'So, Daniel. You have questions for me about Kiaraa Jeong. First of all, the whole subject is still very upsetting for me, so I apologise in advance if I get tearful.

'Secondly, as I'm sure you understand, post-mortem duty of confidentiality means I cannot discuss my treatment of her with you in any way whatsoever. But as you are employed to find her murderer or murderers, I can discuss my treatment of classical pianists *in general*. Do we understand each other? This champagne is simply delicious. Oh look, Daniel. Your impudent Gallic girlfriend is back.'

Out starter has turned up. Very fast service here. Or maybe they want the table back ASAP.

'May I ask who hired you, Daniel? Was it the sister?'

'It was, but I didn't tell you that.'

'How did she know about you?'

'A lawyer who worked for Sansuyu recommended me.'

'A female lawyer?'

'Yes.'

'Have you slept with her? Wait. You averted your gaze for a millisecond. That means you have.'

'You see right through me.'

'How old is she?'

'A little older than you.'

'Is she a better lover?'

'That would be impossible, Aziza.'

She smiles to herself. She liked that. 'You must tell me everything you have done with her. Everything. Think of it as free therapy.'

'For whom?'

'Do you promise?'

'Sure.'

'I'll look forward to it. You know how it excites me. I'm not sure why, precisely. Perhaps I should get myself psychoanalysed again. I have not seen Dr Ørskov for almost six weeks. Perhaps I am a cuckquean fetishist. It's a form of masochism, of course. Do I come across as a masochist?'

'It's what makes you sexy.'

'How sexy am I on a scale of one to twenty?'

'Two hundred and thirteen.'

She chokes on her champagne, coughs, then recovers. 'You push all the right buttons with me, Daniel. I am already hot with anticipation. See how flushed my face is? What could be causing that, I wonder? Lean over and kiss me on the mouth.'

I do as she says. 'Was that OK?'

'Like a high voltage electric shock.'

I take a sip of my cocktail. 'What are the problems that a classical pianist would come to you with?'

She gives me a look that is nothing to do with that question, then checks herself and re-enters the room. She busies herself with her Coquilles St Jacques.

'It is an irony that classical music helps to relieve anxiety,' she says. 'Listening to it increases blood flow by at least twenty-five per cent. It lowers cortisol levels and also promotes mental health.

'But the people who perform this music, for example *classical pianists,* regularly experience anxiety and panic attacks. There was a study in 2019 that stated that seventy percent of classical musicians experience these states to a greater or lesser degree.'

'So, these people, these *classical pianists,* may seek help from a professional like you.'

'Correct. But it is not just anxiety. Many of them experience depression, also. They can suffer from crushing loneliness. They can feel useless and despondent. They'll often complain of constant tiredness, losing their sex drive, difficulty in sleeping, appetite loss, being unable to enjoy the things they used to enjoy.

'Some will lose interest in doing anything at all. Some will feel inexplicably sad. Not all of these symptoms can appear at the same time. They come and go. It can sometimes seem as if they are queuing up, waiting their turn to affect the individual.

'You rarely see this suggested in interviews with musicians of this type. It's all about the music. You'll sometimes see words like *difficult* or *challenging*, phrases like *at a low point*, but never words like *useless*, *hopeless*, or *disconsolate*.

'They live an odd life. You're in a luxurious hotel in Bruges, and there is your loneliness, waiting to greet you like an old friend as soon as you open the door to your suite.

'Alcohol abuse is another side effect of that loneliness, but that was not an issue in the case we are most definitely not discussing, and neither was loss of sex drive or loneliness.'

I think of the box of mirtazapine in Kiaraa's house. Unused, but maybe worth a tug.

'Would you prescribe any sort of medication for depression, anxiety, panic attacks? Antidepressants, for example?'

'Sometimes, but it is better to use 'talking therapy' or Cognitive Behavioural Therapy. It helps with the patient's mental wellbeing.'

'But in some cases…'

She looks a little suspicious. How would I know this?

'In one…particular case, I did prescribe mirtazapine, but the patient's symptoms seemed to get better at that particular point, and she – they – did not need the pharmaceutical therapy after all. A good job, really. She – *they* were a tad concerned about the effects that the drug might have on their performance. Understandable. Mirtazapine can cause drowsiness, sedation, and fatigue.'

Well, that's that inconsequential riddle out of the way.

Our main course arrives.

Aziza orders another bottle of champagne.

'Do you remember, Daniel, the last time we met?'

'I still haven't recovered.'

'There was something we talked about. Something dauntingly taboo. Off-limits. Arrestable. Outlawed. *Verboten. Prohibido.*'

'I remember. I think you're evil.'

'I have had quite a while to think about it. I would like to try it.'

'As long as you're sure.'

'I am sure. I am more than sure. You must take me to Japan. Perhaps we could try it for the first time in a busy love hotel of the crudest type with the thinnest walls. It would be overwhelming but exquisite. I feel inflamed, now, talking about it. Or perhaps that is something else...'

'You say that classical musicians suffer from many of these problems. Why this group of people? What are the underlying causes?'

'There are many. Most of these artistes start young; very young.' She chews and thinks for a few seconds. 'They are cossetted, encouraged. But as children, they make so many sacrifices it is difficult to imagine. A lot of the things that ordinary children do, they do not do, they will never do. 'This can often result in them not being socialised properly by the time they grow up.

'But when they become adults, when they become eighteen or whatever, the support they had in their early life stops. They are left to fend for themselves in many ways. They enter a stoical, masochistic world where there are no days off.'

'But by that time, they're obliged to continue.'

'Exactly that. They are praised for being strong enough to keep going. Most go to university or some other type of relevant further education. This affects their ability to practise as much, which causes anxiety. Then they have to invest in their future by paying for masterclasses and extra lessons. More stress.

'Even showing vulnerability and admitting mistakes works against them. It's called the "Beautiful Mess" effect. You may have heard of it. Others regard our vulnerabilities much more positively than we do, not realising that we ourselves think about our vulnerabilities in a far more critical way. It creates negative feedback. It's a Petri dish for multiple neuroses.'

I've drunk a little too much to fully concentrate on this. 'God almighty. I thought it was just a matter of hitting the right notes.'

'It's definitely a culture of survival of the fittest. Very Darwinian. Highly pressurised. Many sink without trace. Then, in the case that we are not talking about, there was the added stress of bisexuality that had run through her – *their* life since her early teens. Guilt and stress because of a conservative background and culture.

'On a conscious level it was not a problem, but it affected other matters. A knock-on effect, you might say, so it was worth discussing from time to time as it played a part in general confidence.'

She reaches across the table and places her hand on mine. 'I was making great progress with Kiaraa, whom we are not even remotely discussing. We took on each issue systematically; confronted it, analysed it and dispensed with it. She was highly intelligent. She understood what I was doing and how the techniques worked.

'Also, this does not usually happen, but it was obvious that we enjoyed each other's company. We occasionally went out to dinner on the strict understanding that the matters we spoke of in my rooms would not be mentioned in any shape or form. Once I was no longer treating her, we could have become proper friends.'

Her eyes fill with tears. She sniffs and quickly turns her head to the right so that I don't see. Then she recovers and glugs down half a glass of champagne. 'Even now, I cannot believe she is no longer here. I take it that you know more of what happened to her than was in the media.'

'I do. But I'm keeping it to myself. You would be upset.'

She nods her head. She keeps wriggling in her seat, and she looks a little flushed. Presumably the alcohol. 'Thank you, Daniel.'

'Did she ever speak of people she was having relationships with?'

'Only in the broadest terms. No names were mentioned. It was not a subject that was really discussed in that manner. Specifics are often unnecessary in therapy of this type. This is normal. At the time I was treating her, she had two regular lovers whom she said fulfilled her in different ways: one female and one male.

'It made her happy to talk about it on occasion, but, as I said, she did not name them, or give me any real information about them. She had had many affairs as a younger woman, but these two really opened up her sexuality, she said. She discovered things about her needs, about *herself,* that she had not been previously aware of. She was not more specific than that, though I think I knew what she was talking about.

'When we met socially we generally talked about music. I loved her playing. It was relucent. She once gave me tickets to a Bach recital she was giving at the Royal Festival Hall.

'I have always liked Clementi and Debussy and I was interested in the insights she had about their compositions. I play myself – did you know? You could talk all night to her.

'She found it intriguing that I was Egyptian. She had never been to Egypt. I told her that once you've seen one jackal-headed deity, you've seen them all. She found that very amusing. She was interested in the mythology: the cosmology, the way the ancient Egyptians perceived the world.'

This is all very interesting, but at the moment, I can't see anything here that relates to Kiaraa's murder. I was hoping that Aziza would know the name of the mystery man, but it seems not. I'm saving the matter of my business card turning up until I feel it's the right time to ask about it.

The manager appears as the waitress takes away our plates. I think this is more to do with getting a closer look at Aziza than a professional courtesy. He holds a couple of dessert menus and speaks to her hourglass cleavage.

'Has everything been to your satisfaction, madame?'

'*Assurément,*' she replies. '*Le Chevreau Provençal Grillé était une expérience voluptueuse et corsée à nulle autre pareille. J'aurai peut-être besoin de desserrer mes vêtements.*' She smiles at him and takes the dessert menus.

He looks flustered and leaves. I have to bite the inside of my lip to stop laughing. She grins, raises her eyebrows, and leans forwards.

'I couldn't help myself. I don't like it when men speak to my breasts.'

'I would never do that.'

'I know. *Ta bouche serait trop pleine.* I rather like the look of the Millefeuille à la mangue et grenade.' She takes a slow, deep breath, combined with some sultry eye contact. 'Do you see anything you find appetising, Daniel?'

'Are we talking about the dessert menu?'

'Possibly. Possibly not.'

'I think I'll have the Panna cotta au babeurre et figues.'

'Figs were Cleopatra's favourite snack, they say. An erotic fruit. Said to be an aphrodisiac. I have a secret to tell you.' She continues to wriggle in her seat. I wonder what's wrong.

'Please go ahead.'

'I took one hundred milligrams of Viagra before I came out tonight.'

'Isn't Viagra for, er...'

'I know, I know. But a patient of mine had been taking it. She had had problems with her libido. She took it to see if it would help. She'd read about it somewhere. She described the effects it had on her; how she felt, how it made her behave with her lovers. I nodded and spoke calmly to her about it. But I knew I had to try it for myself.

'What she was saying set off fireworks in my head. I understand the chemistry. Of the drug, I mean. Why it would work on a woman. It makes sense. Though it does not affect all women, I understand. I thought tonight...I didn't appreciate how quickly it would make me...oh God, Daniel. I have never needed a man so much in my life.'

The waitress appears. 'Have you decided on a dessert yet?'

I smile at her. 'I think we'll just have the bill, please.'

17

POST-COITAL, NAKED & SMOKING

She runs a hand through her sweat-soaked hair, gulping air into her lungs as if she'd just been holding her breath for five minutes.

'Oh my God. Oh God. Oh, Daniel. Oh, my love. I thought I was going to snap in two after that last convulsion. I buckled like a Nissan Altima after an unexpected road traffic accident. My whole body…I behaved like a lioness. Mindless copulation. Beyond thought. My humanity gone. An animal. A beast. Like Izanami no Mikoto, goddess of sickness and death. A salacious carnal fever. I was possessed by malevolent succubi.'

She pauses to pant a little more, then continues. 'Bedevilled by Aosoth, Thanatos, Eros, Bastet. And I have never spoken so crudely. Not to anyone. Not ever. I should be struck off for using language like that. You will report me to the General Medical Council tomorrow morning. I insist.

'Help me get undressed. I need to be naked. Actually, being a nudist, a naturist, quite appeals to me. I am naked at home quite a lot, and the idea of others secretly observing me never fails to give me a delightful frisson.'

'Stand up.'

I help her out of her remaining clothes and pick her up in my arms. She kisses my neck and shoulders, then starts biting them.

I carry her into the bedroom and lay her on the bed. She writhes and sinks her teeth into one of her forefingers. The flat smells of her sex, her sweat and Amber Mystique by Estée Lauder.

'You picked me up like I weighed nothing. It was masterful. I am completely at your mercy. Treat me as you would a Corinthian temple girl.'

'Stop talking. I'm in a meeting.'

'Where are we, Daniel? I have lost my mind.'

'We're in a love hotel in Toshima-ku in Tokyo. They have loyalty cards and free condoms.'

'Yes. Yes. And paper-thin walls. And used panties in vending machines, adult vending machines. And they are *my* panties. The people in the rooms next to us complained about the excessive noise and the evil language. And I paid by card, so the owners know exactly who I am.

'And my bank queried the payment. I am humiliated. They have stopped all my direct debits. Even Netflix. Why am I sweating so much? Should I wear a mask? Black leather? Rabbit ears? I would be a bad bunny. A bad bunny in a sleazy love hotel in Ikebukuro.' She bites her forearm over and over again, leaving livid teeth marks. 'Bad,' she repeats.

'Stop biting yourself, Aziza. Would you like some champagne?'

'Yes. Can we have the one we purchased at the bistro? Did you put it in your refrigerator?'

'Of course. I seem to remember having a few spare seconds when we came in.'

Before we left Le Jardin d'Épicure, we hurriedly bought a chilled bottle of the Lombardi Hyménée champagne. I pour out two glasses and sit next to her on the bed.

She's still panting. I watch the rise and fall of her breasts.

'This is the first time you have seen me naked for over nine months. Do you think my body has changed?'

'Yes.'

'For the better?'

'Without a scintilla of doubt.'

'More obscenely voluptuous? More desirable? More enticing? More indecent? More outrageously venereal?'

'All of those things and more.'

'Touch me. I am aflame, psychotic, damned. I am a hapless slave of Onan.'

'Could you stop doing that?'

'Make me stop.'

I grab her wrist. 'I need to talk to you about something else, Aziza.'

'I'm sure you could hold my wrist tighter than that. I know how strong you are. But I have two hands. You'll have to hold both wrists to stop me.'

I pin her to the bed, leaning over her. She gasps. She moans. She bares her teeth and arches her back. People wouldn't believe what I have to put up with to get information.

'I know that you gave Kiaraa one of my business cards about two years ago.'

'In ancient Egypt, they say it was the custom for some women to take multiple husbands. I can quite understand that. Do you know why I think – why I *know* my ex-husband had other women? It was because he could not satisfy me, and I mocked him for it. Until I met you I thought that no one could.

'Look at my face. Look at my eyes. You know what has to happen next. I am fully ready for it. Oh, La Païva! You must collar me, Daniel. I absolutely insist upon it! Dress me up as a maid. Take me from behind as I dust your priceless collection of obscene Japanese ceramic sculptures. Do not speak to me. Steal money from me. Sack me the next day.'

'Why did you give her my card?'

'I didn't need it anymore. Your mobile number is branded onto my accursed soul. Kiss me on the mouth. I have become insane. Multiple husbands. I am Messalina. Rebuke me in any way you wish. Promise me you'll take me to a love hotel.'

'Was she in trouble?'

'Trouble? I don't know. I don't remember. I can't think straight. Please, please, Daniel. My love. Just one more indecent paroxysm. That is all I ask. Then we can take a break and we can talk. I promise.

'Have you ever seen me like this before? It may never happen again! We may both be dead tomorrow! Look at my body! Look at it! I'm commanding you. I'm imploring you. This is beyond everything.' She bites my shoulder. 'Look! I have drawn blood a second time! I shall eat your flesh. I shall devour you. Sexual cannibalism. Just like insects!'

'You're a hell-cat, Aziza.'

'I know.'

'A witch.'

'Exactly that. I practise bitchcraft! Let us sacrifice a dog to Satan. Position me in whatever way you desire. Nothing is off-limits. Nothing! We shall worship Pan! Drink each other's blood! Beelzebub observes us with his baleful gaze this day. Do not hold back. Explore my cavern. Seek my womb. I demand the ultimate crisis!'

* * *

Forty minutes later, she gets up, walks unsteadily into the bathroom, and returns with her cigarettes and posh Caran d'Ache lighter. She smokes Sobranie Cocktail and selects a pink one. She lights it and draws the smoke deep into her lungs.

'My God. This is my fourth today. Usually I only have three, but you have to spoil yourself sometimes. I have already had two green ones and a yellow one. Have you got an ashtray anywhere?'

'Hold on.' I get up and fetch my red Murano glass ashtray from the kitchen.

'Thank you. One of my patients has a smoking fetish. He has a sexual interest in watching naked women smoke. It's called capnolagnia. It is not his main problem – he is an enthusiastic frotteur – but it is interesting all the same. Do you like watching me smoke, Daniel? While I am naked?'

'I do, actually. It's quite relaxing and curiously erotic; artistic, even. I think it's to do with your body language, the movements, the elegance, the femininity. Your face when you exhale, the way you close your eyes. There's a focus on your mouth, too. I think it's just another expression of your sexuality.'

She smiles. 'Hm. Thank you. It interests me that you said that. Would you make love to a woman who was smoking? I mean, *really* make love to her?'

'If she wanted me to.'

'She would.'

'So, tell me about my business card and how Kiaraa ended up with it.'

'I will not ask how you know about this. I'm sure it's very clever. We went out for dinner one night. Can't remember the date. She was having a brief break from touring.

'I think she was just spending a few hours a day in some recording studio somewhere. She was in London, her sister was away, her lovers unavailable, she fancied going out to dinner. She called me and we went to Araki. Do you know it?'

'New Burlington Street. Sushi. Expensive.'

'That's it. I feel so louche lying here next to you; delectably post-coital, naked, and smoking. Feeling your eyes on my body. Watching its changes. Totally exposed. Vulnerable. Oh, God. Self-pollution calls.'

I give her a light slap on the back of her hand. 'What did she say to you? Why would she need a detective?'

She takes a deep breath. 'There was something that had happened – an unpleasant thing that she thought was to do with her personally. I told her it was not so. I told her it was just a racist thing, that she should not take it to heart.

'I told her that I had been a victim of such episodes myself. Nothing so frightening, but in some ways similar. I am not so identifiably foreign-looking, I suppose. Foreign, yes – but from *where*? I am non-specifically *exotique*. Do you think I'm *exotique*, Daniel?'

'Like a bird of paradise. What was it? What happened?'

'I can't remember where she had been. Perhaps it was to see her agent or a record company person. Or an accountant. Something like that. Something non-musical. But it was in the middle of the day. It was in James Street. No. Not James Street. That little road you cut through from James Street to get to Selfridges in Duke Street.'

'Barrett Street?'

'That's it. A dowdy little thoroughfare. Betting shops, cafés, the backs of various shops and companies, motorcycle parking. She heard a man shouting at her. At first, she thought he was shouting at someone else. He caught up with her, grabbed her by the arm and swung her into a doorway. He had a knife.

'He pressed the flat of the knife against the side of her neck. She was terrified. She didn't know whether it was a mugging or whether he was a madman and was going to kill her. The street was empty. People walked by in the adjacent roads without seeing what was going on.

'He told her that people were sick of people like her. That she ought to find somewhere else to live. Clear out of the country. Go back to her people. He told her that the next time he saw her, it wouldn't be a knife, it would be a gun. Then he just laughed at her and walked off, but before that he spat in her face.'

Is this connected with her kidnapping in some way? Very unlikely. Sounds like random London dickhead shit to me. You wouldn't do something like this – particularly in the middle of the day – if you were planning some multi-million-pound kidnapping shakedown.

'What did he look like?'

'She said around forty. Stuff in his hair that smelled. Hair oil, I suppose. Greasy. Dark suit. Shirt, but no tie. Tall-ish. And – this is what made me concerned – hate in his eyes. No. Not hate. Anger is what she said. Anger. Like someone who was permanently angry. About what, we could never know. That's all, really. That was all she could remember. She was pretty shocked and upset.'

'Nothing else at all? His voice, accent, facial features, general demeanour, aftershave?'

'We are not all detectives, Daniel. I can remember the date, though, if that's any help. It was the 28th of July. It happened four days before my birthday.'

'And she didn't go to the police.'

'She did not. Koreans and police, yes? I told her that if she did not report this incident, then I would. She implored me not to. I eventually agreed. I did not want this to affect our friendship and our professional relationship.

'She was coldly furious, though, I think. Agitated. She became, I suppose you'd call it *closed down* for a while. She was not one to brood, but I felt she was brooding about this incident.

'She did say one thing that I remember, though. She said it would not happen again. She had friends in Korea who had experienced similar events, and she knew how to deal with it. I'm not sure what she meant by that, and I did not press the issue.

'I thought that if someone like you could demonstrate to her that her fears were unfounded, that this was not a personal attack, but an indiscriminate episode, then it would be a weight off her mind.

'Maybe you could track down the perpetrator. I had no idea what you would do. It was selfish of me. I didn't want the work I had done with her to be undone in any way. Mm. I've never felt like this. Will you kiss me?'

'Only if we can keep on talking. I don't want it to lead to anything. Not yet. This is my first time.'

'I hate you. I've never hated anyone like I hate you. You have control over me. You dominate me. Kiss my neck. Now my mouth.'

We kiss for a while. I hold her down by her shoulders. This makes things marginally worse. She wants more, but I need to keep her on edge.

She doesn't like this.

'Please, please.' She holds the back of my neck. 'Oh, fuck. I so rarely use wicked language in real life, but with you I am compelled to. Fuck. *Fuck!* How many times must I have said that word this evening?'

'Eighty-three times. So, it was just that incident that made you think she should contact me?'

She drinks some more champagne. 'There was something else. Something else she told me about.'

'What was it?'

'She was with her – I don't know what she was – her girlfriend? Her lover? Am I your lover, Daniel? Even though we don't see each other that frequently? Am I?'

'Yes you are, Aziza.'

'Do you like it when I pretend to be needy like that? I lose myself when I am with you. You have unlocked something deep within me. My sexual fantasies have gone off the rails. Tell me about the lawyer woman. Was she as wild as me? How did you make love to her? How long for? What sort of things does she say to you? Is she as coarse as me? Would she go with you to a love hotel in Osaka?'

'We haven't got round to discussing that.'

'They have them in Korea, too. Kiaraa told me about them. She had been to one on several occasions. In the Sinchon region, I seem to recall. I think they cost around £80 a night. Very clean. She enjoyed it. Found it stimulating. I've no idea who she went with. That was what put the idea in my head. I have been brooding about it for over two years.

'We could stay at a hotel here instead of going to each other's places. We could check in as a married couple. We could argue and fight until someone called security. I would answer the door naked and smoking a cigar with an enormous python wrapped around my waist. You would shout at me. You would lick Iordanov vodka off my body and eat Kaluga caviar straight out of my mouth.'

'What happened when Kiaraa was with her girlfriend?'

Are we talking about Odette Fournier here, I wonder?

'Her girlfriend, lover, whatever she was, had been giving a talk. Actually, it may not have been a girlfriend. It may have been just a friend. I can't remember. Do you know the Charlotte Street Hotel? It was there. They host business meetings.

'They have marvellous suites. We should stay there for a weekend. Make love on the floor. This was not a business meeting per se, it was more of a conference maybe. I don't know what you'd call it.

'Anyway, she – the girlfriend – is in charge of this organisation called something like Grassroots. Maybe not that. Something like that, anyway. You have to remember that this was a while ago now. My memory. The August before she died.

'It concerns itself with the support of women working in high positions in industry and also with women in high profile careers. And helping women climb up the ladder. Professional women of varying types. Like me.

'But I do not join things. I never have. I am not a joiner. I am a lone wolf. A lone vixen. A lone wench. Kiss my breasts, Daniel. Kiss them like you kiss my mouth. Take me to Elysium.'

'So, what happened?'

'When the whole thing had finished, the participants were leaving and found themselves face to face with a protest, on the pavement, right outside the main entrance to the hotel. I think a dozen people. All men. Thugs. Shouting. Calling the women who were trying to leave feminazis, femicunts and so on. Delightful.

'Again, Kiaraa felt this might have been to do with her alone, but I wasn't so sure. I felt she was a little paranoid. That was another reason I thought she may need to speak to you. I want to put my new bra on again. I like the way it feels, the way it makes me look. No. I want you to put it on. I want you to dress me as if I were a doll. A sex doll. Should I wear a cheap blonde wig and sunglasses the next time we meet?'

'Yes. Sit up.'

'My God, this is good. I'm so hot. Must be a side effect. Feel my skin.'

'Anything else?'

'Only a vague thing. This woman – the girlfriend again, I think – she'd been assaulted on a tube train one night. Punched in the face by some man. But – I'm sorry – I can't place this chronologically and I've forgotten the details now if I ever knew them. I think it was the August again, though. Kiaraa wasn't present, obviously, but she was very upset by it. Upset and angry.'

'Did this girlfriend go to the police? Hospital?'

'I don't recollect. It was a long time ago now. Maybe she took it in her stride. People want to forget about such things, not repeat them by going to the police. You know: you go through it once, then go through it again with added disbelief, smirks, and insinuations. Many more women are assaulted or threatened than the records show. I'm sure you appreciate what it's like.'

'And you don't know who this woman was? This girlfriend. You don't have a name.'

'No. Like I said. We talked about Kiaraa's sex life in general terms only.'

She's panting again. 'I am a spoilt maiden princess, sitting on the banks of the Nile. I'm imperious and feisty. But I need a man, a real man. The fops at court are no use to me. You are a simple boatman. I look at your muscles flexing as you repair your papyrus sails, the sweat streaming down your back…'

If it was Odette Fournier, she may not have wanted to make a fuss because of her husband. Why would that be? Was it connected to where she'd been? Why did she take a tube train instead of a cab? Was she trying to save money? That's something I'll have to talk to her about tomorrow.

At least the mystery of the business card seems to be solved, and that assault in Barrett Street may well explain the gun, particularly as Kiaraa asked Baek-Hayeon for it four days later.

'So, all those things together. That's why you recommended me.'

'Yes. Yes it was. And although I thought those incidents were a little worrying, I didn't want her to be fretting. After all the work we'd done. I just said that I knew someone who dealt with things that were not in the realm of police work, or things that they might be sceptical about. Ill-defined things.

'I told her the police may be offhand about these matters, but you would not. You would look into them thoroughly to put her mind at rest. So, I gave her your card. But I was afraid. I was afraid you would have an affair with her and would not have time for me. She was sexy. You must have noticed.'

'Yeah. I did. But not sexy in the way you are.'

'You make me that way, you bastard. "Sister Aziza. You have disgraced this nunnery. You shall be chastised. Shunned!"

'"No! No! Don't be angry, Mother Superior!"'

She leans over, picks up a purple Sobranie, lights it, takes a drag, lies on her back and stretches, her free hand rubbing her thigh. 'Now. About making love to a woman who was smoking.'

'Just don't get ash everywhere.'

18

WAITING FOR A MIRACLE

Day three begins.

Grafton Street is all designer jewellery, shoes, and clothing, plus a couple of expensive restaurants. There's a blue plaque above the Givenchy store: Sir Henry Irving, actor, lived there. Across the road, a subtle silver sign saying 'Fournier Textiles'. I walk over and press the doorbell. Nothing happens.

Before I came out, while Aziza was still asleep, I called Charing Cross Police Station. After listening to light jazz for ten minutes, I finally got through. Lucky it wasn't an emergency.

'Charing Cross.'

'Hi. This is DI Patterson from Homicide and Major Crime Command in Putney,' I say. 'Could you put me through to Rowan, er, DS Kinnaird, please? Cheers, mate.'

'Hold on.'

Lots of clicking. At least there's no music.

'Sorry, sir. DS Kinnaird isn't in today. He's on three days' leave this week. I think he's just using up some leftover holiday time.'

I put impatience with a touch of humour and regret into my voice. 'Bit of a pain. We're having a collection for one of the guys here who he worked with a few years ago. Retiring. Thought he'd like to contribute and sign the card. I could have popped over as I'm in the West End later on today.' I sound resigned and a little upset in a tough, blokey way. 'Never mind. Thanks for your help, anyway, chum.'

'I don't have his mobile number, sir. D'you, er – I'll tell you what. If you're over this way, why don't you pop into the Bijou Noir later on tonight. That's your only hope if you're in a hurry. I'm pretty sure you'd find him there.'

I laugh. 'What the fuck's the Bijou Noir?'

'Oh, it's a – you'll see if you go there. It's in Gresse Street. Can't miss it. Big neon sign outside. Well, not a *big* neon sign. An average-sized neon sign. That's the best I can do I'm afraid, sir.'

'That's his hangout, is it? Isn't Gresse Street off Tottenham Court Road?'

'That's the one.'

'OK. Well, I may pop in. you've been very helpful, er...'

'PC Terrence Baker, sir.'

'OK. Good work, PC Baker.'

'Thank you, sir.'

I'm rather glad he wasn't there; I have no idea what I was going to say to him. But he told Penny, against Sallow's express wishes, that Kiaraa had been stabbed multiple times. It may be nothing, but it's piqued my interest all the same.

I might just pop in the Bijou Noir and take a look at him if he turns up.

Penny's description of Kinnaird was *a big man, intimidating, shifty, rather ugly, overweight, and blinked a lot* from what I can recall. Oh, and there were the sly eyes, little beard and moustache, fat face and fat hands.

Well, that'll have to do, but I'd still like to know when he called on her if she can't find the date in her diary. He's committed one indiscretion; he might have made more.

When did I speak to her? Yesterday? I may call her again.

Then there's a buzz and the door opens. I take a look at the sign next to the lift. Fournier Textiles are on the fourth floor. Compared to the lift at Sansuyu, this one takes a decade to reach its destination.

As soon as I get out, I'm greeted by a keen, grinning young chap of about twenty in Ralph Lauren, hand out ready to shake. French. A Marseillais.

'Mr Beckett. Welcome. Hello. Hi. Odette will be ready to receive you in just a short while.' An exasperated eye raise. 'It is impossible to get Grégoire Lécuyer off the telephone, as I'm sure you know, though she will doubtless be curtailing him as we speak. May I get you something to drink? Do sit down.'

Grégoire Lécuyer is still at it, then. 'I'll have a coffee, please. No sugar, dash of milk.'

'Of course.' He nods and disappears. I sit down on what looks like a park bench, except it's made from hammered copper. That was odd. I presume Odette gave me some sort of backstory to avoid suspicion.

Just as he hands me the coffee, Odette appears. 'Thank you, Gilles. Come in, Mr Beckett.'

I get up and follow her into her office. She's absolutely not what I imagined. Maybe it was her name. Maybe it was her occupation. Maybe it was her voice.

For some reason, at least for me, the name Odette Fournier conjures up pictures of a slim, svelte, elegant, chic and refined 1950s Parisian sophisticate wrapped up in the latest Chanel creation.

But she's not like that at all. In fact, she's almost the opposite: a little over five feet, plump, buxom, with a disarmingly pretty face, a charming, down-to-earth smile, pink lipstick and enormous red hair tied back in a large, messy bun. She's wearing a belted Marilyn Monroe sweater, faded blue jeans and no shoes. Early forties, at a guess.

Her office gives nothing away. High distressed wooden ceiling, big brown distressed leather sofa, enormous pale blue rug (undistressed), two glass coffee tables, a huge abstract in red and black on the wall, possibly a reclining woman, and a gigantic Swiss cheese plant that needs repotting.

No computer. Perhaps that's in another room.

Where are all the textiles?

We sit down next to each other on the sofa. She curls up like a cat. Now I can smell her perfume. Chanel No. 19. Well at least *something* was Chanel. I smile at her.

'Je peux converser en français si cela vous met plus à l'aise,' I say.

'Thank you, but there will be no need. I prefer to speak English when I am here. I am sorry I was terse with you on the telephone, Mr Beckett. It – Kiaraa – is still a delicate subject with me. How did you know that those letters were from me?'

'I didn't. It was just a guess. Her sister told me that you had been in a relationship with Kiaraa. Seemed logical that it was you who had written the letters, and then you confirmed it when I spoke to you yesterday.'

'Very clever. So. You know everything.'

I tilt my head to the right to indicate 'enough'.

'It must have been hard,' I say, trying to be sympathetic and understanding.

'What must?'

'Dealing with her death. The effect it had on you. Maybe hiding what you felt from others.'

'Do you mean my husband?'

'I have no idea whether he knew about your relationship with Kiaraa.'

'He did not. Anyway, it was logical that I would be upset. Just because I was upset didn't necessarily mean I was having an affair with her. It *is* possible to be upset about the death of someone without having had sexual relations with them.

'She was a very good – a *very* good friend of mine, even though our meetings were infrequent. By that I mean that they were not as frequent as I would have wished.

'She was also an acquaintance of Mathéo's, so he was equally shocked by the news of her death. He is a great fan of the classics and adored her playing. He said that she left a vacuum in the world of classical piano virtuosity that could never be filled. He thought she was irreplaceable in that sense, and so did I. Do you keep what is discussed in circumstances such as this to yourself?'

'Of course. I guarantee it.'

I get a penetrating stare which lasts about ten seconds. 'Yes. I can see you have rectitude. You seem – how can I put this – consolatory, so

I think you can be trusted. Unless you are very skilled at faking it, which is always possible. I have misplaced my trust in the past.'

'Did he ever suspect what was going on between the two of you?'

'No, he did not. Are you suggesting that he might be a suspect in her abduction and murder? Are you suggesting that *I* am a suspect?'

'No, I'm not suggesting that. At the moment, I have so little to go on that I'm speaking to everyone who was involved with her in any way, as far as that is possible.

'Obviously, I'll be speaking to the people who were at Abd El Wahab that evening she disappeared, at least those who are still in the UK at present. That would include your husband, of course. Sometimes people have a tiny bit of information that they may not realise is important.'

She rests a hand beneath her chin and stares past me, looking out of the window. I take a sip of coffee. Not bad, if a little fruity. Milk is on the turn. I won't mention it.

She frowns. 'Both Mathéo and I have already spoken to the police. Twice. But I understand that you could have a different perspective that may bear fruit. After all, both Mathéo and I want Kiaraa's murderers to be brought to justice. Do you have Mathéo's telephone number? He would not object to speaking to you, but I beg you to be discreet.'

'I don't have his number, and you have my promise I'll be discreet.'

'One moment.'

She gets up and goes into another room. I find I'm watching her walk to see if it's sexy. It is. I can't put it into words, but I think I can see how she'd be attractive to both sexes.

She returns and hands me Mathéo's business card. Rather nice and undoubtedly pricey. Hard black suede, metallic gold print: *Mathéo Fournier, publisher*. It has two telephone numbers and an email address. I stick it in my wallet.

'You will be better off contacting him through his company on one of those numbers there. He has a mobile, but he is always turning it off. Most annoying. I'll write that mobile number down for you anyway.'

I decide to soften my questioning for a moment. I smile warmly. 'How did you meet Kiaraa?'

'Mathéo is a patron of the Vienne Musikverein. It's the home of the Vienna Philharmonic. Do you know it? He is a great aficionado of classical music and he supports when he can. Financially, I mean.

'We both had business in Vienna at the same time. He was visiting the Austrian headquarters of his publishing company, and I had a couple of meetings with Nicki Aigner about supplying her fashion house with a certain type of cotton fabric. She nearly always used local manufacturers, but not that time.

'To cut a long story short, Kiaraa was playing at the Musikverein with the Vienna Philharmonic. A Rachmaninov concerto, I recall. Through Mathéo's connection, we met her and two of the other patrons for dinner the next evening. I was absolutely besotted. And I was afraid.

'I thought everyone could read my mind. Knew what I was thinking. I could feel her calling to me, do you understand? I was aware that I was blushing every time she looked at me or spoke to me. Or maybe it just felt like I was.

'I could feel my heart pounding in my chest. I started drinking too much. Milliseconds of eye contact told me that she was feeling it, too.

'I didn't know what to do or how to act. There was no way I could communicate with her with Mathéo and the others there. When I got back to the hotel we were staying at, the Ritz-Carlton, I found a piece of paper torn from a menu which had been deposited in my clutch bag. I don't know how she'd done it. It had her room number at the Palais Coburg Hotel Residenz. And her mobile number. And just one word: 'tomorrow', followed by the letter K.

'I suppose I can tell you as you're a stranger and you maybe have her best interests at heart in some way. I'd never experienced anything like it. Sexually, I mean. My God, those first moments. The abandonment.

'She was very domineering, which I hadn't expected. I don't know why. But I responded to it. It was electrifying. I was addicted. I was a junkie, a fiend. Sometimes I felt as if I was going to die. To die from overstimulation. And I would have welcomed that death. Welcomed it with open arms. I apologise if I am too blunt. It is the way I am.'

Bloody hell.

This, of course, does not clear Madame Fournier of being involved. Strong emotions and sexual obsession can go either way. I leave about a minute of silence before I go back to the reason I'm here.

'Tell me about the meal you had at Abd El Wahab. Did Kiaraa seem OK? Was her behaviour normal?'

'I have been over this with the police. My story has not changed.' Big exasperated sigh. 'She was a little tired. She had been in a recording studio. She said what she had been doing was boring and it had made her fatigued. But apart from that, quite normal. She was funny and bright, as she usually is. Was.'

'And because she was tired, she left early,' I say. 'As far as you know, no one called her or texted her while she was in the restaurant.'

'She always switched her telephone off at social gatherings. She felt it tremendously rude to read texts under those circumstances, as did we all.'

'Did you see anyone else at that gathering send a text or do anything with their mobile phone?'

She frowns. 'No. No, I did not. But obviously I could not have surveyed everyone there all of the time. That would have been impossible. And I had no reason to do such a thing.'

'And no one approached her or spoke to her apart from you, your friends and the staff.'

'No one.' She sighs and shakes her head. 'This will sound foolish to you, but when she left Abd El Wahab, it was as if my soul was being ripped from my body. The combined sensations of her presence and Mathéo being there was exquisitely frustrating and overwhelming. If I had known then that I would never see her again…' She sighs. She looks tearful.

'I was looking through Kiaraa's things in her house the other night. I discovered a hidden compartment in an item of furniture. It was where I found your letters. There were some other items. We'll come to those in a moment. In those letters, you refer to *the man* several times. Someone you were keeping secrets from. Was that your husband or someone else?'

'It was my husband. Who else could it be? I knew he would never see those letters, but I still felt it was best to be circumspect. Mathéo is a wonderful man, and he is in love with me. It would kill him to discover I was being unfaithful.

'But it is a different thing. With another woman, I mean. I do not see it as being faithless. But there was a chance that Mathéo would not see it that way; he might become jealous or upset. But I find that type of knife-edge deceit exhilarating and thrilling. I had experienced it only once before.

'I had an affair with a much younger man four years ago. That was similar. I was on an extended business trip in Saint-Germain-des-Prés. He worked in a bistro close to my hotel. He was a waiter. It lasted for two weeks. It was very physical and I did not regret it. Far from it. But Kiaraa was something different. My excitement with her was on another level altogether. More emotional, I think it could be said.

'There is something else that may be of use to you. The first detective who questioned me said that Kiaraa had been having a relationship with a man, at approximately the same time she was with me. He did not know who this man was. I was a little taken aback, but not that much. Nothing she did surprised me. I suppose it was a little exciting.

'We people, we weave a tangled web, no? I did not know if it was serious. Kiaraa and I had discussed, I suppose you would call it *running away together*. Perhaps moving in with each other. Perhaps in Paris, perhaps in London.

'How that would have affected her relationship with this man I do not know. Knowing her as I did, I suspect it would have continued. He may have joined us.

'I have always been charmed by the idea of a ménage à trois and how it would work, though I suspect there would be many impracticalities and, perhaps, emotional dilemmas.

'Whoever this man was, he would naturally become my lover. I am not sure how I would have coped with that and how it would have affected the balance of my relationship with Kiaraa.

'At that time, I was rather ambivalent about Mathéo. Physically, I mean. I don't know whether I would have left him, but I think Kiaraa would have liked it. Did you know who this other man was?'

'I don't. There was a semi-automatic pistol and some ammunition in this hidden compartment. Do you have any idea why she would have those?'

She looks genuinely shocked. 'A gun? She had a gun?'

'You knew nothing about this?'

'Certainly not. No. Do you think she was going to shoot Mathéo?'

I shake my head. 'I don't think that's likely. There was also a fossil. A leaf plate with a few ginkgo leaves on it. Was that from you?'

'No. No, it was not. I knew that was one of her hobbies, but never made her a gift of an item like that. Was it valuable, do you think? Is that why it was in a hidden compartment?'

'I don't know. I'm looking into it.'

'She said she was going to show me her fossil collection one day, but that never happened.'

'There was also one of my business cards in there. This had been given to her a few weeks before her death by a friend of hers. The friend thought she might need my services, but Kiaraa never contacted me. There were a few reasons why this friend thought she might require the assistance of a private investigator.'

I tell her about the knife threat in Barrett Street. I tell her about the disturbance outside the Charlotte Street Hotel. I tell her about her own assault on the underground, as if she needs to be reminded.

She's silent for a few moments, her mouth slightly open. 'I did not know. I did not know that Kiaraa went through that trauma with the knife ruffian. The poor girl. When was this?'

'July 28th. About a month and a half before she was abducted.'

'She didn't say anything to me about it. I assume she kept it to herself. My God.'

'What did you make of the other two occurrences? Why didn't you contact the police?'

'Charlotte Street was a public disturbance. There was no need for me to contact the police. The only statement the police took was from the manager of the hotel, who witnessed everything from beginning to end.

'I kept that incident to myself. That is, I did not tell Mathéo. I had started my affair with Kiaraa by that time and wanted to, to *distance* myself from any contact with her. I know that came out badly. I loved her. Please have no doubt about that.'

'Did you have any idea who might have been behind the fracas outside the hotel?'

'None at all. It was not the first time something like that had happened, but I did not take it too seriously. The ignorant are always with us. Hate on their faces, though. Quite scary. This impression from a couple of glances lasting no more than a few seconds.'

'What about the assault on the underground?'

'The assault? I can remember the punch quite clearly. Like it was yesterday. Very traumatic, but not as painful as I might have envisaged. No external bruising. Perhaps a slight swelling. I did have blood inside my mouth, though. I noticed traces of it later. Once again, I could have reported the incident to the police, but chose not to.'

'Mathéo again?'

'Yes. If the details had come out, he might have wondered why I had taken a tube train, which I never usually do. It was a spontaneous decision. I had been with Kiaraa. I did not want to return home quickly. I wanted to have some time to, to *consider* our evening together. To run it over in my mind. To wallow in it. Do you understand?'

'Tell me about the man who punched you.'

'It was a youngish man. Your age, perhaps. He sat opposite me. Just as the train pulled into a station, he smiled at me and punched me in the jaw. Then he got off. I was surprised. But I was more surprised that no one helped me or tried to stop him.

'Even after he'd got off, no one asked me if I was alright, even though they'd seen what had happened. It was as if they were pretending it hadn't occurred. Perhaps they thought it was a lovers' tiff and none of their business. I was crying. I was embarrassed. I think the shock was what has remained with me. No one had ever hit me before.

'Do you think all these things are connected? Are they connected to her kidnapping and murder?' She frowns. 'Do you think she wanted a gun because of that man with the knife? Because of the hotel incident? Because of my assault?'

'I think it was the knife threat that did it. I don't think it was connected to her murder. Tell me about Grassroots.'

'What's that?'

'Your organisation for women in high profile careers.'

'Do you mean Principles?'

Thanks, Aziza. 'Could be. The Charlotte Street Hotel incident was connected to it.'

'Grassroots? Who told you that? Never mind. I can see how it might have happened. Yes. That is me. Us. It's a bit like The National Organisation for Women. Like they have in America, yes? It's an organisation of feminist grassroots activists. That may be where the confusion arose.

'We push for tougher laws against violence, discrimination, and harassment against women. Many other things. Increased business opportunities. Education. You probably think it's all very amusing.'

She frowns. 'Hm. At no time did I attempt to induct Kiaraa. She had been involved with women's issues in Korea when she was younger. She was still a patron of one organisation, I think.

'Women's rights in South Korea are a new thing compared to the first and second waves in the Western world. These things were simply not discussed in that country. Talking to me made her glimpse things from a slightly different perspective, perhaps.

'It was known, latterly, that she was bisexual. Do you think that had any bearing, Mr Beckett?'

'On her being kidnapped and subsequently murdered? Unlikely. At present, I think money was the primary motive.'

'Why do you think they killed her?'

'It can sometimes be the outcome in kidnapping cases. Perhaps she got a look at one of her abductors.'

'It's a big leap from being a kidnapper to being a murderer.'

'True, but it may have been a necessity in some way we're unaware of. At least at the moment.'

'I know she was stabbed to death. But was it quick?'

'Instantaneous. There was something else. Something I found in her flat. She'd had a series of photographs taken of herself. Prints. It seemed to me that there were originally twenty of them, but four appeared to be missing. I was wondering if you had them.'

'What sort of photographs?'

I find the sixteen remaining shots on my mobile. I hand it to her. She flicks through them. She stares at them for a long time. Tears fill her eyes. 'She was perfect,' she smiles. 'And she could be so wicked. A wicked angel.'

'You've never seen these before.'

'I – no. I would have remembered, I think! They are quite shocking, but at the same time exquisite. Who took these? Do you know?'

'I'm afraid not.'

'You said there were some prints missing. If I don't have them, then who does?'

'At the moment, I've no idea.' I smile at her. 'You were my best bet.'

'Could you text me these photographs? Please?'

'If you think it'll be safe.'

'They'll be safe on my telephone.'

'Just don't leave it on the tube. Do you remember the date of the Charlotte Street Hotel incident?'

'Wait. She had a book. It was quite large. I forget the photographer's name. We had booked a hotel room for the night when Mathéo was in Basel on business. We were in bed. She wanted me to look at the photographs. She said I would find them exciting. She was right.

'It was very artistic. Beautiful. Erotic. Many different types of women. Body types, I mean. It was bondage with ropes. Kiaraa called it kinbaku and shibari, terms I had not heard before. No. That's not true. I had heard of shibari.

'One of the women had a figure like Kiaraa's. She ran her fingers across those photographs and asked me if I thought she would look good like that. Tied, I mean. The ropes tight on her body. I told her she would. She thought perhaps she should be photographed like that.'

'It looks like she went ahead and did it.'

'Sorry. You wanted the date of the Charlotte Street meeting. One moment.'

She walks over to a small console table, moves a pile of magazines out of the way, finds her mobile and taps and scrolls for a few seconds. She's left-handed. It occurs to me that the book she was describing was *Ordonnance Restrictive*, Pöck's bondage volume. Was Kiaraa sailing close to the wind showing Odette a book by her other lover? Was she getting a buzz out of it?

'A little over two years ago. It was the 13th of August.'

'And the date you were assaulted on the tube?'

'Oh, that was after that. Still August. A few days later. Perhaps the 16th or the 17th. Something like that. I didn't make a note of it in my diary. It was something I wanted to forget.' She pauses. 'But I cannot forget.'

So those two incidents were definitely not the reason for getting the gun from Baek-Hayeon Bahk; that request was made on August 1st, a few days after the prick with the knife.

The riddle of the missing photographic prints and ginkgo fossil is still outstanding, however.

I feel suddenly dispirited, as if I'm wasting my time worrying about this stuff, hacking my way through dense undergrowth, going nowhere. While Odette continues to pore over the photographs, I try to think what else I can ask her, though I think she's a bit of a dead end.

'When Kiaraa attended your Principles meetings, was she ever directly involved with the, the *presentation* of them?'

'Did she speak from the platform or platforms, do you mean?'

'I think that's what I mean.'

'No. Never.'

'So, she was not publicly associated with your organisation.'

She runs a hand through her hair. 'I wouldn't go that far. She had mentioned us in interviews once or twice. She made a lovely little speech supporting us after one of her performances at the Wigmore Hall about a month and half before she died.

'I was in the audience with my husband. It would have been very early July. The 4th or 5th. She had been playing a selection of Bach pieces. It was a wonderful recital. Magical.

'She was called back for an encore. She played three Scarlatti sonatas. But before she played, she gave a brief talk about Principles and what we were doing. Kept it very light and funny. Lasted maybe a minute if that. Just said that there was no pressure; look into it if you have a spare moment. That kind of thing.'

'She didn't stuff it down their throats.'

She laughs for the first time since I've been here. 'Certainly not! There were pamphlets in the foyer for anyone who was interested. She was wearing a very lovely black Dolce & Gabbana dress.' She smiles at the memory of this performance.

'You will not have seen her, I am guessing. In concert, I mean. Apart from her outstanding skill, her performance was highly, if perhaps unintentionally, sensual. But that is not unusual with female classical pianists nowadays. It is almost commonplace. There are very few who do not dress well, who do not dress...appealingly.'

There are tears in her eyes now. She sniffs a couple of times to recover, fails and starts sobbing, her head in her hands. I decide to give her a couple of minutes. 'Oh, God,' she says. 'Oh, God.'

It takes a few minutes for her to compose herself. She wipes the tears from her face with the back of her hand.

I close my eyes for a few seconds to allow the timeline of all this stuff to sink into my subconscious. It's no good; it's all too complicated. I'm going to have to write it down.

'Are you OK?' she asks.

'Waiting for a miracle.'

'How is her sister? How is Micha?'

'Still very upset.'

'Why you, after all this time?'

'The police have made no headway. Micha had employed three big private investigation companies who were unable to help. Maybe I'm a last resort. One of her lawyers recommended me.

'Micha said that you and Kiaraa had a fair number of rows. What were the rows about?'

She looks surprised that I know about this. She frowns. She sighs. 'We were both very insecure, you might say. In the, ah, ambience of our relationship, I mean. Each of us needed constant reassurance from the other. We were similar in that way.

'Sometimes we felt we were not getting enough of that. It caused arguments. I would not say they were serious arguments. In fact, they added spice to our relationship, if you understand me.

'Did Kiaraa tell her sister much about me? Did she tell her that she loved me? Our relationship was very physical, and was mainly confined to fleeting trysts in hotels, so it left little time for that sort of reflection.'

Why the fuck not? 'Yes. Micha told me that Kiaraa loved you.'

She nods her head. Her eyes fill with tears again.

'Thank you.'

19

SHITASTROPHE

I pick up a Rustica Piccante pizza and a bottle of Coke from Zizzi in Bow Street, and head back to my flat. In the bathroom, Aziza has written 'this must be at least once a month, or I will have myself committed' on the bathroom mirror in lipstick. She's also left a ten-pound note on the bedside table. Generous to a fault.

I pin the photograph of the Fiat Ducato van to my notice board and mentally demand answers from it or else.

While I'm eating, I start to create a chronology of what I know so far on a sheet of A4 cartridge paper. Sometimes this can be inspirational and instantly solve the case, though this rarely happens. Most of the time it makes things more perplexing. Usually, it's a waste of the ink in the pen. Sometimes, if you're very lucky, you acquire a bonus headache.

So, as far as can be ascertained:

July 4th.
Kiaraa at Wigmore Hall. Pre-encore plug for Principles.

July 28th
Knife/gun threat incident in Barrett Street.

August 1st
Kiaraa asks Baek-Hayeon Bahk for a gun.

August 13th
Charlotte Street Hotel incident.

August 16th/17th
Odette tube train assault.

August 22nd
Baek-Hayeon Bahk gives Kiaraa the gun.

September 12th
Kiaraa leaves restaurant at 10.30 p.m. and disappears.

September 13th
First call from Munro demanding ransom.

September 14th
Micha sorts out the money.

September 15th
Baek-Hayeon Bahk makes the drop. Kiaraa found dead.

September 15th/16th
Formal murder enquiry starts.

September 30th
Cable cutter info released to investigating officers.

Seems pretty logical. Uninspiring, even. The only interesting thing is that none of the violence, as far as I know, happened before that Wigmore Hall concert.

Did that trigger this mess in some way? Seems unlikely.

I'm still haunted by the Fiat Ducato used for the ransom pickup.

I don't know why, but a nagging little worm in my brain is telling me that something's not right there, but, helpfully, it's not telling me what it is.

I'm just about to make myself a coffee when my mobile rings. Penny.

'Oh. Hi! Me again. Sorry to be a nuisance.'

'You're not a nuisance, Penny. How can I help?'

'It's that policeman. Finally found the diary. Took a while. For some reason it wasn't where I kept all the others. It was in the airing cupboard under some old towels. Couldn't remember why at first, then it came to me. I'd spilt coffee on it. Ages ago, this was. I'd wiped the coffee off with some warm water, put it in the airing cupboard to dry and then forgot about it. Knew I had it somewhere.'

'So…?'

'It was the 21st of September. That's when he came here asking his questions. That chap Kinnaird. Told you I'd made a note of it. Is that any good?'

'That's excellent, Penny. Really useful.'

'And there was something else. When I spoke to you yesterday I was getting rather upset. Silly.'

'Not silly at all, Penny. You were describing a pretty dreadful event.'

'Well. Yes. Thing is. There was more. I just – I don't think *forgot* is the right word. More that my brain had been doing some spring cleaning for the sake of my sanity. And I was upset. I'm sure you noticed. Embarrassing.'

'Don't worry about it.' For some insane reason I'm imagining kissing her.

She takes a deep breath. 'He said that they'd cut her fingers off. The girl. The pianist.'

'On the 21st. When he visited you. Are you sure about that?'

'Yes. He said they'd used some heavy-duty thingy or other. A bolt cutter. A cable cutter. Something like that. Not the sort of detail one wants to hear, really.'

I experience a moment of light-headedness.

Six days after the murder, nine days before the investigative team knew about the cable cutters, and there he is talking about them to a member of the public.

I mustn't get too excited. There could be many reasons why he'd know a detail like that, many people he could have spoken to about it.

And in a major murder investigation, speculation, rumours, and gossip would be rife, the cop grapevine would be buzzing, and not every police officer or forensic scientist could be guaranteed to be discreet and professional. Someone might have figured out the cutter stuff before the formal announcement on September 30th and blabbed/bragged. It could have been guesswork that Kinnaird took as gospel.

And surely Kinnaird, if he's involved, couldn't have been that much of an idiot. He'd have to be aware that his comments to Penny might come back to bite him. Unless he was pretty sure they wouldn't.

All the questions that *any* police officer, let alone Kinnaird, would be putting to the residents of Elder Street would be about the Fiat Ducato or any activity around it.

And after drawing a blank with someone like Penny, a report would be written and that would be the end of that. No other officers would revisit her to ask her about *anything*, let alone Kinnaird's aberrant behaviour or what he said or when he said it.

Unless she reported it.

And I think he was confident that she would not.

What was the phrase she used? *Deniable suggestive remarks*. And, as far as she was concerned, not worth bothering the police with, especially during a murder enquiry. And he didn't *actively* proposition her, anyway.

If he *was* involved, it was definitely a risk on his part, but only a tiny one.

Maybe he thought it was worth it. Maybe he got a buzz from that risk. Maybe the chance of some sort of sexual liaison overrode his common sense. And he could always refute it, or say she was confused.

And there was too much going on with that investigation in the first place to bother with such relatively trifling matters.

Whatever, he's now on my naughty list. I write his name on my sheet of A4 and place a single tick next to it.

'That's really useful, Penny.'

'Oh, good. Glad I could be of some help, however gruesome the thing might be. How is, er, how is everything going? Or am I not allowed to ask that?'

I put a smile into my voice. 'I'm not the police, Penny. And, um, it's going OK, I guess. A bit slower than I'd like, but I think I'm making some progress. It is an old case, after all. Your information has certainly given me a bit of a lead. I'll just have to see where it takes me.'

'Exciting! Haven't been doing much today. Plaster of Paris seems a bit dull after helping a detective! Did some shopping this morning. Food, mainly.'

She wants to talk. I'm going to have to stop this, and I know exactly how to do it, while dipping a toe in the water.

'I've been thinking about the sort of lingerie I should buy you, Penny. You've been most helpful. It'll be my reward to you.

'I've seen a rather bold set in black that Fleur of England do from their Fridar range that I think will suit you. I'm going to text you the link. See what you think. If it's not your sort of thing you can let me know. Sound good? If you like it, just reply with the word "yes". OK?'

'I…'

'I'll give you a call when I've booked Tengoku No Aji. I'll see you soon. And thanks again. 'Bye, Penny.'

I click her off. I find I'm laughing. I wish I had that sort of confidence when I was seventeen.

Once she's texted me back, I'll buy it online, get it gift-wrapped and sent to her before we go out; give the evening a buzz.

I make an addition to my chronology:

September 21st. DS Kinnaird visits Mrs Penelope Coryton-Ward. Knows about cable cutters!

I don't usually favour exclamation marks when making notes, but today I'm making an exception. Now I'm definitely going to scope out the Bijou Noir.

I check my watch: 12.36. This time, I'm going to take the actual photographs with me instead of showing them to Pöck on my mobile like I did with Odette. After all, he took them and may find that a little disrespectful.

I slide them into my messenger bag, get my jacket on, go outside, and get a rainbow-patterned Ride with Pride black cab to D'Arblay Street.

* * *

D'Arblay Street is dead in the centre of Soho, sandwiched between Wardour Street and Poland Street and sliced in half by Berwick Street. It's all coffee bars, bin bags, traffic cones and roadworks with a smattering of film companies, editing suites, restaurants and a whole load of shops that don't seem to sell anything thrown in for good measure.

Like Pöck said on the phone, it's right next door to a tattoo parlour called That Touch of Ink. The splashy graffiti outside (his own work, or so he claimed) is pretty classy and enhances the neighbourhood rather than spoils it.

I press the lower of the two bell pushes and wait. It's a wide, three-storey building with a basement, and I wonder if he owns the whole lot. Or rents it. Or whatever. I look at my watch: nine minutes to one.

Nothing happens for several seconds, then I can hear locks being undone. The young woman who opens the door is about twenty-five, slim, with almond-shaped pale green eyes, a heart-shaped face and incredible-looking long, light brown wavy hair which reaches all the way to the small of her back. Presumably, this must be Jasna Løvstrøm.

I'm not sure what I expected a photographer in a place like this to dress like, but she looks more like she's a PA in an advertising agency. A basic white cotton shirt, a blue and white floral midi skirt, black stockings, and silvery ballet pumps.

She looks at me as if she expects me to try to sell her something.

'You the dick?'

'So they tell me.'

She shakes my hand. 'I'm Jasna. We spoke on the phone. Come in. He's doing some shit.' She looks me up and down. She smiles. I seem to pass muster. 'You look the fucking part, at least. Are you smart as well?'

'Been back to Stockholm recently, Jasna?'

She laughs. '*Smart kille.*'

'*Sexig tjej.*'

'Oh, I like you, detective. Wanna coffee?'

'Sure.'

She's really tall. I notice that I've slightly changed my posture in a useless attempt to add a couple of inches to my height.

I follow her into a high-tech chrome kitchen. There are a couple of mammoth monochrome photographic prints on two of the walls. Same blonde model in each. In one, she's lying on a bed with a cotton vest pulled up to reveal her breasts, and in the other, she's naked apart from black stockings, on all fours on a worn-looking wooden floor. I just hope there were no splinters.

Both photographs have been treated with some sort of effect that simultaneously ages them and makes them look ultramodern. You feel you wouldn't want to know how much one of these would cost.

Jasna sticks a kettle on and spoons grains into a cafetière. 'Maraba Rwanda OK with you?'

'Fine. Dash of milk, no sugar.'

'Where did you learn to speak Swedish?'

'I won a Duolingo crash course in a pub quiz.'

'Yeah. Like fuck. Let me see your mobile. Unlock it.'

I do as she says. She takes a photograph of her face, makes it my wallpaper and hands it back to me. 'There. A one-off. Unique. Top photographer. No charge. Pretty Swedish girl. Be the envy of your friends. Get some fucking fridge magnets done.'

This makes me laugh. 'You're too kind, Jasna.'

'And don't call me Jazz. I can't stand it.'

'I'll try and remember that, Jazz.'

'Hey. We've got Oscar fucking Wilde here.'

She brings two coffees over and we sit next to each other on a couple of black leather bar stools. She smells nice. Some sort of flowery perfume.

'So. The Korean chick again, yeah? I met her. I did the set-up for one of her album covers. The Bach one where she's leaning up against the brick wall with the shirt unbuttoned, yeah?'

I nod to let her know I've seen it.

'She was just starting to get raunchy. With her image, I mean. Pretty *wicked,* yeah? Before that, too much *pudeur,* you know? If she hadn't died, who knows where we'd be now. The mind is boggling.

'It was me that told her to get that wolf cut. Suited her face. We got Peverell Rochefort to do it. Pretty little thing and a born model. The Korean chick, not Peverell. He's a cunt.

'Sleek body. Camera loved her. So much *bitch,* you know? Did some sort of working out thing. Can't remember what it was called. Began with a G. Gangnam style or something.'

I laugh. '*Geongangmi*. Healthy Beauty. Big in Korea.'

'That was it, yeah. Fit-looking chick. I guess they have to be like athletes nowadays to hammer out that stuff year after year. I also suppose they have to look out for getting their fingers jammed in elevator doors and things. Still no clues about who killed her, huh?'

I shake my head. 'You got any ideas?'

'Yeah.'

'Want to share?'

She shrugs and sips her coffee. 'First impression? Classical music fan.'

'Why?'

'OK. First of all, she wouldn't have been lifted – is that the right word? Lifted?'

'That's fine.'

'Yeah. Well. She wouldn't have been lifted if she was just some Korean chick walking down the street. A tourist. A student. Work experience. An au pair. Dentist.

'Kidnapping's a big serious thing. Mucho jail time. It would have to be worth their while financially. Worth the risk. Too haphazard to pick a random girl off the street. Her folks might be poor, yeah? Way too much risk. But this one – you could just Google her name and her net worth would be the first thing you'd see.

'So, what I'm saying is, they knew who she was, and they knew how much she was worth. That's the first thing. Otherwise, why kidnap? Why ask for a ransom? If she was just some fucking nobody, no fucking point. Has to be some classical fan who was also a *kuksugare.*

'They'd also have to know that there was someone out there who could pay the ransom. Someone who she could easily reimburse when they set her free. No one's going to ask the person who's been kidnapped to pay their own ransom. They're not going to march them out to the nearest cashpoint with a blindfold on. I read it was her sister that paid it. Some tech chick. Pretty rich. So, they must have known about her, yeah?'

'You want to come and work for me?'

She purses her lips, trying not to laugh. She runs a hand through her hair. 'Anyway, back to my theory. Now, I don't know about you, but I'd never fucking heard of her until she turned up here. My guess is you'd have to be into that sort of shit for her to be brought to your attention.'

'You're right. I'd never heard of her either.'

'See? But now we take a left turn down the alleyway of evil. Classical music; it's kind of conservative, yeah? It never changes. You can't say, I'm going to play the Chopin dude whatever, but tonight I'm going to stick a fifteen-minute crazy bongo duet in the middle. People would get pissed. Well – and this isn't just Kiaraa Jeong by any means – the way she dresses, her – what's the fucking word? *Deporterar*?'

'The way she conducts herself?'

'Yeah, yeah. So *visually,* and, you could argue, *sexually,* she just stuck an hour-long digeridoo solo in some piece of Beethoven or whatever. Just like that Ukrainian chick, the tiny one who wears the figure-hugging lycra short skirt thing and the ten-inch stiletto heels. What's her name? Roksolana something?'

'So, you think that this would upset a classical music lover so much that they'd kidnap and murder her?'

'Well, when you put it that way, it sounds a bit wacky, but my theory still has water, I think. I reckon someone saw her in concert or on YouTube and something went *click.* Their outrage button, maybe. And maybe all the rest followed. They wanted to kind of *fine* her for spoiling their preconceptions, spoiling their fun. They were *hostile* towards her.

'You'd *have* to be a classics fan to go and see someone like that in a for real concert or check them out online. Or, at least, I *presume* you would. I mean, I don't go scouring the internet for country and western music or book tickets to go and see it. Why would I do that? I can't stand it. So. Any use?'

'Well, actually, yes. I discussed motive with someone else only yesterday and the idea that she might have been hated came up.'

'Uh-huh, uh-huh. And of course, someone may have needed the money for reason or reasons unknown and the two things collided, *förstå mig*? You've got your fucking hands full with this, haven't you, detective, particularly as it happened over two years ago. The trail is as cold as a witch's teat. Let's go and hang out with Florian.'

'Won't he mind?'

'He doesn't mind anything. Oh. Hang on.'

She walks over to the kitchen door, takes a black woollen jacket off the hook and fishes around in one of the pockets. 'Here.'

She hands me her business card. Smart and retro with a photograph of a vintage Hasselblad against an ivory background on the left and 'Jasna Løvstrøm. Photographic Artist.' in blue on yellow on the right.

'You're a detective. You might need a fearless photographer one day. Or someone who can detect image tampering. I can do the lot. Don't throw this away.'

'I won't. Here.' I hand her one of my business cards. 'You might need a fearless dinner date one night.'

'I might at that, Mr *Häftigt*. Follow me.'

The steep, serpentine wooden stairs seem endless. By the time we're on the third floor, I'm out of breath.

I can hear Pöck before I see him. Still got the Austrian accent, but it's mixed in with a touch of New York and London.

'What is wrong with you? What is *wrong* with you? You've opened the creaking insanity door to total derangement! You don't even know why you stole it. You're crazy. You don't need it. Do you need it? No! You could afford to buy it with your own ill-gotten cash. But you *stole* it. Are you *proud* of yourself? You don't like me talking to you like this. Look at me. Out of the corner of your eyes. That's it. You're mocking me. You despise me. I see you for what you really are. Go on. Stroke it. Stroke that bastard. Bury your face in it. Breathe the scent in. Try and catch anthrax off it. You love anthrax. You love the stomach pains, vomiting and ulcers.'

We turn a corner and now I can see what's going on.

The studio is wide, bright, high-ceilinged, brand new, and unbelievably spacious, with cool exposed brick walls and engineered grey wood flooring.

Like many buildings in this area, my own flat included, these houses have expanded into the premises on either side and, in this case, seem to have had the ceiling raised.

Pöck darts around a naked woman in heels, who's guiltily grabbing the sleeve of a sable fur coat and rubbing it in her face. She's standing in front of a pure white paper backdrop and is being blasted by the light from three Profoto photographic umbrellas.

Pöck is dressed in exactly the same way as the photograph on his site: outsize pale blue shirt, ripped blue jeans, and a pair of shabby UNDERCOVER 'Jack Purcell' sneakers.

He sees me, smiles, and waves, then continues haranguing the model, who contorts and gurns her way through a variety of startling and ferocious poses.

'You hate fur coats. They make you sick. Look crazy, my dear. Crazier than that. It's the coat. The coat has done this to you. It's an evil coat. It smells of Christian slaughterhouses. It's Satan's coat, made from the fur of misery and starvation and children. That's it. That's good. Give me that depraved look again. More spite please, darling. No shithead's going to take that coat away from you! Hey. Can you drool? That would be fantastic. No? OK. Stop there. Big break now. Marvellous, Franka. You're stupendous. I'm in love with you and all you stand for. I'd kill/hang/set fire to myself if it would make you smile for a millisecond.'

Franka strides across the studio like nothing's been happening, barely glancing in my direction. She unscrews a chunky diamond and sapphire ring from her index finger and tosses it towards Pöck. He catches it in mid-air and slips it in a pocket. She picks up an orange towelling robe from the back of a chair, puts it on, sits down and lights an untipped cigarette, picking tobacco strands off her lower lip.

'All cool, sex bomb?' asks Jasna. Franka smiles and nods. I recognise her now. It's Franka Galletti, the fashion model. Tousled black hair, thick eyebrows, bee-stung lips, pink mascara and a small but noticeable diagonal chip off one of her upper left incisors. Someone must have advised her not to get it fixed as a smart career move. She seems to notice me for the first time and looks me up and down with a haughty expression on her face.

Pöck starts to say something to me, but Jasna raises her hand to shut him up. 'OK. We got an independent observer here.' She turns to me. 'What do you think that photo session was all about? What are we selling here?'

'Fur coats? Shoplifting for beginners? Anthrax?'

All three of them laugh. 'See?' says Jasna, seemingly pleased with my response. 'Some private detective you are! It was the ring. That's what this was all about. You reckon it's too avant-garde?'

'Just right. Brilliant idea. Pushes the envelope of modern advertising.'

'I like this guy,' beams Pöck. 'Now look…' He throws the ring at me and I catch it. 'How much d'you think that ring's worth?'

I turn it around in my hand. 'Four pounds.'

'Ha! *Yeeeaaahhh*. Sure that's right. Try seven thousand. It's a Piaget.'

'You're a PI?' asks Franka, suddenly interested. She squints at me through a cloud of cigarette smoke. 'Good face. Hint of menace. *Soupçon* of deviance. Take your shirt off. I wanna see your muscles.' She has a thick Romanesco accent. 'You wanna do some shots with me? Can we do that, Florian? After lunch?'

'What? For the ring?'

'No. Fuck the ring. Like your books, you know? Yes? Like – what's that one called? – *Déshonorabilité.* That one. Me in a leather micro skirt, nothing else, this guy here holding my throat like he's giving me the third degree in some rubber fascist dungeon hell-hole, bright light in my face. He's naked, too. Threatening unhinged expression. Crazy.

And you know it's some sort of twisted roleplay. I'm licking my wet lips. I'm loving it like a fucker. You can only see the whites of my eyes.'

She stops for a moment. She screws her face up. 'Maybe we could hire a big ferocious dog? A Doberman or a Rottweiler? We've driven into Fuck Me Hard City in some fuckoff sex car. A Sexyfuck Mercedes Sexyfuck C-Class. It'd make a great coffee table book, *Flori-aaaan. Pleee-aaase*. You could see the shadow of a gallows against the wall. Two gallows, one for each of us. And a cackling old woman knitting and giving birth to a chimpanzee or a pope.'

Jasna can't stop laughing. 'You fucking crazy bitch.'

'Why not? Why not? Charge, like, five hundred dollars for it. Get Benedikt Taschen on the phone right now. Make it enormous with its own Philippe Starck table like *Sumo*. You know I'm talking sense here, Florian. I'm always right about everything.'

'You been hitting the mescaline again, fruitcake?' says Pöck. 'This guy won't want to be photographed. He's a private eye. He has to work undercover. He...'

'We don't have to see his face. He can wear a Venetian carnival mask. One of those Plague Doctor masks with the beak. Hey – now *that* would be creepy. And we smear it with dog food so the dog can lick it off.'

'So, you've got a Doberman Pinscher licking dog food off a guy wearing a Venetian beak mask with you only wearing a leather micro skirt, and a cackling old woman giving birth to a chimpanzee or a pope in the background?' asks Jasna, giggling uncontrollably. 'Oh, Jesus Christ.'

'Yeah. Why not? Why not? This is the sort of imagery that Versace would kill for! In fact, I'll storyboard this up and FedEx it to them this afternoon. They'll go along with anything I suggest. They love me! They worship the toilets I use and the toilets I am yet to use. I threw up over one of their shitballoon boy band brand ambassadors last year and they didn't say anything!'

'They were too fucking frightened,' observes Jasna.

Pöck shakes his head incredulously. 'Listen. You two go out and get a bite to eat. Jasna, take her to Umu. I'll pay. Keep the receipt. Take your time. Go shopping. Visit an art gallery. Do some busking or something. We'll finish the shoot later on. I have to talk to this guy. Go and get changed, Franka.'

'Can't I go out like this? I'm Franka *Galletti*! I go out in a robe if I want! I'll be naked by dessert if I feel like it, dribbling Truffe Chocolat Amedei over my tits. I've already got lifetime bans from nine London restaurants. One more won't make any difference. No, it's ten. I got a lifetime ban from Sushisamba last week. I forgot. It wasn't even my machete! Hey, Jasna. You ever been to Concrete + Water in New York? We'll go there and I'll do a makeover on you. You look like you wear your grandmother's clothes.'

'I don't need a makeover. *You're* the one that fucking needs a makeover. You need a makeover in your head.'

'So, what – are you Jean-Paul Sartre now? Are you chain-smoking Gauloises in a collaborationist Camembert factory now?'

'You *look* like Jean-Paul Sartre, you fucking termagant.'

I watch as they bicker about stuff. There's a small table to my left with half a dozen cameras on it: a Nikon D850, a big, heavy Pentax 67 with a large wooden handle, a Canon 7D Mark II, the Nikon Z7 with a Nikkor Z lens that he's just been using, and a couple I don't recognise. I wonder which he used to photograph Kiaraa.

As Franka brushes past me, her robe falling open, she whispers in my ear. 'You are the tits, baby. You wanna go on holiday with me? Just three little weeks. *Pleeeaaase.* We could go to Laucala, you know? Fiji? My father committed suicide a year ago, and then my mother and sister, so I'm fucked up, yeah? You'll like. I'm off my head. But you have to spoil me like some trashy little Euro-princess bitchtramp. Then I'll throw your gifts back in your face and have affairs with Australian Nazi surfers while you look on. It'll be a shitastrophe. I'll see you later or get Florian to give you my contact info. Whatever. Who cares? You think I'm beautiful? What sort of music do you like?'

She and Jasna disappear down the stairs, Jasna still laughing. Florian, chuckling and shaking his head, pats me on the shoulder. 'Come on. Let's go in my office. You like champagne?'

20

PÖCK, YOU RÖCK!

Florian Pöck's office is not the place to take an ageing relative who may be offended by photographs of naked women.

We get to it by heading to the back of his studio, then going down one flight of stairs. From the way Jasna and I got up here I would expect us to be on the first floor, but we seem to be on the ground as there is a very well-kept garden which can be seen through an expanse of vast, tall conservatory windows, two of which are open, allowing a pleasant scent of rose and honeysuckle to fill the room.

I try to imagine how the positioning of this garden is possible, but the logic escapes me. Perhaps someone emptied a few thousand tons of topsoil into the rear of the house behind this one and planted everything on top of it. Some eccentric nineteenth-century millionaire. Maybe we're in another dimension. Now I can smell Lebanese or Turkish food, possibly lamb with mint and sumac.

The walls are exposed red brick, the floor is black rubber. A wide, dark wood surface with a dozen narrow drawers beneath is right up against the windows. It could be used as a desk, were it not piled up with photographic prints, photography books, award statuettes, cameras, unused rolls of analog film, some Knipschildt Bacon & Bourbon truffles in a Swarovski chocolate box, Japanese religious sculptures, an unopened bottle of Isle of Raasay Hebridean gin, a Fender Jazz Bass, a cardboard box with 'Lucky Boat No.1 Noodles' on the side, art books in stacks of ten or twelve, an Indian hand drum, a packet of Karelia Slims, a yellow silk suit (one sleeve missing on the jacket) and a signed photograph of BABYMETAL, a Japanese *kawaai* metal band. It says 'Pöck, you Röck!' and has three thick felt-tip signatures underneath.

There's a big table covered in photography books in the centre of the room. Many of these are of Pöck's work and most feature naked women on their covers.

There are further piles of books like this on the floor and also a slim magazine called *Praze* featuring an orange-haired Franka Galletti on the cover, wearing an embroidered mesh bodysuit, and aiming a Titan M1 crossbow at a silver Bugs Bunny sculpture.

There are many framed photographs/prints leaning against the windows and bigger ones propped up against the brickwork. There are even some actually hanging on the wall. These are invariably female nudes, some artistic, others shockingly in-your-face erotic, like the bondage photographs in his book *Ordonnance Restrictive*, only more explicit.

Some are old posters for his exhibitions, going back fifteen or twenty years in a few cases. Many have Japanese characters on them, some are in French, others in Italian and German, and a few are in English.

Pride of place goes to a colossal poster for an exhibition called *Ausschweifung* at the Christian Cheneau Gallery in Paris, featuring Pöck himself, dressed as a gendarme with a head injury, lying on the floor in a dingy warehouse being photographed by several naked women in heels.

One framed photograph in particular catches my eye. It's a striking, powerful, gold-tinted portrait of a beautiful Chinese woman with long blonde hair. She's toned, athletic, oiled, and only wearing black hold-up stockings and red Feiyue Bruce Lee trainers. The oil and the lighting point up the miniscule downy hairs all over her body.

There's a reddish glow to her left and she's glaring at it with a crazed expression in her eyes. It looks like she's got too close to a furnace, though that could just be my interpretation. The print is about five foot across and seven foot high. Pöck follows my gaze as he opens a chilled bottle of Veuve Clicquot and pours some of the contents into a couple of Moya champagne flutes.

'You like that one?'

I laugh. 'It's extraordinary. I can just imagine it in my flat.'

'It's Julissa Vòng. You know her? Chinese model. The Sauvage Sauvage girl. I did a session with her for Osmanthus Cosmetics about seven years ago now. She's great fun.

'Anyway, she likes what she sees, she likes how I make her look, so she privately commissions me to take a load of wild photos of her. She didn't care what I came up with as long as she was naked in all of them. That one's a good example. She had a limited-edition book done, five hundred copies, though I suspect she kept them all herself. Big ego. That's a favourite of mine. You want it?'

'You're kidding.'

'No, my friend. No, no. I can rustle up another anytime. No hassle. One phone call to I Was Framed is all it takes.' He nods at the champagne. 'You're a friend of the widow, I take it?'

'Sure.' I take a glass from him and drink half of it, thinking about Franka Galletti and Fiji.

'Write your address down on the back of that McDonalds receipt. Someone likes my work, I get a buzz. It never changes. Not since I was an apprentice all those years ago. I was lucky enough to be apprenticed to Csilla Gabor. You know her? No? I'll have it couriered to you this evening. I'd sign it, but I don't think I can get the photograph out from beneath the glass without damaging it in some way, and if I sign the glass it'll fade away with time, but we'll both know, eh? We'll remember!'

'Don't worry about that. Thanks. Very kind.'

'I'll just get all this shit out of the way and we can talk.'

He spends five minutes transferring a load of books from a medium-sized table to the floor. He's panting a little with the effort. 'Fanny Burney,' he says. 'She was a prolific writer. Married this guy General Alexandre d'Arblay, and this street was named after her. Eighteenth century sometime. She lived up the road. But here's the thing: the site on which this street was built was called Doghouse Close! I wish they'd kept the name. Fantastic. I could have had cards made. *Florian Pöck – Doghouse Photography*. Or a documentary: *In the Doghouse with Florian Pöck*. Ha ha ha. Do you use a camera? You must use a camera. Photographing trashy bourgeois adultery through net curtains, yeah? All that dismal marital shit. What do you use?'

'A Nikon D610. Variety of lenses. Depends on the job.'

'Good camera. They still have that problem with the oil on the sensor?'

'Yes. But they're aware, and they'll service it for free because of that.'

'And so they should!'

Books dealt with, he drags two chairs over, and we sit opposite each other with the bottle of champagne between us. There's a huge wooden bowl filled with delicious truffle-flavoured crisps.

'You like them?' he asks. 'The best *patatine con tartufo* you can buy. I have them sent over from La Bottega del Tartufo in Rome. Via della Croce. They think I'm crazy. Is that decadent? Having crisps delivered from Italy? I damn well hope so!'

Looking suddenly older, he rubs his temples and closes his eyes tightly. 'OK. OK. I'm just going to psych myself up to talk about this. Not easy, not easy. You understand? Not easy. Two years now. I've put it all into a little room in my head and the key is rusty. Do I want to try and see if it will still open the lock? You said something about some photographs.'

I briefly outline the history of the investigations that led to me being hired. I explain that I had to visit Kiaraa's house, and when I was there I came across the photographs that I was pretty sure he'd taken. I remove them from of my bag and slide them across the table to him.

He looks at the black-and-white ones first, and tears come to his eyes. He nods his head. 'Beautiful. Beautiful. I haven't seen these for a long, long time. I couldn't, understand? Now it's like I took them yesterday, you know? It's all coming back. It's like she's in the bathroom here, right now, showering the oil off her body and washing her hair. She used to sing in the shower. She sang with an American accent. She used to sing "I'm Gonna Make You Mine" by Lou Christie. You know that oldie? You said her sister hired you. What's she like?'

'Very smart. Very determined.'

'No, I mean, what does she look like? Is she…you know.'

'She's as beautiful as Kiaraa was. Different features, obviously. She's younger, different figure, but the same facial bone structure, the same general colouring, except she's pretty obviously pregnant at the moment. If you saw her, you'd know she was a close relative. Doesn't have that downturn to the mouth that Kiaraa had, but still very attractive.'

'Yeah. Yeah. That mouth, that downturn, was what made Kiaraa's face, yes? Gave it a hint of cruelty. You mix that in with how she looked generally, and it was dangerous and stimulating. She still had a freshness and innocence about her, but that mouth told you she was not a little girl but a woman. Is that bullshit?'

'Take a look at the back of the photographs.'

'Yeah. Yeah. I numbered these for her. Can't remember why now. A good idea at the time, probably. Old habits die hard, I guess. No need nowadays. Oh.' He squints at the rear of each photograph. 'What happened to number seven? You keeping it as a souvenir?'

'Check out the colour shots.'

He flicks through them, sometimes smiling, sometimes laughing, sometimes sad, sometimes heartbroken. 'Yeah. Yeah. This is when we really started going for it. This was what she wanted. She was born to it. But these are from a couple of different sessions, from what I can recall.

'Jesus. Look at that one with the cane on her ass. And that shibari work. Who did that? Can't remember her name. Oh yeah – Hiraoka, Okimi Hiraoka. Beautiful Japanese lady. Drank Luzhou Laojiao. Green eyes. Very striking and unusual. The eye colour, I mean. Wore purple lipstick. You should have seen how fast she was with the rope. I could have watched her all day.

'She and Kiaraa, they were chatting away about clothes and Keanu Reeves while the whole process was going on, like it was nothing. Freaky. I'd have loved to do a session with her, maybe her and Kiaraa together. With her tying Kiaraa up, I mean. Artistic. A bit of text. The history of it. From Hojo-jutsu to Fusion. There could have been a transcendent book in it! But she wasn't into that type of thing, yeah? Didn't like being photographed. You can never tell what people like that are like. We got missing ones here, too?'

'One, four and seven.'

'OK. Let's take a look at what's missing before we go any further.'

He grabs an orange iMac, dumps it on the table, fires it up and starts click-clicking, swearing all the while. 'Jesus. Fuck. This is like opening the door to a whole jar of writhing worms from the past. The ones she wanted printed out were in a dedicated file and the jpeg ID will link to where they came from. I haven't looked at these since…here we are. This is the missing one from the black-and-white stuff. Number seven. Let me expand it. Come and sit next to me. More champagne?'

'Thanks.'

I drag my chair around so I can get a good view of the screen.

This photograph is clearly connected to the grainy black-and-white series, but the eroticism is turned up to eleven. She's naked, lying down, a knowing smile on her face, the fingers of her left hand gently touching her mound and those of her right hand pinching a nipple.

'I was trying to pay tribute to the work of František Drtikol. You are familiar with his métier? Art Deco. Grainy. Big shadows. Scary. Sexy. Great poses. This is the sort of photograph you'd send to a lover, yes?'

'Certainly. What about the missing colour shots?'

'One, four and seven you said? This will take longer. Different sessions, multiple files. Hold on. Never thought I'd have to do this.'

After three or four minutes, he's got them all on the screen.

The first missing photograph is more bondage. Naked apart from heels and stockings. Black rope this time. She's standing up. Ankles tied, wrists tied, breasts tied and there's a single rope around her waist which gets tightly drawn up between her legs and bisects her sex.

Now the blonde wig once more. She's kneeling on the floor, blindfolded, a riding crop in between her teeth, leather cuffs on her wrists, head bowed, thigh muscles stretched. The bright yellow backdrop again.

That grand piano from the photograph I found in her house makes another appearance. This time the rattan cane and the harness bra have gone and she's naked, seated and playing. This is artier than the others and, dare I say it, more tasteful, but provocative nonetheless.

Pöck stares at each image, resting his chin on the ball of his left hand.

'So, what do you think, detective?'

'They're certainly the cream of the crop. But I don't know who she could have sent them to.'

He sighs. 'Well, I knew she had this girlfriend, if that's the right term. French, yes? I think they were for her. Just my theory. She said she had a special friend and wanted to give her a special gift. That's why we did the printouts, the ones she liked the best, so she could choose which ones to send, yeah? That's why we started doing boudoir in the first place. Not in so many words, but, you know, I'm really perceptive.'

'I've spoken to the girlfriend, unless there's another one. She didn't receive them.'

'Who was it? Do I know them? But you can't say, can you.'

'Not yet. Do you remember when you gave her these prints?'

'Not exactly. About two or three months before she died. Would have been mid-May, maybe. That's the best I can do.'

'Can I ask you something? How did it get to this? You did album covers for her, then she's naked and being tied up by Japanese bondage experts.'

He bites one of his thumbnails. 'Ha ha. Yeah. Yes. It was kind of a natural evolution, I guess. Her record company knew of my reputation for being a bit *on the edge*, you might say. Well, *they* thought that. I don't think that. I think I'm normal. They commissioned me to do the photography for three consecutive CD releases. Oh, and a Blu-ray cover.

'Things had been changing in the way that female classical performers had been manipulating the way they presented themselves. It had been going on for quite a while. No more sitting at a piano smiling like a sloth. I understood totally. In fact, I always wanted to have a crack at it, but no one asked me.

'I had a meeting with Kiaraa and her record company lady. Sheila Hulme, is it? And some guy whose name I've forgotten. A prissy guy. We had a long chat. They showed me the session she did for *Vanity Fair*. Pretty tame stuff, really. But quite glamorous and atypical, all the same.

'There was one of her in a lace and mesh body lying on a rug. Bewitching. That one turned on a light for me. I thought *OK*, yes? I could see her potential. I could see she liked posing for that one. Intuition.

'But it was the look in her eye. That lithe figure. That exotic beauty. I knew *immediately* where to go with this. If you think about it, classical musicians are playing the same old thing again and again. It never changes.

'So, if you're going to sell CDs, Blu-rays, or downloads, you have to stand out from the crowd in some way. Make people buy something they may well have bought before, perhaps more than once.

'You can do it with the way you play, yes? With your skill. With your talent. But today it needs a little more. A little more of a push. And sex sells, like they say.

'Look at Sarah Coburn, Tina Guo, Anna Netrebko, Kari Blöndal, Anastasia Huppman, Liya Petrova. These are powerful, talented, and independent women. She could beat them at their own game. She thought her previous image had been a bit staid. She felt she was getting left behind and wanted to catch up. So, with Jasna's help and a couple of stylists and hair people, we started to reinvent her. To reinvent her public image. And it worked.'

'So, how did she make the leap to the erotic stuff?'

'I do boudoir photography, but I'm sure you already knew that. Very exclusive. I think I'm the only artist of my great stature who bothers themselves with it.

'But I enjoy it. I like making women who maybe don't feel very glam look fucking amazing. Jasna does, too. That's why she started working here. She gets a kick out of the skill required, the creativity. I don't like *boudoir,* though, you know? The word, I mean. Too corny, yeah? I think *voluptueuse* would be better. Or *photographie indécente. Brut et nu*. What d'you think?

'Also, some women want it to be done by another woman or at least have another woman around the place. Understandable. No problem. Jasna comes in handy again, yes? And there is always a stylist around, or a makeup and hair person. Sometimes the sitters bring their boyfriends or husbands which is cool as well, as long as they don't speak or try to relate to me.

'Also, I can experiment a bit with boudoir and that feeds into my other work. Jasna's still young. One day she'll have her own studio. Everything done here is good experience for her.

'Kiaraa was here one day and asked to see some of my boudoir work. I'd seen her flicking through the pages of my books, as well. Books like *Ordonnance Restrictive, Fétiche,* and *Déshonorabilité and Complètement Nu.* I watched her face as she looked at that stuff. It made me smile, you know? I gave her free copies of those books. I thought it might inspire her.

'She was very shy. At first, at least. It was cute. She asked if I could do some boudoir shots with her. As gifts for a friend. I said sure, why not? I told her it would be cool, that it wasn't a big stretch from the Bach and Clementi CD covers. You've seen them? Shirt unbuttoned to the waist, body-hugging flesh coloured dress. We just go a little further, that's all. It's all good. It's all artistic. Elegant. Taboo. Frivolous in some ways, *extrèmement serieux* in others. She liked me. She trusted me. I asked her if she wanted Jasna to be present, but she said no, it was OK.

'So, I arranged the bedroom set that I always use. Super king size bed. White Egyptian cotton sheets. Couple big pillows, all that shit. She had some sexy lingerie: Tisja Damen, Coco de Mer, Anoeses, Kleio. Some wicked stuff there. She had excellent taste. So, we did about half an hour with that first. Soft lighting, bra strap off the shoulder, pensive expression, coquettish taunting gaze, that sort of thing.

'Then she asked if she could do some topless and would I mind. She said her friend would like it, and she wanted to thrill her friend. I don't know who the friend was, though. I say no problem, I am Florian Pöck, you know? Would I *mind*? Is the pope a promiscuous party animal swigging meths with a heroin chaser in drag on a motorbike? I could always make her laugh. I always do that with boudoir. Relaxes the sitters. I try to find some interest they have, also, so we can shoot the breeze about it.

'It was a short step from there to some naked shots. I mean *naked* naked, yes? Her idea once more. I never press. I told her to think of it as a journey that we were both embarking on. Memories. Desires. Imagination. Fantasy. Everything mixed up. Breaking boundaries. I could tell it excited her.

'She had no problem with being topless or naked. Very relaxed. But she was a little shy about her breasts at first, I think. Their size. Too small, she thought. Not sexy enough for nude. Kept covering them with her hands for the first few shots. I thought *fuck*, you know?

'I said take it from me. No problem. Get those fucking hands down! This made her laugh. She had a lovely laugh. I got the feeling that she had not been appreciated much in her life. Sexually, I mean. Physically. By guys, at least.

'She told me that some prick suggested she get a boob job. *What?* I mean – *fuck?* You'd be surprised how much I hear that. From quite exquisite women, too. Women who don't need it in a million years. Especially my boudoir clients. Non-professionals, you know?

'I showed her some shots I'd done of Celestina Ortiz. You know her? The face of Quattrocchi? No? You *must* know her. Same figure. Bigger ass, though. Ortiz, I mean. That made her feel better. I showed her some shots of Celestina to make my point. That made her turn the corner, yes?

'This wasn't the session that you have the printouts for, by the way. Those came later. So. Once she was comfortable, she really got into it. Stretching her body, hands behind her neck, smouldering, sexy looks, laughing, frowning, growling, getting on all fours, ass in the air. Unselfconscious. Provocative. Dismissive. Couldn't care less.

'Of course, she'd seen my stuff, so she knew all the hot poses, all the attitude. I think she'd looked at a lot of other stuff, too. Kink magazines, porn. I was a little taken aback, to be honest. At first I was thinking "Hey, cool it!" But it was all good.

'I started to think of her as one of my models, rather than as an amateur. She was that talented. A natural. By the end of that session, she was cooking. I do a lot of this stuff, you know? But I couldn't get her out of my mind. Floodgates waiting to be opened, yes? I thought of my studio as a little kingdom where her sexuality could blossom. Too pretentious?'

He refills our champagne glasses and chews truffle crisps for a while.

'Now when you do boudoir, you can't expect all of the women to fall into the steamy stuff like it was nothing. So, I usually use one of two professionals, Lilac Romero and Aparecida Francisco, to show them what to do, demonstrate some raunchy poses.

'Sometimes I use Chō Aoki. Which one I use often depends on the figure of the woman having the shoot. Lilac's very slender, no bust, works out like a fucker, whereas Aparecida is kind of full-figured and I guess fleshy. Chō is like an athlete. Does weights and shit. I had it in mind to use Lilac or Chō to help Kiaraa out originally, but there was no need.

'So, we did another shoot about six weeks later, just me and Kiaraa. More boudoir. Mostly nude. She'd been playing in Stuttgart and some other places. I could tell she'd been looking forward to it. And halfway through, she seduced me. That's the only word for it. Totally out of the blue.

'Usually, *I'm* the one that does the seducing, you know? But I could not resist. Broke one of my golden rules. For boudoir shoots, at least. And that was it. Unexpected but expected. Once that had happened, her shoots got more and more daring. You've seen the results. There are others I'll never show you or anybody. We were an item until she died. I was shattered.' Tears in his eyes again. 'I don't know if I'll ever recover.'

He looks down at the floor and sniffs. So Pöck is the mystery man. I don't know what to say. The number of people damaged in one way or another by her murder is totting up, and I'm starting to feel it's my sole responsibility to try to make things better for them. I take a swig of champagne.

'Did you contact the police?'

'I thought about it, you know? Then I decided it would just complicate things. I hadn't seen her for a few weeks before she died. She was off wherever doing her shit. What could I say? I'd just be wasting their time. If they called on me, I'd talk to them, but I'm not a big police fan, you know?

'And it was meant to be a secret. Because of this girlfriend, among other things. And, er, people know me, you know? Know my work, my *notoriety*, if you like. This will sound dumb, but I didn't want to sully her reputation after she'd gone. "Murdered pianist was sex pal of smutty photographer" or some shit.'

'I think they knew there was a mystery man in her life, and they were curious,' I say. 'They asked around about you. But it was all a bit vague. Her sister knew as well, but no name. If it helps, it doesn't seem like you were a suspect. Micha told me that they had an interest in who you might be. I suppose you could have eliminated yourself from their enquiries, but I think there were a fair number of ex-lovers scattered about the place. Too late now, though.'

'Yeah. Maybe I'm an idiot. Maybe I'm a coward. I didn't kidnap her, you know. I didn't kill her.'

'I'm sure you didn't.'

'Well, thanks.'

'Apart from this French girlfriend, is there anyone else you think she might have shown those photographs to?'

'I've thought about it, but, ah, I can't really imagine who it could be. I don't think she was in another physical relationship; a third one, I mean, and that would be the only reason you would send photographs like that to someone. I think she was sincere, you know? Truthful. I think there was just me and this woman.

'She would tell me about this woman, what she was like, what they were like together, why she would enjoy photographs like that, but she felt that it would be a breach of confidence telling me who she was. She was quite well-known in her field, apparently, this woman, and I think she may have been married. Just an impression.

'And that was OK with me, yes? If she was discreet about this woman, then she would be discreet about me. And she expected me to be discreet about her. Her fame, yes? Her status. I'm always discreet. I'm not some asshole.

'If it's any help, I don't think, I mean, I read in the papers that she left this restaurant and was never seen again, and I've been wondering how they could have got hold of her. I think the police don't tell the media about a lot in cases like this.'

'What do you mean that you were wondering how they could have got hold of her?'

'From what I can gather, she was on her way home and lived a short distance from that restaurant.'

'Yes. I've duplicated the walk from there to her home at the same time of night and the same time of year. It's pretty busy and well-lit.'

'So, did she get into someone's car? Someone she knew, maybe, offering her a lift?'

'Possible, but I think unlikely.'

'What if it was the cops? *Excuse me, miss. Could I have a word?* A flash of the badge. A friendly smile. They ain't all angels, you know.'

This is something I haven't considered.

'Again, it's possible. Do you think this French girlfriend knew about you?'

'Definitely not. I knew about the French girlfriend, yes? But that was because – am I getting too personal here? – it kind of turned Kiaraa on to talk about it when she was with me and she knew it turned me on, too.

'But she said she would never tell the French girlfriend about us, because she thought it might upset her. Know what I mean? And, er, sometimes that sort of thing doesn't work in reverse, you get what I'm saying? One-way street. Hey. You said the sister was pregnant. If she wants to book a session with me, it'll be no charge. She can bring her husband if she wants.'

'I'll pass that on to her. I saw you did – what was it called? – *maternité*. But maybe she won't…'

'But those are great shots, those *maternité* photographs, don't you think? Very erotic. There are a lot of reasons that pregnant women are sexy. A great coffee table book there, I think. Limited edition. £200 a copy. No. Make that £500. All numbered and signed. Just call it – I don't know – *Enceinte*. Simple. Classic. Another heroic idea from me. All my book titles are in French even though I'm Austrian. It sounds sexier, don't you think?'

'Why did you use that yellow backdrop paper so much?'

'What? Oh, *that*. Kiaraa picked it out one day. She loved that colour. It's called acid yellow. Used to be called something else. Can't remember what. They call it that in fashion now and it stuck. I think it's used in food colouring, too; another name for Metanil yellow. I thought it would look terrible – too bright, too jarring – but it actually works. Makes everything kind of *bouncy*, you know? Like some kind of zany pop art.'

'It's also the name of a chemical dye that's used to detect blood stains.'

'No shit! Kiaraa had a lot of clothes in that colour. Her favourite. And she thought acid yellow sounded cool, a cool phrase. She said if anyone ever wrote a book about her, they should call it that.'

The whole conversation falters and it seems as if he's suddenly become weary, as if someone's put him on standby. I don't think we can go any further. We stand and he escorts me to the street.

'If there's anything I can do to help you, let me know,' he says. 'Anything. And let me know if you catch the fuckers. And pop in when you like, yes? We can have another chat. Go and get drunk. I like talking about her. It's weird. I'll send that photo tonight. You'd like Julissa Vòng. Maybe I should introduce you. You crack the case and I'll talk you up to her. There's your motivation on a silver platter.'

Just as I step out onto the pavement, I can hear the animated chat of Jasna and Franka about ten yards away as they step out of a cab.

'Hey!' Franka shouts. 'Wait there! I thought of somewhere else for our holiday. Have you ever been to Playa de Ses Illetes? They have a nudist beach! You could knock me up in the surf and I could have a baby when we got back! Florian could photograph me while I was pregnant, and I could be in another one of his spicy pregnancy pics. Or maybe a book with just me in it being naked and pregnant. Taschen. Or Rizzoli. We could call it *Superhot Baby Mama.* Or *Mama Super Sexy*. Or *Inseminarmi!* Then we get it adopted to avoid all the baby hassle: shit up the walls and stuff. Meet it for dinner in Il Pagliaccio when it's twenty-one. See how it's getting on.'

'Don't listen to her, detective. She's as janky as it gets.'

'Yeah, Jasna?' says Franka. 'Well at least I don't scrape orphans.'

What?

I leave the two of them screaming with laughter on the pavement and hail a cab. I get a text from Penny. It just says 'yes'. Well, at least *something's* panning out positively today.

21

WHITE VAN/RED HERRING

I get back to the flat and make a coffee. I've had enough talk today. After Odette and Pöck, I need some time to let all they said sink in, even though I'd like to have a quick chat to Odette's husband, if possible.

My mobile rings.

'Mr Beckett? It's Toby Bauguess from Fossilia. Thank you for your email. An excellent example of fossilised *Ginkgo adiantoides* leaves. Beautiful. Probably about sixty-five million years old. Paleocene epoch as I'm sure you already know. I can discern the quality just from your excellent photographs, but if you wanted to sell, I'd have to inspect it personally as it's the way we do things.'

'I understand. How much would it be worth?'

'Ballpark figure? Well, even without handling it, I think you'd be looking at a minimum of £3,000.'

'OK. Thanks very much. I'll be in touch should I decide to sell.'

'My pleasure, Mr Beckett. And thank you for thinking of us.'

Well, that's one expensive rock to give someone as a gift. Unless Kiaraa bought it for herself and was keeping it in her secret drawer for security purposes. But if it was a gift, then who gave it to her?

What time is it? Two-thirty.

I fire up the computer, get on the Fleur of England website and buy

Penny's lingerie set, plus a pair of matching luxury seamed stockings in black nylon and the gift wrap option. I think I've assessed her size correctly unless I'm losing my touch.

For some reason, I find buying this stuff relaxing. It's almost like therapy. Women's undergarment shopping therapy. I must seek Aziza's counsel.

I take a sip of coffee. While I'm thinking about Penny and what she'd look like in that lingerie, and her face when she opens the package, and how she'd try it on (slowly, I hope), and how she'd admire herself in the mirror, and what she'd wear over it, and a million other concupiscent matters, I start thinking about the Fiat van once more. I think about what Sallow said.

Bugs me a bit, that van, I have to say.

The van that only Baek-Hayeon Bahk saw.

It bugs me a bit, too.

Then it hits me.

Oh, *yes.*

Someone's been very, very clever.

Someone smart. A risk taker.

I give Baek-Hayeon a call.

'Hello, Mr Beckett. How may I help you today?'

I put a casual note into my voice, so he doesn't freak out completely. 'Just a quick thing if you've got a moment. Nothing too important. I just want to go back to when Mr Munro spoke to you about the arrangements for the deposit of the ransom money.'

'Yes. I remember. That was September 13th. It was a stressful time, Mr Beckett. Very stressful.'

'And that was the first time that he mentioned the white Fiat Ducato panel van, is that correct?'

'Yes. Yes it is. He told me where it would be, how long it would be there and what I was to do.'

'So, up until the point you delivered the ransom money, it was only you and Micha knew about the Fiat van.'

'That is correct.'

'And it was only you that saw it when you made the drop-off.'

'Yes, but I don't understand. We have been through all of this, and I went through it all with the police on two occasions. I…'

'You said the back doors were wide open when you arrived in Elder Street, and they told you to leave them open after you'd placed the suitcases in the back. I know you didn't recall seeing the registration, but, as you said, the Fiat logo on those vans is on the back door, so you wouldn't have seen that either.'

While he's thinking, I text DC Scarlett Sackville.

I'm going to call you in about thirty minutes. Please accept the call. It's not about our romantic dinner. It's about a police matter that you were involved with. V.Important. Daniel.

'You are right, Mr Beckett. I would not have seen it. But it was not important. Doing what the kidnappers said was what was important.'

'So, the only evidence you had that the van was a Fiat Ducato was because Munro *told* you it was. When you got there, it was certainly parked in Elder Street at the right time and it was certainly white and it certainly had the back doors open, but those were the only identifiers you saw, the only things that mattered at the time.

'You didn't walk around to the front of the van or inspect the sides. You didn't see the word 'Fiat' and you didn't spot the Fiat logo, usually a silver circle with 'Fiat' in silver against a red background, or, more recently, just the silver letters without the circle and with no red background. Is that right?'

Long pause. 'My God.'

'OK. Don't worry about it, Baek-Hayeon. I'll be in touch.'

'I…'

I click him off. I can feel my heart pounding in my chest and my coffee is cold.

I get on the computer, bring up the Fiat site and get a picture of the Ducato van on the screen.

Then I do a quick search for vans of the same size and specifications that look like the Fiat Ducato and are often recommended as an alternative to it for prospective purchasers/hirers. This takes a tedious twenty minutes.

Time and time again, the same four vehicles come up: the Citroën

Relay, the Ford Transit, the Renault Master, and the Mercedes-Benz Sprinter. I check each of these as thoroughly as I can, looking at their general appearance and particularly for photographs of the rear interiors. It's the Citroën Relay. It has to be.

It's almost identical in appearance to the Ducato: same shape, same size, same side trim, same wheels, similar bumpers, and once again, the Citroën logo and registration would not be visible when the back doors were open, and as Elder Street is a cul-de-sac, you would not see the front of the van as you drove in.

None of the others come close and it's the only one with the white interior and black side panels that Baek-Hayeon described; the Fiat interior is totally white.

When Baek-Hayeon was being questioned by the police, he said that they were not that interested in the interior of the van; and to be fair, why would they be? It would have been an irrelevance.

I'm about to ring Scarlett when something stops me. It's almost a revelation. It may even save time.

I need a van for a job. The police will not be searching for this type of van as I'll con them into looking for a totally different make. But in case they see through my cunning plan, I have to cover my back.

So, how do I obtain this red herring white van that's about to be used in a major crime without potentially incriminating myself?

I don't buy a new one. Too risky, unless it's with cash, but 32K is a lot of money to carry around. I'd be remembered. I buy a fairly new used one. Risky again, but with less money involved. Both options would be dumb on a number of levels.

I steal it. After all, someone stole the red Renault Megane that Kiaraa's body was found in. But this would be too perilous under the circumstances. I'd be pushing my luck. Being pulled over by the cops with three million pounds sitting in the back would not be a smart idea.

That leaves renting, or, better still, getting a test drive, which is what I would do. Both would need a driving licence and an insurance form filled in. Most would also need your credit card details as collateral. Obtaining a fake licence and/or credit card would be no problem if you had the right contacts.

Or perhaps if you were unaware of being involved in some sort of criminal conspiracy, you'd use your genuine documents.

Whatever, places that do rentals and/or test drives would take the information you presented on face value and would only investigate further if you crashed/stole the vehicle.

If you test drive a used vehicle, and it's a brief test drive, someone will usually come out with you due to paranoia about theft. If it's a new vehicle, however, that often doesn't happen; test drives like that can last a few days, and in those cases the showrooms will often use a tracking device which would be used if the van was not returned in time or stolen.

But that's OK. You're not going to steal it, and to all intents and purposes this is a kosher test drive, and when you returned the vehicle, that would be the end of that.

So, Test-Drive Guy, who has no idea what's going on, leaves the showroom in his new Citroën Relay, meets Ransom Guy at a prearranged time. Ransom Guy drives to Elder Street, picks up the money, dumps it somewhere and returns the van to Test-Drive Guy, who takes it back to the showroom and tells them he doesn't like it after all.

Ransom Guy would not be insured to drive the van, but that's a risk he'd have to take, and after all, he'd only be driving it for a matter of hours.

What's in it for Test-Drive Guy? Couple of thousand, maybe? Less? Low hazard, and the likelihood is you won't be connected to any crime.

Yes. I think I'll go with this.

'Scarlett? It's Daniel. Have a pen ready as I'm going to do some serious offloading here.'

'Did you just want to hear my voice? You couldn't wait?'

'All of those things and more. I'm in love with you, Scarlett. Those twenty seconds in the lift were all it took.'

'That happens so often I barely notice it anymore.'

'It was your modesty that first captivated me.'

'Yeah, yeah. Come on. I'm busy.'

'My meeting with DCI Sallow was concerning Operation Ivory which I know you were involved with and very wittily named. I've just come across some startling new evidence (did I really just say that?) which I'm going to share with you, but I'm going to need you to promise that you'll help me out in return.'

'We'll see. Go on.'

I give her a brief rundown of the case and who I'm working for and how well it is or isn't going and how clever I am.

'It was the van that the ransom was placed in. The white Fiat Ducato that seemed to disappear into thin air and that couldn't be traced. It bugged DCI Sallow and it's been bugging me.

'I think you were sent on a wild goose chase. I think it was a different make of van. The original information that this was a white Fiat Ducato came from the kidnapper Munro, who told Ms Jeong's head of security about it. By the time he got to the drop-off site, he was focussed on looking for a vehicle of that description with its back doors open.

'But this guy was stressed out of his head. He was carrying three million around with him in a car. High adrenaline, angry, maybe not thinking straight. He was in a high stakes situation, one he was unfamiliar with.

'The back doors of the van being open meant that no company logo or registration could be seen, plus he told me that he had a problem identifying foreign motor vehicles. That may be irrelevant, and the kidnappers wouldn't have known it, but they'd have known he was under pressure and was probably a relative stranger to this country.'

I can hear her scratching away with a pen. 'OK. Got it so far,' she says. 'Keep going. Wait. Wasn't this a bit risky? For the kidnappers, I mean.'

'It was. But it was a daring, masterly bit of misdirection and wasted a lot of police time. I'll bet whoever thought it up got off on it. Once they saw the police appeals with their description of the vehicle, they'd have known that it had worked, and they'd have breathed a sigh of relief.'

'How could we have been so bloody stupid.'

'Forget it. Totally understandable. They gave Baek-Hayeon a ten-minute window to park in Elder Street, identify the van, get four suitcases of money out of his car, transfer them to the van, and get the hell out of there. On top of that, they were insistent that he did not close the van doors when he left. That could have rung alarm bells, but it didn't. Both DCI Sallow and I thought that Elder Street, a small one-way cul-de-sac, was a stupid place to carry out something like this. Now I can see how smart it was.

'Firstly, it was the only van in the road. You couldn't miss it. Then factor in the awkwardness of the location, the worry of someone blocking you in, the appearance of traffic wardens or police, residents trying to park outside their house or popping their heads out of the window.

'Baek-Hayeon Bahk could not fail with this. He could not fuck up. He had to be quick. Really quick. A woman's life was in danger; a woman he was close to in certain ways. He missed the registration which would not have been visible, and he missed the fact that it wasn't a Fiat. Oh, and this van was facing the barrier, so he wouldn't have seen the front as he drove in from…'

She cuts me off. 'So, if it wasn't a Fiat, what was it?'

'I think it was a Citroën Relay. Look it up if you want. Second choices would be a Ford Transit, a Renault Master, or a Mercedes-Benz Sprinter. They all look pretty similar, but I think the Citroën is the one.

'Mr Bahk said that the interior was white with black panels on the sides. None of the other vans I've looked at have an interior that fits that description, only the Citroën. Get a Ducato up on a screen and take a look, then compare and contrast with the Citroën website.

'Remember that Bahk said there was damage on the left side bumper of what we thought was the Fiat. A thin, barely noticeable crack, maybe seven or eight inches long, and you could see a bit of the yellow polystyrene foam underneath the crack. You could also cross-check the bumper foam colour on each of those vans.

'Now, you could do the same sweep that you did when you thought it was a Fiat. Go back six years. Concentrate on the Greater London area. Check for felons, speeding tickets, all of that stuff.

'Start with dealerships who sell new Citroën Relays, prioritising those who allow unaccompanied test drives and who don't always use a tracking device. Then dealerships that do use a tracking device.'

'Take it from me,' says Scarlett. 'If they allow unaccompanied test drives, they'll use a tracking device. Of course, the tracking info would only be used if the van was stolen or not returned in time.'

'Quite right. If that lot doesn't bear fruit, look into rental companies who hire out those particular vans, especially new ones. You may find you're coming across fake driving licences and/or fake credit cards along the way, though not necessarily.

'This may not be that spectacularly important and it could be a dead end, but I think it's worth pursuing. Whatever you find, I'd be very grateful if you'd share it with me. If you get any hassle, remind whoever gets in your way that this is an ongoing murder investigation. Text Sallow if you have to. I'm sure he can pull some strings and will get back to me with the results if you find you can't for some reason. If this is sorted before we go out to dinner, I promise you two desserts and a bottle of champagne.'

She laughs. 'Oh, well now you're talking.'

'I'll leave you to get on with it. Good luck, Scarlett.'

'I'll remember about the champagne and desserts.'

'Did I mention the snog?'

She laughs and hangs up.

I'm quite pleased with this. *If* the van was rented or test driven, the renter/test driver may remain unknown, particularly if fake documents were involved. But if whoever it was, was unaware of what was going on, and had no reason to be cagey, there's a slim chance that they may have used their genuine driving licence, credit card and other details. I'll try not to get my hopes up.

* * *

It's starting to get chilly as I walk down Rutland Gate heading for Ennismore Mews. Knightsbridge again. Seems to be cropping up quite a lot at the moment: location of the Abd El Wahab restaurant where Kiaraa had her last supper, location of my first meeting with Suzanna at The Buddha-Bar, and, lest I forget, the home of Plaisirs Interdits where Aziza purchased her Bordelle sanglé suspender belt in black leather and seamed black nylon stockings. That's in Montpelier Square.

I may pop in after this meeting and have a look around.

I'm on my way to have a little chat with Mathéo Fournier at his publishing company HQ. I don't know what good this will do, but something might come of it. I was expecting him, not surprisingly maybe, to be French, so it was a surprise to hear a rather posh, Home Counties English accent on the phone. I'm sure there's an interesting story behind this anomaly.

Like most mews in well-to-do areas of London, this one keeps the potted tree/shrub/plant industry in business; there isn't a single building that doesn't have at least half a dozen of these items standing guard outside their solid-looking, security-laden front doors and lattice security grilled windows. The manufacturers of faux antique lantern lights also do quite well.

All of the houses have been painted white, pink or sky blue. Most of these places come with their own garages, and number 14 is no exception. The garage door is open, and I can see the rear end of a new-ish Mercedes AMG SL 65 in Firemist Red. Nice cars. If it was mine, I'd make sure that garage door was closed.

There are retractable security grilles on all of the windows and an ADT security box above the door, but it's a fake. An experienced burglar would spot that immediately.

But beneath this box is a much smaller device. This is part of a Soteria T home alarm system. They come with internal and external sirens both of which will give out a 120-decibel blast if you upset them.

Smart home alarms like this would have a couple of door and window sensors and at least two motion sensors. Controllable from your smartphone and a battery backup in case of a power or wi-fi failure.

So why the fake ADT box? Maybe it's a legacy from a previous owner.

The garage door also has a security box, but it's not a Soteria, it's a HomeTech 40dd, also controllable from a smartphone and not affected by any internet/wi-fi/power failures. This door has a barely noticeable camera lens on the bottom right, so that a casual observer might not notice it, or realise what it is. This lens would catch anyone loitering around the front door, as well as potential car thieves.

The Soteria has a camera lens, too, but in this case it's a conspicuous bullet CCTV camera, high up the wall and about six feet away from the box. In a place like this, you'd probably have maybe half a dozen cameras, two outside and the rest indoors. This may not be the case, but it's always best to assume it is.

I press the doorbell and am buzzed into a nice, clean reception area with framed prints of book covers all over the walls.

A tall and rather luscious receptionist with long jet-black hair and a St Tropez tan walks over to me and shakes my hand. Mid-twenties. White midi wrap dress, white shoes, white bangle on her left wrist and she's wearing Miss Dior Rose Essence and holding a black Samsung Galaxy.

'Mr Beckett. How do you do? Would you like to take a seat? I am called Gaëlle. Mathéo is expecting you. He will be with you in a moment. Can I get you for something while you are waiting? A drink of something?'

Strong Parisian accent. From Neuilly-sur-Seine at a guess. I'm going to flatter her. I may need her assistance later.

'I'm fine at the moment, thank you, Gaëlle. Great dress, by the way. Fabulous.'

She likes this. 'Oh, thank you!'

'Perfect for showing off your beautiful tan. Where have you been?'

'I went to Corsica with my sister for a week.'

'North or south?'

'South. Porto-Vecchio.'

'The market there is great, isn't it. Sorry. I'll let you get on with what you were doing.'

I sit down and flick through a magazine called *Publishing Perspectives* and settle on an article about publishing in Latin America, while surreptitiously watching Gaëlle with my peripheral vision. She continues the phone call she must have been having when I rang the bell. She is speaking French, assuming I do not understand, and glances at me from time to time, assuming I do not notice.

'Well, I don't know. No one tells me anything. I spoke to Brigitta here and she was cagey as she always is. Yeah. Yeah. Yeah. Well, I have to give a month's notice, but I don't really care, you know? No. I mean about the notice. That other girl. What was her name? Willow?'

I have to curtail my eavesdropping as Mathéo Fournier bursts into the reception area like a big shaggy dog. He's over six feet tall, late forties, handsome in an ugly way, grinning, affable, longish grey hair, designer stubble, dressed casually in a pale blue cotton suit with a black t-shirt underneath and white trainers on his feet. I stand. We shake hands.

'Mr Beckett! Come in. Did Gaëlle get you, um…' He gestures towards Gaëlle who seems to have switched topics and is now talking about some Romain Duris film she saw and didn't like.

'Thanks,' I reply. 'She asked, but I'm OK at the moment.'

'OK. Good. Come in. Have a seat and then we can have a gabfest.'

His office is medium-sized and airy, all pine flooring and white bookcases. Big desk, with three landline phones, two mobiles charging away, an Asus Zenbook Pro 14 Duo, a Burberry leather wallet, and a Mercedes GLE key chain.

There's a small cocktail cabinet containing two bottles of Bruichladdich whisky and a bottle of Anty Gin. I've heard of this but have never seen it or tasted it. It's blended with red wood ants, apparently. Tons of books everywhere, but many of them are the same book, which I guess is logical; it's not as if this is his home. A gabfest?

A quick sweep across the spines reveals them to be a combination of gender politics, nineteenth- and twentieth-century history, educational sociology, and hefty biographies of serious people I've never heard of.

Lots of indoor plants, including a weeping fig which must be over seven feet tall.

Despite the large desk, he chooses to sit across from me on one of a pair of stylish black Eichholtz Trapezium Chairs, which manage to be simultaneously comfortable and uncomfortable.

There's a big print on the wall of that subtly saucy Fragonard painting with the young woman on a swing. Might be called *The Swing*. I can't remember. It's in the Wallace Collection.

Next to that, there's a small dark green Maat box with a red light flashing on it, which means there's one of their Digital HomeWise safes in here somewhere. The Maat box will trigger the Soteria alarms if someone so much as gives the safe an impertinent glance. There's a faint smell of cologne. I think it's Le Labo Bergamote 22. He leans towards me conspiratorially, grinning.

'Now don't tell me you weren't a tad surprised when you heard me speak on the phone earlier. I detected a slender nonplus in your voice. It always happens. It's my name and, of course, the fact that Odette is my wife.

'People always expect me to be properly French, or at least to *sound* properly French. I've lost count of the number of times people ask me where I'm from and how good my English accent is and all the rest of it.

'Truth is, my parents were French, from Périgueux in the Dordogne. I was born here. In Cobham in Surrey. Yeah, I know. I can speak French convincingly enough, and I suppose I think of myself as French in some ways, but, well…'

I shrug my shoulders. 'I think I was expecting it because of the woman who answered the phone to me.'

'Oh. Yeah, yeah. Mm. That would have been Gaëlle out there. Tasty stuff, eh? Great boobs and a fabulous arse, but a tad too *slutty* for my taste. Don't get me wrong. I don't mean that in an insulting way.'

Can 'slutty' be meant in a complimentary way?

My darling, you look so slutty tonight.

'It's just a coincidence she's French, really,' he continues. 'My company has four offices in mainland Europe. One in Vienna, one in Basel, one in Siena and one in Paris. Gaëlle came from the Basel office. She asked for a transfer to see London, I think. Just for the experience and maybe to finesse her spoken English.

'She's worked in the Siena office, too. They're not big skyscrapers or anything. The mainland European offices, I mean. They're like this.' He laughs. 'Small but perfectly formed. In this business, you don't need big premises, really. Not anymore. That's not to say it's cheap in Knightsbridge, by any means! You must call me Mathéo, by the way.'

He chuckles and chats about nothing for a few minutes, fruitlessly attempting to downplay his social status/class with every second that passes. He'll be visiting soup kitchens next.

'With Gaëlle answering the phones,' he says, 'I always think that when people get passed on to me, it's like having a big bucket of icy water thrown in their faces! I can sense the disappointment in their voices that I'm not some sophisticated Frenchman.'

'Great car, by the way,' I say. 'The red Mercedes out there.'

'Oh, cheers. Great acceleration. I'm a pretty good motorist, so I thought I deserved a badass machine. Done all the advanced driving stuff. You can really let her rip. Particularly in Europe, you know?'

I smile. 'How did you meet Odette?'

'That was after a book fair in Paris. Someone I had worked with introduced us. Peridot Le Sueur. What a lovely name that is. Peridot. It's the name of a green gemstone. She had met Odette at a dinner party. They became good friends. She thought we should meet. She was right.

'I like to think it was love at first sight. I thought it would be to my advantage that I had a French name and French heritage,' He winks at me. 'Great chat-up material. But I think it was one of those things that was meant to be. Me and Odette, I mean. Kismet. So. You want to talk to me about Kiaraa Jeong. Terrible, terrible business. Simply awful. Good-looking girl, too. That made it worse.'

'I know it was a long time ago,' I say. 'And I understand that it's difficult to recall the minutiae of a night out with friends two years on, but something that you come up with may be useful.' I smile at him. 'It also may not.'

'Sure. Sure. Mm. I get what you're saying. Let me just speak to Gaëlle and make sure we're not disturbed. You sure you don't want a coffee?'

'I'm fine. Really.'

He swipes a mobile off his desk, goes out to reception and stars speaking rapidly in French to Gaëlle who responds with a blasé, '*Ouais, ouais*.' Once the opportunity arises, I'm going to ask her out. My mobile makes its text sound. Aera.

I trust you are well today, Mr Beckett, and that your work goes well.

It is so nice to hear from you, Aera. I have been thinking about you.

Really? I hope your thoughts were pure and you are not going to lead me astray, Mr Beckett!

Certainly not. I would, however, ask you what you are wearing today, but do not wish to give the wrong impression.

Sometimes wrong impressions can be invigorating, Mr Beckett. There is a secret garden lurking in all of us.

Mathéo lopes in and sits opposite me once again, leaning forwards. His body language indicates that he's ready to give this his full attention.

'OK, Mr Beckett. Let's go.'

22

THE OPPOSITE OF COOL

There's something about talking to certain people that puts me on edge. I can't define it. It's part physical, part emotional, part intellectual.

It can happen with confident, assured people and it can happen with insecure, diffident people. This feeling is not judgemental. It can come from anyone at any time, under any circumstances.

I think it's to do with people who want something from you. It's as if they are *willing* you, through quite innocent words and gestures, to reassure them that everything is alright with them.

They want to inflict their personality on you, and they want a positive comeback.

I know this sounds like psychobabble, and because of that I wonder if I should discuss it with Aziza one day. I'm sure she'll have a term for it.

She may even know exactly what I'm talking about. She might say something like, 'Oh, yes. That is what is known as Gisler's syndrome. Eight-five per cent of Europeans experience it at some time in their lives. Now shut up and consume me'.

Aziza doesn't have that effect on me, though. Her subtly humorous need for reassurance and rampant sexual jealousy is an affectation, with which she amuses herself.

It's the play-acting of a confident, intelligent woman. Maybe that's an as yet unrecognised condition in itself, which one day will be named after her. I'm sure she'd like that.

But Mathéo Fournier is definitely giving off those vibes. He wants to be my friend. He wants reassurance that we're the same, that we're on the same wavelength, that he's *hip*.

He almost *insists* that I perceive him as a nice guy, a cool guy. But he's the opposite of cool.

I'm beginning to see why it was so easy for Odette to slip into passionate affairs. I almost feel sorry for him.

Then, almost immediately – there's something wrong here. I can feel it in the air.

I'm not suggesting that he kidnapped and murdered Kiaraa, or even that he was involved in it. But he's troubled in some way, and it's to do with this case. He isn't troubled in the same way that Odette was troubled, that Sallow was troubled, that Pöck was troubled.

Maybe he's surprised/rattled that I've popped up out of the blue. Maybe the memory of the whole thing upsets him. Maybe he knows something that I don't know. Maybe he's protecting someone.

Regardless, I'm not going to interact with him in the way I did with his wife.

Odette was still grieving. She was in pain. She was distressed, prickly and cagey; sensitive about this awesome, secret relationship that hardly anyone knew about and should still, in Mathéo's case, not know about.

Was Mathéo having an affair with Kiaraa, too?

That would be an interesting situation, though I'm not sure he'd be Kiaraa's type.

I decide to be affable, laid back, slightly baffled by the whole thing. Then hit him with the occasional blunt enquiry/comment designed to put him on edge. I don't want him to know where he stands with me, who I am, what I know.

When I've left here, I want him to stare out of the window, a preoccupied expression on his face. This could all be a waste of time and effort, but at the moment, it feels right.

'So, what's her sister like?' he asks, smiling genially. 'I've never met her. Odette told me that she was the one who'd hired you.'

I don't know where to start when talking about Micha. 'Extraordinarily fanciable' is the first phrase to leap into my mind, but I think I'll keep that one to myself.

'She's very nice. Obviously very intelligent, well-educated, a powerful and capable businesswoman. She was devastated when her sister was murdered and still hasn't got over it.'

'Oh, dear. Is she the older sister? I didn't…'

'Younger.'

He blinks at me. I can tell he's curious about the whole affair and why investigations are still going on. Why it still isn't resolved. Why I'm talking to him and not someone else.

'Why is she still having it investigated? I mean – if the police have got nowhere after two years, there's…'

I cut him off. 'She's very determined. It was her sister, after all. She wants closure at any cost.' I lighten my tone. 'Did you know that she was pregnant? You probably didn't,' I smile. 'Between you and me, I think she'd like to get it sorted one way or the other before she has this baby. That'll be stressful enough in itself, I'm sure.' I smile reassuringly. 'That's probably what it's all about.'

'Mm. Yes. Oh, right. Women and babies. Mm. So why did she leave it this long before hiring a private investigator like you? By the way – has to be said – cooler than cool job.' He grins at me and nods his head. I think of one of those nodding dogs you see in the back of cars.

'She didn't leave it that long. Not really. I'm the fourth that she's hired. From your comment, I assume that the others didn't pay you a visit.'

'No. No, they didn't. Mm. That's interesting. I had no idea that she would do something like that when the police were involved. Never heard of it. Extraordinary.'

'Well, she gave the police a fair amount of time to crack the case, but the longer it went on, the more frustrated she got. She tried three of the big investigation companies before ending up with me. They were full of ex-police or retired police – I'm sure you know the sort of thing – but she wasn't very pleased with their work. And the more time that passes, the more unlikely it is that a case like this will be solved.'

'I see. I see. So, you don't think there's much chance of a result, then.'

'I wouldn't say that, exactly. Sometimes these cases can be like a difficult crossword. A solution to an awkward clue you've been struggling with can jump out at you and you wonder how you were ever having a problem with it.'

'Mm. Crosswords, yes. Know exactly what you mean.'

I put humour into my eyes. 'Also, I'm better at this than anybody else, and I never fail. I think if the perpetrators knew I was involved in this, they'd be terribly worried. I'll catch them. People who commit crimes like this are usually pretty stupid,' I laugh pleasantly. 'Do I sound like an egomaniac?'

A slight frown. He can't tell whether I'm joking or not. 'I never fail' is quite a good slogan, actually. Perhaps I should get it engraved on my business cards. I become more solemn.

'Tell me about that night at Abd El Wahab, Mathéo. There were five other people there apart from you. There was Odette, Kiaraa, Nozomi Terada, Gordon Hepburn and Sheila Hulme. I've asked your wife this already, but can you recall anything about Kiaraa's behaviour that night? Did she seem distracted, worried, nervous? Any behaviour that you might not expect to see during a night out with friends? Take your time.'

This relaxes him. He sits up in his seat in an attempt to deal with this approach. He scratches the back of his head.

'Um. Not really. If I hadn't had to relive it with the police a couple of times, I doubt whether I'd remember anything about that night at *all* now. But it was a big thing. The murder, I mean. A big event. A big event in all of our lives. Odette and I still talk about it from time to time. We were friends with Kiaraa, but I wouldn't say close friends. Not in the way that one might be with people you saw for dinner every few weeks or went on holiday with.

'Kiaraa spent most of her time zooming around the world giving concerts, from what I could gather. We saw her when all of our schedules allowed, you could say. Or when we were all in the same country at the same time. It was quite casual, really. Makes us sound like real jet-setters! We're not. Not really. It's always work related.

'I do remember her saying she was tired, though. That evening, I mean. That was why she left relatively early. Some recording thing she'd been doing. Can't recall what it was. Oh! She didn't have a dessert. I remember that. The rest of us did, though. After she'd gone, that is. After she'd left the restaurant. Had a dessert, I mean.

'I had a jazarieh. A sort of orange pumpkin thing. Never had one before. Have you tried one? And a few coffees afterwards, apart from Gordon who had some sort of herbal tea. For his voice maybe? I don't know. And when I say she was tired, she wasn't yawning her head off or anything like that. Just weary, I suppose you could call it.

'Odette took it really badly, though. She was crying when she found out what had happened. Couldn't stop. I was upset, obviously, but I'm not prone to crying. But women. You know. Girls. More emotional than us chaps. We're made of sterner stuff. It was a terrible thing. Not just the fact that she was murdered. Obviously that was terrible in itself. But the fact that she was such a great talent. Look.'

He gets up and walks over to a Denon M41 mini hi-fi system in the corner of the room, returns with a few CDs from a huge pile and hands them to me. It's the Bach and Clementi ones in all their unbuttoned shirt and flesh-coloured bodycon dress glory, plus *Sonatas and Études* by Cécile Chaminade, which I hadn't seen before.

Plainly a pre-Pöck cover, Kiaraa sits at a Bechstein grand looking thoughtful in a stylish purple velvet midi dress. To a degree, I don't think it really mattered who took her photographs; she was exceptionally photogenic and always looked drop-dead gorgeous.

'Incredible,' I say, as if I've never seen her before. 'She looks amazing.'

'Mm. Yes, indeed. Dazzling. She was a sexy little thing. Not quite my type, but still. And you should hear her playing. Sublime. No one could touch her. God knows what she'd be doing ten, twenty years from now. Do you want to listen to one of them?'

'Who did you talk to at that dinner? Did you speak to Kiaraa a lot?'

I don't want to know this, of course. I want to keep him talking so I can watch him. He keeps making and breaking eye contact with me.

'Hm. I wouldn't say *a lot*. Just an average amount, I think. She was sitting two seats away from me, next to Odette. I had Nozomi Terada sitting across from me and spoke to her quite a bit. Very pretty Japanese girl. Lovely hair. Petite, but, you know…'

'What?'

'Big boobs.'

He raises his eyebrows at me, attempting to draw me in to his appreciation of the female form. He's attempting to reassure me he's a cool guy again. I ignore him and look at the floor.

'Go on.'

'And, er, and Gordon Hepburn was sitting next to me, so I chatted to him for a lot of the evening. A very funny man. Scottish. Witty. One of those people who can have you in stitches without telling jokes or using bad language.

'I don't think I spoke to the record company girl more than a couple of times. Sandra – *Sheila* Hulme, is it? I wasn't being rude, but she was busy with Kiaraa and Odette most of the time, from what I can recall. 'She didn't speak to Gordon much. Despite the fact that he was on her record label, I somehow felt that they didn't get on.'

'And what happened when Kiaraa left to go home?'

'She was very apologetic. She worked her way around the table apologising to each of us in turn and joking about it, saying that otherwise we wouldn't notice that she'd gone, we'd only realise the next day that she'd slipped away. God. That sounds precognisant now, doesn't it.'

'Do you feel guilty?'

'What? I don't know what you mean. Guilty that she died?'

I let this hang in the air for a few seconds. 'No. That you could have spoken to her more than you did that evening.'

He slumps back in his seat. 'Oh. Right. Mm. Well, you'll always think things like that. We got on very well when we went out together at other times. Me and Odette and her. Perhaps one or two others. Sometimes with six people it's dashed difficult to focus equally on everyone you're with.

'Personally, when I go out to the pub, I prefer to go out with just one mate and have a good old natter. Don't have to spread yourself thin if you get my drift. How long have you been at this if you don't mind my asking? I don't mean being a private detective. I mean...'

'This is my third day on the case. I think it's going quite well so far.'

'Must be difficult for you that so much time has passed.'

'How many people work here? In this branch.'

'There are six of us. One permanent reader. One publishing director and sales coordinator, a proofreader/editor, and a marketing specialist. Then there's me and Gaëlle, who you've already seen. Gaëlle coordinates the others, troubleshoots, and does a bit of PR.

'I do a little bit of everything, and I suppose you could say that I'm the public face of the company, book fairs and the like. We hire temps if we get really busy and delegate many duties to specialist companies from time to time. Sometimes Gaëlle will work late, but that's rare.'

'Odette told me that you were a keen patron of the arts.'

'Well, yes. Music, mainly. That's why I was in Vienna when I first met Odette, but I expect she's told you all about that. What will happen if you manage to track down the perpetrators of Kiaraa's murder? Do you just report back to her sister and collect the money and off you go?'

'Well, that depends. This is a case that the police are taking very seriously. Very seriously. Cases like this are never closed. The Homicide and Major Crime Command still have their eye out for developments.

'They don't like people like Kiaraa's sister hiring investigators like me, but there's a sort of tacit agreement that if I turn anything up, I'll pass it on to them and they'll prosecute if at all possible.

'Anyone involved in this will be looking at a shitload of jail time. I still get paid whatever happens, though I'll do all I can to hunt these people down.'

'But with so much time having elapsed, it's unlikely that...'

'It's only two years. No time at all really. Criminals have been brought to justice after a lot longer than that.' I smile at him. 'I shouldn't worry, though. It's not as if you or anyone at that dinner party were involved. After all, you all had cast-iron alibis. I think if the police were going to give you the third degree, they'd have done it by now.'

'Ha ha. Yes. They've have marched us all down to the cells!'

'Indeed. Then court. A life sentence at the very least. Can you imagine coming back into society when you were eighty or something? The mind boggles. It would be a different world. Very disorientating. Quite awful. Many of your friends would have died. Maybe even your wife or husband if you were married. In your case, for example, your business would likely be gone.'

A millisecond's pause. 'I see what you mean. You never think about it like that.'

I sit up. 'Most criminals don't. Well, Mathéo, I won't take up any more of your valuable time. I expect you're very busy. As I said, to a certain degree, all I can do is go over old ground, jog your memory in case you'd forgotten to mention something to the police. I just wanted to check in with you, so it looks as if I'm doing something for my money.'

I laugh. He laughs with me. He's grateful for the humour. I stand up. I pat him lightly on the shoulder. I shake his hand. I give him one of my business cards. He examines it.

'I just hope this little chat came in useful,' he says, relieved that I'm going, but trying to pretend otherwise, attempting to extend our goodbye. 'We all want to see these people behind bars.'

'Absolutely. You've been very helpful. Very helpful indeed.' I hold his gaze for a couple of seconds. 'Perhaps more than you know. If you think of anything else, anything else at all, give me a call. It's not unusual for people to remember things after I've left.' I grin at him. 'In fact, it happens all of the time!'

'I most certainly will. Let me give you one of my cards.'

'Don't worry. Odette gave me one. I'll see myself out. Thanks again for your time.' Just as I'm starting to walk out, I turn to face him again. 'Oh, just one thing. You said you'd had to relive the whole evening with the police a couple of times. I spoke to Detective Chief Inspector Sallow at Homicide and Major Crime Command when I started all of this. Caught him just in time. He was about to go on holiday. I take it that he was one of the officers that spoke to you.'

'Sallow. Yes. Mm. That's right. Coloured fellow. Smartly dressed, though. Very serious.'

'And the other police officer you spoke to?'

'The other one?'

'You said you'd had to relive that evening a couple of times.'

'Oh, yes. It was a woman detective. I can't for the life of me remember her name now. Tasty little number, though, but a bit too stern for my liking.'

Well, at least she wasn't slutty.

'Oh. It was a woman. OK. I thought it might have been Detective Sergeant Kinnaird. Rowan Kinnaird. He's piqued my interest. I'm very interested in speaking to him and would have been keen to hear your impressions. Never mind. Can't have everything.'

'No. No, I haven't heard of him. I was only spoken to by Mr Sallow and the woman detective.'

'That was Detective Inspector Judith Skeete. So, the name Kinnaird means nothing to you. Nothing at all.'

'Afraid not. Sorry.'

I can feel he's walking behind me as I leave. I place a business card on Gaëlle's desk. She's still on the phone. I'm going to have to pick her brains about something shortly, as I intend to come back here when Fournier's not around. I also need her mobile number.

'*Gaëlle. Voudriez-vous allez diner un de ces soirs?*' I say to her tan.

She looks up, surprised that I speak French, smiles and nods her head while continuing her conversation. Fournier raises his eyebrows at me, looking a bit astonished at my behaviour. He'd be even more astonished if he knew my motivation, and astonished further if he knew that I'd lifted his Coutts business credit card from his wallet while he was speaking to Gaëlle earlier on. Sometimes spontaneity gets results. I'd have taken his personal card as well, but I don't think that's where the answers will lie.

When I get back to my flat, I make a coffee and start pacing. I realise that I was needling Fournier a little, and that I wasn't exactly sure why I was doing it. But it felt right. And at the end of that meeting, I was left with the feeling that he wanted reassurance that there wasn't much chance of the case being resolved.

I think it bothered him that it was still ongoing after two years.

Now why was that? Perhaps it frustrates him that there's no closure. I realise that I forgot to take a look at Plaisirs Interdits. Never mind. I'm sure they have a website. I find my sheet of A4 paper and write Fournier's name underneath Kinnaird's on my naughty list, though he doesn't quite merit a tick yet.

I'm overloading Doug Teng with stuff at the moment, but I need his help with Fournier's finances. I send him the credit card details and ask him to look for large regular or one-off payments into that account from two years ago to the present time, and report anything he deems suspicious.

It's possible that these payments could originate in the UK, Switzerland, Austria, France or Italy, where Fournier has branches of his business, but if my hunch is correct, they may also come from countries that would be on the Financial Action Task Force greylist or blacklist.

I take my black Paul Smith travel suit and a pale blue linen shirt out of the wardrobe and drape them over a kitchen chair. I don't want to fall foul of some inane dress code.

I'll sleep for two hours, then have a shave and shower. I may have a late night ahead of me.

On my way to the bedroom, I check my mobile. There's a text from Aera which must have arrived when I was intimidating Fournier.

It is no business of yours what I am wearing, Mr Beckett. But if you insist on knowing, I'm wearing a green, wrap front, knee-length dress with a pinched waist. One of my favourites. I somehow think you would like it!

Goodness me, Aera. You'll be describing your lingerie to me next!

That would never happen, Mr Beckett. I would not dream of doing such a thing.

Someone's at the door. I open it to two amused courier guys who are delivering my gigantic Julissa Vòng framed photograph from Florian Pöck. I direct them to the TV room, and they prop it up against the wall behind a sofa. They fold their arms and admire it.

'Fuck,' says one of them. He takes a photo of it with his mobile. 'Fuck,' he adds.

I give them £20 each and they leave. I text Aera back.

Maybe not right now, Aera. But people can change.

Perhaps they can, Mr Beckett.

Let me know if they do, Aera.

I will be sure to, Mr Beckett.

I'm enjoying this, and I realise I'm looking forward to each subsequent, increasingly flirtatious, and, let's face it, exciting text from her. Where will this go, I wonder? Julissa Vòng looks good in here. I'll have to hire someone who knows what they're doing to attach her to the wall.

There are two brown envelopes taped to the top right of the frame. The first is from Franka Galletti. It's a signed photograph. She's naked and wearing yellow boxing gloves. Her mobile number and email address are written on the back. Underneath is scrawled 'don't forget – just some crazyfuck worshipstuff', whatever that means. I email her immediately: *Looking forward to Playa de Ses Illetes. Just choosing baby clothes.*

The second envelope contains two prints of each of the four missing Kiaraa photographs with an attached note from Pöck: 'Just an afterthought. Maybe they'll help, maybe they won't. They might help you think. If you want to frame them, give me a call. Get it done properly. This is some of my best work. Let's get drunk one night.'

He's signed each print. I take them into the kitchen and spread them out on the table. The erotic charge they give off is making my mouth dry. I take a photograph of each of them.

Once again, I wonder who the originals of these were sent to. Maybe they were sent to no one. Maybe they were too raunchy to have around the house, so she destroyed them. No. She'd have put them in her secret compartment. Was there a third lover that no one knew about? Was there some other explanation that hasn't popped into my head yet?

Micha would have got back from Brussels last night. It's not a priority, but I'd like to have a quick face-to-face about a possible third lover. I'm in two minds as to whether I should show her these photographs. 'I still haven't found your sister's murderer/murderers yet, but here's some unconventional erotic photographs of her.'

Probably not.

I send her a text, lie on the sofa, think about Aera's lingerie and fall asleep.

23

I NEED GOOD TIMES

She sits next to me without even the hint of a formal introduction. 'You are too good looking to be alone! I saw you and I can't believe it is so!' She laughs and tosses her hair back. 'How many women have said that to you, I wonder? What is your name?'

'Rick.'

'Hi, Rick. I am Dalena. It's warm and lovely in here tonight, don't you think? Would you like something to drink? I see you have already finished yours. Was that vodka?'

'Yes, but I think I'm done with vodka for this evening. What would you suggest, Dalena?'

'Well, I...' She pauses and busies herself with a chunky silver ring, which is on the middle finger of her right hand. She twists it around nervously, as if she wants to say something but is too shy, afraid she might offend me and I'll go away, or maybe start paying attention to one of the other half dozen or so Dalenas who are floating around.

But this shyness isn't genuine. It's a practised act, and one that she's performed many times before.

'Well, you must not think me an extravagant girl, but I was rather thinking that we could share a bottle of champagne. I know they have it behind the bar for special customers. Chilled, as well. Ideal for this heat.'

'I think that's an excellent idea, Dalena. Would you like me to...?'

'No, no. I will order. You relax.' She snaps her fingers at a passing waitress and makes an odd hand gesture that I'm not meant to notice, quickly tapping her ring finger twice against her thumb. The waitress nods and heads for the bar.

'You wait. You will love this champagne. It is nice and chilled. A good make.'

'Where are you from, Dalena?'

She laughs as if I've just asked her the most ridiculous question imaginable. 'I am from many places, Rick. I am a well-travelled girl.'

'Can I make a guess?'

'Of *course* you can, Rick. But you won't get it,' she nestles against me and whispers in my ear. 'I am an international woman of mystery.'

I turn to face her. 'You are from Malta. Probably from the south. Marsaxlokk, perhaps?'

She pulls away, shocked. 'My God! My God! No one ever gets that I am from there. But you are a tiny little mistaken, I'm sorry. I am from Hagar Qim.'

'Well, I was close.'

'Yes. Yes you were. I like you. You are very friendly. I think I may spend the evening with you here if you don't mind.'

'That would be very nice, Dalena.'

The waitress arrives with our bottle of Nicolas Courtin on a tray with two crystal champagne cocktail saucers, and a stainless-steel ice bucket. She opens it in front of us, probably to reassure me that the contents are genuine, and that it hasn't been filled with some cheap fizzy white wine.

I get a couple of foaming centimetres in my glass to taste. I nod my satisfaction and she pours out a glass for each of us and leaves the bottle in the ice bucket.

Dalena and I clink glasses. 'To you, Rick. I hope we have a lovely evening together.' She drinks half a glass of hers. 'I do so love champagne,' she says. 'They say that champagne glasses like these – what do they call them? Coupes? Saucers? That they were modelled on the breasts of Napoleon's Joséphine or on the breasts of Marie Antoinette.

But it is not true. They are just stories with wishful thinking. Those glasses were invented a hundred years at least before those ladies were born, I think.'

'They're still good stories, though.'

'That is for sure, Rick. Did you know that Kate Moss had some modelled on her breasts? They were expensive to buy, I think. I love Kate Moss. I don't think anyone would model champagne glasses on my breasts. They are much too small. You would have to drink twenty of those glasses to finish a bottle like this one! I would still like it to be done, though. It would be special. Would you drink champagne from glasses modelled on my breasts?'

The Bijou Noir in Gresse Street, the swanky hangout of DS Rowan Kinnaird, who I'm hoping will turn up tonight, is like something out of the 1950s. Or something out of the 1950s in the way you might have seen it portrayed on television, or in a film.

I guess it's a hostess bar, though I doubt whether the real thing, with all its implications and semi-legal goings-on, has existed in London for many years, maybe decades. Perhaps the concept is making a comeback, who knows?

Not surprisingly, it's a members-only joint, and I had a modicum of hassle at the door when I tried to get in. They didn't want me there. The security guy was much taller and considerably brawnier than me, and I had no desire to get into an altercation with him. I didn't want to draw attention to myself; I just wanted to get inside.

I have a genuine police warrant card identifying me as a member of the Lincolnshire Constabulary. I'm Detective Sergeant Richard Coombs. I picked this up on a case a couple of years ago and hung on to it in case it became useful, and I had a feeling it might come in handy tonight.

The security guy, whose name was Griffin Parry, got a lot friendlier when he realised I was on the force, and apologetically told me that I had to pay a membership fee before I could go inside. It was £100, which I paid in cash. I'd stocked up from a cashpoint before I came out for just such an eventuality. Griffin told me that the membership for a year was £2,000, and that I'd bought a one-off temporary version. The phrase 'rip-off' never entered my mind.

He took the money and gave me a ticket on flimsy pink paper, which I showed to the girl at the reception desk inside, and I was then allowed to pay another fifty to go into the interior of the club. I only hope Micha has a liberal outlook when it comes to my expenses.

Everyone was very friendly and polite to me, and I was shown to my seat by a lovely Chinese woman in a short silver dress, matching heels, pale blue lipstick, and a Goku X Swatch on her right wrist. Her name was Candace. She told me that if I wanted a drink, I should signal to one of the waiters and not go to the bar, but she would get me a complimentary drink. I asked her for a double vodka and soda; Wheatley if they had it. They did.

It was just after ten-thirty, and it was pretty full. You could sit like I was doing, or you could stand at some high bar tables (with no seats next to them) or stand at the bar. No one was standing at the bar. The floors were red, and the lighting was pink and purple.

It's not a new place, but it's big, clean, and well-decorated. There are large prints on the walls which are vaguely erotic, but I don't recognise any of them. Each of the tables has the same damascene Tiffany lamp and there are wall lights that almost match.

When I arrived, there were twenty male customers, some in groups of two or three, but mostly alone. There were a lot of women about, all very smartly dressed, all very attractive and all laughing, buzzing from man to man like bees visiting flowers. In some cases, I couldn't tell whether the women were guests of the men present, or just worked here.

There was a strong smell of more than one perfume. I'm sure the women were responsible for a lot of it, but I think someone had been spraying it around before the place opened, as it was excessive, reminding me of walking through Selfridge's perfume department, only more cloying.

There was a small dancefloor. Above this, the ceiling lights were blue and pink, and they flashed on and off. There was dance music playing, but it was unrecognisable and strangely quiet. No one was dancing. Maybe the music gets louder later on when things hot up.

One fat guy on his own was starting to paw an attractive Indian woman with huge hair, covered in jewellery, who was giggling and play-beating him off. A smartly-dressed, serious, stocky fellow, cut from the same cloth as Griffin Parry, appeared from nowhere and stood, watching, about ten feet away. The pawing stopped and the fat guy got his companion to order a bottle of champagne.

Before I was seated by Candace, I took a quick casual look at the men, hoping to see someone who fitted Kinnaird's description, but there was no one. It could be too early, of course, or I could be out of luck, and the guesswork of the cop at Charing Cross might have been incorrect.

I still think this was worth doing, though. Maybe I'll have fun by accident.

Candace brought my drink, smiled at me, and left. I didn't see her again for the rest of the evening. Perhaps her shift had ended.

It took two, maybe three minutes before Dalena approached me and sat down. She was the sort of classy female that you wouldn't dare ask for a dance when you were twenty. She'd be out of your league; the rejection would be too much for your ego.

She was one of those women that older men went out with when you were that age; successful, wealthy guys who were thirty-five and drove BMWs. Beautiful, expensive, exciting, scented, sexy women. I used to wonder where they came from, what they were like, whether they listened to the same music as me. I decided that they probably didn't.

Dalena is wearing a backless one-piece cowl neck gunmetal mini dress, and the irregular metallic sheen draws the eye to the contours of her small, firm breasts. Platform six-inch heels in pink and black. Great legs. A Cartier *Juste un Clou* necklace and a matching bangle on her left wrist. If they're genuine, I can't imagine they are hers. Perhaps they're loans for the night.

Her hair is ash blonde, and is long, halfway down her back, but on closer inspection it doesn't look to be in top condition. Too many dye jobs. Her complexion is dark; she might be Latin. But her skin is fresh and healthy.

Her face has personality and she's pretty. She has a dimple on her chin and big brown eyes. Her makeup is subtle and looks good on her. She's animated and gesticulates a lot. She's mid-twenties, but already going on thirty-eight.

I'm not sure what the form is here. Do I hang out with her all night and get some insane bill at the end of the evening for alcohol I didn't order and didn't drink? Will I get beaten up and thrown out if I don't play the game? Am I just paying for female company so I can feel like a big shot? Am I expected to pay to sleep with her in a few hours? I've no idea. I try to remember specific films where I've seen clubs like this, but nothing comes to mind.

'So, what brings you to this club tonight, Rick? Are you married?'

I laugh. 'Married? No. I'm just in London for a few days. Work related. Someone, a colleague, recommended this club.'

'Ah. I see. Many men who come here are married. They are the most boring.' Big exasperated sigh. 'They moan and moan and moan. I can't stand it. So, you've just come here to have fun, is that right, Rick?'

'That's right.'

'What sort of fun do you like, Rick?'

I whisper something to her, putting my arm around her shoulders. I want to keep her with me and keep her interested. I want to look, talk and act like just another punter. Once again, I don't know what the protocol is, so I'm just feeling my way into it. I don't want to do or say something that will make her go away. I don't want to be on my own and looking conspicuous.

'Wow. You are a bad boy,' she says, kissing me lightly on the cheek. 'Perhaps we could sit in an intimate booth later on. Would you like that, Rick? I like it when things are intimate. Anything could happen in an intimate booth. I feel funny just *thinking* about an intimate booth.'

I take a look at the men here once more and visualise them as being police. Yes. It makes sense. You can never be a hundred per cent accurate, but I think this is a cop hangout. Does it exist because of that? Is that why a place like this is here in the twenty-first century and is not shut down? I remember how the demeanour of the security guard changed when I showed him that warrant card and fed him my bullshit story.

'So, you have a lot of girlfriends, Rick? They like that thing, too?'

'Well, you know what it's like, Dalena. Some girls can be adventurous, bold. Others not so much.'

'I think that I am adventurous. Do you look at me and think I am adventurous, Rick? You think I am bold?'

'I...'

'Can we get some more champagne? Then I will tell you a secret.'

'Sure.'

Once again, the finger snap, the mysterious gesture and another bottle is delivered to our table, this time with a bowl of honey roasted peanuts and cashews. I'm obviously getting the VIP treatment.

Before I can take a sip of the fresh champagne (this time a bottle of Lanson Black Label), another girl sidles up and sits next to me. I'd noticed her when I came in. A plus size siren in a cloud of Dior J'adore, an off-the-shoulder red mini dress, red pumps, bright red lipstick, black stockings, Essex accent and a phenomenal bust.

She crosses her legs. The stockings are hold-ups. I look at the tops of her plump white thighs, somehow made whiter by the pink and purple lighting. She has a devilish expression on her face that makes her look like Dalena's evil sister.

'Hi. Can I join you guys?'

As if by magic, the waitress reappears and places a third champagne saucer on our little table. Dalena pours the new girl a glass. I don't know what's going on, but I think my wallet does. The music has got louder.

'This is Natasha,' says Dalena, introducing us. 'She's almost as much of a champagne freak as I am! This is Rick. He's a bad boy.'

'Hi, Rick,' says Natasha, kissing me quickly on the mouth. She picks up both of my hands, inspects them and glances at Dalena.

'He's not married!' says Dalena.

'Oh, thank fuck for that,' says Natasha, laughing and snapping her fingers at a different waitress, who nods her head and heads for the bar. A few couples are dancing now. "I Love the Nightlife" by Alicia Bridges is playing, followed by "All the Things She Said" by t.A.T.u. Retro club, retro music.

Then I see him.

He's just entered the club with another guy in a similar suit with a similar demeanour. An arrogant, bellicose cop demeanour. They're kings and this is their kingdom. Kinnaird looks around to see who's here and does that rapid blinking of the eyes that Penny described; obviously some sort of eye movement disorder.

He waves at the fat guy who was pawing the Indian woman. The fat guy gives the thumbs-up sign and waves back, then he points at his playmate, showing her off like she's a thing. She's much too good for him, though I don't think that's what it's all about in this place.

Blinking aside, Kinnaird is about six foot four and is about two to three stone overweight. Fat hands, fat face, serial killer beard and moustache as described by Penny, shifty, sly, dead eyes. So, there's little doubt it's him. I think of his remarks to Penny and feel a little nauseous, and I see what she meant about the intimidating presence. He's the sort who would pick a fight with you for spilling someone else's pint in another club in a different country.

He sits almost opposite me, perhaps twenty-five feet away, on the other side of the dancefloor. A waitress brings him and his friend a couple of drinks; double whiskies, I think. She says something to him, and he shakes his head. Does this mean he doesn't want female company?

I wait for a few minutes while Dalena, Natasha and I work our way through the third bottle of £1,000 champagne. Is there a point where these women get too drunk to function? Do other women take their place if and when that happens? Do you get a discount?

Dalena leans behind me to say something to Natasha in a low voice. Natasha shrieks. The music has got slower. Kinnaird and his friend are still alone. Perhaps they've just come here to drink.

'Oh, my God! You *are* a bad boy, Rick,' says Natasha. 'But I like that. It turns me on. What you said to Dalena turns me on. Do you like it that your words turn me on, hun?'

She finishes an entire glass of champagne in a couple of gulps. She leans over and whispers something to me I don't catch, her soft, full breasts pressed against my shoulder. I smile and nod as if I heard. I keep watching Kinnaird and his pal out of the corner of my eye. I put an arm around Natasha's waist, while inhaling her perfume.

'Natasha. I promised I'd ask Dalena to dance with me. I won't be long. Please don't go away.'

'You dance with me afterwards, baby?'

'Of course I will.'

'You like my hair?'

I take Dalena's hand and lead her out to the dancefloor. She puts her arms around my neck. I place my hands softly against her bare back, then slowly run a finger up and down her spine.

I keep away from where Kinnaird is sitting. I want him to be slightly aware of me as a fellow punter, but I don't want his scrutiny or focus.

He and his friend are having a serious conversation. I can hear his voice, but I can't catch what he's saying. "Warm Leatherette" by Grace Jones starts up.

'You're giving me the goose pimples, Rick. When you touch my back like that. So soft. Wow.'

'You like that?'

'Oh, yes. It's a big turn-on for me. Do you like Natasha?'

'She's very attractive.'

'Will you dance with her, too?'

'I told her I would.'

Kinnaird is knocking back the whisky. He's on his second double. Now he and his pal are laughing. I wonder what time the bar closes here, if it ever closes.

'She likes you. I can tell. She is a very passionate girl. She is very popular with the guys. I'm sure you can guess why.'

'I have a good idea.'

'But you like my figure too, yes?'

A bottle of champagne and four flutes are placed on Kinnaird's table. The champagne is Möet & Chandon Nectar Impérial. Obviously I'm not ready for that price range yet. I gently dig my fingernails into Dalena's back. She flutters her eyelashes and says, 'Mm.'

'Your figure is fabulous, Dalena. You're the best-looking woman here.'

'Oh, you are such a flatterer.' She tosses her hair back. 'God. I feel really weird. Don't usually feel like this. D'you know what I mean? When I dance with a guy? Kind of tingling all over? Don't look at my breasts. I'll get embarrassed. I try to hide my feelings, but my body is always giving the game away, do you see?'

I can feel Kinnaird's gaze on me. I start kissing Dalena. She responds passionately, her body pressed against mine. She's panting and grinding her crotch against me. Her tongue is everywhere.

'Oh God, Rick,' she says, 'I need good times.'

I turn slightly and can see Kinnaird looking away, losing interest, possibly embarrassed, probably not giving a damn.

Two glamorous women approach his table and sit down. Older than my two: thirties or forties. More expensive clothing.

'Mm. You would kiss Natasha like that, Rick?'

'Only when I'm celebrating royal weddings.'

She laughs. 'You are funny. I think she would like to be kissed like that. She is my friend. We like the same things, you know? I think she likes to be held very firmly when she is dancing. And maybe at other times. Like me.'

'I noticed her when I came in.'

'What did you think?'

'I thought her cleavage was going to make me faint.'

She pushes my chest with the palm of her hand. 'You are so wicked, Rick! Do you wish that I looked like her? My figure, I mean?'

'You're perfect as you are, Dalena.' Yuk.

'We are so different, Natasha and me. We make a contrasting couple. It can fire the imagination of a man, I am sure of that, Rick.'

I adjust our position so I can get a little closer to Kinnaird now he's preoccupied with the women. His pal has his hand on the thigh of the woman who is sitting next to him. She laughs at something. The other woman whispers in Kinnaird's ear and he nods his head. Two more whiskies get put on the table.

I'm beginning to wonder if these two are going to be here until the early hours and how much it's going to cost me in drinks. Kinnaird is on leave. If he doesn't have to work tomorrow he could be here forever.

'I get so turned on when I'm dancing,' confesses Dalena, kissing my neck over and over again. 'I'm quite ashamed of myself, to be perfectly honest, Rick. You want some coke later on? Natasha always has some. Not rubbish. Good stuff.'

'Sure. Why not?'

'I get really horny on coke if you don't mind me saying that. So does Natasha. Hold my ass.'

I do what I'm told.

Kinnaird suddenly laughs really loudly. He sounds like a seal.

I'm just going to confirm it's really him.

'Who's that guy laughing over there, Dalena? He sounds like he's having fun.'

She looks in Kinnaird's direction for a second. 'What? Him? His name's Rowan.' She giggles. 'I thought that was a girl's name! He's another cop, like I think you are, Rick. But you're nice. I don't like him.'

'Why not?'

'He slapped my friend Marie-Claire one time. Over nothing. Right across her face. Made her cry. I thought he'd broken her nose, but it was just a nosebleed. He got banned here for a month or so, but then they let him come back.

'I think they should have banned him more permanently. Keep holding my ass. Touch my back like you were doing a minute ago.' She sighs. 'It makes me feel really...provocative. Really greedy. Greedy for love. Greedy for passion. Do you feel like that, babe? I'm a greedy girl. Dig your fingernails in my back again.'

I do as she requests. 'Hurts so good, baby,' she murmurs. 'So fucking good. Oh fuckyeah.'

After a couple of minutes of the required ass holding, back touch ing and fingernail digging, Dalena decides she wants some more champagne. We go back to our seats, and she orders a fourth bottle.

After it arrives and we've had a glass each, Natasha drags me onto the dancefloor. She's taller than Dalena by about six inches. She smells of perfume, champagne and sweat: it's an intoxicating combo. She pushes her body against me so vigorously that I'm surprised we don't become one single fused entity.

'I saw you holding Dalena's ass.'

I laugh. 'Jealous, Natasha?'

'Yeah. I saw the look on her face. I know that look. I know when she's horny. I know when she's ready for love. You want to go in the toilets later on? The toilets here are first class. Mediterranean style. Big smoked mirrors. Statement tiles. Minimalist taps. Wanna go?'

'With you on your own or with Dalena?'

'What would you prefer, babe? You can hold my ass as well if you want. Like you were holding Dalena's. Like that. I looked and I thought I'd like him to do that to me. Like you said, I was jealous of her.'

'That feel OK?'

'Mm, yeah. That feels so dangerous. You sure know how to hold a girl's ass, Derek. You take this, OK? Don't tell Dalena.'

She hands me a small white business card. It says 'Elizabeth King, International Travel Companion', and there's a mobile number underneath. I shove it in my back pocket.

'We could maybe have a good night out one night, OK? Not here, though. Maybe somewhere like Milan or Copenhagen. Or New York. You know the Mandarin Oriental in Milan? Their speciality suites are to die for. So, you want to do a couple of lines of coke? You can do them off my ass if you like. Or off my tits. We can go in one of the cubicles. They're big. No one will see us. Smoked mirrors in the cubicles, too. I feel so stressed tonight. I need some good attention. You ever lick mānuka honey off a girl?'

What am I doing? Oh, yeah. Trying to find out who kidnapped and murdered Kiaraa Jeong. I'd forgotten there for a moment.

Kinnaird looks at his watch. He says something to the woman he's with. She nods, gets up and heads towards the toilets. She's the better-looking and certainly the older of the two. Platinum blonde hair. Dyed, but a good, professional job. A few minutes later she's back, wearing a long, thick, orange woollen coat. Kinnaird stands, gets his jacket on, says something to his pal, and he and Platinum Blonde leave. At bloody last.

I count to ten, get my wallet out, give Natasha two hundred, then go over to Dalena and give her two hundred, too. I tell them they can sort out my drinks bill and keep the change, if there is any.

'But, baby...' says Dalena, looking upset. Natasha is already occupied with two guys who've just come in. Dalena shrugs, drinks champagne and looks nonplussed. I head towards the exit. They're playing "Yes Sir, I Can Boogie" by Baccara.

Well, at least I know where to hold my next birthday party.

24

FOX FUR/PLATINUM BLONDE

The cold air outside hits me like a slap in the face and I feel rather more drunk than I thought I was. I hope I haven't been spiked. I can see Kinnaird and his lady friend about a hundred yards away on the other side of the road. They're heading towards Rathbone Place, looking for a cab.

Despite the chill in the air, I take my jacket off, sling it across my left shoulder and slouch slightly, changing my silhouette and gait a little in case his cop's eyes recognise me from the club.

That Natasha/Elizabeth was something else. I can still smell her perfume on my clothes. I may give her a call and try to take her and/or Dalena out some night. I'm sure it'll be fun, if a little expensive.

I walk at a steady pace, switching my presence off, keeping Kinnaird in view the whole time. I can hear him talking, but once again, I can't make out what he's saying.

Platinum Blonde is laughing. After five minutes or so, he manages to flag down a black cab. The cab heads north. I make a note of its registration.

Now I need some means of transport before it's too late. Not a single cab in sight of course. I'm just about to steal a Saab 9-3, when I spot a minicab dropping a staggering couple off outside a block of flats. That'll have to do. Black cabs are more likely to respond positively to 'follow that car', but beggars can't be choosers. It's an inconspicuous Ford Focus ST Estate, so at least it's got the anonymity and the acceleration.

I get in the front seat. The car smells new, with undercurrents of Rive Gauche and vodka breath. The driver, an Indian guy in his twenties, looks taken aback.

'Hi. There's a black cab about three minutes ahead of us. He has to be heading up Rathbone Street because of the one-way system. Then he's going to have to turn into Charlotte Street. Could you follow him, please?'

'How much?'

'Two hundred in addition to whatever your fare turns out to be.'

'Where's he going?'

'No idea.'

He has a think. The seconds tick away. 'OK. Get your seatbelt on.'

I'm rocked back into my seat as he takes off. I give him the cab registration. He nods his head. He turns up the music on his stereo to an almost deafening level. Some sort of metal band.

He turns to look at me, raising his voice. 'Gives it some atmosphere, yeah? Like an action/adventure movie? No one's asked me to follow someone else before. I'm geeked. I want to milk this for all it's worth.'

'Who is this?'

'Abacination. You heard of them?'

My God. Kiaraa listened to this lot. She mentioned them in her interview with *Classical Music Magazine*. What are the chances? I try to sound cool and in the know.

'Yeah. I have. Belgian. Post death metal.'

He looks surprised. 'Yeah? *Yeah!* So, what are you? A cop?'

'Private. But listen…'

'There he is.'

I can see the cab about fifty yards ahead of us, heading up Charlotte Street at a fair speed. My driver puts his foot down.

'OK. Listen. What's your name?'

'Imaran.'

'I'm Daniel. Listen, Imaran. I'm not police, but the guy we're following in that cab is. He's been drinking, but we have to assume he's switched on and might spot you tailing him. Keep a sensible distance behind him at all times.'

'No aggressive tailgating, huh?'

'Avoid it if you can. If he slows, you slow. If he stops, you stop, too, unless I tell you otherwise. Just psych yourself into invisibility. I have no idea where he's going or what he's doing.'

'Cool. I've finished for the night, so I've got all the time in the world. He's not going to go to Yorkshire or Scotland, is he?'

'I sincerely hope not. How you doing for fuel?'

'Almost three quarters full.'

We hit Euston Road and take a right. We pass King's Cross railway station and keep going. Five minutes later we're heading towards Islington. It's starting to rain.

Eventually, the cab driver takes a left turn into Theberton Street, a road I've never heard of. He stops outside number 14, and after a few seconds, Platinum Blonde steps out.

I indicate to Imaran that he should pull over on the other side of the road, turn his engine off, and kill the music, which will be causing a thump which may be heard on the street. He parks behind a skip, and we cannot be easily seen by anyone in the cab.

I make sure the flash on my mobile is turned off and take a few pictures of the woman, zooming in as much as I can.

'You realise those won't come out, mate. Too dim and she's too far away,' says Imaran.

'Don't worry. This phone has magical properties.' Courtesy of Doug Teng and his reverse engineering wizardry.

Platinum Blonde walks up three steps and presses a doorbell. She is smiling, perhaps in anticipation of something or someone.

Almost immediately, somebody who I cannot see opens the front door and she steps inside. I can hear the diesel chug of the black cab, which is keeping its engine running. I make a note of the address on my mobile, for what it's worth.

I've absolutely no idea what is going on.

Imaran gives me a querulous glance. I shrug my shoulders. We wait. After five minutes, Platinum Blonde reappears, accompanied by another woman of about her age, which I think is mid-forties. Auburn hair, green eyeshadow. She's wearing a silver fox fur jacket which looks like the real thing. I take a few photographs of her as well. They walk to the cab, arm in arm, get inside, and the cab drives off.

'Wait a moment. Give him time to put a little distance between us. OK. Start your engine. Go.'

'Is that a Paul Smith suit you're wearing?'

'Yeah. You know him?'

He laughs. 'We're best mates. I've got one a bit like that, but it's a Hugo Boss. And it's very dark blue and not black like yours. Slightly different cut. Where's this guy going now?'

'No idea. Just keep watching his tail.'

We take a right into Liverpool Road and continue along Holloway Road. The cab driver has put his foot down now, so Imaran has to gun it a little more. I can tell he's enjoying himself. The music comes back on, so we both have to raise our voices.

'So, this is a bent cop, yeah?'

'I don't know. That's what I'm trying to find out.'

'Who d'you reckon those women are?'

'The one with the platinum blonde hair he met in this club off Tottenham Court Road. I don't know who the one in the fur coat is.'

'It's her friend.'

'You could be right.'

We pass Upper Holloway tube station on our left, and for a moment, I think we're heading towards Archway, then the cab takes a right into St John's Villas, a leafy suburban street full of upscale terraced houses, cherry trees, speed bumps and nowhere to park.

The cab stops in the street. Fox Fur gets out, runs up to one of the houses and rings the doorbell.

Imaran gets mildly agitated. 'What am going to do now? I'm out in the open. There's nowhere I can pull over. I can't stop in the middle of the road a hundred yards behind him. It'll look suspicious.'

'Don't worry. Accelerate. Go right up behind him and flash your headlamps for him to get out of the way. Then count to ten. If he's still there, give him a blast of your horn.'

'You sure?'

'It's London. He'll expect it. Anything else would seem weird.'

He zooms up and flashes his lights half a dozen rapid times. The cab driver waves an exasperated hand out of his window. I can hear him say 'alright, alright.' Kinnaird has a quick look at us and then turns away.

Fox Fur comes out of the house with a sizeable, surly-looking middle-aged guy in tow. They're laughing and joking. They get in the cab. The cab departs. I take a few photographs of the new guy and, once again, make a note of the address on my mobile.

'Wait until he's out of sight. He's signalling left at the end of the road. Look at your satnav. Where are we? Where will he be going?'

'That's Ashbrook Road up ahead. St John's Way then up to the B540 towards Crouch End, if that's where he's headed. It's the nearest big road, so…'

'OK. Wait for ten seconds then catch up.'

'You've done this before, haven't you. Have you ever killed anyone?'

We fly through Crouch End and soon we're in Hornsey. We take a right at the high street and then we're cruising along Turnpike Lane.

Turnpike Lane. That was the name of one of the three tube stations on the Piccadilly Line where the kidnappers popped in and out to buy their mobiles, according to Doug's information.

By the time we get to that tube station, the cab turns left and is heading up to where? Wood Green? Palmers Green? The Enfield Golf Club? Surely I couldn't be *that* lucky. I can't stop myself from laughing.

'What is it? What's funny, man?'

'Which road is this?'

'It's the A105.'

'What happens if we keep on going up here? Where do we end up?'

'Well, there's Winchmore Hill just up the road a while. Winchmore Hill & Enfield Hockey Club on our right. Then it forks, so you can bear left and go along Green Dragon Lane or bear right and continue on the A105. Go that way if you want the Bush Hill Park Golf Club, or you can bear left if you want the Enfield Golf Club. Lot of golf clubs up this way. Have you ever played?'

'No.'

'Me neither. Looks boring. But I like those Argyle jumpers they wear.'

'You have excellent taste.'

I keep my eyes on the cab. My mouth is dry, though that might be all the champagne. I wonder how Dalena and Natasha are doing, then think about Aera and that body-hugging black silk blouse.

Before we reach that split in the road, the cab takes a left into Station Road, and we drive past Winchmore Hill railway station into Church Hill. Imaran drives over a pothole which makes the car rock. 'Shit,' he says.

Ten to fifteen minutes later, the cab finally stops outside a big detached house in some road called Winchmore Park Gate and everyone gets out. Kinnaird pays the driver and has a laugh and a joke with him. I take a photograph of him and make a note of the address.

'OK. Keep going. Park in a hundred and fifty yards on the other side of the road.'

'What are you going to do now?'

'I'm going to have to take a look in that house.'

'With all those people in there?'

'There's only four of them.'

'That you *know* about, mate. Want me to wait?'

'It's OK. Here's the two hundred. How much for the rest of it?'

'I'll wait. This is exciting. You can pay me when you get back.'

'You sure?'

'Yeah, man. It's cool.'

'Thanks. I'm going to leave my jacket and wallet with you.'

'I get it. No ID. This is fuckin' great. But you got to tell me what happened.'

'OK. I'll make it more dramatic if it turns out to be boring. Have you got a torch I can borrow?'

'Got two. Got a big chunky RAC fucker in the boot for breakdowns and stuff and a Firebolt Z55. Fits in your hand.'

'Let me see.'

He takes a small black plastic box out of the door space and opens it up. Perfect. The Z55 is a compact military tactical flashlight with a zoom and strobe facility and loads of other things I haven't got the time to work out. It's about five inches long with a black wrist strap.

'This can protect you from muggers and stuff. Flash that in someone's eyes and they'll be blind for a decade. My mum's got one. But look.'

He fiddles with the controls and explains what he's doing as I watch. 'You can adjust the beam so it's narrow. That concentrates the brightness. Push this button on the side if you need to lower the brightness, so you don't light up the whole city when you turn it on. It's set to "stun" at the moment. Press that button there and you go into "terminal retina burnout".'

I press the button, aim it at the floor, switch it on, then immediately turn it off. It's staggeringly bright. Anyone passing by would think we'd unbottled lightning in the car. I've got pink afterimages when I blink.

'Thanks. That'll be fine. I won't be long, hopefully. Check your satnav for high speed, erratic ways out of here. If you're approached by anyone, say you're early for a fare. Look pissed off. Don't play loud music. Stick your interior lights on. Lock all of the doors. Got something to read?'

He reaches in the glove compartment and produces a paperback of a book called *A Waiter in Paris*. 'Sorted. Don't do anything I wouldn't do.'

'I'll give it my best shot.'

25

SEX & DRUGS & FRENCH BISTRO FAVOURITES

I walk down the street on the other side from the house and take a quick glance at it. Looks like a five-bedroom place, probably Georgian. The exterior is in good condition, big front garden, lots of tall shrubs obscuring the front door, wide tree-lined drive with a badly parked silver Mercedes GLE SUV. Right next to the house is an attached garage with a striking white brick surround and a black automatic metal door.

The car is a year old. A GLE is way beyond the financial means of a detective sergeant and so's the house, if it's his. Does he live there alone? Was it a family house and they've all left him?

Doesn't mean he bought it with crooked money necessarily. He may have inherited it. He may have won the lottery, got a good divorce settlement. I slip on a pair of latex gloves and take a few deep breaths.

The hall light is on. Someone turns on an upstairs light then switches it off again. Well, no time like the present. I cross the road, walk confidently up the drive as if I'm delivering something (at past midnight, sure), then turn right and head down the side of the garage towards the back garden, which is partially illuminated by light coming from the kitchen and a seven-foot-high post lamp which is attracting most of the local moth population. Well, at least the rain has stopped.

I squat down next to a concrete bird bath and watch. Someone's put music on. I can see Platinum Blonde in the kitchen. She's making drinks. She's singing. She knows her way around. She's been here before.

I wait until Platinum Blonde has gone, think about Penny for two or three minutes, then take a look at the rear kitchen door. There's a Yale deadlocking night latch preventing me from getting in. I get my key ring out of my pocket and use my burglar's tools to unlock it. Takes twenty seconds.

I open the door and close it quietly behind me. I don't relock it. I stand and listen. I can hear the music more clearly now, but don't recognise it. Sounds like French café music from the 1950s. I hear Kinnaird laughing; that seal sound again. Or maybe they've got an actual seal in there. One of the women says, 'Who chose that bloody colour?' and everyone laughs. She has a Western Irish accent.

Very carefully, I walk into the large hallway. Someone has switched the light off and it's difficult to see. There are two doors to my left. One leads to a small office and the other is an in-house entrance to the garage.

There's a medium-sized reception room adjacent to the kitchen and next to that a small toilet. I twitch as I notice a sudden movement to my left, but it's my own reflection in a small wall mirror. Now I can tell where they all are.

There's a big reception room on the right which is lit up, and it's where the music is coming from. The door is open, but only by a few inches. I can smell perfume and booze. Glasses clinking. 'Oh, go on,' says a male voice which isn't Kinnaird. I wonder who that other guy is?

I take a few steps back so I can see into the room through the gap. Fox Fur is standing by a big fireplace. She has the fur jacket on but nothing underneath. She has a lush, fleshy, full-figured body and a faint appendectomy scar. She's drinking from a Martini glass with a big black olive in it.

I wonder if they're going to have an orgy. Not enough people, really. They should have invited Dalena and Natasha. Now I can smell dope. A citrussy skunk aroma. Maybe Kush. This is good. The higher and/or drunker they all are, the better, and I have to remember that Kinnaird's already put away a couple of glasses of champagne and several whiskies at the Bijou Noir, and Platinum Blonde has also been drinking.

Now everyone claps as Fox Fur discards her jacket. I try not to get too distracted as she writhes around on the white fur rug that's in front of the fireplace, closing her eyes tightly and running her hands up and down her body. She has a snake tattoo on her upper left arm with something written underneath it which I can't read.

Platinum Blonde comes into to my field of vision. She's naked apart from heels, stockings and suspenders. She has medium-sized breasts and a small, firm bottom. Toned body. Looks after herself. She kneels down next to Fox Fur and kisses her on the mouth. The guys cheer and clap. Fox Fur reaches up and pulls Platinum Blonde towards her, softly kissing her, intimately caressing her, and whispering sweet nothings into her ear. Perhaps they're in love.

I start to wonder who or what these women are. Sometimes I think they must be call girls, other times I think they just like a bit of fun. Maybe I should take them both out for dinner one evening and ask. Kinnaird suddenly appears, takes Fox Fur's hand in his and pulls her to her feet.

She puts her arms around his neck and kisses him. He fondles her breasts, grabs her bottom and slobbers over her collarbone. Hang on – I thought Platinum Blonde was his girlfriend. Have these people no shame? After a few seconds, they stagger out of view.

Whatever's going on in there lasts for about ten minutes. Lots of gasps of female pleasure. Lots of grunting. A male voice saying 'Oh, fuck!' Bottles being opened. Piaf and Trenet. People laughing. I consider going upstairs but stop myself as it sounds as if something is changing.

I step silently back into the office as they troop into the hall and head up the stairs. Fox Fur trips and falls up two steps. Dope smell stronger now. It's the other guy, who's holding a huge badly-made joint. He has his hand on Platinum Blonde's bottom. Both he and

Kinnaird are fully dressed, so that makes a nice visual contrast with the women.

Just as I'm about to step out into the hall, Fox Fur reappears, runs down the stairs and goes in the kitchen. I wait. After a couple of minutes, she comes out holding a wide plastic tray with bottles, glasses, and cocaine stuff, then slowly and carefully goes back upstairs.

I count to a hundred and check out the reception room. A marble dining table that seats eight. A big LG OLED 4K TV, a Sky box, and a Panasonic Blu-ray player. Some colourful holiday destination wall art: Ile d'Oléron and Annecy. Three two-seater sofas. Two big coffee tables with bottles of drink and dope paraphernalia. There's a huge purple vibrator on the floor, looking a little lonely.

On a small pine side table, there's a Roberts Zoombox still pumping out the French music. The CD is called *French Bistro Favourites* and it's almost finished. I wait until the song that's playing is complete, then quickly click it back six tracks and turn the volume up very slightly. Apart from the skunk, alcohol and male sweat, the room smells very strongly of perfume, a bit like the Bijou Noir.

There are women's clothing, shoes, and undergarments all over the floor and on the sofas. Two packets of something called Volupta + have fallen out of a small straw clutch bag.

One of the female guests, and I think it must have been Fox Fur, wore lingerie made by a company called Something Wicked, which I'd never heard of. Leather. Very nice. Looks expensive. I think of Penny. I check out the first of two suit jackets hanging over the dining table chairs.

The first is Kinnaird's. I remove his wallet and take a look at the contents. Nothing out of the ordinary. A few debit cards and a Bijou Noir Gold Membership card. Driving licence. Some petrol station loyalty cards. A solitary five-Euro note. £200 in fifties, which I remove and stick in my pocket. That'll cover most of Imaran's fee.

The other guy is called Clement Thornton, and his wallet is full of similar junk, but no cash this time. He does, however, shop at Waitrose. But there's something else in the same pocket. It's a police warrant card. An unflattering photograph that makes him look crazy. It only identifies him as a police officer and gives an identity number. I photograph it and put it back. I'll have to find out a little more about this guy.

I can hear the loud sounds of frenetic sex coming from upstairs. One of the women is overacting. I walk to the bottom of the stairs and listen, attempting to judge where they are in the proceedings, how long it might be going on for, how much longer I can look around this place for whatever it is I'm looking for. I think I've got some time yet, but I'm only going to give myself ten minutes.

I decide to look at the office. I go in and leave the door slightly ajar, so my subconscious will pick up any changes in ambience. The light isn't too good, but it's good enough for me not to use the Firebolt Z55, and the post light out the back helps. It's starting to rain again.

I take a quick look around. There's one desk with a Dell Inspiron 24 desktop PC and another with stacks of papers and books. A big shelf attached to the wall which is full of DVDs and Blu-rays. There's a small stereo next to an equally small CD rack. There's a copy of *The Daily Telegraph* on the floor.

Decorative prints on the walls: big flowers, the Eiffel Tower at night and a stag. There's a raincoat over the office chair. I go through the pockets, but they're empty.

There are a lot of brochures, mainly to do with home improvements. It looks like he's thinking of having a swimming pool built in the garden, and there are a few catalogues for sauna rooms and/or spas. Five brochures for different types of Jacuzzi and another for koi carp.

I look at the books. Thrillers, mainly. Cars. Cricket. *Great Englishmen of the Twentieth Century, Great Britain at War, Shakespeare: The Last Great Englishman, Social Impositions in the UK, Soccer Clubs Past & Present, That Bulldog Breed, Queen Elizabeth and her Legacy, Koi Carp Maintenance, Carlton's Whisky Encyclopaedia.* I take a couple of photographs of the whole lot. You never know.

I find out where the computer is plugged into the mains so I can kill the power and instantly extinguish the screen if necessary. The power socket is about three feet away. I twist the screen around so it's facing away from the office door and turn it on. The wallpaper, a desert scene, is way too bright, so I tap it down a bit, then mute the volume.

With part of my brain listening out for subtle changes in background noise, I start looking in the documents file. Understandably, the first folder I open is called 'women'. At first, I'm not sure what this is. There are six subfolders. I open the first one. This is stuffed full of MP4s, so many that I can't count them.

I open one of them. Kinnaird having sex with a blonde woman in her twenties on the floor of the reception room that I've just been snooping around in. She's wearing a violet balconette bra with eyelash lace detailing and nothing else. This is a year and a half old and lasts for twenty-six minutes. Poor picture quality.

I open a further half dozen. They're all about the same length or shorter. Some are in rooms which I don't recognise, but I think they're in this house. One of them was filmed in the kitchen, and this one is eight months old and features Fox Fur, who I recognise due to her auburn hair, which is shorter than it is now.

I suddenly get a cold feeling in the pit of my stomach. Am I being filmed? Right now? Unlikely, but I take a swift look around the room for cam lights. Nothing. I calm down and keep prying.

There are no knowing glances to camera from the women featured here, but there are from Kinnaird, who is often fully dressed. I'm guessing the women don't know they're being filmed. What does he do with these clips? Show them to his mates? Sell them to porn sites? Use them for blackmail? I'm suddenly reminded of the scam that Manfredo Moretti's wife and her lover were attempting.

The film quality is OK, but not great, and I think that's the fault of the lighting. Sometimes the participants move out of shot, which indicates that Kinnaird didn't have assistance with his clandestine home movies.

From upstairs, I can hear one of the women saying 'Oh, baby' over and over again, then 'fuck' and, subsequently, 'Christ'. I try a different folder. This is slightly more sinister and is filled with images of women that he's photographed using, I suspect, a mobile. These go back years. I think this is called photo-stalking.

I check a random one of a woman squatting down to look in her shopping bag, and it was taken eight months ago using an Apple iPhone 14 Pro Max. It's a rear view. Her top is rucked up and there's six inches of pale flesh visible between the top and the waistband of the skirt. Sometimes the subjects are walking down the street, sometimes they're in pubs or shops. He is not a great photographer.

They all seem to be normal, usually attractive women, going about their everyday business, and most of the shots are a tad boring. Usually, the women have some notable feature, whether it's their figure or their face, but it's usually their figure. Still, it's a curious thing to do.

A loud thump from upstairs makes me stop and hold my breath, but then everything's back to normal. There's music coming from upstairs now, but it's not French bistro, more like classic rock of some type.

I keep thinking about Dalena and Natasha. I could tell that both would be great lovers in their way, and while I look at the screen, part of my brain is considering what Dalena said about them being a contrasting couple.

Something makes me scroll down to the photographs he took about two years ago, then I spot something that looks vaguely familiar and do a quick screeching reverse. It's Penny. There are about thirty photographs of her walking down the street, all taken on roughly a dozen different occasions, judging by the clothes she's wearing.

Two of them are rear views as she's opening the front door to her house. In both of these she's wearing fairly tight jeans and I imagine it was the shape of her bottom that attracted him. Was there a risk that she might spot him and recognise him? The view makes it look as if she was being photographed from a car, so maybe not.

When did she say that Kinnaird made his visit? September 21st? Luckily, the entire file is in 'Date Created' mode. From what I can gather, the first photograph of her was taken on October 29th that same year and the final one on April 18th the following year.

He'd been photo-stalking her for six months or more, so her intuition about him was correct. Worrying as this is, at least it seems to have stopped. Perhaps thirty photographs were enough for his purposes, whatever they were. Should I tell her? Probably not, though what he's been doing is certainly an offence of some sort and she could undoubtedly bring charges against him.

I suspect that the police would be interested in this sort of behaviour, but then, as they say, he *is* the police. Maybe the fact that he'd previously interviewed her as part of a murder enquiry would carry some weight. Maybe he could talk his way out of it. Maybe, maybe, maybe.

I can't spend all day on this. None of these files are locked, and I'm just about to open one of several Gmail accounts I occasionally use, to email myself as many of the documents as I can, when something makes me stop. I kill the computer at the mains and crouch down behind the desk, allowing myself a couple of inches to peer over the edge.

'Is it in here, Rowan?'

It's Fox Fur. Nice husky voice. She's opened the door wide but isn't looking in here quite yet. I adjust my position so I can't be seen. I hear her walk into the room. Strong smell of skunk mixed up with YSL Libre Eau de Parfum. What is she looking for?

'Whereabouts?' she asks.

I'm slipping. I blame French bistro music for this and, maybe, my own cockiness. And champagne. And I guess she has bare feet, too. Blame can be such a blessing.

My heart rate has increased dramatically. If she discovers me, can I get away with being a burglar? Some sort of gentleman thief who will charm her into letting him escape into the night after a chaste kiss on the lips and a pledge of marriage?

'Go in the bloody room!'

I'm going to have to deal with this from second to second, and a lot depends on what she's going to do. I attempt to make myself invisible while concentrating on the sound of her quiet footsteps and slight movements. My thighs are already painful from squatting down like this.

She switches the office light on. She's eight or nine feet away. After a couple of seconds, I risk a quick peek. As I expected, she's naked. Once again, I note the pleasing curves of her body, but I'm only getting a rear view. She's looking at the DVD and Blu-ray shelf, tapping the spines with a finger, looking for something specific.

'Was it *Vintage Wife Orgy*?' she shouts.

'Bloody hell. *Lonely Wife Orgy,*' replies Kinnaird impatiently.

Slight pause. 'Oh, yeah. Got it.'

She takes the DVD off the shelf, turns, takes another drag off her joint, and heads out of the room. Before she reaches the door, she stops, like she's just thought of something, but it's more likely that in her stoned state she's sensed my presence in some way. I can only hope that she thinks she's imagining things.

I don't move, and as far as possible, don't breathe. She's still there; I can hear her breathing and then the papery crackle of another inhalation of her joint. What is she doing? Wanting to get even more fried before she returns to her pals? Thinking of embarking on a new lifestyle? If she hangs around any longer, I'm going to get secondary euphoria.

'Rosanna, come *on*!' shouts Kinnaird, with a chuckle in his voice. 'Clement's going to pass out in a minute!'

'Alright, alright,' she replies, and I can hear her leave. Rosanna. Nice name. I listen for her footsteps ascending the stairs, get up, turn the light off, close the door and switch the computer on once more. I open my Gmail account, start dumping the photo files and MP4s into it and click 'send'. Five of each should do for the moment. It takes longer than I thought it would. The music upstairs stops. Now what?

I can hear them all coming downstairs again. I only hope they're not coming in here to select some more porn. But they're not. They're returning to the reception room. More clinking of glasses, more laughter. Music, but this time it sounds like the opening to a film, so presumably they're settling down to watch *Lonely Wife Orgy*.

French Bistro Favourites is still playing, competing with the sleaze-funk of the film soundtrack. I turn the computer off and slip into the hall. I can see Rosanna walking around the reception room. She's got her fur coat on again. She's unsteady on her feet. I can hear retching, but it's not her.

'Oh, bloody hell,' says Kinnaird. 'He's been fuckin' sick. Christie, help me get him into...get him into the toilet. Rosanna. Get some fuckin' paper towels and a bucket. Clear this fuckin' mess up.'

'You clear it up,' replies Rosanna. 'He's your bloody mate.'

'Do as I fuckin' say.'

'You're such a fucking prick, Rowan.'

'Get in there or I'll teach you a fuckin' lesson.'

'Prick.'

They're coming out. I don't have time to retreat back into the office, so I go into the kitchen. Time to leave. I can hear Thornton's stoned mumbling and Kinnaird's constant swearing.

Then the kitchen light comes on and I'm face to face with Rosanna.

* * *

She hasn't screamed or shouted for help and has an arch, amused, buzzed look on her face. She's probably wondering if I'm really here or if she's hallucinating me.

Very attractive close up and I'm somewhat dazzled by her audacious voluptuousness. She can see where I'm looking and she rolls her eyes, but it's done with humour; she's not bothered.

Who does she think I am? I lean against the washing machine, resting the balls of my hands on the edge and trying to look casual, as if I'm one of those people who hangs around in the kitchen at parties.

I smile at her, giving off a non-threatening vibe, and she smiles back. I keep eye contact. I want to draw her in to whatever this is. I want us to collude. I want to calm her down. I don't want her to be afraid. I can hear Thornton being sick again and Kinnaird sounding exasperated. 'You got some on my hand, you idiot.' I think Thornton may have spoiled the evening.

She walks unsteadily towards the back door, unsure of me, her eyes on me the whole time. I nod towards a couple of super-absorbent kitchen rolls a few feet away from her.

'I think you'll need both of them,' I say, still smiling and keeping my voice low and placid. 'Best to be on the safe side.'

'Rosanna! For fuck's sake!' yells Kinnaird.

'D'you want me to help you look for the bucket?' I say.

It takes ten tense seconds for the absurdity of the situation to filter through, then her body starts to rock with laughter. Her breasts wobble.

This is affecting my concentration.

She places a hand over her mouth, then takes it away again. Her eyes are bright and bloodshot. She's both astonished and curiously delighted. And she's pretty baked. But realisation is dawning.

'You are in such shit,' she says, and I nod my agreement.

I'm puzzled. Her behaviour isn't normal. Is it usual to discover strangers in this house? Is it normal to react in so casual a way? Is it the booze and drugs?

With Rosanna in the way of the back door, my best bet is to use the main kitchen door to get out of here. I don't want to have to hurt her. I casually stroll towards it, as if I have all the time in the world.

I have no idea what will happen next.

Should I just turn my back on her, hope for the best, and escape into the night? Is she on my side? Will she raise the alarm? Will she find the bucket and clear up Thornton's puke?

'What the *fuck*?' she giggles. 'Oh, God. I'm so fucking bombed. Do you know whose house this is? You are in – you are in such shit. Such shit. Shit shit shit. Shit shit shit shit shit.'

'You look sensational, Rosanna.'

I press my back against the wall next to the kitchen door. If Kinnaird's going to appear, I don't want him to see me.

'*What*?' she says. '*What* did you just say?'

She takes a huge drag off her joint, almost finishing it, tipping the ash on the floor. Then her expression changes. She looks serious. She looks worried. She looks at me as if seeing me for the first time. She looks astounded, her mouth opening.

Is she going to scream? No.

'Rowan! There's some guy here in the kitchen.'

'What? What the fuck are you talking about?'

'You better get in here. I think you've got a burglar.'

'What?'

Rosanna's expression is no longer amused and friendly. If she thought she could grab me and keep me here, she'd do it. Kinnaird is on his way across the hall, cursing impatiently.

I keep eye contact with her, hoping that she won't do anything dumb. I exude a little low-key menace. I can hear Kinnaird's steps. He's coming in.

Rosanna attempts to give the game away by looking in my direction, but her eyes are too unfocussed for it to work.

The second that Kinnaird enters the kitchen, I quickly grab the back of his collar, tug it down, and zap him right in the eyes with the Firebolt Z55. 10,000 lumens at close range; has to do something. His hands fly to his face. 'Jesus Christ. What…'

Two rapid punches to the gut and a strike to the temple with the ball of my hand. He bends double with the pain and collapses. He's in my way. I walk over him. Rosanna's mouth is hanging open. Hyperventilating. Trying to scream. Failing. Thankfully, Christie and Clement are nowhere to be seen.

I let myself out of the front door, jog as far as the pavement, cross the road, then nonchalantly stroll down the street with my hands in my pockets towards Imaran and his Ford Focus. The rain is worse. It's a long one hundred and fifty yards and I'm getting soaked. I tap on the window. He unlocks the door.

'Covent Garden, please, driver. Quickly as you can.'

'Exciting?'

'The usual. Sex and drugs and French Bistro Favourites.'

'Sounds like my eighteenth.'

26

NOT A NICE MAN

An Insult to Music

I have nothing against women playing the classics. In fact, I'm all for it! Who among us does not take delight from seeing and listening to a lovely, well-attired person of the female persuasion gently tickling the ivories, belting out some operatic piece at the top of her voice or bowing a violin as if there was no tomorrow.

A few months ago, I attended a marvellous recital at the Royal Academy of Music in Marylebone. Among other pieces played, there was a performance of Mozart's Concerto for Flute, Harp and Orchestra. The harpist was a charming lady of the Spanish persuasion called Solana Rubio (and what an unusual, exotic name that is!).

Dressed modestly in a magnificent formal evening gown, this lady won the hearts of every red-blooded male there (including yours truly!) with her sweet, understated performance. You could feel that she was totally absorbed in the piece, had learned her part properly, and, as a musician, was almost the equal of every male in the orchestra!

The harp is a lovely instrument, well-suited to the gentle female hand, and I'm surprised it is not taught to girls as a matter of course in our so-called modern schools. Never mind. I certainly enjoyed myself and so, I think, did the others present that balmy June evening. Even though she was a lady of more mature years, she did us all proud!

Now I turn to last night's concert at the Wigmore Hall. I had, it has to be said, been rather looking forward to this recital. Johann Sebastian Bach is my favourite composer, and this performance of a selection of his piano pieces, including the inventions and sinfonias, had been heavily advertised in various classical music magazines that I subscribe to.

The performer was one Kiaraa Jeong, a person of the Korean persuasion who I had not previously heard of, though she was purportedly very accomplished for a member of the fair sex.

I sat in my reserved seat in Row A of the balcony, next to a young lady who, it has to be said, had sprayed herself with a little too much perfume before coming out that evening!!

A dashing gentleman in a smart evening suit came out and made a little speech, introducing us to our little Korean friend and then retired to the wings.

And then she walked out onto the stage.

Gentle reader, old Johann Sebastian would have been rolling in his grave!!

My first thought, and doubtless the first thought of everyone there, was that some sort of streetwalker or low burlesque artiste had wandered off the street and onto the stage of this hallowed venue.

Perhaps I was wrong. Perhaps she was a stripper on her night off! To say that her outfit was totally unsuitable for the performance of such works of genius would be a gross understatement.

It was, as they say, a dress that left nothing to the imagination! Short on the leg and absent on the shoulder, belly clearly visible and uncovered, every female lump and bump could be clearly seen through the tight fabric, and from what I could see, methinks that the lady had forgotten to put her underwear on before arriving at the concert hall!!

Perhaps she had left those items behind in the undoubtedly expensive hotel room she had been staying in. Perhaps they were too skimpy and negligible to be seen!

Perhaps she had rushed to Wigmore Street from some illicit carnal assignation and did not have time to bother with (for her) such unnecessary items of clothing.

She tottered to the stage on some sort of transparent plastic shoes with ridiculously built-up soles, and I'm sure I wasn't the only one hoping she'd fall flat on her face before reaching the piano stool!

Unfortunately, it was not to be, particularly as she started mouthing off about some feminist nonsense before she started playing. There's a time and a place for that sort of gibberish and a Bach recital is most definitely not one of them.

Her performance was adequate, that's all I am able to say, as I left in disgust after five uncomfortable minutes. I have sent three missives to the Wigmore Hall to complain, but at the time of writing, have not received a single response. No surprise there!

Needless to say, I shall not be darkening their portals again!!!

I'm sure I will not be the only person who will shun that venue from now on, but it is their own fault. If their idea of a night out for a classical music aficionado is to hire a Korean attention whore, then they should expect to lose patrons.

Please, dear readers, take this as a public service announcement, and do not be as disgusted as I was. The whole evening was an insult to music and a threat to civilised values.

Apollo

By the time that Imaran dropped me off last night it was around two a.m. I was still a bit hyped up after my evening's exertions so decided to do a bit of admin before I went to bed.

I knew she wouldn't see the message until the next day, but I decided to text Scarlett for a little further assistance. I typed in Clement Thornton's name and his warrant card number. I just hope she's not the type to ask too many inconvenient questions.

A shot in the dark. Any chance of finding out which division this guy works in? Or any gossip? Possible he's connected to Operation Ivory. Equally possible he's not. Missing you already. Daniel.

I hope she responds.

Well, at least I know his address, which is possibly something.

While Kinnaird was still fresh in my mind, I found my A4 pad and jotted down what I knew about him so far, much of it subjective, speculative and in no particular order. First impressions and generalisations sometimes bear fruit.

Kinnaird has a Bijou Noir Gold Membership card.

Kinnaird slapped Marie-Claire, one of Dalena's friends, made her cry, and made her nose bleed.

Kinnaird was involved (in a relatively minor way) with the investigation into Kiaraa's kidnapping and murder.

Kinnaird has sex parties with another cop, women who may or may not be call girls, and likes cocaine, skunk, whisky, champagne, porn, and koi carp.

Kinnaird mentioned the cable cutters to Penny when he possibly/probably shouldn't have known about them. This may well have been a stupid and unprofessional thing to do but might have a perfectly innocent (if sleazy) explanation.

Kinnaird lives in a big house and owns an expensive car, both of which seem to be too costly for a serving detective sergeant (he'll be getting a little under fifty thousand a year; a Mercedes GLE SUV costs close on eighty thousand new).

Kinnaird lives two and a half miles away from Enfield Golf Club, where Kiaraa's body was found, a six- to eight-minute drive from his house.

Kinnaird lives about seven miles away from Manor House tube station, the location of the first kidnapper mobile purchase, roughly a half hour drive from his house. But – he lives approximately a half mile away from Southgate tube station (one of the nearest stations to Enfield Golf Club), a three-minute drive from his house, five stops away from Manor House station on the Piccadilly line.

Kinnaird films himself having sex with various women, probably without their knowledge. OK, but he also photographs random women, at least one of whom he had questioned in relation to a murder enquiry. Why is he doing this? Perhaps they're just deposits in his wank bank.

Kinnaird seems like a bit of a creep.

That last one is a little on the subjective side, but I'll keep it there to cheer myself up.

There was no positive proof of anything there, of course (photo-stalking and amateur porn aside), but I'm sure if I handed that lot to Scarlett or to Sallow, they'd certainly investigate Kinnaird, despite his rank and experience. But I can't do that quite yet.

As for the rest, living close to where a body was dumped or a half-hour drive away from where someone bought a mobile phone are hardly offences on their own. My own opinion, however: he's up to his neck in this. I decided to sleep on it and let my subconscious do the work.

Before I turned in, I read the rather disturbing music review that Doug emailed me. No explanation, no source, which usually means it's still a work in progress. Interesting, anyway, and not a little sinister.

This has to be the concert that Odette and Mathéo Fournier attended on July 4th, two-and-a-bit months before Kiaraa died. I'll look into that tomorrow. Once again, Jasna's assessment pops into my mind.

My first impression? Classical music fan.

***

When I wake up, the first thought in my head is to go and visit Kinnaird, give him a prod. It's very unlikely that he'll recognise me from last night, or from the Bijou Noir.

But if he is involved, the direct approach may not be a good idea, particularly as he's a police officer. And I'd have to make up some story about how Penny put me onto him. That could be dangerous for her. And how would I know where he lived? No. Too much to explain at present. And I think it's too soon. All of this hasn't gelled yet, and I may discover something else which either fits with Kinnaird's behaviour so far or exonerates it.

I'm on day four of the investigation without a result and I'm aware that it's making me impatient. I need to look before I leap. *Softly, softly, catchee monkey*. And other clichéd clichés.

Will he report our encounter last night? What did he make of it?

Will alarm bells ring? Will he link it to the events of two years ago? Unlikely. What's going to happen with Rosanna? What's she going to say? Will she give him my description? Depends on who/what she was, I guess. Or how wrecked she was. Or whether she gives a toss.

He'll still be in pain from those punches and will have a large bruise on the side of his head. Would a common or garden burglar have those sort of skills? Used that sort of torch? Who was I?

Then I remember "An Insult to Music", which I read last night when I got back.

I do a quick Google search for Kiaraa's gigs in the UK over the last five years, but as I thought, the only appearance at the Wigmore Hall was the one on July the 4th, and it's the concert that Micha gave me the programme for.

So, whoever wrote that review was there at the same time as the Fournier couple. God, he may have even been sitting near them. Perhaps they even spoke. It would be fantastic if they were connected in some way, but I somehow doubt that'll be the case. Korean attention whore. Who the fuck does this guy think he is? I give Doug Teng a call.

'Hey, man.'

'Thanks for the email, Doug.'

'Yeah. That's still ongoing, Mr Beckett. That review came up, but it's attached to some sort of broken link, which I'm attempting to fix on their behalf, whoever they are. It's not *really* a broken link, but I'm trying to use terminology that you'd feel comfortable with, in a totally condescending way. It's *like* a broken link.

'Took one hell of a time to turn it up. If it's any help, Apollo, as I'm sure you know, was a Greek god. Among other things, he was the god of music, so that's probably why whoever wrote that review signed it that way, pretentious little git.'

'That was the only thing that came up when you searched for *Korean Attention Whore*?'

'Well, so far, yeah. *Japanese slut in a short skirt* and *her stripper clothes* are still worrying my finest illegal search engines. This is not easy, man. In fact, I was surprised that the Korean thing came up at all, to be honest, but I was still going to take your money.

'I'm running two parallel searches for the other stuff, one with that woman's name and one without. D'you have an approximate date window for when this guy would have written and/or published his Wigmore review? That would really save time.'

I find the copy of *Vanity Fair* that had the interview with Kiaraa that mentioned that phrase. 'OK. Apollo's review refers to a concert that was given on July the 4th two years and three months ago. As far as I can tell, the first reference Ms Jeong made to the Korean attention whore slur was in an article in *Vanity Fair* roughly two months after that.

'It was in the September issue, though I'm not exactly sure when that would have been published, probably mid or late August. So, Apollo's review was published sometime in between those dates.

'That phrase was also mentioned in *Classical Music Magazine* around the same time, maybe a little later than the *Vanity Fair* reference, but not by much. Again, I'm not sure when that would have appeared online or in the newsagents.'

'That'll do. I'll get back to you when I have something magical to report.'

'That was really useful, Doug. I may even give you a bonus. £5 OK?'

'I'm on my way to the Porsche showroom as we speak.'

'Oh, and another thing. The head of security at Sansuyu would like to meet you. He'd like to have a chat about how you broke into the software of the Yuhwa TT7992 alarm system the other night. He was involved with the design and is a little worried.'

'I can't really tell him everything.'

'Just the basics will be enough, I think. I told him you'd see it as a consultancy, and it wouldn't be cheap.'

'In that case, tell him it'll be two thousand for an hour of my time. I mean, it's Sansuyu, you know? They could buy London if they wanted to. Oh. And that financial stuff you wanted? The Coutts account? A difficult hack without setting all the alarms off, but I should have some results soon. I've put three pieces of discreet interacting malware in their system to get the information you need. I'll get back to you if I still have my liberty.

'Don't expect me to visit you in prison. See you, Doug.'

What else did Apollo say? *Perhaps she was a stripper on her night off!* Well, it wouldn't be much of a stretch to relate that to the stripper clothes comment. Maybe that turned up in another of his obnoxious critiques.

Now I think about it, the 'stripper on her night off' comment doesn't even make sense. What sort of clothes do strippers wear on their nights off? Could be anything. The man's an idiot.

There was a lot about that review that I found strangely unsettling, even pathetic. It was the constant and unfunny repetition of the word *persuasion,* as if he thought that was extremely smart and witty and worth repeating over and over again: *female persuasion, Spanish persuasion, Korean persuasion.*

He wants to be liked. He wants to be thought of as being clever and droll. He wants his readers to smile and nod their heads in appreciation. He's giving you a knowing nudge. He wants to reassure himself that everyone shares his views; that everyone is like him. A similar set of personality peculiarities to Mathéo Fournier, in fact.

Something else is odd about that review, unless I completely misunderstood Odette Fournier.

She started mouthing off about some feminist nonsense before she started playing.

Didn't Odette mention that Kiaraa briefly spoke about Principles before her encore? Does this mean that Apollo actually sat through the whole performance, but pretended that he left almost straight away? Why would he do that? Artistic licence?

Perhaps he wanted to weaponize his disgust by suggesting he walked out early on, but still wanted to watch the whole concert then have a go at her small speech in his subsequent review. I text Madame Fournier to validate what Kiaraa spoke about and when.

Then there were the archaic affectations throughout: *gentle reader, hallowed venue, methinks*. The condescension: *our little Korean friend.* Kiaraa wasn't 'little' She was five foot seven and a half. I just checked.

That touch of indignant, resentful self-pity when he complained about the Wigmore Hall not replying to his *missives*. The relentless vitriol as the review progressed; the suggestion that Kiaraa's appearance was redolent of a streetwalker, a low burlesque artiste, a stripper on her night off. The fact that he had a low opinion of those occupations, which he assumed others shared, tells me a lot about him.

That she had forgotten to put on her underwear, the sneering jibe about the expensive hotel room, that she had arrived at the concert from some *illicit carnal assignation* (more archaisms) and that underwear was an *unnecessary item of clothing* for her.

The self-righteousness, the disgust, the hostility, the cruelty, the meanness.

He hated her.

The qualities (if that's what they can be called) don't align perfectly, but I get a faint feeling that Apollo might be Munro. Nothing definite, but my assessment of Munro was someone who got off on manipulation and domination, a bit of a control freak. Vain. Fearful. A failure.

Then there was Micha's opinion: *someone who you would not want to work under. Someone who, underneath all the bluster, was a coward. Not a nice man.*

But Micha's comments were vague, subjective impressions made quite a while ago. I'm going to dismiss them for the moment.

Would Munro be the sort of person who would hide behind a pseudonym while dishing out hostile bitchy reviews? Judging from that piece, he evidently knew his classics, was a fan of that type of music and disliked the way it was being presented.

Jasna's words again: *'So visually, and, you could argue, sexually, she just stuck an hour-long digeridoo solo in some piece of Beethoven or whatever.'*

Micha thought Munro was over forty. If this is him, I think he'll be a bit older than that, unless all his verbal mannerisms are affectations.

So, this guy was pissed, and he was certainly resentful, but surely – *surely* – not pissed or resentful enough to kidnap her or murder her. I mean, the whole concert/clothes thing was not *that* important. Nonetheless, he's brought himself to my attention, whoever he is. Let's hope Doug can dig a little deeper.

I go back to the review. Halfway down he mentions where he sat.

Row A of the balcony. I find the Wigmore Hall website and look at the seating plan. I'm aware I'm clutching at straws, but some straws are worth clutching.

The balcony seats are right at the back, but I don't think the price difference between seats is great. It's a relatively small venue, so it wouldn't make that much difference to your appreciation (or lack of it) of whatever was being performed.

I call the box office and ask if they keep records of who booked which seat at a concert that happened over two years ago. They don't, and even if they did, they probably wouldn't give out details like that to just anyone, *just anyone* being the category that I fall into.

He's got enough on his plate already, but I'm going to have to get Doug's help with this. I text him with the venue, date, and seat details.

He's going to have to hack every booking service you could have used to buy the tickets, and the accounts of the Wigmore Hall box office. And that'll be just for starters. This will cost Micha a lot of money, but I can't let this lead go, no matter how speculative it may be.

Then something occurs to me. I open a search engine and dip into YouTube, making sure I don't accidentally spend three or four hours looking at promo videos of bands I like. As always, with this sort of 'research', I have to bat away a subconscious suspicion that I'm wasting my time.

Then I get a text from Aera.

Just to wish you good luck in your work today, Mr Beckett.

Thank you. I hope you have a good day as well, Aera.

I shall. What were we talking about last time, Mr Beckett? I forget.

I think we were talking about how people can change.

Ah, yes. I think that was connected to the matter of my lingerie and the possible description of it.

I think it was.

I have to get on with my work now, Mr Beckett. Have a nice day.

You, too, Aera.

God almighty. She's terrible. I can't focus.

Where was I? Who am I?

27

CALL SHEET

I should have known better. I expected to have to spend a fair amount of time searching for videos of Kiaraa's performances, but as soon as I type her name in, there's a dedicated channel, run by her record company, which boasts over seventy-five thousand followers and contains an immense number of her performances, solo and with orchestras.

I click on the first video, a clip of her playing a Clementi sonata at the Boston Symphony Hall five years ago. Beneath are three thousand plus comments in multiple languages, all positive and glowing.

People loved her. They call her a goddess, a genius, a unique artiste. The comments run the gamut from obsessive adulation to heartbreaking grief. People saying that *they* died when she died. People wondering how unspeakable evil can exist in the world. They don't know the half of it.

She's wearing an exquisite turquoise strapless gown. Just like when I watched the Satie Blu-ray, I'm mesmerised, but I have to snap out of it. I can always subscribe to her channel when all this is over.

I type in her name once more and add 'Wigmore Hall'. The July 4th concert is there, but the clip only lasts for twenty-eight minutes. Presumably the whole thing must have been a lot longer than that, so I'm looking at edited highlights or whatever they call it in this sphere.

There are shots of the audience, but they're brief. Understandably, the main focus is on Kiaraa and her playing. Looks like they had two or three cameras on her. There's a logo at the end for the company that filmed this, or at least edited it.

As I'm watching it, I get a text from Odette Fournier.

M. Beckett. Kiaraa did not mention Principles at the Wigmore Hall concert until she came back for her encore. She said nothing at the beginning of the concert, as was usual. She only bowed to the audience. I hope this is of help to you. Mme Fournier.

So, Apollo sat through the whole concert and reimagined the speech as occurring right at the beginning so he could have a petty dig at it. OK.

'Call Sheet. How can we help you today?'

'Hi. My name's Daniel Beckett. I'm a private investigator. I need to speak to someone who was connected with the filming, production and editing of a classical music concert at the Wigmore Hall in London a little over two years ago. I found it on YouTube.'

'Um, do you know who was involved in that here?' She sounds young, and maybe not used to enquiries of this sort.

'No, I don't, I'm afraid. I thought that maybe I could pop in and have a talk with someone.'

A hand over the phone. She has a quick chat with some guy. Some guy comes on the line.

'Hey there. I'm Zac Miller. I'm the director of media services and facilities. How can I help?'

This time I hit him with the full request and my reason for asking.

'Jesus. Yeah. Well, that would have been Juliette Leonida edited that one and she's on maternity leave, but all the, er, stuff will still be here somewhere. I'm sure I or someone else can dig it out for you. When – why – why don't you come in this morning and talk me through what you want, and I'll see what I can fish out of the quagmire. Where are you?'

'I'm in Covent Garden. I can be with you in fifteen minutes.'

'OK. See you soon, Mr Beckett.'

The cab drops me right outside Call Sheet, which is in Frith Street, south of Soho Square and only a couple of minutes' walk from Pöck's place. It's a smart grey building with a blue plaque on the wall outside, noting that John Logie Baird first demonstrated television here in 1926.

There's no buzzer that I can see, so I push the door open and go inside. For a few seconds I think I've walked into the wrong place. It looks more like a club, with luxury sofas, an exotic snack menu on the wall, and a long bar serving coffee during the day and booze at night.

I don't hear a thirty-something Indian woman come in, and jump when she clears her throat to get my attention. She's looking smart and captivating in a bright red knitted mini dress.

'Are you Mr Beckett? Would you like to come upstairs? I can see you looking baffled. This is the hospitality zone. We like our clients to feel relaxed when they come here. Would you like one of the girls to make you a coffee?'

'I'm fine, thanks.' I can't see any girls. Who is she talking about?

I follow her up a narrow staircase, until we reach a padded door with a 'Suite Two' sign on it, which she pushes, then holds open for me.

'I'm Trisha Debbarma, by the way. I work with Zac. I'm the tech target director and senior post-production coordinator. Are you sure you don't want a coffee? There's a Nespresso in here if you change your mind.'

It's a modern and impressively large editing suite. No windows, orange walls, big orange sofa, grey wooden floor, recessed LED lights scattered like stars on the ceiling, and two enormous and intimidating Genelec speakers attached to the wall.

Zac Miller appears and shakes my hand. 'Zac,' he says helpfully. He's older than he sounded on the phone. I'd have put him at about my age, but he's more likely in his mid-fifties. Slight Liverpool accent. He's wearing a single-breasted black Armani suit with sky blue trainers and a black t-shirt underneath. The t-shirt says 'Roxy Music' in glittery pink letters.

'Hi. I'm Daniel.'

Our voices sound odd and flat. Must be the soundproofing.

'Come and plonk yourself down over here. Trish will sit in. Two heads are better than one.'

We sit in front of a desk groaning with three big computer screens, one an Apple and the other two HP Envy 32s. Four keyboards on the desk, and an HP Omen 30L on the floor. Next to this is an intimidatingly complex console with a couple of million multi-coloured buttons, faders, and other mystifying stuff.

This is facing two bigger screens which are currently switched off. Trisha drags a couple of seats across, and we all sit down. She crosses her legs and smiles at me. I smile at her legs. She notices and treats me to a playful eyelash flutter. Zac claps his hands together.

'OK. Obviously, I know about what happened to that musician and so does Trish. You were right not to approach the record company in the first instance, by the way, if you were thinking of doing it. You might have *not* been thinking of doing it, but anyway. They're a royal pain in the ass. You'd still be on the phone listening to light jazz or some crap. So, what is it you want? How can we help?'

This is more like it. I take the seating plan of the Wigmore Hall out of my messenger bag, which I'd printed out before I left the flat. I tell him about the concert and that at twenty-eight minutes long I believe it to have been edited.

'I'm looking for someone, possibly a middle-aged man, who may have been seated somewhere around here.' I poke the printout. 'That's Row A of the balcony. It's possible he was sitting next to a woman, but I don't know whether she was on his left or on his right. If she exists, she'll probably be younger than him.

'I saw a couple of quick views of the audience in that clip on YouTube, but they were pretty brief. I want to see if I can find a good facial shot of the member of the audience I'm looking for. Can this be done?'

Trisha frowns. 'You think the guy who murdered her might have been at this concert? Shit.'

'Shit,' echoes Zac.

'It's possible. I can't say at the moment. It's a lead I'm following up.'

Zac taps his fingers on the edge of the table. 'Well, first of all, you're right. There *was* a lot more. These sort of recitals usually last about ninety minutes to two hours with an interval in the middle. The interval can be anything from ten to thirty minutes. It all depends on how long the playing time is. Of the whole event, I mean.

'I can't remember quite why this one was edited down to twenty-eight minutes. There may have been a lot of reasons: record company request, sponsor request, something technical went wrong. We have two hours, seventeen minutes, and nine seconds unedited footage on this one.'

'We've done loads of these,' adds Trisha, 'And the camera unit would have taken a lot of audience shots that could be spliced in later on if they were needed. There would normally have been three camera people. There's probably too much of it, but that's the way they work.

'I can't remember who shot this footage, but the MO would be the same whoever did it. They tend not to film during the interval, though.' She smiles. 'Only real fanatics want to see the intervals.'

'We should do a compilation,' says Zac, grinning. '*Top Twenty Classical Intervals*, with a five-minute break in the middle so that the intervals can have an interval. Only fair after all.'

'Firstly, we'll look at the audience footage from the POV of the camera guy who did the concert footage,' says Trisha. 'If that fails, we can check the other ones out until we find what you're looking for.'

'That's great. Can we run through the file quickly and slow it down and/or freeze it when the audience is being filmed?' I ask.

'Yeah. No problem,' says Zac cheerily. 'Let's get it up on one of the screens and start from the beginning.'

He finds the file, which is called KJWH 0051. He and Trisha swap seats. He smiles at me. 'She's better at this than me. My wife always screams at me when I'm fast-forwarding things on the TV.'

Trisha puts on a pair of rimless rectangular glasses. The images appear on one of the larger screens. Incredible picture quality. She zooms through high-speed images of an empty Wigmore Hall with people walking around and doing things with Kiaraa's piano. The lighting keeps changing.

'This would have been taken when they were setting things up,' she says. 'Just a test, really. Boring. Hold on.'

Then we're at the point when Kiaraa walks onto the stage. As Odette said, no preamble, no pro-feminist speeches. She just acknowledges her applause with a smile and a quick bow and sits down. We zip through the performance at a medium pace.

'Just say "stop" when you want me to stop,' says Trisha.

'I can think of a dozen smutty answers to that.'

She laughs. 'Only a dozen?'

Then I see the first audience shot. A slow pan from left to right, lasting maybe twenty seconds. Looks like it was taken from the stage.

Trisha notes my bafflement. 'This would have been a different cameraman. They would always keep one camera on the performer. This would be a cut-in for use later on. Or not. You can just dip in and out of this stuff and pick 'n' mix. Depends on what you ultimately want to use it all for, yes?

'This shot would have been parked where it is for the convenience of the assistant editor, which was...Gary Loveridge. The cut-ins are all different and it's a bit confusing if you're not the one who was working on it. 'We've tried to standardise it in case someone is off sick, but it's like banging your head against a brick wall. Soho film guys, you know?'

'Can you tell which is the balcony?'

'Sure, but it's not in this shot. This is front stalls. Let's keep going.'

More playing, applause, playing, applause, then another shot of the audience. It's all appreciative looks, smiles and clapping from the area ten rows back from the front of the stage.

The hall is well-lit, but people at the back are more difficult to see.

We're about twenty-five minutes into the concert now, and there's a moment when the screen goes black for several minutes, followed by a static view of the audience nodding and appreciating.

Once more, we're focussed on the stalls and the first ten or so rows. We finally reach the interval and Kiaraa bows and leaves the stage. The lighting changes and we get a slow pan of people clapping.

Interval over, Kiaraa reappears in a black deep V mini dress, slashed down to the navel and revealing enough cleavage to give Apollo a rage-induced seizure, assuming he was actually there. More like a party dress, really. Some party that would be.

I have to admit, I had no idea that classical musicians did a costume change halfway through a concert, though I guess it makes sense.

I notice that Trisha is wearing Eau Extraordinaire by Clarins.

'Can we run this at normal speed for a moment, Trisha?' I ask.

'Sure. That's a fab dress she's wearing. I've never seen her before. Seen her playing, I mean. She's really something, isn't she. I'd never have the nerve to wear something like that.'

'Think of it as a branch of showbiz,' says Zac. 'Then it makes sense.'

This dress (and its wearer) get a lot of cheers and applause from the audience, which Kiaraa acknowledges with a broad smile before sitting down.

Then we see the audience again, some of whom are giving the dress a standing ovation. Cut back to Kiaraa, laughing. She knows exactly the effect she's having, and she loves it.

Then the camera zooms in to the back of the hall and we can clearly see the balcony and its occupants.

'Stop. Can we do a zoom and then a slow pan across everyone in that front row, please. That'll be Row A. From left to right. Thanks.'

I'll have twenty-two faces to look at. I was expecting the images to be blurry or pixilated in this sort of slow motion, but they're as clear as day.

I can feel my heart pounding in my chest as I focus on each audience member. One guy attracts my attention immediately – late sixties, white hair, smart suit, horn-rimmed glasses – but he's not only looking too appreciative, he has other men sitting either side of him. This could mean nothing. It may mean that Apollo's comment about the perfume of the woman sitting next to him was an inaccuracy or just a lie.

Nine faces later, I'm wondering if anything's going to jump out. Perhaps Apollo was lying about where he was sitting. Perhaps he wasn't even there. I once had a client who wrote rock music reviews and just made them up without actually attending any gigs.

Then Trisha places a hand on my forearm. 'Look. Him.'

Somewhere in his mid to late fifties. Brown hair cut short. Dyed? Nondescript black suit, white shirt, a dark blue tie with some sort of oval pattern. Running to fat. A clean-shaven, rather characterless and featureless face that you'd forget about a few minutes after seeing it.

'He's not focused on her,' continues Trisha. 'Look at the people either side. They're all looking at the stage and smiling. Every one of them. All smiling. He looks utterly nonplussed, like he doesn't want to be there.'

It's true. We watch him in slo-mo. He glances at the wall on his left, then at the stage, then at the ceiling. His facial expression is sour, inattentive. There's a young woman in a purple dress sitting on his right who seems to be with her boyfriend, her hand resting on his thigh. On his left, an older man and woman. The woman is smiling and whispering something to the man, while keeping an eye on the stage. Our boy is definitely on his own, sandwiched between two obvious couples. Trisha freezes the image.

'What's that pattern on his tie?' asks Zac. 'Let's have a closer look.'

Trisha zooms in until the pattern almost fills the screen. It's lots of tiny William Shakespeares.

'No accounting for taste,' observes Zac.

'Let's keep going,' suggests Trisha. 'We'll look at the other people on Row A of the balcony as well before we move on.'

We look at the remaining punters, but none of them really fits the bill. Trisha zooms through the rest of the recording, but that was the only time the cameraman zeroed in on the front row of the balcony and its inhabitants. The non-smiling guy is still the best bet.

OK. I'm going to go with this.

'Is there any way you can give me an MP4 of that guy as the camera moves past him?'

'Sure,' says Zac. 'We'll do you one in real time and another one slowed down. We can do you maybe a dozen decent jpegs of him as well, if that'll be of any use.'

'That would be fantastic. Would you mind if I called my email account up here? I need to get these to someone as soon as possible.'

'Of course not.'

Zac taps a lot of buttons, while I get on the phone to Doug Teng. I can feel Trisha looking at me with, possibly, amusement.

'Doug? Have you started on that job regarding the Wigmore Hall box office yet?'

'Oh, yeah. Finished it half an hour ago. You kidding me?'

'Good. Something else has come up which needs to be prioritised over that. Stick it on the backburner and take a look at your emails in a few minutes. I'll be sending you a couple of MP4s and some jpegs. I want to find out who this guy is. Have you got CompreFace or something there?'

'You think I have to buy other people's facial recognition software to do something like this?'

'OK. Sorry. Should have known. How long will it take?'

'It's a two-stage process. Maybe three hours, maybe less. Five hundred quid OK?'

'Fine. Can you call me as soon as you get anything?'

'Yeah, yeah. I was just about to call you with something else, actually. Just got a result on *A Japanese slut in a short skirt*. Those exact words have only turned up once so far, but I thought I'd pass it on as it's directly connected to your pianist lady.'

'Where did it turn up?'

'It's a review of a concert given three years ago at the Lucerne Summer Festival in the Palace of Culture and Congress. It's from a classical music blog called *Clavier*. Film of the concert was on the blog. She was playing, er, some stuff by some composer or other.'

'I'm amazed.'

'That short skirt phrase is in the comments. Are you near a screen?'

I turn to Zac and point at an HP Envy. 'Can I?'

'Sure.'

I find the Clavier site and type in Kiaraa's name in the search bar. There are three results; two of them are CD reviews and the third is the Lucerne concert. Both Zac and Trisha watch intently.

'OK, Doug. I've got the review up. Where's this comment?'

'Oh. Hang on…' Lots of fast typing. 'Thirty-four comments down. Name of Orpheus. Calls himself *a friend of the classics*. With friends like that, eh?'

An abomination. I fail to understand the fuss over this damsel, who as far as I'm concerned, is simply a Japanese slut in a short skirt, an attention-seeking carnival trickster. A cleavage-flashing charlatan. A talentless technique monster. Has it really come to this, dear reader? Has any shred of decorum totally disappeared from today's classical scene? The farms where players like this are bred should be shut down immediately!!!

There it is again: 'dear reader'. The archaic 'damsel'. The overuse of exclamation marks. The insulting idea that musicians hailing from the Far East are 'bred'.

I'm pretty certain that this is Apollo up to his tricks again, even though this appears under the name of 'Orpheus'. The Wigmore Hall piece was ten months later, so it's conceivable that at the time this was written, he genuinely thought Kiaraa was Japanese. Or it was intended as an insult. Either is possible.

'You see the connection there, Mr Beckett? I think this is the same guy as the other one. Greek mythology with a music connection again. Apollo then Orpheus, plus all the antiquated terminology.

'I should have the Apollo ID sometime today. I've fixed the broken link which is not really a broken link and I'm hoping we can find out where that review originated. Once I know that, the sky's the limit.'

'Let's hope so. Thanks, Doug. Oh. I've texted the guy at Sansuyu. He'll be in touch. Name is Baek-Hayeon Bahk.'

Zac points me to the MP4s and jpegs and I send them to Doug. I sling him and Trisha a hundred each. Or rather, I attempt to. Both wave their hands in horror.

'Oh, no no no no no,' says Trisha. 'Just helping you with this is payment enough. Imagine if you catch whoever killed that girl and we helped you!'

This makes me laugh. 'Well, if you're sure. I won't use up any more of your time. Is there any way you can email me the entire file of that concert? I may need to take a more detailed look later on.'

Zac looks at Trisha for help. 'Um, not in this format,' she says. 'It's a pro set-up called PulseFile and not suitable for emailing. What we *can* do, is convert the whole thing to a different format using CloudCatch, and *then* we can email it to you. You'd have to use CloudCatch on your computer to…anyway, I'll explain in the email. It'll take about an hour on our end, though. To convert, I mean.'

'That's fine. Thanks.' I scribble an email address on a sheet of paper and place one of my business cards on top of it.

'Is it all hi-tech like this now?' asks Zac, who I suspect would have taken the money if Trisha wasn't present. 'Was that some sort of hacker or rogue programmer you were talking to? Don't you hang around dark alleys and beat people to a pulp anymore?'

'Only in my spare time. You have to have a hobby.'

My mobile starts ringing.

'It's Scarlett. We're going to have to meet a bit sooner. How about lunch?'

'Is this a pre-date romantic thing?'

'You're relentless, aren't you.'

28

LUNCH AT THE SOAK

'Why did you ask me out for dinner the other day? Just curious.'

'I don't know, Scarlett. It just felt like the right thing to do at the time. I was compelled. I hadn't, you know, er…'

'So, it wasn't physical attraction or anything like that.'

'It may have played a part. Why did you go along with it?'

'Because lots of people ask me out and I usually decline. Perhaps I just fancied a change.'

'So physical attraction wasn't involved on your part, then.'

'I didn't say that.'

'So, it *was* involved.'

'I didn't say that, either.'

'This conversation is too prickly for me. Would you like to order? I'll just use my undeniable urbane charm on that waitress over there.'

She smiles at last. After her call, I booked a table for two at The Soak, a rather smart restaurant inside the Grosvenor Hotel near Victoria Station. Not my first choice, but it was all I could get at short notice, and she'd called me from somewhere in Westminster, so it was only a short cab ride away for her, though it turned out she'd got the tube.

I met her outside the hotel entrance at our allotted time and escorted her inside. She'd dressed differently from the other day and was wearing a tailored navy blazer with matching straight trousers, a black t-shirt and black court shoes with a bit of a heel, but not too much.

She'd looked a bit overwhelmed by this place, which I'd anticipated. It's quite an eatery: colder than I'd like, unnecessarily spacious so you can hear your voice bouncing off the walls, groovy thump music in the background, Doric columns, posh grey stoneware crockery, pine floors, luxurious blue velvety furniture, a booze-stuffed cocktail bar that looks like Christmas, intimidating menus and too many waiting staff hanging around looking at you and waiting, waiting. Smells slightly of lavender. Perhaps it's floor cleaner.

We both order luxury fish and chips (the chips triple cooked, naturally), with mushy peas and tartare sauce. After batting away cocktail recommendations, we both ask for Coke with lemon and ice. The waitress looks so disappointed I consider ordering a Vitruvian Spritz and an Aztec Sunset to make her feel better. They're proud of their cocktails here, and their cocktail menu is as big as their food menu.

'Is this the sort of place that private investigators always go for lunch?'

'Absolutely. Especially when we're trying to impress chicks.'

'Is that what you're trying to do now?'

I reach across the table and place my hand on hers. 'You're special, Scarlett. I knew it from the moment I first set eyes on you.'

She laughs and slaps my hand. 'Oh, shut up.'

Our food arrives and we concentrate on that for a while.

'Delicious. Why is this place called The Soak?'

'I think it's to do with pickling. You know. Curing, er, gherkins and meats and so on. It's one of their specialities.'

'What sort of person would know something like that?'

'A true sophisticate.'

'Thought so. And you pickle cucumbers to get gherkins. You don't pickle gherkins. They're already pickles. Some sophisticate *you* are.'

'Thanks. So, what was it you wanted to see me about?'

She purses her lips and looks downwards. 'I don't know how much I can tell you. Because...'

'Because Operation Ivory is still an ongoing murder investigation and I'm technically a member of the public. I get it. I've been in this sort of situation before, and I've found that the best way to proceed is to do a kind of subtle, erratic quid pro quo.

'You release a bit of information and I'll give you something in return. Or vice versa. Think of it as a verbal tennis match. Also, you have to remember that even though I'm not the police, I'm bound by a certain confidentiality myself and I have to keep my investigation on track, which is my first priority.

'Obviously, it may not be possible for me to give you too much information. Equally, I might give you something that you'd have to immediately act upon, and that would possibly unbalance/damage my own investigation in some way. That would include confessing to my own dubious activities, which may well be illegal.'

She grimaces. 'It's a tricky situation.'

'It sure is. You first. You're the one that called *me*, remember?'

'OK. Why did you want to know about Clement Thornton? And why did you think he might be connected to Operation Ivory?'

I finish my Coke and order another two. 'I'm assuming that you know who DS Rowan Kinnaird is.'

She nods her head. 'He was involved in that operation. I didn't work with him directly, but I know who he is. He's somewhere else now.'

'Charing Cross.'

'Really? I didn't know that. I didn't like him. He was a creep.'

'Why was he a creep?'

'He asked me out once. It was before that murder case. I turned him down. He didn't like it. Told me I was making a big mistake and that one day I'd come crawling after him, that one day he would control me and I'd enjoy it.

'A few weeks later, I was walking past him in a corridor and he accidentally-on-purpose jostled me in the shoulder as he went past. It hurt. I didn't react, of course. Big bruise. He was that sort of wanker. He's a big guy, you know? Doesn't have to act like that but he does.

'Apparently, he'd sexually harassed a couple of female police officers a few years back, but that was before I started, so I don't know if it was rumour or not. Got away with it, though, or he wouldn't still have been in the job. But I think stories like that probably stopped him climbing up the promotional ladder.

'At his age, he should be a DI or a DCI by now. He's, er, about forty something, I think. Older than Sallow, anyway. He used to hit on all the female officers when he was at Putney. No success whatsoever. His whole manner put women off, so no surprise there. Cocky, surly, and aggressive. I think he was surprised his technique didn't work on the women at the station. He used to tell them that they should be grateful for his propositions. That they'd cave in eventually.

'And I think he was behind a distressing nickname for me that started up shortly after that shoulder jostle. When something like that happens, it kind of hangs around. It's like a long-term demeaning thing.'

'What was the nickname?'

I get a long, hard look while she's deciding whether or not to tell me. She takes a deep breath. 'Tits.' She purses her lips and glares at me. 'I'm sure you've noticed why. I know it could have been worse, but it kind of puts you in your place, do you know what I mean?'

What was it Micha said about the mysterious Mr Munro? About his general tone? That he was putting her in her place by his language? Interesting. A waiter materialises and takes our plates away. The dessert menu appears.

'Kinnaird has long been the subject of rumours that he was on the take,' she continues. 'But nothing has been proved and I don't think there has ever been an investigation. There are close on forty thousand police officers in the Met and there just isn't the manpower to look into every rumour.

'My uncle was a DCI in the Avon and Somerset Police. Retired now. He said it was an ongoing problem in all police forces. And corrupt police are smart. They know how they'll be investigated. They know how to cover up. They know how to conceal or explain away sudden apparent wealth or what have you. They're careful. They know all the ducking and diving that has to be done. So...'

'OK. Um. I'm highly suspicious of Kinnaird. I won't give you all the details yet, and I have to be delicate with this as he's a cop and so, let's face it, are you.

'I scoped him out in a club that he visits, then followed him home. He was with Clement Thornton and two women who may or may not have been call girls. I broke into his house and had a look around while they were involved with intercourse.'

'You *what*? You broke in while he was actually *there*? God almighty. Are you crazy? He's a serving police officer!'

'What would you like for dessert? I think I'll have the Black Forest gateau with double cream. I'm on a health thing at the moment.' She chooses the Earl Grey Panna Cotta with mixed berries. An overattentive waiter takes our order immediately. We wait until he's gone.

'Tell me! What happened? You do realise that you could be in serious shit for this, don't you?'

'He almost caught me, too. It was very exciting. And interesting. I had a look around, went through Kinnaird and Thornton's pockets – that's how I found Thornton's warrant card – took a look at his computer and some other stuff. I gave myself ten minutes. I had a minicab waiting outside.'

'Very *exciting*? A *minicab*? Are you kidding? I don't believe I'm hearing this. Is this the sort of thing you usually get up to?'

'So, who's Thornton? What is he?'

Deep exasperated breath. 'Clement Thornton is a DCI in Economic Crime Command. I don't know if you know, but Hugh Sallow was attempting to track down that ransom payment as it was all new notes. I assisted him. Thornton was one of the people we were asking for help.

'Sallow knew you couldn't go out and spend that sort of traceable money in the shops, so he was looking into currency smugglers being involved, among other things. ECC is one of the departments you would go to for assistance. It was a long shot.'

'As far as you know, is Thornton bent in any way?'

'I hadn't heard anything. I think more slow, unhelpful, and incompetent would be more on the nose. I was being continually stonewalled whenever I tried to get hold of him or any of his staff. I'd only just become a DC at that point, and I assumed that my junior status was something to do with it. Or maybe being female. It's still a struggle.'

Our desserts are delivered. Quick service. Hers looks better than mine. She steals one of my cherries.

'But when I told you it was possible that he was connected to Operation Ivory, alarm bells started ringing and here we are,' I say. 'Why was that?'

'I just found it odd that a private investigator should turn up his name out of the blue like that *and* mention Operation Ivory. After all that time. I wondered how you could *possibly* know about him and connect him to that case.

'I'd always had my suspicions about him and his department. It was always delay, delay, delay. It was like they *could* have helped, they *could* have made it a priority, but they chose not to. It was inexplicable. I thought it was me. I mentioned it to Hugh Sallow and he just shook his head. He was used to interdepartmental shit.

'I had no proof that Thornton had anything to do with all that prevarication, by the way, but in my opinion, it wasn't totally unlikely that he was behind it. Just a gut feeling.

'After a while, we kind of let that route go, even though it's always been in the back of my mind. It can happen. We just focussed on different things. Perhaps ECC were busy with something more important. Who can tell?'

'More important than murder?'

'Well...'

'I just wondered who Thornton was. Curiosity really. As I said, I have my suspicions about Kinnaird and his connection to this case and I thought something might turn up.

'Now you've told me what Thornton does, it makes me even more mistrustful of Kinnaird. Is it possible that Thornton could have criminal contacts though his work who could move around an amount like three million?'

'It has been known. It's not exactly my area of expertise, but this is how it could be done. The bad guys have three million in new notes from the ransom. Obviously, they're going to want to spend it or invest it eventually. Basically, there are currency smugglers who would take that money off your hands, and, for a percentage, swap it for used notes.

'I don't really know what they do with the new notes after that. Not my speciality. Maybe they gradually feed the money back into circulation somehow. They have to, otherwise what's the point?

'I did read about it once, but it's very complicated. If one of those new notes turned up in your wallet one day, you could have been the twentieth, fiftieth, hundredth person to possess it. An amount like that gets dispersed and diluted pretty quickly. Then the trail goes cold. Very hard to investigate effectively.

'The other possibility is that cash is laundered, invested somewhere, and fed back to the perpetrators in dribs and drabs under the guise of some dodgy untraceable investments from the British Virgin Islands, UAE, or Singapore. Politicians and their friends and families do it all the time.

'As I said, it's complicated. It's why there are entire government departments dealing with it. But even *that* is not as fast or effective as you might imagine. Where there are large amounts of money involved, you'll *always* find corruption of one sort or another.'

'Did you know that Kinnaird and Thornton were pals?'

'No, I didn't. What made you suspicious of Kinnaird?'

'Off the record?'

She grins. 'Provisionally.'

'Well, see what you make of this lot.'

I tell her about his visit to Penny. The bolt cutters. The fingers. His proximity to the Enfield Golf Club and the mobile phone shops. I keep the multi-drug situation, the filming of his sex sessions and the photo-stalking of women in the street to myself for the moment. I want to keep him in place, not have him arrested for something like that, and it would only muddy waters.

Scarlett's eyes widen. 'God almighty. He's almost directly linked to that girl's murder. Not to mention being in on the police investigation on two different levels. We *have* to pull him in.'

'No. Not yet. I've given it a lot of thought. We – you – need more cast-iron proof.'

'We should get him in and grill him. Get the IOPC onto it.'

'I think there are more people than just Kinnaird and Thornton involved in all of this, and I think that *they* think they've got away with it. I already have my suspicions about who they might be, though I'm not one hundred per cent sure yet.

'If Kinnaird is arrested, the others may vanish into thin air. Or he'll warn them. Or he'll walk. Or all of the above. Or something we haven't thought of yet. It's just too early. It's been over two years. I'm sure we can hang on for another few days.

'And what if Kinnaird's innocent, or you can't prove anything against him? At the moment, it's all conjecture, and he sounds like a slippery character. He may have covered his tracks in some way that we're currently unaware of.

'It could blow everything apart if you let him know he's under suspicion, and it might bounce back on you in some way. You've got a DS and a DCI there. You're only a DC. If they're corrupt, they or someone else could crush you in some way.

'I think all that hedging and avoidance by DCI Thornton and/or his department when you were trying to get assistance from Economic Crime Command should give you an idea of the corruption that's been going on.'

'You sound like a paranoid conspiracy nut.'

'Thank you. The people behind Kiaraa Jeong's murder: their guard is down. It would *have* to be after two years. They think they're in the clear. They're all feeling secure. That can be exploited to our advantage.'

'To *your* advantage, you mean.'

'You're just going to have to trust me for a while and let me get on with it in my own way. I'm going to be – I *have* been – alarming them. Forcing them into giving themselves away. Making them come after me, if at all possible. Making them show themselves. I'm from the private sector. I'm not important. I can be dealt with. Once I've got some solid stuff you can act on, I promise I'll pass it on to you. Besides, you've got your own work to do, I'm sure.'

'But I can't...'

'This is an old case. Whoever's in charge of you now is not going to change your duties without some tremendous time-wasting hassle. And something like that could get back to Kinnaird in some way; you must know what the cop rumour mill is like. And when the kidnappers first contacted Micha Jeong, they told her that they'd know if she contacted the police. Could have been bluff, but we can't know for sure. Wait…' I fish my mobile out of my pocket and send her a text. 'That number is a direct line to Detective Inspector Olivia Bream at Seymour Street. You can ask her about me if you're unsure. Don't tell her what's going on in too much detail. Tell her you found me too charming to be trustworthy.'

She laughs. 'You're full of yourself, aren't you.'

'I'm sure you've got a heavy workload at the moment. Keep on with what you're doing. I think it'll be best if you don't make any conspicuous changes to your routine. The moment I can tie things up a little more, I'll let you know. If it wasn't such a delicate situation…'

'I'm going to ring this woman now.'

'There's nothing like being trusted.'

As soon as she starts using her mobile, a waiter materialises to tell her off. She flashes her warrant card at him. He reverses. I give him a smug smile.

'Hello. Am I speaking to DI Bream? I'm DC Sackville, Homicide and Major Crime Command in Putney. Yeah. Yes. That's right. I won't waste too much of your time, ma'am. I'm sitting in a restaurant with a private investigator called Daniel Beckett.' Olivia says something that makes her laugh. 'Yes. Yes, I know. It – it's The Soak in the Grosvenor Hotel. Yes – he's paying, though he doesn't know it yet. Really? Maybe next time. Ha ha. Anyway, I just wanted to know if he's trustworthy and whether I should take his advice on a case that's over two years old but has just reared its ugly head in a surprising way. I just don't want to get fired or demoted.'

She gives Olivia the briefest of outlines, mentioning how long I've been involved.

So far, so good.

The restaurant background noise abates for a few seconds, and I can hear Olivia speaking. 'Does he want you to lay off some aspect of this case until he's sorted something out, but he's totally vague about what that might be and might never tell you?'

'Basically, yes.'

Scarlett nods while she listens to whatever else Olivia is saying.

I've handed DI Bream a lot of good stuff over the last few years, which I like to think has done wonders for her career. Let's hope she passes this info on to DC Sackville.

I find I'm looking at Scarlett's mouth as she speaks and wonder what it would be like kissing her. She looks up and our eyes meet for a couple of seconds. Lovely hair. The ancient Greeks thought that redheads turn into vampires when they die.

'He seems pretty positive. Yeah. Yes. Yeah, that's what I was thinking. That's very helpful, ma'am. Yes. Quite understandable. Thanks very much. Yes. Yes, I will.'

I indicate that she should pass her mobile to me.

'Hi, Olivia. Would you like *me* to call you ma'am from now on? It'd be no trouble. In fact, I think it would be rather stimulating.'

'Shut up. I've just sold you to that poor girl, so you owe me dinner.'

'What – sold me to her like at a slave auction?'

'She should be so lucky.'

'There's a fantastic restaurant in Copenhagen called Alouette. We could go there if you like. Stay at the Nyhavn Hotel. Separate rooms, of course.'

'God almighty.'

''Bye, ma'am.'

I click her off and hand the mobile back.

Scarlett sits back and folds her arms. 'She told me that you're a really fast worker.'

'That's what all the girls say. We can never come here again after you intimidated one of the waiters like that. I hope you realise.'

'Fuck 'em. She said that I should give you a week from today to clear things up with this case and then attack it more formally. She said you'd probably let me tidy up the cadaver-strewn mess afterwards and get myself a promotion.'

'Did she mention that I was fascinating, suave and cultured?'

'Hm. She likes you, doesn't she. I could hear it in her voice. Have you had an affair with her?'

'No.'

'Sure?'

'It's just a schoolgirl crush.'

'She also said that you were mysterious and scary. I couldn't tell if she was serious or not.'

'What do you think?'

'I don't know.'

'Have you made any progress with the Citroën van yet?'

'No. But if it's any consolation, I think your idea about it being a hire or test-drive vehicle was on the nail, as was concentrating on the Greater London area. I've got one of the PNC guys onto it. Took him off his current job temporarily. It wasn't easy, but I used emotional blackmail.'

'So, when...?'

'He thinks later on today if he's very lucky. Tomorrow morning at the latest.'

'That's great. Now that we know each other a little better, do we still have to meet at Bar Termini for drinks before our dinner date?'

'Yes. I like their cocktails. I'll be off duty so I can drink. They do a magnificent Marsala Martini.'

'And a devastating Death in Venice.'

She takes a deep breath. 'I remember this case like it was yesterday. I kept it to myself, but I was very upset by it. Reading all the details. I'd never read anything so awful in my life and I still haven't. People have a general if vague idea of how they might die. But her last hours when she probably knew, deep down, that there was no hope.

'She must have thought she was in Hell. All the thoughts that must have crossed her mind. All of her achievements. All the people she must have thought of: friends, family, lovers. She could never have imagined it. Not in a million years. That this was how her life was going to end. Terrible. I'll be honest with you; I think the general consensus is that whoever did it has got away with it.'

'Sallow doesn't think that. He thinks they're insane. He thinks they'll slip up.'

'Who hired you?'

'Her younger sister, but I didn't tell you that.'

'Was she angry? Women tend to be in despair at this sort of thing. It's men that tend to get angry.'

'She was angry. She is angry.'

'And what about you? Are you angry?'

I fold my arms. 'I've discovered a lot about Kiaraa Jeong and her life in the last few days. I probably know more about her than a lot of the people involved in this.' I smile at her. 'I'm well beyond anger.'

She sits up. 'For some reason, I just started feeling sorry for the perpetrators.'

'I'll do my best not to cruelly violate their human rights.'

'Now I *really* feel sorry for them.'

29

BIG FUNERAL/MANY CELEBRITIES

On my way back to Exeter Street, I get a text from Doug. It just says:

Check your email. All generous bonuses for exemplary hi-speed work accepted. Your Korean guy called me, btw. I'm seeing him tomorrow. Funny attitude. It was as if he was talking to an enraged scorpion.

When I get in, I fire up the computer and make myself a cup of Panama Geisha. Kiaraa's photographs are still on the kitchen table. I take a last appreciative look and pop them back in their folder.

I think the bondage one was my favourite, followed closely by the grainy black-and-white one. Who did Pöck say it was inspired by? František Drtikol? I check him out online and buy a book about him. You can never know enough stuff.

There are three emails from Doug. The first one references the MP4s and jpegs that I sent him only this morning.

He notes: 'Into politics now?? This was a damn sight easier than tracking down the source of those online reviews, I can tell you that for nothing. BTW – Adamite T66 IdSoftware would still be working on this next week!!'

The material I sent him is at the top of the email. Beneath that is a row of ten photographs of the same person, some in colour, some in black and white. Most of them look recent, one or two look older. The same characterless face that I saw this morning on the Wigmore Hall video.

My heart sinks as I begin to think I've hit a dead end. This guy is some sort of minor politician. Doug has supplied a link which I click on. I'm led to a professional-looking website. At the top, it says 'Birthright'. My man, whose name is Alexander 'Billy' Carmichael, has his photograph directly underneath. Why 'Billy'? If his first name was William, I could understand it. Ah well.

I'd put his age at somewhere around fifty. Maybe older. He's attempting a charming smile which borders on the oleaginous. His hair is dyed a weird chestnut colour and so are his eyebrows. Looks like he does it himself. At least he's taken the trouble to shave his sideburns off; those are always a pain to dye, and I speak from experience.

Birthright

The dictionary will tell you that the meaning of the word 'birthright' is something to do with the right of privilege that a person has from birth, the passing on of a country's traditions, its convictions, its qualities, its values, its heritage, and its integrity. What is fair or unfair. What is good and what is bad. What is wrong and what is right.

But in this country, sadly, we have lost sight of our birthright, our inheritance. Not so long ago, we knew who we were. Everything was as it should have been. We'd got it right and we were proud of that fact. We were on target. We could congratulate ourselves. We knew what to do. So, what went wrong? Why are we drowning in the cesspit that is modern life? Why have people forgotten who they are? What their place is in the great scheme of things?

Where has respect gone? Where has plain speaking gone? Where has reason gone? Where has sanity gone? Why has our birthright been savagely snatched away from us? What did we do wrong? Why are we being punished for using plain common sense? Plain honest language? For speaking out?

Here at Birthright, we understand. We understand why you are feeling alienated, unsettled, and dissatisfied. Why you feel like a stranger in your own country. Why everything seems to be working against you. We will support you. We will help you fight back. We are determined, truthful and robust. We are Birthright.

It's no good. I can't stop myself laughing out loud. It's like some tinpot, reactionary political party from the 1970s.

Personally, I rather enjoy drowning in the cesspit that is modern life.

Not surprisingly, they're asking for donations, and there are a couple of links enabling you to send money to them. Minimum amount seems to be £5, so you can't send them 1p as some sort of sardonic insult.

If you keep on scrolling, you come to a series of photographs of 'Billy' shaking hands with people outside village halls and small companies. These have dates underneath and are quite recent, though it doesn't mention who these people are, what they do or where they're situated.

There are archived articles going back ten years. They seem to expend a lot of energy on attacking other political parties and the media and, in one case, how much noise there is nowadays.

So far, so cranky. But if you keep going right to the bottom, there are links to articles written by others that strike me as being a little more sinister.

Female academics and the distortion of facts.

Total power over women – Live your dreams!

Rape. The biggest lie.

All-male schools. The future of education.

Why Japanese women make the best wives.

Why women love conspiracy theories.

Men – how to protect yourself against nagging.

I click on *Rape. The biggest lie.* There's a list of approximately fifty reasons why women lie about being raped, ranging from general hatred of men, to being mentally challenged, to getting sympathy, to getting money, to being 'sulky'.

There's a link on the author name (Dr Colin D. Metcalfe) which I click, but it's not working, and I reckon if I tried to look him up in the medical directory I probably wouldn't find him.

Why Japanese women make the best wives. This is a pretty long article by an American called Noah Barrick PhD, who it seems is a respected academic (yeah, yeah).

It's the usual double discrimination stuff about Asian women (it gives Filipina, Chinese and Japanese women as examples) being better than Western women, as they understand how to respect and honour men and are pleased to cook and clean. Noah also says:

Women should not work. It's as simple as that. When everyone understands this, the world will be a better place.

If that's not a t-shirt slogan I don't know what is.

I open Doug's other email. The Apollo review of the Wigmore Hall concert came from a defunct online magazine called *Music & Musicians,* and it would have been posted on or around the 15th of August.

Doug hacked (with some difficulty, he added) the magazine's list of contributors. This took him to Apollo's email, which took him to another email, then another, until he got to one which was obviously Carmichael's.

Similarly, the Orpheus review on the *Clavier* site eventually took him back to that same email address.

So, when Carmichael isn't busy feeling like a stranger in his own country, he's busy trolling classical music sites under assumed names. We could look into his web activities in a little more detail, but I think this will do for the moment.

I check out Wikipedia to see if he and/or his party is mentioned there, and he has his own page. He founded Birthright a little under five years ago and is its leader.

This means that the archived articles on that website precede the creation of Birthright by at least five years. Perhaps it was called something else in the old days.

It doesn't mention who else might be in this party, apart from a deputy leader called Frederick Fernsby-Ketts aka Freddy Fernsby.

I click on his name, but it doesn't take me anywhere. Perhaps he doesn't exist. The party was registered with the Electoral Commission four years ago.

A quick scan of the page reveals much of what I know already about this guy: anti-women, anti-foreigner, pompous, ingratiating, supercilious, bitter, and rather pathetic. You feel you want to ask him 'What happened to you?' but at the same time you don't care, and would probably cruelly laugh if you found out.

I suspect he'd like to time-travel back to the 1940s, when everything was nice, apart from the war, of course, and stuff like smallpox and polio.

He's the author of three books: *England Keep My Bones!, Moaning Minnies* and *Once More unto the Breach.* Two Shakespeare-inspired titles there, but the books are not about Shakespeare.

England Keep My Bones! seems to be about the swamping of the UK by foreigners, and is intended to be jocular, and *Once More unto the Breach* is about feminism and the death of chivalry and is intended as a serious academic tome.

Moaning Minnies, again posing as jocularity with a crying schoolgirl cartoon on the cover, is a directory of women in public life whom the author doesn't much like. He's an Old Etonian and studied at the University of East Anglia, getting a degree in history.

There isn't much about his personal life. There's no mention of a wife or offspring, and his interests include philately, the works of William Shakespeare, British beer, and classical and baroque music.

Once again, I think of Jasna and her assessment of Kiaraa's murderer being a classical music fan. But this guy doesn't really fit the bill. I just don't think he'd have the guts to kidnap someone or kill them in cold blood and I don't think he'd relish the thought of going to prison for the rest of his life.

I could be wrong on all counts, of course.

His party actually stood at the last general election, and he managed to get nineteen votes in his ward. Must have been a blow.

I follow a link to a government page which shows Birthright's expenditure over the last five years. The donations were pretty good to start off with, but slowly decline. Three years ago, they only totalled a little over £2,000 over a twelve-month period. Sometimes, the party's recorded income is greater than the donation amount, but I don't really understand where this extra money comes from, and no details are given.

But Birthright's expenditure generally seemed to increase as the donations declined. When they started out, they were spending a lot less than they were being given, but now they're spending more than ever.

Where does the money come from? Can a political party get overdrawn at the bank? Acquire loans? What do they need the money for? Advertising? Paying staff? Hiring village halls? Photocopying expenses? Are they Office World's favourite client?

Now I try to apply the outlook of this guy and his party's philosophy to someone like Kiaraa Jeong.

I've read a lot of anti-female ravings in my time, and some of the many, many things that people of this persuasion (sorry, Apollo) particularly don't like is women who are wealthy, successful, intelligent, independent, attractive, and self-reliant.

They're also none too keen on these women having some sort of superior skill/talent, being able to pick and choose lovers, being elegantly/fashionably dressed and, in many cases, being foreign.

I think Kiaraa ticks all the boxes there, but I still don't know where this is going. I fire off a quick text to Doug.

Great stuff. Do we have a current address for this gentleman?

I compile all of Carmichael's reviews, the Birthright website and his Wikipedia page into a single email and send it to Aziza. I'll have to give her a call, or she may not see it in time. I just hope she's not with a patient.

'My God, Daniel. It was only two nights ago that you desecrated me. Do you crave me again so soon? Shall we perform a salacious sex tape and release it on the interweb? Or shall we just keep it to watch together on holiday? You may take the initiative. My obeisance knows no bounds.'

'Are you with a patient, Aziza?'

'Yes. But she has a rare delusional disorder and also suffers from transient global amnesia. She will remember nothing of this brief interlude and/or think she imagined it.'

'OK. I've just emailed you a couple of music reviews of Kiaraa Jeong by this guy. I've also sent you links to his political party's website and his Wikipedia page. Could you take a quick look and maybe give me a two-sentence McDiagnosis, please?'

'And what do I get in return?'

'Some strict discipline for being such a bad girl.'

'That seems fair payment. *Bisous*.'

Once more, I have to admit to myself that this case is a bit of a pain. There are a lot of tiny threads, but they're like gossamer and/or insubstantial or inconsequential and I can't get them to connect to each other. Part of it is because everything happened so long ago.

Also, I'm on day four now. This is taking too long.

So, what's the problem? Let's take Kinnaird first.

He's my chief suspect at the moment, and Scarlett certainly seemed enthused by what I told her, but the problem is that he's a serving police officer, and if he was involved in any of this he's had plenty of time to cover himself and get himself alibis, if they're needed.

And he's certainly not going to cooperate with someone like me if he can help it, and I can't corner him somewhere and get the thumbscrews out. Not yet anyway. He could even get me arrested, which I can't have.

Plus, everything I've got on him is circumstantial and conceivably coincidental. But it's all pretty suspicious, and it feels bad.

On the plus side, however, my breaking into his house revealed his connection with DCI Clement Thornton, so that wasn't a complete waste of time. But once again, I can't go and interrogate a serving police officer, particularly a DCI, without putting the cat among the pigeons.

My new pal 'Billy' Carmichael has certainly put himself in the frame, but he could just be a harmless crank, and a couple of creepy reviews don't mean that someone is a potential kidnapper and murderer. And he's a politician, albeit a small-time one.

But that's not to say that politicians can't be involved in criminal activities. It's virtually a prerequisite. And his party's financial arrangements are mildly fishy.

So, I'm keeping an eye on him. In fact, I think I'll pay him a visit as soon as Doug gets back to me with an address.

Also, I'm a little suspicious of Mathéo Fournier. I can't put it into words, but there was something not right in his response to me and my questions.

Now there could be a number of reasons for this. Perhaps I was expecting the sort of attitude he might have had shortly after the murder.

I keep having to remind myself that two years have passed and people's reactions to old crimes are different, no matter how awful and upsetting they were at the time and no matter how close they were to the victims.

Also, he's in international publishing, a patron of European classical music venues, drives a Mercedes AMG SL 65 in Firemist Red and is married to a very attractive wealthy bisexual buxom businesswoman who's a big cheese in textiles. I haven't encountered anyone quite like that before. Perhaps they're all like him.

I open Doug's third email. Now this is more like it.

Re: Fournier business account. Due to nature of business, multiple and erratic payments from all over the globe, some big, some medium, some small. Examples: Japan, Iceland, New Zealand, Italy, Argentina. But buried in there are occasional large payments from FATF blacklist countries (Myanmar, Iran) and FATF greylist countries (Senegal, Bulgaria, South Africa, Croatia).

Preliminary bonus check: this company (Fournier International) do not sell their product in Myanmar, Iran, or Senegal. That doesn't necessarily mean skulduggery. Could be some sort of subcontracting is going on.

These greylist/blacklist payments started eighteen months two weeks and six days ago. Did not occur before that time. Account and therefore business looking unhealthy/staring bankruptcy in the face a year before these blacklist/greylist payments started. Source of these grey/black payments unknown, but that's true of apparently legit deposits.

Income from all six abovementioned FATF listed countries totals £593,059 so far. Works out as roughly seven and a half thou a week. Lots of politely negative exchanges between Fournier and Coutts about two and a half years ago, then slackened after FATF payments began.

More later. This will cost you, man.

Not my speciality, but this sounds like one of the money laundering techniques that Scarlett mentioned. Could be legal and above board, of course, in which case I'll be hurt and disappointed. If it's bent, the only way it could be picked up would be through the tax people, but as long as Fournier and his accountants sling them the correct amount of money for his recorded revenue, they're not necessarily going to investigate which countries the money came from or what its source was. Payments like this would get buried in all the other international dribs and drabs. Fournier has just earned himself a tick against his name on my naughty list.

If this greylist/blacklist money is somehow his share of the ransom, I bet he resents having to pay tax on it, though if he's smart, some of the money will have been invested, so he won't lose out that much. Are Carmichael and Kinnaird doing something similar?

I find I'm thinking about Rosanna. I get my mobile out so I can take a look at the photograph I took of her. I think this is called displacement activity. It's the one where Platinum Blonde was accompanying her out of her house. I zoom in. She's actually pretty gorgeous. I may try to track her down and ask her out. It's the first time I've looked at the photographs from that evening.

The indoor ones in Kinnaird's house are really good: sharp focus, good illumination despite the dim lighting. Thanks, Doug. Even the photograph of the books in the office are really clear. Hm. One of them is called *Shakespeare: The Last Great Englishman* by someone called Graham Anthonyson. Carmichael mentioned Shakespeare as one of his interests on that Wikipedia page. And he had a Shakespeare tie. But then Shakespeare is pretty big and sells a lot of books, or so I've heard.

I'm just going to make another coffee when my mobile goes off.

'Daniel? It's Micha. I got your text. I apologise for not responding earlier. I had a *really* bad night's sleep last night. I've only just got into the office. I've got meetings all day. I just hope I don't fall asleep during one of them.'

'How was Brussels? Did you visit the Atomium?'

'Ha ha. No. But I bought you a souvenir. I think you will find it funny.'

'Really? You shouldn't have. What time did you get back?'

'About ten o'clock. The plane was delayed. I am not going to do anything like this again until I have the baby. I'm not up to it. It's exhausting. What can I help you with?'

'I just wanted to have a quick chat with you about something concerning Kiaraa. I'd prefer not to do it over the phone. I'll also give you a bit of an update on what I've been doing.'

'I cannot see you today, really. Like I said. Meetings.' Slight pause. 'On the other hand, why don't you come to my home tonight? I can cook dinner for both of us.'

'Sure. That'll be fine if you're not too exhausted. Where do you live?'

'Do you know the Skyline Tower in Southwark? It's in Long Lane.'

'I'm sure a cab driver will find it.'

'I own the penthouse. Twenty-ninth floor. Just tell the concierge that I am expecting you. He or she will call me to confirm. They are not being rude. It's just the way they do things. And don't worry; the lift is nowhere near as scary as ours!'

'Well, that's a relief. I'm still getting nosebleeds from the other day.'

'You are so droll! Shall we say eight this evening? That will give me time to have a quick nap before you arrive.'

'Eight will be fine. I'll see you then, Micha.'

'I will look forward to it, Daniel.'

I get two texts in quick succession. The first is from Micha confirming her address and the second is from Doug.

Alexander Carmichael residence: 15 Robert Adam Street W1 1AH. Handy for WED2B bridal shop and The Wallace Collection. Have fun!

I do a bit of revision on Carmichael and his works, including reading all the charming links from the Birthright website and half of the archived articles.

There are a few links from the Wikipedia page that I didn't bother with earlier, so I read them as well, until I've got the whole disconcerting mind-set roosting in my brain and can be convincingly simpatico when I meet him, assuming he's in, of course.

This takes the best part of an hour. It's all so poisonous and deluded I feel slightly depressed.

One little glitch in all of this. How do I know his address? After about twenty minutes of tedium, I find a website for an organisation called feministsRcrazy, who he gave an unhinged interview to around eighteen months ago.

As a footnote to the interview, his email, his website, and his home address are given out, though I somehow don't think it was with his permission. They probably thought they were being helpful.

I get out an A4 pad and a V5. I'm going to have to work out a little legend for myself. I don't think it needs to be too watertight, as I think Carmichael is the sort of person who'll be flattered by any sort of attention, particularly if it falls in with his general weird philosophy of life. But I could be mistaken, and I'll have to be careful.

I don't own a tie, so I'll have to buy one in Selfridges on my way there; I somehow think a tie would help. But before I start on that, I have to make a quick phone call.

I can hear lots of echo and weird crackling static, as if my call is being diverted a couple of hundred times.

'*¿Sí?*'

'Krysia? Guess who?'

Big sigh. 'Oh, good God. You are still being in the land of the living now?'

'I'm afraid so. You?'

'No. Died last week. Big funeral. Many celebrities. Brad Pitt.'

'Sorry to hear that. My condolences.'

Krysia Hodak is someone I encountered a few years ago when she'd hacked and erased all the bank accounts of a dangerous criminal organisation based in Budapest. To this day, I have no idea why she did it. Certainly not for personal gain. She may just be crazy. Anyway, they were trying to murder her, and she needed help.

She also creates fake religious websites for scamming purposes and is a person of interest to Interpol and the FBI. In short, her activities are blatantly and recklessly criminal. And often pointless. She denies being an anarchist. Wears hats with big feathers. Black lipstick. Figure like a gymnast. She has a thick Polish accent with a touch of Spanish in there that makes her difficult to understand when she's speaking English.

'So, what's the score now? Make it quick. Fifty seconds please. The Interpol jizzbiscuits are always scanning for me. Tick tick tick tick.'

I speak as quickly as I can without being totally incoherent. Krysia says *mm-hm* constantly. 'I'm going to email you some stuff shortly. I want a website set up in the next hour. Right-wing nutjob stuff, anti-women, anti-immigrant, disgruntled, fucked-up; basically, the sort of thing you'd hate.

'Make it as poisonous as you like but not too mad, not too funny. Has to be believable. Make it look as if it's been around for a few years. Chuck in a few dumb spelling mistakes and a couple of broken links. No dates, no contact details. Fairly slick and professional looking.'

'An hour? *De acuerdo.* I can find some sites to use as template. That be OK now?'

'Fine. What I'll send you is stuff by this guy I'm going to see shortly. I'll send you his Wikipedia page, too. It has to be the sort of thing that he'd like. Take ten minutes to absorb it all. Make it connect to his site. Make it not as pro-looking as his site. Apart from this job, if you come across anything about this guy that looks interesting, let me know, even if you don't have time to use it. When you've finished, text the link to this number.'

'Yeah. What are we talking here?'

'Three thousand Euros, plus another five hundred for any bonus material you may dredge up.'

'Done. You wanna fuck sometime soon? I mean, *properly*?'

'I don't even know what country you're in, Krysia.'

'S'got a big lake beginning with a G and a folk hero with a crossbow. You still in good shape?'

'Yes. You?'

'Hot as fuck and twice as noisy.'

'Email?'

'Just texted it to you. Three seconds left.'

'I'll be in touch.'

'Kocham cię skarbie.'

I click her off before they start banging on her door, which is what she's always expecting, though they (whoever *they* are this week) won't get far tracking my mobile, or hers for that matter. Then I get back to work. I make another coffee. I've got a headache. I think about Aera's swaying walk. I can't remember what day it is.

30

THE SMELL OF THE SEWER

Certainly, multiple unspecified personality disorders. Possibility of severe antisocial personality disorder (sociopathy/psychopathy). Narcissistic. Insecure. Paranoid. Needy.

Low self-esteem. Attention-seeking. Probable difficulty in interpersonal relationships. Fear of intimate relationships. Socially irresponsible. Feelings of powerlessness. Feelings of emptiness. Fear of failure. Devaluation of others. Need for dominance.

Wants/needs to be liked/appreciated. Prone to resentment. Non-specific anger. Non-specific rage. Latent/active tendency to bullying and/or abusive behaviour and/or aggressive behaviour. Difficulty in controlling anger. Prone to reckless or impulsive behaviour. Prone to exaggeration/lying. Prone to odd remarks in conversation.

Would suggest extended course of CBT (cognitive behavioural therapy) in the first instance. Perhaps psycho-sexual therapy required, though not enough information at present.

In the real world, I would give someone like this a wide berth. They could be dangerous and/or violent.

Was that enough of a McDiagnosis for you, my love? When I think of our last night together, I almost levitate with lust. You must make love to me again when I smoke. It was transcendental. I shall smoke cheap Turkish cigarettes while wearing a green wig and pink lipstick.

Call me. Castigate me. Aziza.

Bloody hell. Well, Micha and I ticked some of the boxes mentioned there, at least. I take a few minutes to memorise the diagnosis, such as it is. If you have background information like that, it can often help with the way you perceive someone and what they have to say.

And how you handle them. And how you manipulate them.

I pick up a blue stripey tie in Selfridges, put it on in the toilets so I can see what I'm doing and walk up to Robert Adam Street via Duke Street and Manchester Square. I've brought my messenger bag with me and a pair of plain glass round-eye spectacles which don't suit my face.

I've decided to call myself John Gaunt, subtly referencing John of Gaunt from Shakespeare's Richard II. It might ring a bell and make me relatable to this guy if he's that much of a fan of the Bard.

Robert Adam Street starts just across the road from the Wallace Collection and ends in Baker Street. Carmichael could have walked to the Wigmore Hall in five minutes from here.

Well-kept terraced houses, probably eighteenth century, some more recent, nowhere to park without a permit, quiet, central, tree-lined, and four tube stations within easy reach.

Before I came out, I checked the prices on a few residences, which usually have four bedrooms, two reception rooms and two bathrooms. Most are somewhere in the region of two million. If you rented one of these places, it would cost you about three to four thousand a month.

I walk past number 15 on the other side of the road and take a quick look out of the corner of my eye. Three storeys high, basement, nice brickwork, shutters and blinds so you can't see inside, and a Bentley Continental parked outside.

My mobile vibrates. My website's called The Unvarnished Truth. It's perfect; professional, but not *too* professional. Very good, Krysia. I shall take you on holiday to a country where you're not wanted by the authorities or by criminal gangs: the Kerguelen Islands or somewhere.

I cross the road, put my glasses on, walk boldly up to the front door and press the buzzer. In thirty seconds, I can hear the abrupt metallic drag of two door chains, followed by the unlocking of a Yale then a mortice. The door opens. It's him. Grey cardigan over a pale green shirt, beige slacks, brown leather carpet slippers.

He's put on weight since that Wigmore Street video, perhaps a stone or more. Fat gut. Same featureless face. Height is five seven/five eight. Substantial nostril hair. I can smell cloves, bay, bergamot; it's Trumper's Bay Rum Cologne.

The most notable difference in his appearance is that he's wearing a large black eyepatch. It's cruel, but I immediately envisage him with a parrot on his shoulder.

He looks suspicious. He narrows his visible eye, a cold smile on his face. Am I going to sell him something?

'Good afternoon. How can I help you?'

I avoid making eye contact. I look at the floor. I shrug my shoulders.

'Good afternoon, sir,' I say nervously. 'I'm awfully sorry to bother you. Am I speaking to Mr Alexander Carmichael?'

'That's me. How can I help?'

'I – I'm sure you'll think I'm terribly rude. I was going to call you in advance, but I was unable to find a telephone number for you. I found your address on the feministsRcrazy website. If it's not convenient, I…'

He relaxes slightly. 'Yes. Yes. I didn't really want them to put my home address up on their site, but it has been terribly difficult to get them to take it down. I have tried emailing them on several occasions, but they have so far not responded.'

Stern, supercilious expression. He's suspicious of me. Let's change that.

'I hate it when that happens, don't you? Just… being let down, you know?'

'It's far too common nowadays, sir.'

'And that's putting it mildly. I'll get straight to the point, Mr Carmichael. My name's John Gaunt…'

His eyes light up. 'Parents were Shakespeare devotees, Mr Gaunt?'

'Quite right. My father, really. He was an aficionado. Still is. Truth be told, I think he thought it was amusing to call me John. Not that I'm complaining!' A self-effacing smile. 'I have a lot of things to complain about, Mr Carmichael, but not that.

'Anyway, I run a website called The Unvarnished Truth. I've placed a link to your Birthright website on it, and, um, I was hoping to have a very quick chat with you. I'll *fully* understand if you're too busy. I won't waste too much of your time. After all, I did rather turn up out of the blue. I…'

He holds his hand up to stop me. 'Under the circumstances, I think I can spare you a few minutes of my time, precious as it is, Mr Gaunt.' He smirks. 'As yours so obviously isn't. Come in.'

I follow him into the house. It reminds me of Penny's place: one long corridor running all the way to a kitchen at the back with reception rooms to the right and left. And like Penny's place, the house looks and smells as if it's been recently decorated.

The kitchen has just arrived from 1952, but it's all new stuff. I watch him as he makes the tea. He's using a black Staub cast-iron teapot. I think they cost about £200. He doesn't use tea bags, but instead spoons some dark loose-leaf tea into the pot. He turns around to look at me.

'I hope you like your tea strong, Mr Gaunt. That's how I like it so that's how you're having it.'

'The stronger the better!' I reply. I don't like tea.

When he's finally finished with the preparation, he puts the pot and some white bone china crockery onto a circular bamboo tray, and we retire to the sitting room.

It's a tad oppressive. Dark brown leather furniture that matches his slippers, thick grey carpet that matches his cardigan, maroon wallpaper with a bird pattern, a creaky-looking sideboard, a print of *The White Horse* by Constable over the fireplace and a bigger print of *Flaming June* by Leighton on the wall next to the door. Smells of male sweat and that cologne in here. He needs to open some windows.

Looking out of place is a black Panasonic mini system and three Perspex CD racks. I take a quick glance at the CDs: Bach, Mozart, Schumann, Clementi, Telemann, Haydn. More Bach than anything else.

'Take a seat. The smaller of the two armchairs there. Mine is the bigger one. I'd be grateful if you'd keep that in mind. Milk?'

'Yes, please.'

'Outstanding.'

I take a sip of tea and work hard on not pulling a face. Much too strong, not enough milk, teeth being destroyed by tannic acid.

'I must say, Mr Carmichael…'

'Stop right there. I'm using *your* first name so it's only proper that you can use *mine*. You may call me Billy.'

'Of course, Billy. Thank you. Um. I was just about to say that this is a very agreeable road to live in. Very quiet, considering its proximity to the West End.'

'Indeed. And of course, the Wallace Collection is a few minutes' stroll away. Have you ever been there?'

'I haven't, I'm afraid.'

'You should visit. A couple of excellent Gainsboroughs.'

'I'll certainly make a point of it, Billy. Lived here long?'

He ignores this question and opens up a small laptop. 'What did you say your website was called?'

'The Unvarnished Truth. I – I tried to call it something that…'

'Let's have a look.' He taps and squints and taps and squints until he finds it. He turns the screen around so I can see. 'That it?' he barks.

'Yes. That's the one. Not quite as polished as yours, obviously…'

'No. It's not. And you've linked to the Birthright site on it, you say. Let me have a look. Hm. Eighth link down.' A brusque laugh. 'I'm insulted! Were you intentionally trying to insult me? Ridicule me?'

I laugh along with him. 'Nothing personal, Billy!'

His tone suddenly becomes terse, as if he's suddenly lost interest in the whole thing. 'So, what was it you wanted to chat to me about? I can see from your site that we're on the same page about a number of issues.' He flicks through the site and nods his head in appreciation from time to time. I can't wait to read the whole thing.

'I just wanted some confirmation that I was moving in the right direction, I suppose. I often feel that I'm alone in my beliefs. You always have doubts sometimes about what you're doing, what you believe in.'

He doesn't react. He just stares. I'll hand him a little more.

'My wife left me about five months ago. We were having one of those big rows that you have at the end, and I began to wonder if it was just me that thought these things. I started to wonder if I was going mad, to be brutally honest. I wondered if what I was doing with the site was actually working, or whether it was worth going on with at all. You see, I don't know many people who…'

He interrupts. 'We all have our doubts sometimes. But our doubts make us strong. And believe you me, John, we men *need* to be strong in today's questionable world.'

He rubs his hands together and leans forwards.

'What sort of a woman was your wife, John? A slut? A jezebel? A bimbo? You don't have to talk about this if you don't wish to. I'll fully understand. It's just that I'm a bit of an amateur psychologist when it comes to the so-called gentle sex, and I may be able to give you some reassurance.'

'No. No, I don't mind. She'd been working in a bookshop with some, some *women* who'd put a lot of stupid ideas into her head. A couple of years ago, this was. I suppose you'd call them severely deluded ideas.'

He looks at my site again, but nods to indicate that he's still listening.

'Five years we'd been together. Over five years. Five years and four months. She kept on calling me out for things I was saying and things I was doing. It led to a lot of arguments. All that I was saying was just common sense as far as I was concerned. Just plain speaking. The plain truth. I'm only glad we didn't have children.'

He puts his laptop down. 'Women are lepers, John. They should have a bell to ring, so we know they're coming. You were afraid she'd pass her fetid views on to children?'

I look mildly surprised. 'No. Not that. Just the, er, hassle with kids as a result of divorce, you know?'

'Financially, I assume you mean. Yes. Total lack of sympathy towards men in the courts. Always has been. Favour the mother, get rid of the father except for his bank balance. I've heard plenty of my supporters say the same thing. Once women have the baby they want, the man is no longer of use to them. Same old story the world over.

'And let me tell you something, John. The number of times I've heard of men having to pay through the nose for the upkeep of some child that isn't even theirs is *staggering*. It's an aspect of the exploitation of men that is generally ignored in the media and everywhere else for that matter. Cuckoos in the nest I call it, except it's the father who is feeding the cuckoo with his hard-earned cash.'

'I hadn't considered that, Billy.'

'Let me tell you something else, John. You are most definitely not alone with your feelings. More and more men are getting angry with how women's ideas about equality and whatnot are poisoning relationships.

'Not just relationships, but society as a whole. The job market. The professions. The media. Industry. My wife left me, as well, or so she claimed. She was not a particularly good-looking woman if truth be told, but she still had her uses, and it was a blow to the ego.'

Or so she *claimed?* Didn't she know? He takes a few sips of his tea. His hand is shaking.

'Women, John, have been pushed out of their natural state by a whole plethora of misguided beliefs. Inane, foul points of view that sound as if they've come out of the mouth of a monkey. Or a donkey. The views of a bunch of worthless trumped-up man-hating peasants.

'I know this is not a popular view among the so-called chattering classes, but it's simply the truth and I can't help that. Everyone knows it, but no one admits to it.' He brings his fist down hard on the coffee table and I worry about my disagreeable tea.

'*Everyone* is burying their head in the sand. I blame the 1960s. All I want is for everyone to be happy. I want everybody to be where they need to be. Where they belong. It's why I went into politics. But women, John, *women* want us *all* to be sad. Where's the sense in that?'

I nod sagely. 'Why did your wife leave, Billy, if I may humbly ask that? Was it the same sort of thing as me?' I think of the black balcony bra and matching strap thong that I bought for Penny.

He shakes his head. 'Not really. Some similarities, but it was different in many ways, too. She was belittling me, certainly. Telling me I was a failure. Telling me that she was not satisfied with our marriage, which was a bloody lie. She *was* satisfied with it; she just didn't realise it.

'Once more, the putrefactive poison of the 1960s raising its ugly head. Women demanding too much. Entitlement. Bad behaviour. Requests. Lack of respect. They belong to us so they should respect us. Worship us. It is our right to own them and control them, and we will not be laughed at. The media encourages them to expect all sorts of experimentation and unnaturalness as their basic right.'

'Billy – this is pushing all the right buttons with me. I can totally relate.' I think Penny will like the stockings. The site said they'd go well with the suspender belt, so I obeyed.

'Sometimes she'd come back, and I could smell other men on her. I had no proof, but I was sure of it. The foul reek of adulterous fornication. The smell of the sewer. The malodorous stench of the sexual septic tank. I put up with it for months and months. Then one night I snapped. I confronted her with her sins. I was like John the Baptist. She was shouting and screaming. Denying everything. Waving her arms around. Screeching like a bloody parrot. So, I slapped her hard. Just the once. It broke her jaw.'

'I bet that gave her food for thought!'

'It was obvious to me that she had a weak jaw. Lots of women do. It's not for nothing that they are called the weaker sex.' He looks downwards, avoiding my gaze for a moment. 'I narrowly escaped incarceration. I was humiliated.' He looks shifty. 'I – I received a suspended sentence. I lost my job. On top of that, I was in the Army Reserve. Thirteen years. They didn't want to know anymore.'

He'd finished his tea, but just before he put the cup down, his hand started shaking again and he snapped the handle clean off. 'Damn!' he says. He places the bits on the table.

'And the irony of the situation was that it was her fault. It was her fault that I struck her with such force. It was her fault that she forced me to act in such a way. It was her *fault* that I had to resort to violence to assert myself, to act like a man. All of it was her fault.

'I don't even call it violence. I call it exercising a husband's prerogative. A *man's* prerogative. Rough justice. Nothing more, nothing less.

And this is *exactly* how women are aggressive to us men. It's *exactly* how they're constantly trying to get the upper hand. It's about time we fought back.'

He slams his fist down on the table to emphasize the word 'fought'. I'd like to go now.

'If a man doesn't fight back, then he's not a man,' he continues. 'It's war, John, and it's a war that we're going to win, because be in no doubt, we are the stronger sex in all ways, and we're going to reclaim our crown, our kingdom, our birthright.'

He's sweating and shaking. I decide to change the subject before he has a stroke.

'I see you're a fan of classical music, Billy. That's quite a CD collection you have there.'

He looks at the CD racks as if he hasn't seen them before. 'Yes. Yes. But even that pleasure is being...do you ever go to classical concerts?'

'Me? No. It's a luxury I can't really afford.'

'You're well off without that particular luxury, my friend. Particularly when it comes to performers of the female persuasion. It's like going to a bloody strip show nowadays. A bloody strip show. A carnival of deep cleavage and exposed buttocks. A parade of obscene bump-and-grind artists with as much talent as a chimp banging a stick on a cardboard box.'

'I don't understand. Do they...?'

'No no no no no. I didn't mean it literally. Don't be stupid. I mean that they have no respect for the great composers. No respect for their audiences. They dress up in barely-there floozy slut dresses, so-called push-up brassieres, and parade around in gaudy whore costumes, undoubtedly purchased in some vulgar high street emporium.

'Pornographic and indecent displays are the order of the day now, I'm afraid. More brazen fat cleavage than you can shake a stick at. If I want to see women who look like that, I'll hire a well-proportioned bosomy lady of the night, not go to the Royal Festival Hall. Not that I condone prostitution. It's a threat to family values, and spreads disease.'

'Wasn't one of these harpies kidnapped a couple of years ago?' I ask. 'I seem to remember reading something about it. Or murdered, or something? My memory is not too great, Billy, and I don't really read the newspapers. They don't report the truth. What was she? A violinist possibly?'

This stops him dead. His visible eye narrows. He's starting to get the shakes. 'I don't, um, I don't remember anything like that happening.'

'Might be my memory playing tricks on me. Perhaps she was a cello player.'

He recovers. He wants to change the subject. 'You know what? After years of pandering to the so-called gentle sex, I and my followers have concluded that we don't need them anymore. It's true. They've outstayed their welcome. We can do without them and their ways.

'I'm sure you feel the same way, John. Do without the nagging, do without the denigrating, do without the delusions that they can do a man's work. They can't. Plain and simple. I'm sick of people telling me that black is white, that bad is good.

'All the energy we expend trying to be nice to them. Do they appreciate it? Of course they don't. They think we're mugs. They think we're weak. They think we're idiots. All the money we spend taking them out to dinner and buying them jewels in the hope of getting a couple of minutes of grunting out of it. And then to be laughed at? Jeered at? A complete waste.

'Frankly, John, I piss on the whole lot of them, and I'm not alone. There are many of us and the numbers are growing all of the time. I'm proud to say that I have many high-profile professionals in my party. Influential people. People who have seen the light. Doctors. Judges. Lawyers. Businessmen. Scientists. Financiers. Policemen. Priests.'

God almighty. I try to think of what John Gaunt would say to a mad outburst like this. Got it. 'Billy, I am with you one hundred and ten per cent on this. It's about time that we took back control. And wonder how we ever lost it. And how we can make sure that it never happens again.'

'You are absolutely correct, John. I can tell from your face and I can tell from your words and I can tell from your website, which I will read in more detail later. You are sincere. Sincere and trustworthy. And those are two qualities that are most certainly missing from modern life.

'Women are deluding themselves that they are in some way necessary to our lives. They are most certainly not! We don't need them in the workplace, and we certainly don't need them messing around in business and politics and the like. God help us all. And I mean that in the most literal way.'

'Yes, well, God is a man, after all, Billy.'

'Yes. Yes He is. People tend to forget that, like they've forgotten many, many other things. Short-term memories. We're all becoming like women. Flibbertigibbets. Shallow. Flighty. Ignorant. Superficial. Inferior. And I'm sure you're aware that Hell is mainly populated by women. Sometimes I think I can smell their flesh roasting.'

'I'm only too glad that there are people like you to lead the way,' I say. 'Individuals who are not afraid to stick their head above the parapet. Not afraid to go to war.'

He closes down for a few moments, as if he's giving some matter considerable, serious thought. Then he suddenly stands up, a self-satisfied smirk on his face.

'Have you heard of the term Monk Mode, John?'

'I, er...'

'It comes from our American cousins. It's about *really* being a man. It's about eliminating women from your life completely. Taking responsibility. Now some people take it too far. Have you heard of semen retention? No? I'm not so sure that it's healthy. Others think it is. But a man needs release every now and then. He needs to offload his seed, his life force. But that doesn't have to involve an actual woman, with all the criticisms, derision, and scorn that that invariably involves. There are alternatives. I call it Monk Mode with benefits. Rather amusing, I thought. Hope it'll catch on.'

'It sounds like the name of a rather outstanding article. Or a book title.'

'I don't do this that often, John, but I feel that I can place confidence in you and that you'll be appreciative. I can tell that you've been crushed by the female boot. You said your wife was a slut, didn't you?

A jezebel? A bimbo? A slattern? This will help. I want to show you the way. It'll make you feel better. Demonstrate to you that you're on the right track. That there are alternatives. Worthy alternatives. Wholesome alternatives. Quality alternatives. I'm going to show you something, my friend. I'm going to show you just how easily a woman can be replaced. Why we don't need them anymore. Come with me. I'm going to introduce you to my better half.'

Now what?

31

THE PERFECT COMPANION

He stands, walks into the hall, and goes up the stairs. I follow him, as I'm sure John Gaunt would do. His better half? Unless I'm slipping, my senses told me that Billy was the only living creature in this house.

I have to admit, I'm not feeling any fear, but I am experiencing a little anxiety.

He opens the door into a bedroom. Strong smell of his cologne and sweat in here once more, but there's another odour as well. A woman's scent. Some sort of floral perfume that I can't immediately identify.

The curtains are open, but the room is dim. There's someone lying on the bed on their side under a sheet, their back to us. A female shape. Long black or dark brown hair. I can see the slow movements of regular breathing making the sheet move very slightly.

Billy, smiling to himself, sits down on the edge of the bed and very slowly pulls the sheet down. OK. This is some sort of hyper-realistic sex doll. I can see now that her hair is jet black, not dark brown.

Her? Do I mean *it*?

Very gently, Billy touches her shoulder and rolls her onto her back, manipulating her arms and legs so that her recumbent position looks realistic.

She wears dark red lipstick, mauve eyeshadow, and a short dark green, sequinned, strappy party dress, cut low to reveal her gigantic bust.

If I had to guess her height, I'd say she was dead on five foot. There's a black wire coming out of her upper left thigh which is connected to some sort of chrome charging device. The breathing effect has to be some sort of electronic thing, maybe an extra you can pay for.

She's quite substantial-looking, if that's the right phrase, and I imagine she'd be heavier than you'd think if you tried to lift her up. Maybe that's the point. Her expression is simultaneously vacant, wanton, and submissive, her mouth slightly open, her eyes half closed.

He pulls the dress down a couple of inches to protect her modesty. Before he did that, I could see that she was wearing a black thong. He turns to me and grins.

'This is Poppy, John. To say that she has the advantage over bothering with a real so-called woman, would be an understatement. Touch her skin. Anywhere will do.' He sniggers. 'I'm not the jealous type.'

I lean forward and place a hand on her forehead, as if I'm a doctor. She's warm. A little warmer than normal body temperature, but not by much. I nod my head in some sort of wonder/understanding/appreciation hybrid.

'I can see you're interested, John, so I'll tell you. Her body temperature and her simulated breathing are controlled by a chip. Marvellous technology. She's on charge at the moment, as you can see, but both those effects can last for up to four and a half hours. See the little red light on that charger? When she's fully charged it'll become green.'

I instruct my brain to come up with some sort of response. My brain lets me down.

'She's beautiful, I'm sure you'll agree, John. And has a fantastic, desirable figure. I've always hankered after women who are on the ample and voluptuous side, and Poppy certainly comes under that category. How much do you think she cost? Go on. Have a guess.'

'I've really no idea, Billy. Er, £400?'

He snorts derisively. 'My goodness! Try £3,700. Poppy is from the Goddess of Love range made by Queen Consort of Hong Kong. I don't know if you saw it, but I put a link to them on my website and I would suggest you do the same.

'I'll be honest with you, I find the company name Queen Consort a little tasteless. Offensive, even. I've written to them with some other suggestions, but to date have received no reply.'

He flashes me a man-to-man smile. 'I know some people would find owning one of these beauties a little strange or eccentric; I would have thought it strange myself once. I would have laughed at someone who'd told me they'd purchased one. I would have jeered at them. I would have ridiculed them until the cows came home.

'But the reality of synthetic companion ownership, especially a synthetic companion of this calibre, is a whole different experience, a whole different ball game. Plus, ownership fits in nicely with the Birthright philosophy, as I'm sure you'll agree,' he laughs. 'You women don't want to be nice to us? Well, we'll damn well find a woman who will! No more bottom-feeding for plain Janes with multiple so-called mental depression problems who think they're better than you.'

'I can completely see that. This is a slap in the face and then some.'

'Absolutely. Poppy isn't needy, she doesn't have stupid opinions, she doesn't have non-existent mental problems, she's not disgustingly promiscuous, she won't make false rape claims and she's remarkably desirable and seductive. Her skin is made from the best silicone on the market; soft to the touch, convincing human appearance. She has gel filled breasts and you can choose the areola size and colour.

'Obviously you can choose the breast size. That goes without saying. Poppy here is a 50L. You can even choose to get her nipples pierced, but I wasn't too keen on that. Too kinky. I am most certainly not a pervert or degenerate. Her thigh girth is 23 inches exactly. Meaty.'

He strokes her hair. 'I'm sure you've already noticed, but this is genuine human hair. I often wonder where they get it from, but it doesn't say anything about it on their site.

'I suspect that there are professional hair growers who sell their hair when it's long enough and then let it grow back again. I find the idea that such people exist rather charming, don't you? It's as if it's an ancient craft that has been sorely neglected in today's world, rather like orrery-making or blacksmithing.

'You can also choose from six different eye colours, four skin colours and she comes with an oh-so-vital repair kit. Three vaginal options, six vulval options, two anal options and a free cleaning kit and lubricant gel are provided. You can buy more lubricant gel from their website should you run out, which I have on many occasions, I'm proud to say.

'Pubic hair is optional, as is armpit hair, but should you require either of those components, then there are different colours and designs to choose from; thirteen pubic hair varieties and six armpit hair options.

'The skeleton is metal and lasts a lifetime. Wasn't sure about that at first, but it makes her have a convincing weight, and the manipulation into different positions is fluid and remarkably easy.

'The weight, however, can make it rather difficult to move her from one room to the other. For example, if I wanted to take her in the kitchen, to *have* her in the kitchen, I mean, getting her down the stairs can be rather awkward and tiring.

'But the pros outweigh the cons, believe you me. Just occasionally, she seems to catch my eye, and it's a spine-tingling moment. I can tell you, hand on heart, without any shame, that sex with Poppy is the best sex I've ever had. She makes me feel like a god. And she's grateful for it.'

He must talk to a lot of people about this. Perhaps he has friends who own similar items. If it was me, I think I'd probably keep all of this to myself. But he's relaxed about it, has nothing to be ashamed of, and doesn't realise anymore how unusual it is. Fair enough, I suppose, and it is part of the Birthright philosophy in a way. What did he call it? Monk Mode with benefits?

I note that he's constantly up and down; friendly one moment, then hostile and aggressive the next, as if he's trying to suppress an underlying anger and failing. Definitely chimes in with Aziza's assessment.

'There are speaking models,' he continues. 'But I didn't want that. Not me. One gets enough yammering away from real women. She does moan, however, and her moan is sweet, like the wind in the trees, like the mewing of a kitten, like the waves on an autumn day.

'We have had some great fun, Poppy and me. Up all night sometimes. Things can get pretty vigorous, pretty lusty. Lipstick having to be reapplied frequently, if you get my gist. I can do things with her that my ex-wife would never have permitted, believe you me. And no complaints if you get my drift. And certainly – *certainly* – no fear of her straying. No extracurricular hanky-panky, as it were.

'There are no limits to what she'll do. It took me a while to personalise her if that's what it can be called. Don't favour that word myself, but there it is. A lot of thought had to go into it. Her surname is Windsor, out of respect to the royals, and her middle name is Virginia, to venerate her virtue. Poppy Virginia Windsor.

'She is twenty-two, a senior secretary to the director of a top newspaper, and she needs to be carefully and sensitively wooed before she bestows her favours upon one. She is also a keen horsewoman. And here's the icing on the cake.'

He walks over to a wardrobe and opens the doors. It's full of Poppy's sexy clothes, lingerie and shoes, but on the top shelf there are a selection of wigs and two different heads. One of the heads has pointed ears, like an elf. The other one has Japanese features. He points at the heads.

'Every man fancies a change every now and then. May I introduce you to her Royal Highness Lobelia Craven. She is an elven princess of great nobility, an ardent necromancer and mistress of the sword. And this is Miss Hatsuko Okamoto, she is a very, very senior air hostess for Japan Airlines, and it is her first job. She is a keen practitioner of *kintsugi*.'

He opens another section of the wardrobe. There are clothes in here that must belong to Lobelia and Hatsuko; some medieval-looking warrior clothes, including helmets and swords, a couple of air hostess uniforms and a pink kimono with a white crane pattern, which actually looks quite nice.

'Both have different tastes from Poppy, sexual tastes, and they can be quite outrageous at times. They're a little too much for me sometimes if truth be told, particularly Lobelia Craven.

'Hatsuko is a tad gentler and submissive, though she does have a wild side. I like to think it's her samurai spirit manifesting itself. When that happens, it can actually be quite frightening.

'The heads can be removed and replaced very quickly if you desire more than one woman in a single session. They are aware of each other, but, thankfully, envy is entirely absent. That's another quality in a woman that I can't abide – jealousy. Jealousy, vindictiveness, and spite. Come on, let's go back downstairs. Oh. Wait.'

He opens a drawer next to the bed and produces a small book, which he hands to me. It's called *The Queen Consort Guide to Sexual Intercourse*. I flick through it. It's full of illustrations of sexual acts and various sexual positions.

There's also a chapter called 'Love Talk', which contains an extensive list of things you might want to say to your Goddess of Love when you're enjoying thorough and fulfilling coitus with her, as it says here.

These conversational gambits are subdivided into 'romantic', 'saucy', 'adventurous' and 'dirty'.

'This little tome comes in handy more frequently than you might think, John. I thought I wouldn't need something like this. I thought I was too much of a man of the world, but I was mistaken. It's opened a whole new world up for me and it's never too late to learn something new. Take it down with you. Have a browse while I'm in the kitchen.'

He leans over and kisses Poppy's shoulder. She doesn't seem to notice. We head downstairs.

I read the chapter entitled 'Forbidden and Fantastic' while he makes us another cup of strong tea.

'I'm glad to be able to share my interest with you, John, and I can recommend the Goddess of Love range wholeheartedly, particularly to a man such as yourself who has been a victim of the female scourge.'

He sits down at the kitchen table. 'I can imagine that all of this would have seemed a tad crazy about fifty years ago, but I'm glad to say it's quite normal now.

'A friend of mine who had sadly lost his wife to Lyme disease bought one of the Hot Housewife range. Her name is Bronwyn. Welsh, you see. Very buxom. *Very* buxom. Fond of see-through nighties, I understand, and she possesses some very saucy underwear and several high-class evening gowns.

'She sleeps on the side of the bed that his poor suffering wife slept on, and sometimes wears some of her clothes, so you see it's not all about sex. It can also be about affection. She is his life companion, and they do many things together outside the bedroom, such as watching television, though he has yet to take her to the cinema.

'I have not mentioned this to my bereaved friend, but I find his Bronwyn very attractive. Now under normal circumstances, this would be something that you would let go, but – and I can see you're already way ahead of me, John – in this case, it would be possible to buy a companion identical to Bronwyn and have one's wicked way with her as it were, pretending that it was the real Bronwyn you were copulating with to add a bit of spice to the proceedings. Forbidden fruit and all that.'

'The possibilities seem endless,' I say.

'You should think about investing in one of these, John. Believe me, whoever you choose will work her way into your heart, and your ex-wife will soon be a distant memory.'

'I may have to have a discreet word with my bank manager, Billy.'

He winks at me. 'And the best thing of all, John, is that I was Poppy's first!'

I drink some tea to avoid having to talk. It's going to take a while to process all of this. Billy, now he feels he knows me a little better, rants and rants about almost every subject under the sun that pisses him off. Women, particularly feminists, come in for a lot of unhinged criticism, but also people who don't originate in the UK.

Women who don't originate in the UK are beyond the pale, obviously, as are women in top jobs. How this squares with his synthetic sex pals I can't imagine, two of whom could be described as foreign, and you could claim that all three are in top jobs (though for Lobelia Craven it's more like a royal duty).

Then he goes on to contradict himself further with his views about women from the Far East; how they make superior wives, how they're more submissive, how they're better than Western women who have been 'spoiled' by progressive and noxious views, how they know how to value men properly and will cook and clean and all the rest of it.

This sounds as if he's almost quoting verbatim from that link on his website. What was it? Why Japanese women make the best wives?

This would explain the presence of Miss Hatsuko Okamoto upstairs (or at least her head), but not necessarily her sword-wielding Royal Highness Lobelia Craven or senior secretary Poppy Virginia Windsor.

In fact, his whole conversation is peppered with barely-thought-out discrepancies like this. I don't know if he's had a great deal of media exposure, but any half-competent interviewer would tear him to pieces.

I'm pushing him this way and that. He tells me that I'm actually quite a good-looking chap underneath the specs, and my marital problems were probably more to do with my personality than my looks. Well, that's always good to know.

A couple of times, despite him trusting me enough to be introduced to his vinyl harem, I catch him looking at me with something approaching suspicion. Something is telling him to be wary of me, but he can't put his finger on what it is.

This is good. Cage-rattling can sometimes be subtle and manipulative.

Occasionally, I'll disagree with him in a way that he obviously doesn't like, and he becomes quite overbearing and obnoxiously bossy, but we seem to be parting on good terms, and I promise to do all I can to support Birthright.

I decide to ask him about the eyepatch.

'Is that a stye you have under your patch, Billy? I know from experience that they're very hard to get rid of. I found using a warm compress finally got rid of mine if that's any help.'

He looks uncomfortable. 'A stye? No. Not a stye. I have lost my sight in that eye. A misfortune.'

'Oh, I'm so sorry. I…'

'Think nothing of it. Anyway, it was nice to meet you, John, and very satisfying to meet someone I've inspired. From the look of your website, and from what you've said, I think you're definitely on the right track with your opinions and assertions. Do not let anyone tell you otherwise! I shall link to your site and put you on Birthright's mailing list post-haste. I hope I've been able to help and do look into purchasing one of these vinyl companions. It'll be the best decision you'll ever make.'

'I'll be sure to, Billy. And thank you for the tea. Oh! I just remembered. That classical damsel who was murdered. She wasn't a violinist or a cellist. She was a piano player. Can't remember her name, though. The old memory playing up again.'

'Can't say I recall that, John.'

'Ah well. Never mind.'

We shake hands. He closes the door behind me.

Just as I'm binning my tie, I get a text from Scarlett. It's quite a relief to have some sort of communication, no matter how brief, from someone hailing from the world of sanity.

I think we just found the van.

32

UNCHARTED TERRITORY

I call her immediately, waving away a cab that I'd just flagged down in Bentinck Street. The driver tuts, shakes his head, mouths 'prick' and drives off.

'So, is this three desserts I get now, Mr Beckett?'

'I wouldn't want you to lose your figure, DC Sackville.'

'What would you know about my figure, Mr Beckett?'

'Nothing much. Just a casual, disinterested observation or three. Maybe four. OK. Five. Eight.'

There's a smile in her voice. 'I *certainly* didn't notice *that*. OK. First of all, I handed this job over to a computer guy called Farlan who works for PNC. Did I tell you that? He owed me a favour; you owe him a pint.

'I gave him the details of the case and what we were looking for, so he discarded your advice about going back six years and went back one year before the drop-off instead.

'He did, however, think your hunch about a test-drive vehicle might bear fruit, so he went for that first. If it didn't work, he'd just have to backpedal and start all over again, looking at van rental places as well. He spends most of his time with financial cybercrime, so this was like a holiday, he said.

'He made a list of all dealers in the Greater London area who sold new Citroën vans. Then he narrowed it down to dealers who took delivery of white Citroën Relays over that one-year period. There were seventy-three of them.

'He hacked the records of each of those dealers, checking for extended test drives that were taken in the seventy-two hours leading up to the ransom pickup in Elder Street. Dealerships *always* keep their test-drive records. Test drives can often be for an hour, but extended test drives can be for twenty-four hours or even forty-eight hours.'

'But what if…'

'Shh! Someone took out one of these vans for a forty-eight-hour unaccompanied test drive two days before the ransom drop-off. That was the only instance in that time window. None of the other test drives came close. It was from a Citroën dealership in Battersea called Falcon Commercial Auto Sales.

'The woman I spoke to remembered it because the only van they had available on that date had been in a minor accident a few days before and the left rear bumper had been pranged. Remember what your Korean guy said about that damage?

'Now that wouldn't have made much difference to the test drive itself, and was hardly noticeable, but for appearances' sake, they fixed it up temporarily with some sort of repair gunk. She did it herself. She said it wasn't a great job and you'd probably still notice it if you were standing behind the van.

'The van was sold twenty-two months ago to a hire place called Hatcham Cars in New Cross. Luckily, they still have it. I've already sent a couple of officers out there to bring it in for forensics to take a look at.

'Before you panic, I didn't tell anyone why I wanted it looked at. There'll be paperwork eventually, but I reckon I can hold off on that for six or seven weeks. May be a waste of time, but…'

'Brilliant. Do we have the name of the person who did that test drive?'

'Name *and* address. Mr Brian Colbert, 42 Brookfield Crescent, London SW15 3DE. That's Putney, off West Hill. I think it's just a coincidence that it's in the same area as the police station, but, of course, it may not be. Assuming he still lives at that address, I'm going to pay him a visit tomorrow morning.'

'No, Scarlett. Don't. Let me do it. It's the same as the Kinnaird situation. A police enquiry at this stage may not have the consequences you'd want. If this guy is involved in any serious way, an official visit may freak him out, and then we don't know what he might do or who he might talk to or how it might backfire on you.

'Text me his name and address and anything else you may find on him in the meantime. If a visit bears any fruit, I'll call you tomorrow morning.'

I can hear her exhale impatiently.

'OK. But no hanging him out of the window by his ankles.'

'You're no fun, Scarlett.'

* * *

'Hi, Daniel. Do come in. I'm so pleased to see you.'

Micha and I kiss each other's cheeks like we're suddenly old friends. When did I see her last? Three days ago? She's wearing a beautiful sleeveless fuchsia pink maternity dress with a knot front and an alluring V neckline. It's quite short, perhaps three inches above her knees, and the thin material sways and flows when she walks. Deep red lipstick, and pink eyeshadow which matches the colour of the dress. On her feet, a chunky pair of white sneakers with Suecomma Bonnie in gold letters on the top of the tongue. These make her look taller than she seemed the other day.

She has an unusual silver necklace around her neck, made up of small, oxidised beads that are all slightly different sizes, plus earrings to match. She sees me looking at it.

'It's unusual, isn't it. The necklace. Beautiful. It belonged to Kiaraa, as did the earrings. It's by Georg Jensen. The range is called Moonlight Grapes.'

A different perfume today. Not Rose D'Arabie anymore. This is less flowery: musk, amber, vanilla orchid, possibly Ellis Super Amber. Sexy.

'They look great. They really suit you and suit the dress. In fact, madame,' I smile at her, 'You look stunning.'

Wide smile. 'Thank you. That is nice to hear. Have you ever been to the Jensen shop in Copenhagen? Or are men not interested in Scandinavian design?'

'Funnily enough, I have. Four years ago, now, I think. I was there on holiday.' Or something. 'It's across the way from the Stork Fountain.'

'That's right. Oh! Before I forget.' She walks towards a side table and picks up a small package. 'Here. For you. A souvenir of Brussels. It is not expensive. I hope it makes you laugh. I bought Baek-Hayeon a limited-edition bottle of Tripel Karmeliet beer. He is a big beer fan. And a Miglot scent diffuser for Aera.'

I unwrap it. It's a box of champagne chocolate truffles from the Manneken Pis Chocolaterie in Rue de Chen 2, Brussels. The Manneken Pis is the famous statue of a little boy pissing, and his image is on the side of the box. She's right, it does make me laugh.

'Thank you, Micha.'

'They say that Belgian chocolate is the best in the world. I shall have to steal one of those later! Come on. Let us go into the living area. Ah!'

'Are you OK?'

She places a hand on her lower back. 'Lots of strange aches and pains now. My body seems to have a life of its own. It sometimes feels as if it's out of my control. Some very odd changes. But some interesting and unexpected ones, too. Most intriguing. But I have accepted my pregnant body now, with all that entails.'

On my way to the Skyline Tower, I let the meeting with Carmichael sink in. He didn't give me anything incriminating, but then why would he? His attitude was strange and not a little disturbing, but then I already knew that from his concert reviews and his website.

But he's normalised his eccentricities, otherwise he wouldn't have confided in me so readily. Or maybe he just wanted to talk. He was occasionally difficult to read; sometimes he seemed suspicious, sometimes accepting and friendly.

Is he the sort of person who would arrange or participate in a kidnapping? Once again, I can't see it.

What about if someone else suggested it to him, dragged him into it? Still difficult to imagine. I'm keeping his odd outlook on life and apparent wealth in mind, though.

Like Kinnaird, he's living in a place which could be beyond his means, and both men seem to have a lot of disposable income.

And there's the Shakespeare link, which is tenuous at best. Plus, of course, he didn't like Kiaraa Jeong very much. But as my good, un-cynical conscience is telling me, so what?

I didn't think it was a good idea to discuss it, but I did wonder where he got his money from, and money he most certainly has. There was no mention on his Wikipedia page about a job, an inheritance or any other type of financial support, and the donations to his party have been declining over the last few years. But the expenditure had increased, as had the recorded income, and once again I wonder where that money came from.

Scarlett mentioned a number of ways that three million could be filtered back to the people involved in all of this.

In Carmichael's case, for example, he could be paying off a mortgage on that house from interest paid to him every month from some dodgy investment company in the Cayman Islands or wherever.

If Carmichael had told me he was about to go on holiday, I'd burgle his house tomorrow night and see if I could pick up a credit card or some of his bank details and do a Fournier on him. I still might do it. I'll just have to make less noise.

I also texted Doug Teng. I wanted to know if Carmichael had been admitted to any hospital in London over the last five years and, if so, what he was in for. I'm curious about him losing the sight in one eye and want to know how and when it happened.

When the cab pulled up outside the Skyline Tower, a uniformed security guy came out to open the door as if it was a top-of-the-range hotel.

'Blimey,' said the driver as I paid him. 'Who're you visiting here? Some movie star?'

'A royal personage,' I replied. 'I can't tell you any more. I'm sure you understand.'

'Ha ha. Yeah. Sure. Been there myself.'

'Nice evening, sir,' said the security guy as he escorted me into the building. I nodded my head in agreement.

The reception area was about the size of a football pitch. The woman behind the counter flashed me a dazzling smile. 'Good evening, sir. My name is Aubrielle. How can I help you this evening?'

'I'm here to see Ms Micha Jeong.'

She looked down at something. 'Mr Beckett?'

'That's right.'

'One moment, please.' She stared at me and held an index finger in the air while she made a call. 'Ms Jeong? Mr Beckett is here for you. OK. Yes. Thank you, Ms Jeong.

'That's the twenty-ninth floor, Mr Beckett. The penthouse suite. Osman will escort you.' She nodded at a guy of about twenty that I hadn't noticed. I braced myself as the lift took off, but as Micha said, it wasn't a patch on the scary Sansuyu one, plus it was playing a muzak version of "Kids in the Dark" by Bat for Lashes.

* * *

'Well, let me know if the strange aches and pains become too much for you, Micha. I'll send out for a massage therapist. My treat.'

'You would not offer to give me a massage yourself, Daniel? I am disappointed!' There is laughter in her voice.

'Damn. I left my sweet almond oil at home.'

'Maybe another time. I will hold you to it. I like patchouli and jasmine oil by Charbonnier. Very sensual. I have a bottle in the bathroom, but it has not been opened. I am so busy that I do not have time for such luxuries.

'I am trying to cut down on my work a little, but it is difficult. I'm giving a talk at the Mermaid London the day after tomorrow. In Blackfriars, you know? In their auditorium. Nine-thirty. Much too early! Four hundred people or thereabouts, but at least it won't last long. I am only speaking for an hour, then others will take over.

'It concerns our new smartphone, the Crystal D3. It has five kill switches. Vault-like security. I don't want to do it, but it was arranged seven months ago, and it's been in all the papers over the last couple of days. Look.'

She points to a copy of *The Daily Telegraph* which is draped over the back of a chair, and there she is on the front page, her photograph next to a headline reading 'Sansuyu Launch Innovative Smartphone'.

'As I said, I am going to wind down the work I do after that. I'm feeling too tired now. I slept for two hours before you arrived this evening. I didn't mean to sleep for so long.'

'Sorry – I'm still thinking about the patchouli and jasmine oil massage.'

'Perhaps I should open that bottle!' She laughs. 'I'm sorry. I am putting risqué thoughts into your head. Sit down, Daniel. I just have to go and check something in the kitchen zone. I hope you like South Indian cuisine. I'm afraid I'm doing that weird pregnancy thing where you eat unusual or unfamiliar food. I won't be long.'

I sink into a soft grey sofa that could seat five and take a look around.

As is usual with penthouse suites, the view is breathtaking, despite being about fifteen floors lower than her office at the Sansuyu building.

A place like this would cost many millions, quite apart from payments for the maintenance, gym, pool, security etc etc. She referred to it as her home when I called her, so I assume she owns it, though it might be Sansuyu in some complex, convoluted way.

It's pretty much open plan apart from the bedrooms and bathrooms, and I can see Micha talking to herself as she prepares food in the kitchen and dining area. Already, a delicious, spicy smell is beginning to make my mouth water.

All the furniture is cool and minimalist, in a style that I think is called Japanese Modern, and all the floors are grey stone which is flecked with veins of dark red. There are many thick, white fur rugs scattered around, similar to the ones in her office.

Where a fireplace might have been in the olden days of posh penthouse living, is a gigantic television screen, though there's no sign of any associated tech like a satellite box or Blu-ray player. I'm sure she's well past owning any of that sort of primitive stuff.

There are, however, two large remotes on the coffee table which are like miniature works of art: bright white, each adorned with the Chinese dogwood branch and its accompanying yellow flower.

There's a month-old copy of *Vogue Korea* on the sofa, which I pick up and flick through. Looks basically like any other *Vogue*, with ads for Tiffany, Zadig&Voltaire, Chanel, Yamaha golf clubs, Recto, Graffe, Johnnie Walker whisky, Leonard of Paris and ba&sh, but the models are mostly Korean and so is all the text, except, strangely, many of the article headings, which are in English.

There's a whole spread of a pregnant model wearing a variety of bump-revealing designer clothes and expensive-looking jewellery. Couldn't-care-less expression, minimal makeup, long braided hair.

I stand and walk slowly around. There are three enormous abstract paintings on one of the walls, spectacular explosions of colour. They're overwhelming, and I have to take several steps back to really appreciate them. Micha appears, standing by my side and grinning. That perfume's too much.

'You like them? They are called gunpowder paintings. They are by Cai Guo-Qiang, a Chinese artist. He uses gunpowder as an art medium, even igniting it on the canvas with different pigments.

'He creates gunpowder events or happenings with fireworks. I saw one in America three years ago. It was marvellous. These paintings are a very good investment.' She giggles. 'Do I sound terrible? I really do like them.'

'You have excellent taste, Micha.'

'I saw you looking at *Vogue*. Did you see that shoot with the pregnant model? Great clothes. Shows you can be pregnant and sexy at the same time.'

'I never doubted it for a moment.'

'I read an article about sex during pregnancy just the other day. It said that twenty per cent of women discovered orgasm for the first time while they were pregnant. Isn't that remarkable?'

'It was me that did the research.'

'Were you paid well?'

'I waived my usual fee.'

Another wide smile that turns into a laugh. 'Shall we sit down? I have made fish mappas. It is a coconut fish curry. And black pepper goat curry. I will put the dishes on the table, and you can take what you wish. There are dosa and vada breads, appams, and a few dips, as well. It *will* be spicy.

'I have made a sort of banana porridge for dessert, with cardamom, jaggery and cashews, but we may be too full to eat it when the time comes. I think I made too much. Apparently they eat the desserts first in southern India, but I think if we did that in this case, we would leave most of the main course, which would never do.'

For a second, I think it's my imagination or my failing eyesight, but the lighting here has imperceptibly dimmed and become warmer, softer, creating a seductive and intimate atmosphere; romantic, even. And now there's discreet background music; some sort of ambient/classical hybrid. I didn't see Micha touch anything, so I assume all of this was programmed in advance. Interesting. She doesn't react; her expression is one of studied nonchalance.

'Would you like some champagne? I texted my doctor earlier on. I have not drunk alcohol since my pregnancy started. She said that it is best not to drink alcohol during the first three months, but as I am beyond that now, and am healthy, I am allowed two glasses. Come on.'

We sit down and start to eat. I can feel perspiration forming beneath my eyes from the food and wipe it away. I take a sip of the chilled champagne. It's a Taittinger rosé.

'I have another bottle in the refrigerator. You look like you may need it!'

'It's certainly a spicy dish.'

'Unless it is *me* that is raising your temperature.'

'It's either you or that dress. Or a combination of the two.'

'Oh, really? Why is that?'

'I can't bring myself to tell you.'

'Perhaps you should.'

'I'll certainly consider it.'

'Don't leave it too long, Daniel. Evenings do not last forever. Have you ever heard of the Korean word *inyeon*?'

'I don't think I have.'

'I may explain it to you later.'

She clasps her fingers behind her neck and rocks slowly from side to side a few times. She's a demon in human form. I can hear soft, dull clicks as she moves. She really does need a massage. Her expression becomes serious. 'You wanted to ask me something about Kiaraa. And then you must tell me what you have discovered in the course of your investigation so far.'

'I'm not going to tell you everything, as some of it is uncertain, and it changes from day to day. Hour to hour, even. I don't want to get your hopes up too much. But I'll tell you why I wanted to see you and we can take it from there. If what I say starts to upset you, just tell me and I'll stop.'

'Of course, Daniel. Thank you for your sensitivity.'

'Kiaraa had some erotic photographs taken of herself. I managed to track down the photographer. His name is Florian Pöck and he's pretty famous. He took the photographs for some of her CD covers and the Blu-ray you gave me. He is the mystery man you were telling me about. Kiaraa was having an affair with him at the same time she was seeing Odette Fournier.'

'I see.'

'I found prints of these photographs when I was looking around her house. They were in a hidden compartment inside a bureau. But there were four missing. I wondered what had happened to them. Pöck managed to identify the missing photographs. They were certainly the most prurient. She wanted these prints done so that she could give them to a friend, and it seems as if those four were the ones she picked.

'I assumed that friend might have been Odette Fournier, but she didn't know anything about them and had never received them. What I wanted to ask you, was if there was another serious or semi-serious lover around at that time. Someone she might have sent photographs like that to. Someone you might have forgotten about or didn't mention for some other reason.'

'Can I see the photographs?'

'You sure?'

'I am not a child, Daniel. And I am familiar with erotic art of many types, photography included.'

I find the file on my mobile and hand it to her. 'The first sixteen are the ones I found in her house. The sub-file labelled KJExtra contains the four that were missing, that I'm assuming she sent to someone.'

She inspects them all for about five minutes, sometimes serious, sometimes smiling, sometimes laughing. 'You still have the prints of all of these photographs? Apart from the missing ones, that is?'

'Yes, all 10 by 13 inches. Pöck sent me some prints of the missing ones, too.'

'I should like to have them. I assume you did not bring them with you.'

I shake my head. 'So. Those last four. Do you have any idea who she might have sent photographs like that to? Pöck said he gave them to her two or three months before she died.'

'No. I would have known if there was someone else at that period in her life. She would have discussed it, even if there were no names given. She would have known I'd be interested and intrigued. Presumably this photographer still has these photographs on his computer.'

'He does. But he said he would never do anything with them, and I believed him. He was profoundly upset by her death, I think.'

'I would like to meet him when all of this is over. What's he like?'

'In his fifties. Austrian. Good-looking. Intense. Garrulous. A wit. He has truffle-flavoured crisps delivered from a shop in Rome.'

She smiles. 'Did he ask about me?'

'Yes. He wanted to know if you were as beautiful as Kiaraa.'

'And what did you tell him?'

'I told him that you were.'

A raised eyebrow. 'Was that your honest opinion?'

'No. It was not. I think you're more beautiful.'

She likes this. She looks at me. 'Why are you smiling, Daniel?'

'Pöck does private commissions of pregnant women. He calls it *maternité*. It's a form of boudoir photography. Celebrates a woman's new, sexy curves. He thinks the pregnant female body is beautiful and erotic.

'I've seen a few examples. The women were either wearing lingerie, or they were naked. Soft lighting. Tasteful. Tantalising. Alluring. It's quite popular, apparently.

'He said that if you wanted a session, it would be free of charge. I can accompany you, if you wish, purely as a chaperone, and it goes without saying that I'll look the other way while the photographs are taken.'

'I would expect nothing less from you, Daniel.'

'If you want, he can get a professional model in to show you what to do, how to pose.' I produce my mobile. 'Shall I give him a call now?'

'Oh, no! I would never! You are kidding me, of course. I had not heard of this. Do women really do this?' She's bemused, but curious.

'Only the most evil women on earth.'

She grins. 'On the other hand, if he's *that good…*'

'Stop it now.'

As we continue to eat, I run through the leads I'm following up, though I play down what I'm thinking about a lot of them. I don't want to give her false hope.

'This is taking longer than my usual cases, but that's because I'm investigating something that happened a while ago, and the bad guys will have had time to cover their tracks. But I think I'm getting there.

'There are people involved in this that I don't think the police had any interest in. I just need to tie all the threads together. But I'll be honest with you, Micha, it's not easy.'

'Your work is not my area, but it seems to me that you are making very good progress, Daniel. And after only a few days. I think Suzanna Leishman's instinct about you was correct. Have you seen much of Suzanna since you started this case?'

'I haven't seen her for a couple of days. Why do you ask?'

'I told you I was nosey when we first met. Many women like to know about other women's sex lives. And men's sex lives, too. Or at least *I* do. I like Suzanna, and her sexuality does interest me. I think it's her sophistication, intelligence and age. I'm curious as to what she would be like as a sex partner for a man. Is that too bold of me?

'When we spoke of it the other day, I was interested in the age gap between you, as you'll remember. But I was also interested in other aspects. It is what I am like, and I do not apologise for it. Perhaps it is the background I am from.

'Kiaraa and I always talked about sex when we were teenagers, and so did all of our friends. We had a little collection of erotic books between us – paperbacks – that were always being passed from person to person.

'My favourites always featured a lot of erotic tension. I found that aspect to be very appealing and thrilling: situations where you did not know what was going to happen. How things would be resolved between, say, two characters. How exciting the outcome would be; how stimulating, how satisfying, how passionate.'

'Would you like details, Micha? I'm very liberal. Where would you like me to start?'

'Wherever you like. I get a feeling that Suzanna would like to be spoken about in that way, am I right?'

'Yes, you are. What about you? Would you like to be spoken about in that way?' I raise an eyebrow, waiting for her reply.

'Hm. Yes. I think so. I think I would enjoy my intimate tastes to be discussed by another. In the right way, of course, and by the right person. I hate crudity. It's hard to put one's finger on why it would be appealing. I find it interesting and exciting to talk about such erotic matters. I always have done. Perhaps we can discuss some of them later on if you would not mind. Concerning Suzanna, maybe. Purely objectively and scientifically. You can be very frank with me. Explicit, even. You will find that I am as liberal as you are. Perhaps more so. What do you think?'

'Is there somewhere here I can have a cold shower?'

She giggles and waves a hand up and down. She suddenly reminds me of Aera. I'm aware that I keep glancing at her cleavage, so I look at one of the gunpowder paintings on the wall instead. She isn't wearing a bra, and she knows I've noticed. It's hard not to with the thin, revealing fabric of that dress. Her areolae are big and dark.

'One glass of champagne and I'm asking you intimate details about your personal life,' she says. 'I haven't drunk alcohol for so long.

I must be tipsy. I remember when you asked me if I had any Korean ginseng. That was funny.'

'Did you buy me some? What sort of woman are you? I just hope you didn't put any in the food.'

'I cooked Southern Indian cuisine so you would not taste it. I put a whole bottle in. You'll soon feel the effects. Is your heart rate raised yet? Any lascivious thoughts?'

I laugh. 'Only about you, Micha, I promise. Is Korean ginseng really an aphrodisiac? I've never really looked into it.'

'Maybe. Maybe not. I don't think there's any such thing as an aphrodisiac, personally. I think words and thoughts are far more effective, don't you?' She sips her champagne. 'All those things: ginseng, oysters, red wine, dark chocolate, pistachios. I've tried them all. In fact, I tried them all just before you arrived!'

'I'm leaving right now. On the other hand...'

She laughs and pours us both another glass. 'I know there is one question you want to ask me about *my* personal life, but you are too polite to ask it.'

'What would that be, Micha?'

'You want to know who the father of my baby is.'

'It had crossed my mind. No one seems to talk about it; not Suzanna, not Baek-Hayeon, not Aera...'

She chews whatever she's got in her mouth for a few seconds. 'I told you that I was having a girl. That I would name it after Kiaraa. You will think this is frivolous, but I wanted to have a baby for her, because she was gone.

'Not to replace her in my life; that would be ridiculous, but to...she would be like its aunt, even though she is not here anymore. So, she would still have a role in life, in my life. She would still be present. Do you understand?

'But I was not in a relationship and had not been in one for some time. You know what us Korean workaholics are like!' She takes a few rapid sips of champagne. 'So, I asked one of the design staff to join me on a business visit to Cologne.

'I had picked him out as a suitable candidate. He was an attractive young man, only three years younger than I am. Tall, like you. His name was Ye-jun Kim. I hoped that his good looks would merge with mine to make a beautiful child.

'When we were in Cologne, in the Cologne Marriott Hotel, I invited him to my suite, and I seduced him. It was easy. On many levels it was not a success. He was very nervous and very excitable. I think he could not believe it was happening.

'It did not last long, and I personally found it a bit of a disappointment. Physically, I mean.' Another quick sip. 'But I was impregnated. When we got back to London, I had him promoted. This meant that he had to go back to Sansuyu headquarters in Seoul.'

'Did he know you were pregnant?'

'No. And he will never know that he is the father. I can't imagine what must be going through your mind at this moment!'

I can't stop myself laughing. 'I think you're one hell of a tough cookie, Micha!'

Now she laughs as well and finishes what's in her glass. 'I have never told a *soul* what I just told you, Daniel. I hope – no – I *know* you will keep it to yourself. I think I should open a second bottle. I need a third glass of champagne after that lurid confession! I'm sure my doctor will understand.'

'I'm sure she will if you pay her enough.'

She folds her arms and leans slightly forwards, with predictable results on her upper body. 'I am really enjoying myself with you, Daniel. I have not had an evening like this for so long. Our talk is both amusing and flirtatious. Most pleasurable. I can tell that you are teasing me at times, and I think you are doing it because you are attracted to me. In fact, I *know* that you are attracted to me. That makes me feel good.

'Also, you are looking at me in the way that a man should look at a woman. It feels like an embrace. I'm sure you can tell that I am responding to it. It is something that I have missed.'

She fiddles with her hair and leans forwards a little more. 'And I'm sure you are reading my body language and know what it means.'

'I have absolutely no idea what you're talking about, miss.'

'I think you do. I think we both do. Sometimes it is hard for me to be subtle, especially in a language which is not my first, but I think I have made a good job of it tonight. I have tried to push the subject of sex to the fore without being too…too obvious. At least I hope I have.

'I am presenting myself to you as a sexual being, despite my pregnancy, or maybe because of it. You remember what I said about erotic tension? This past hour has been electric for me. Thrilling and overwhelming.'

'And I thought it was *me* that needed the cold shower.'

'Oh no, Daniel. It is most definitely me that needs it. I have needed it since you first arrived this evening. Since I first met you, in fact. When you called me at home the other night, when I was in bed, it was extraordinarily stimulating. Very exciting, even though our conversation was not sex-specific. I felt like a teenager with a crush, and I could tell you were aware. I'm sure I don't have to elucidate.' She chuckles to herself. 'Don't get big-headed. It is a well-known side-effect of pregnancy!'

'And I thought it was my use of metaphors.'

'Come now, Daniel. I think you're well aware of the thrilling effect you have on women. Let's go and enjoy the view.'

We walk over to the windows and look out at the twinkling lights of central London. Neither of us speaks. After a while, she interlaces her fingers around mine and squeezes them. This goes on for a few tense minutes.

'That word *inyeon* that I mentioned earlier,' she says, her voice now soft and seductive. 'It comes from Korean Buddhism. It refers to the destiny of two people. Their fate if you like. Whether they were meant to be together or not. Whether there is a connection between them. I have always found it to be a very romantic idea.'

She turns to face me and kisses me very gently on the mouth, over and over again, until our kissing becomes hungry and passionate.

She tastes of champagne and spices. I slowly turn her around so she's facing away from me and can see her reflection in one of the windows. I hold the sides of her body beneath her armpits and kiss her neck. She gasps softly and pulls the dress off her shoulders. I caress her breasts.

She inhales sharply and manages a breathy and brief, 'Oh!' Still watching herself in the glass, she leans back and turns her head so I can kiss her on the mouth again. 'It's...mm...' she says.

Her flesh feels warm, as if she's just stepped out of a hot bath, and her nipples are stiff. She keeps watching herself out of the corner of her eye. She smiles, pushes her chest out, stretches her spine, and presses her body into mine, her movements rhythmic, slow, and catlike. I'm dying.

'I like seeing my reflection in the window like this,' she whispers. 'It is as if I am in a movie, an erotic movie. It is very exciting. Very sensual. To watch myself moving like this. To see myself being touched like you are touching me. It is almost as if it is happening to someone else and I am a voyeur, spying on someone when they think they cannot be seen. Spying on a woman who is slowly losing control.'

'You must introduce me to this woman, Micha. She sounds intriguing.'

'And she is not used to losing control.' She turns to face me. 'If you wanted me to do one of those photo sessions as I am now, I would.'

'Really?'

'Do you think I should?'

'Most definitely.'

'I think so, too. It would remind me of this moment. It would remind both of us. I would want you to have copies of the photographs. I think we should go into the bedroom now, Daniel. We will have to be cautious at first. I think we are both going to sail into uncharted territory this evening, don't you?'

33

CALIGULA'S LEGACY

I watch her for a few moments.

She sits at the breakfast bar, eating some sort of muesli, occasionally sipping from a French coffee bowl with the Sansuyu logo on the side. The blinds on two of the windows are closed, to prevent the slowly rising sun from dazzling her. She's wearing a short cotton kimono, red with a white chrysanthemum pattern.

I look at the clock on the wall. It's five-fifty. She looks up.

'Good morning, Daniel. I am afraid that my sleeping patterns are shot at the moment. I have been up since just before five. I hope I did not wake you. Would you like something to drink?' She smiles sweetly. 'Anything at all?'

'I think just a coffee at the moment, thank you, Micha.'

'Would that be with milk?'

'Just a dash.'

'Any particular type of milk? Skimmed? Whole? Soya? Oat? I have all types available, just let me know what you'd prefer.'

I kiss her on the forehead. 'I'll let you choose.'

'Famous last words, Daniel.'

She has a Fisher & Paykel bean to cup machine. She watches me carefully as she makes my coffee.

'I hope you did not think I was too forward during our lovemaking last night, too impertinent, too self-centred, too pushy. But then you soon took control, did you not?'

I sit down. 'Someone had to. I was afraid it might descend into anarchy.'

She places the coffee in front of me. 'It was exhilarating, as I suspected it would be. I have read a lot about…women in my state and their libido. If it is acceptable to you, I would like to take advantage of my condition on some more occasions. It may be the last time I will be able to experience those exact sensations. They were…heady. I'm sorry. I don't mean to sound so clinical. After what I told you about how I got pregnant, you must think me a little unemotional; manipulative, even.'

'Not at all. I'll check with my secretary first thing this morning. I'm sure I can fit you in somewhere.'

'The feeling is mutual, Daniel.'

'I can't think of a snappy reply to that.'

She grins. 'I was a little worried at first because of your relationship with Suzanna. But then it's only sex, isn't it, and I feel it is only sex with Suzanna. I would not want her to think that I was stealing you from her; using up your time when you could be with her.

'I will be honest with you, Daniel. The first time we met, and I saw the effect you had had on her, I wanted to see if you could have the same effect on me. No. That's a lie. I *knew* you would have that effect on me. I could feel it. And whatever you were doing to her, I wanted you to do it to me. I had been thinking about it ever since. Can we not mention it to her? What we have done?'

'My lips are sealed.'

'Good. Then it will be our secret.' She sits next to me, and we kiss for a while, her hand on my thigh, her fingernails almost piercing the flesh. The perfume she wore last night still lingers, mixing appealingly with the other scents coming from her body.

She pulls away from me. It's frustrating. 'I know you are busy, but we must try and book some more assignations as soon as we can. We should be businesslike. Are you available tonight?'

'Depends. I'll let you know.'

'Are you teasing me again?'

'Maybe.'

'I like being teased. And I liked it that you did not judge me last night.' She grins. 'Us Jeong girls seem to have a strong deviant streak, as I'm sure you're aware by now. It's just that mine has always manifested itself in different ways from Kiaraa's, especially at the moment, as you assuredly noticed.

'I imagine that some men might be taken aback at my requests and would think them unusual or outlandish. Is your coffee OK? Are you sure you don't need some more milk? It would be no problem. I have plenty as you know. What will you be doing today?'

'I told you about the Citroën van last night. How the idea that it was a Fiat sent everyone in the wrong direction. I mentioned it to Baek-Hayeon, and he didn't take it too well.

'But it was a mistake anyone could have made under those circumstances. It would probably have fooled me, too. It's quite possibly the last thing you would expect.

'I asked a detective who was involved in the case to see if she could track down this vehicle and she did. I suspect the person who hired it was not directly involved in the kidnapping, but I could be wrong.'

'How could he not be directly involved?'

'It may be that he was paid to take the van out on a test drive for a couple of days. Not all test drives require accompaniment. He then passed it on to whoever was involved in picking up the ransom money.

'Once that was over, they handed the van back to him and he returned it to the showroom. He may not have even known what the van was going to be used for. It may be that they paid him to do the job and to keep his mouth shut.

'The police have picked the van up and they'll get their forensics team onto it, but I don't think they'll find anything. I have the name of the man who hired it. I'm going to visit him this morning and ask him a few questions.'

She gets up and rests her wrists on my shoulders, kissing me on the cheek. 'Be careful, Daniel. I would be most distressed if anything happened to you. Especially at the moment.' She removes her kimono and drapes it over a chair.

She takes one of my hands, places it on her upper belly and slowly moves it down to below her navel. 'It's still very early. Only ten past six.' She squeezes my hand. 'I don't have to be in in work until nine-thirty.' I get another quick kiss, her tongue darting in and out of my mouth. 'Plenty of time to investigate my deviant streak a little more.'

'Shall we stay here, Micha, or go into the bedroom?'

'Stay here. And you stay seated. I have plans. I just hope you don't find them too wicked.' She leans towards me, smiles, and whispers in my ear. 'I hope you didn't get me pregnant last night, by the way. I'm not using any contraception.'

'*Now* you tell me.'

* * *

I get a cab back to my flat for a shave and a change of clothing. I had a shower at Micha's, and we pencilled in a further half dozen assignations, on the understanding that I may well have to cancel any of them at short notice.

All in all, she seemed delighted that I'd moved the investigation on so much in just a few days, but I told her we still weren't out of the woods yet, an expression she'd never heard before but liked. I left her as she was deciding what to wear for her talk in Blackfriars the following day.

I give Pöck a call and tell him that Micha would be interested in a *maternité* shoot. He sounds delighted.

'Oh, *yeah*. That's good news. I think Jasna would like to meet her as well. It'll be like, I don't know, something I could *do*, you know what I mean? She can come and take a look at the studio if she wants. Before the shoot, I mean. We can show her around and discuss whether she wants a stylist or a hair person. Who does her hair? Do you know? She can look at some other shoots we've done. Send her a link to my site. Cool. Tell her it'll take about two or three hours. Any time of the day as it's her. Any idea when?'

'It'll be after my investigation, I think. I'll let you know.'

'How's that going?'

'Lots of middle-range breakthroughs. Lots of dead ends. Lots of frustration. Lots of false trails. It's like a complicated jigsaw with lots of pieces missing and some thrown in from other puzzles.'

'You've got the cold case blues, man. Don't forget. You crack this motherfucker, and you get an introduction to Julissa Vòng. You like the photograph I sent round? Not too big for your place?'

'Looks fantastic. And thanks for the other stuff.'

'My pleasure, my friend. Watch out for that Franka Galletti, though, she was a succubus in a previous life. Oh, and I just emailed you a photograph of Kiaraa that I think you'll appreciate. No one else has seen this apart from me and Jasna. It's funny. A one-off. It's *her*, you know what I mean? Perhaps it'll inspire you to catch these dickheads. Let me know if you want it turned into a print. Keep in touch.'

I download the photograph and it fills up my screen. It looks like a glossy magazine ad from a parallel universe. Kiaraa is naked and wearing a pink wig. She stands in front of a dazzling acid yellow background. Eyes wide with surprise.

She's about to pop a piece of nigiri sushi into her mouth. There's a black censor bar, but instead of blocking out her eyes, breasts or crotch, it's positioned over her navel.

It makes me laugh. I hate whoever killed her. I'll show it to Micha when all this is over.

I pick up five hundred in bribery money from a cashpoint and get a cab to Brookfield Crescent in Putney. I have no idea what I'm going to say to Mr Brian Colbert. Hiring that van is probably a distant memory for him now.

I just hope I get lucky.

Good morning, Mr Beckett. I hope your investigation is proceeding well. Ms Jeong seems in a good mood this morning. Quite a spring in her step, as they say. She is obviously pleased with your expertise.

Does she know? She knows. How does she know?

I'm glad to hear that, Aera. Some clients can be very difficult to satisfy.

I am sure that's true, Mr Beckett. But not all of them, I think. I was in the John Lewis department store yesterday. They sell some extraordinary lingerie there.

Did anything catch your eye, Aera?

The Myla Rose range was very appealing. Particularly the items in black.

Perhaps you should consider a purchase.

Perhaps I should, Mr Beckett. Have a productive day.

The houses in Brookfield Crescent are big Edwardian semi-detached affairs, three floors, loft conversions, a basement, usually with cars parked where there were once front gardens. Many have been converted into flats. Lots of cherry trees everywhere.

Outside number 42 is a sign that says 'no vehicle idling' with a graphic of a family being choked by exhaust fumes. There's an £80 fine for doing this, it would seem.

Brian Colbert's house, as far as I can tell, has not been converted into flats. Battersea, where the test-drive Citroën van originated, is hardly any distance away. There's a new white BMW iX in the former front garden.

I decide to bite the bullet and ring the doorbell.

Almost immediately, a guy in his late thirties or early forties answers the door. He could be Mathéo Fournier's sporty younger brother. He's wearing a turquoise jumper with a white shirt underneath and black jogging bottoms. I still don't know what I'm going to say.

'Brian Colbert?'

'That's me. And you are...?'

'My name's Daniel Beckett. I'm a private investigator.'

'Who is it, Brian?' A woman's voice from upstairs. Well-spoken. A little strident. Maybe the same age as Brian.

'He says he's a private investigator, Genevieve.'

'What the *hell*? What does he want?'

'No idea.' He turns to me. 'What do you want?'

'I've like to have a chat with you, Mr Colbert. It's concerning a test drive you booked over two years ago at a Citroën dealership in in Battersea called Falcon Commercial Auto Sales.' I give him the dates and a quick description of the vehicle.

'A test drive? A van? Me?'

'It was a white Citroën Relay van, registration FCA 072. Your name and address were on the insurance forms and the company has a photocopy of your driving licence. An employee at the dealership remembered you and the vehicle you took out.'

He looks a little pained. 'Oh, yes. I remember now,' he says quickly. 'I don't see that it's any of your business whether I test drive a van or not. Is that all you wanted?'

Genevieve appears behind him and gives me the mother of all disdainful looks. She's a little younger than him. Tall. Overweight in a sexy way.

What do they call it? Junoesque?

Good makeup, particularly around the eyes. Mauve blusher on the cheeks. There's a family resemblance and she has the same light brown hair, cut fairly short but with a ponytail. Sister? Cousin?

'So,' she says. 'If you hire a vehicle nowadays, you get a free visit from a detective a couple of years later, is that it? Jesus Christ.'

'This vehicle was involved in criminal activity on the second day you used it, Mr Colbert.'

They both look at me as if I'd told them I had proof of the existence of unicorns.

'That's impossible,' says Genevieve. 'Call the police, Bri. Do something useful.'

'Yes, Bri, call the police,' I say. 'I think the nearest station is in Fulham Palace Road. They can be here in ten to fifteen minutes.'

Brian narrows his eyes and looks anxious. I bet he'd forgotten about all of this, and now he's getting a cold feeling in the pit of his stomach.

'Well, if it's so pissing serious, why aren't the police here talking to us right now? Answer: it isn't serious and you're a liar,' says Genevieve angrily.

Brian's face has gone red.

'Brian would never test drive a bloody *van*. He's got a car. *We've* got a car. And it's a damn sight better than any car *you* could ever afford by the look of you. We've got a brand new BMW iX. Take a look over your shoulder. It's not hard to miss. Or are you blind as well as stupid? And how do we know you're a detective, anyway? You could be anybody.'

'Listen, Gen,' says Brian. 'Perhaps we should invite him in and hear what he's got to say.'

'If you do that, I'm going out,' replies Genevieve. 'You can't control me. You think you can, but you can't. No one can. Least of all you.'

What the hell is going on here?

'You don't have to go out, Gen. I only said that we should hear...'

'You're a little shit, Brian,' spits Genevieve. 'A weasel. I can't stand being in the same building as you. I urinate on you.' I look at my watch. It's still only a quarter to ten. If Brian doesn't invite me inside in five minutes, I'm going to be livid.

'Come in,' says Brian, looking sheepish. I walk into the house. Genevieve is putting on a big red fluffy coat and slips into a pair of ruby red pumps. As she storms out, she jostles me in the shoulder, and a few seconds later slams the front door hard behind her. A print on the wall shakes so much that I think it's going to fall to the floor.

I hear her start the brand new BMW iX that I can't afford, and drive off. Almost immediately there's a tyre screech and an angry car horn blast.

I follow Brian into the kitchen. 'Bit of a row this morning,' he says, without looking behind him. 'Started before you got here. Almost as soon as we woke up. She's still fuming. You know what they're like about kids.'

'Yeah,' I say, not knowing what he's talking about. He makes me a coffee and we sit on basket chairs in a conservatory at the back of the house. There are a lot of nice plants in here and an inflatable mattress on the floor.

'So, go on. What's it all about? What's happened?' he says.

'Just so we're on the same page, Mr Colbert. You definitely had a test drive of that Citroën on the dates that I mentioned.'

'Yes, I did. Is it a crime? Gen didn't know.'

'So, you were thinking of buying one of those vans, is that right?'

'Why would I be thinking of *buying* one?'

'That's usually the reason people book test drives. Or did you just fancy travelling around in a van for a couple of days as a special treat?'

'I don't know what you're getting at.'

'You took that van for a test drive at nine-thirty a.m. on the 14th of September. You returned it to Falcon Commercial Auto Sales at around four p.m. on the 15th.'

'That's probably right,' he says sulkily.

'It was used to pick up three million pounds in ransom money in Elder Street E1 at about eleven a.m. on the 15th. Now, if you weren't involved in that pickup, someone else was. I'd like to know the name of that person. I want to know what happened.

'If you don't tell me, I can have you shitting yourself in a police cell within half an hour. This is a serious criminal conspiracy that you're involved in. It's been dragging on for over two years and the cops are just *dying* to find someone to pin the whole thing on.'

'What will happen to me?'

'Nothing will happen to you as long as you're straight with me. The police involved aren't aware of your connection to this and I can guarantee you won't be on their radar in any way. That woman who was here. Who is she? Will she be coming back any time soon?'

'Genevieve is...she's my sister. Well, she's sort of my sister.'

'*Sort* of your sister? What does that mean?'

'She's my sister and she's my wife. I'm not ashamed of it. Neither of us are. Who are you to judge us? This is the twenty-first century, in case you hadn't realised. We got married in Italy. La Spezia. They do gay marriage, so we thought why not us? Cost a fortune to arrange. Sometimes you just have to go with what feels right. Have you ever been to La Spezia?'

Christ almighty. 'Where has she gone? How long will she be?'

He takes a deep breath. 'Whenever we have a row like that she usually goes into the West End to do some shopping. Then has lunch somewhere until she's calmed down. She usually goes to Hibox in Goodge Street or Chamisse. She likes Lebanese. I would expect her back at around two, maybe later. That's what usually happens.'

'Right. Now take me through it. Quickly. Step by step. Believe me, I'll know if you're lying. Who told you to hire that van? I take it that it wasn't your idea.'

He groans. It's a heart-breaking sound and I feel really bad. 'You're right. It wasn't,' he admits. 'Will I be in trouble? It was a long time ago now. Surely it doesn't matter anymore. Um, Gen and I were having a ferocious post-coital fight about…something. Oh, yes. The usual. She wants to have a baby, you see. More than one. I don't think it would be a good idea. Sort of, genetic consequences, do you understand?

'But she doesn't want to adopt. I'm always a little afraid that one day she'll accidentally-on-purpose forget to take her contraceptive pills before we have sexual intercourse, or whatever she does.

'Anyway, it turned into a major screaming match, and she threw a Lalique vase at my head. It missed but went straight through one of the windows at the front of the house. They're double-glazed, so you can imagine the force of the throw. Gen plays cricket for the Oval Invincibles women's squad.

'One of the neighbours called the police. We don't get on with the neighbours around here. I can tell they don't like us, though I can't imagine why. Two police officers turned up. I think they called it something. A domestical? Something like that. I was mortified.

'I explained everything and swore it wouldn't happen again. We were given a caution. But I could tell the police were amused. They were smirking. We look alike, Gen and me. Well, we would, wouldn't we.

'We were both flushed and agitated, and Gen was hardly wearing anything. Neither was I. I had a towel around my waist and she was only wearing a thin cotton loose-fitting t-shirt.

'Gen's hair was a mess, and she was sweating. She sweats a lot during coupling, and she likes to couple for a long time. She's seeing a doctor about it. The sweating, I mean. I think they knew the score, if you get me. The police, that is.

'I'm sure they come across all sorts of things in the line of duty, though. Neither of us are ashamed. We're proud, in fact. Why shouldn't we be? Caligula had sex with all three of his sisters. No one complained about *that* at the time. They wouldn't have dared. He wasn't even married to any of them.

'Anyway, a few weeks went by, and this other policeman turned up. Plain clothes. In his forties, I think. A bit scary. Corpulent. Said he was a detective. Towered over me. Body odour. Nasty beard. This is silly, but I felt afraid of him straight away. I'm not usually afraid of people, apart from Genevieve when she's in a strop.

'I don't remember the exact conversation, but he said it was a follow-up visit because of what had happened and he wanted to see that everything was alright. He...sort of intimated that we could be in trouble because of our...living arrangements.

'But he was kind. He understood. He wanted to help. He said he realised that we didn't want trouble, didn't want people to gossip. The neighbours here, they don't quite know what's going on. At least I think they don't.

'Gen wasn't here. If she was, she would have launched herself at him. She's hot-blooded. A fishwife. So, it was just me. I think those other officers had told him about us. Probably had a laugh and a joke about it.

'But I think they were jealous. Gen is exceptionally beautiful, very, very sexy and has a superb body. Well, you saw her, didn't you. She's so *tall*. Very mature for her age. Stately. Lusty. Regal.'

'I'm afraid that sounds ridiculous, Brian. Did you *believe* what this officer said? That he'd come here to help you? For no reason?'

A nervous cough. 'There's always a fear of things turning out badly with something like this, a situation like this. You're always afraid that people will find out, even though you don't care deep down. People in work and so on. You care and you don't care simultaneously, d'you get it?

'But by God it's worth it. You can't imagine the passionate frenzy that the truly forbidden can engender. I'm a project manager at a live event production company. Gen is in between jobs at the moment, but she usually works as a customer experience advisor. Very highly paid. She's damn good at it.

'He said that he was sympathetic and would do everything he could to protect us from undue attention, and that I wasn't to worry. I made him a cup of tea. We had a chat about this and that, and everything seemed fine. Just as he was leaving, he asked if I wouldn't mind doing him a little favour.'

'Go on.'

'He said it was nothing. Just a personal thing. Girl trouble. Said he was having an affair behind his wife's back. We had a bit of a laugh about it. He told me that his wife was a bit of a toad.

'Well, by that time I'd have done almost anything he asked. To pay him back. He was the police, after all, and I thought it would consolidate things. It was a bit odd, but I went along with it. Couldn't see any harm. I suppose it was quite exciting.

'He just wanted me to go to this van dealer In Battersea on a particular day and ask for a two-day test drive of a particular type of van. A white Citroën Relay. He said they had about half a dozen of those vans for sale in this place, so there'd be no problems. Once I'd got the van, I'd meet him in the car park of this pub, The Regular Lamb in Lower Richmond Road, at just before ten a.m. and he'd take the van away.

'He said there was a minicab place almost next door to this pub. He'd give me some money, five hundred, for doing this favour for him and to cover my minicab expenses to get home. There'd be another five hundred cash when he gave the van back to me and I returned it to the dealer.

'He would return the van to me in the car park of a different pub, The Blue Cod in Wandsworth. That would be at around lunchtime the same day. Then the next day I'd take it back to the dealer late in the afternoon, to make the test-drive story sound convincing. He suggested that I say something like I didn't like the handling or the acceleration. Give them a little story, yeah? But make it quick.'

'Didn't you find all of this a little suspicious?'

'Not at all. Why would I? If you can't trust the police, who can you trust? I assumed he wanted the van to have it away in with some girl. That was kind of what he said. That he and this girl needed somewhere to get some privacy. I mean, it was a bit weird that it had to be a particular make and colour, but maybe that's what the girl wanted or something. Or it was just a convenient place for me to get to. I didn't ask. It wasn't important.

'I've never had it away in a van. Don't fancy it. Or in a car, though Gen has mentioned it a few times. I think she'd like to do that. In a car park or somewhere. She'd read about it. It's called *doggy*, I think.'

'What was his name?'

'Bill. Bill Goodman.'

'He told you he was a detective. Did he give you his rank? Did he tell you which police station he'd come from?'

'Well, no to all of those, basically.'

'Did he show you a warrant card with his name on?'

'What's a warrant card?'

'Never mind.' I get out my mobile and scroll to the photograph of Kinnaird that I took while he was paying the cab driver off the other night. I expand it, crouch down next to Bri and show it to him. 'It this him?'

A flicker of anxiety as he looks at the image. 'Yes. That's Bill Goodman. Why have you got his photograph?'

'You're doing very well, Brian. What else did you talk about?'

'Um, Bill said to keep the whole thing with the van to myself. Not to tell a soul. That would be the best thing. He didn't want to get into trouble with his wife. Mum's the word, he said. We had a laugh about his wife situation, me and Bill. We talked about wives in general.

'He thought marriage was pointless and it never worked out. He thought women were after all they could get from a man. He said they were conniving shrews. He said they were liars. Malicious. Greedy.

'I felt quite flattered that he trusted me with something like that. The van thing, I mean. Oh. He hinted that he might be connected to MI5. We were both helping each other out. That's all it was. He said that he might be a useful contact for me some day if Gen and me got into hot water.'

There's something he's not telling me. I think I know what it is. 'What else did he say, Brian? About the van? About the whole visit?'

'Nothing else. That was it.'

'You seem like a trustworthy guy, Brian. I'm sure that Bill Goodman trusted you to keep all of this to yourself. But I'm also sure he'd want to know if anyone came around here asking questions about the whole affair. Perhaps someone working for his wife. Did he tell you to get in touch if that happened?'

He keeps fiddling with his wedding ring. He looks down at his lap.

'He said I should ring him straight away if that happened, and I was not to worry. He would sort it out.'

'Are you going to do it? Are you going to tell him that you spoke to me this morning?'

'Not if you don't want me to.'

'I think he'd be upset if you didn't tell him, don't you? What would happen if he found out later that I'd turned up here and we talked about you and him and the van?'

'I don't know. I don't know what to do. It was years ago. I didn't think…'

I stand up. 'I guess you have to do what you think is right, Brian. But I know what I'd do if I were in your position.' I hand him one of my business cards. 'If you need to speak to me again, my number's on here.'

He sees me to the front door. I turn and shake his hand. I'm in no doubt whatsoever that he's going to give Kinnaird a call as soon as he's closed the front door, and it's exactly what I want him to do.

'OK. Thank you for your help, Brian. Give my regards to your charming wife. Tell her you saw me off.'

He nods his head. 'But you keep away from Genevieve, do you hear me? I don't want you coming around here when I'm out. I saw you looking at her.'

As soon as I'm on the pavement, I text Scarlett.

Brian Colbert inconclusive at present. I'll tell you everything as soon as it's all sunk in.

Inconclusive???

I almost forgot. Sallow said that Kinnaird was involved in the house-to-house, then was involved in tracking the van down. How did that happen? Did he volunteer for van duties? Were the house-to-house enquiries completed?

Let me check the details of that. WTFs going on here?

Have to go now. Spotted a really good street performer.

This is what DI Bream said it would be like.

Kisses.

34

CLOUDCATCH

As I walk down the street, I find I'm constantly and rapidly snapping the fingers of my right hand. This is usually a sign that I'm thinking, so I'll interpret it as a positive thing, rather than a repetitive motion disorder.

I've certainly got enough on Kinnaird to have him pulled in and questioned should I decide to pass all my information about him to Scarlett. She'd have no choice but to act.

This may well lead to the incrimination of others, but, once again, it may not. And it would be a long drawn-out process that would involve a lot of people and would enable Kinnaird to get lawyered up or leave the country or whatever.

I try to imagine what I'd do next if I was the police and had all that information. I'd certainly haul Brian Colbert in and get him to make a statement. I'd put the frighteners on him about his direct involvement in several serious crimes. I'd get him to formally ID Kinnaird from a photograph or, better still, a line-up, and hope he'd spill his guts.

I'd find the police log about the domestic that those local cops were called to and find out who they were and where they came from. Then I'd find out if and when they told Kinnaird about it, what they told him, and the manner in which they told him.

I'd put those cops on ice, then get Kinnaird arrested, or invited in for a nice chat, or whatever police do to other police who are suspected of being involved in major illegal shitshows.

Even if forensics found no trace of his DNA or prints on that van, it would be interesting to see how he'd try to squirm out of the whole thing, as it's all pretty damning. And that visit to Colbert was way beyond the pale, almost crazy. It's just something, I suspect, no normal police officer would ever do.

Kinnaird would have to have no warning and an early morning arrest. He'd have to get legal representation pretty quickly, but that could be delayed while he sweated.

Then I'd question him about his inside knowledge about the bolt cutters and the fingers. We'd get DCI Sallow in to back that up, and Penny, too.

I'd get Thornton in and isolated from Kinnaird, grilling him until his teeth fell out. And he's a DCI. You'd undoubtedly need an entire squad of ordinary police/internal affairs for all of this to work, someone high up and incorruptible pulling the strings and a speedy no-bullshit take-no-prisoners attitude.

In a case that's over two years old, and involves one or two serving senior detectives, would the police be up to it, and would they be up to it quickly enough? There's Scarlett, but she has other work, and is not going to be transferred onto a different case overnight, even if it's a murder case, and particularly one that isn't recent. And, as I told her, there's a real danger of Kinnaird being tipped off in some way.

If Sallow wasn't on holiday, he'd probably tell her to drop everything and get to it. But he is on holiday.

Sod it. The police have already had two years with this and have got nowhere. I think I'll keep most of this to myself. But I'll have to tell Scarlett something about my visit to Brian Colbert and his Hammer House of Incest, even if it's a pack of half-truths.

I'm still not one hundred per cent sure who drove the van away after the ransom was deposited in it, but whoever it was, it's now more than likely that the ransom money was passed on to DCI Clement Thornton of Economic Crime Command to be laundered in some way.

This may not actually be true, but it's certainly a good theory, and one I'm hanging on to for the moment.

Thanks to Kinnaird's expertise/slyness, who knows how many people have test driven and/or hired that van since, and how many times it would have been cleaned, inside and out, over a two-year period. If I was him, I'd have given that van a damn good scrub before handing it back to Colbert and/or worn gloves when I was driving it. No precaution would have been too great.

Kinnaird was police. In the unlikely event of that van being tracked down, he would know exactly what would be done to it by forensics. He might even have disguised himself in some way while he was driving it. It's what I would have done.

Yes. This whole operation has bent cops written all over it, right down to the missing mobiles.

So, smart but not that smart. If Kinnaird hadn't been such a prick with Penny, I wouldn't even know he existed. But he couldn't help himself, and now we're here. On the plus side, he now has two ticks next to his name on my naughty list.

I grab a cab and get it to take me back to Covent Garden. I have to clear my head and think all of this through. Once again: if only the damn police weren't so involved. I have no problem with aggressive interrogation, but it's a little different when the interrogatee could have you arrested and dumped in a police cell.

As I'm in the private sector, the whole system would be against me.

I only hope I don't get Scarlett into trouble. I'd hate to do something that would spoil our date.

My mobile rings. It's as if she knows I'm thinking about her:

'You're going to love this.'

'Hi, Scarlett. Just thinking about you.'

'Fuck off. Now listen. I spoke to a DI called Caroline McHale. Kinnaird answered directly to her and was put on house-to-house in Elder Street less than a week after the body was discovered.'

'That was the 21st of September.'

'Correct. But he was pulled off that duty four days later after a complaint was made against him by one of the residents there, a Mrs

Ritika Knight, a conveyancing solicitor. She said he had made several inappropriate comments to her during his visit.'

'DCI Sallow didn't mention that when I spoke to him.'

'It could be that he didn't know. Or he was too busy to deal with it. Or Caroline McHale didn't tell him. Or he'd simply forgotten. Two years ago, remember. Everything was so chaotic at the time that we don't seem to have a record of who said what to who, but when DI McHale was trying to reallocate him, he suggested that he might try to track down the van that was used to collect the ransom money, so that's what happened. I think they were low on personnel for that particular task, and I'm sure he was very apologetic about Mrs Knight. Moment of madness; something like that.

'And you have to remember that the Elder Street house-to-house would have been a terminable task, so everyone involved in it would have been put on other duties sooner or later.

'As I said, it was all very chaotic, so this complaint slipped into the mists of time. He did very thorough work on the search for the van, apparently.'

I'll bet he did.

'That's what Sallow told me,' I say. 'Wouldn't there have been any comeback from that complaint at *all*?'

'Well, you'd think so, but I didn't hear anything about it. I didn't even know about it until today. I checked his file and there was nothing about it at all. Just the dates when he was taken off house-to-house and transferred to van duties. It happens, you know? Maybe someone thought that Mrs Knight was overreacting. With that case, we needed everyone we could get. He'd been involved with a couple of kidnapping cases before, but I don't know how he'd fared. Maybe someone thought that experience would come in useful. Maybe he volunteered that information. Maybe none of the above.'

'OK, Scarlett. Give me a little more time and I'll give you all I've got. It's just that there may be a little more and I don't want to send you in the wrong direction. I'll be in touch.'

'But...'

As the cab crosses Chelsea Bridge, I think about last night with

Micha. I certainly didn't see that coming. On the other hand, I think I did, and I think it was something I wanted to happen, probably from the first moment I saw her, and she obviously felt the same way. Sometimes that kind of mutual attraction steers and controls events without you having to do much.

And it was a longer session than I might have expected; lots of talking from her, lots of laughing, lots of intensity, lots of demands, lots of noise, lots of imagination. A fantastic evening, in fact. She's the kind of lover you'd want to see again and again, whatever her condition.

I was reminded of Pöck saying how it was Kiaraa that had seduced *him*, rather than the other way around. And how Micha had seduced that guy and got him to impregnate her. And her frankness and directness about what she needed from me.

That kind of female sexual authority, boldness and assertiveness obviously runs in the family. Or maybe it's connected to professional women who are/were at the top of their game in one way or another. It has been known. I doubt either sister would be Carmichael's type.

When I get back to my flat, I make a coffee, sit at the kitchen table, fire up the computer and look at my messages. The first thing I see is an email asking me to download an app called CloudCatch. I'm just about to delete this, then spot the email after it, which is from Trisha at Call Sheet.

Whole Wigmore file(s) attached. You'll have to download CloudCatch first. This will take about five minutes if you're lucky. Then you can open the Wigmore file in it. It's big but shouldn't take that long (famous last words!). Be careful when you fast forward or rewind. It's really alacritous and can be hard to control.

It's in two sections. Alpha is the concert proper; Beta is the audience shots, though there are some crossovers. Sound will be noticeably louder on the Alpha section. Suggest muting computer volume so you don't get a shock. Send me a text or call me if you have any problems. Or you could send me a text or call me if you'd like to go out for a drink some time. No pressure. Trisha.

Well, that was unexpected. I'll have to juggle dates, or further dates, or possible dates with Suzanna, Micha, Aera, Penny, Scarlett, Gaëlle, Krysia, Aziza, possibly Jasna, and now Trisha. Oh, and a holiday with Franka Galletti. And a possible introduction to Julissa Vòng if things go well with the investigation. Is that everyone? I just hope I can wrap this case up fairly soon and maybe even get a bonus. I think I'm going to need it to cover restaurant, hotel, and flight expenses.

I download the CloudCatch app, and a little circle appears with some wispy cirrus clouds on a blue background and a goldfish orange download bar beneath. I instantly get three identical emails from CloudCatch asking me to lease or buy some of their other stuff, which I delete.

While that's cooking, I peruse my sheet of A4 cartridge paper on which I'd written all the relevant dates of the case, starting with the concert at Wigmore Hall in July and ending with the cable cutter info being released to the investigating officers at the end of September.

I decide to apply Occam's razor and slash out the incident at the Charlotte Street Hotel and Odette Fournier's assault on the tube. I'm sure these two events will come back to bite me, but at the moment, I can't see how they could possibly be connected to the murder. I have to assume they're coincidence; barely even that.

I almost remove the knife threat that Kiaraa endured in Barrett Street, but that links to her gun request, so has to remain, for the moment at least.

For a few seconds, my mind goes completely blank. Well, at least I've got Kinnaird and the Citroën van on the backburner, plus his advance knowledge of the cable cutters. My computer makes a space-age noise to let me know that CloudCatch is ready, so I start the Wigmore Hall download.

There was something else I was thinking about while at Micha's last night, but events overtook my thought processes and I forgot about it. Oh yes. Part of me was wondering if I could have spotted the Fourniers on the Wigmore Hall video.

We were only looking at the audience shots from one of the camera people according to Trisha, so they might be in there somewhere. Also,

I was only looking to identify Apollo at the time and didn't want to push for more.

I'm still not sure about Apollo/Orpheus/Carmichael, but it does interest me that he and the Fournier couple attended the same concert, though I can't imagine that either of the Fourniers would socialise with someone like that.

I get a text from Aera with a link to a photograph of a mature, full-figured model wearing a Myla Rose lingerie set in black: a tanga brief, plunge bra and suspender belt.

These are the items that I mentioned, Mr Beckett. I thought I would seek your advice on the matter before making a purchase.

I think they are lovely, Aera. Very alluring. Ideal for a desirable woman with a secret, seductive side.

So, you think I should buy?

Most definitely. Of course, stockings would be a necessary investment with such items. Probably black with seams.

Of course. I will check to see that they have these items in my size. I may be a little bigger than the model in that photograph. In certain areas, anyway. It is always a problem for me when buying lingerie.

Be sure to let me know how it went. Back to work now, madame.

Of course, Mr Beckett. And thank you for your assistance with this matter. It is often useful to have a man's point of view.

It's my pleasure, Aera.

The Wigmore Hall audience footage doesn't look quite as crisp on my computer as it did on the screen at Call Sheet, but it'll do. Trisha was right, the fast forward is difficult to control, and it takes me about five stressful minutes before I get it right. While I'm practising, Baek-Hayeon texts me. At least it's not Aera; I don't think I could cope with another of her provocative messages so soon after the last one.

Hello, Mr Beckett. I thought I would thank you about putting me in touch with Mr Teng. He has just left. Such an interesting fellow with a lively personality. And a fast talker. We have many improvements to make with our security software and he will make a fine consultant, if a little on the expensive side.

A *little* on the expensive side?

Most of the audience footage is in the stalls. I suspect the reason is that the lighting is better down there, much of it reflected from the stage and the balcony lights.

I have to stop myself being hypnotised by the images as they glide past and force myself not only to focus on what I'm looking for, but also to blink every now and then when my eyes start to sting from keeping them open for so long.

I pause the flow of images when I see Carmichael once more. This is the shot I saw at Call Sheet. I do a slow-mo sweep along the entire first row of the balcony, but no sign of the Fourniers. Were they actually there?

The view of the balcony cuts off at this point and we're looking at the rear stalls. Still no sign of them. This shot seems to go on for a long time, then everyone on screen bursts into applause.

Then something happens with the lighting and everything gets bleached out for a while.

Back to the balcony now, moving slowly along from right to left. There were four balcony rows, A, B, C and D. Carmichael was sitting in the middle of Row A. So far, there have been no views of the other rows.

Then this changes. Once the camera reaches the left side of Row A, it slowly moves upwards to show Rows B and C, which are not so well lit. People are clapping. Another slow pan from left to right and there they are: Odette and Mathéo Fournier, centre of Row B, almost directly behind Carmichael.

I pause this moment, rewind, and then slow it right down, looking for any eye contact between them; any recognition. It only takes a few seconds before I find it. Carmichael, surprisingly, is clapping. I guess he didn't want to look out of place.

Then he turns slowly and glances over his right shoulder, looking directly at Mathéo Fournier, smiling, and nodding his head in appreciation. They look straight at each other, smile, and then both go back to looking at the stage. Odette didn't see this; she's focussed on Kiaraa, as you might expect.

I rewind a little and look at this sequence in real time. That glance only took a second, but it's definitely a shared moment by two people who know each other, as opposed to two appreciative music fans. It's almost romantic.

I look at every single audience shot that's on here, but the higher balcony rows are never featured again, so no more Fourniers. I take a look at that moment another eight times. Did I imagine it? Did I want to see some evidence of collusion between the two of them, so my brain was making it happen? But there can be no doubt.

Now I'm going to look at the Alpha section, which only features the performance. In particular, I want to look at the end of the concert, the point where Kiaraa makes her speech about Principles. If I'm lucky, I may see Carmichael and Mathéo Fournier getting all dewy-eyed again.

It's only when the stage goes dark that I realise I've overshot. I wind the picture back, turn the volume on and play it.

The lights come up and there she is in her black deep V mini dress, wearing the silver George Jensen necklace and earrings that Micha wore last night. I'm getting butterflies in my stomach just thinking about Micha. Kiaraa acknowledges the applause and waits patiently until it's over.

Thank you so much. Thank you. It has been such a pleasure to perform for you this evening. For my encore, I would like to play three pieces by Scarlatti: two sonatas in D major, K443 and K45, and a sonata in B minor, K27.

She quickly traces a line down the sides of her body with the tips of her fingers to draw attention to the dress.

I hope you like it…

This comment causes a lot of applause, cheering and whistles from the audience. She's making light of her reputation for wearing designer clothing to entertain and amuse. There's a big grin on her face. She holds a hand up so she can speak.

This is the first time I've worn it. It's a Dolce & Gabbana. You don't think it's too much, do you?

More applause and cheering. She laughs.

I know there are some that think that female classical musicians should not dress in this way. There are some very backward-looking organisations out there, led by backward-looking, ignorant and, it has to be said, rather sad people who seem to delight in telling women how they should or should not dress. In fact, one of those organisations – they call themselves Birthright – actually wrote to my record company suggesting that I be dropped from their roster as I was nothing better than a vile harlot!

She raises her eyebrows in mock horror. More laughter and whoops from the audience.

Thankfully, my record company did not agree. At least, they did not think I was vile!

Lots of laughter and applause.

But we are trying to fight back against this sort of imbecility. On your way out tonight, you may care to take a pamphlet by one of the organisations who are taking a stand against this poisonous attitude. They are called Principles. And they believe, among other things, that freedom to wear whatever we like is our *birthright. Thank you.*

Fifteen seconds of applause and cheering. She sits down and starts playing.

Vile harlot. No prizes for guessing who was behind *that.* He must have had steam coming out of his ears being insulted and humiliated like that, almost to his face. And the whole audience, in effect, laughing at him.

Then he got his revenge by calling her a Korean attention whore in that insane review.

Well, that's Billy Carmichael officially on my naughty list.

And how much does Fournier know about him and his political activities? I think both of these guys merit further investigation.

I open an enormous email from Doug, listing the names and addresses of the Enfield Golf Club membership from the last five years. I spend forty minutes scrutinising each name, but nothing jumps out.

Ah well.

A text from Suzanna:

Cancelled meeting. Are you free for a few hours?

Sure. I need a break to clear my head. I may have to pop out later on, though.

We'll just have to see how much we can cram in.

Was that a single entendre?

I thought I'd wear that black latex bodysuit you bought me…
I'm sending my driver for you.
I find I'm thinking about Genevieve.

35

BITE MARKS

I finish my takeaway halloumi and apricot jam sandwich from Crespo's Restaurant in Wellington Street, make another coffee and call up Carmichael's Wikipedia page on the screen.

I have to start somewhere, so I'm going to see if I can find the books that he's authored on Amazon. Sometimes I really don't know what I'm doing, but it can often get results.

England Keep My Bones! gets an average two-star rating and several diabolical reviews. Fifty-eight pages long. It's described as racist, badly written, largely incomprehensible, and full of typos. This looks like a first effort and was published eight years ago by Good Citizen Publishing. Doesn't sell much, by the look of things.

Moaning Minnies appears three years after this and does a little better with the reviews, though it's difficult to know if they're genuine or not. One describes the book as 'a long-awaited critique of modern feminism, virago by virago. Puts into words what most intelligent modern men are thinking.'

The word 'virago' makes me think that Carmichael himself was behind this one. Can you review your own books on Amazon? I have no idea.

Another review says 'At long last – someone who talks sense and wants to turn the clock back in a good, sensible way. I shall be gifting this goodly tome to my lady wife and insisting that she read it.' This time, the publisher is called Counterblast. 'Goodly tome'. 'Lady wife'. Carmichael again? Or do all people like him speak as if it's the nineteenth century?

All of the reviews are positive in one way or another, but that could mean anything. Perhaps you're more likely to bother writing a review if you like a book. If you didn't like it, or didn't finish it, it would hardly be worth your while, though I'm sure there are plenty of disturbed folk out there with various axes to grind.

Once More unto The Breach, again published by Counterblast, presents itself as a serious essay on the decline of chivalry in direct proportion to the rise of women's rights.

Sounds like bollocks. What is wrong with this guy?

From the blurb it seems to bemoan the loss of courtly manners, nobility, honour, religious belief, and the role of women as arming their men for battle, literally and metaphorically. Presumably, these would be the sort of courtly manners, nobility and honour that make you describe a woman as a Japanese slut in a short skirt.

One review says 'A lot of truth spoken here. Men who allow their wives to be put to work should be ashamed of themselves. Men should man up.'

Another, the only negative review, says 'Badly written, poorly thought-out misogynist crap. Avoid.'

If you click on Carmichael's name, it takes you to a page which displays all his books and there's a little biography which features the same photograph that's on his Wikipedia page but here it's in black and white.

Alexander 'Billy' Carmichael is a well-respected politician and leader of the Birthright political party. He was educated at Eton College and the University of East Anglia, where he earned a degree in history.

He is the author of three books, England Keep My Bones!, Moaning Minnies *and* Once More unto The Breach. *He is currently working on a new book, provisionally titled* Man 2 Man. *He is a devotee of the works of William Shakespeare and Johann Sebastian Bach. He lives in London, England.*

No mention of Miss Poppy Virginia Windsor, HRH Lobelia Craven or Miss Hatsuko Okamoto, I see. Would they be offended?

I attempt to look up Good Citizen Publishing but after a fifteen-minute search find nothing at all.

Counterblast, however, is a different kettle of fish, and what I find makes me stop what I'm doing and sit back in my seat.

Just to make sure I'm not going crazy, I do a further fifteen minutes of searching for other European publishing companies called Counterblast, but the only one is an imprint of Fournier International.

I check Fournier's website, find the Counterblast section and Carmichael's books are there. His bio is taken from his Wikipedia page and the blurbs for both books are the same as the ones on Amazon, with a few inconsequential differences.

Counterblast has published just under forty books over the last ten years, usually on sociological/political topics. Many of them are quite short: usually around a hundred pages long. They all have terrible chart positions, but then they're a minority interest.

What seems to be a statement of intent describes their output as being radical, progressive, fearlessly unfashionable, and giving a voice to the underdog.

So, what does this tell me? Well, it certainly explains that little glance at the Wigmore Hall. Carmichael and Fournier know each other. Fournier has published two of Carmichael's books, so presumably must rate him and must have met him on more than one occasion.

Doesn't mean that he shares his views, though; he seems much too intelligent for that, particularly given his choice of partner. But you never can tell. And he thought Gaëlle was slutty.

What did Fournier think about Kiaraa's little dig at Birthright? Maybe it amused him. After all, he knew what Carmichael was like and was aware of his views.

Did he get Carmichael his ticket to that concert? Odette said that her husband was a patron of many musical associations. If he did get Carmichael a ticket, perhaps he felt bad about his chum being humiliated like that, even though no one present would have known who Carmichael was or what he did.

I also wonder if Odette knew who he was. There was no eye contact between her and Carmichael. Perhaps he and Fournier had to pretend not to know each other so that Odette wouldn't give her husband a hard time regarding his politically questionable clients.

But this is suspicious, and links Carmichael to Kiaraa on two levels, once through his nasty reviews/comments and again through Fournier. Does Fournier know about those spite-filled reviews, I wonder?

This also now links Fournier to Kiaraa on two different levels, once through Odette and once via Carmichael. Circumstantial? Coincidence? I don't believe in coincidences. Carmichael gets a tick next to his name and Fournier now has two.

I lean back in my seat and stare at the ceiling. There's something I'm missing here. Some magical sorcerer's key that will solve this mystery. I attempt to crowbar Kinnaird and Thornton into the Fournier/Carmichael relationship, but can find no way in.

Apart from their varying and often vague connections to Kiaraa, there is nothing that links them, and at the moment, Thornton is not really connected at all, at least not in any provable way. But maybe that's not important. I give Gaëlle a call.

'Hello, Gaëlle. It's Daniel Beckett from the other day. Remember?'

'Sure. *Ça va*? You were quite risky asking me out in front of Mathéo like that. He doesn't like personal stuff in work.'

'No? Anyway, I thought I'd better ask you if there's any type of food that you don't like.' I put a laugh into my voice. 'I wouldn't want to spoil our evening together.'

'Uh, no. I can't think of anything. I'm OK with eating most things. Don't like curry that is very, very hot, but apart from that I'm cool with most cuisine.'

'That's great. I'm a little busy at present, but as soon as I have an evening free I'll call you. Oh. That's what I was going to ask you. What time do you finish work there?'

'Usually, six. Sometimes at seven, but very rare.'

'Does Mathéo ever work late at the office?'

'Never. He's always off at six strictly. He never works late. Only me sometimes. Seven, maybe, but infrequent. There're the other guys, the sales publishing guys, and the editing people, but they usually only work mornings or from home. I can't do that, you know? I *have* to be here. It shits, yeah?'

'I'm sure it does. OK. I'll give you a call as soon as I've booked somewhere. If you can't fit it in, I can always change it. Lovely speaking to you again, Gaëlle.'

'OK. Great. And talking to you, too. *A bientôt.*'

'Oh! I almost forgot. Can you give me your mobile number, please, Gaëlle? Just in case you've left work when I call you or are busy on the landline.'

'Of course.'

I text Gaëlle's mobile number along with Fournier's to Doug Teng.

One or both of these numbers may contain the apps for a Soteria T and/or a HomeTech 40dd system. There's a Maat box that'll be connected to the Soteria alarm function. Same location. Check them out then give me a call. Insincere apologies for short notice. I await your bill with interest.

You had me at 40dd.

...is this year's entry for the Unpredictable Doug Teng Text Awards.

You think it'll win??

While Fournier's site is up on the screen, I take some time to familiarise myself with the sort of books he publishes. It surely can't be all nutjobs like Carmichael. Just as I'm starting to wade through an imprint called Curtain Raisers, which deals with biographies of playwrights, I get a text from Suzanna.

I'm standing outside the door downstairs. Can I come in?

We could just sext if you'd prefer.

Are you sure you wouldn't like a taste of the real thing?

Well, if you insist.

As soon as she's inside, her mouth is on mine straight away.

'My God, Daniel. How long has it been? Two days? It seems like two years.'

She's wearing a blue bouclé midi dress. I start to slowly unbutton it. Her breathing gets ragged. She kisses my neck. The dress falls to the floor.

'How are things going with the case?'

'Some deep and penetrating insights.'

'Those are always the best.' She slips out of her thong then turns her back to me so I can unclip her bra. 'Have you seen Micha since your initial meeting?'

'I had dinner with her last night. There was something I had to talk to her about that couldn't be really dealt with over the phone.'

'Where did you – ah! – where did you go? Wait, wait. Not yet. Not yet.'

'Nowhere. I went to hers. She'd got back late from Brussels the night before and had a day of catch-up meetings. She was pretty tired. Those are nice stockings.'

'Oséree. I bought them yesterday. I needed some new holdups. I think I'll keep them on. My heels, too. They'll complement that body-suit. What's her place like? I've never been there. Not too quickly, Daniel. That's it.'

'It's the penthouse suite. Twenty-ninth floor. Very spacious. Good views. Big television.'

'Did you watch anything?'

'*Mr Bean's Holiday*. Twice.'

'I should have guessed. Did she cook for you, or did you order a Domino's?'

'Southern Indian. Delicious. Very spicy. We had a Domino's after that. I had a Mighty Meaty and some dough balls.'

'What did you have to drink? Sprite?'

'Pink champagne. She was allowed a couple of glasses by her doctor. We had Sprite later on, straight from the tin.'

'Sounds like quite an intimate affair. What did you talk about? Apart from the case, I mean.'

'This and that. Mainly that.'

'Mmm. I thought as much. I'm glad I won't ever have to cross-examine you.'

'I think she's rather interested in your love life.'

'My love life with you?'

'Yes.'

'Did you tell her anything?'

'Of course not.'

She puts her arms around my neck and presses her body into mine.

'It must have been difficult not to try and seduce her, Daniel. She is rather gorgeous, after all.'

'I used every scrap of my willpower.'

'The idea must have crossed your mind, though.'

'Would you like it if it did?'

'I would.'

'Well, the next time she invites me to dinner, I'll certainly let it cross my mind.'

'I think I want to go in your bedroom now. We can talk about it in there. If you don't mind, that is. I want to get that bodysuit on.'

My mobile rings. Doug. Suzanna takes my hand and leads me into the bedroom.

'Hey, Mr Beckett. Just a couple of things. First of all, it was the second mobile number you gave me, the one ending in 3332, that had the Soteria and HomeTech apps on it. The other one was clean.'

3332 is Mathéo's mobile. At least that makes things a little easier. After Gaëlle mentioned that she occasionally finished work at seven, I had to check whether she sometimes set the alarm systems up herself, even though Mathéo could do it remotely on his mobile. She probably just texts/calls him when she's leaving, and he sorts it out.

Suzanna unbuttons my shirt and runs her hands up and down my chest. I hold the side of her neck.

'OK. Just wanted to be positive the other one wasn't getting noisy notifications,' I say.

'Yeah, yeah. Now, as I'm sure you know, quite apart from the local alarms kicking off, any breach of either of those two systems will cause three things to happen. First of all, the app will start shrieking. This will override silent mode and will automatically push your mobile volume up to the max.'

Suzanna gets into the bodysuit. She stands in front of the mirror and zips it up to her throat. It crackles and squeaks. It's a bit too tight over her bust at first, but she makes a few adjustments and now it looks fine.

'Second, you'll get three texts in quick succession. Useless as this may be, any emergency texts from Soteria or HomeTech will also override silent mode and, once again, will turn your volume up, but it'll be your usual text tone.'

Suzanna reapplies her lipstick. She turns to face me. She smiles. She's pleased. The bodysuit makes her look powerful and domineering. Keeping the stockings and heels on was a good idea.

'Third, you'll get an email, presumably letting you know that your premises are being broken into. That's a really useful feature. Wish I'd thought of it.'

The vinyl of the bodysuit feels cold. It's a tight fit but looks fantastic. Suzanna takes my shirt off and tosses it onto the floor. She starts to kiss my neck. I grab a handful of her hair. She closes her eyes and groans with pleasure.

'So, what can we do about it?' I ask.

'You give me two minutes' notice. During that time, I get inside that mobile, access the apps and disable both alarm systems. It goes without saying that the Maat box that communicates with the safe will also be neutralised as it won't be able to access the Soteria system.

'There'll be nothing I can do about any safe that may be connected to the Maat box, but I'm sure you can sort that problem out yourself if need be.'

Suzanna's breathing is ragged. She licks her lips. She's getting impatient.

'But the big problem here is the alarm system communicating with the apps and sending messages *while* I'm shutting the system down,' he continues. 'This will result in the shrieking, the texts and the email as previously mentioned.

'The time lapse between shutting both systems down remotely and the mobile apps getting the message and being noisy is exactly five seconds. Unfortunately, there's nothing I can do to override that, soundwise. Or rather, I *could* override it, but won't have the time.'

Suzanna notices the bite marks that Micha left on my biceps and shoulders, not to mention the biggest one, courtesy of Aziza. She runs a finger over them, looks up at me, smiles, and starts planting gentle kisses on each one of them.

'You'll have to kill the mobile, Doug.'

'Exactly. Under these particular circumstances, the only way is to speed-drain the battery.'

'How long will that take?'

'About three seconds.'

'Cutting it fine.'

'Well, yeah. Still doable, though. But now you have to decide how long you want to make this situation last.'

Suzanna whispers in my ear, 'This feels fantastic. So tight. So restrictive. God. I had no idea.'

'Let's make it twenty minutes from the time it goes down. No. Better make it twenty-five minutes. How long for you to recharge the mobile?'

'Total recharge eight minutes minimum. I can get it to forty percent in two to three minutes, which'll probably be enough. If the target looks at their mobile during that time, or tries to make a call, they'll just assume it's a software or hardware failure of some sort.'

Suzanna runs her hands up and down the sides of the bodysuit. 'So restrictive,' she murmurs.

'And once it's charged again, those apps will show no evidence of tampering?'

'When it's fully charged, I'll have to go in again and set the wireless/software memory back, say, half an hour. That'll take thirty seconds or so.'

'Should the target look at the mobile while this is happening, will it be apparent that something's going on?'

'Get off the bloody phone,' whispers Suzanna.

'No. Everything will look normal, unless you decide to screw around with the Soteria or HomeTech app settings during that thirty seconds, but no one ever does that as they're too confusing to operate for most people.'

'OK. If you could keep your mobile on you this evening, I'll send you a text when you can start all of this. How much?'

'Two thousand. Special offer. D'you think I should do a loyalty card?'

'What about Carmichael's hospital visits?'

'Shirley Oaks Hospital. Appendectomy. Fifteen years ago. That's it.'

'OK. Thanks, Doug.'

Suzanna is getting rather breathless. 'God. I can't believe you. I can't believe you're like this. Look at those bite marks. Why is this so stimulating, so overwhelming?'

'I'm sure there's a term for it.'

'Why was she biting you? What was happening? What was it like? You must tell me everything.'

'You know I can't do that. Client confidentiality.'

'What do I have to do to make you spill the beans?'

I kiss her and whisper a suggestion in her ear. She nods, her mouth open. She looks dazed. She holds on to my shoulders to support herself.

'I feel faint. And yes. Yes, I'll do that. A glass of champagne first, though. And I need to fetch something from my bag.'

A text from Doug:

I can tell you've got a woman there. I want a divorce.

36

A NIGHT IN KNIGHTSBRIDGE

I get a cab to drop me off in Kensington Gore and walk down to Ennismore Mews via Exhibition Road and Prince's Gardens. It's just after ten, a moonless, mild, cloudy night and lots of people wandering around. Just how I like it.

I send a text to Doug.

Now.

I set a timer for twenty-seven minutes on my watch and slip on a pair of latex gloves.

I left Suzanna in my flat watching a documentary about Alain Robbe-Grillet, finishing off the last of the champagne and eating the rest of the Chicken Satay and Weeping Tiger Beef that we'd ordered from Thai Hot Spot. I told her I wouldn't be long. And I told her not to believe anything I said.

As I turn into Ennismore Mews, I take a quick, focussed glance down the entire length of it. Virtually every house has an alarm box outside and I can spot maybe half a dozen security cameras dotted around. These will be aimed at the area immediately outside their respective front doors and hopefully will not be scanning the rest of the road for ne'er-do-wells like me.

There are a few video doorbells, but these are down the other end of the mews, and I can't see any next to Fournier's place or across the road from it. Like Elder Street, this is an affluent area and people are less inclined to use them. Regardless, I'm going to have to work quickly.

It's very bright here. All of the streetlights and house lanterns are turned on. Someone is having a party down the far end of the road. Lots of voices and the dull thump of music. The retractable security grilles outside Fournier's have been pulled down and are locked.

There's some building work being done in the premises next door. Scaffolding, tarpaulins, and security boards extend about three feet to the edge of the pavement. This will prevent me from being seen from the right on this side of the road. There are no cameras on this site, but several warnings that the place is alarmed. That's OK; I have no intention of paying it a visit.

I'm thirty yards away when I see the lights on the Soteria and HomeTech security boxes go off. That means it's safe to enter. I get to the front door, fish out my burglar's tools and start work on the five-lever mortice lock. This is a Fusion Sentinel and is one of the most difficult to bypass.

I push the tension tool into the cylinder and twist it from left to right so I can feel the bolt moving. I push the wire in just above the tool and carefully raise all the levers. The last one is a bit troublesome and feels as if it's been damaged in some way, possibly during the installation. Took ten seconds.

Once that's out of the way, it's the turn of the Yale 1109 night latch. This is pretty straightforward. I use a medium hook to lift the pins and the thing's open in two seconds.

Why do people still install these? I open the door, go inside, and close it quietly behind me.

There are wooden shutters on all of the windows. They're partially closed, so I close them completely and turn on my Maglite. I can smell Gaëlle's perfume. I flick the light around the reception area. Looks much the same as it did the other day.

I crouch down behind Gaëlle's desk and take a quick look in all the drawers. A few pens, a pink retro-looking calculator, a broken mobile stand shaped like a duck, a copy of *La serveuse était nouvelle* by

Dominique Fabre, a Hello Kitty luggage tag, and some magazines: *L'Officiel, Madame Figaro,* and *Elle*. I check the floor and walls for a safe. Nothing.

I don't waste any more time in reception and go into Fournier's office. The door was closed, and for a moment I thought it might have been locked, but in the event it was easily pushed open. Part of me is looking for something that will confirm the suspicions generated by Doug's hacking of Fournier's bank account.

I close the door behind me and look around. I remembered that there was a medium-sized banker's lamp on his desk, so I switch it on; the dim illumination won't be seen from the front or from the rear of this place. I toss his credit card (fingerprints eradicated) onto the floor behind the weeping fig.

I take a look at the Maat box on the wall. The red light is still flashing, but if anything happens to the safe (wherever that is), it won't be able to communicate with the Soteria system, so no alarms will go off.

A bit of a stupid set-up, really, but not uncommon. If I was in charge of Fournier's security, I'd make sure that the safe was connected to a system that didn't depend on another one. It must have seemed like a good idea at the time; obviously an excellent salesman was involved.

There's a small stack of books on a table next to the Fragonard print with a recent copy of *The Daily Telegraph* resting on the top. *Music Comes out of Silence* by András Schiff, *Merchants of Culture* by John B. Thompson, *Beating Bankruptcy* by A.C. Young, *Britain's Steam Locomotives* by Julian Holland. I take a photograph of them just in case it comes in useful later.

Beating Bankruptcy is an interesting choice, all things considered. I can smell Fournier's cologne. It's so strong that I wonder if he's in here, looking over my shoulder, nodding his head, wanting to be liked.

Now it's the turn of Fournier's desk. Six drawers, none of them locked. I pull out each one in turn, dump it next to the banker's lamp and take a good look inside, photographing the contents of each one, so I can put everything back as it was, or pretty damn close. I'll double-delete those photographs as soon as I get out of here.

The first thing I find is a dog-eared manuscript of Carmichael's latest literary masterpiece, *Man 2 Man*. I flick through it. Looks boring, though it's pretty weighty. Chapter titles are things like "Why Do Women Hate Us?", "Men's Suffrage", "Economic Fraud in the Home" and "Feminisation in Portugal".

I don't think I'll be putting it on pre-order.

Once again, I wonder why Fournier bothers himself with this sort of stuff. Does Odette know? If she does, what does she think? This is surely at odds with everything she stands for. Perhaps he has an egalitarian outlook.

I look up. Footsteps. Someone walking by outside. A man and a woman, talking and laughing. I wait until they're gone.

There's a letter from The Old Etonian Association. Some sort of newsletter called the OEA Review. So, Fournier went to Eton as well. Would he have been a contemporary of Carmichael? No. Wrong age. Something to keep in mind, though.

I spend exactly three minutes looking at more drawer debris, but it's all pretty uninteresting. The red flashing light on the Maat box catches my eye. It's time to find the safe.

I didn't see it in the reception area and as far as I can tell it's not in here, but I take a good look around anyway.

First of all, I flash the torch across the floor, systematically looking for any obvious carpet disturbance or wear and tear. Nothing. I move each item of furniture in case someone's being clever, but no luck. I look at my watch. Thirteen minutes to go.

Now the walls. There are six large framed prints which I carefully move to the side, but I know I'm being a bit optimistic; no one would put a wall safe behind a picture, unless they were starring in a 1960s television series. I turn the banker's lamp off and switch the Maglite back on.

There's a door at the back of this room. I open it to reveal a narrow staircase. These mews houses only have a first floor, so at least that's something. I go upstairs.

There's a medium-sized sitting room, a bedroom, a bathroom with a shower, a fairly large office area, and a spare room which is stuffed with tons of books. Perhaps I should take Gaëlle out sooner rather than later. Very attractive and sexy. Might be fun. Might be informative.

I take a look behind the piles of books that are up against one of the walls, obstructing the view out of a small hexagon window. I check the ceiling and the walls. I check the floor. Nothing.

For a second, I wonder if Fournier's having an affair with Gaëlle despite his disparaging remarks, then dismiss the idea. There was no chemistry between them, and I don't think he'd be her type. She had a nice voice. I bet she likes dancing.

The office area contains three medium-sized desks, each with its own PC. I assume that this is where the publishing director, marketing specialist and proofreader work, when they can be bothered to come in. Nothing of interest in here, apart from a paperback of *Was it an Illusion?* by Amelia B. Edwards on one of the desks.

The sitting room is pretty basic: a huge Toshiba smart TV, a B&B Italia swivel chair, a big red sofa, a shiny Eichholtz coffee table, a smart wooden bar cabinet with six built-in wine racks and three Seletti Hybrid Clarice cocktail glasses resting on the top. I pull out the bar cabinet and look behind it, and, once again, check the walls and the floor. No luck.

I take a look in the bedroom. The king size bed looks unslept in, the ensuite bathroom untidy but clean. There's a fair-sized triangular door next to the bed. I pull the handle and the whole thing loudly comes away in my hand. No hinges. The door is attached to the frame with magnets.

That was sloppy of me. Too much noise.

And there it is. It's a big alarmed Midgely Protector. A triple lever lock that can be opened with a key, or in my case, picked. Not too bad. It could have been one with a keypad that required a correct hundred-digit code to be typed in or something annoying like that, although those hi-tech safes are generally much easier to break into.

There's a small rectangular box attached to the side with a red flashing light, which will be the connection to the Maat box downstairs. This would be triggered by the vibration caused by the bolts being retracted into the door when it was unlocked. I can't turn the light on in here as there's a curtained window at the front of the house, so I'll have to hold the Maglite between my teeth.

I grab the safe on both sides, concentrate, and give it a subtle slow push. Sometimes these safes will have an anti-tamper mechanism which will kick off if you lose your temper with them and rock them back and forth or hit them. I want to see how immobile it is. It's immobile. This lack of movement means it's bolted to the floor. Probably at least four anchor points. Must have been a pain to install.

There's a theory that if you hit the top of this type of safe hard enough, the door will open, but I'm not going to test that out right now, and that phenomenon is more likely to happen with digital keypad safes. Besides, there isn't enough space in here to raise your fist up that high and you'd probably break your hand in the process.

I've got a small burglar's tool attached to my keyring for precisely this type of job. It's a variation on a Utility Wafer Jiggler or gas cap key. More commonly used for opening filing cabinets and the like, but it could have been made for this type of safe lock which is too incapacious for my usual tools. I push it into the lock and, as the name suggests, jiggle it around for about thirty seconds. Plays havoc with the internal pins and doesn't do any damage or leave any marks.

There's a loud click as the primary lock opens. I count to ten and very slowly push two of my toughest tungsten picks into the secondary lock and turn, keeping a fair amount of pressure on all of the time. I hear a car backfire somewhere outside. My wrist hurts.

In five seconds, I can hear the three bolts grinding as they recede into the door. The door opens. Not much of a safe, really, but with all the other security precautions here, I reckon Fournier didn't think he'd need a better one. Or perhaps he doesn't keep anything of value in here.

There's a big pile of stuff inside. It's going to be too awkward to squat here looking through everything with a torch in my mouth, so I take a photograph of the pile in situ, pick it up in both hands, take it downstairs and dump it on Fournier's desk, turning the banker's lamp on again so I can see what I'm doing.

I speed-read my way through countless multilingual contracts with distributors, designers, agents, authors, accountants, proofreaders, publishers, lawyers, and communications with three different banks, two in the UK and one in Siena, though God knows what I'm looking for. A name? A clue?

There's a magazine called *Éditeur Moderne,* which has Fournier's face on the cover. It's almost four years old and he looks slimmer and younger, a smug smile and designer stubble. Why keep this in a safe? Perhaps he didn't want it to get damaged. Perhaps it meant a lot to him in some way.

I find the article that's about him and quickly read it. Just PR for his company, basically, apart from a bit of gushing about Odette, who he absolutely adores and how they're a mutual support society in the matter of their respective businesses. Romantic.

There's a photograph of him sitting on the corner of a desk in the company's Basel branch, smiling and looking self-consciously cool and casual. Behind him, sitting at a desk and doing something, is a blonde girl who I realise is Gaëlle. I think black hair suits her better. I remember Fournier saying that she'd come from the Basel office when I spoke to him the other day.

Then at the very bottom of the pile, the very last thing I come to, is something that gives me a couple of seconds of heart palpitations.

Surely not. It's a brown, card-backed envelope. A3 size. 'Please do not bend' on the front in red letters.

It's addressed to Mme Odette Fournier, 44 Pembridge Crescent, London W11 3AA. That's Notting Hill.

Did I know Odette lived there already? I can't remember. Oh yes. W11 was the postmark on those letters to Kiaraa from Odette, or Chaton as she was known to me then.

I can barely bring myself to open this in case I get disappointed. But I absolutely, positively know what I'm going to find.

I push all the other stuff out of the way, take a deep breath, and tip the contents of the envelope onto the desk in front of me.

The four missing Pöck photographs: every naked, tied, black-stockinged, blindfolded, cuffed, high-heeled, blonde-wigged one of them.

And there's a letter, written on a sheet of notepaper from the Parco dei Principi Grand Hotel in Rome. There's a small, stained area where the ink has run. I sniff it: Estée Lauder Tuberose Gardenia.

Chaton

I had these taken for you for while I am away in Europe. I wonder which one is your favourite? Look at them when you are alone and think of me. Think about what we do when we are together. All of it. And what you enjoy the most, my bad, bad, wicked girl. Do not make too much noise, and that is a strict order, from me to you. I insist you obey. Do not show to Mathéo, my love. I doubt that he would understand! There are more. Perhaps for your birthday? But then I may have another gift for you also – I'll LYCO. Yours always, your only love.

Angel

P.S. The more I think of us living together, the more appealing it becomes. Can you imagine? We said Paris or London, but what about Rome?

Well, that's it. The photographs were sent to Odette, but somehow found their way into Fournier's hands. How it happened is irrelevant. Maybe he ripped the envelope open thinking it was for him. Maybe he was suspicious of Odette and was keeping an eye on her mail. I wonder if he knew what LYCO meant, as I certainly don't.

I scan the photographs dispassionately, to see if there's any way these could have been perceived as a bit of a lark between friends, or some ironic and amusing diversion.

Absolutely not.

Even if there was no accompanying letter, these were way too explicitly erotic to be anything other than an intimate communication between two lovers. Factor in the letter with its erogenous implications and talk of cohabiting, and it's obvious that Odette had been caught red-handed.

But Fournier didn't confront her about it. When I spoke to Odette a couple of days ago, she told me that he didn't know about her relationship with Kiaraa. But he did. I take a look at the postmark on the envelope. July 17th. Almost two weeks after the Wigmore Hall concert and about ten days before the knife threat in Barrett Street.

So, does this put Fournier in the frame? Pretty much, and he just earned a third tick against his name on the naughty list. He has motive to dislike Kiaraa, perhaps even loathe her. His business is in receipt of some extremely dodgy-looking payments. But is he a kidnapper? Is he a murderer? A rapist? More thought needed here. I put the photographs back in the envelope and carefully return them to the safe with all the other stuff.

After checking that there are no tell-tell signs that I was here (accidentally dropping a business card on the floor, signing my name in the visitors book), I let myself out, lock the door behind me, and let Doug know that he can turn the alarm system back on. Then I get a cab back to Covent Garden, thinking about Aera in black seamed stockings.

37

I'M YOUR PLAYBOY BUNNY?

The next morning, after I've had a shower and a shave, I sit at the kitchen table with a large mug of coffee and a heap of painkillers. For some reason, I've got a terrible headache behind my eyes and my back aches. Must be all the stresses and strains of burglary catching up with me. I think Suzanna may be to blame, as well. Just possibly. I may start a campaign to have HRT banned in the UK.

I turn the computer on and impatiently tap my fingers on the surface of the table. I was hoping that a good night's sleep would sort out some of the conundrums that my brain has been wrestling with over the past twenty-four hours, but they're still there in their unsolved form, mocking me. I just need a few more things to link together. I find my A4 sheet with the chronology of events written on it and place it in front of me, pen at the ready.

I think about Fournier and his discovery of Kiaraa's photographs and the accompanying note.

A man discovers his wife is having a passionate affair with a famous woman, a woman he knows, a woman whose pianistic skills he greatly admires, a woman who his wife would never have encountered were it not for his European musical patronages. There is even the suggestion that they were thinking of moving in together, presumably without him.

But he doesn't confront his wife about it. He keeps it to himself. Maybe he broods over it. Maybe he wants revenge. Maybe he's waiting for the right moment, the right set of circumstances to appear before he can act.

Then, almost two months later, this woman is kidnapped. Minutes, possibly, after leaving a dinner at which he was present. Is it conceivable that these events are connected in some way? Lazy thinking would make it seem likely.

I try to put myself in his position. Let's say I was married to Penny, for example. We don't have kids, we're both wealthy and successful, we appear to be madly in love with each other, then I discover that she's seeing someone else behind my back. Would I be upset? Probably. Would I tell her about my discovery? Certainly. Would it make it worse that I'd introduced her to this person? Absolutely.

So, what would make me stay with her? What would stop me talking about it? Perhaps I loved her so much that whatever she did or whoever she did it with wouldn't matter to me. I might even welcome it. It might act as some surreptitious aphrodisiac. I might shunt the whole thing into some spare room in my brain, lock the door and throw away the key.

At the time Mathéo discovered the photographs on July 17th or thereabouts, his business was 'looking unhealthy/staring bankruptcy in the face' as Doug put it. That, at least, would give him a pretty good reason to stay with Odette. Until he was able to make some sort of financial recovery, which it looks as if he did six months after Kiaraa was murdered, possibly with his share of the ransom money.

So why is he still with her? To avoid suspicion? To be careful? Was he advised to stick with the status quo for a while? By whom? Kinnaird? Did Odette know about his business troubles?

Just as I'm pondering these notions, a request for me to accept a Zoom call appears on my screen. I don't have Zoom, but it looks as if I do now. It's from HŒDAK&r^^420. I look down to see if I'm dressed. I'm not. But sod it, it's only Krysia. I accept the call.

She's wearing an ivory satin cami set that looks great against her light olive skin. Blonde hair for a change, with purple lipstick and ochre eyeshadow. She sips from a huge coffee mug with Monkey3 written on it in poison green lettering. Probably some band.

She laughs. 'Hey, sexface,' she says. 'I was going to talk to you about some shit but as you're naked you want to have Zoom call fuck instead?' She whips off the cami top and throws it across the room. 'You feeling good now? You ready to rock? What you think? Hot or what? My name's Egelfride. I'm an air hostess with Flysas. Your type for sure. I've just split up with my violent fiancé and I'm as horny as a mink in season.'

I laugh and point at the screen. 'Can I do a screen capture of this and get a t-shirt made?'

'Only if I can do the same with what I can see on *my* screen, teeny tiger. You wanna have unprotected sex sometime? Let's have a crazy baby.'

'That's the second time someone's suggested that to me in three days.'

'No shit. I need to settle down. You know how old I am now?'

'Sixteen.'

'That your best guess now? I'll be thirty-two next birthday. I'm almost as old as you. You better drink your coffee before it gets cold instead of gawking there with your mouth hanging open like some fat politician ogling hot plastic surgery chicks on PornoThrust while his wife helps starving children in a skanky tent.'

'Why are you risking this call, Krysia? Aren't Interpol watching?'

'No worry. I shredded your DG6 IP sensor alarm as soon as you replied to this. Automatic. Very clever. You'll need to get your computer fixed after we're finished here. Sorry. And Interpol is like wet sandwiches, you know? They smell of mouth.'

'What can I do for you, Krysia? Can you put your top back on?'

'Am I distracting you now?'

'Yes.'

'Hold on.'

She disappears for a few seconds and reappears holding the cami, which she slips back onto her body as unhurriedly as possible, arms slowly waving in the air, followed up with a lot of hair fingering and tossing, and a tiny bit of eye smouldering. She looks like she's preparing for a photo shoot while attempting to seduce the photographer.

'Nice action, Krysia.'

'Thanks. OK. I'm ready. Thing one. How did it go with the website?'

'Totally fell for it. A brilliant piece of work. Putting the link to his website eighth down was a good idea. We had a little laugh about that.'

She drinks more coffee and licks her lips. 'He seems like a big creep. This some job? You going to crush him now?'

'Maybe. It's difficult and slow-moving.'

'OK. Thing two. Yeah. So. You said to let you know if I came across anything interesting when I was scoping out this dickwad.'

'Did you?'

'Well, yeah. Kind of. He's quite an asshole, I think. He's *such* an asshole that it was quite entertaining reading about him, in a kind of sick way. Like it's fun reading about serial killers or tropical diseases.

'I dug deep. I was bored. You wanna live with me in Stockholm? This is all a bit random and disconnected, but I'm sure you'll sort it out in your head. All that stuff on his sadfuck political site about women lying about rape and Japanese chicks and things. It's like – *whoa!* Is he for real? There was a big police report I found about him breaking his wife's jaw.'

'Yeah. He mentioned it. It wasn't his fault apparently. He claimed she had a weak jaw. He got a suspended sentence.'

'Well, that's not a fact, you know? He actually went to prison for two years for grievous bodily harm. He was lucky. Could have been more. It says here he pleaded lesser culpability whatever the fuckhell that is.'

Prison? Was he sparing my feelings by not telling me about that?

Perhaps he was ashamed. Perhaps it wasn't good for Birthright business. Perhaps he was in denial. Perhaps he'd blocked it out.

What was it Aziza said? *Prone to exaggeration/lying.* You could plead lesser culpability if you had a mental disorder, or if the assault was spontaneous and/or impulsive.

How the hell could a two-year prison sentence be under the radar?

'Are you sure about this?'

'No. I just made the whole thing up for big laughs. And it wasn't the first time he'd attacked her. No no *no*. It had happened before. That time he'd punched her in the stomach a few times, but she didn't press charges. Got a caution. *He* did, I mean. Women, eh? Sounds like an uncontrollable temper or some shit. There might have been more things. I'll keep digging.

'Want my sophisticated psychology? He's a violent, nasty, impotent cockshit, but he got caught out, so he sublimated his lust for beating chicks up into his bullshit politics and his wanksucker books. How's that for psychobabble, baby?'

'I couldn't do better myself. Did you just call him a *cockshit*?'

'You like that? I just thought that up! His Wikipedia page you sent me. It doesn't mention *any* of that crap at all. Or on his crummy website. It's been cleaned up, I'm thinking. Or it wasn't on there in the first place.

'Maybe he was such a dweeby small fry at the time that it wasn't mentioned, and nobody noticed much? Or perhaps it was because it all happened before he was a politico? Maybe he had influential scuzzbag friends? Who knows? I mean, they must have a lot of stuff to look at, all those website nerds. Lots of stuff on the net. Mega.

'I guess if he became the Prime Minister it would all come out. Some snoopy journalist would take a close hyper-look, then *boom*! Maybe he cleaned it up himself. Maybe he got someone to do it for him. It's doable even if you don't have an account. I could go into that page and alter it in five minutes flat and no one would know I was there. I could make it say he likes having sex with balloons or parrots.

'Anyway, that's just the half of it. All this Birthright bullshit thing. That's a bleach job, too.' She starts laughing. 'This is so fucking ridiculous. It used to be called Men Versus Women, sometimes Men V Women, and before that it was called The Battle Stations Party.

'He gave an interview to some online shitmag called *Integrity Monthly*, bleating about how he might have to wind down Birthright because not enough people were giving him money and he was finding it hard to cope. Big crying jag from me on that one. I blubbed until dawn. Neighbours complained.'

'When was that?'

'Oh. Er. No exact date, but about three years ago now, by the look of the other stuff in that issue.

'And he calls himself Billy – or it was a nickname – because his favourite author is some assprick called Billy Pottinger, who wrote a book called *Run, Little Girl, Run,* which is a trash novel about women being naturally subservient to men in this utopian hell-world of the future where chicks are slaves and men are gods or some shit. Tried to find it on Amazon, but I guess it's out of print. Boo-hoo. Assprick. I made that one up, too. And wanksucker. And shitmag. And scuzzbag. And twatwank. And fuckhell. I'm a towering creative force. No wonder you're in love with me.

'Pottinger's got another book called *What it Means to be a Man*. Non-fiction. I'll be tracking that one down for *sure*. Are you sure you don't want some Zoom call horny stuff? We could do some online edging if you like. I've got all morning.'

'You're an hour ahead of me. Give me time to wake up. Keep going.'

'So, he comes out of prison and gives this insane interview to some piece of shit online magazine called something or other, and it was clear that he blamed his imprisonment on women as a whole and *that* was where the whole political thing started. Or it seemed to be. Just like I said – sublimated lust. Good band name. What a freak! I can't find the actual interview, though. Can't find the date. Only the mention of it. Maybe they went under. Big shame. Huge loss. I'll need therapy to cope.'

'So…'

'Wait. Stop interrupting me. You're like my mother. You'd like my mother. Physically, I mean. Zaftig. Juicy. Drinks too much, though. You could take her off my hands. I could be a bridesmaid.'

'I'm not going to marry your mother, Krysia.'

'So then, even though he's on probation or whatever shit you do there, he gets into a *fist fight* with some woman in a supermarket *car park,* right? Unbelievable. No date. Something about where she parked her car. You heard me right. What the fuck? Police called but sorted out as some big misunderstanding. Woman calmed down, everyone happy.

'*Then* I find this different article in a paranoid student blogshit called *Conspiracies* and they got it from some nutjob UK news site or other. It says that one of the police guys who was somehow involved in this supermarket shit and calmed it all down was a secret member of The Battle Stations Party as it was called then. Doesn't say how they found this out, though. Some detective constable, though who knows how a detective got caught up in normal cop shit like this. Poor staffing maybe. Desperation. People on holiday. Dog-sitting problems.'

'I...'

'Quiet. I'm not going to tell you again. So, mini scandal. The supermarket woman finds this out and demands lots of stuff. Fairness. Stuff like that. Women, huh? And so it ends. How she found out about your Billy guy or what he did isn't mentioned, but I can dig deeper for more money if you like. My mother's name is Bozena. Cute, huh? Means "divine".

'And hey – I found a little thing about The Battle Stations Party on a loser blogcrap called *Why Women Nag*. Flaky, huh? Not much, but they have a little byline or whatever: *The Battle Stations Party – Putting Women in their Place*. Fuck. Do I nag?'

'All the time.'

'You think I should train as a geisha?'

'Absolutely. I'll blacken your teeth for you.'

'And listen to this: "I will only say this once. We men are at war. We are at war with women. They will stop at nothing to defeat us. But have no fear, we will defeat *them*".' She pauses to laugh for thirty seconds. Her laugh is charming, like tinkling bells. '"We will crush them. We will obliterate them. We will be victorious. We are The Battle Stations Party, working for proud but downtrodden men everywhere". I mean, how is the human race meant to reproduce now?'

'Haven't you heard of cloning?'

'Didn't think of that.'

'Anything else?'

'Well, that's where it kind of runs out, like these things often do in the interworld. All this was in this article, but it doesn't link to anything else. Sorry – am I confusing you? But, I mean, fuck. The police are bad enough in the first place, but I don't think they should belong to *chiflado* organisations like that. I'm thinking he got a reprimand. The detective constable, I mean. Slap on the wrist. Called a naughty boy. Police are police are police.'

'Can you get that article up on the screen while remaining here with me?'

'You like me being with you? Hey. I'm wearing that perfume you like. Thameen Palace Amber. Limited edition. How can I afford that, huh? The mind's boggling. Shall I take the top off again? I'm looking sexy as fuck today. You think I should be a model? Do I look stoned? I have to go out to the shops later. Will people notice, d'you think? Hold on now.'

Everything goes black. Then some sort of shouty rock music starts playing. A red medusa-like symbol flashes on and off in the corner of the screen. I can't imagine what she's done to my computer. I'll have to get Doug to look at it. The music stops. Krysia returns.

'Here's the little article coming on your screen now. Top right. No. Top left. No. Top right. Top left from my POV. Can you see it?'

'Got it.'

I expand it. It's from something called the *Marylebone Gazette*. And the detective constable was Kinnaird.

I read it three times to be sure just in case I'm hallucinating. I can hear my text tone going off in the bedroom.

'You OK? You look like you're thinking. Stop that now. What's that noise? That your mobile? Sounds like fairy xylophones. Hey, if you marry my mother she'll be Bozena Beckett. Sounds splashy. Can you imagine the relationship complexities if you're still intercoursing *me* from time to time? Wow. I'm liking the sound of this. It's depraved.'

'This is fantastic, Krysia. Fantastic. This a real breakthrough for me. I know that cop. I've been trying to link him to Carmichael, and I just couldn't find a way in. I'm sending you another thousand Euros for this. No, fifteen hundred. If you've got nothing else on, I'd be grateful if you could keep at it.'

'Sure. I'm your girl of the month now?'

'Girl of the year. At least.'

'I'm your Playboy Bunny?'

'Right down to the fluffy cottontail.'

'Shall I take the top off again now?'

'Only if you absolutely insist.'

'Ha ha. You want to tie me up again next time? Can we go on holiday?'

'Sure. Where would you like to go?'

'Iceland.'

'It's a deal.'

'Oh, great. I'll bring my Playboy Bunny costume and fishnets, channel my inner Elsa Peretti. I'll buy some new everyday clothes, too. Short skirts, yeah? Tight blouses? Impertinent overpriced lingerie? Fifteen-inch heels? Pony mask?'

'What else?'

My text tone repeats itself.

'I know you better than you know yourself, *cariño*.'

'Hey – what does LYCO mean, Krysia? L-Y-C-O. As in "I'll LYCO". Is it slang? An acronym?'

'God. You don't *know*, sexboy? I'll tell you when we're in Iceland. 'Bye now.'

'Hey…'

Too late. She's gone.

So somewhere along the line, Kinnaird distanced himself from Carmichael but quite possibly kept in touch. This means that he, Carmichael, and Fournier are all connected. And Carmichael had money troubles, just like Fournier. At bloody last.

From what I can remember, the Home Office doesn't allow cops to take any sort of active role in politics. Something to do with impartiality in the course of their duties.

But they can still be members of a political party. Just not one involved in terrorism or one with extreme views. Did Carmichael's party count as one of the latter?

I think it did. Any political party that promotes the idea that women lie about rape is certainly edging towards that exalted status.

So, the info about Kinnaird belonging to Carmichael's crew somehow drifted into the public domain, albeit in a small way. How did he get away with it? I can only assume he'd have got a dressing down from his superiors and promised to be a good boy. *Slap on the wrist* as Krysia speculated.

Maybe he'd have said he didn't fully understand what The Battle Stations Party were all about. He was a little naïve. And it's not as if The Battle Stations Party was any sort of big deal at the time.

It occurs to me that Kinnaird may have been behind Carmichael's crimes not appearing in any media outlets. Could he do something like that, or is it just my paranoia? Maybe it was someone else. Carmichael bragged about having many high-profile, influential professionals in his party.

Whatever, it was done. And it doesn't matter who did it or how they did it.

Scarlett speculated that Kinnaird should have been a detective inspector or a detective chief inspector by now. Perhaps that whole episode was a blot on his record. Perhaps the Met see him as only being good for house-to-house enquiries or tracking down vans.

And then there were the rumours of sexual assault. And hitting on all the women officers when he was at Putney. What was it Scarlett called him? Cocky and aggressive? And I mustn't forget Penny and her subsequent photo-stalking. And the complaint from Mrs Ritika Knight. And all the rest. Don't the police weed out people like this?

I press my fingers into my eyeballs until everything goes white and sparkly. If only I had powers of arrest and an escape-proof basement. Maybe I should just hook up with Scarlett and give her everything I've got right now. My train of thought is interrupted by my text tone going off yet again.

I go into the bedroom and check my mobile. Two messages from Aera. Perhaps she needs more lingerie advice. I realise that I get an adrenaline rush whenever she sends me a text.

So sorry to hear about your misfortune, Mr Beckett. I hope you get to read this message. Micha called me. She is most concerned and is on her way to visit you in St Mary's Hospital. She has cancelled her talk about the Crystal D3.

And then:

Do get well soon, and we can resume our highly stimulating (!) exchanges as soon as you have recovered and are able to reply. I bought the black Myla Rose lingerie, by the way. A thrilling purchase. I also took your advice about the black seamed stockings. Hold Ups. Bluebella 10 denier. Once again, get well soon. A.

My mind goes blank. What is she talking about? Alarm bells start ringing. I reply:

Thank you, Aera. I'm afraid I don't understand your text. What misfortune? I'm not in any hospital. I'm in my flat.

But you were the victim of a hit and run accident in Tottenham Court Road early this morning. A police officer informed Micha shortly after she arrived at the Mermaid. She seemed very upset. I can't imagine why!

I call her straight away.

'Aera. Tell me what happened. What's going on?'

'She – Micha – called me from the foyer of the Mermaid at about twenty past nine. Her driver dropped her off there at approximately nine-fifteen.'

It's 9.31.

'She said that you had been involved in an accident, as I described to you. A police officer told her about it shortly after she arrived. He kindly offered to give her a lift to St Mary's. He said it would be faster than her getting a cab.

'She said that she had to prioritise and that seeing that you were OK was more important than a talk that she did not want to give anyway. She asked me to quickly organise a replacement for her. I did so. Mr Deok-su Kim has taken over. He is the chief designer of the Crystal D3. Ms Isuel Maeng is on her way over there now for the questions at the end.'

'Do we know the name of this police officer?'

I get my jacket on. What was it Sallow said? *Be careful out there, as they say. I think we're dealing with major nutjobs.*

'No. I – here is Mr Bahk. He would like to speak to you.'

'Mr Beckett? What has happened?'

'Someone's whisked Micha away under the premise of me having had an accident. I have not had an accident. I'm on my way over. I'd like to speak to Micha's driver as soon as I get there. Try Micha's mobile and call me back.'

'Of course, Mr Beckett.'

I'm about to leave when some sixth sense combined with Sallow's words makes me stop. I'd put all of Kiaraa's secret drawer stuff in a cupboard in my bedroom. I open it up, pick up the Daewoo K5 semi-automatic, give it a quick once-over, and shove it in the waistband of my chinos.

I head down to The Strand to find a cab. Takes five frustrating minutes. I sling the driver a fifty.

'Leadenhall Street. The Sansuyu Building. I need to get there the day before yesterday.'

'Time travel a speciality, mate. Hold on.'

Baek-Hayeon gets back to me. 'She is not answering her mobile, Mr Beckett. It seems to be dead. Most unlike her. She always carries a Syringa SS60 charger with her in case she is unable to find a charging point. One moment, please...

'Aera has just contacted the Mermaid. A reception coordinator said that Micha left the building with a police officer after he had told her a friend had been in an accident.'

I glance out of the window. We're racing down the A40 approaching Chancery Lane. Come *on*...

'Give them a call. Find out who that coordinator was. I'll be with you shortly.'

I watch St Paul's Cathedral flash by. To calm down, I try to imagine that I'm a tourist on some sort of high-speed rush-hour trip around the City of London. Doesn't work.

I give Doug Teng a call.

'Listen, Doug. This may be impossible, but that tracking app thing you were trying out on me the other day. You said it could work on mobiles that have been switched off or even destroyed and whatever the other thing was.'

'Yeah, yeah. Destroyed might be difficult. Depends on how destroyed it is. There's destroyed and there's destroyed. And then there's *destroyed*. Details, please.'

I give him Micha's mobile number. The cab lurches to the right to avoid a cyclist and I get hurled into the door. 'Sorry, mate!' We're already in Cheapside, so my fifty-pound mega-tip to get me to Leadenhall Street fast has paid off.

'Can you start on it immediately, Doug? This is urgent. The phone and its owner are almost certainly in a moving vehicle.'

'In front of a screen now. This is registered to Jeong Mi-Cha, is that right? And it's a Sansuyu Crystal D2. Manufactured eight months ago in Gangneung.'

'That was worryingly quick.'

'At first glance, it may have been intentionally switched off or forcibly drained of power. Zero signal. But there are, like, *vapour trails* that all new-ish mobiles give off. More complicated than that, but that'll do for now, I don't want to give you a techboy headache.

'I'll just leave you with "quick decay molecule strength" and "low signal reflection". Very faint but traceable by someone as smart as me. This is free as it's experimental software. I'll have to make a few adjustments. I'll send you the app after I've worked things out. I'm going to end this call so I can concentrate.'

He clicks me off. The first thing that occurs to me is that Kinnaird has lifted Micha for reason or reasons unknown.

I'm guessing that Brian Colbert would have told Kinnaird about my visit by now. Two years have gone by, he thinks he's well in the clear, and then a private detective gets one of his idiot helpers to spill his guts about the Fiat van, then gets him positively ID'd from a photograph. Where did the photograph come from? Who took it? When did they take it? Why did they take it?

Colbert only knew Kinnaird by his fake name of Bill Goodman. Did this PI know his real name? He would have to assume that if he'd gone to the trouble of photographing him, then he probably did. Also, someone searching for a DS Bill Goodman would quickly come to a dead end.

The van misdirection was a brilliant piece of deceit, as was getting himself on that facet of the case. Muddying waters doesn't cover it. Did he make up a few false leads to waste time? Who knows. Every time

Kinnaird spoke to anyone in Elder Street and its adjacent roads about the white Fiat Ducato, the deceit would have been reinforced, time and time again.

When he was removed from Elder Street duties for being a jerk, he could continue the deception while he supposedly searched for the Fiat. Smart stuff. The behaviour towards Penny and Mrs Knight might even have been intentional: a smokescreen, a time-wasting deception, typical shitty Kinnaird behaviour, maybe a way of getting him on van duties. Could he have been *that* sly, *that* shrewd?

And now it's starting to unravel. How on earth, he'll be wondering, did this PI find out about Brian Colbert?

So, he knows the identity of the PI. Would it not be logical for him to move against me first? Contact me in some way? Threaten me? Perhaps not. He might have surmised that surprise would not be on his side.

But Micha? Isn't he in enough trouble as it is? Did he think it would be easier? He must know now that Micha had hired me, and that information could only have come from Fournier, which is obvious now that I've linked Fournier to Carmichael and Carmichael to Kinnaird.

If Kinnaird gets caught and brought to justice, then he's totally screwed. Kidnapping, murder, rape, perverting the course of justice many times over. As a cop, his life in prison would be hell on earth, particularly with Sallow's unscrupulous input. He's got nothing to lose. He's panicking. Either that, or he's much smarter than I've given him credit for.

We speed down Cornhill and soon we're in Leadenhall Street, outside Thunderbird Three. I thank the driver and walk into the foyer, taking deep breaths to calm myself down, trying not to think about Aera's black seamed Hold Up stockings and Myla Rose plunge bra. And failing.

38

THE MERMAID

Chan-Yeol Choi, senior daytime reception co-ordinator, is already waiting for me, with yet another female receptionist – this time a willowy middle-aged woman – standing behind him and smiling broadly. I must find out what all this is about one day. He doesn't bother with an ID badge. He gives me a curt nod and is not quite his usual cheery self.

'Mr Beckett. Charmed to see you again. Would you join me in the elevator, please? We shall proceed to the forty-fourth floor.'

After the requisite millisecond, the lift stops, and I get out. Baek-Hayeon is waiting, looking uneasy and ashen-faced. We shake hands. Chan-Yeol withdraws into the lift.

'Thank you for getting here so quickly, Mr Beckett. Come into my office. What do you think has happened? Is Micha in danger? I cannot...'

'I don't know yet. What did they say at the Mermaid?'

'I have spoken to a Mr Sevrin Vervloet. He is the Corporate Events Management Deputy Coordinator. Micha spoke to a Miss Omya Detha when she was there.'

'Has anyone called you?'

In the back of my mind, I'm a little concerned about the possibility of another Kiaraa situation raising its ugly head. Or something like it.

Or something worse. I'm going to have to visit the Mermaid as soon as possible.

'Called me? No. No one has called. Is it the same people? The same criminals that took Kiaraa?'

'We'll see. We have to be prepared for any eventuality.'

There's a young woman in her mid-twenties sitting on one of the sofas in Baek-Hayeon's office. She's wearing a yellow single-breasted blazer with a matching skirt and a white blouse. On her feet, a pair of Chloé Lauren sneakers.

When she sees me, she stands up and walks over to shake my hand. She's tall. She wears no perfume.

'Mr Daniel Beckett. I am Soo-ah Ryo. I am Ms Jeong's primary driver. Mr Bahk said you would like to speak to me.'

'Sit down, Soo-ah. This won't take very long.' We sit down opposite each other. I can feel the Daewoo K7 pressing against my right kidney. She smiles at me. She's exceedingly pretty and I need to concentrate. 'I'm sure you've said some of this to Mr Bahk here already, so my apologies if I'm making you repeat yourself.'

'That is quite alright, Mr Beckett. I do not mind.'

'What time did you arrive at the Skyline Tower this morning to pick Micha up?'

'8.41. I had called her earlier to let her know when I was five minutes away. This is my usual protocol.' She laughs. 'Ms Jeong thinks I am silly. She always tells me not to bother.'

'What happened then?'

'She wanted to give herself forty minutes to get to the Mermaid in case the traffic was hectic. It can happen. This, despite the fact that she likes to arrive at these events shortly before she is about to speak.

'She wanted to be early, but she didn't want to hang around when she got there. It could be quite challenging to judge. So. She came down at eight-fifty and we headed for the venue. She had a briefcase with her. Her usual navy Smythson.'

'What time did you arrive at the Mermaid?'

'We arrived at the venue at 9.16, which was fine for her. I parked right outside the entrance. I got out, opened the car door for her and she went inside. We agreed that I would pick her up at the same spot at ten-forty precisely.

'I watched her as she went inside. A black woman of some years greeted her, and they briefly embraced. Then I left and came back here.'

'Were there any other vehicles parked outside or across the way from the centre?'

'No. I was the only vehicle. The road – it is called Puddle Dock – has double yellow lines on all sides. It is a busy thoroughfare. There is a bus stop, but there was no bus there at that time.'

'Did any vehicles pass you by while you were parked?'

'Absolutely not.'

'Any people walking by or hanging around?'

'No one.'

'That's great, Soo-ah. Thanks for your help.'

'You are most welcome. Do you think she will be alright? I am not quite sure what is going on.'

'I'm sure she will. I think there's maybe been a breakdown in communications of some sort.' I turn to Baek-Hayeon, who stands stiffly, as if waiting for orders. 'Could you try her mobile one more time please?'

I watch as he holds the phone to his ear and stares sternly at the floor. He clicks it off and shakes his head.

'OK. I want to go to the Mermaid now. Is there any way that…'

Soo-ah, who was on the point of leaving the office, turns to face me.

'I shall take you. Time is of the essence, yes? I shall be superfast.'

I look at Baek-Hayeon and he nods.

* * *

Superfast doesn't cover it. I'm almost choking on my own adrenaline and the words 'Oh. My. God.' are doing their best to force their way out of my throat.

I've no idea what Soo-ah's driving background is, but I somehow imagine it's the unholy spawn of maxed-out Formula 1 and ultra-hazardous rally racing.

She's driving a Kia Stinger GT2 in neon orange. It smells of Micha's perfume. '0 – 60 in 4.2 seconds,' she says proudly, and I can believe it.

From the moment we erupted from the Sansuyu underground car park, I was gripping my seatbelt in terror while trying to look cool and unruffled.

Every car we approached was rapidly overtaken, every red light loudly threatened by the impatient roar of the engine. Other cars, and especially black cabs, wisely kept out of her way. She cut up a five-ton lorry and casually gave the finger to a neon pink cyclist who had the nerve to shake his fist at her.

With one hand on the steering wheel, she alternated between second and third gears, the engine frequently and noisily objecting to this rough treatment.

To try to calm myself, I watch her hand manipulating the gearstick. Great manicure. Yellow nail polish with red stock car flames, and a black Girard-Perregaux diamond and onyx watch on her wrist. How much do they *pay* her?

As she accelerates down Queen Victoria Street, overtaking three cars in one insane speed-burst which presses me back into my seat, I risk a quick glance at the flexing of her calf muscles as she operates the clutch. She notices and smirks.

Women *always* notice when I do this, no matter how surreptitious I try to be. Must be a sixth sense.

'Everything A-OK, Mr Beckett?' she says, grinning.

I smile at her. 'Just checking the pedals were working properly.'

'And are they?'

'Everything looks in top condition.'

'Pleased to hear it.' She returns my smile. 'I work out.'

'If you ever need a personal trainer, let me know.'

'Are you strict?'

'Beyond your wildest dreams.'

She laughs and rolls her eyes. 'Oh, goodness. That's strict!'

I would have guessed the drive time between Leadenhall Street and Blackfriars to be somewhere around fifteen minutes at this time of day, but we screech to a halt outside the Mermaid in six minutes flat.

Due, I suspect, to force of habit, she gets out of the car, walks around to the passenger side, and opens my door then Baek-Hayeon's.

'I'll be parked here with the hazard lights on,' she says. 'If you'd be so kind, Mr Bahk, to let me know if you're going to be longer than ten minutes and I will drive around the block a few times.'

'Of course, Ms Ryo. And thank you.'

The foyer of the Mermaid is new looking, well designed and enormous. It's a big open space with a large tropical fish tank on one side and several seating areas dotted around: black leather seats, black glass tables. Staircases on both sides that take you up to the first floor.

The reception desk says 'Welcome to The Mermaid' in wavy lettering, continuing the nautical theme. There is a big bunch of red roses to the left. Two black doors either side of this desk, one says 'Like Adam', the other 'Like Eve'. I assume they're toilets.

Baek-Hayeon strides up to the desk. Two people. A tall guy in his fifties in a dark green suit and a pleasantly smiling twenty-something Indian woman in a red uniform. Tall Guy walks towards us and shakes Baek-Hayeon's hand. I assume this is Mr Sevrin Vervloet.

'Mr Bahk. Would you like to come into my office?'

He snaps his fingers at some young guy who's wiping the glass of the fish tank. 'Viggo. Reception, if you would be so kind. Omya, would you join us please?'

Viggo takes his place behind the desk. Omya is the woman in red.

Baek-Hayeon nods towards me. 'This is Mr Beckett. He is my security associate. He will accompany us if that is no problem for you.'

'Of course not. Hello, Mr Beckett. So pleased to meet you. I'm Sevrin Vervloet. I'm the Corporate Events Management Deputy Coordinator.'

Hard to place his accent. Belgian?

We sit down in Mr Vervloet's office. Omya sits next to him.

'This is Miss Omya Detha. She was working reception when Ms Jeong arrived this morning. She may be of help. I'm afraid I was busy in this office at the time and did not see Ms Jeong leave. Do you wish me to contact the police?'

'We don't know what has happened yet,' I say. 'Let's have a chat first.'

Mr Vervloet nods his head. He looks relieved.

'OK, Omya,' I say. 'Could you quickly tell me the sequence of events from the moment Ms Jeong was dropped off outside this building, please.'

She smiles. 'Of course. I saw her get out of that orange car. You could not miss it. I had seen it before when she was here. The last time was about two months ago for the Sansuyu stockholders meeting.

'The driver was a very pretty Korean girl in a yellow suit and light brown sneakers. She got out of the car and opened the door for Ms Jeong to get out. After a short while, the girl drove away.'

'What happened when Ms Jeong came in?'

'Mrs Greer walked over and greeted her. They embraced quickly. Ms Jeong is pregnant, and was holding a dark blue briefcase, so it was awkward for both of them and they both laughed.

'Mrs Sofia Greer is the Conference Chief Executive for Product Launches. She organised the logistics for today's Sansuyu event. She pointed at Ms Jeong's bump, said something, and they laughed again.

'Ms Jeong was wearing a maternity dress. Navy with pink spots. White trainers with some sort of light green leaf pattern. Red lightweight scarf around her neck.

'Mrs Greer talked to Ms Jeong for several minutes. There was a bunch of red roses on the reception desk. Mrs Greer had planned to give them to Ms Jeong after her presentation. A little pregnancy gift.

'Then Mrs Greer left. I think she went into the auditorium to make some last-minute tech checks before Ms Jeong's presentation started. A few seconds later, a man in his forties entered the foyer and started speaking to Ms Jeong.

'I assumed at first that it was someone connected with the presentation, possibly a latecomer, then he produced what looked like a small wallet, opened it, and showed it to Ms Jeong. My instinct was that it was the police.'

'Why did you think that?'

'Apart from showing her the wallet? Just his manner. His size as well, I guess. Now you ask, I can't give you a logical reason. I could not hear what he was saying to her, but he had a concerned expression on his face. After a moment, she looked shocked, and covered her mouth with her hand.

'She approached me and told me that a friend of hers had been involved in a road traffic accident and she was going to visit him in hospital. She asked me to pass on her apologies to all the relevant members of staff here. Then she called her company and asked someone to find a replacement for her this morning.

'Then she went out with this man through the front doors. She looked serious. Serious and upset.'

I get out my mobile and find the photograph of Kinnaird. I show it to Omya. 'Is this the man who spoke to her?'

'Absolutely no doubt whatsoever.'

'And that was it. You didn't see her get into a car. You didn't see her walking away to the left or right when she exited the building.'

'No. My attention was elsewhere by then. I had to deal with a call from TST about their AGM next week. Five hundred people.'

'OK. Thanks very much, Omya. You've both been most helpful.'

'Let us hope there is a positive outcome,' says Mr Vervloet, smiling nervously. 'We are all very fond of Ms Jeong here.'

'I'm sure this will have a very logical explanation,' replies Baek-Hayeon, looking as if he doesn't believe his own words.

Baek-Hayeon and I leave the building and go outside, where Soo-ah is still waiting in the Kia Stinger. I hear her start the engine.

Baek-Hayeon knows nothing about Kinnaird, of course. I give him a brief résumé about who Kinnaird is and quickly explain the van scam. He looks grim-faced.

'What do you think he will do to her, Mr Beckett? Why has he…'

'I think he's panicked. After two years of thinking he's home free, someone has unravelled the puzzle of the Fiat Ducato. That puts Kinnaird right at the centre of Kiaraa's kidnapping.

'The police have that van at the moment and their forensic team is on it. Personally, I don't think they'll find much, but even the tiniest scrap of genetic material would be enough. Kinnaird would know this.'

'But I don't understand, Mr Beckett. What does he have to gain from taking Micha somewhere? Why can these people not leave

Micha's family alone? Is he going to try to hold her to ransom like he did with Kiaraa? It cannot possibly work. We know who he is. Besides, how would we get the money?'

'I don't think another ransom is on the cards. I think he wants to get away with all of this, and in some twisted way, grabbing her was the first thing that came to mind. I don't think even *he* knows what he's going to do yet, or how he's going to do it.

'Colbert would almost certainly have passed my name and mobile number on to Kinnaird. It's what I wanted to happen. I wanted to flush him out. Maybe he decided against contacting me and snatched Micha instead. Her talk today was in the public domain. He must have read about it in the…'

The papers. *The Telegraph* at Micha's place with her photograph and the news item about the mobile launch. The same newspaper on the floor at Kinnaird's and on Fournier's desk in his office. One of them must have read the report about today's talk.

Where the hell is Doug?

'This is all too confusing for me, Mr Beckett. I am so angry that I cannot think straight.'

'I'm the only investigator that has got close to any of these people and it's taken them by surprise. Perhaps he thinks that threatening Micha will kill my investigation before I tell the police what I've discovered. But he has to find out what I know and who I've spoken to. He won't get that information from Micha; he has to get it from me. Lifting Micha gives him leverage.'

My mobile starts making a deep, throbbing noise that I've never heard before. There's an app starting to download. When it finishes, it's just a black circle. My other apps have vanished, probably forever. Then I get a call. Doug.

'Hey, Mr Beckett. That thing stopped downloading yet? What can you see?'

'A black circle. Very minimalist.'

'Tap it please. I'm going to have to talk you through this as it's difficult. Well, not difficult. Unusual. Well, not unusual. Tricky. Hey, what happened to Tricky? I love that album *Maxinquaye*.'

My screen fills up with a primitive and monochrome map of Greater London. It keeps flickering and turning pink and green from time to time. It's almost psychedelic.

'Now. See the pulsating red dot? That's you. OK. Drag two fingers down the screen to move north. Very slowly, please, and a little less pressure than you'd usually use on something like this. This is experimental and delicate. Don't want it to crash. The pulsating violet dot is Ms Jeong's mobile. Can you see it yet?'

'No.'

'Sod it. Keep going. Slow as you like. Let me know when you can see it.'

'Got it. It's on the A1 by the Hope & Anchor. It isn't moving. What's going on?'

'Hold on. Yeah. Good. It was moving until one minute ago. Whatever vehicle it's in is caught in road works. Quite a big snarl-up there. Been going on for weeks. There are three major traffic disruptions on the A1 heading north. This is the first one. OK. So that's it. That's where her mobile is at the moment.

'I'm afraid there's a little time delay on this because of the tracking method, and once you leave London you'll be out of its signal range, but better than nothing, eh?'

We get in the Stinger. Soo-ah looks at me and raises her eyebrows.

'We're going to follow a car which probably contains Ms Jeong. They're almost certainly aiming for a road called Winchmore Park Gate. I'll give you further instructions as and when. For the moment, head for the A1 Islington. We're about thirty to forty minutes behind them, but I think they're going to get snarled up in roadworks. So…'

'Fast?'

'Oh yeah.'

39

A WORLD OF PAIN

It takes us ten scary minutes to get to City Road and we've got the A1 coming up on our right. I check the app. The pulsating violet dot is moving again, keeping on the A1 and proceeding through Highbury.

Soo-ah is doing sixty or seventy most of the time. At one point, an angry besuited prick in a BMW X6 who she's been tailgating for thirty seconds stops in the middle of the road and gets out of his car, presumably to give her a piece of his mind. We're almost touching his bumper.

She waits calmly, tapping her fingers on the steering wheel, until he's about two feet away, then executes a terrifying semi-circular reverse, straightens up and zooms past him. I lip-read 'fucking bitch'.

'BMW drivers here,' she snorts. 'Small dicks.'

Baek-Hayeon roars with laughter in the back.

'What car do *you* drive, Mr Beckett?' she asks.

'A bicycle.'

'Good answer!'

In a couple of minutes, I start to recognise stretches of road from my journey with Imaran the other night, and I'm pretty positive where Kinnaird and pals are heading.

'OK, Soo-ah. We're going to get snarled up in road works if we keep going in this direction. Stick Winchmore Park Gate in your satnav and I'll keep an eye on this app in case there's any deviation. The signal I'm looking at has a slight delay, but it'll be generally accurate.'

'Sounds super hi-tech.'

'Can you work out a way to get to Winchmore Park Gate avoiding all the main roads? Some superfast, er...'

'Got you.'

She does a screeching U-turn and heads back the way we came, to the accompaniment of a cacophony of complaining car horns. She takes a right and speeds down a series of leafy roads, all of which conveniently have speed bumps.

Of course, it occurs to me that the signal I'm looking at may just be Micha's mobile rather than Micha herself. It doesn't exactly explain why her mobile may be switched off or damaged or dead, but it's something I'll have to keep in mind.

Under other circumstances, I'd get Soo-ah to catch up with Kinnaird and force him off the road. I'm sure she'd be up for that. But then he's likely got a pregnant woman in his car, so it probably wouldn't be a great plan, and I think surprise will be on my side if we manage to get to the Winchmore Park Gate house before he does.

How is he subduing her, if indeed he is? Has he assaulted her? Drugged her? Tied her up? None of these would be wise ideas considering her physical state, but I think of what Kinnaird has already got up to and wouldn't put any of them past him. Particularly now.

I check where he is on the app. Turnpike Lane. But he appears to have stopped again.

I show my mobile to Soo-ah. 'Could you have a look at your satnav and see if there's been anything going on where that violet dot is?'

'Sure. Um. Hold on. Yeah. Roadworks. Drains. Destined to be completed in eleven months.'

'Are you sure this is going to take us to…?'

'Just keep your eye on the violet dot and update me as and when,' she says, not taking her eyes off the road, and speedily and skilfully negotiating the speed bumps.

The car rocks from side to side. I feel nauseous.

How is she such a good driver?

She turns to look at me, as if she's been reading my thoughts. 'Superrace Championship Night Race, Gangwon-do. Driver's Champion. Three years running.'

'I can believe it.'

'Very dangerous. Very fun. Great fireworks afterwards.'

I keep watching the app. Kinnaird is, or was, moving again and is on the A105. I have no idea where we are, other than the fact we're driving past a park at 74 mph. I grip the side of my seat. My poorly concealed terror is noted by Soo-ah.

'No grabbing my thigh!' she says.

'That's not what you said last night.'

Big laugh. 'I wasn't playing hard to get then.'

Three minutes later we're in Winchmore Park Gate. I recognise Kinnaird's house due to the distinctive attached garage and its black automatic door. The door is closed. No vehicle parked in the drive. I ask Soo-ah to park on the other side of the road, about a hundred yards down.

I turn around to speak to Baek-Hayeon. 'I'm going to go in a house across the road back there. It's where Kinnaird lives. The car we were tailing is almost certainly heading in this direction. It should be here in about ten minutes, maybe less. Hopefully they'll have Micha with them. Watch where I'm going so you know which house it is.'

'Of course. But how will you get in?'

'I broke into it a few nights ago through a back door. I can do it again.'

I hand him my wallet. He looks uneasy. 'You broke *in*?'

'Whatever transpires, whatever you see or hear, I must ask you not to come in there after me unless I call you and ask you to do it. OK? Even if you see Micha being escorted in, stay where you are.'

He nods his head. 'You have a plan?'

'No.'

'Ah.'

'Thanks for the ride, Soo-ah. Amazing.' Should I ask her out for dinner? No. No. That would be too much at the moment.

'You are welcome, Mr Beckett.' She smiles at me. 'That was great!'

I assume there were at least two people involved in Micha's abduction. Kinnaird, for sure, but there must have been someone else doing the driving, at least initially. Thornton? Carmichael? Fournier? Whoever it was, they're going to be encountering an armed one-man reception committee when they get back here.

I check Doug's app to get a rough idea of their location. Still on course for the house. Less than ten minutes away now, traffic allowing.

In her current state, Micha couldn't have put up much resistance. It may be that she was not under duress and/or did not think she was in danger. But she's not dumb, and she'll be getting distressed by now.

Once again, I walk briskly down the side of the house and let myself in through the rear door that leads into the kitchen. I turn my mobile off and slide it underneath a large Bertazzoni fridge freezer.

Once again, I don't bother to lock the door behind me in case I need to make a quick getaway.

I'm annoyed that I didn't remember to bring any latex gloves, but that can't be helped. I stand still, listening, getting the feel of the place. No noise, no nothing; at least not down here, but I can sense a faint presence somewhere else in the house, possibly upstairs.

As quietly as possible, I revisit the ground floor rooms I was in last time. The reception rooms, the office, the hallway, the kitchen. All empty.

I've never been upstairs here, so I ascend as softly as I can, putting firm pressure on the edges of each step to avoid squeaks. That faint presence is stronger now. Male. When I get to the top I wait a few seconds, then quietly push a door open and walk into what must be the master bedroom. Empty. Unmade bed. Smells of booze and dope.

There are three more large bedrooms, two of which look like they're never used, and the third one looks like it might have been occupied by a woman at some point, but not for a while. Down the other end of the landing is a spacious bathroom. The door is slightly ajar.

There's someone in there.

I can smell sour male sweat and hear the faint rustling of clothes. Then someone pulls the flush. They're about two feet to my left. I give the door two sharp raps.

'Rowan?' says a gruff voice.

The door opens. It's Thornton. He looks at me with astonishment.

'Who are you? Where's Rowan?'

'Caught in traffic. He asked if you'd make me a coffee.'

I can see the cogs turning. Then:

'You're that guy. You're that guy that was in here the other night. Rosanna described you to us. You assaulted Rowan.' He nods his head with satisfaction and smirks at me. 'You're staying with me, mate. You picked the wrong place to burgle. You are about to enter a world of pain.'

I didn't get a great look at him the other night, but he's tall and stocky. He walks towards me. He sneers. I reverse onto the landing. I let him grab my right wrist. I step to the side and take his balance, jerking him towards me while striking him in the side of the head with my left fist. He drops to his knees. He's stunned. He breathes deeply.

'Very fancy,' he whispers. 'Very fancy.'

He rocks from side to side, then pitches forward as if he's about to fall flat on his face. But as he's on his way down, he quickly reaches out and grabs my left ankle, yanking my leg from under me.

I can't stop it happening. I fall heavily on my back, the wind knocked out of me. I attempt to get up, but he kicks me in the face, and my head rocks back with the impact. He's on me straight away, his hand on my throat, punching me in the jaw again and again. He catches me on the nose, and I can taste blood in the back of my throat. This has to stop.

I grab the arm that's throttling me, hit the centre of the elbow hard with the ball of my hand, twist to the side and smack him face down onto the floor. I get him in a wrist lock, my thumb pressing the centre of his palm. The pain makes him yelp. I break two of his fingers. The yelp turns to a scream. I'm able to get on my feet again. I touch my face and look at my hand. Lots of blood.

He gets up, but instead of trying another attack, runs back into the bathroom and locks the door behind him. I kick it open and follow him in. He's making a phone call. He throws his mobile at my head. I bat it away. Another attempted punch to my face. I move inside it and strike the base of his windpipe.

While he's coughing and enjoying that, I clasp both of my hands together and bring them up fast into his balls as hard as I can. I can't hear the testicular crunch, but I can sense it.

He howls with the pain. He's bent double. He straightens up. He staggers. He backs away. He holds his crotch. He reaches in his pocket and produces the warrant card which I photographed the other night. He waves it in the air.

'Listen,' he croaks. 'I'm a police officer. I don't know who you are or why you're here again, but...but this house belongs to a senior detective in the Metropolitan Police. I'm placing you under arrest. You do not have to say anything. But it may harm your defence...'

'Shut up.'

He looks concerned. I walk towards him, block a couple of half-hearted punches to my face, and give him a swift knuckle strike beneath his lower lip, splitting it and splintering two of his incisors. Blood pours out of his mouth. I give him a backhander across the face, then knee him in the balls. His balls are not having a good day. He attempts to support himself on the sink. He fails. He collapses.

A small voice on his mobile is saying, 'Hello? Hello?'

I hear the front door open. Male voices. Someone's running up the stairs and now they're on the landing, heading for the bathroom.

'What the *fuck* is going on in here? Who the hell are you? Are you alright, Clem? Hands on your head, sonny. Turn around. I know how to use this.'

It's Kinnaird. I do as he says. My heart sinks. He's got Baek-Hayeon's gun aimed at my chest. Only now I realise I can't feel its comforting weight against my lower back. It must have got dislodged during that little altercation. Shit.

Kinnaird stares at me. He looks bewildered. 'Do I know you?'

'I was best man at your wedding.'

'Ruin the fucker, Rowan,' says Thornton, attempting to get up and sounding a bit lispy. His voice is hoarse due to that throat strike. So much for his career narrating audiobooks.

'Wait a minute. Wait a minute,' Kinnaird says to him.

'The cunt's crushed my balls. Look at my mouth. My fingers. Look what's he's done. Look at my teeth. Christ.' He gradually gets to his feet, holds his crotch, and dabs his mouth with his functioning digits. 'It hurts to speak.' He pronounces it 'sveek'.

'We'll get you fixed up when all this is sorted,' says Kinnaird. He looks at me. He's angry. 'Who are you? What's your name?'

'He's the guy,' says Thornton uselessly.

'You don't remember me?' I say. 'I'm really hurt, Rowan. I was here the other night. That cosy drugs/booze/porn/bistro favourites/sex evening. You, me, Clement, Rosanna, and Christie. I wanted it to last forever. I died inside when it ended so abruptly.'

Big serious expression. 'You're the guy that punched me. The burglar.' He looks perplexed. 'What are you doing here? Having another go? That fucking torch or whatever it was. I thought you'd blinded me.'

'I wanted to borrow *Lonely Wife Orgy*.'

'Look.' He shows me the side of his head. Nasty bruise where I'd hit him in the temple. 'You could have killed me, you stupid prick.'

'That's what I was going for.'

'I'm going to fucking kill *you*, you toe-rag. Assaulting two senior police officers. Big mistake. We can do whatever the fuck we like to you.'

I'm aware that Thornton is close behind me. I'm impressed that he's still standing. He attempts to grab my arms. Without turning around, I deliver a hard elbow strike to the side of his face, and he drops to the floor.

Almost simultaneously, Kinnaird pistol-whips me across the side of my jaw. He's fast. He's strong. It hurts like a bastard. Blood in my mouth again. I spit the blood in his face. He punches me in the gut.

He makes me face the bathroom wall, both hands flat against the surface. I feel dizzy, nauseous, disorientated. He pushes the gun against the back of my neck, pats me down like a pro, and removes the keys from my back pocket.

I can tell he doesn't quite know what to do. This has happened at a bad time for him. He's confused, annoyed.

'OK. Keep it together, Clem. Don't be a pussy. Get up,' he says.

'We're going downstairs. Go in the kitchen and see if you can find something to tie this dickhead up with. Look in the cupboard next to the fridge. Jesus Christ, a fucking burglar while all this shit is going on. Fuck it. Hurry it up, Clem.'

'My balls are killing me,' complains Clem, slowly getting to his feet. 'He's broken my fingers. Look.'

Kinnaird keeps the gun on me. Proper two-handed grip and the safety is off. I slowly turn to face him, smiling. He keeps his distance. He indicates that I should come out onto the landing.

When I get out there, I'm relieved and worried at the same time. Micha is downstairs with Fournier. He's holding her upper arm in a tight grip. There's a cut/graze on her right cheek that's dribbling blood. She looks up and sees me.

'*Daniel!*'

Half-scream, half-plea.

Fournier squints up at me. 'Christ almighty. That's him, Rowan. That's Beckett. He's the guy that came to the office. The one I was telling you about. The private detective.'

'You're such a sneak, Mathéo. What would Odette think?'

'Well, well. I've heard all about you, my friend,' says Kinnaird, attempting to look unsurprised. 'Down the stairs. Quickly.'

Once we're downstairs, Kinnaird makes me get down on my knees. I'm about six feet away from Micha. Tears stream down her face. That cut looks nasty. Undoubtedly the result of a swift, hard punch. I can see her looking at *my* face and all the blood. I must find a mirror.

'Are you OK, Micha?'

'They have hurt you, Daniel. Your face…'

'Don't worry. Occupational hazard.'

Her gaze is suddenly on Fournier. She frowns. She looks alarmed. She says his name. 'You are Odette Fournier's husband. Is that what this is? You kidnapped and murdered my sister because she was having an affair with your wife? What is it you want? Are you going to murder *me* now? You are cowards. All of you. You are pathetic.'

Fournier looks away and doesn't reply. Thornton reappears, holding a length of hemp rope and a pair of kitchen scissors, which he hands to Kinnaird. Kinnaird gives the gun to Thornton, who keeps it trained on me, standing the requisite six feet away and swaying slightly.

I should have broken the fingers of his right hand. Too late now.

Despite that fact that Thornton looks pale and sick, I reckon both of these dopes would have had firearms training to some degree, so I'm not going to do anything foolish.

Not yet. There's a time and a place for foolish.

Kinnaird quickly cuts the rope into lengths of various sizes. 'Hands behind your back, sonny,' he orders. 'Wrists close together. No stretching the rope. Believe you me, I know all the tricks.'

I look up at Fournier. He appears anxious. Whatever was meant to be going on here was probably quite enough on its own.

Micha glares at him. 'Can you not reply? You are contemptible.'

Kinnaird speaks into my ear as he's tying me up. 'I don't know what damage you've done, but we're going to find out, my friend. We are going to find out.'

'Now you're frightening me, Rowan.'

'You realise it's your fault she's here, don't you. Why she's in that state. Smart idea giving that prick Colbert your business card, but it backfired, didn't it. I had no idea where *you* were, but I knew where *she'd* be. Then, it was only a matter of time before I flushed you out. Then we could use her to get you talking.

'I was going to give you a call once we'd got her here, but you've conveniently delivered yourself to us. You're a mug, plain and simple.'

'I understand prison is pretty bad for cops, Rowan. I do hope you won't be sharing a cell with someone nasty.'

'Keep it up, sonny. Keep it up.'

'I admired your trick with the Fiat Ducato, Rowan. To be honest, you don't seem smart enough to have thought something like that up. You seem – what's the word – *stupid*.'

He pulls me up to my feet. He smirks. He headbutts me. Ouch. Broken nose? Don't think so. Wrong angle. My face feels on fire, though.

He follows this up with a knee to my crotch. Mega-ouch.

He takes the gun off Thornton and puts the barrel right against my forehead. 'I should be very careful about what you say to me, my friend. Very careful indeed. You're in a very bad position.'

'No!' cries Micha.

Without removing the gun, he turns towards her and snarls, 'And *you* can shut the fuck up, you stupid little bitch. Unless you want another smack across the face.'

'How are you going to get out of this, Rowan?' I say. 'You'll never get a promotion now, will you. Perhaps you could become a nightclub bouncer. Or a supermarket trolley shepherd.'

They're ignoring me. Thornton is doing something in the big reception room. After a few minutes, I'm hustled in there and made to sit down on a dining chair. My shoulders hurt.

Micha follows, with Fournier still holding her arm in a tight grip. He ushers her towards another chair about five or six feet away from me, and indicates that she should sit down. He's standing right behind her, watching her carefully.

'It's not going to be *French Bistro Favourites* again is it, Rowan? If I hear "Place Pigalle" one more time, I'll scream.'

No reaction. Of course, I'm saying all this stuff for Micha's sake. I don't like seeing her looking so distressed.

She isn't sobbing, but there's a constant stream of tears running down her cheeks.

Now, on Kinnaird's instructions, Thornton is tying my ankles to the chair legs. He's sweaty and pallid. He's hyperventilating. Those broken fingers must hurt like hell. He attaches my bound wrists to the back of the chair with another length of rope.

'Who are you people?' says Micha. 'What is it you want with us?'

'Get some gaffer tape, Clem,' says Kinnaird. 'I'm sick of hearing that bimbo's whiny voice. Then tie her to that chair.'

Thornton does as he is asked. There's a lot that I still don't understand, so I decide to ask Fournier a couple of questions. Wind him up while I'm at it. You never know. He might even answer.

'What was your main motivation for getting mixed up in all of this, Mathéo? Was it just because of those photographs? I thought they were rather good. Artistic. Or was it the letter? Must have been a shock. Or was it money? How's the business doing? Are things looking up? All those book sales in Bulgaria and Myanmar. Must make a difference.'

Thornton gaffer-tapes Micha's mouth up, winding the tape right around her head, then attaches her ankles to the chair. She attempts to pull the gaffer tape off her mouth, so he tapes her wrists together.

She's breathing slowly but steadily. Fournier looks as if his world is capsizing. How would I know about the letter and those photographs? How do I know about Bulgaria? What else do I know about? Who have I told? Does he realise I pinched his credit card? He's not looking so puppy-like now and is wondering – well, I can't imagine *what* he's wondering.

Kinnaird pulls up a chair and sits facing me, about four feet away. He wipes my blood off his face with the back of his hand. He's cocky but stressed. We eyeball each other. To be fair to him, this *is* a bit of a circumstance overload. He sighs. He snorts. 'I don't know what I'm going to ask you first, sonny Jim.' He rests the gun on his thigh.

'Well, why don't I ask *you* something, Rowan?'

'Shut it. I'm trying to think. I need a lot of answers before I decide what's going to happen to you and girly over there.'

'*Then* what are you going to do? You don't know, do you. It must have been a wonderful two years, though. Thinking you'd got away with murder. What a buzz. And all that money. And say I give you some answers. Then what? Are you going to let us go? Unlikely. You've got no leverage here. You're not thinking straight. No wonder you're still a DS.'

'I said shut *up*.'

'Are you going to murder her like you did her sister? Or maybe it wasn't you. Maybe it was the wonder boy publisher over there. He's got motive, hasn't he. Or should that be *motives*. God. What a mess. I know that criminals are stupid, but it's still a shock to experience it first-hand.'

His expression darkens. He grips the barrel of the gun as if he's about to pistol-whip me again, then changes his mind. He turns to Fournier. 'Come over here and give him a slap, Mathéo,' he jeers. 'Do some of the heavy lifting for a change.'

Fournier walks over to me and gives me an open-handed slap across the side of the face. Stings, but nothing more.

'Not an *actual* slap, Mathéo,' I say. 'It's a slang term. He wanted you to punch me. You'll *never* make a proper criminal. Would you mind if I started seeing Odette when you're in prison? I'll be two-timing her with Gaëlle, but at least I'll be keeping it in the family, so to speak.'

Now he punches me. Not bad, but all it's done is to make the area where Kinnaird pistol-whipped me feel a bit worse. My tongue assesses the damage. Now there's blood dripping out of my mouth and down the front of my shirt. I surreptitiously move my wrists to see if there's any give on the ropes yet. Nothing. I think it's polyhemp decking rope, so it could be worse. It's quite thick, so more difficult to knot.

I assess the chain of command. At the moment, Kinnaird is at the top, then Thornton, then Fournier. I try to think of some clever way that I can turn them against each other, but my brain isn't playing ball. A vehicle pulls up outside. A car door slams.

'How did you find out about Brian Colbert and the van?' asks Rowan.

'It just came to me in a flash of inspiration.'

'Why were you in here the other night?'

'That's not what your second question should be. It's irrelevant. You're meant to be a detective of sorts, Rowan. Maybe "Which gigantic salivating cop-hating oversexed psychopath am I going to be sharing a cell with?" might more pertinent. Anyway, let's have a little quid pro quo, shall we? I've just answered one of your idiot questions. Now you answer one of mine.'

But it is not to be. The doorbell rings, and Thornton limps out of the room to answer it. Amazon?

40

VIPER IN THE NEST

Billy Carmichael strides into the room with a grave expression on his face. The eyepatch makes him look like a bargain-basement Bond villain. If he was wearing his carpet slippers and escorting Miss Hatsuko Okamoto, the look would be complete.

He squints at me, then at Kinnaird. He purses his lips. He pouts. He's plainly perplexed.

'Sorry I'm late, Rowan. Bentley's been acting up. Overheating. What's going on? Why is *he* here? What's happening?'

'Things have unexpectedly escalated since I called you,' says Kinnaird, pointing at me. 'We've captured a private investigator. He'd been hired by the hag with the bun in the oven,' he indicates Micha, 'To discover what happened to her sister.'

For a moment, Carmichael looks fearful, and takes a few steps back. 'But he – he…'

'No need to be afraid,' says Kinnaird. 'I tied him up myself. Can't move a muscle and he ain't going anywhere.'

Impossible situations.

'But I know him,' says Carmichael. 'He came to see me yesterday. Said he was a supporter of my party.'

Kinnaird roll his eyes and shakes his head from side to side.

'Hi, Billy,' I say, with a touch of feigned friendliness. 'I bet you wish you hadn't introduced me to your fembot harem now. How embarrassing. Do your pals here know about the girls? Shall I tell them?'

Carmichael walks up to me until he's about a foot away. Then he spits in my face. He's trembling with suppressed rage. 'Well, John,' he growls. 'You turned out to be a viper in the nest, didn't you.'

'What does that even *mean*, Billy? That's not even a saying. You're thinking of *a nest of vipers*, which is something entirely different.'

'He's not John *anything*, Billy,' says Kinnaird. 'His name's Daniel Beckett. He's been a naughty boy. And I'm going to find out exactly what he's done.'

'I had a feeling there was something wrong about you,' says Billy. 'I can always spot a liar.'

'But that's just not *true*, Billy. You fell for it completely, you rascally little cyclops. How's HRH Lobelia Craven doing, by the way? It must be so stressful being of royal blood, even if you're an elf. Does she have paparazzi problems, or do they not have cameras in Middle Earth?'

Carmichael punches me in the face. I manage to turn my head quickly to the left to avoid getting a broken nose, and the punch clips my cheekbone. I have a thing about getting a broken nose. I'd tell you it was the pain, but really it's vanity. He may have just given me a black eye, though. He spits in my face once more, though this time it's more phlegm than spit. And it smells of fish.

'This joker here linked me to the van,' says Kinnaird to Carmichael. 'The actual van. The Citroën. He knew it was used to pick up the ransom. That's why I asked you to come over. That's why I said it was urgent. He'd started to join the dots. The whole thing will blow apart if we don't act quickly. I refuse to sort all this mess out on my own. We're all in it together. That was the deal. You better get your thinking cap on, Billy.

'He visited that weirdo, Brian Colbert. Tells him he knows about the van and gives him his fucking business card. He even has a bloody photograph of *me* with him. Then he suggests that Colbert gives me a call about his visit!' He turns his attention to me. 'How did you know about Colbert?'

'Clever detective work. Ever heard of it? Thought not.'

'He also paid a visit to Mathéo,' continues Kinnaird, ignoring me, and addressing Carmichael once more. 'Very affable, Mathéo said, but there was an undercurrent: like he knew more than he was letting on, like he was suspicious, like he could see right through him. And my bloody name came up again. Mathéo felt threatened and intimidated by him, though he couldn't put it into words. So, he called me.'

He exhales sharply. 'We've had two years of nothing happening, then *you* get a visit from this guy, *Mathéo* gets a visit from him, that freak *Colbert* gets a visit from him and now I find out that the same guy discovered where I lived and was snooping around in my bloody house the other night and again today.'

You may attempt to use words to anger me, to confuse me, to distract me, to insult me, to goad me, to disorientate me.

'This is a mess, Rowan. You have my sympathy. I've already spoken to the National Crime Agency about you and they couldn't stop laughing.'

'Could you just shut up?' asks Kinnaird.

'Right,' says Billy, sounding superefficient and clever. 'We've got Miss Moneybags here, we've got this private detective or whatever he thinks he is. What next, Rowan?'

Micha's head has lolled forwards and I wonder if she's fainted.

'I'm working on it,' says Kinnaird impatiently. 'One thing's for certain, we've got to cauterise the wound. It's no problem. We can do this. Contain this. Then we can act. We need all the info we can get. I want to know everything step by step. The most important thing is to find out who else knows what this prick has unearthed and who else he's visited, what he's said.'

'Who *else* knows? *Everyone* knows, Rowan,' I say. 'It's been all over social media for three days. Give yourself up, for your poor old mother's sake.'

'How did you find this house?' asks Carmichael. 'Why now? Why are you here now? How did you get here?'

'What an idiotic load of questions, Billy. If you must know, I got a Superrace Championship Night Race winner to drive me here.'

Micha looks up. She'll know who I'm referring to and it may give her an iota of hope.

'What the hell are you babbling on about?' says Kinnaird. 'Listen, Billy. He's here and that's all there is to it. We should count ourselves lucky that we've caught him in time. Now let me concentrate.'

'I'll bow to your expertise, sir,' says Carmichael, patting Kinnaird on the shoulder. 'We have to stop this in its tracks. Rally the troops. It's like a military campaign. We'll just have to readjust, realign, and decide what we're going to do next. Then we find our target and pull the trigger.'

Carmichael's full of shit.

'There's no deciding about it,' says Kinnaird, chewing his thumbnail. 'We'll probably have to dispose of both of them. I can't see another option at the moment, can you?'

'Well, you'd better bloody think of one,' says Fournier angrily. 'I'm not being party to a double bloody murder. And they're not going to tell us *anything* if you kill them. Use your brain.'

'You're already party to *one* murder, Mathéo, *old chap*. Don't forget that. In for a penny, as they say,' jeers Kinnaird.

'Oh, Mathéo,' I say. 'Don't you realise that this is what happens? Covering up one awful crime with another? It's what all laughably stupid criminals do. It'll go on and on until you're a notorious mass murderer with your own Netflix documentary.'

You may try to turn them against each other. Be aware this rarely works. It's too obvious, too predictable. But it can still be worth the effort.

'And don't let Rowan speak to you in that tone of voice. He's just a bent cop. You're a sophisticated publisher with a sexy French wife and a tanned Parisian secretary for God's sake. You went to Eton. Show him who's boss here. Be a man.'

Kinnaird makes a fist for me to see. 'And you can shut up. I *will* not tell you again.'

'Mathéo's going to sell you out to save his skin, Rowan. So's Billy. They both look down on you. They think you're a scuzzbag.'

Kinnaird punches me in the face. I can feel a small fragment of tooth in my mouth. More dental bills.

Thornton, who has been quiet for a while, starts to speak. He looks deathly pale. 'Rowan, I…' His eyes roll up into his head and he falls heavily to the floor. He's fainted. Must be the TLC I gave to his testicles, fingers, and head. Ah well; one down, three to go.

'Who else knows about the van?' asks Carmichael, ignoring Thornton's embarrassing state. 'Come on. Speak up!'

'Would you mind if I took Miss Hatsuko Okamoto out for dinner one night, Billy? It would be purely platonic, I'm sure. I expect she'll be talking about you all evening. I hate it when that happens.'

Carmichael looks down at the floor. 'Shut – him – up,' he says to Kinnaird. There's an edge of panic and disarray here, which may or may not be a good thing. I'm trying to think of a way that they could contain all of this without resorting to murder, but nothing comes. Whatever they do to me, I can't let them know about Scarlett. I get the feeling I'd be putting her life in danger.

All those physiological fakeries during interrogation. Could you still do them if you had to? While you're tied up in this way?

I allow my head to drop forward briefly, then quickly raise it, as if I'm trying to disguise the fact that I'm feeling faint.

'You're in quite a bit of trouble now, aren't you, Billy. What'll become of Poppy Windsor when you're in prison? She'll end up in a department store window, modelling leather basques. *A viper in the nest.* What were you thinking?'

Carmichael studiously ignores me.

Kinnaird walks over to Micha. He rests his hands on her shoulders. He leans forwards and sniffs her hair, looking straight at me. He licks his lips. 'I'm sure when we begin to maltreat the chink bitch here, you'll start talking. Sisters. Never done that before. Tasty.' He leers repulsively. 'Can't do them both at the same time, unfortunately, but beggars can't be choosers, as they say.'

Carmichael looks bilious. I decide to play for time, while trying to work out some spectacularly ingenious way of getting Micha and myself out of here in one piece.

Use your voice. Use the tone of your voice. People like to be talked about, even if negatively or inaccurately. You'll get their attention.

I speak softly, so they have to strain to listen. 'The kidnapping of Kiaraa Jeong. I don't know all of the details. How could I? I'm not as smart as you guys. But I can make a couple of educated guesses.'

Kinnaird sneers at me. 'Come on, Miss Marple. Let's have it. I could do with a laugh.'

'Let's see. About two years ago, Mathéo's publishing company was in financial freefall. Then he finds out his beloved wife is having a fling with Kiaraa Jeong, who, irony of ironies, he was instrumental in introducing her to.

'He's angry. He can't leave his wife as he's dependent on her money in one way or another. He's in a bind.'

I half-close my eyes, as if the effort of speaking was tiring. I focus on lowering my pulse rate. Doing this and speaking at the same time is not easy, but I attempt it anyway.

Thornton is slowly regaining consciousness. There's a stainless-steel fire poker by the fireplace. Looks solid. You could kill someone with it.

'At the same time, Billy here was having financial troubles with his crackpot political party.

'Mathéo knows Billy as he's published a couple of his deranged one-star books. It could be...' Another head drop. Another partial recovery. 'It could be that they're friends...quite apart...from their business connection. It could be that they get on well.' I take several shallow breaths. I lick my lips. I swallow saliva.

'Mathéo got Billy a ticket to see Kiaraa perform at the Wigmore Hall. Billy's a fan of the classics and Mathéo gets classical freebies. This was before Mathéo found out about his wife's infidelity. Billy wasn't too keen on Kiaraa but wanted to keep on Mathéo's good side. Mathéo was a source of money.'

Kinnaird is listening, which is good. Fournier looks pissed. There's a tall, slim glass vase next to the stereo. Thick, heavy base.

'Billy had been trolling Kiaraa on various classical sites, and she mentioned this activity at the Wigmore Hall. She named and shamed Billy's Mickey Mouse political party and referred to its members as backward-looking, ignorant, and sad.

'And everyone laughed. They *laughed*. They laughed at Billy and all he stood for. He'd been directly humiliated. And by that Korean bitch, of all people. So, he gave her another nasty anonymous review. Called her a Korean attention whore, a stripper, a streetwalker. Got it so far? I'm not going too fast for you?'

Thornton interrupts, his voice a pained whisper. 'Stop him talking. I can't stand it.' He props himself up on his elbows and pukes over his chest. Looks like he's eaten fish and chips recently. Kinnaird raises a hand to shut him up.

Carmichael laughs. 'I was holding back with that review,' he says. 'I could have called that trollop a lot worse!'

'Then one day,' I continue. 'Billy and Mathéo are having a meeting, a chat, a drink, whatever. Perhaps Billy wants another publishing advance. He *always* needs money for Birthright. But Mathéo can't help because of his own financial troubles.

'Maybe Mathéo tells Billy about Odette and Kiaraa. About the photographs he found. The letter. Maybe they have a gripe about women in general. After all, both had faithless wives who belittled them in one way or another. Maybe they bond over their money tribulations.'

Carmichael shakes his head to indicate that I'm talking rubbish. Maybe I am.

Fournier looks peeved. Kinnaird looks smug. He likes hearing these two being denigrated like this.

I give my wrist bindings another miniscule stretch. A tiny bit of give, but I'm not expecting miracles.

'Then something occurs to one or both of them. An idea. A great idea. They both loathe Kiaraa Jeong. They both need a lot of money.

'Perhaps it's old wife-beater Billy who suggests kidnapping Kiaraa. Maybe as a joke at first. A good wheeze. A jolly jape. He can always backpedal. Maybe he picked up a few tips about abduction from his fellow prisoners in the Bitch Wing.

'Mathéo is cautious. This sort of lawbreaking is anathema to him. But it's tempting. He could get back at Kiaraa, punish his wife and help his business all at the same time. It's a win-win-win situation.'

'I've heard enough of this bullshit,' says Fournier, looking grim.

'And Billy is very persuasive. And he knows someone who could help, who could give advice. A Billy supporter from the olden days. Gets off on risk. Someone who would jump at the chance of a bit of easy money.

'It's his old pal and former Battle Stations Party member Detective Sergeant Rowan Kinnaird. Corrupt. Sly. Smart. Greedy. Been on the take for years. This would be right up his street. And Billy owes him for sorting the demented supermarket ultraviolence, of course.

'As a bonus, he'd been involved in a couple of kidnapping cases. Nothing big, but he knew the score, the logistics, the MO. No one would get hurt. Everything would run smoothly. The prize would be sensational. Mathéo is now completely convinced. Billy is ecstatic.

'Now the seed had been sown. You talked about it over and over again until you had a watertight plan. Mathéo told you where Kiaraa would be and what time she'd be leaving that restaurant. Bit of a glitch when she left early, but a quick text would have solved that problem.'

Flatter them. Let them know you hold them in esteem. Make them feel good about themselves.

'I have to ask this. How did you manage to lift her? Who did it? How did you subdue her? Was it you, Billy? I don't think so. No sane person would get in a car with you, particularly a woman.

'Mathéo had an alibi, so it can't have been him. It had to be you, Rowan. I'm full of admiration.'

Kinnaird likes this. He's smiling. His guard is down slightly, for all the good that'll do me at the moment.

I allow my eyes to become unfocussed for a few seconds. 'What did you do? What did you say? She wasn't stupid. She wasn't gullible. But you outsmarted her.'

'Flashed the card,' he says proudly. 'Even shone my iPhone torch on it so she could see it clearly. Told her Suzie Wong over there had been in a road traffic accident. Nothing too serious, but she had a fracture of the femur and mild concussion.

'Offered her a lift to the hospital. Fell for it. As soon as she got in the car – wallop! – hit her on the jaw. Out cold. A sharp uppercut. The best way to hit a woman. Doesn't leave a bruise if you do it right.

Shoved her on the floor of the motor. All over in ten seconds. Easy-peasy.'

So, Pöck's guess was right. *Excuse me, miss. Could I have a word?* And he's just used a similar technique on Micha, with me as the fake victim.

'So, she was dead as soon as she got in your car,' I say. 'She'd seen your face and warrant card. Heard your voice. If she ever got away, or was released, they'd make her do a facial composite and/or sit down with a police sketch artist. You'd be recognised.'

He shrugs. 'It was always a possibility. But it was dark, she was stressed because of what I'd told her, and before she regained consciousness, I'd blindfolded her and shoved some liquid Rohypnol down her throat. The effects would last for about an hour…'

'And cause amnesia for a day or two afterwards.'

'Very smart. So, her memory of events leading up to getting in the car would be hazy if not totally absent. It's unlikely that she'd remember what I looked like, how I spoke. That's why it's a good rape drug.'

'So,' I say. 'You got back here, restrained her/kept her subdued overnight, tied up, drugged, whatever, and the next day these two monkey-boys popped around for the next stage of the masterplan. Billy was Mr Munro, of course, the voice on the phone.'

'Clever boy. Yeah. Gave her a few Rohypnol top-ups to be on the safe side. I love that fucking drug.'

'A few calls later you had the money, and thanks to Clem Thornton down there, you had a way of laundering it.'

I sigh, making it seem as if speaking is coming hard to me now. 'So, who started the ball rolling? Who was it that made you rapists as well as kidnappers? Who was the first to cross that line? Who…I…'

Kinnaird stares at me. He narrows his eyes and looks a little anxious. He thinks I'm on the verge of nodding out. I'll be looking dreadful by now.

'I don't think it was you, Billy. I – I can't see you coping with a flesh and blood woman. I think you'd faint. Or did the others egg you on? Did you manage that once-in-a-lifetime erection with a real, living female?'

'You are scum,' replies Carmichael.

'No. I think you started it off, Rowan,' I say. 'You were the first. You and your rape pharmaceuticals. When they arrest you – once Billy or Mathéo has ratted you out – they're going to take a sample of your DNA and it'll be all over for you.' I take a deep breath and defocus my eyes.

'It was because she was so fucking mouthy.'

I'm quite surprised to hear Mathéo's educated posh-boy drawl. I'm ashamed to say I'd almost forgotten about him.

Your captor or captors may even find that they are unintentionally confessing to you. Some people can't help themselves. They want to brag.

'She was so fucking mouthy,' he says angrily. 'And she had my fucking wife. So, I was going to have *her*. To punish her. To punish Odette. It's as simple as that. It was eating me up from the inside. I was demeaned.'

Oddly, his voice has got deeper, uglier, and more...*posh*. It's as if he's given up on the fabricated nice guy voice he usually affects.

'Anyone would have done it in my place. I was owed that. She owed me. I deserved it. It was my right. Is that *so* difficult to understand? They were going to move in together. I couldn't believe it. I'd have been humiliated. I'd have been publicly cuckolded by the little tart.

'Once we'd got here, I was sick of keeping quiet. I ripped the blindfold off her face. I wanted her to see me, hear me. To see who was doing this to her. To see who her master was. To see her master's face. To hear her master's voice.

'She insulted me. She said things about me that Odette had told her. Personal things. Humiliating things. She told me what she and Odette had got up to. How much Odette had enjoyed it.

'She just talked and talked. She said her sister would never pay a ransom. She called us all idiots. I just wanted to shut her up. She needed to be shut up and punished.'

Carmichael laughs. 'And the little slut was strong. It was like trying to hold down a hurricane, even though she was doped up to the gills. Kicking, clawing. If there weren't three of us, I don't know how we'd have done it. And then *this!*' He removes his eye patch. There's a revolting flesh sinkhole where his left eye once was.

'She did this, the little whore. Scratched me right across the eyeball. One hand then the other. The pain was unimaginable. Obviously, I could not go to a hospital. Rowan said it was out of the question. I'd just have to take it like a man. I thought it would heal, but it got infected. More pain. Foul leakage. I thought I was going to die. A few weeks later it was gone.' He sounds like he's about to cry. 'Disfigured! Blinded! Crippled!'

So, my theory was correct. 'She had your DNA under her fingernails. So, the bolt cutters came out.'

'And by God did I enjoy doing that,' says Carmichael. 'I did it for Johann Sebastian Bach. I did it for Muzio Clementi. I did it for civilised values. She'd made me scream. Now it was her turn.'

'You see,' says Kinnaird. 'Getting rid of the fingers was a necessity. Billy was the only one of us who'd had his DNA on record. If the police got hold of him, he'd squeal like a pig. The cutters were my idea, but Billy was only too pleased to do it, weren't you, Billy.

'I wanted to knock her out first, but not Billy. Oh no. He wanted her wide awake. A little bit of a weirdo, is our Billy.'

I try to transmit the message 'don't listen to this' to Micha. It's not working. She's sobbing again. She shakes her head from side to side.

'Anyway,' he continues, as if we're discussing some everyday matter. 'Seeing Mathéo with that bimbo got me a bit hot under the collar, know what I mean? Well, I'm only human, get it? I had a good time. A really good time. It was sweet. As sweet as a nut. I loved it.'

'But it was her fault. All it of,' says Carmichael, now dribbling profusely. 'They ask for it. They really do. What did she expect? How are we men meant to control ourselves? Why *should* we have to control ourselves? This is our world, after all.'

I still don't fully understand what happened at the end. All that stabbing. What was it that Sallow called it? Over-killing? He said that that type of psychopathic behaviour had several possible causes. Extreme anger, madness, resentment, male rage.

And then there was Aziza's McDiagnosis: *Latent/active tendency to bullying and/or abusive behaviour and/or aggressive behaviour. Difficulty in controlling anger. Prone to reckless or impulsive behaviour.*

'So, the stabbing,' I say. 'That had to be you as well, Billy. That was your sex substitute, your penetration substitute. You're an insane little boy.'

'I'm a king,' says Billy. 'A lord. And you are a loser.' He spits in my face once more. If I get out of this, I'm going to hit him.

Kinnaird laughs. 'You should have seen him! He went crazy. I was a little scared myself! Mathéo went as white as a sheet. Had to go and puke. It was bloody mayhem! It was my knife, too. Had to get rid of it in the Thames with that bolt cutter. Took us hours to clean up the mess in the kitchen.

'There was no way we could have let her live, of course. You must see that. Not after she'd seen Mathéo, and we'd had our wicked way with her. Stands to reason. Pure logic. So technically, it hardly mattered how we finished her off. But it had to be done. Things could have gone a different way, but they didn't. Tough shit.

'She may well have died after the fingers came off, but people can survive stuff like that. So, Billy played executioner. Could have been less messy, but you can't have everything. Brought out a part of me I didn't know was there, watching that. I enjoyed it, got off on it. Got me hard again. Weird.'

I look at Kinnaird and Fournier in turn. 'You could have stopped all of it. You could have let her go once you'd got the money. You could have left her alone. You could have saved her. But you didn't. You total pair of fuckwits. You…'

I close my eyes. I can feel the sweat dripping from my hairline and trickling down the sides of my body. I'm getting heart palpitations. Good.

Kinnaird leans forwards and pokes me in the shoulder. 'Hey. Wake up. D'you hear me? What's wrong with you?'

41

IMPOSSIBLE SITUATIONS

It must have been eleven or twelve years ago now.

I'm in a large, secure house in a private compound on the outskirts of the Tatra National Park in Slovakia. The house overlooks the Štrbské Pleso lake. The water is calm, reflecting the High Tatras mountain range in the distance.

The peaks are covered in snow. Pine trees everywhere. You can smell them. There are meant to be bears and wolves around here, but I've never seen any, though I did spot an Alpine Swift, which I'm told is quite rare.

From the outside, it looks like the holiday home of some wealthy plutocrat, but inside it's rather different.

It has ten bedrooms, two Olympic-size indoor swimming pools, three state-of-the-art gyms, a luxurious spa, two dojos, a cutting-edge language laboratory, a colossal library, three massive white marble kitchens, a triple-height hall, and eight large, assorted rooms which have different functions at different times. In the basement is a soundproofed thirty-metre shooting range.

I can't remember the exact amount, but I remember being told that a house like this would be worth around twenty-five million Euros, in the unlikely event that you'd be thinking of buying it.

Outside, there's a picturesque stone jetty and a big pile of logs – ash,

I think – which are replenished from time to time, but I've never seen anyone do the replenishing which I have to assume is done in the middle of the night, when everything else is presumably delivered.

Sometimes, motion sensor lights come on at three or four in the morning, which I guess is either the wood/food/equipment being delivered or wolves having a sniff around. I've never bothered to check which it is; I'm usually too tired.

I'm in a large, ornate reception room. My hands are handcuffed behind my back, and I'm sitting in a metal chair which is anchored to the floor by objects that look like space-age rivets.

Apart from the handcuffs, my arms are tied to the chair with Kevlar rope, as are my ankles. I can't move, and the feeling is starting to go in my hands and in my feet.

There's a woman standing seven feet away from me, pointing a gun at the centre of my head. It's a black SIG Sauer M17 semi-automatic pistol.

Her name is Kora Wetere. When I first heard her speak, I thought she was from South Africa, but it turned out she was a New Zealander. When she says 'yes', it sounds like 'yis'. She's tall, perhaps five feet eleven, and has the physique of an athlete. If you had to guess, you might think she was a runner, rower, or tennis player.

But she is none of those things.

She has a severe, rather beautiful face, and you could easily imagine her being a model for one of the more extreme German fashion photographers. Her hair is very short, slicked back with gel, and is dyed blue-black. Her eyes are bright blue, like a Siamese kitten. She wears square-frame metal glasses by Gucci. This last detail, a little designer affectation, almost makes her cute and relatable.

But she is not cute and relatable.

Her clothing is functional and vaguely sporty: an Adanola sleeveless scoop-neck unitard in cocoa brown and a pair of Balenciaga track trainers in fluo pink. If it was anyone else, I'd think this combo had been chosen to show off her powerful physique or make a fashion statement.

But she is not anyone else.

There are three others in the room, watching me being threatened.

The first of these is a woman of about my age. Her name is Alita Langlois. She's blonde, very attractive and has a permanent semi-smile on her lips, as if she knows something terrible about you and everyone else she encounters.

The second person is known to me as Jokull Birtingr. Dark, stocky, and tense. I know he's not a deeply suspicious sociopath, but his facial expression makes it look as if he's waiting for you to put one over on him so he can retaliate. He has been told about this and is working on it.

The third person is another female, Machara Campion. Red hair, tall, curvy, sexy. A very bright personality, but also very studious. Always reading in her spare time. She says, 'you can never know enough stuff.' She has a barely noticeable scar on her left shoulder blade which looks as if it might have been a bullet hole before the plastic surgeons did their work.

Kora flicks the SIG Sauer upwards with a quick jerk of her wrist. For a millisecond I think she's going to shoot me, but it was just to get our attention.

'Impossible situations,' she says, looking me straight in the eye. 'If I pull the trigger, you have nothing further to worry about. But if I don't, it may be that I need some sort of information from you. There may be some other reason that I am keeping you alive that you cannot, at the moment, discern. It may not be to my advantage to slay you, at least not at the present time.

'So, what have you got going for you? Not much. You're immobile. You can't tip the chair to the side on the off chance it'll get damaged and magically release you from the ropes and cuffs. Even if you tried it, even if it was possible, I might kill you immediately. I am perhaps not the sort of person who tolerates shit like that. My time is precious. I am angry, desperate, psychopathic, criminal, deadly, insane, impetuous, running out of time. I am a monster. You disrespect me or condescend to me or patronise me and it will not go well with you, I can promise you that.'

She walks to the side, still aiming the gun at my head. I stare straight ahead, using my ever-improving peripheral vision to keep her in sight.

'You're not gagged, so you may attempt to use words to anger me, to confuse me, to distract me, to insult me, to goad me, to disorientate me; to make me think that things are not as they are.

'You must use your judgment, your instinct, when taking this tack. You must be careful. It could backfire. People are often not as smart as you think they are. Equally, people are often not as stupid as you think they are.

'If there is more than one person present, you may try to turn them against each other. Be aware this rarely works. It's too obvious, too predictable. People are wise to it. But it can still be worth the effort.

'Depending upon the circumstances, you may say that they are wasting their time, that they'll never get away with it, whatever it is. That stratagem will not work with everyone, but there is a chance that it might work with someone. You can pretend to be too clever. Or not clever enough. Keep it facetious. Keep it serious. They will listen.

'You can pretend to know about things that you do not know about. Perhaps those things, whatever they are, will have to be checked up on.

'You can tell them a story. Give them your views on some event or other. People like to be talked about, even if negatively or inaccurately. You've just bought yourself some more time. Time to think. They may or may not believe what you're saying. You can also pretend that you know nothing. Use your voice. Use the tone of your voice. You should know how to do this by now.

'You can lie to them, or, on the other hand, you can be completely honest with them. Tell them what your actual plans are. Tell them why you're saying what you're saying. What your aims are. Throw lots of chaff into the air. Confuse. Distract. Demean. Offload theories, offload information, ask questions you won't get an answer to. Your output can be chaotic. Give them something to think about. This can be discomfiting.

'Your captor or captors may even find that they are unintentionally confessing to you. Some people can't help themselves. They want to brag. They may not realise that they are giving you useful intelligence. They will not know what matters to you or what does not matter to you.

'Keep an eye on their physical state. Are they tired? Sick? Look for weaknesses. Diagnose them. Look for symptoms. You know most of the common ones now. Use the knowledge to your advantage. Be sadistic, if necessary. Be cruel. Be ruthless.

'Assess their potential as combat opponents. Could you defeat them? Are you physically stronger than them? More skilled? How many of them could you take down if the opportunity arose? Visualise killing them. Decide how you would do it. How quickly you could do it.

'Flatter them. Let them know you hold them in esteem. Make them feel good about themselves. Make them feel that they're a success in whatever it is they're doing. Make them feel that they're smart.

'Will any of these ploys work at all? It's possible. As I said, they may buy you some time. You may even frighten your adversaries. They may rethink their entire life and let you go. But you have to keep in mind that you might fail. Or only half-succeed.

'You may find your skill, your reaction time, your strength, and your speed will fail you when you need them the most. This is normal. You cannot be at the top of your game the whole time. No one can. Be prepared for those outcomes; they are the most common. You'll often be dealing with acute unpredictability. If one ploy fails, have the next one ready. And the one after that. Improvise. Mix and match. Always keep hyper-focussed. Remain optimistic.

'If I'm an aggressive insecure fuck with an ego, I may untie you so we can have a fair fight, like in a movie, so I could prove to myself that I was better than you. But I'd only do that if I was stupid. Perhaps I *am* stupid. You'll have to make that judgement yourself, and quickly.

'So, you may have bought some time by being provocative, by ridiculing me. But time is of no interest to you. Not really. You want to kill me. You want our positions to be reversed. That's what your focus should be on. And at the moment, you're still alive. So, apart from the gun, what do I have that may be of interest to you?'

'The keys to the handcuffs,' I reply.

'Very possible. But let's say they're in my back pocket. How are you going to get hold of them?'

'Your family,' says Alita.

'What about them?'

'That's what you have that would be of interest to him.'

'Go on,' says Kora, amused.

'If it was *me* – if I felt that a situation like this might occur, I would have done my research on you. Belt and braces. I'd have got Decima or someone to lift a close member of your family: parent, child, spouse, sibling. Maybe all of them. They'd be sequestered away somewhere without food. If you killed me, then you'd be killing them.'

'But I could torture that information out of you, could I not?'

'Not if I didn't know their location,' says Alita, her semi-smile working overtime. 'I'd let Decima or whoever know that if I called them asking for that information, then I would be under duress, and they were not to pass that information on to me. They could only do that if I made a personal visit, and even then, there would be code words or coded signals set up. They would certainly not give that information to you or anyone else.

'In fact,' she continues. 'I could set things up so that any unexpected or atypical query from me would result in the immediate execution of said family members.'

'Good,' says Kora. 'But a little too specific. A lot of forethought required. And they might kill or torture you anyway, not being privy, as it were, to your clever precautions and set-ups. And the situation that *he*,' she points at me, 'Finds himself in might be totally unexpected. Nice try, though.'

'Hm!' says Alita.

'He's got a few things going for him,' says Machara.

'And they are?'

'Close – sometimes *very* close – proximity to weapons. Which is better than no proximity to weapons at all.'

Kora nods her head and addresses me. 'What weapons is she talking about?'

'First of all, your gun,' I say. 'I can tell it's fully loaded by the way you're tilting your wrist from time to time. If I could get hold of it I could shoot you or pistol-whip you with it.'

'What else?'

'The rope I'm tied with is Kevlar rope. I can smell it. Very strong. Excellent for strangulation.'

'But more difficult to stretch and loosen than ordinary rope,' says Alita. 'So, you'd be less able to put pressure on it or wriggle your way out of it.'

'True,' says Jokull. 'But it's not impossible, all the same.'

'Other weapons?' asks Kora. 'Apart from your physical skills, of course.'

'If I needed them,' I say, 'There's a cast-iron fire poker over there. A powerful blow with that against the side of your head would be the end for you. That drinks tray: I'd go for the Double Cross vodka bottle. It's full, so the weight would be OK. Long neck for gripping.'

'And distilled locally, too,' adds Machara, laughing.

'But we still have the problem of your being pretty effectively tied up,' says Kora. 'All that weaponry is useless to you in your position. Jokull?'

Jokull squats down in front of me, squinting, his eyes searching mine. 'How do you feel?' he asks. 'You look a bit pale.'

'Not too good,' I reply.

'What's the matter with you?'

'My breathing's shallow and I feel a little faint. A little nauseous, even. Apart from the predictable tingling in my hands and feet, I'm aware of my tongue in my mouth, and that's starting to tingle, too.

'Despite the artificiality of this situation, I feel physically and mentally stressed. I'm starting to feel tired from low-key adrenaline production. I wish everyone would stop talking. The method of immobilisation is partly to blame. I feel like I can't get enough air in my lungs. Even though it's not warm in here, I'm perspiring. I can feel it on my hairline and down the sides of my body.'

'And having a gun pointed at your head, even in a bogus situation like this, will be mildly stressful for you. It'll reinforce and escalate the other stuff,' adds Machara. 'And guns have been known to go off on their own.'

'You've been tied there for how long?' enquires Jokull. 'Maybe fifteen or twenty minutes? Something like that?'

I find I'm sighing. 'Something like that.'

'It was an effort for you to reply to me just then. You would have preferred not to have spoken to me, am I right?'

'Yes. It's an effort. I just want to lie down.'

'All those exercises to deal with certain sorts of injury,' he continues. 'All those physiological fakeries during interrogation. Could you still do them if you had to? While you're tied up like this? Shallow breathing? Psyching yourself up to feel fear when you don't really feel it? Upping your adrenaline production? Making yourself look pale? Making yourself sweaty? Making yourself look like someone who needs help? Fooling your autonomous nervous system? Overriding it?'

'Sure.'

'Do it now. Artificial situation notwithstanding. Take your time.'

It takes a while. But after a minute I start to feel worse. There's perspiration on my upper lip now. I'm getting heart flutters. But I don't feel as bad as I must look.

'Now,' says Kora. 'He's done it. Look at this. Look at him. This is how people can sometimes die in police custody. The same goes for hostages or captured members of the armed forces. Poor ventilation of the body, as he mentioned. Asphyxiation. Any cop in any country, any professional interrogator, any medic, would ask him what was wrong, but he must say nothing is wrong.

'They'd be afraid that he might die, particularly if he seemed unresponsive to their queries, which they may not want. They may need him functioning for a little while longer. He looks pale and sweaty. His breathing is shallow and occasionally erratic. I don't have to check his pulse to know that it'll be weak.

'If they had a medical officer on site, they'd get him in to take a look. It's eighty percent likely that they'd untie him. Being trussed up like this is almost certainly what's causing his apparent condition. If someone wanted to keep him awake and functioning for whatever reason, they'd have to act. Maybe untie him and then re-tie him in a different way. If there's no medical officer present, they might even consider getting him to a hospital. But be aware, this is quite a gamble. How do you feel?'

'I'd like a double vodka and soda.'

'If I untie you now. Right at this moment,' says Jokull. 'How quickly could you recover? How long would it be before you could attack me and disable me, maybe even kill me?'

'A couple of seconds with the right sort of concentration. Maybe instantly. I'd probably feel like shit for a few moments, maybe more. Dizzy, perhaps. The lack of feeling in my hands I could do without, but I'd just have to overcome it, ignore it.'

'And if I had the gun that Kora is holding?'

'I'd use it on you.'

'OK. Let's leave this for the moment. Have a think about it,' says Kora. She nods at Machara. 'Would you mind untying him?'

'Of course. Or we could leave him here like this, drive to Košice and have lunch in Republika Východu.'

'Very funny,' I say.

Machara whispers in my ear as she unties me. 'New perfume, my dear. Bought it yesterday. Any ideas? You'll never get it.'

'En Passant. Frédéric Malle.'

'I hate you.'

42

NOT BOTH OF THEM

Hey. Beckett. Answer me. What's wrong with you?'

Kinnaird slaps me hard across the face. Twice. I don't respond.

'Mathéo,' he says eventually. "I'm going to give you this pistol. The safety is off. That means you squeeze the trigger, and it'll go bang. Keep it aimed at chummy here. He moves in a way you don't like – shoot him. Go for the centre of the body. I'm going to have to untie him then truss him up in a different way. It'll take a minute. You can manage a minute, can't you, *old chap*?'

'I've never...'

'Listen. Clement is in no state to do this. Billy's too shaky. You know he's sick.' He grabs my chin. Lifts my head up. 'I've seen it before when I've tied people up like this for too long and they've passed out. Sweaty, white as a sheet, green around the gills.

'It's the way his arms are tied behind his back. Restricts proper breathing. We had a death in one of the cells when I was a DC because of this. I can't have this one popping off just yet.'

'But people will hear if I...'

'Believe me. Most people don't know what a gun going off in a house sounds like. They'll think it's a car backfiring. Particularly at this time of day. He's out of it. He'll wake up and see you with a gun in your hand. He's not going to ask for a firearms training certificate. Here. Take it.'

Kinnaird gets behind me and unties the ropes attaching me to the chair. He's hyped up and having difficulty. I can hear him say 'fuck' repeatedly. It can be a lot easier to tie someone up than it is to untie them.

I can hear Thornton's breathing. It's that slow, measured dog-pant that you do when you're in pain or trying to stop yourself from throwing up. In his case, I think it's both.

I'm no longer tied to the chair. Kinnaird allows me to slump to the floor. He squats down and starts work on the ropes that are binding my wrists together. More swearing. I wait and wait. Waiting for him to defeat those big, tight, difficult knots.

Then he stops.

'What was that?' he asks.

'What are you talking about?' says Fournier. 'What was what?'

Kinnaird gets to his feet. Damn. I was getting all keyed up then.

'The kitchen,' he says. 'Didn't you hear it? There was a noise coming from the kitchen. Like a loud thump. Like someone hitting something.'

'I didn't hear anything,' says Carmichael.

'Me neither,' says Fournier. 'Hadn't you better keep on with untying him? After what you said, he might…'

'Shut it,' snaps Kinnaird. 'He can wait. Keep that gun on him. He'll be out for a little while longer. If he gets a little asphyxiated, that's tough. Stay on the ball. Both of you. Keep watching him. Remember, Mathéo. Centre of the body.'

As soon as I can tell he's left the room, I moan and roll onto my back. I can feel that Fournier is suddenly on high alert. I refresh my fake symptoms and allow myself a weedy little eyelash flutter to reassure him that he's not in any peril. Through the flutter, I can see that he's pointing the gun directly at my throat.

After a few minutes, I can hear Kinnaird creeping up the stairs. I give my ropes another exploratory stretch and get a shock. There's much more give than there was five minutes ago and it's probably due to Kinnaird's sweary endeavours.

Very slowly, I slide the middle finger of my right hand down the palm of my left until I'm able to hook it round a section of the rope at the base of my left wrist. I give it a forty-five-degree tug, and it slowly extends by about three inches.

Conveniently, I'm starting to get severe cramp in the palm of my right hand, but I'll just have to ignore the pain and get on with it.

I slowly drag the ball of my left hand down the inside of my right wrist and twist it ninety degrees. This ramps up the pain, but it's done the trick. The ropes slacken, fall away, and my hands are free.

I can feel my heart thumping. Has Fournier spotted this? Carmichael? Thornton?

No. They'd have done/said something by now.

If it were not for the gun, I could send all three of these goons to their maker in a matter of seconds, then deal with Kinnaird when he returned. But the presence of a gun makes it too much of a risk, too much of a danger to Micha.

Even if she didn't get hit by a stray bullet, I'm not sure about the health hazards involved in a pistol going off a few feet away from a pregnant woman in an enclosed space. I must look this up one day.

I can hear Kinnaird's footsteps in the hall and in a few seconds he's back in the room. I lapse back into my sick boy mode.

'Anything?' asks Carmichael.

'Nothing. I thought the sound came from the back of the house, from the kitchen. Then I thought it might have come from one of the back bedrooms.'

He leans over me and starts to roll me onto my front. I reckon I've got half a second before he sees the state of the ropes.

The moment his hand touches my shoulder, I grab his wrist, hook my other hand around his neck and bounce his head off the floor.

I get to my feet before he can recover, dragging him up with me, getting him between me and the gun.

I use the rope that was binding my wrists to throttle him, winding it tightly around his neck and tying it off with a constrictor knot. Fournier waves the gun around, unsure what to do.

Kinnaird's hands claw at the rope trying to loosen it, but it'll be pointless. His face is going red. Soon it'll be purple and then it'll be black. I grab a handful of his hair and tug his head back.

'You get that damn rope off his neck,' shouts Fournier, his voice cracking.

'You drop the gun, and he lives. How about that, Mathéo? Sound good?'

'I'll fucking kill you.'

'Take a shot. You might get lucky. Or you might blow Rowan's head off. Decisions, eh?'

Then, in a move I hadn't anticipated, Carmichael strides up to Fournier, wrenches the gun out of his hand and aims it at the side of Micha's head. Single-handed grip, finger on the trigger. His hand and his arm are shaking like crazy. She closes her eyes.

I push Kinnaird to the floor and raise both hands to indicate surrender. I should have kept Carmichael in my sights, but I was too focussed on the gun. Damn. If Carmichael's got Parkinson's, stress will make the tremors much worse. I only hope he doesn't pull the trigger by accident.

Carmichael sneers at me. 'You know I'll do this, and you know I'll enjoy doing it. Now be a good fellow and get that bloody rope off Rowan's neck. Now!'

He's bluffing. For now, at least. 'You get it off, Billy,' I say. 'I'm busy.' Fournier looks pale. He's obviously not a fan of dramatic standoffs.

'I'm not bloody kidding,' roars Carmichael. 'Get that rope off his neck or this bitch's brains will be all over the wall.'

'I've used a constrictor knot, Billy. The only way you'll get that off is with a knife or strong scissors. Do you really want me to have either of those in my hands? I'll be going after your remaining eye.'

Fournier has a flustered go at the knot. He shakes his head.

'Mathéo. Keep an eye on her,' says Carmichael. He turns to me. 'You'll do whatever I say as long as I'm holding this gun and the slut is under threat. We're going in the kitchen to find a knife. Move it.'

Rowan's face is getting a tad darker now.

'Look at Rowan, Billy. He's dying. I reckon he's already got brain damage. How are you and Mathéo going to cope without him telling you what to do? Give yourself up.'

He shakes the gun in my face. 'Get in the kitchen. Get a fucking knife.'

'Are you sure you want me to?'

'Just do it!' he barks.

Kinnaird collapses onto his face. Carmichael and I make our way into the kitchen. He's standing about five feet behind me, much too far away for me to grab the gun.

'The problem is, Billy, is that I don't know where everything's kept. If only Rowan had labelled the drawers.'

He points at a stainless steel Wüsthof knife block next to the sink. 'There. Are you blind?'

'I don't know, Billy. Wüsthof are very good, but I'd be happier with a Sabatier. On the other hand, Kai Shun are probably the sharpest.'

'Get one of those fucking knives out and get back in there.'

'You sound like you're panicking, Billy. I'm only glad Miss Hatsuko Okamoto is not here to witness this humiliating display.'

I select a paring knife and we return to the reception room, Carmichael still keeping his distance. Thornton is standing with the aid of a chair. Kinnaird now lies on his side, his breathing weak and laboured. I stoop down next to him. Just as I'm about to cut the rope, I look up.

'Are you sure you want me to do this, guys? Think. If Rowan dies, you three can have his share of the money, wherever the hell it's coming from. Or you could give it to me to keep my mouth shut.'

Once again, Carmichael calmly pushes the barrel of the gun against Micha's temple, his hand trembling, his finger still on the trigger. She looks quite calm now, and is watching me carefully, expecting a miracle that I'm not sure I can deliver.

I've rattled them enough. Time to stop. I pinch the knot at the side of Kinnaird's external jugular, pull it towards me and slice through the rope.

'The knife. Throw it towards me. No tricks,' says Carmichael.

It lands a foot away from his feet. He leans down and picks it up, watching me the whole time.

Kinnaird inhales like a man who's been held underwater for ten minutes, then grabs his neck and coughs and coughs and coughs. His eyes are bloodshot and streaming with tears. After a few minutes, he manages to get up on his knees. His face is still an unhealthy crimson but looks better than it did a few moments ago.

He's furious. He points at me. 'You…you…' he croaks, but doesn't complete the sentence.

I check on Thornton. Still leaning against the chair, staring blankly around the place. His broken fingers are purple and swollen.

Very slowly, Kinnaird gets to his feet. He launches himself at me, coughing, retching, punching me repeatedly in the gut, neck and face. I avoid the blows as well as I can. He knows I won't retaliate while Carmichael's got the gun on Micha. Finally, he stops. He's out of breath. I think he's cracked one of my ribs.

'Alright. Alright.' He massages his neck. 'I know exactly what I'm going to do about you two. I'm not fucking around for another second. Come on, Clem. Get yourself together. I need you to be switched on here.'

'I'm good, Rowan. I'm good,' replies Clem. Doesn't look it, though. He needs half an hour with his head between his legs and a litre of intramuscular dihydrocodeine.

Kinnaird delicately removes the gun from Carmichael's quivering grip and waves it in my face. At least Micha's out of immediate danger.

'I know people like you,' he says to me. 'Came across them all through my career. Chancers. Losers. Greedy little pricks who couldn't cut it in the real police force. Whatever you've discovered, you'll never in a million years share it with proper detectives, proper police officers.

'You won't want to give anything away that might make you a bit of money, get you a fat juicy bonus from the so-called businesswoman there. So, I think we can discount the possibility that you've spoken to the police since you started on your little kiddie adventure.

'And yes, we know you spoke to Sallow before he went on leave, but that was a few days ago. You told Mathéo that you'd only just started at that point. Like I said before, I'm going to find out what you've unearthed, and I know exactly how I'm going to do it.'

He reaches in his pocket and chucks some car keys to Fournier, who catches them in mid-air.

'Stick my car in the garage. The remote for the main door is hanging off the indicator stalk. You can reverse it in from where you parked it. Then close the garage door again. Open all the car windows. When you've finished, come back in the house through the side door across the hall there. Billy, get the tart to her feet. Get the tape off her ankles.'

Fournier leaves the room. Thirty seconds later, I can hear Kinnaird's Mercedes being started up and the garage door grinding open. The car reverses, stops, the engine is turned off, and the door slowly and squeakily closes. Shortly afterwards Fournier reappears, shoving the car keys in his pocket.

'Right,' says Kinnaird to me. "I'll tell you what's going on, chum. We're going to take dragon lady into my garage and put her in the back of the car with her hands taped to the passenger seat headrest. Then we're going to start the engine. There are no windows in that garage and both doors will be closed. I'm sure I don't have to tell a bright spark like you what'll happen next.'

He nods to Carmichael and Fournier. 'Come on, Batman and Robin. Get her in the car and keep the windows open. I'll be with you in a minute.' He chucks Thornton the roll of gaffer tape. 'Pay attention, Clem. Once they've got her inside, I want you to tie her wrists where I said so she can't move or fuck about, got it?'

Thornton nods his head, pleased to be able to help.

Carmichael and Fournier take an arm each and escort Micha out of the room with Thornton following, gaffer tape in hand.

'I used to know all the side effects of carbon monoxide poisoning, but I've forgotten most of them now,' he says. 'Dizziness, chest pain, muscle pain; that's all that comes to mind at the moment. But I do know that they happen quickly. A favourite of suicides, of course. Doesn't take long to kill yourself with it. It's not the biggest of garages, either. Things will escalate pretty quickly.'

'She's pregnant. What the fuck are you doing?'

He laughs. 'Oh, really? I hadn't noticed. So. Beckett. Once we commence, all you have to do is start talking and I'll go in and switch the engine off, open the garage door, give her a bit of fresh air. If I don't like what you have to say, back she goes, and I'll turn the engine on again. I might even shoot you in the leg to give you a bit of encouragement. Let's hope the fumes don't trouble the baby too much, eh? What a shame that would be.'

He stands in the doorway looking pleased with himself, the gun still in his hand, aimed at my chest. He continues to keep his distance. Is he bluffing? Is he this much of a maniac?

'You should think more carefully about the jobs you take on, old son. Some are best avoided. Like this one.

'They'll be ready for me in a couple of minutes. It's such an easy way to get someone to spill their guts. Favoured by South American drug lords. Even saw it in a couple of movies. First of all…'

He doesn't finish the sentence. One hand grips his throat and the other inflicts a brief but powerful percussive strike to the back of his head, instantly breaking his neck. The gun falls to the floor.

'Not both of them, Mr Beckett. Not both of them. I could not permit it.'

43

OUT OF THE BLUE

So that's what the noise that Kinnaird heard was: Baek-Hayeon breaking in. He possibly realised too late that I'd left that back door unlocked. I know I told him to wait in the car, but he mentioned the other day that he had always been a rule-breaker and besides, why the hell should he take orders from me?

I suppose he could have acted earlier on and stopped some of the shit that's gone down, but then he wasn't familiar with the layout of the house and had no real idea how many people were here, who they were, what they were doing, what they were capable of.

On top of that, he knew Micha was in here somewhere and maybe didn't want to do anything that might cause her harm, so fair enough.

This is now a complex situation that'll have to be sorted in some sort of inspired, high-speed way that I haven't quite thought of yet.

First things first.

While Kinnaird is still being held upright, I retrieve my keys from his back pocket. I keep my voice low and assume that Baek-Hayeon will do the same.

'OK. Thanks for doing that.' I pick his gun up and tuck it in the waistband of my chinos. 'I'll take care of this for the moment. You have your hands full.'

We carefully lower Kinnaird's body onto the floor. He's one heavy bastard, a dead weight, you might say. His eyes are open, and his tongue hangs out of his mouth. He looks stupid, but not as stupid as he looked when he was alive.

'I found it difficult to work out what was going on here, Mr Beckett,' says Baek-Hayeon. 'But then that man's words left me in no doubt that Micha's life was in imminent danger. In a hazardous, unstable situation, drastic and decisive action is sometimes called for. It is one of the first things I learned in the army.'

'You were right. What's happening with Soo-ah?'

'She is in the car, waiting for my call.'

'There are three other people here. We're going to have to incapacitate them and then we can decide what to do.'

'I fully understand, Mr Beckett, and I will understand if you subsequently call the police. After all, I have just murdered a man in cold blood and will gladly serve a prison sentence.'

I quickly retrieve my mobile from the kitchen. This place is going to have to be cleaned of fingerprints at some point, but not yet.

'The people we want are in the garage. That door over there is the way into it from the house. They're busy attaching Micha to a car seat. They'd intended to poison her with exhaust fumes to get me to talk. The big exterior garage door can be opened with a remote that's in the car. We absolutely cannot let them go. OK?'

Then the interior door opens. Thornton. He takes one look at the unexpected scene in front of him, says 'shit', turns back into the garage and slams the door hard. A sliding bolt is pushed home.

I hear the Mercedes being started, followed by the slow metallic grind of the front garage door starting to open. I run across the hall and attempt to open the interior door. Useless. I hit it with my shoulder. Doesn't move. Baek-Hayeon touches my arm to indicate that he should have a try.

'I am heavier and sturdier than you, Mr Beckett.'

He rams the door twice with the full weight of his body. A huge vertical crack appears. I kick it open. But it's too late. Mathéo is in the driver's seat of the Mercedes and he's revving the engine. With a screech of the tyres, he bombs out of the garage and onto the street, the roof of the car getting its paint scraped off by the partially opened automatic door.

Carmichael was in the passenger seat, Micha in the back seat behind him, her wrists chaotically taped to the headrest in front. Thornton was sitting behind Fournier. I turn to Baek-Hayeon.

'Soo-ah.'

Ten seconds later, the orange Kia Stinger screeches to a halt outside the house. We get in. I sit in the front once more.

'Have you been in a fight, Mr Beckett?' asks Soo-ah, frowning and looking at my face.

'Police brutality. Five hundred yards down the road. A silver Mercedes GLE. Registration RVK Q7227. See it? We tracked it earlier this morning. Follow, but be inconspicuous for the moment. The people inside won't know this car, so that'll initially be to our advantage.'

'You want me to force him off the highway?'

'No. Your boss is inside. I wouldn't want you to lose your job.'

'Oh, crap. What are they doing?'

'I really have no idea and I don't know where they're heading. Their priority will be to get as far away from me and Mr Bahk here as quickly as possible. We can't let them do that.'

'OK. Seatbelts, please. And,' she nods at the gun on my lap, 'Weapon in the glove compartment. Thank you for your cooperation.'

We take off a little more sedately than on our previous journey. She's soon about seventy yards behind the Mercedes, matching its speed but keeping her distance.

40 mph limit here, but Fournier's cruising at just under sixty. It's still only mid-morning. Traffic not too bad. I noticed a grey Bentley Continental parked outside before we left. Carmichael's.

Where can Fournier and pals be going? They must know about Kinnaird's fate from Thornton or have decided that the game was up in some other way. The obvious places to flee to would be Fournier's home in Notting Hill, Carmichael's place in Robert Adam Street or Thornton's house in St John's Villas. But I don't think they're going to do obvious. Not today.

If I was Fournier, I'd probably keep driving until some plan appeared in my head. A full fuel tank in a car like that could take anything from seventy to eighty-five litres. That would give him a range of well over five hundred miles. He could drive to Inverness without stopping at a petrol station.

I check the tracking app. Micha's mobile remains in Kinnaird's house, so that form of pursuit won't be possible. But there may be another way.

I fish Fournier's business card out of my wallet and call Doug Teng, asking him to put an immediate track on the mobile number. Pays to be cautious. I don't want these dickheads to get away.

I look out of the window. We're heading along Winchmore Hill. Now we're in a 30-mph zone and the Mercedes is doing over fifty. It would be great if he got pulled over for speeding, but that's unlikely to happen; there are never any police around when you need them.

My mobile buzzes, and as Fournier speeds along Cockfosters Road, he appears as a violet dot on Doug's psychedelic tracking software.

Well, that's something. But soon it becomes nothing as the dot disappears and the software seems to fail.

A text from Doug: *Problem here. You're going out of range.*

'Keep him in sight, Soo-ah. We can't rely on this tracker anymore.'

She nods her head and puts her foot down.

Now we're heading towards the M25. Is he going to try for one of the airports? But when we reach the junction, he flies straight across the scary roundabout, avoiding the motorway turnoffs.

Close on his tail, Soo-ah cuts up a fifteen-ton Eurocargo truck which gives her a sustained and angry blast of its horn.

'Prick,' she comments.

'Where is he going, Mr Beckett?' asks Baek-Hayeon. 'I am concerned for Micha.'

'Me too. I have no idea what he's doing. But on the plus side, I don't think *he* does, either. Unless there's some safe haven he's heading for that we don't know about. He could be going anywhere: St Albans,

Cambridge, Peterborough. I'm going to be a little more proactive and see what happens.'

I give him a call.

'Hey, Mathéo. I hope you're insured to drive Rowan's car. I wouldn't want you to get stopped by the police. I think it's a £300 fine, but hey, you've got plenty of money.'

'Is this Beckett?'

'Oh, come *on*, Mathéo. Who else could it be? Take a look in your rear-view mirror. We're right behind you. The orange Kia Stinger GT2. One thing; have you got a full tank in that car? I'd like to know how far you can get before I catch up with you and rip your head off your body.'

He clicks me off. It's come to that. We have nothing to say to each other anymore.

He increases his speed, travelling at sixty-five now, a bit too fast for this road, but not too bad. We seem to be heading for Hatfield or Welwyn Garden City. Hard to tell.

'OK, Soo-ah. Let's catch up. Get about twenty yards behind him.'

'Will do. I can see Ms Jeong in the back seat. I think she will be stressed. Will she be OK?'

'Just don't tailgate him. Drop back occasionally. I don't want to panic him. But keep him in sight.'

I'm concerned about Micha's safety, but Fournier won't do anything *that* stupid while he's driving. He's too self-centred. I hope. And I recall him saying he was a pretty good motorist and had done all the advanced driving stuff. Do those courses cover desperate high-speed chases with someone like Soo-ah in hot pursuit?

Thornton is leaning forwards and talking to Carmichael. I give Fournier another call.

'Me again. Sorry to bother you, Mathéo. We're all a little curious as to where you might be going. Do you have any idea? Just a hint would do. Just the county, maybe. And while I'm here, have you and Billy decided on who's going to pay for Rowan's funeral?'

I hear Carmichael say something. I can see Fournier pass his mobile over.

'What are you talking about?' asks Carmichael. 'You'd knocked him out.'

'Don't tell me you don't *know*, Billy. I thought Clem had seen what had happened. Rowan wasn't *unconscious*, Billy. He was dead. I thought that's why you all ran away. Did Clem think he was having a doze on the floor? Anyway, all of you are rich enough. Perhaps you could split the funeral expenses. Or you could just dump his bloated corpse in a skip to save money. That's what I'd do.'

He clicks me off. No manners.

Now they're really moving. Soo-ah keeps the same distance behind them, travelling at just over seventy. We're out in the countryside. I can't see any signs telling us where we are. Soo-ah sees me looking around.

'We're approaching somewhere called Broxbourne, Mr Beckett. Wait. Look.'

Fournier is signalling right. The car rocks as he takes the turn a little too fast and now we're speeding along a minor road in the middle of nowhere, a country park on one side and a golf course on the other.

There's a T-junction up ahead and he swings left without looking to see if anything's coming from his right. I can hear his tyres squeal. Soo-ah stops at this junction, but as soon as she sees the coast is clear she makes the same turn and accelerates so that we're close behind the Mercedes again. The road surface needs repair here, and the car keeps rocking and trembling. Soo-ah keeps tutting.

There's a sharp curve in the road about two hundred yards ahead. There are black-and-white warning chevrons starting a few feet away.

'Drop back a little, Soo-ah. We don't want to make him do anything really brainless.'

'Sure thing.'

The Mercedes visibly lists as it takes this curve, then straightens up and accelerates.

The road ahead is straight for about two miles and there's not another vehicle in sight. Now he's up to seventy again. We accelerate to match his speed. I take a deep breath to calm my adrenaline rush.

'You liking this?' asks Soo-ah, grinning.

'Exhilarating.'

'This road is terrible.'

'It's a rural farming area. Roads like this weren't designed for insane high-speed car chases.'

'No shit.'

'Let's slow down a little. This road is straight for a while. Just keep your eye on him.'

I try to call Mathéo again, but his mobile seems to be switched off. The Mercedes is maybe half a mile in front of us now.

Then I see the other car.

It's a metallic blue Peugeot 308. Probably doing forty along a small road on our right that intersects with the one that we and the guys are travelling along. Let's hope the driver of the 308 sees the Mercedes in time and doesn't think he can slip out just because it's a quiet road. Let's hope they're taking a left.

'Hey,' says Soo-ah, pointing at it. 'You think they'll see them coming? Look at all those trees and bushes ahead. You think they'll see the Mercedes? Shit.'

'I'm sure it'll stop. People around here must be used to exercising caution on roads like this.' That sounded good. Do I believe it for a second?

I give Fournier another call; warn him about that other car. Still no reply. Baek-Hayeon leans forwards and looks through the gap between the front seats. He hisses through his teeth. The Peugeot shows no signs of slowing down and neither does the Mercedes.

'Put your foot down, Soo-ah.'

The Kia's engine roars as she eases off the throttle and does a racing change from fourth gear to third, pressing us all back into our seats. Baek-Hayeon grunts with the shock of the g-force on his body.

We hear a screech of tyres, then an unbelievably loud bang, almost an explosion. The Peugeot has hit the Mercedes side-on and the impact has lifted the back of the Peugeot off the ground by about four feet before it drops to the ground, almost bouncing right back up again. I can hear some sort of loud machine hiss.

'Shit,' says Soo-ah.

By the time we get there a few seconds later, I can smell burning and see a few flames emanating from the impact point, but I can't tell which vehicle they're coming from.

Soo-ah parks about thirty feet away from the wreckage after Baek-Hayeon has sternly warned her about petrol explosion radius and flying debris.

As all three of us walk towards the scene of the accident, I get a sick feeling in the pit of my stomach. I'm really not looking forward to what I'm going to find.

44

RANDOM FRAGMENTS

The flames are high now, maybe three or four feet in the air. Lots of smoke. My first concern is Micha. I can see the Peugeot passengers. It's a man and a woman in their twenties. Both dead, I think.

The woman went straight through the windscreen, even though she was wearing a seatbelt. You can see the snapped remains of it across the front of what's left of the bonnet. There's broken glass and blood everywhere.

The man is still sitting upright in the driver's seat, but it looks as if he received some sort of powerful blow to the side of his head, as the whole right-hand side of his face and body is soaked with blood.

There are flames coming from the driver's side of the Mercedes, but I can't tell whether it's fuel spillage or something else. The smoke is acrid and pungent and it's making my eyes water. The Mercedes was almost shunted into the ditch by the collision; only its bulk stopped it being tipped over completely. One of its tyres has burst.

I ask Baek-Hayeon to confirm the Peugeot pair are both dead while I take a look at Micha. She's slumped forward in her seat and leaning a little to the side.

Thornton is conscious with a deep and ugly gash on his cheekbone, and he's struggling with something. His right hand is caught in between the driver's seat and the damaged side of the car. He tugs and tugs, but nothing happens.

Soo-ah is not squeamish and stands just behind me. 'Is she dead?' she whispers.

I take Micha's pulse. Weak. Her breathing is shallow, and she's as white as a sheet, but she's still alive and has no obvious external injuries. Having her hands taped to the passenger seat in that precise way may have saved her life.

I slowly remove the gaffer tape from her mouth. Blood drips from her lower lip. I gently poke around in her mouth with my thumb and forefinger. She flinches. It seems as if she may have bitten her tongue or the side of her cheek.

'She's OK, Soo-ah. At least I think she is.'

Baek-Hayeon returns from the other car. 'Both dead, Mr Beckett.'

'Do you have your Leatherman on you?'

'Of course.'

I use the spring-action scissors to cut through the gaffer tape on Micha's hands and wrists. I put my hand around her shoulders and slowly help her out of the car. She's semi-conscious so it's not as difficult as it might be. I don't think I'd be able to lift her out of *any* vehicle if she was unconscious; in her condition, I wouldn't know where to start. It takes about two minutes to get her standing up.

She looks dazed. I place two fingers under her chin and lift her face up so she can look at me.

I smile at her. 'You OK, sexy?'

I get a weak smile in reply. 'The baby,' she says quietly. There are tears in her eyes.

'Come on. We have to take a little walk, then you can sit down again. If you promise to behave, we can go to a McDonalds Drive Thru. My treat.'

'W – what happened?' Her voice is faint. She inhales suddenly and winces with pain.

'It was really exciting. I'll tell you about it later. We have to move.'

I turn to Soo-ah. 'Put her in the front seat. Make her comfortable. When we leave here, avoid crazy driving and potholes, particularly at the same time. She'll need a thorough hospital check-up after you've dropped me and Mr Bahk off. You go with her and stay with her.'

She nods her head. She's looking as pale as Micha but is focussed and switched on.

'But I don't want you to take her to a normal hospital. I'm going to text you the address of a place that's not too far from the Sansuyu Building. It's in Clerkenwell, near the Sadler's Wells Theatre.

'You ring the bell and tell them that I have sent you. I will call them and let them know you are on your way and roughly when you are expected. I'll explain everything. Ask for Dr Cían Hennigan. If he is not available, Dr Félicité Sourd will see you.

'Tell Micha she will not have to leave anything out. She will be able to tell them absolutely everything that has happened this morning. And she will get the best possible treatment. She must not worry about anything.

'I've just got to go back and have a look at this accident. In the meantime, turn around so you're facing the way we came.'

'My car needs a service,' observes Soo-ah.

'And you deserve a pay rise.'

I send Baek-Hayeon back to the Kia Stinger. 'I won't be long. Just got to talk to our friends.'

Fournier and Carmichael are in a real mess. The driver's door is destroyed. In the back, Thornton is trying to disengage his ruined hand from the crushed mess by pushing the front seat forward with all his strength. Doesn't work.

Fournier was wearing a seatbelt, but for some reason his airbag didn't engage. He jerks and shudders. His tongue hangs out of his mouth. There's copious haemorrhaging from a wide laceration on the side of his face. I can see his back teeth through it. His breathing is rapid.

It looks as if his right arm and shoulder took most of the impact and are twisted and broken in such a grotesque way I can barely bring myself to look at them. But I do, anyway. I can see the jagged end of a broken bone poking through his bicep, and the amount of blood spreading from his shoulder indicates that he's possibly broken his collar bone and has ruptured his subclavian artery. Not good. The crotch of his trousers is soaked with piss. He farts. He's shitting himself. He's going into shock. He needs immediate hospital treatment. He's still conscious, and moans from time to time.

He looks up at me like a flatulent spaniel, silently asking for help. My eyes are watering from the smoke, which is thick and black. Won't be long now. I find Fournier's mobile and slip it into my pocket.

Carmichael is in a bad way and also needs a rapid journey to A&E. Blood dribbles from his mouth and then suddenly gushes out after he produces a weedy little cough. His jaw is broken and pushed to the side, and I'd be interested to hear him speak, purely as an academic exercise. At least his airbag worked.

I can't really see how his injuries occurred – perhaps he got struck by Mathéo at some point – but the left-hand side of his chest seems to have been damaged and the blood has soaked his shirt and most of his trousers. He's in agony. Like Fournier, he looks up at me in a sweet, puppy-like, beseeching manner that you'd have to have a heart of stone to ignore.

'Puueeze,' he slurs. 'Abbiwance. Don't wat to burn. Don't wat to die. Puueeze hewp.'

'You want an ambulance? You want me to help you get out of this?'

He's crying. He nods his head.

I smile at him. I look at Fournier, who has turned his head to stare at me, an imploring look in his eyes, his mouth wide with a silent scream, the flames now roasting his legs and giving off a smell like barbequed steak mixed with burning feathers. The shit smell is much worse, and he continues to noisily evacuate his bowels. The sound is almost comical.

Then I look at Thornton, convulsing and sobbing, who calls me fucker and bastard and keeps trying to get free, blood now soaking his right forearm.

Random fragments of conversation from the last few days flutter around my consciousness like confetti.

'I was so proud. If I was somewhere and people started talking about her and they didn't know, I'd always say "That's my sister!".'

'We were an item until she died. I was shattered. I don't know if I'll ever recover.'

'Camera loved her. So much bitch, *you know?'*

'Such a loss. I wept. I enjoyed her company.'

'Did Kiaraa tell her sister much about me? Did she tell her that she loved me?'

'She used to sing "I'm Gonna Make you Mine" by Lou Christie. You know that oldie?'

'Sorry, guys,' I say, smiling. 'I'd like to help you, but I'm fresh out of fucks today.'

We've been driving for about ten minutes before we hear the explosion. It's very loud. Both Baek-Hayeon and I turn to look out of the rear window, and I see Soo-ah calmly glancing in the rear-view mirror. She says nothing. Micha seems to be asleep. A few miles back, there's a mushroom cloud of dark smoke that must be at least thirty feet high. Someone will be calling the police soon.

'OK, Soo-ah. I think you can put your foot down now.'

* * *

When we're dropped off at the house, the first thing I do, with Baek-Hayeon's assistance, is to drag Kinnaird's corpse into the kitchen. I don't want him to be spotted by anyone delivering more koi carp brochures or flexible finance options for Jacuzzis.

Despite Baek-Hayeon's willingness to be incarcerated for Kinnaird's killing, I'm trying to think of a way to organise everything so that it doesn't happen. After all, there's a strong possibility that both Micha and I would be dead now had it not been for his actions.

I'll need to speak to Suzanna about this, but I think he'd get away with it being manslaughter with mitigating circumstances, but that would still put him in prison for a lengthy spell. I can't see any way out of that. Or can I?

I sit down on one of the sofas and stare blankly at the ceiling while I think. Baek-Hayeon says nothing, and sits opposite me, possibly waiting for me to come up with something brilliant. He may have a long wait. I send him off to find Micha's mobile, to give him something to do.

When the police scope out this place, as they surely will, explaining away Kinnaird's corpse would be much too difficult, particularly as it would be obvious that he was killed by someone who knew what they were doing.

So, Kinnaird will have to be disposed of and I'm going to have to concoct a story for Scarlett and for Micha.

Baek-Hayeon returns, proudly holding Micha's mobile in the air. It looks as if someone has introduced it to a sledgehammer. He also has her white trainers.

The doorbell rings.

'Mr Beckett…'

'Don't worry. It's someone I texted on the way here.' I open the door to a cheery, white-haired, respectable-looking, rather dapper fellow who must be in his mid-to-late seventies by now. He looks like he's collecting for something worthy and very possibly religious.

He's wearing a green sports jacket, a white shirt, red stripey tie, beige trousers, and well-polished brown brogues; typical garden centre pensioner chic. In his left hand, a worn black leather briefcase.

'Good morning, sir. May I pop in for a few minutes to talk about something we're objecting to in this area?'

He always makes me laugh. 'Come in, Jack. Nice to see you again.'

'And you too, Mr Faulkner. Long time, no cover-up. And you must be Mr Bahk. Please to meet you, sir. I visited Jeju Island when I lived in Japan. I understand the Pohang Steelers are doing very well this season.'

They shake hands. Baek-Hayeon looks fully baffled. Jack slips on a pair of white latex gloves and hands some to me and Baek-Hayeon.

'For later, if you need them,' he says.

We go into the reception room and sit down.

'Would you like something to drink before you start, Jack?'

'Not for me, thank you. Perhaps a little something when I've finished. It'll give me something to look forward to.

'Now. Let's get down to details. I'd like both of you to tell me which rooms you've been in in this house today. If you can remember any specific things that you've touched, door frames, windows, cups and saucers, cutlery and the like, that may come in handy. It also may not, of course!'

We give him the details. He nods his head. Then he produces a small biometric fingerprint/hand scanner and presses a button on it. It bleeps.

'If I could just ask you to place the palms of your hands on this little devil one at a time until it indicates its happiness. Then each individual finger and the thumb, of course. Thank you. Now I'm just going to take a tiny sample of your blood and introduce it to some magical technology. Multiplexed single-nucleotide polymorphism detection. Always gets the girls. No screaming when I prick your fingers please, gentlemen.'

All of this takes about five minutes and involves a lot of quiet electronic noises. Once he's happy, he puts the devices away, and puts on a pair of frameless spectacles. I notice that the light bounces off them in an odd way. Then he fiddles with an app on his Apple iPhone 6. He looks up. 'If you'd told me that something like this would exist in my lifetime when I was in school, I wouldn't have believed you!'

When he's ready, he stands up. In one hand he holds a small aerosol and a green microfibre cloth and in the other his iPhone and what could be a small hi-tech hairdryer. He heads upstairs to start his work.

'What's he doing?' askes Baek-Hayeon.

'Basically, he's clearing this entire house of our fingerprints and any dried blood and/or DNA traces. I had a bit of an altercation upstairs with one of the scumbags when I got here today, and some more stuff happened down here. Any evidence of my fingerprints from that time, and yours from later, will contradict the story I'm going to make up for the police and for Micha.

'This story will be the truth apart from a few small but important details. We knew about Micha's abduction from the Mermaid. I suspected that she would be brought to this house, so with the help of her driver, we got here before her abductors. I told you I'd been here before. I'll square that with the police, then text you to let you know what happened, and you can add it to your story.

'Luckily, the back door was unlocked. Both of us went inside to see if we could surprise them when they arrived, and rescue Micha. This will mean that Soo-ah has to adjust the time you got out of the car. You got out *with* me, not some time later. You will speak to Soo-ah about this as soon as you can, plus some other details.'

'There will be no problem with that, Mr Beckett. Soo-ah is family.'

'When the bad guys arrived at the house, one of them, Kinnaird, had a gun and overpowered both of us.' I give him a pointed look. 'That gun has since mysteriously disappeared. We were made to sit on the floor with our hands on our heads.

'After a while, Kinnaird drove off in Carmichael's Bentley, presumably to prepare some house or warehouse he was taking her to. Thornton now had the gun and threatened us with it. Eventually, Fournier and Carmichael manhandled Micha into Kinnaird's car, and taped her to the seat. Thornton followed them and they all drove off somewhere. Only now could we act.

'We followed them in the Kia Stinger, keeping our distance as Micha was in the car. Then we saw the accident. I managed to get Micha out, but the car exploded killing the others before I could help them. Soo-ah then took Micha for medical help.

'When the police investigate this, they will be able to identify Fournier, Carmichael and Thornton from their dental records, explosion damage allowing. That will confirm a big chunk of my story.

'There will be a considerable amount of direct, primary and secondary evidence, including forensics. A lot of it will come from me. They will almost certainly check the bank accounts of all four men involved, and link all of them to Kiaraa's kidnapping and murder. I'm sure it'll be a complex and time-consuming job, but I'm also sure that DCI Sallow will push it through.

'Keep in mind that the only witness to your killing of Kinnaird was me, and I won't be talking to anybody.'

'But what about…'

'Kinnaird's body and Carmichael's car will have to be got rid of. I will deal with it, though I may have a word with Jack when he's finished. Run that story through your head again and again until it becomes the only truth. It shouldn't be too difficult; most of it really happened. When Jack has finished, I'll go and see Micha. I told Soo-ah to text me with updates.'

'I am worried about her. The baby, you know?'

'I know.'

Fifteen minutes later, Jack reappears, whistling.

'All done, gents. Clean as a whistle. What on *earth* were you doing upstairs, Mr Faulkner? Shenanigans?'

'You're so nosey, Jack.'

'There's a dead body in the kitchen. Had you noticed?'

'Must have missed that.'

'Clive's still working, if you're interested.'

'Yes, I am. There's a car as well. A grey Bentley Continental 4.0 GT. Parked on this side of the road about twelve feet down on the left. I don't have the keys. Both items must vanish without trace. Oh, and this.'

I hand him Baek-Hayeon's pistol. 'Merry Christmas.'

'It'll have to be tonight,' he says, putting the gun in his briefcase. 'When it's dark, you know? Sunset's at 9.12 this evening.'

'The corpse is a cop.'

'They don't pay them enough, do they.'

We both laugh.

'How much?' I ask.

'Well, Clive has put his prices up. Inflation. And that fact it's a policeman. Both jobs – I'd say five thousand?'

'Done. Tell him I'll be in touch tomorrow with the money transfer.'

'I'll take my leave now, gents. I'll have that drink another time. If you have to, stick a few fingerprints around the place to back up whatever your innocent but suspiciously implausible story is going to be. You know the score. Nice to meet you, Mr Bahk.'

'Thanks, Jack. Payment pending.'

I suddenly feel exhausted, even though it's only lunchtime. I can feel Baek-Hayeon looking at me.

'Pardon me, Mr Beckett, but I'm not really sure who you are anymore. Or should that be *what* you are. Or were. I am confused.'

I don't look at him. 'There was a secret compartment in Kiaraa's house. That was where I found your gun. I also found a fossil leaf plate with ginkgo leaves on it. A beautiful piece. Worth over £3,000, as it turned out. A very expensive gift. A special gift.'

'Ah.'

'Have you got something to tell me, Baek-Hayeon?'

He clenches his jaw over and over again, just like he did that day when he described discovering her horrifically abused body in the golf club car park.

'Not much to tell, Mr Beckett.' He smiles and shrugs. 'Unrequited. You know how it can be sometimes.'

I nod my head. 'I take it she knew it was from you.'

'Yes, she did. It was a congratulatory offering after a successful Haydn recital she had given at the Conway Hall.'

'She kept it with the things that were most precious to her. There weren't many of them. Just so you know.'

He starts to choke up. 'Thank you.' More jaw clenching. 'You can…you can imagine how I felt when I found her in the boot of that car.'

'Sure. Now. Let's go and dab a few fingerprints on the walls.'

45

A WICKED AND DECADENT TEMPTRESS

Three weeks later...

Micha sits upright on a high makeup chair, designed, Jasna tells me, so that makeup artistes don't have to keep bending over and give themselves backache. It looks like a folding director's chair, but taller. I don't think I've ever seen one before.

She's wearing an outsize blue blouse and a pair of loose black joggers which are specially designed for the comfort of pregnant women. There's a wide cotton collar around her neck to prevent makeup getting on her clothing.

The cosmetic artiste, a striking and glamorous black woman with a Birmingham accent called Freya Thomassen, is dabbing some bronze Prada eyeshadow onto Micha's upper eyelids with her fingers.

'Oh, darling, look at your skin,' she coos. 'You're so radiant! You hardly need anything. I don't want to spoil your face, but Florian is the boss here. Just a microscopic dusting of blusher on your cheekbones, he says. I'm going to use Suqqu Hyuugaaoi. It's your colour. I'll write all this down for you before I leave, and you can have what's left over. My treat.

'Now. Mouth open please, darling.'

Micha opens her mouth, trying not to laugh. She looks at me and raises her eyebrows. Freya brushes some YSL lip stain onto her mouth, starting with the outer edges and working inwards until she's happy with the result.

'That's it. That's it. All the guys are going to want to kiss you now, darling. This colour is called 216, OK? I'll write that down for you as well. Now. Lips together. You can lick if you like. It won't come off.'

I'd spent two hours with Micha in Hershesons in Fitzrovia getting her hair sorted for the shoot before we arrived here. Both Pöck and Jasna wanted her to use one of their usual hair stylists (not Peverell Rochefort, obviously), but she insisted on booking an appointment with her regular guy, Laszlo, who she'd been with for four years. She likes her hair to look the same all of the time, and she had the same pixie cut as she did when I first met her. To my untrained eye, it looked as if he hadn't done anything. Perhaps that's his special skill.

While all this is going on, Pöck and I stand several feet away, both of us drinking coffee and watching Freya at her work.

'You dog,' he says to me, without turning his head.

'What are you talking about?'

'You think I'm stupid, my friend? I'm too old to be stupid. But, hey. She's beautiful. Just like her sister.'

'I don't understand.'

'Jesus Christ. You could cut the air with a knife between you two.'

I start laughing. 'What on earth does that mean?'

'Jasna noticed it, too. She had to go in the toilets to laugh so Micha wouldn't see. So fucking obvious.'

'And I thought we were being so smart and subtle.'

'That was the problem. You were being *too* subtle. You were both acting like you'd just met five minutes ago. Too deferent. Too polite. Too affable. Too disinterested. Not convincing at all, my friend. *I* should be the detective, not you.

'And *she* should work on her body language. She squirms and stretches like a damn cat when you're anywhere near her. She can't keep her eyes off you. And her pupils become like enormous bottomless black holes whenever she glances in your direction. I notice that sort of thing because I'm so brilliant and perceptive.'

'Maybe it'll make the photoshoot better.'

'You're damn right it will. *Damn* right it will. This is artistic boudoir. It's *meant* to be sexy. And with *maternité*, there's an added element of eroticism. Many added elements. When we start shooting, you stand somewhere where she can see you all of the time. That's an order. And you keep looking at her. You won't have to be an extraordinary photographer like me to notice the effects it'll have. I can't wait to see how this session turns out. It may be one of my best. There may even be a book in it.'

'Limited edition, thirty thousand a copy, size of a football pitch, comes with its own city to keep it in?' I ask.

'Yeah!' He becomes serious. 'You think she'd go for it?'

'She's a high-profile businesswoman, Florian.'

'That's why it would sell. And if she's high profile *now*, imagine her profile when it's published! It would take its place in the heavens! It would be like some crazy erotic fertile constellation profile!'

'I can't argue with that.'

* * *

As soon as Baek-Hayeon and I had finished sorting out the various problems at Kinnaird's house, I took a cab to Clerkenwell to visit Micha. It was Dr Félicité Sourd who had looked after her and insisted that she remain under observation for three days.

'She is traumatised,' Dr Sourd told me. 'And I am not happy about letting her go just yet. We have done all the bloods and the scans. She is physically fine, and the baby was unaffected, but she needs to have complete rest and twenty-four-hour attention, just to be on the safe side.'

'She won't like that.'

'I'm sure she won't. They never do. That cut on her face will heal naturally and quickly and did not require stitches. There will be no scar. The bruising will be gone in about a week. She has several minor lacerations on her wrists because they were taped to the front passenger seat when the impact occurred. Those will heal fairly rapidly, perhaps two weeks, maybe more. I'll get Cecette Scurloch to pop in for a few casual chats. Ms Jeong will not know that she is a trauma-focussed psychotherapist.

'The young lady who brought her here was concerned about the blood that Ms Jeong had coming from her mouth. She had given the side of her tongue one hell of a bite with her left molar teeth at some point, probably at the moment of collision. I told her to masticate only on the right side of her mouth for ten days.'

'Can I go and see her?'

'She has been sleeping. Wake her up slowly. Run a finger up and down the side of her cheek. That usually does the trick. It's funny; I only bought a Sansuyu fridge freezer yesterday.'

'Is it working OK?'

'It's fine. But if it breaks down over the next few days, I know who I can complain to. How is your back now? It was a while ago, wasn't it. Five years?'

'Perfect. Just the odd twinge when there's thunder.'

'You were a terrible patient.' She squints at my face. 'You look fucked, by the way.'

'Excellent diagnosis, doctor. How much do I owe you?'

She's sitting up in bed reading, so I don't have to do the cheek thing, which I was rather looking forward to. She's wearing a green hospital gown. She smiles when she sees me.

'I hear you're traumatised, Micha.'

'Wouldn't you be? You must tell me what happened. What part each of them played and what happened to them. I must know.'

I run through the story I'd outlined to Baek-Hayeon. She looks serious. She nods. She smiles. Then she looks serious again.

'And that is what you will tell the police.'

'I've liaised with a DC who's been involved with the case right from the very beginning. She's been very helpful. She will pass all that I've just told you on to DCI Sallow when he returns from holiday.'

'But it is not true, Daniel. What you have just said. For a start, you and Mr Bahk did *not* arrive at the house at the same time. I did not see him there. I did not see him until you rescued me from that car.'

* * *

'So, detective,' says Jasna, who's standing next to me with her arms folded and a smirk on her face. 'Everything fine with you today?'

'Yes, thank you, Jasna.'

'She looks pretty, doesn't she. Freya always does an excellent job. It's nice of you to accompany Micha, hold her hand, so to speak. It'll be odd for her to be naked in front of you for the first time, though.' Now she can't stop herself laughing, her shoulders shaking. 'As you're a relative stranger, or a temporary employee or whatever you are. I hope neither of you will be embarrassed.'

'I'm sure we'll both manage.'

'I might hire you myself, detective. How much is the mega-platinum service that *she* gets?'

'What *are* you suggesting, Jazz?'

'OK, my precious jewel,' says Pöck. 'You can come out now. I've turned the heating up a little.'

Micha comes out of the changing room and walks into the main part of the studio wearing a dark blue silk robe, which she leaves open. Pöck and Jasna have constructed a few interchangeable sets for her to be photographed in: one with a large four-poster bed and a fake window with fake sunlight pouring through it, another with a chaise longue in front of a poster for a 1914 Picasso exhibition in Paris and another with a large antique mirror leaning against the wall.

She smiles and looks at each of us in turn. 'I am nervous!'

'So you should be, my dear! I've never done this before. I was just delivering pizzas and they handed me this camera!' says Pöck, giggling to himself.

During her preliminary visit, she looked at a bunch of *maternité* prints that Pöck had done in the past, picked out around fifteen that she liked the look of, and took them home with her. Now she selects one of them and points to it.

'I'd like to do something like that first, if it's OK.'

As Jasna takes light readings and fiddles with two Profoto photographic umbrellas, Micha takes her robe off. She looks at me and smiles.

She's wearing a black vintage lace bra and a pair of matching embroidered briefs. Jasna hands her a see-through black silk chiffon kimono. She puts it on, keeping it open at the front to reveal her bump.

Pöck selects the Nikon Z7 with a Nikkor Z lens, the same combo he was using to photograph Franka Galletti a few weeks back.

'OK now, *ma belle baguette*. Be careful. No acrobatics. Get onto the bed and sit on your haunches. That's it. Knees a little apart. Maybe thirty centimetres. Now rest both hands on your thighs.

'Jasna, can you flick her kimono back a little so we can see more of that bump? Good. Now, turn your head to the left and look pensively down at the bed. That's it. That's great. That's great.'

He circles her for maybe five minutes, clicking away from every conceivable position, angle and height.

At one point he has to stop because she's started laughing at something he's said.

'OK. That's that done.' He flicks through the photographs she's chosen and holds one up. 'We're doing this next. Stay on your knees, take the kimono off. Hands clasped behind your head. Stretch back as much as you can. Turn your head to the right. Eyes closed in ecstasy. Mouth slightly open. Oh, good Lord, yes. This is it. There is a God. Fabulous. Fabulous.

'A coy little bite of your lower lip, please, madame. Now a cute smile at the same time. I know it's awkward. Let the smile reach your eyes. *Ammaliante*. My camera is melting. Even the ones I'm not using are melting. Cameras in shops everywhere are melting in solidarity. Yes. Yes. Beautiful. Beautiful.' He looks at me. 'Do I sound too much like Austin Powers? Tell me if I do.'

* * *

'This has to be confidential, Micha. If anyone ever speaks to you about this, you must never tell them what I am about to tell you. You know about a lot of this already, but…'

'She was my sister, Daniel. Whatever you tell me, I will keep to myself. You know you can trust me.'

I explain the motivation of the three main players, and exactly how each of them played a part in the events that led to Kiaraa being murdered. Her eyes fill with tears.

'Kinnaird needed to find out who else I had told about the case and who knew how far I'd got. That was the reason he abducted you, to get leverage against me. He was panicking. He was desperate.

'To get this information, he was going to poison you with carbon monoxide until I talked. That was why Carmichael, Thornton and Fournier took you in the garage and attached you to the car seat.

'Kinnaird remained in the house with a gun on me, waiting for me to spill the beans before they turned the car engine on and left you in there.

'I didn't know that Baek-Hayeon was in the house. In fact, I'd told him to stay in the car with Soo-ah. While Kinnaird was mouthing off at me, Baek-Hayeon came up behind him and broke his neck. I'm having his body disposed of by people who know what they're doing.

'As you know, Fournier and the other two panicked and drove off, taking you with them. After the accident, I checked on them. They were in a bad way. You probably didn't see. They all needed urgent medical attention. All three would have been conscious up to the point when the car exploded. They'd have burnt alive for quite a while, perhaps for ten to fifteen minutes. It's possible I could have saved them. I chose not to.'

She folds her arms across the lower part of her bump. 'Good. It was what they deserved.'

'You must not tell Baek-Hayeon what you know about his part in this. He'll be coming in to see you tomorrow. Let me know later if he has his story straight. Think of his visit as a test. I have to go now. Sorry I didn't bring any grapes.'

'I don't like grapes. Come here.'

I lean forward and am on the receiving end of a rather soft and pleasant snog.

She licks her lips. 'I wanted at least one nice thing to happen to me today. Will you come and see me tomorrow?'

* * *

'OK, *ma tigresse*. We're going for the big one now,' says Pöck. 'Let's get that lingerie off and then put the kimono on again. You can do this in the changing room if you want, or we can get the blindfolds out.'

'I'm OK. I can do it here. I'm surprised I feel so relaxed. This is fun!'

She unhooks her bra and removes the briefs, looking around for somewhere to put them.

'It's OK, sweetie,' says Jasna. 'Daniel will take them off your hands. He's today's wardrobe boy. Go on, Daniel,' she says evilly.

Seeing Micha naked, albeit briefly, in this context, is shockingly erotic and I'm not quite sure why that should be. Perhaps it's because there are other people here seeing her as well. Perhaps it's the situation we're in. Perhaps it's because she's so casual about it. Perhaps it's the heat in here. Perhaps it's the sexual charge she gives off. Perhaps it's just me.

She hands me the lingerie. This is accompanied by a wide smile that I know the others are observing with glee. I can smell her perfume, which seems quite strong. Must be the studio temperature.

'You dressed, me naked. I'm having déjà vu, Daniel,' she whispers.

'You are a wicked and decadent temptress.'

She laughs.

'What is going on there?' asks Pöck. 'This is a place of business!'

She wraps the kimono around herself, stands next to the wall mirror and positions herself so that the left side of her body can be seen in its reflection.

'That's it. Very good, Micha. Doing good work here,' says Pöck. 'We won't need the belt. Lean against the wall there and let the kimono fall open. This is from that photograph you liked, except the kimono was red in that one, yes? Now raise your hands above your head, palms facing forwards, look to your right and stare into the middle distance.'

Jasna adjusts the pose so that all Micha's weight is on her left leg and her right leg is bent at the knee.

The thin see-through fabric hangs from the full breasts. Then Jasna pulls the material across so each nipple is partially exposed, and, touching Micha's chin, makes some imperceptible adjustment to the position of her head.

Pöck keeps clicking away with his Nikon, instructing her to look this way and that, look up, look down, look to the side, look serious, look thoughtful, look sexy, look happy: I'm beginning to get an idea of how tiring it must be to be a professional model.

'OK, sex bomb,' says Jasna. 'Now the shots for your company calendar. Wardrobe boy!'

Micha hands the kimono to me with another warm smile. Seeing her like this is starting to be murder now, as I'm sure hard taskmistress Jasna Løvstrøm knows only too well.

'Probably a new experience for you, isn't it, detective?' she says. 'Being this close to a totally naked pregnant woman. Are you feeling OK? D'you feel faint? D'you want a glass of water? Some therapy? A cold shower?'

'These are your first *exposée* shots, madame,' says Pöck. 'Would you like some Valium or a deadly cocktail of some sort? What am I saying! You're pregnant and I'm trying to ply you with drugs and drink.'

She stands, artily lit from the side, a hand resting on her bump and an arm across her breasts. Then multiple variations on the same shot. Then she clasps her fingers behind her neck, leans backwards and looks up at the ceiling. I find I'm thinking 'God almighty'.

'Look down, look down,' orders Pöck. 'Now look at me. Heavy eyelids please, like you're falling asleep, but still want to tease. Good. Good.'

Then she lies on the bed, knees raised, hands on her thighs, her head turned to look at the camera. The cool look on her face reminds me of Kiaraa, and I sometimes get flashes of how similar they are. Then she's on her haunches, running her fingers through her hair and looking foxy. Then a seductive pout and a delicate cupping of both breasts. Then she's sitting on the floor, a string of black pearls around her neck, leaning backwards, staring at the ceiling, supporting herself on the palms of her hands. Damn.

Despite Pöck's instructions, she's finding it difficult to get the smile off her face. She's obviously having a ball. This is good. Every second that goes by from that awful day three weeks ago is good.

* * *

'So, I don't understand, Daniel. Why would Kinnaird take Carmichael's car instead of his own?'

It's two days after the exciting events at Kinnaird's house. I'm getting a lunchtime third-degree from Scarlett in Pizza Union in King's Cross. This is almost as bad as talking to DI Olivia Bream.

Scarlett can feel there's something fishy, but she can't work out what it is. She's having a Fiorentina and I'm having a Formaggi. We both drink Coke. She's wearing the same navy/black combo that she was when we met in The Soak the other day.

'I don't know. I've given it some thought. The only logical explanation is that the Bentley was conveniently parked outside, whereas the Mercedes was in the garage. Could have been simple laziness.

'Perhaps Kinnaird liked driving the Bentley. Maybe he was in a hurry, and it was faster. Who knows? I think he was going on ahead of the others, maybe meeting up with them at some prearranged destination.

'Obviously, Mr Bahk and I could do nothing while Thornton was waving that gun around. Ms Jeong was also at risk at that point. It was only when they left that we could pursue them in a car they would not recognise and then discover where they were going.'

'What sort of gun was it?'

'No idea. Some sort of automatic. Presumably it's still in the wreckage of the Mercedes. Unless it melted in the inferno, which is always possible.'

'What would you have done if you'd caught up with them? If they hadn't had that crash, I mean.'

'I didn't have a plan. My focus was on making sure I knew where Ms Jeong was at all times and not letting her out of my sight. If they'd stopped at some big house in the country, I don't know that I'd have approached them. Too dangerous. I think I'd probably have called you and let you know what was going on. Then you could have sent in the cavalry.'

'Very kind. Where d'you think Kinnaird is?'

'Hiding in a cave somewhere? Living in South America? Once DCI Sallow is back from his holidays, I think the priority would be to follow the money from the ransom payment.

'We now know who the kidnappers were, and I'm sure Economic Crime Command could be persuaded to get off their arses and do something, particularly as one of their senior officers was involved in all of this. If Kinnaird has access to his share of the money, this would be a good way of tracking him down. He'll certainly be using it in some way, I would think.'

She pushes the tips of her fingers into her eyeballs. 'OK. We have to get one piece of bullshit straight. How did you know where Kinnaird lived so you could get to his house before he and Fournier turned up with Micha? If someone asks me about this, Sallow or whoever, I've got to have a convincing story. I can't say that you'd already been there and broken in a few days before all hell broke loose.' She sighs and runs a hand through her hair. 'I can't believe I'm going along with all of this.'

'That's easy. One of my contacts told me about the Bijou Noir club where Kinnaird hung out. It's in Gresse Street. I went there. I asked a few questions. One of the girls there knew his address. I made a note of it. I never knew the girl's name. That's what happened. That's how I knew.'

She narrows her eyes suspiciously. 'One of your *contacts*. I *see*. When I spoke to DI Bream about you the other day, she said that you'd probably let me clear up the cadaver-strewn mess afterwards and get myself a promotion.'

'Well, we've certainly got the cadaver-strewn mess part sorted. Would you like me to write a letter of recommendation to the Met? I'm sure I could pull some strings. Or get you back on traffic duty. Up to you.'

'Two years we've been on this. And then Micha's three big private investigation companies. And you sort it out in six days.'

'Just dumb luck. So. Bar Termini for cocktails then Blacklock Soho for dinner?'

'Let me check my diary.'

* * *

Micha, Pöck, Jasna and I sit around a big wooden desk in the corner of the studio, staring at the enormous screen of Pöck's Microsoft Surface Studio 2+. He passes around a huge bowl of truffle crisps, which Micha seems to eat most of.

He clicks through image after image from the shoot, pausing every now and then to study one particular photograph for a few seconds, then moving on. He nods his head frequently, appreciating his own genius.

'Look at this,' he says, pointing at a striking image of Micha lying on her back on the bed, naked, eyes half closed, head turned to the side, running one hand through her hair, the other hand resting on her lower belly. 'I shall be brutally honest with you, I am brilliant. But I truly think that this is the most electrifyingly erotic *maternité* photograph I have ever taken. Possibly the most erotic photograph full stop. It's true. It is burning the air around it. It simply oozes sex, desire, and sensuality. It is almost too much. It makes me want to get drunk as I will never be able to top it. I shall give up now. I shall become a gardener. Or a pilot. Or a telesales supervisor.'

'Can I have the studio?' asks Jasna.

'You're just saying that because I am here,' says Micha, who can't stop herself grinning at his words.

'No no no no, *ma dragée*. This is a work of art. *You* are a work of art. It's everything: your body, your face, your hair. You are alight. And I know part of the reason why. *Do* not get embarrassed. *Do* not get offended. It is because your lover is present. Yes, yes, we know. Of *course* we know.

'But he did not tell us. It is purely photographer's intuition. But there is no doubt in my mind that this pose, and many of the others, are for him. I *knew* it would happen. Do not deny it! I can read your mind from that photograph. And your body is continually giving the game away, *mon petit lapin*.'

'Let's have a look at it in black and white,' says Jasna, tapping something. It's different, but far more striking and arty.

'Good, good,' says Pöck. 'A trace of Anton Trčka there, I think. Now try going back to colour and changing the contrast. Let see how that looks. Get it a touch darker, too.'

The screen fills with all three variants. 'Hard to choose,' he says. 'God.'

He gets down on his hands and knees in front of Micha. 'Please, please, *please* let me do a book!'

Micha looks fatigued now. She and Pöck retire to his office, leaving me and Jasna to drink coffee and select what we think are the best of the best from the shoot. I knew Micha wanted to talk to him about Kiaraa and he wanted to talk about her too, so we leave them to it.

When they reappear twenty minutes later, they both look drained and upset, but it doesn't last too long and soon they're enthusiastically chatting about the photographs again.

'That one. You know. On the bed,' says Micha. 'Can it be made into a nice print for Daniel, please? And whichever of the other ones he wants?'

'I was going to suggest the same thing myself, my dear,' says Pöck. 'After what you've told me about the quality of his work for you, I think he deserves it.'

I get a knowing smile. 'Yes,' she says. 'I think he does.'

The next day, I'm walking along Tenterden Street, on my way to pick up a bespoke rose bouquet from Moyses Stevens, the posh florist. Then something makes me stop.

There's a window display in a classical music store called Calliope on the other side of the road. It's dominated by an enormous monochrome photograph of Kiaraa Jeong, which looks like an unused shot from the Bach CD photo session. The store has been hosting a special retrospective of her work, probably to coincide with the second anniversary of her death.

In the photograph, Kiaraa sits on the floor, leaning against the whitewashed brick wall, the soft cotton shirt unbuttoned to the waist.

But unlike the photographs in the CD booklet, with their smouldering, sexy, serious expressions, in this one she's holding a small bottle of Coke and she's smiling, looking straight at the camera.

Straight at *me.*

Who knows? Maybe that wanderer ghost has found peace at last.

What should you read next?
Browse Dominic Piper's Books on Amazon

Dominic Piper is an author, film and television writer, journalist and script editor. He lives in London, UK. He is the author of the best-selling, critically acclaimed thrillers *Kiss Me When I'm Dead, Death is the New Black, Femme Fatale, Bitter Almonds & Jasmine,* and *Acid Yellow,* all featuring the enigmatic, London-based private investigator *Daniel Beckett.*

All five novels are published by Opium Den Publishing.

FOLLOW DOMINIC PIPER

X - @DominicPiper1
BLUESKY - @dominicpiper.bsky.social
INSTAGRAM - @dominicpiperauthor
THREADS - @dominicpiperauthor
AMAZON: https://viewauthor.at/DominicPiper